LAUGHING SPACE

LAUGHING SPACE

FUNNY SCIENCE FICTION

CHUCKLED OVER BY

Isaac Asimov and J. O. Jeppson

Introduction and Headnotes
by Isaac Asimov

HOUGHTON MIFFLIN COMPANY BOSTON

1982

Library of Congress Cataloging in Publication Data

Main entry under title:

Laughing space.

1. American wit and humor.   2. American wit and
humor, Pictorial.   3. Science fiction, American.
I. Asimov, Isaac, date.   II. Jeppson, J. O.
PN6231.S42L38   817'.54'08   81–7146
ISBN 0-395-30519-5   AACR2

Printed in the United States of America

V   10   9   8   7   6   5   4   3   2   1

"Et Tu," by John Stallings. Copyright © 1979 by John Stallings. First published
in *Isaac Asimov's Science Fiction Magazine.*
   "Creation," by L. Sprague de Camp. Copyright © 1969 by Ultimate Publishing
Co., Inc.
   "Stag Night, Paleolithic," by Ogden Nash. Copyright 1948 by Ogden Nash. First
appeared in *The New Yorker.*
   "An Epicurean Fragment," by Robert Hillyer. Copyright 1933 and renewed 1961
by Robert Hillyer. Reprinted from *Collected Poems* by Robert Hillyer, by permis-
sion of Alfred A. Knopf, Inc.
   "Spaced Out," by Russell Baker. © 1975 by The New York Times Company.
Reprinted by permission.
   "The Coffin Cure," by Alan E. Nourse. From *Tiger by the Tail.* Copyright © 1965
by Alan E. Nourse. Reprinted by permission of Brandt & Brandt Literary Agents.
   "Silenzia," by Alan Nelson. Reprinted from *The Magazine of Fantasy and Sci-
ence Fiction.*
   "The Agony of Defeat," by Jack C. Haldeman II. Reprinted by permission of
author's agent, Kirby McCauley, Ltd. First published in *Isaac Asimov's Science
Fiction Magazine.*
   "Epitaph on Ceres," and "Epitaph on Rigel XII," by Sherwood Springer. Copy-
right 1977, Mercury Press, Inc. Reprinted from *The Magazine of Fantasy and
Science Fiction.*

To: The Sense of Humor,
working uphill
to make humans humane,
healthy, happy, and busy
creating comedy

Contents

Part III Comedy on — or from — Other Worlds

Part IV Wacky Time Travel Problems

Part V "Writing (The Crowning Heights of Civilization) and Criticism (The Pits)"

Part VI The End?

Introduction

ISAAC ASIMOV

I tend — I think with justification — to take science fiction seriously. We live in a time of crisis and there is too much cause for supposing that the human species stands a good chance of witnessing a breakdown in its civilization within the lifetime of the present generation.

The one way we can cope with the dangers of nuclear war, overpopulation, resource depletion, pollution, and social unrest is to undertake vast changes in our way of living and in our outlook that may offer us new kinds of solutions to defuse these deadly risks. It means, if we are to survive, that society must change more in the next thirty years than it has changed in the last three hundred — and it must do so shrewdly, deliberately, and with forethought.

But people resist change, and it is difficult to blame them for that. Change is uncomfortable — even frightening. We like what we are accustomed to; we feel warm in our pleasant cocoons of habit. To alter this, we have to accept the very notion of change — its desirability, its inevitability. That's where science fiction comes in. It doesn't predict the future in detail (except occasionally by accident), but it does take for granted that the future will be different from the present, and that much is crucial.

Consequently, the more we turn our thoughts to science fiction, the more easily we can make the adjustments necessary to solve our vast problems, and the more likely we will be to solve them and survive.

So, in brief, runs my argument. Yet just because science fiction serves a serious, even vital, purpose, it doesn't mean that science fiction must be universally serious. Humor has power too — look at Cervantes and Swift.

My co-editor, who suggested this anthology of humorous science fiction, is J. O. Jeppson — a psychiatrist and psychoanalyst, writer (two novels plus short stories and articles), and a woman of sound judgment — else why would she have married me? She is also a lover of laughter and is interested in its psychiatric and medical applications.

The power of humor was described by Norman Cousins in his recent best-selling book, *Anatomy of an Illness.* He restored himself to normal health largely by seeking occasion for laughter, and says:

> I was greatly elated by the discovery that there is a physiological basis for the ancient theory that laughter is good medicine . . . it creates a mood in which the other positive emotions can be put to work, too. In short, it helps make it possible for good things to happen.

We need good things to happen in this crazy world we inhabit, and if we all laughed more, perhaps the world would get better. While laboring with heart and soul to correct the injustice, the misery, and the physical suffering of millions, why should we not also find occasion for laughter when possible? Is not part of the injustice and suffering the result of the frowns and scowls that close the heart against the appeals of compassion and brotherhood and might not fun and merriment help let them in?

And if so, why should not science fiction also offer the occasion for laughter?

So Janet and I scrabbled through our science fiction library searching for items we could agree were funny — decisions that are primarily subjective. It is relatively easy to come to some consensus on what is suspenseful, or dramatic, or poignant, or thoughtful — but there are wide and almost unbridgeable differences in what people think is side-splittingly humorous. Combatants cannot demonstrate the right or wrong of the argument by logic or reasoning. There is no way out but flat assertion.

Janet and I, fortunately, had only mild differences on what is funny; when such disagreements arose we wasted no time in arguing, since the rule was that any entry must amuse both of us. Our editor and friend at Houghton Mifflin, Austin Olney, offered a third opinion.

All three of us realize that a sense of humor is a highly individual creature, if not an endangered species, so that what we think is funny may not leave *you* limp with laughter. We realize that there have been other anthologies of humorous science fiction, but this one is composed of stories all three of us like.

Janet suggested that we include light verse and cartoons, and Austin and I agreed enthusiastically.

So here we are with ample scope for merriment, or *Laughing Space* — Janet overbore her natural suspicion of puns (the one blight on our marriage) and invented the title. She also asked me to remind you that curmudgeonly old Martin Luther said it best:

"If you're not allowed to laugh in heaven, I don't want to go there."

PART I

Beginnings — Comic?

Now, honestly, has it been worth the effort?

"Did it! Arrived in upper atmosphere approximately 4:05 Standard Oceanic Time. Fantastic view. Funny, cold feeling on my closed gills. New breathing apparatus working satisfactorily; all life-support systems go. Feel humbly conscious of the greatness of the occasion. Millions of years of evolution necessary to prepare for this day. No deed of living creatures ever so well rehearsed as this first step into the Unknown, or requiring the cooperation of so many patient millions of the Team."

A Fuller Explanation
of Original Sin

ISAAC AND JANET

In the innocent, primeval sea
Terra's cells lived quite singly — and free
    From all risk of perdition
    Since they used only fission
Reproducing — but suffered ennui.

Some adventurous cells said, "We'll grow —
Not alone, though, for that's status quo.
    Let's become he and she,
    Multicellularly —
So hold on to each other — let's go!"

Then together they clung; grew complex.
Fully half went concave, half convex;
    And it all proved complete
    When each came into heat
And announced the invention of sex.

Crises began early . . .

"You'd better make a decision — the continents are starting to drift!"

"Look, kid, we're aware of the problems besetting our society. We're working on them."

Et Tu

JOHN STALLINGS

I met a lizard who said to me
Although you're king over all you see
Remember
   there was once a time
When all of this was truly mine
And God was green
         with scaly skin.

"The way I look at it, I live one century at a time. Why worry about the future?"

Creation

L. SPRAGUE DE CAMP

That Yahveh manufactured man from dust, the Hebrews tell;
In Hind they said that Varuna had formed him by a spell;
The Norse believed that Odin made the breath of life indwell
    His torpid trunk.

Of all Creation legends, though, the one I like the best —
A myth from ancient Sumer, where perhaps the truth was guessed —
Asserts the gods created man one day, in cosmic jest,
    When they were drunk.

"It could never work out for us; you're at the end of the Pleistocene period, and I'm at the beginning of the Mesozoic period."

Stag Night, Paleolithic

OGDEN NASH

Drink deep to Uncle Uglug,
That early heroic human,
The first to eat an oyster,
The first to marry a woman.

God's curse on him who murmurs
As the banquet waxes moister,
"Had only he eaten the woman,
Had only he married the oyster!"

"Go back! Go back! The cost of being human has gone up sky-high!"

An Epicurean Fragment

ROBERT HILLYER

As part of an exploding universe,
Our bit of fragmentation might be worse.
Seated beneath companionable stars,
Small beneficiary of cosmic wars,
I must admire how well our atom split
When once the Scientist exploded it.
Aeons ago an overwhelming fission
Blew the existing order to perdition,
But luckily so long before my birth
I need not mourn the burst that made the earth;
And, furthermore, I shall not be about
When, aeons hence, our fragment flickers out.

Spared both the introductory detonation
And the finale of annihilation,
With snug millenniums on either side,
Through the brief pleasantries of life I ride,
Remote from the beginning and the end.
I must regard that bombardier as friend,
Who, on an impulse, pulled the switch — or cork,
And gave us Earth, the Seasons, and New York.
Should I myself face atomized disaster,
At least I've profited from one far vaster,
And trust that equal happiness befall
Those who will benefit from one so small.

Our favorite "B.C."

PART II

Onward — and Upward? — with Terran Civilization

B.C. by permission of Johnny Hart and Field Enterprises, Inc.

Spaced Out

RUSSELL BAKER

One day when — as is my wont — I was smiling happily to myself while typing up a science fiction story, a sixteen-year-old girl phoned me and, between sobs, asked me if it were really true that the universe might come to an end after a hundred billion years or so.

Maybe it's better to avoid thinking heavily about such things, unless you can achieve Russell Baker's profound philosophical perspective and move rapidly on to Allen Nourse's Coffin Cure.

I AM SITTING HERE 93 million miles from the Sun on a rounded rock which is spinning at the rate of 1000 miles an hour,

and roaring through space to nobody-knows-where,

to keep a rendezvous with nobody-knows-what,

for nobody-knows-why,

and all around me whole continents are drifting rootlessly over the surface of the planet,

India ramming into the underbelly of Asia, America skidding off toward China by way of Alaska,

Antarctica slipping away from Africa at the rate of an inch per eon,

and my head pointing down into space with nothing between me and infinity but something called gravity which I can't even understand, and which you can't even buy anyplace so as to have some stored away for a gravityless day,

while off to the north of me the polar ice cap may,

or may not,

be getting ready to send down oceanic mountains of ice that will bury everything from Bangor to Richmond in a ponderous white death,

and there, off to the east, the ocean is tearing away at the land and wrenching it into the sea bottom and coming back for more,

as if the ocean is determined to claim it all before the deadly swarms of killer bees,

which are moving relentlessly northward from South America,

can get here to take possession,

although it seems more likely that the protective ozone layer in the upper atmosphere may collapse first,

exposing us all, ocean, killer bees, and me, too,

to the merciless spraying of deadly cosmic rays.

I am sitting here on this spinning, speeding rock surrounded by four billion people,

eight planets,

one awesome lot of galaxies,

hydrogen bombs enough to kill me thirty times over,

and mountains of handguns and frozen food,

and I am being swept along in the whole galaxy's insane dash toward the far wall of the universe,

across distances longer to traverse than Sunday afternoon on the New Jersey Turnpike,

so long, in fact, that when we get there I shall be at least 800,000 years old,

provided, of course, that the whole galaxy doesn't run into another speeding galaxy at some poorly marked universal intersection and turn us all into space garbage,

or that the Sun doesn't burn out in the meantime,

or that some highly intelligent ferns from deepest space do not land from flying fern pots and cage me up in a greenhouse for scientific study.

So, as I say, I am sitting here with the continents moving, and killer bees coming, and the ocean eating away, and the ice cap poised, and the galaxy racing across the universe,

and the thermonuclear thirty-times-over bombs stacked up around me,

and only the gravity holding me onto the rock,

which, if you saw it from Spica or Arcturus, you wouldn't even be able to see, since it is so minute that even from these relatively close stars it would look no bigger than an ant in the Sahara Desert as viewed from the top of the Empire State Building,

and as I sit here,

93 million miles from the Sun,

I am feeling absolutely miserable,

and realize,

with self-pity and despair,

that I am

getting a cold.

The Coffin Cure

ALAN E. NOURSE

I rarely get colds. I don't say that in a spirit of triumphant crowing: merely stating a fact with the proper condescending sympathy for the rest of you poor souls. But once I had one, in 1962, that outdid all of yours. I went through each messy symptom, and my olfactory system blocked off completely just at a time when, I had every reason to suppose, I was being offered a record series of gourmet meals. Life wasn't worth living. And then one day there was a rift in the olfactory fog, and in the middle of some glum chewing I smelled and tasted what I was chewing. Quite ordinary, I suppose, but not to me. It was like the Sun poking over the hill after a week-long night. Nourse must have lived through the same sort of moment.

WHEN THE DISCOVERY was announced, it was Dr. Chauncey Patrick Coffin who announced it. He had, of course, arranged, with uncanny skill, to take most of the credit for himself. If it turned out to be even greater than he had hoped, so much the better. His presentation was scheduled for the final night of the American College of Clinical Practitioners' annual meeting, and Coffin had fully intended it to be a bombshell.

It was. Its explosion exceeded even Dr. Coffin's wilder expectations, which took quite a bit of doing. In the end, he had waded through more newspaper reporters than medical doctors as he left the hall that night. It was a heady evening for Chauncey Patrick Coffin, M.D.

Certain others were not so delighted with Coffin's bombshell.

"It's idiocy!" young Dr. Phillip Dawson all but howled in the laboratory conference room the next morning. "Blind, screaming idiocy! You've gone out of your mind — that's all there is to it. Can't you see what you've done? Aside from selling your colleagues down the river, that is?"

He clenched the reprint of Coffin's address in his hand and brandished it like a broadsword. " 'Report on a Vaccine for the Treatment and Cure of the Common Cold,' by C. P. Coffin *et al.* That's what it says — *et al. My* idea in the first place, Jake and I pounding our heads on the wall for eight solid months — and now you go sneak it into publication a full year before we have any business publishing a word about it — "

"Really, Phillip!" Dr. Chauncey Coffin ran a pudgy hand through his snowy hair. "How ungrateful! I thought for sure you'd be delighted. An excellent presentation, I must say — terse, succinct, unequivocal — " he raised his hand — "but *generously* unequivocal, you understand. You should have heard the ovation — they nearly went wild! And the look on Underwood's face! Worth waiting twenty years for . . ."

"And the reporters," snapped Phillip. "Don't forget the reporters." He whirled on the small dark man sitting quietly in the corner. "How about that, Jake? Did you see the morning papers? This thief not only steals our work, he splashes it all over the countryside in red ink."

Dr. Jacob Miles coughed apologetically. "What Phillip is so stormed up about is the prematurity of it all," he said to Coffin. "After all, we've hardly had an acceptable period of clinical trial."

"Nonsense," said Coffin, glaring at Phillip. "Underwood and his men were ready to publish their discovery within another six weeks. Where would we be then? How much clinical testing do you want? Phillip, you had the worst cold of your life when you took the vaccine. Have you had any since?"

"No, of course not," said Phillip peevishly.

"Jacob, how about you? Any sniffles?"

"Oh, no. No colds."

"Well, what about those six hundred students from the university? Did I misread the reports on them?"

"No — ninety-eight percent cured of active symptoms within twenty-four hours. Not a single recurrence. The results were just short of miraculous." Jake hesitated. "Of course, it's only been a month. . ."

"Month, year, century! Look at them! Six hundred of the world's most luxuriant colds and now not even a sniffle." The chubby doctor sank down behind the desk, his ruddy face beaming. "Come now, gentlemen, be reasonable. Think positively! There's work to be done, a great deal of work. They'll be wanting me in Washington. Press conference in twenty minutes. Drug houses to consult with. How dare we stand in the path of Progress? We've won the greatest medical triumph of all times — the conquering of the Common Cold. We'll go down in history!"

And he was perfectly right on one point, at least.

They did go down in history.

The public response to the vaccine was little less than mass scale. Of all the ailments that have tormented mankind throughout history, none was ever more universal, more tenacious, more uniformly miserable than the common cold.

It respected no barriers, boundaries, or classes; ambassadors and chambermaids snuffled and sneezed in drippy-nosed unanimity. The powers in the Kremlin sniffed and blew and wept genuine tears on drafty days, while senatorial debates on earthshaking issues paused reverently upon the blowing of a nose, the clearing of a rhinorrheic throat. True, other illnesses brought disability, even death, in their wake, but the common cold brought torment to the millions, as it implacably resisted the most superhuman of efforts to curb it.

Until that rainy November day when the tidings broke to the world in four-inch banner heads:

COFFIN NAILS LID ON COMMON COLD!

"No More Coughin' "
States Co-Finder of Cure

SNIFFLES SNIPED; SINGLE SHOT TO SAVE SNEEZERS

In medical circles it was called the Coffin Multicentric Upper Respiratory Virus-inhibiting Vaccine, but the newspapers could never stand for such high-sounding names and called it, instead, "The Coffin Cure."

Below the banner heads, world-renowned feature writers expounded in awesome terms the story of the leviathan struggle of Dr. Chauncey Patrick Coffin et al. in solving this riddle of the ages:

How, after years of failure, they ultimately succeeded in culturing the true causative agent of the common cold, identifying it not as a single virus or even a group of viruses, but rather as a multicentric virus complex invading the soft mucous linings of the nose, throat, and eyes, capable of altering its basic molecular structure at any time to resist efforts of the body from within, or the physician from without, to attack and dispel it; how the hypothesis was set forth by Dr. Phillip Dawson that the virus could be destroyed only by an antibody which could "freeze" the virus complex in one form long enough for normal body defenses to dispose of the offending invader; the exhausting search for such a "crippling agent" and the final crowning success, after injecting untold gallons of cold-virus material into the hides of a group of cooperative dogs (a species which had never suffered from colds and hence endured the whole business with an air of affectionate boredom).

And, finally, the testing. First, Coffin himself (who was suffering a particularly horrendous case of the affliction he sought to cure); then his assistants, Phillip Dawson and Jacob Miles; then a multitude of students from the university — carefully selected for the severity of their symptoms, the longevity of their colds, their tendency to acquire them on little or no provocation, and their utter inability to get rid of them with any known medical program.

They were a sorry spectacle, those students filing through the Coffin laboratory for three days in October: wheezing like steam shovels, snorting and sneezing and sniffling and blowing, coughing and squeaking, mute appeals glowing in their bloodshot eyes. The researchers dispensed the material — a single shot in the right arm, a sensitivity control in the left.

With growing delight, they then watched as the results came in. The sneezing stopped; the sniffling ceased. A great silence settled over the campus, in the classrooms, in the library, in classic halls. Dr. Coffin's voice returned (rather to the regret of his co-workers), and he began bouncing about the laboratory like a small boy at the fair. Students by the dozen trooped in for checkups with noses dry and eyes bright.

In a matter of days, there was no doubt left that the goal had been reached.

"But we have to be *sure,*" Phillip Dawson had said emphatically. "This was only the pilot test. We need mass testing now on an entire community. We ought to go to the West Coast to run studies — they have a different breed of cold out there, I hear. We'll have to see how long the immunity lasts, make sure there are no unexpected side effects . . ." And, muttering to himself, he fell to work with pad and pencil, calculating the program to be undertaken before publication.

But there were rumors. Underwood at Stanford, it was said, had already completed his tests and was preparing a paper for publication in a matter of months. Surely, with such dramatic results on the pilot tests, *something* could be put into print. It would be tragic to lose the race for the sake of a little unnecessary caution . . .

Phillip Dawson, though adamant, was a voice crying in the wilderness, for Chauncey Coffin was boss.

Within a week, though, even Coffin was wondering if he had bitten off just a trifle too much. They had expected that the demand for the vaccine would be great — but even the grisly memory of the early days of the Salk vaccine had not prepared them for the mobs of sneezing, wheezing, red-eyed people bombarding them for the first fruits.

Clear-eyed young men from the Government Bureau pushed through crowds of local townspeople, lining the streets outside the Coffin laboratory, standing in pouring rain to raise insistent placards.

Seventeen pharmaceutical houses descended with production plans, cost estimates, colorful graphs demonstrating proposed yield and distribution programs.

Coffin was flown to Washington, where conferences labored far into the night as demands pounded their doors like a tidal wave.

One laboratory promised the vaccine in ten days; another guaranteed it in a week. The first actually appeared in three weeks and two days, to be soaked up in the space of three hours by the thirsty sponge of cold-weary humanity.

Express planes were dispatched to Europe, to Asia, to Africa with the precious cargo, a million needles pierced a million hides, and with a huge, convulsive sneeze, mankind stepped forth into a new era.

There were abstainers, of course — there always are:

"It doesd't bake eddy differets how buch you talk," Ellie Dawson cried hoarsely, shaking her blonde curls. "I dod't wadt eddy cold shots."

"You're being totally unreasonable," Phillip said, glowering at his wife in annoyance. She wasn't the sweet young thing he had married, not this evening. Her eyes were puffy, her nose red and sore. "You've had this cold for two solid months now and there just isn't any sense to it. It's making you miserable. You can't eat, you can't breathe, you can't sleep — "

"I dod't wadt eddy cold shots," she repeated stubbornly.

"But why not? Just one little needle. You'd hardly feel it — "

"But I dod't like deedles!" she cried, bursting into tears. "Why dod't you leave be alode? Go take your dasty old deedles ad stick theb id people that wadt theb."

"Aw, Ellie — "

"I dod't care, *I dod't like deedles!*" she wailed, burying her face in his shirt.

He held her close, kissing her ear and making comforting little noises. It was no use, he reflected sadly. Science just wasn't Ellie's long suit; she didn't know a cold vaccine from a case of smallpox, and no appeal to logic or common sense could surmount her irrational fear of hypodermics. "All right, sweet, nobody's going to make you do anything you don't want to."

"Ad eddyway, thik of the poor tissue badufacturers," she sniffled, wiping her nose with a pink facial tissue. "All their little childred starvig to death — "

"Say, you *have* got a cold," said Phillip, sniffing. "You're wearing enough perfume to fell an ox." He wiped away her tears and grinned at her. "Come on now, fix your face. Dinner at the Driftwood? I hear they have marvelous lamb chops."

It was a mellow evening. The lamb chops were delectable — far the best he had ever eaten, he thought, even with as good a cook as Ellie for a spouse. Ellie dripped and blew continuously, but refused to go home until they had taken in a movie and stopped by to dance a while.

"I hardly ever gedt to see you eddy bore," she wistfully explained. "All because of that dasty bedicide you're giving people."

It was true, of course. The work at the lab was endless. They danced, but came home early nevertheless. Phillip needed all the sleep he could get.

He awoke once during the night to a parade of sneezes from his wife, and rolled over, frowning sleepily to himself. It was ignominious, in a way

— the wife of one of the cold-cure discoverers refusing the fruit of all those months of work.

And cold or no cold, she surely was using a whale of a lot of perfume.

He awoke suddenly, began to stretch, and sat bolt upright in bed, looking wildly about the room. Pale morning sunlight drifted in the window. Downstairs, he heard Ellie stirring in the kitchen.

For a moment, he thought he was suffocating. He leaped out of bed, stared at the vanity table across the room. *"Somebody's spilled the whole damned bottle —"*

The heavy sick-sweet miasma hung like a cloud around him, drenching the room. With every breath, it grew thicker. He searched the vanity top frantically, but there were no open bottles.

His head began to spin from the emetic effluvium.

He blinked in confusion, his hand trembling as he lit a cigarette. No need to panic, he thought. She probably knocked a bottle over when she was dressing. He took a deep puff — and burst into a paroxysm of coughing as acrid fumes burned down his throat to his lungs.

"Ellie!" He rushed into the hall, still coughing. The match smell had given way to a caustic stench of burning weeds. He stared at his cigarette in horror and threw it into the sink. The odor grew worse. He threw open the hall closet, expecting smoke to come billowing out.

"Ellie! Somebody's burning down the house!"

"Whadtever are you talkig aboudt?" Ellie's voice came from the stairwell. "It's just the toast I burned, silly."

He rushed down the stairs two at a time — and nearly gagged as he reached the bottom. The smell of hot, rancid grease struck him like a solid wall. It was intermingled with an overpowering oily smell of boiled and parboiled coffee. By the time he reached the kitchen, he was holding his nose, tears pouring from his eyes.

"Ellie, what are you doing in here?"

She stared at him. "I'b baking breakfast."

"But don't you *smell* it?"

On the stove, the automatic percolator made small, promising noises. Four sunnyside eggs were sizzling in the frying pan; half a dozen strips of bacon drained on a paper towel on the sideboard. It couldn't have looked more innocent.

Cautiously, Phillip released his nose, sniffed. The stench nearly strangled him. "You mean you don't smell anything *strange*?"

"I dod't sbell eddythig, period," said Ellie defensively.

"The coffee, the bacon — come here a minute!"

She reeked — of bacon, of coffee, of burned toast, but mostly of perfume.

"Did you put on fresh perfume this morning?"

"Before breakfast? Dod't be ridiculous."

"Not even a drop?" Phillip was turning very white.

"Dot a drop."

Phillip shook his head. "Now wait a minute. This must be all in my mind. I'm — just imagining things, that's all. Working too hard, hysterical reaction. In a minute, it'll all go away." He poured a cup of coffee, added cream and sugar.

He couldn't get it close enough to taste it. It smelled as if it had been boiling three weeks in a rancid pot. It was the smell of coffee, all right, but a smell that was fiendishly distorted, overpoweringly and nauseatingly magnified, pervading the room and burning his throat; tears gushed to his eyes.

Slowly, realization began to dawn. He spilled the coffee as he set the cup down. The perfume. The coffee. The cigarette . . .

"My hat," he choked. "Get me my hat. I've got to get to the laboratory."

It grew worse all the way downtown. He fought down nausea as the smell of damp, rotting earth rose from his front yard in a gray cloud. The neighbor's dog dashed out to greet him, exuding the great-grandfather of all dog odors. While Phillip waited for the bus, every passing car fouled the air with noxious fumes, gagging him, doubling him up with coughing as he dabbed at his streaming eyes.

Nobody else seemed to notice anything wrong at all.

The bus ride was a nightmare. It was a damp, rainy day; the inside of the bus smelled like the locker room after a big game. A bleary-eyed man with three-days' stubble on his chin flopped down in the seat next to him, and Phillip reeled back in memory to the job he had held in his student days, cleaning vats in the brewery.

"It'sh a great morning," Bleary-eyes breathed at him. "Huh, Doc?"

Phillip blanched. To top it, the man had had a breakfast of salami. In the seat ahead, a fat gentleman held a dead cigar clamped in his mouth like a rank growth. Phillip's stomach began rolling; he sank his face into his hand, trying unobtrusively to clamp his nostrils. With a groan of deliverance, he lurched off the bus at the laboratory gate.

He met Jake Miles coming up the steps. Jake looked pale, too pale.

"Morning," Phillip said weakly. "Nice day. Looks like the sun might come through."

"Yeah," said Jake. "Nice day. You — uh — feel all right this morning?"

"Fine, fine." Phillip tossed his hat into the closet, opened the incubator on his culture tubes, trying to look busy. He slammed the door after one whiff and gripped the edge of the worktable with whitening knuckles. "Why do you ask?"

"Oh, nothing. Thought you looked a little peaked, was all."

They stared at each other in silence. Then, as though by signal, their eyes turned to the office at the end of the lab.

"Coffin come in yet?"

Jake nodded. "He's in there. He's got the door locked."

"I think he's going to have to open it," said Phillip.

A gray-faced Dr. Coffin unlocked the door, backed quickly toward the wall. The room reeked of kitchen deodorant.

"Stay right where you are," Coffin squeaked. "Don't come a step closer. I can't see you now. I'm — I'm busy. I've got work that has to be done — "

"You're telling *me,*" growled Phillip. He motioned Jake into the office and locked the door again carefully. Then he turned to Coffin. "When did it start for you?"

Coffin was trembling. "Right after supper last night. I thought I was going to suffocate. Got up and walked the streets all night. My God, what a stink!"

"Jake?"

Dr. Miles shook his head. "Sometime this morning. I woke up with it."

"That's when it hit me," said Phillip.

"But I don't understand," Coffin howled. "Nobody else seems to notice anything — "

"Yet," Phillip said. "We were the first three to take the Coffin Cure, remember? You and me and Jake. Two months ago."

Coffin's forehead was beaded with sweat. He stared at the two men in growing horror.

"But what about the others?"

"I think," said Phillip, "that we'd better find something spectacular to do in a mighty big hurry. That's what I think."

Jake Miles said, "The most important thing right now is secrecy. We mustn't let a word get out — not until we're absolutely certain."

"But what's *happened?*" Coffin cried. "These foul smells everywhere. You, Phillip — you had a cigarette this morning. I can smell it clear over here and it's burning my eyes. If I didn't know better, I'd swear neither of you had had a bath in a week. Every odor in town has suddenly turned foul — "

"*Magnified,* you mean," said Jake. "Perfume still smells sweet — there's just too much of it. The same with cinnamon; I tried it. Cried for half an hour, but it still smelled like cinnamon. No, I don't think the *smells* have changed any."

"But what then?"

"Our noses have changed, obviously." Jake paced the floor in excitement. "Look at our dogs. They've never had colds — and they practically live by their noses. Other animals — all dependent on their senses of smell for survival — and none of them ever have anything even vaguely reminiscent of a common cold. The multicentric virus hits primates only — *and it reaches its fullest parasitic powers in man alone!*"

Coffin shook his head miserably. "But why this horrible reek all of a sudden? I haven't had a cold in weeks — "

"Of course not! That's just what I'm saying," Jake persisted. "Look, why do we have any sense of smell at all? Because we have tiny olfactory nerve endings buried in the mucous membrane of our noses and throats. But we've always had the virus living there too, colds or no colds, throughout our entire lifetime. It's *always* been there, anchored in the same cells, parasitizing the same sensitive tissues that carry our olfactory nerve endings, numbing them and crippling them, making them practically useless as sensory organs. No wonder we never smelled anything before! Those poor little nerve endings never had a chance!"

"Until we came along and destroyed the virus," said Phillip.

"Oh, we didn't destroy it. We merely stripped it of a very slippery protective mechanism it had against normal body defenses." Jake perched on the edge of the desk, his dark face intense. "These two months since we had our shots have witnessed a battle to the death between our bodies and the virus. With the help of the vaccine, our bodies have won, that's all — stripped away the last strongholds of an invader that has been almost a part of our normal physiology since the beginning of primates. And now, for the first time, those crippled little nerve endings are just beginning to function."

Coffin groaned. "God help us. You think it'll get worse?"

"And worse. And still worse," said Jake.

"I wonder," said Phillip slowly, "what the anthropologists will say."

"What do you mean?"

"Maybe it was just a single mutation somewhere back in prehistory. Just a tiny change of metabolism that left one line of the primates vulnerable to an invader no other would harbor. Why else should man have begun to flower and blossom intellectually — grow to depend so much on his brains instead of his brawn that he could rise above all others? What better reason than because, somewhere along the line, *he suddenly lost his sense of smell?*"

"Well, he's got it back again now," Coffin said despairingly, "and he's not going to like it a bit."

"No, he surely isn't," Jake agreed. "He's going to start hunting very quickly for someone to blame, I think."

They both looked at Coffin.

"Now don't be ridiculous, boys," said Coffin, beginning to shake. "We're in this together. Phillip, it was your idea in the first place — you said so yourself! You can't leave me now — "

The telephone jangled. The frightened voice of the secretary bleated, "Dr. Coffin? There was a student on the line just a moment ago. He — he said he was coming up to see you. Now, he said, not later — "

"I'm busy," Coffin sputtered. "I can't see anyone. And I can't take any calls — "

"But he's already on his way up," the girl burst out. "He was saying something about tearing you apart with his bare hands."

Coffin slammed down the receiver. His face was the color of clay. "They'll crucify me! Jake — Phillip — you've got to help me!"

Phillip sighed and unlocked the door. "Send a girl down to the freezer and have her bring up all the live cold virus she can find. Get us some inoculated monkeys and a few dozen dogs." He turned to Coffin. "And stop sniveling. You're the big publicity man around here — you're going to handle the screaming masses, whether you like it or not."

"But what are you going to do?"

"I haven't the faintest idea," said Phillip, "but whatever I do is going to cost you your shirt. We're going to find out how to catch cold again if we have to die trying."

It was an admirable struggle, and a futile one. They sprayed their noses and throats with enough pure culture of virulent live virus to have condemned an ordinary man to a lifetime of sneezing, watery-eyed misery. They didn't develop a sniffle among them.

They mixed six different strains of virus and gargled the extract, spraying themselves and every inoculated monkey they could get their hands on with the vile-smelling stuff. Not a sneeze.

They injected it hypodermically, intradermally, subcutaneously, intramuscularly, and intravenously. They drank it. They bathed in it.

But they didn't catch a cold.

"Maybe it's the wrong approach," Jake said one morning. "Our body defenses are keyed up to top performance right now. Maybe if we break them down, we can get somewhere."

They plunged down that alley with grim abandon. They starved themselves. They forced themselves to stay awake for days on end, until exhaustion forced their eyes closed in spite of all they could do. They carefully devised vitamin-free, protein-free, mineral-free diets that tasted like library paste and smelled worse. They wore wet clothes and sopping shoes to work, turned off the heat and threw windows open to the raw winter air. Then they resprayed themselves with the live cold virus and waited prayerfully for the sneezing to begin.

It didn't. They stared at each other in gathering gloom. They'd never felt better in their lives.

Except for the smells, of course. They'd hoped that they might, presently, get used to them. They didn't. Every day it grew a little worse. They began smelling smells they never dreamed existed — noxious smells, cloying smells, smells that drove them gagging to the sinks. Their nose plugs were rapidly losing their effectiveness. Mealtimes were nightmarish ordeals; they lost weight with alarming speed.

But they didn't catch cold.

"*I* think you should all be locked up," Ellie Dawson said severely as she dragged her husband, blue-faced and shivering, out of an icy shower one bitter morning. "You've lost your wits. You need to be protected against yourselves, that's what you need."

"You don't understand," Phillip moaned. "We've *got* to catch cold."

Ellie snapped angrily, "Why? Suppose you don't — what's going to happen?"

"We had three hundred students march on the laboratory today," Phillip explained patiently. "The smells were driving them crazy, they said. They couldn't even bear to be close to their best friends. They wanted something done about it, or else they wanted blood. Tomorrow we'll have them back and three hundred more. And they were just the pilot study! What's going to happen when fifteen million people find their noses suddenly turning on them?"

He shuddered. "Have you seen the papers? People are already going around sniffing like bloodhounds. And *now* we're finding out what a thorough job we did. We can't crack it, Ellie. We can't even get a toehold. Those antibodies are just doing too good a job."

"Well, maybe you can find some unclebodies to take care of them," Ellie offered vaguely.

"Look, don't make bad jokes — "

"I'm not making jokes! I don't care *what* you do. All I want is a husband back who doesn't complain about how everything smells, and eats the dinners I cook, and doesn't stand around in cold showers at six in the morning."

"I know it's miserable," he said helplessly. "But I don't know how we can stop it."

He found Jake and Coffin in tight-lipped conference when he reached the lab.

"I can't do it anymore," Coffin was saying. "I've begged them for time. I've promised them everything but my upper plate. I can't face them again. I just can't."

"We only have a few days left," Jake said grimly. "If we don't come up with something, we're goners."

Phillip's jaw suddenly sagged as he stared at them. "You know what I think?" he asked suddenly. "I think we've been prize idiots. We've gotten so rattled, we haven't used our heads. And all the time it's been sitting there blinking at us!"

"What are you talking about?" snapped Jake.

"Unclebodies," said Phillip.

"Great God!"

"No, I'm dead serious." Phillip's eyes were very bright. "How many of those students do you think you can corral to help us?"

Coffin gulped. "Six hundred. They're out there in the street right now, a blood-seeking mob howling for a lynching."

"All right, I want them in here. And I want some monkeys. Monkeys with colds — the worse colds, the better."

"Do you have any idea what you're doing?" asked Jake.

"None in the least," said Phillip happily, "except that it's never been done before. But maybe it's time we tried following our noses for a while — "

The tidal wave began to break two days later . . . only a few people here, a dozen there, but enough to confirm the direst newspaper predictions. The boomerang was completing its circle.

At the laboratory, the doors were kept barred, the telephones disconnected. Within, there was a bustle of feverish — if odorous — activity. For the three researchers, the olfactory acuity had reached agonizing proportions. Even the small gas masks Phillip had devised could no longer shield them from the continuous barrage of violent odors.

But the work went on in spite of the smell. Truckloads of monkeys arrived at the lab — cold-ridden, sneezing, coughing, weeping, wheezing monkeys by the dozen. Culture trays bulged with tubes, overflowed the incubators and worktables. Each day six hundred angry students paraded through the lab, arms exposed, mouths open, grumbling but cooperating.

At the end of the first week, half the monkeys were cured of their colds and were unable to catch them back; the other half had new colds and couldn't get rid of them. Phillip observed this fact with grim satisfaction and went about the laboratory mumbling to himself.

Two days later, he burst forth jubilantly, lugging a sad-looking puppy under his arm. It was like no other puppy in the world. This one was sneezing and snuffling with a perfect howler of a cold.

The day came when they injected a tiny droplet of milky fluid beneath the skin of Phillip's arm and got the virus spray and gave his nose and throat a liberal application. Then they sat back and waited.

They were still waiting three days later.

"It was a great idea," Jake said morosely, flipping a bulging notebook closed with finality. "It just didn't work, was all."

"Where's Coffin?"

"He collapsed three days ago. Nervous prostration. He kept having dreams about hangings."

Phillip sighed. "Well, I suppose we'd better just face it. Nice knowing you, Jake. Pity it had to be this way."

"It was a great try, old man. A great try."

"Ah, yes. Nothing like going down in a blaze of — "

Phillip stopped dead, his eyes widening. His nose began to twitch. He took a gasp, a larger gasp, as a long-dead reflex came sleepily to life, shook its head, reared back . . .

Phillip sneezed.

He sneezed for ten minutes without a pause, until he was blue-faced and gasping for air. He caught hold of Jake, wringing his hand as tears gushed from his eyes.

"It was a sibple edough pridciple," he said later to Ellie as she spread mustard on his chest and poured more warm water into his foot bath. "The Cure itself depedded upod it — the adtiged-adtibody reactiod. We had the adtibody agaidst the virus, all ridght; what we had to find was sobe kide of adtibody *agaidst* the adtibody." He sneezed violently and poured in nose drops with a happy grin.

"Will they be able to make it fast enough?"

"Just aboudt fast edough for people to get good ad eager to catch cold agaid," said Phillip. "There's odly wud little hitch . . ."

Ellie Dawson took the steaks from the grill and set them, still sizzling, on the dinner table.

"Hitch?" she said.

Phillip nodded as he chewed the steak with a pretense of enthusiasm. It tasted like slightly damp K-ration.

"This stuff we've bade does a real good job. Just a little too good." He wiped his nose and reached for a fresh tissue.

"I bay be wrog, but I thik I've got this cold for keeps," he said sadly. "Udless I cad fide ad adtibody agaidst the adtibody agaidst the adtibody — "

Silenzia

ALAN NELSON

Our apartment affords us a magnificent view of all of Central Park. We watch the changing of the seasons; we see the strollers and joggers and ballplayers and kite-flyers and the automobile ballet and, on special occasions, the marathon runners. But there's a catch. If the weather permits, and frequently when it shouldn't, there's something called "music" for something called "people." I used quotation marks for both words because I cannot believe that real people mistake the sound for real music. To hide the false notes, gravel voices, and amateur talent, this "music" is amplified — and, it seems, aimed directly at our apartment. Since the law unaccountably forbids us a rifle with a telescopic sight aimed at the loudspeakers, we need — we want Silenzia. So where is it?

A T   F I R S T, I wasn't permitted to relate the story of Silenzia at all, in any form, to any person. Now, however, I have convinced the Society that no harm will come of it. People eventually will hear about Silenzia; certainly the authorized version, with names and places disguised, is better than wild stories . . .

It started the day I decided to leave Edith. She didn't know it, of course — didn't even suspect it. But I was through.

She was a good wife, I guess, but the sounds she made! I just couldn't stand them: the harangues about my being nothing more than a shorthand teacher in a business school; the shrill laugh which was a noise like someone with long fingernails slipping off a tin roof; the constant piano playing, grim and vigorous, as though she were hacking her way through a jungle with a dull knife; the hollow *scru-r-unch-scrunch* as she scratched her haunches just before getting into bed at night.

There was a little cabin in the Siskiyou mountains, a job in a service station nearby, chipmunks for companions.

Then I found Silenzia — beautiful, wonderful Silenzia. It was in the back room at Ziggert's, a little pawn shop off Third Street, while I was looking at trunks. I reached into the bottom of an old iron-bound model and came up with an Air Wick bottle lying under some old rags. An Air Wick bottle, yes, but filled with something very special indeed — a milky, opalescent fluid boiling ever so gently around some coiled copper wires.

I unscrewed the lid, lifted the wick. Immediately I was surrounded with a glorious silence. The street noises, the twang of Ziggert's sales talk up front, the plink-plink of a customer testing a banjo — these sounds all disappeared completely. I pushed the wick back into the bottle. The noises returned.

Blinking, I looked at the label on the bottle. In red pencil someone had scrawled *Silenzia* over the Air Wick label. Could it possibly be, I wondered, that someone has invented a Sound Wick, and that it does to unpleasant noises what an Air Wick does to unpleasant odors?

Excitedly, I screwed the lid on, put the bottle in my vest pocket, paid Ziggert for the trunk, and left.

I walked all the way home through the five o'clock traffic with Silenzia's wick extended and I was covered with a glorious tent of silence. Epileptic juke boxes, sirens, clanging signal lights, froggy howls of news vendors — Silenzia blotted them all out for me completely.

It was as I fumbled with my front door key that I first encountered the squat man with the anxious face and the gray homburg. He'd been puffing up the hill behind me, and now he tipped his hat and said breathlessly, "I beg your pardon, sir. My name is Emmett Dugong. It is important that I talk with you."

I was too excited to bother with peddlers and I brushed by him and went inside.

We lived in a three-story Telegraph Hill flat — a wooden soundbox — chosen by Edith for its Bohemian atmosphere which, unfortunately, crowded us closely from all sides. On our left was a xylophone player with strong wrists and a perfectionist complex who had been learning "Anitra's Dance" for seven months; on the other side, a retired cabinetmaker had for three years been constructing something that required sledge hammers and an electric sanding machine; above, an insecure teenager was well along with a correspondence course in weightlifting; and directly below was a Mr. Snitling, forever trying to hush them all up by pounding on his ceiling with a broomstick.

My long fight with them had been a losing one. Maybe now things would be different; for today, with Silenzia, I didn't hear a thing.

I could hardly wait to try it on Edith and for fifteen minutes sat impatiently in the kitchen playing with the noises, tuning them in and out at whatever volume I fancied by pulling the wick in and out.

Finally over my shoulder I saw she'd arrived and was standing in the doorway taking off her hat. In silence I watched her lips bouncing off each other, arms gesticulating in seven directions, tiny facial muscles twitching — Edith was talking.

A powerful instinct warned me it would never do to let Edith know about

Silenzia; unobtrusively I folded my coat over the vest pocket where the Sound Wick rested and pretended to understand what she was saying.

Ever watch someone speak without hearing what's being said? It's like listening through a plate-glass window and can be a very pleasant sensation indeed. How well I could imagine the gist of her monologue: the detailed description of her afternoon ceramics class; what she told the grocery man when he tried to overcharge her; the 2000-word exposition on how I was wasting my life at Modern Business College. As if I enjoyed working for the bald and lipless Amos C. Schmuckbinder and his pimply faced student body!

When Edith's lips finally slowed down I wondered suddenly if my voice would reach out through the cushion of silence — whether Silenzia was unidirectional.

"Why don't you play the piano for me?" I asked.

She looked at me suspiciously, led me into the front room, and began playing, attacking the keys like a clever welterweight warming up on a punching bag. Stretched out in an armchair, I watched the performance with complete enjoyment.

"I don't think you're putting enough into your left," I said at the end of her first selection. She looked disconcerted and on the second opus almost sprained her wrist. I requested — I insisted on! — another selection, then two more, and finally after still another she was too exhausted to continue.

Dinner that night was a charming little affair; I didn't tune Edith completely out, just down low enough to catch the general drift of the conversation. How pleasant to sit there like that in the cool spring silence! How enchanting to make up my own words to fit those tireless lips moving with such fierce energy across the table from me!

I think the weeks that followed were the most satisfying of my life. Sometimes at night I'd wander through the city — the brilliant, mute city — gazing at the swarms of people and cars moving through hushed streets in soundless, swirling patterns, a fantastic ballet without music, and I'd wonder how I'd ever done without Silenzia. Sweet Silenzia . . .

Why, you may ask, if I was so sensitive to noise, didn't I puncture my eardrums long ago and be done with it? The answer is simple, of course. There were still a few things in the world very much worth listening to: the sound of oars in the water, the pop of sparkling burgundy corks, the Beethoven concertos, the sound of bacon sizzling . . .

Sometimes I wondered vaguely if all the world's troubles were not simply noises, and that all the bloody explosions which forever rocked the world — the blasts of field artillery and atom bombs — were they not simply the accumulated sounds of a thousand petty bickerings, snotty words, and ponderous speeches from balconies, all gathered throughout the years, compressed into a single instant and detonated with a thunder that never quite died out?

Even Edith seemed different to me now. At times, sitting across the table from her, when I had her turned down low, I'd gaze at her as I did in the days long ago — at the soft brown hair, at the smile that used to make my heart jump so, and I'd tell myself possibly I wouldn't have to retreat to the mountain cabin after all.

I guess it was inevitable. I guess it happens to anyone who has too much of any one thing: power, money, silence. I became cocky, arrogant. I was like a man with a new rifle who cannot rest until he has used it — proved it on tin cans, rabbits, even human beings. I started gunning for noises, and the act of blotting them up, of *unhearing* them, as it were, gave me a glorious feeling of triumph.

I took to standing my ground as Buick convertibles tried to blast me off the pavement with prolonged explosions of their triple-tone horns.

At school I took to such petty practices as baiting my boss, Schmuckbinder, a man who loved to make speeches more than he liked to eat. I was the tortured soul upon whom he rehearsed these evil recitations.

"Hilkey, I'm guest speaker at the Rotary Friday night," he'd say, trapping me in his office. "You don't mind checking me on this for time, do you?"

Then without waiting for an answer, he'd strike out, and his words were sad and soggy, like an endless string of sour dumplings slogging down a rusty kitchen drain.

Now it was different. Now I egged him on, found ways to make him repeat each speech four times, five times, even more, until his voice croaked, until the saliva turned to glue in his mouth, while I, cozy in an armchair, focused my eyes on the YWCA across the street where there were always a number of interesting sunbathers lolling on the roof top.

I even took to using Silenzia on Miss McKenzie, a student in my intermediate stenography class, a depressingly competent girl, robust and eager, with heavy glasses and loose guitar strings for vocal chords, a girl who was forever twanging away at me over some technicality or other, raising impossible questions, starting arguments I could never hope to win because of my short temper.

"I don't know why I shouldn't have a higher grade on this," she whined one day, handing me the previous day's shorthand speed test I'd just returned.

"I'll tell you why," I answered, glancing at the page of dashes, curlicues, and looping symbols. "Allow me to read what you have written here, Miss McKenzie. According to your shorthand symbols the following is a literal translation:

Dear Sirs:

Your letter of the 25th has been regloofered and in simping we wish to stoot that all our preefgers and boxes of bim sergles have been exhorted. However, may we steet that notwinching, the clergs and shermgaroofles, eeble crates and zimpuggle oorflumit if bill of lading.

Sincerely,

Then I turned the Sound Wick up high and let her talk. Finally when I saw her lips stop I said, "You're absolutely reemsly."

Then I placed the paper back into her limp hand and went out humming.

That's the way it started, and from then on, there was no holding me back. Edith loved loud, gay things — by God I'd give them to her! Eagerly I attended all the screwy social functions she was so fond of, dug up a few of my own. We spent a great deal of time at civic improvement lectures, benefit teas for indigent young poets, the Schmuckbinder Optimist Club lecture series. I dragged her to bowling alleys, high school commencement exercises, political rallies, amateur string quartet groups.

No longer was I the mild, soft-spoken man shrinking in the corner. Wherever there was noise, I was in the middle of it, adding to it with wild abandon, sopping it all up with Silenzia.

It was at one of these many affairs — a cocktail party, I think — that I encountered the man in the gray homburg once more. Vaguely I remembered seeing him at some of the other affairs too.

"My name is Emmett Dugong," he began. "It is important that I talk with you."

The wick was only partially extended; I could just barely hear him. I was half drunk. He looked like a bore. I didn't feel like talking about anything important. Unobtrusively, I pulled the wick out all the way, waited patiently for him to finish — raising my eyebrows every now and then to show I was listening — then drained my glass and left him.

Then one afternoon I came home to find Edith packing.

"Where are you going?" I asked, pushing Silenzia's wick in so I could hear.

"I'm leaving you, Matt," she replied, grimly.

Well, that gave me a start. I'd grown used to Edith these past few weeks of silence; as long as I kept her turned off, I figured we might even make a go of it.

"But why, Edith?"

She had a great deal to say on that. Briefly, it was a matter of sound: the noises I made, my loud voice, my shrill laugh. I'd changed these past weeks, and all that. There was a little cabin in the mountains somewhere, a job in a restaurant nearby. She was getting out.

I decided the time had come to tell her about Silenzia. Reluctantly I launched into it, but instead of placating her, my words of explanation only enraged her.

"You mean you haven't heard a word I've said this past month?" she shrilled.

Edith's words scraped unpleasantly against my nerve endings — I'd almost forgotten how much her voice reminded me of someone chewing on steel wool. Any tenderness I had been building up toward her began to evaporate.

"If you promise to get rid of that obscene little gadget," Edith was saying, "I may change my mind about leaving. But it's either that . . . that bottle, or me. You'll just have to make your choice."

Well, after Edith moved out, I went to work on the neighbors. I brought home a set of drums, a couple of tuba players. I learned to accompany the xylophone player in "Anitra's Dance" with a ship's siren.

Then after *they* moved out I began thinking of bigger things. The idea of manufacturing Sound Wicks for general distribution had occurred to me before, of course — the demand from baby sitters and music lovers alone would be tremendous. But until now, I had always revolted against commercializing. Silenzia was essentially a *secret* instrument. Mass production would be fatal for Sound Wicks. Radio advertisers, speechmakers, horn manufacturers, and every other noisemonger in the world would soon find a way to counteract Silenzia's effectiveness; somehow they'd break through, and lovers of quiet would have at best only a few months' respite before Sound Wicks were as dated as sachet bags.

The first man to put it on the market would, of course, make a million dollars. But why *hadn't* it been put on the market? Suppose someone were to beat me to it?

That decided me. I might be selling Silenzia down the river, but I could certainly buy a lot of peace and quiet with a million dollars.

I held Silenzia up and gazed at the bottle affectionately. Suddenly I frowned and examined it closer. Was it my imagination or had the bottle been getting warmer these past few days? And the milky fluid, was it boiling just a trifle harder? I shrugged — possibly I'd been overworking her a bit. Well, if I were going to be a Sound Wick tycoon, I'd better get started. The man to see was Charlie Mook, president of Engineers Associates — he'd get the contents of the bottle analyzed for me.

I put my hat on and started out the door, then stopped short. Across the street, waiting patiently, was the squat man with the gray homburg. Damned little guy was beginning to get on my nerves. I didn't have time to talk to him now. I came inside, left through the rear door.

C. J. Mook was a tall, thin man who seldom spoke and then without moving a muscle in his face. His trousers bagged at the knees so badly that whenever he stood, he appeared always on the verge of a tremendous leap.

I told him my story and allowed him to examine Silenzia. He sat there a few minutes playing with the noises and getting very excited over it; one corner of his mouth twitched and a single bead of perspiration appeared on his left eyebrow. He didn't want to analyze it; he wanted to buy it.

"Give you one-hundred thousand dollars for it. As is," he said, drawing out a check book. "Two-hundred thousand dollars then."

I laughed at him.

"Look, man!" he cried. "I want it for myself. I've got four kids ages two to eleven. They have toys. They listen to radio programs. They have friends who play at my house. Besides, there's an Irish tenor right across the hall. Doesn't that mean anything to you?"

I laughed it off again.

Well, it finally turned out I couldn't have it analyzed right then; their head research engineer was away for a week and Mook begged me to leave the Sound Wick until he got back. He'd take such excellent care of it! Once more I laughed at him. I'd return in a week; meantime I had factory sites to look for.

I sauntered home that afternoon with my feet scarcely touching the pavement. What a wonderful world! What a wonderful Sound Wick! Nothing could happen now to spoil my happiness. Nothing!

But something *did* happen. It was a shot, and the slug bit into the brick building beside me, kicking up a small spray of red dust just six inches from my head. I ducked, looked around wildly — just in time to see a squat figure in a gray homburg scuttle around the far corner.

When I reached home my nerves were thoroughly unstrung. Who *was* the little man who'd been following me around, and why should he want to kill me now? If only I'd listened to him before. For almost an hour I paced the floor trying to figure it out.

Then I felt a warmth against my chest. I removed Silenzia, looked at her, and was seized by a new fear. Something was very *definitely* wrong with Silenzia. She was badly overheated, there was a perceptible buzzing, and when I unscrewed the cap a slight hiss leaked out as though some kind of internal pressure were building up.

I had never stopped to consider what happened to all the noises Silenzia swallowed — could it be there was a saturation point?

The next two days were completely miserable ones. First I was still edgy about the shot, and second I was really concerned about Silenzia's condition. Now she seemed better, now worse. Thinking perhaps rest was what she needed I left her at home all day now, wrapped in cold cloths in a dark and silent closet.

Even aside from these worries, I was completely lost without the little bottle; for Silenzia was like alcohol or opium: You used it all the time or not at all, and now my nerve endings felt raw and peeled back and the slightest sound made me jump.

It was at dusk on the third evening that another attempt was made on my life. I had just stepped off the curb at Stockton and Greenwich when a large black sedan swerved out of nowhere, bore down on me with tires screaming. The fender just grazed my trousers as I lunged for safety. From the pavement where I lay I caught sight of the driver as he careened around the corner — he wore a gray homburg.

I was still shaking when I climbed the two flights of stairs. My mind was made up: I'd sell Silenzia to Charlie Mook for $200,000, and get out of the city for a while.

I reached into the closet and brought the Sound Wick into the kitchen. Now I was *really* alarmed. The bubbling and sizzling were louder, more ominous, a slimy froth dribbled out from the edges of the cap, and the bottle was almost too hot to hold. I scurried for ice cubes, got blankets to protect her from stray street noises, loosened the cap to allow pressure to escape. An ugly rumble erupted as I unscrewed it. Tiny jets of fluid spat upward.

It was at this point the accordionist started. He was a new neighbor, and he went from "Over the Waves" to "La Paloma" and back again with a piercing whine that raised the hackles on my neck. With each squeaky blast, Silenzia sputtered more desperately.

I guess I lost my head. I rushed across the hall, pounded on the man's door, demanded he stop playing instantly. We had a terrible argument — shouts, threats — and by the time I got him hushed up and had returned to my apartment, I heard something that chilled me to the bone.

"... *why can't you make something of yourself!*" Edith's voice coasted out of the kitchen at me, tinny and distorted like an old phonograph record. "*You're just wasting yourself working for Amos Schmuckbinder . . .*"

I rushed into the room. There was no one there. No one.

"*Scru-r-unch-scrunch.*" I looked at the Sound Wick on the table. Could it possibly be?

"*Get off the street you damned jaywalker!*" the bottle shrieked at me. There was a screech of brakes, a claxon horn, the ping of signal lights, a clashing of gears. Another voice faded in — Schmuckbinder's:

"*... it is a signal honor to be with this distinguished group this evening, paying tribute to the ideals, the dreams, and hopes of. . .*"

"*Scru-r-unch-scrunch . . .*"

"*You take the whites of two eggs, mix them with . . .*"

Horrified I seized the cap and tried to screw it back on the stricken bottle. Some of the hot liquid spurted out and landed on my coat. An ugly burble of sound oozed out of the spot on my sleeve.

"*... and in simping we wish to stoot that all our preefgers and . . .*"

With brute strength I forced the cap back on. The noise was muffled but still leaked out. But I couldn't keep the cap on; the whole interior of the bottle churned more violently than ever, and the wick swelled and thrashed like a strangulated tongue. Once more I removed the cap.

The tinny notes of "Anitra's Dance" roared out, along with the sound of billing machines and typewriters which buzzed and clacked like a closet full of insane geese. Most revolting of all was the intermittent blare of my own voice — a silly, high-pitched sound, squeaky and insistent.

I simply couldn't stand another minute of it. I looked around wildly for my hat.

"*. . . you mean you haven't heard a word I've said this past month?*" Edith's voice leapt out at me as I closed the front door.

On the first landing I pulled up short. Directly across the street, in the shadows of a deserted alley glowed a single cigarette. Gray Homburg again! Waiting for me. I returned to the bedlam inside, grabbed the phone, and dialed Charlie Mook's number.

"Where in thunder are you calling from?" he demanded. "Sounds like the middle of Times Square."

"It's Silenzia," I shouted. "She's vomiting up every noise she ever swallowed."

Charlie listened to the racket a moment.

"You've evidently overworked it," he finally stuttered. "Just keep cool."

"Cool!" I screamed. "This could keep up another month or so. And when I try to put the cap on, it looks like it's about to explode. I'm going to throw it out the window."

"Don't do that!" he implored.

"Well, do something then!"

He thought a moment.

"Look," he said, "get your car. Pick me up in ten minutes. Bring the Sound Wick. We'll take it down to the lab. Maybe we can figure something out."

He hung up. I hesitated a moment, thinking about Gray Homburg. Maybe I could sneak out the back again.

"*. . . you get rid of that obscene little gadget immediately . . .*" Edith's voice shrieked as I crept down the back stairs in utter blackness.

"*Scru-r-unch-scrunch . . .*" as I pushed open the rear door.

"*Mr. Chairman, Mr. Principal, members of the graduating class, parents, teachers, friends, and fellow students . . .*" an adolescent voice whined as I crept across the backyard.

"*I'LLLLL taaaaake yeeeou HOME again, Kaaaaathleeeeen . . .*" came an Irish tenor as I climbed the back fence.

In the car I just had to force the cap back on Silenzia — a cocktail party was coming on the air and Gray Homburg would be able to follow that sound three blocks. Then I laid the bottle on the seat beside me, stepped on the starter, and roared away.

I looked in the rearview mirror. Another car, large and black, pulled out from the curb. I turned the corner at Grant. The car turned. After two more blocks, there was no doubt of it — I was being followed.

How long I dodged and turned through the night streets, I'll never know. I remember that at last I found myself on a lonely mountain road which bordered the ocean. I remember only my deep despair, which grew deeper with every passing second. I was frightened, yes. Frightened of the man relentlessly following me. Frightened of the bottle which verged on explosion at any moment. But above all was the terrifying prospect of life without Silenzia.

I wouldn't have her much longer. There was no doubt about that. Charlie couldn't help her. No one could. She was too far gone. Bitterly I heaped curses on myself for squandering Silenzia the way I had, frittering her life away on xylophones and cocktail parties.

I glanced down. Silenzia was so hot the seat cover was beginning to smolder. An evil phosphorescent glow flickered inside. The metal cap bulged with the ever-increasing internal pressure. A low ominous growl fairly shook the whole bottle.

It was only a matter of seconds, now, I knew, before the whole thing went up. Quickly I pulled to the side of the road, removed my coat, wrapped Silenzia in it, gingerly carried it across the road to the cliff's edge, which dropped away a hundred feet to the ocean below. From within the throbbing bottle, a muffled, distorted voice oozed out. I held it closer to my ear:

"... *my name is Emmett Dugong ... important that I talk to you ...*"

It was the voice of the man in the gray homburg. A convulsive shudder passed through the bottle. Unless I tossed the thing off the cliff this very moment, I would be blown to bits — yet I had to listen.

"... *must return the Sound Wick to me, sir ... No other way, sir. You'll never be able to retain it, sir. Never ... We will go to any lengths to keep it from ...*"

A hideous gurgling drowned out his voice a moment. The heat from the bottle singed my hair as I drew closer. The voice returned:

"... *actually belongs to the Society ... have commissioned me to track the lost instrument ... I had traced it to the pawn shop before you stumbled on it ... must be returned ...*"

I couldn't hold on to the thing any longer. My coat was beginning to smolder. Once more I leaned over the guard rail to drop it. Once more I hesitated.

"... *simply cannot allow a single Sound Wick to fall into the hands of anyone outside the Society ... danger of misuse ... danger of commercialization ... danger of ... danger ...*"

The bottle gave a convulsive jerk. My smoldering coat leapt into flames. I dropped the bottle. There was a moment of dead silence as it plunged downward.

Then came the explosion.

Is it possible to imagine a blast that rips the air apart with whistles, barking dogs, taxi horns, clinking glasses, sirens, alarm clocks, and the roar of a thousand laughing, shouting, mumbling voices? That is what it was. And even after the echo of it died away, I leaned numbly at the rail, staring down into blackness, weary and sick at heart.

Finally I tore myself away and turned. A short, squat man blocked my path — a man in a gray homburg.

"My name is Emmett Dugong," he said. "It is important that I talk with you."

There is little more I am permitted to say about Sound Wicks at the moment, except that my anguish at losing Silenzia has been tempered with the knowledge it was not the only one in existence — there are one thousand eight hundred and seventy-six to be exact, all issued and controlled by the International Silence Lovers Society.

But I *must* not say more; my probationary membership is on a shaky enough basis as it is. In another three years, after the complete indoctrination and instruction period, if things go well, I should be a full-fledged member with a registered Sound Wick assigned to my exclusive use.

How can you too obtain membership? Unfortunately I am not permitted to answer that either. No society was ever more exclusive, more dedicated to the protection of silence. No society ever culled its prospective members more carefully, guarded its device more fanatically. I, of course, was forced upon them — they had to take me. I am still watched, naturally, by a man with a gray homburg and anxious face, and I should be killed in cold blood were I again to attempt the commercialization of Sound Wicks.

No, I cannot tell you how to join. If you're lucky, you will be approached. Watch for a happy-looking man, a man with a slight bulge in his vest pocket, a man who sometimes hears what you say and sometimes doesn't. Watch for a silent man . . .

The Agony of Defeat

JACK C. HALDEMAN II

A number of years ago, someone in a crowd said conversationally, "Well, I see Joe Namath will be playing football again next season."

A young innocent piped up and said, "Who's Joe Namath?"

That's hard to top, but I managed, for I followed instantly with, ". . . and what on Earth is football?"

But you'll be asking the same question in a moment.

ALBERT HUFF couldn't stand losers. Every player on his team knew that only too well. It was a fact for sure. Big Al ran the Castroville Artichokes with an iron hand and a terrible temper. He didn't get where he was by being Mr. Nice Guy, no indeed. Even the defensive line trembled when he walked by, although each of them was three times as large as Al and strong as an ox.

Matter of fact, they *were* part ox.

Genetic engineering sure spiced up the game. It also made for a powerhouse team, and their opponents, the Daytona Beach Armadillos, being mere robots, were running scared.

Big Al wanted this one. He wanted it bad.

It was billed as the game of the century. Of course every Superbowl was called the game of the century, but that didn't matter much. This was it — the *big* one, the whole ball of wax. Bulldog Turner Memorial Stadium was filled to overflowing, a sellout crowd. Scalpers got fifty bucks for crummy end-zone seats. Anything near midfield was simply unobtainable at any price.

It was a glorious day for football.

Cashing in on some of the glory was the Hawk, interviewer *extraordinaire* and nosy S.O.B. *par excellence.* He was down on the field finishing his pregame show by throwing loaded questions at Bronco, the Armadillos' star quarterback. Bronco was a crackerjack passer and a third generation Mark IV robot, sports model. He was also a nice guy.

The Hawk wasn't.

"Tell me, Bronco, how does it feel to know that you're going to get clobbered by eight hundred pounds of pure muscle? The Artichokes led the league in quarterback sacks, you know."

"Well, Mr. Hawkline — "

"Just call me Hawk." He poked the mike closer to Bronco and turned a little so that his best side would be facing the camera.

"Well, Mr. Hawk, those are the risks, part of the game. But I wouldn't be honest if I didn't admit that I'm a little nervous. Nobody likes to get hurt, not even a robot."

"You mean you can feel pain?"

"Of course. I've got a program for it buried in my chest right next to the one I use for my shaving commercials. Robots hurt just like everyone else. I've seen my share of pain. I wouldn't be human if I hadn't."

"What about the scandals?" pressed the Hawk. "The illegal will-to-win circuits?"

Bronco blushed. He had a program for that too.

"If you don't mind, Mr. Hawk, I'd rather not get into that." Poor Gipley Feedback. His heart had been in the right place even if his head hadn't. He was doing five to ten at the state prison. Poor guy had tampered with the system in order to restore the glory of football and now he was paying the price. Bronco hoped they'd let him watch the game.

"I'll bet you wouldn't," said the Hawk. "But the public has a right to know, and we'll get to the bottom of this even if — "

"Up to your old tricks, eh, Hawk?" It was Big Al, cutting across the field with Moog and Quark, halfbacks for the Artichokes. Not only were the two players part ox, they were part gazelle too. They looked funny, but they sure could run.

"What's this I hear about you selling your team by the pound if they lose today?" countered the Hawk.

"Your nose is out of joint, Hawk."

The Hawk's nose was a sore point with him, being of the wooden variety. His natural-born nose had been bitten off by an Arcturian. It hadn't exactly been the Hawk's finest moment, but it had saved the day for Earth.

Big Al was one of the few who could get Hawk's goat.

"Would you like to explain to our viewers, Mr. Huff, how you think you can get away by playing with a genetically engineered squad when the rules clearly state that football is too dangerous to be played by humans?"

"Come on, Hawk, get off it. You know as well as I do that these guys ain't hardly human. Wouldn't take a court to figure that out. How 'bout it, Moog, you human?"

"Irg."

"Quark? How 'bout you?"

"Mug mug."

"See?" said Big Al. "Dumb as rocks. Added together they couldn't scrape up twelve points on an IQ test, not even on a good day. They may not be smart, but they can play football."

"But — " A tuba knocked the Hawk flat on his back. The band was coming on the field from the sidelines. A clarinet stepped on his hand.

"That's the latest from down here," he said, getting to his feet and trying to make his way through the percussion section. "Now back to the booth and Roger Trent." He stepped on an armadillo. Seemed to be thousands of them on the field.

There were only a couple hundred, actually.

From the opening kickoff it was obvious that the Armadillos were in trouble, big trouble. The Artichokes' front line was as tough as a brick wall and just as impenetrable. It was rumored that they were part cinderblock, but that had never been proved.

It was 21 to 3 when the second quarter opened. Castroville was threatening to run away with the game.

Roger Trent sat in the broadcast booth with the Hawk, shaking his head. He was an Armadillo rooter from way back and it didn't look like it was going to be his day. He suspected the Hawk would like to see both teams lose.

As humans go, Roger was old, really old. He had been a superstar for the Baltimore Colts back in the days when flesh-and-blood people were still allowed to play the game. He kept trim and youthful because he had a lot of money, more than enough for rejuvenation treatments. The money came from a film based on a book he had written about his days as the last human quarterback in a field being taken over by robots. The book was called *Hell's Alley,* and it was about football, but when the movie finally came out it had a different title and was full of monsters.

"Second and five. Bronco takes the ball and hands off to Woods." Roger Trent called the plays, and the Hawk provided the color and irritating remarks. "He tries to find a hole up the middle and is smothered by a pile of Artichokes."

"Gonna be a bad day for Woods," said the Hawk. "He averaged four point three seven yards a carry for the year, but he won't be able to get near that today. That line is tough. They wouldn't let their own mothers through."

Their mothers were test tubes, thought Trent, but he didn't say it out loud because it might get the Hawk mad. He wanted all the best lines for himself. Best lines were probably part of the Hawk's contract.

"Third and long," he said instead. "Bronco's going back for the bomb. He's trapped. He's down."

The Hawk had missed the play. He had his nose in a thick book.

"Woods is a third-year veteran with the Armadillos. Prior to that, he played two years with the Key West Jellyfish."

"They're going into punt formation. Devin gets a good one away, taken on the ten by Garth for Castroville."

"During the off season, Woods sells insurance and plays flamenco guitar at an Italian restaurant."

". . . brings it out to the thirty before he's brought down."

"Who was that?" asked the Hawk, looking up from his book.

"Garth," sighed Trent.

"Seventh in the league in punt returns last year," said the Hawk, leafing quickly through the book. "Averaged thirty-two point seven three yards per return. Garth is ten percent cheetah. You can tell by his whiskers and the way he growls when the ball is snapped. In his career he has run seven punts back for touchdowns, although two were called back when the films showed he had bitten a potential tackler. Only last year against Philadelphia, as I recombulate my memory, he . . ."

The Hawk talked through three straight plays. He did that a lot.

"I like your nose," said Trent in exasperation.

"Sit on it, Roger."

The Hawk was hitting his stride.

Unfortunately, the Armadillos weren't hitting theirs. By the half they were down by two touchdowns. It was only by frantic heroics that the point spread wasn't more than that. They were getting clobbered.

The halftime show was a double-barreled extravaganza, even bigger and better than last year's double-barreled extravaganza. It was dutifully ignored by the spectators who spent the time crowding around beer stands and jamming into rest rooms. The players spent the halftime getting patched up and reprogrammed for the second half. The Hawk spent the halftime trying unsuccessfully to sneak into the dressing rooms. He had to be satisfied by interviewing a man dressed in an artichoke costume who was about to dive from a fifty-foot ladder into eighteen inches of melted lemon butter. The dive was a success, but the interview was a flop. The Hawk liked his artichokes with hollandaise sauce, not lemon butter, and his prejudice showed.

The second half unrolled like a carbon copy of the first. Casualties mounted for the Armadillos as they tried to bring down the mighty Artichokes. Woods went out of the game with a dislocated circuit board. Bounds was on the bench with every fuse in his chest blown. Pope's arm kept falling off.

In their huddles, the Artichokes congratulated themselves, patting each other on the back and picking small bugs from their partners' mangy pelts. They had everything under control and they knew it. They hooted a lot.

Only with extreme effort did the Armadillos manage to keep the margin of defeat down to two touchdowns. They were playing their hearts out, just managing to hang on. It was a pitiful sight as one by one they were hauled off the field on stretchers, tears welling up in their optical scanning devices.

They wanted to win this one, win it for the memory of dear old Gipley. It would take a miracle.

The miracle got a nudge just as the two-minute warning was flashed. Someone unlocked the cage that held the Daytona Beach mascots. Two hundred armadillos scuttled onto the field. It was in the middle of a play and confused things a lot. The Castroville Artichokes, not being very bright, mistook the armadillos for loose footballs and pounced on them. Taking advantage of the chaos, Bronco tossed a long bomb to Tucker in the end zone. The Artichokes protested, but there was nothing in the rule books against armadillos on the playing field. Castroville tried to get revenge by rolling artichokes around at the line of scrimmage, but nobody would confuse an artichoke with a football, not even a robot. The kick was good, and Daytona Beach trailed by seven points. But with a minute and a half left in the game, all Castroville had to do was take the kickoff and sit on it, letting the clock run out.

Devin's kick was deep and taken in the end zone by Glunk for Castroville. He elected to run it out in order to use up more time. It was a mistake. Heading toward him with murder in his electronic eye was Wild Bill. As dedicated as any robot on the squad, Wild Bill had fury in his plutonium heart. He wanted the ball. They collided on the twenty with a crunch heard all the way to Rockville.

Glunk went down, hard. Wild Bill disintegrated in a shower of cogs and levers. The ball was loose, bouncing end over end. There was a frantic scramble for the ball, but when the dust cleared it was Rusty who came up with the pigskin for Daytona Beach. The crowd went wild. The Armadillos had been four-touchdown underdogs. Too bad there wasn't enough left of Wild Bill to share in the excitement. He had given his all.

Two plays later, Bronco ran the ball across the end zone on a perfectly executed quarterback sneak just as the final gun sounded. All that remained was the kick for the extra point. But Bronco was worried. That would just tie the game and they'd have to go into a sudden-death overtime. Castroville had never lost a sudden death. They'd be murder. They might even block the kick. As they went into the huddle he decided it was all or nothing. They'd go for the two point conversion.

"They're lining up in kicking formation," said Roger Trent from the booth. "The ball is snapped. Wait! It's a fake. They're going for two. Bronco has the ball, he's moving fast. It's a reverse. No, a *double* reverse. He's going back to pass. *Look at that!* The old Statue of Liberty play. Carter takes the ball from Bronco. He's going around the left side of the line. The Artichokes seem confused."

"*I'm* confused," said the Hawk.

"He's in! They've done it. The Daytona Beach Armadillos have snatched victory from the jaws of defeat."

"The Statue of Liberty play went out with spats," grumped the Hawk.

Bronco was flat on his back. He'd been hit hard. With tremendous effort he raised himself up far enough to look over the three sides of beef that had clobbered him to see Carter go in for the big one. He smiled. Victory was sweet.

Big Al was furious. He flattened his quarterback with one punch. The loss would cost him his job. He beat his tailback silly. He kicked the bench over.

The Hawk was down on the field, trying to grab an interview. The only person he could get close to was Big Al. Everyone with any sense at all was staying well away from him.

"Well, Huff," said the Hawk, jamming a microphone into Big Al's nose. "How does the bitter taste of defeat go down?"

Big Al took one look at the Hawk and there was nothing but raging fury in his eyes. He bit off one of the Hawk's ears. The left one.

Not again, thought the Hawk. *Why me?*

Big Al's mind had snapped at last.

"Not bad," he said, chewing away.

"Could use a little lemon butter," he added, loyal to the end.

Epitaph on Ceres

SHERWOOD SPRINGER

Here lies the body of Black McGinnity,
Freebooting pirate from out of the void,
Slain by an Amazon empress the minute he
Tried to lay hands on her asteroid.

Epitaph on Rigel XII

SHERWOOD SPRINGER

Here lies the body of Zebulon Shore
Whose mutinous conduct we cannot defend.
He laughed off orders when told to explore
The Horse-Head Nebula's opposite end.

The Snowball Effect

KATHERINE MAC LEAN

The story is humorous and clever. I smiled all the way through it. It was only after I finished that I thought of — No, I don't want to spoil your fun. Maybe you won't think of a crackpot political party that grew until it nearly destroyed the world.

"ALL RIGHT," I said, "what *is* sociology good for?"

Wilton Caswell, Ph.D., was head of my sociology department, and right then he was mad enough to chew nails. On the office wall behind him were three or four framed documents in Latin that were supposed to be signs of great learning, but I didn't care at that moment if he papered the walls with his degrees. I had been appointed dean and president to see to it that the university made money. I had a job to do, and I meant to do it.

He bit off each word with great restraint: "Sociology is the study of social institutions, Mr. Halloway."

I tried to make him understand my position. "Look, it's the big-money men who are supposed to be contributing to the support of this college. To them, sociology sounds like socialism — nothing can sound worse than that — and an institution is where they put Aunt Maggy when she began collecting Wheaties in a stamp album. We can't appeal to them that way. Come on now." I smiled condescendingly, knowing it would irritate him. "What are you doing that's worth anything?"

He glared at me, his white hair bristling and his nostrils dilated like a war horse about to whinny. I can say one thing for them — these scientists and professors always keep themselves well under control. He had a book in his hand, and I was expecting him to throw it, but he spoke instead:

"This department's analysis of institutional accretion, by the use of open system mathematics, has been recognized as an outstanding and valuable contribution to — "

The words were impressive, whatever they meant, but this still didn't sound like anything that would pull in money. I interrupted, "Valuable in what way?"

He sat down on the edge of his desk thoughtfully, apparently recovering from the shock of being asked to produce something solid for his position, and ran his eyes over the titles of the books that lined his office walls.

"Well, sociology has been valuable to business in initiating worker efficiency and group motivation studies, which they now use in management decisions. And, of course, since the depression, Washington has been using sociological studies of employment, labor, and standards of living as a basis for its general policies of — "

I stopped him with both hands raised. "Please, Professor Caswell! That would hardly be a recommendation. Washington, the New Deal, and the present Administration are somewhat touchy subjects to the men I have to deal with. They consider its value debatable, if you know what I mean. If they got the idea that sociology professors are giving advice and guidance — No, we have to stick to brass tacks and leave Washington out of this. What, specifically, has the work of this specific department done that would make it as worthy to receive money as — say, a heart disease research fund?"

He began to tap the corner of his book absently on the desk, watching me. "Fundamental research doesn't show immediate effects, Mr. Halloway, but its value is recognized."

I smiled and took out my pipe. "All right, tell me about it. Maybe I'll recognize its value."

Prof. Caswell smiled back tightly. He knew his department was at stake. The other departments were popular with donors and pulled in gift money by scholarships and fellowships and supported their professors and graduate students by research contracts with the government and industry. Caswell had to show a way to make his own department popular — or else. I couldn't fire him directly, of course, but there are ways of doing it indirectly.

He laid down his book and ran a hand over his ruffled hair.

"Institutions — organizations, that is — " his voice became more resonant; like most professors, when he had to explain something he instinctively slipped into his platform lecture mannerisms, and began to deliver an essay — "have certain tendencies built into the way they happen to have been organized, which cause them to expand or contract without reference to the needs they were founded to serve."

He was becoming flushed with the pleasure of explaining his subject. "All through the ages, it has been a matter of wonder and dismay to men that a simple organization — such as a church to worship in or a delegation of weapons to a warrior class merely for defense against an outside enemy — will either grow insensately and extend its control until it is a tyranny over their whole lives or, like other organizations set up to serve a vital need, will tend to repeatedly dwindle and vanish and have to be painfully rebuilt.

"The reason can be traced to little quirks in the way they were organized, a matter of positive and negative power feedbacks. Such simple questions as, 'Is there a way a holder of authority in this organization can use the power available to him to increase his power?' provide the key. But it still could not be handled until the complex questions of interacting motives and long-range accumulations of minor effects could somehow be simplified and formulated. In working on the problem, I found that the mathematics of open system, as introduced to biology by Ludwig von Bertalanffy and George Kreezer, could be used as a base that would enable me to develop a specifically social mathematics, expressing the human factors of intermeshing authority and motives in simple formulas.

"By these formulations, it is possible to determine automatically the amount of growth and period of life of any organization. The UN, to choose an unfortunate example, is a shrinker-type organization. Its monetary support is not in the hands of those who personally benefit by its governmental activities, but, instead, in the hands of those who would personally lose by any extension and encroachment of its authority on their own. Yet by the use of formula analysis — "

"That's theory," I said. "How about proof?"

"My equations are already being used in the study of limited-size federal corporations. Washington — "

I held up my palm again. "Please, not that nasty word again. I mean, where else has it been put into operation? Just a simple demonstration, something to show that it works, that's all."

He looked away from me thoughtfully, picked up the book, and began to tap it on the desk again. It had some unreadable title and his name on it in gold letters. I got the distinct impression again that he was repressing an urge to hit me with it.

He spoke quietly. "All right, I'll give you a demonstration. Are you willing to wait six months?"

"Certainly, if you can show me something at the end of that time."

Reminded of time, I glanced at my watch and stood up.

"Could we discuss this over lunch?" he asked.

"I wouldn't mind hearing more, but I'm having lunch with some executors of a millionaire's will. They have to be convinced that by 'furtherance of research into human ills' he meant that the money should go to research fellowships for postgraduate biologists at the university, rather than to a medical foundation."

"I see you have your problems too," Caswell said, conceding me nothing. He extended his hand with a chilly smile. "Well, good afternoon, Mr. Halloway. I'm glad we had this talk."

I shook hands and left him standing there, sure of his place in the progress of science and the respect of his colleagues, yet seething inside because I, the president and dean, had boorishly demanded that he produce something tangible.

I frankly didn't give a hoot if he blew his lid. My job isn't easy. For a crumb of favorable publicity and respect in the newspapers and an annual ceremony in a silly costume, I spend the rest of the year going hat in hand, asking politely for money at everyone's door, like a well-dressed panhandler, and trying to manage the university on the dribble I get. As far as I was concerned, a department had to support itself or be cut down to what student tuition pays for, which is a handful of overcrowded courses taught by an assistant lecturer. Caswell had to make it work or get out.

But the more I thought about it, the more I wanted to hear what he was going to do for a demonstration.

At lunch, three days later, while we were waiting for our order, he opened a small notebook. "Ever hear of feedback effects?"

"Not enough to have it clear."

"You know the snowball effect, though."

"Sure, start a snowball rolling downhill and it grows."

"Well, now — " He wrote a short line of symbols on a blank page and turned the notebook around for me to inspect it. "Here's the formula for the snowball process. It's the basic general growth formula — covers everything."

It was a row of little symbols arranged like an algebra equation. One was a concentric spiral going up, like a cross section of a snowball rolling in snow. That was a growth sign.

I hadn't expected to understand the equation, but it was almost as clear as a sentence. I was impressed and slightly intimidated by it. He had already explained enough so that I knew that, if he was right, here was the growth of the Catholic Church and the Roman Empire, the conquests of Alexander and the spread of the smoking habit and the change and rigidity of the unwritten law of styles.

"Is it really as simple as that?" I asked.

"You notice," he said, "that when it becomes too heavy for the cohesion strength of snow, it breaks apart. Now in human terms — "

The chops and mashed potatoes and peas arrived.

"Go on," I urged.

He was deep in the symbology of human motives and the equations of human behavior in groups. After running through a few different types of grower and shrinker type organizations, we came back to the snowball, and decided to run the test by making something grow.

"You add the motives," he said, "and the equation will translate them into organization."

"How about a good selfish reason for the ins to drag others into the group — some sort of bounty on new members, a cut of their membership fee?" I suggested uncertainly, feeling slightly foolish. "And maybe a reason why the members would lose if any of them resigned, and some indirect way they could use to force each other to stay in."

"The first is the chain letter principle," he nodded. "I've got that. The other . . ." He put the symbols through some mathematical manipulation so that a special grouping appeared in the middle of the equation. "That's it."

Since I seemed to have the right idea, I suggested some more, and he added some and juggled them around in different patterns. We threw out a few that would have made the organization too complicated and finally worked out an idyllically simple and deadly little organization setup where joining had all the temptation of buying a sweepstakes ticket, going in deeper was as easy as hanging around a race track, and getting out was like trying to pull free from a Malayan thumb trap. We put our heads closer together and talked lower, picking the best place for the demonstration.

"Abington?"

"How about Watashaw? I have some student sociological surveys of it already. We can pick a suitable group from that."

"This demonstration has got to be convincing. We'd better pick a little group that no one in his right mind would expect to grow."

"There should be a suitable club — "

Picture Professor Caswell, head of the Department of Sociology, and with him the president of the university, leaning across the table toward each other, sipping coffee and talking in conspiratorial tones over something they were writing in a notebook.

That was us.

"Ladies," said the skinny female chairman of the Watashaw Sewing Circle. "Today we have guests." She signaled for us to rise, and we stood up, bowing to polite applause and smiles. "Professor Caswell, and Professor Smith." (My alias.) "They are making a survey of the methods and duties of the clubs of Watashaw."

We sat down to another ripple of applause and slightly wider smiles, and then the meeting of the Watashaw Sewing Circle began. In five minutes I began to feel sleepy.

There were only about thirty people there, and it was a small room, not the halls of Congress, but they discussed their business of collecting and repairing secondhand clothing for charity with the same endless boring parliamentary formality.

I pointed out to Caswell the member I thought would be the natural leader, a tall, well-built woman in a green suit, with conscious gestures and a resonant, penetrating voice, and then went into a half doze while Caswell stayed awake beside me and wrote in his notebook. After a while the resonant voice roused me to attention for a moment. It was the tall woman holding the floor over some collective dereliction of the club. She was being scathing.

I nudged Caswell and murmured, "Did you fix it so that a shover has a better chance of getting into office than a nonshover?"

"I think there's a way they could find for it," Caswell whispered back and went to work on his equation again. "Yes, several ways to bias the elections."

"Good. Point them out tactfully to the one you select. Not as if she'd use such methods, but just as an example of the reason why only *she* can be trusted with initiating the change. Just mention all the personal advantages an unscrupulous person could have."

He nodded, keeping a straight and sober face as if we were exchanging admiring remarks about the techniques of clothes repairing, instead of conspiring.

After the meeting, Caswell drew the tall woman in the green suit aside and spoke to her confidentially, showing her the diagram of organization we had drawn up. I saw the responsive glitter in the woman's eyes and knew she was hooked.

We left the diagram of organization and our typed copy of the new bylaws with her and went off soberly, as befitted two social science experimenters. We didn't start laughing until our car passed the town limits and began the climb for University Heights.

If Caswell's equations meant anything at all, we had given that sewing circle more growth drives than the Roman Empire.

Four months later I had time out from a very busy schedule to wonder how the test was coming along. Passing Caswell's office, I put my head in. He looked up from a student research paper he was correcting.

"Caswell, about that sewing club business — I'm beginning to feel the suspense. Could I get an advance report on how it's coming?"

"I'm not following it. We're supposed to let it run the full six months."

"But I'm curious. Could I get in touch with that woman — what's her name?"

"Searles. Mrs. George Searles."

"Would that change the results?"

"Not in the slightest. If you want to graph the membership rise, it should be going up in a log curve, probably doubling every so often."

I grinned. "If it's not rising, you're fired."

He grinned back. "If it's not rising, you won't have to fire me — I'll burn my books and shoot myself."

I returned to my office and put in a call to Watashaw.

While I was waiting for the phone to be answered, I took a piece of graph paper and ruled it off into six sections, one for each month. After the phone had rung in the distance for a long time, a servant answered with a bored drawl:

"Mrs. Searles' residence."

I picked up a red gummed star and licked it.

"Mrs. Searles, please."

"She's not in just now. Could I take a message?"

I placed the star at the thirty line in the beginning of the first section. Thirty members they'd started with.

"No, thanks. Could you tell me when she'll be back?"

"Not until dinner. She's at the meetin'."

"The sewing club?" I asked.

"No, *sir,* not that thing. There isn't any sewing club anymore, not for a long time. She's at the civic welfare meeting."

Somehow I hadn't expected anything like that.

"Thank you," I said and hung up, and after a moment noticed I was holding a box of red gummed stars in my hand. I closed it and put it down on top of the graph of membership in the sewing circle. No more members . . .

Poor Caswell. The bet between us was ironclad. He wouldn't let me back down on it even if I wanted to. He'd probably quit before I put through the first slow move to fire him. His professional pride would be shattered, sunk without a trace. I remembered what he said about shooting himself. It had seemed funny to both of us at the time, but . . . What a mess *that* would make for the university.

I had to talk to Mrs. Searles. Perhaps there was some outside reason why the club had disbanded. Perhaps it had not just died.

I called back. "This is Professor Smith," I said, giving the alias I had used before. "I called a few minutes ago. When did you say Mrs. Searles will return?"

"About six-thirty or seven o'clock."

Five hours to wait.

And what if Caswell asked me what I had found out in the meantime? I didn't want to tell him anything until I had talked it over with that woman Searles first.

"Where is this civic welfare meeting?"

She told me.

Five minutes later, I was in my car, heading for Watashaw, driving considerably faster than my usual speed, and keeping a careful watch for highway patrol cars as the speedometer climbed.

The town meeting hall and theater was a big place, probably with lots of small rooms for different clubs. I went in through the center door and found myself in the huge central hall, where some sort of rally was being held. A political-type rally — you know, cheers and chants, with bunting already down on the floor, people holding banners, and plenty of enthusiasm and excitement in the air. Someone was making a speech up on the platform. Most of the people there were women.

I wondered how the Civic Welfare League could dare hold its meeting at the same time as a political rally that could pull its members away. The group with Mrs. Searles was probably holding a shrunken and almost memberless meeting somewhere in an upper room.

There probably was a side door that would lead upstairs.

While I glanced around, a pretty girl usher put a printed bulletin in my hand, whispering, "Here's one of the new copies." As I attempted to hand it back, she retreated. "Oh, you can keep it. It's the new one. Everyone's supposed to have it. We've just printed up six thousand copies to make sure there'll be enough to last."

The tall woman on the platform had been making a driving, forceful speech about some plans for rebuilding Watashaw's slum section. It began to penetrate my mind dimly as I glanced down at the bulletin in my hands.

"Civic Welfare League of Watashaw. The United Organization of Church and Secular Charities." That's what it said. Below began the rules of membership.

I looked up. The speaker, with a clear, determined voice and conscious, forceful gestures, had entered the home stretch of her speech, an appeal to the civic pride of all citizens of Watashaw.

"With a bright and glorious future — potentially without poor and without uncared-for ill — potentially with no ugliness, no vistas which are not beautiful — the best people in the best-planned town in the country — the jewel of the United States."

She paused and then leaned forward intensely, striking her clenched hand on the speaker's stand with each word for emphasis.

"All we need is more members. Now get out there and recruit!"

I finally recognized Mrs. Searles, as an answering sudden blast of sound half deafened me. The crowd was chanting at the top of its lungs: "Recruit, Recruit!"

Mrs. Searles stood still at the speaker's table and behind her, seated in a row of chairs, was a group that was probably the board of directors. It was mostly women, and the women began to look vaguely familiar, as if they could be members of the sewing circle.

I put my lips close to the ear of the pretty usher while I turned over the stiff printed bulletin on a hunch. "How long has the League been organized?" On the back of the bulletin was a constitution.

She was cheering with the crowd, her eyes sparkling. "I don't know," she answered between cheers. "I only joined two days ago. Isn't it wonderful?"

I went into the quiet outer air and got into my car with my skin prickling. Even as I drove away, I could hear them. They were singing some kind of organization song to the tune of "Marching through Georgia."

Even at the single glance I had given it, the constitution looked exactly like the one we had given the Watashaw Sewing Circle.

All I told Caswell when I got back was that the sewing circle had changed its name and the membership seemed to be rising.

Next day, after calling Mrs. Searles, I placed some red stars on my graph for the first three months. They made a nice curve, rising more steeply as it reached the fourth month. They had picked up their first increase in membership simply by amalgamating with all the other types of charity organizations in Watashaw, changing the club name with each fusion, but keeping the same constitution — the constitution with the bright promise of advantages as long as there were always new members being brought in.

By the fifth month, the league had added a mutual baby-sitting service and had induced the local school board to add a nursery school to the town service, so as to free more women for league activity. But charity must have been completely organized by then, and expansion had to be in other directions.

Some real estate agents evidently had been drawn into the whirlpool early, along with their ideas. The slum improvement plans began to blossom and take on a tinge of real estate planning later in the month.

The first day of the sixth month, a big two-page spread appeared in the local paper of a mass meeting which had approved a full-fledged scheme for slum clearance of Watashaw's shack-town section, plus plans for rehousing, civic building, and rezoning. *And* good prospects for attracting some new industries to the town, industries which had already been contacted and seemed interested by the privileges offered.

And with all this, an arrangement for securing and distributing to the club members *alone* most of the profit that would come to the town in the form of a rise in the price of building sites and a boom in the building industry. The profit-distributing arrangement was the same one that had been built into the organization plan for the distribution of the small profits of membership fees and honorary promotions. It was becoming an openly profitable business. Membership was rising more rapidly now.

By the second week of the sixth month, news appeared in the local paper that the club had filed an application to incorporate itself as the Watashaw Mutual Trade and Civic Development Corporation, and all the local real estate promoters had finished joining en masse. The Mutual Trade part sounded to me as if the Chamber of Commerce was on the point of being pulled in with them, ideas, ambitions, and all.

I chuckled while reading the next page of the paper, on which a local politician was reported as having addressed the club with a long flowery oration on their enterprise, charity, and civic spirit. He had been made an honorary member. If he allowed himself to be made a *full* member with its contractual obligations and its lures, if the politicians went into this too . . .

I laughed, filing the newspaper with the other documents on the Watashaw test. These proofs would fascinate any businessman with the sense to see where his bread was buttered. A businessman is constantly dealing with organizations, including his own, and finding them either inert, cantankerous, or both.

Caswell's formula could be a handle to grasp them with. Gratitude alone would bring money into the university in carload lots.

The end of the sixth month came. The test was over and the end reports were spectacular. Caswell's formulas were proved to the hilt.

After reading the last newspaper reports, I called him up.

"Perfect, Wilt, *perfect*! I can use this Watashaw thing to get you so many fellowships and scholarships and grants for your department that you'll think it's snowing money!"

He answered somewhat disinterestedly, "I've been busy working with students on their research papers and marking tests — not following the Watashaw business at all, I'm afraid. You say the demonstration went well and you're satisfied?"

He was definitely putting on a chill. We were friends now, but obviously he was still peeved whenever he was reminded that I had doubted that his theory could work. And he was using its success to rub my nose in the realization that I had been wrong. A man with a string of degrees after his name is just as human as anyone else. I had needled him pretty hard that first time.

"I'm satisfied," I acknowledged. "I was wrong. The formulas work beautifully. Come over and see my file of documents on it if you want a boost for your ego. Now let's see the formula for stopping it."

He sounded cheerful again. "I didn't complicate that organization with negatives. I wanted it to *grow*. It falls apart naturally when it stops growing for more than two months. It's like the great stock boom before an economic crash. Everyone in it is prosperous as long as the prices just keep going up and new buyers come into the market, but they all know what would happen if it stopped growing. You remember, we built in as one of the incentives that the members know they are going to lose if membership stops growing. Why, if I tried to stop it now, they'd cut my throat."

I remembered the drive and frenzy of the crowd in the one early meeting I had seen. They probably would.

"No," he continued. "We'll just let it play out to the end of its tether and die of old age."

"When will that be?"

"It can't grow past the female population of the town. There are only so many women in Watashaw, and some of them don't like sewing."

The graph on the desk before me began to look sinister. Surely Caswell must have made some provision for —

"You underestimate their ingenuity," I said into the phone. "Since they wanted to expand they didn't stick to sewing. They went from general charity to social welfare schemes to something that's pretty close to an incorporated government. The name is now the Watashaw Mutual Trade and Civic Development Corporation, and they're filing an application to change it to Civic Property Pool and Social Dividend, membership contractual, open to all. That social dividend sounds like a Technocrat climbed on the bandwagon, eh?"

While I spoke, I carefully added another red star to the curve above the thousand-member level, checking with the newspaper that still lay open on my desk. The curve was definitely some sort of log curve now, growing more rapidly with each increase.

"Leaving out practical limitations for a moment, where does the formula say it will stop?" I asked.

"When you run out of people to join it. But after all, there are only so many people in Watashaw. It's a pretty small town."

"They've opened a branch office in New York," I said carefully into the phone, a few weeks later.

With my pencil, very carefully, I extended the membership curve from where it was then.

After the next doubling, the curve went almost straight up and off the page.

Allowing for a lag of contagion from one nation to another, depending on how much their citizens intermingled, I'd give the rest of the world about twelve years.

There was a long silence while Caswell probably drew the same graph in his own mind. Then he laughed weakly. "Well, you asked me for a demonstration."

That was as good an answer as any. We got together and had lunch in a bar, if you can call it lunch. The movement we started will expand by hook or by crook, by seduction or by bribery, or by propaganda or by conquest, but it will expand. And maybe a total world government will be a fine thing — until it hits the end of its rope in twelve years or so.

What happens then, I don't know.

But I don't want anyone to pin that on me. From now on, if anyone asks me, I've never heard of Watashaw.

Pâté de Foie Gras

ISAAC ASIMOV

This story, written a quarter-century ago, was carefully designed to allow one rational answer to the question that was asked at the end. To my pleasure, I got a number of answers (correct ones) over the next decade or so, with everyone marveling at the ingenuity of the problem.

Imagine my chagrin, however, when the advance of science made possible another answer that was better than any I had imagined. I found myself beginning to get that better answer from more and more people who were astonished (since the new answer was an obvious one) that the character in the story had any trouble at all.

I am seriously considering a lawsuit against the scientific establishment for the crime of making unauthorized scientific advances. The least they might have done would have been to clear the whole thing with me first.

I COULDN'T TELL YOU my real name if I wanted to, and, under the circumstances, I don't want to.

I'm not much of a writer myself, so I'm having Isaac Asimov write this up for me. I've picked him for several reasons. First, he's a biochemist, so he understands what I tell him — some of it, anyway. Second, he can write — or at least he has published considerable fiction, which may not, of course, be the same thing.

I was not the first person to have the honor of meeting The Goose. That belongs to a Texas cotton farmer named Ian Angus MacGregor, who owned it before it became government property.

By summer of 1955 he had sent an even dozen of letters to the Department of Agriculture requesting information on the hatching of goose eggs. The department sent him all the booklets on hand that were anywhere near the subject, but his letters simply got more impassioned and freer in their references to his "friend," the local congressman.

My connection with this is that I am in the employ of the Department of Agriculture. Since I was attending a convention at San Antonio in July of 1955, my boss asked me to stop off at MacGregor's place and see what I could do to help him. We're servants of the public, and besides we had finally received a letter from MacGregor's congressman.

On July 17, 1955, I met The Goose.

I met MacGregor first. He was in his fifties, a tall man with a lined face full of suspicion. I went over all the information he had been given, then asked politely if I might see his geese.

He said, "It's not geese, mister; it's one goose."

I said, "May I see the one goose?"

"Rather not."

"Well, then, I can't help you any further. If it's only one goose, then there's just something wrong with it. Why worry about one goose? Eat it."

I got up and reached for my hat.

He said, "Wait!" and I stood there while his lips tightened and his eyes wrinkled and he had a quiet fight with himself. "Come with me."

I went out with him to a pen near the house, surrounded by barbed wire, with a locked gate to it, and holding one goose — The Goose.

"That's The Goose," he said. The way he said it, I could hear the capitals.

I stared at it. It looked like any other goose, fat, self-satisfied, and short-tempered.

MacGregor said, "And here's one of its eggs. It's been in the incubator. Nothing happens." He produced it from a capacious overall pocket. There was a queer strain about his manner of holding it.

I frowned. There was something wrong with the egg. It was smaller and more spherical than normal.

MacGregor said, "Take it."

I reached out and took it. Or tried to. I gave it the amount of heft an egg like that ought to deserve and it just sat where it was. I had to try harder and then up it came.

Now I knew what was queer about the way MacGregor held it. It weighed nearly two pounds.

I stared at it as it lay there, pressing down the palm of my hand, and MacGregor grinned sourly. "Drop it," he said.

I just looked at him, so he took it out of my hand and dropped it himself.

It hit soggy. It didn't smash. There was no spray of white and yolk. It just lay where it fell with the bottom caved in.

I picked it up again. The white eggshell had shattered where the egg had struck. Pieces of it had flaked away, and what shone through was a dull yellow in color.

My hands trembled. It was all I could do to make my fingers work, but I got some of the rest of the shell flaked away and stared at the yellow.

I didn't have to run any analyses. My heart told me.

I was face to face with The Goose!

The Goose That Laid The Golden Eggs! My first problem was to get MacGregor to give up that golden egg. I was almost hysterical about it.

I said, "I'll give you a receipt. I'll guarantee you payment. I'll do anything in reason."

"I don't want the government butting in," he said stubbornly.

But I was twice as stubborn, and in the end I signed a receipt and he dogged me out to my car and stood in the road as I drove away, following me with his eyes.

The head of my section at the Department of Agriculture is Louis P. Bronstein. He and I are on good terms, and I felt I could explain things without being placed under immediate observation. Even so, I took no chances. I had the egg with me, and when I got to the tricky part, I just laid it on the desk between us.

I said, "It's a yellow metal and it could be brass only it isn't because it's inert to concentrated nitric acid."

Bronstein said, "It's some sort of hoax. It *must* be."

"A hoax that uses real gold? Remember, when I first saw this thing, it was covered completely with authentic unbroken eggshell. It's been easy to check a piece of the eggshell. Calcium carbonate."

Project Goose was started. That was July 20, 1955.

I was the responsible investigator to begin with and remained in titular charge throughout, though matters quickly got beyond me.

We began with the one egg. Its average radius was 35 millimeters (major axis, 72 millimeters; minor axis, 68 millimeters). The gold shell was 2.45 millimeters in thickness. Studying other eggs later on, we found this value to be rather high. The average thickness turned out to be 2.1 millimeters.

Inside *was* egg. It looked like egg and it smelled like egg.

Aliquots were analyzed, and the organic constituents were reasonably normal. The white was 9.7 percent albumin. The yolk had the normal complement of vitellin, cholesterol, phospholipid, and carotenoid. We lacked enough material to test for trace constituents, but later on with more eggs at our disposal we did and nothing unusual showed up as far as contents of vitamins, coenzymes, nucleotides, sulfhydryl groups, et cetera, et cetera, were concerned.

One important gross abnormality that showed was the egg's behavior on heating. A small portion of the yolk, heated, "hard-boiled" almost at once. We fed a portion of the hard-boiled egg to a mouse. It survived.

I nibbled at another bit of it. Too small a quantity to taste, really, but it made me sick. Purely psychosomatic, I'm sure.

Boris W. Finley, of the Department of Biochemistry of Temple University — a department consultant — supervised these tests.

He said, referring to the hard-boiling, "The ease with which the egg proteins are heat-denatured indicates a partial denaturation to begin with, and, considering the nature of the shell, the obvious guilt would lie at the door of heavy-metal contamination."

So a portion of the yolk was analyzed for inorganic constituents, and it was found to be high in chloraurate ion, which is a singly charged ion containing an atom of gold and four of chlorine, the symbol for which is $AuCl_4^-$. (The "Au" symbol for gold comes from the fact that the Latin word for gold is *aurum*.) When I say the chloraurate ion content was high, I mean it was 3.2 parts per thousand, or 0.32 percent. That's high enough to form insoluble complexes of "gold protein," which would coagulate easily.

Finley said, "It's obvious this egg cannot hatch. Nor can any other such egg. It is heavy-metal poisoned. Gold may be more glamorous than lead, but it is just as poisonous to proteins."

I agreed gloomily. "At least it's safe from decay too."

"Quite right. No self-respecting bug would live in this chlorauriferous soup."

The final spectographic analysis of the gold of the shell came in. Virtually pure. The only detectable impurity was iron, which amounted to 0.23 percent of the whole. The iron content of the egg yolk had been twice normal also. At the moment, however, the matter of the iron was neglected.

One week after Project Goose was begun, an expedition was sent to Texas. Five biochemists went — the accent was still on biochemistry, you see — along with three truckloads of equipment and a squadron of army personnel. I went along too, of course.

As soon as we arrived, we cut MacGregor's farm off from the world.

That was a lucky thing, you know — the security measures we took right from the start. The reasoning was wrong, at first, but the results were good.

The department wanted Project Goose kept quiet at the start simply because there was always the thought that this might still be an elaborate hoax, and we couldn't risk the bad publicity if it were. And if it weren't a hoax, we couldn't risk the newspaper hounding that would definitely result over any goose-and-golden-egg story.

It was only well after the start of Project Goose, well after our arrival at MacGregor's farm, that the real implications of the matter became clear.

Naturally MacGregor didn't like the men and equipment settling down all about him. He didn't like being told The Goose was government property. He didn't like having his eggs impounded.

He didn't like it but he agreed to it — if you can call it agreeing when negotiations are being carried on while a machine gun is being assembled in a man's barnyard and ten men, with bayonets fixed, are marching past while the arguing is going on.

He was compensated, of course. What's money to the government?

The Goose didn't like a few things either — like having blood samples taken. We didn't dare anesthetize it for fear of doing anything to alter its metabolism, and it took two men to hold it each time. Ever try to hold an angry goose?

The Goose was put under a twenty-four-hour guard, with the threat of summary court-martial to any man who let anything happen to it. If any of those soldiers read this article, they may get a sudden glimmer of what was going on. If so, they will probably have the sense to keep shut about it. At least, if they know what's good for them they will.

The blood of The Goose was put through every conceivable test.

It carried 2 parts per hundred thousand (0.002 percent) of chloraurate ion. Blood taken from the hepatic vein was richer than the rest, almost 4 parts per hundred thousand.

Finley grunted. "The liver," he said.

We took X rays. On the X-ray negative, the liver was a cloudy mass of light gray, lighter than the viscera in its neighborhood, because it stopped more of the X rays, because it contained more gold. The blood vessels showed up lighter than the liver proper, and the ovaries were pure white. No X rays got through the ovaries at all.

It made sense, and in an early report Finley stated it as bluntly as possible. The report, paraphrased, went in part:

"The chloraurate ion is secreted by the liver into the blood stream. The ovaries act as a trap for the ion, which is there reduced to metallic gold and deposited as a shell about the developing egg. Relatively high concentrations of unreduced chloraurate ion penetrate the contents of the developing egg.

"There is little doubt that The Goose finds this process useful as a means of getting rid of the gold atoms which, if allowed to accumulate, would undoubtedly poison it. Excretion by eggshell may be novel in the animal kingdom, even unique, but there is no denying that it is keeping The Goose alive.

"Unfortunately, however, the ovary is being locally poisoned to such an extent that few eggs are laid, probably not more than will suffice to get rid of the accumulating gold, and those few eggs are definitely unhatchable."

That was all he said in writing, but to the rest of us, he said, "That leaves one peculiarly embarrassing question."

I knew what it was. We all did.

Where was the gold coming from?

No answer to that for a while, except for some negative evidence. There was no perceptible gold in The Goose's feed, nor were there any gold-bearing pebbles about that it might have swallowed. There was no trace of gold anywhere in the soil of the area, and a search of the house and grounds revealed nothing. There were no gold coins, gold jewelry, gold plate, gold watches, or gold anything. No one on the farm even had as much as gold fillings in his teeth.

There was Mrs. MacGregor's wedding ring, of course, but she had only had one in her life, and she was wearing it.

So where was the gold coming from?

The beginnings of the answer came on August 16, 1955.

Albert Nevis, of Purdue, was forcing gastric tubes into The Goose —
another procedure to which the bird objected strenuously — with the idea of
testing the contents of its alimentary canal. It was one of our routine searches
for exogenous gold.

Gold *was* found, but only in traces, and there was every reason to suppose
those traces had accompanied the digestive secretions and were, therefore,
endogenous — from within, that is — in origin.

However, something else showed up, or the lack of it anyway.

I was there when Nevis came into Finley's office in the temporary building
we had put up overnight — almost — near the goosepen.

Nevis said, "The Goose is low in bile pigment. Duodenal contents show
about none."

Finley frowned and said, "Liver function is probably knocked loop-the-loop
because of its gold concentration. It probably isn't secreting bile at all."

"It *is* secreting bile," said Nevis. "Bile acids are present in normal quantity.
Near normal, anyway. It's just the bile pigments that are missing. I did a fecal
analysis and that was confirmed. No bile pigments."

Let me explain something at this point. Bile acids are steroids secreted by
the liver into the bile and via that are poured into the upper end of the small
intestine. These bile acids are detergentlike molecules that help to emulsify the
fat in our diet — or The Goose's — and distribute them in the form of tiny
bubbles through the watery intestinal contents. This distribution, or homogen-
ization, if you'd rather, makes it easier for the fat to be digested.

Bile pigments, the substances that were missing in The Goose, are something
entirely different. The liver makes them out of hemoglobin, the red oxygen-
carrying protein of the blood. Worn-out hemoglobin is broken up in the liver,
the heme part being split away. The heme is made up of a squarish molecule
— called a porphyrin — with an iron atom in the center. The liver takes the
iron out and stores it for future use, then breaks the squarish molecule that
is left. This broken porphyrin is bile pigment. It is colored brownish or greenish
— depending on further chemical changes — and is secreted into the bile.

The bile pigments are of no use to the body. They are poured into the bile
as waste products. They pass through the intestines and come out with the
feces. In fact, the bile pigments are responsible for the color of the feces.

Finley's eyes began to glitter.

Nevis said, "It looks as though porphyrin catabolism isn't following the
proper course in the liver. Doesn't it to you?"

It surely did. To me too.

There was tremendous excitement after that. This was the first metabolic
abnormality, not directly involving gold, that had been found in The Goose!

We took a liver biopsy (which means we punched a cylindrical sliver out of The Goose reaching down into the liver). It hurt The Goose but didn't harm it. We took more blood samples too.

This time we isolated hemoglobin from the blood and small quantities of the cytochromes from our liver samples. (The cytochromes are oxidizing enzymes that also contain heme.) We separated out the heme and in acid solution some of it precipitated in the form of a brilliant orange substance. By August 22, 1955, we had 5 micrograms of the compound.

The orange compound was similar to heme, but it was not heme. The iron in heme can be in the form of a doubly charged ferrous ion (Fe_{++}) or a triply charged ferric ion (Fe_{+++}), in which latter case the compound is called hematin. (Ferrous and ferric, by the way, come from the Latin word for iron, which is *ferrum.*)

The orange compound we had separated from heme had the porphyrin portion of the molecule all right, but the metal in the center was gold — to be specific, a triply charged auric ion (Au_{++}). We called this compound "aureme," which is simply short for "auric heme."

Aureme was the first naturally occurring gold-containing organic compound ever discovered. Ordinarily it would rate headline news in the world of biochemistry. But now it was nothing — nothing at all in comparison to the further horizons its mere existence opened up.

The liver, it seemed, was not breaking up the heme to bile pigment. Instead it was converting it to aureme; it was replacing iron with gold. The aureme, in equilibrium with chloraurate ion, entered the blood stream and was carried to the ovaries, where the gold was separated out and the prophyrin portion of the molecule disposed of by some as yet unidentified mechanism.

Further analyses showed that 29 percent of the gold in the blood of The Goose was carried in the plasma in the form of chloraurate ion. The remaining 71 percent was carried in the red blood corpuscles in the form of "auremoglobin." An attempt was made to feed The Goose traces of radioactive gold so that we could pick up radioactivity in plasma and corpuscles and see how readily the auremoglobin molecules were handled in the ovaries. It seemed to us the auremoglobin should be much more slowly disposed of than the dissolved chloraurate ion in the plasma.

The experiment failed, however, since we detected no radioactivity. We put it down to inexperience, since none of us was an isotopes man, which was too bad since the failure was highly significant, really, and by not realizing it we lost several weeks.

The auremoglobin was, of course, useless as far as carrying oxygen was concerned, but it only made up about 0.1 percent of the total hemoglobin of the red blood cells, so there was no interference with the respiration of The Goose.

This still left us with the question of where the gold came from, and it was Nevis who first made the crucial suggestion.

"Maybe," he said at a meeting of the group held on the evening of August 25, 1955, "The Goose doesn't replace the iron with gold. Maybe it *changes* the iron to gold."

Before I met Nevis personally that summer, I had known him through his publications — his field is bile chemistry and liver function — and had always considered him a cautious, clear-thinking person. Almost overcautious. One wouldn't consider him capable for a minute of making any such completely ridiculous statement.

It just shows the desperation and demoralization involved in Project Goose.

The desperation was the fact that there was nowhere, literally nowhere, that the gold could come from. The Goose was excreting gold at the rate of 38.9 grams a day and had been doing it over a period of months. That gold had to come from somewhere, and, failing that — absolutely failing that — it had to be made from something.

The demoralization that led us to consider the second alternative was due to the mere fact that we were face to face with The Goose That Laid The Golden Eggs, the undeniable GOOSE. With that, everything became possible. All of us were living in a fairy-tale world, and all of us reacted to it by losing all sense of reality.

Finley considered the possibility seriously. "Hemoglobin," he said, "enters the liver and a bit of auremoglobin comes out. The gold shell of the eggs has iron as its only impurity. The egg yolk is high in only two things: in gold, of course, and also, somewhat, in iron. It all makes a horrible kind of distorted sense. We're going to need help, men."

We did, and it meant a third stage of the investigation. The first stage had consisted of myself alone. The second was the biochemical task force. The third, the greatest, the most important of all, involved the invasion of the nuclear physicists.

On September 5, 1955, John L. Billings of the University of California arrived. He had some equipment with him, and more arrived in the following weeks. More temporary structures were going up. I could see that within a year we would have a whole research institution built about The Goose.

Billings joined our conference the evening of the fifth.

Finley brought him up to date and said, "There are a great many serious problems involved in this iron-to-gold idea. For one thing, the total quantity of iron in The Goose can only be of the order of half a gram, yet nearly forty grams of gold a day are being manufactured."

Billings had a clear, high-pitched voice. He said, "There's a worse problem than that. Iron is about at the bottom of the packing fraction curve. Gold is much higher up. To convert a gram of iron to a gram of gold takes just about as much energy as is produced by the fissioning of one gram of U-235."

Finley shrugged. "I'll leave the problem to you."

Billings said, "Let me think about it."

He did more than think. One of the things done was to isolate fresh samples of heme from The Goose, ash it, and send the iron oxide to Brookhaven for isotopic analysis. There was no particular reason to do that particular thing. It was just one of a number of individual investigations, but it was the one that brought results.

When the figures came back, Billings choked on them. He said, "There's no Fe^{56}."

"What about the other isotopes?" asked Finley at once.

"All present," said Billings, "in the appropriate relative ratios, but no detectable Fe^{56}."

I'll have to explain again: Iron, as it occurs naturally, is made up of four different isotopes. These isotopes are varieties of atoms that differ from one another in atomic weight. Iron atoms with an atomic weight of 56, or Fe^{56}, make up 91.6 percent of all the atoms in iron. The other atoms have atomic weights of 54, 57, and 58.

The iron from the heme of The Goose was made up only of Fe^{54}, Fe^{57}, and Fe^{58}. The implication was obvious. Fe^{56} was disappearing while the other isotopes weren't, and this meant a nuclear reaction was taking place. A nuclear reaction could take one isotope and leave others be. An ordinary chemical reaction, any chemical reaction at all, would have to dispose of all isotopes just about equally.

"But it's energically impossible," said Finley.

He was only saying that in mild sarcasm with Billings's initial remark in mind. As biochemists, we knew well enough that many reactions went on in the body which required an input of energy and that this was taken care of by coupling the energy-demanding reaction with an energy-producing reaction.

However, chemical reactions gave off or took up a few kilocalories per mole. Nuclear reactions gave off or took up millions. To supply energy for an energy-demanding nuclear reaction required, therefore, a second, and energy-producing, nuclear reaction.

We didn't see Billings for two days.

When he did come back, it was to say, "See here. The energy-producing reaction must produce just as much energy per nucleon involved as the energy-demanding reaction uses up. If it produces even slightly less, then the overall reaction won't go. If it produces even slightly more, then considering the astronomical number of nucleons involved, the excess energy produced would vaporize The Goose in a fraction of a second."

"So?" said Finley.

"So the number of reactions possible is very limited. I have been able to find only one plausible system. Oxygen-18, if converted to iron-56, will produce enough energy to drive the iron-56 on to gold-197. It's like going down one side of a roller coaster and then up the other. We'll have to test this."

"How?"

"First, suppose we check the isotopic composition of the oxygen in The Goose."

Oxygen is made up of three stable isotopes, almost all of it O^{16}. O^{18} makes up only one oxygen atom out of 250.

Another blood sample. The water content was distilled off in vacuum and some of it put through a mass spectrograph. There was O^{18} there but only one oxygen atom out of 1300. Fully 80 percent of the O^{18} we expected wasn't there.

Billings said, "That's corroborative evidence. Oxygen-18 is being used up. It is being supplied constantly in the food and water fed to The Goose, but it is still being used up. Gold-197 is being produced. Iron-56 is one intermediate and since the reaction that uses up iron-56 is faster than the one that produces it, it has no chance to reach significant concentration and isotopic analysis shows its absence."

We weren't satisfied, so we tried again. We kept The Goose on water that had been enriched with O^{18} for a week. Gold production went up almost at once. At the end of a week it was producing 45.8 grams while the O^{18} content of its body water was no higher than before.

"There's no doubt about it," said Billings.

He snapped his pencil and stood up. "That Goose is a living nuclear reactor."

The Goose was obviously a mutation.

A mutation suggested radiation among other things, and radiation brought up the thought of nuclear tests conducted in 1952 and 1953 several hundred miles away from the site of MacGregor's farm. (If it occurs to you that no nuclear tests have been conducted in Texas, it just shows two things: I'm not telling you everything, and you don't know everything.)

I doubt that at any time in the history of the atomic era was background radiation so thoroughly analyzed and the radioactive content of the soil so rigidly sifted.

Back records were studied. It didn't matter how top-secret they were. By this time, Project Goose had the highest priority that had ever existed.

Even weather records were checked in order to follow the behavior of the winds at the time of the nuclear tests.

Two things turned up.

One: The background radiation at the farm was a bit higher than normal. Nothing that could possibly do harm, I hasten to add. There were indications, however, that at the time of the birth of The Goose, the farm had been subjected to the drifting edge of at least two fallouts. Nothing really harmful, I again hasten to add.

Second: The Goose, alone of all geese on the farm — in fact, alone of all living creatures on the farm that could be tested, including the humans — showed no radioactivity at all. Look at it this way: *Everything* shows traces of radioactivity; that's what is meant by background radiation. But The Goose showed none.

Finley sent one report on December 6, 1955, which I can paraphrase as follows:

"The Goose is a most extraordinary mutation, born of a high-level radioactivity environment which at once encouraged mutations in general and which made this particular mutation a beneficial one.

"The Goose has enzyme systems capable of catalyzing various nuclear reactions. Whether the enzyme system consists of one enzyme or more than one is not known. Nor is anything known of the nature of the enzymes in question. Nor can any theory be yet advanced as to how an enzyme can catalyze a nuclear reaction, since these involve particular interactions with forces five orders of magnitude higher than those involved in the ordinary chemical reactions commonly catalyzed by enzymes.

"The overall nuclear change is from oxygen-18 to gold-197. The oxygen-18 is plentiful in its environment, being present in significant amount in water and all organic foodstuffs. The gold-197 is excreted via the ovaries. One known intermediate is iron-56, and the fact that auremoglobin is formed in the process leads us to suspect that the enzyme or enzymes involved may have heme as a prosthetic group.

"There has been considerable thought devoted to the value this overall nuclear change might have to the Goose. The oxygen-18 does it no harm, and the gold-197 is troublesome to be rid of, potentially poisonous, and a cause of its sterility. Its formation might possibly be a means of avoiding greater danger. This danger — "

But just reading it in the report, friend, makes it all seem so quiet, almost pensive. Actually, I never saw a man come closer to apoplexy and survive than Billings did when he found out about our own radioactive gold experiments, which I told you about earlier — the ones in which we detected no radioactivity in the goose, so that we discarded the results as meaningless.

Many times over he asked how we could possibly consider it unimportant that we had lost radioactivity.

"You're like the cub reporter," he said, "who was sent to cover a society wedding and on returning said there was no story because the groom hadn't shown up.

"You fed The Goose radioactive gold and lost it. Not only that, you failed to detect any natural radioactivity about The Goose. Any carbon-14. Any potassium-40. And you called it failure."

We started feeding The Goose radioactive isotopes. Cautiously, at first, but before the end of January of 1956 we were shoveling it in.

The Goose remained nonradioactive.

"What it amounts to," said Billings, "is that this enzyme-catalyzed nuclear process of The Goose manages to convert any unstable isotope into a stable isotope."

"Useful," I said.

"Useful? It's a thing of beauty. It's the perfect defense against the atomic age. Listen, the conversion of oxygen-18 to gold-197 should liberate eight and a fraction positrons per oxygen atom. That means eight and a fraction gamma rays as soon as each positron combines with an electron. No gamma rays, either. The Goose must be able to absorb gamma rays harmlessly."

We irradiated The Goose with gamma rays. As the level rose, The Goose developed a slight fever, and we quit in panic. It was just fever, though, not radiation sickness. A day passed, the fever subsided, and The Goose was as good as new.

"Do you see what we've got?" demanded Billings.

"A scientific marvel," said Finley.

"Man, don't you see the practical applications? If we could find out the mechanism and duplicate it in the test tube, we've got a perfect method of radioactive ash disposal. The most important drawback preventing us from going ahead with a full-scale atomic economy is the headache of what to do with the radioactive isotopes manufactured in the process. Sift them through an enzyme preparation in large vats and that would be it.

"Find out the mechanism, gentlemen, and you can stop worrying about fallouts. We would find a protection against radiation sickness.

"Alter the mechanism somehow and we can have geese excreting any element needed. How about uranium-235 eggshells?

"The mechanism! The mechanism!"

We sat there, all of us, staring at The Goose.

If only the eggs would hatch. If only we could get a tribe of nuclear-reactor geese.

"It must have happened before," said Finley. "The legends of such geese must have started somehow."

"Do you want to wait?" asked Billings.

If we had a gaggle of such geese, we could begin taking a few apart. We could study their ovaries. We could prepare tissue slices and tissue homogenates.

That might not do any good. The tissue of a liver biopsy did not react with oxygen-18 under any conditions we tried.

But then we might perfuse an intact liver. We might study intact embryos, watch for one to develop the mechanism.

But with only one goose, we could do none of that.

We don't dare kill The Goose That Lays The Golden Eggs.

The secret was in the liver of that fat goose.

Liver of fat goose! *Pâté de foie gras!* No delicacy to us!

Nevis said thoughtfully, "We need an idea. Some radical departure. Some crucial thought."

"Saying it won't bring it," said Billings despondently.

And in a miserable attempt at a joke, I said, "We could advertise in the newspapers," and that gave *me* an idea.

"Science fiction!" I said.

"What?" said Finley.

"Look, science fiction magazines print gag articles. The readers consider it fun. They're interested." I told them about the thiotimoline articles Asimov wrote and which I had once read.

The atmosphere was cold with disapproval.

"We won't even be breaking security regulations," I said, "because no one will believe it." I told them about the time in 1944 when Cleve Cartmill wrote a story describing the atom bomb one year early and the FBI kept its temper.

"And science fiction readers have ideas. Don't underrate them. Even if they think it's a gag article, they'll send their notions in to the editor. And since we have no ideas of our own, since we're up a dead-end street, what can we lose?"

They still didn't buy it.

So I said, "And you know . . . The Goose won't live forever."

That did it, somehow.

We had to convince Washington; then I got in touch with John Campbell, editor of the magazine, and he got in touch with Asimov.

Now the article is done. I've read it, I approve, and I urge you all not to believe it. Please don't.

Only —

Any ideas?

"Inflation is here! I just laid a golden egg!"

The Available Data
on the Worp Reaction

LION MILLER

Does there live and breathe a science fiction writer who hasn't dreamed up something like this particular story? There can't be because I myself wrote one once, and if I can do it, you can bet everyone can. My story was called "Robot A1-76 Goes Astray"; you'll find it in my book, The Rest of the Robots. *But don't look for it. Miller's story is shorter, better, and lots funnier.*

THE EARLIEST CONFIRMED DATA on Aldous Worp, infant, indicates that, while apparently normal in most physical respects, he was definitely considered by neighbors, playmates, and family as a hopeless idiot. We know too that he was a quiet child, of extremely sedentary habits. The only sound he was ever heard to utter was a shrill monosyllable, closely akin to the expression "Whee!" and this only when summoned to meals or, less often, when his enigmatic interest was aroused by an external stimulus, such as an odd-shaped pebble or a stick.

Suddenly this child abandoned his customary inactivity. Shortly after reaching his sixth birthday — the time is unfortunately only approximate — Aldous Worp began a series of exploratory trips to the city dump, which was located to the rear of the Worp premises.

After a few of these tours, the lad returned to his home one afternoon dragging a large cogwheel. After lengthy deliberation, he secreted said wheel within an unused chicken coop.

Thus began a project that did not end for nearly twenty years. Young Worp progressed through childhood, boyhood, and young manhood, transferring thousands of metal objects, large and small, of nearly every description, from the dump to the coop. Since any sort of formal schooling was apparently beyond his mental capacity, his parents were pleased by the activity that kept Aldous happy and content. Presumably, they did not trouble themselves with the aesthetic problems involved.

As suddenly as he had begun it, Aldous Worp abandoned his self-imposed task. For nearly a year — again, the time is approximate due to insufficient data — Aldous Worp remained within the confines of the Worp property. When not occupied with such basic bodily needs as eating and sleeping, he moved slowly upon his pile of debris with no apparent plan or purpose.

One morning he was observed by his father (as we are told by the latter) to be selecting certain objects from the pile and fitting them together.

It should be noted here, I think, that no account of the Worp Reaction can be complete without certain direct quotations from Aldous's father, Lambert Simnel Worp. Concerning the aforementioned framework the elder Worp has said: "The thing that got me, was every (deleted) piece he picked up fit with some other (deleted) piece. Didn't make no (deleted) difference if it was a (deleted) bedspring or a (deleted) busted eggbeater, if the kid stuck it on another part, it stayed there."

Concerning usage of tools by Aldous Worp, L. S. Worp has deposed: "No tools."

A lengthier addendum is offered us by L. S. Worp in reply to a query which I quote direct: "How in God's name did he manage to cause separate parts to adhere to each other to make a whole?" (Dr. Palmer). *A.* "The (deleted) stuff went together tighter'n a mallard's (deleted), and nobody — but *nobody,* mister, could get 'em apart."

It was obviously quite stable, since young Aldous frequently clambered into the maze to add another "part," without disturbing its equilibrium in the slightest.

The foregoing, however sketchy, is all the background we have to the climactic experiment itself. For an exact report of the circumstances attendant upon the one "controlled" demonstration of the Worp Reaction we are indebted to Major Herbert R. Armstrong, U.S. Army Engineers, and Dr. Phillip H. Cross, A.E.C., who were present.

It seems that, at exactly 10.46 A.M., Aldous Worp picked up a very old and very rusty cogwheel . . . the very first object he had retrieved from oblivion on the junk pile, so long ago when he was but a lad of six. After a moment's hesitation, he climbed to the top of his jerrybuilt structure, paused, then lowered himself into its depths. He disappeared from the sight of these trained observers for several minutes. (Dr. Cross: 4 min. 59 sec. Maj. Armstrong: 5 min. 02 sec.) Finally Aldous reappeared, climbed down, and stared fixedly at his creation.

We now quote from the combined reports of Maj. Armstrong and Dr. Cross: "After standing dazed-like for a few minutes, Worp finally came very close to his assembly. There was a rod sticking out with the brass ball of a bedpost fastened to it. Aldous Worp gave this a slight tug. What happened then was utterly fantastic. First, we heard a rushing sound, something like a waterfall. This sound grew appreciably louder and, in about fifteen seconds, we saw a purplish glow emanate from *beneath* the contraption. Then, the whole congeries of rubbish arose into the air for a height of about three meters and hung there, immobile. The lad Aldous jumped around with every semblance of glee and we distinctly heard him remark 'Whee!' three times. Then he went to one side of the phenomenon, reached down and turned over the rusty wheel of a coffee mill, and his 'machine' slowly settled to earth."

There was, of course, considerable excitement. Representatives of the armed services, the press services, the A.E.C., various schools for advanced studies, et al. arrived in droves. Communication with Aldous Worp was impossible since the young man had never learned to talk. L. S. Worp, however profane, was an earnest and sincere gentleman, anxious to be of service to his country; but the above quotations from his conversations will indicate how little light he was able to shed on the problem. Efforts to look inside the structure availed little, since the closest and most detailed analysis could elicit no other working hypothesis than, "It's all nothing but a bunch of junk" (Dr. Palmer). Further, young Worp obviously resented such investigations.

However, he took great delight in operating his machine and repeatedly demonstrated the "reaction" to all beholders.

The most exhaustive tests, Geiger et al., revealed nothing.

Finally, the importunities of the press could no longer be denied, and early in the afternoon of the second day telecasters arrived on the scene.

Aldous Worp surveyed them for a moment, then brought his invention back to earth. With a set look on his face, he climbed to its top, clambered down into its bowels, and, in due course, reappeared with the ancient cogwheel. This he carefully placed in its original resting place in the chicken coop. Systematically, and in order of installation, he removed each part from his structure and carefully returned it to its original place in the original heap by the chicken coop.

Today, the component parts of the whole that was Worp's Reaction are scattered. For, silently ignoring the almost hysterical pleas of the men of science and of the military, Aldous Worp, after dismantling his machine completely and piling all parts in and over the chicken coop, then took upon himself the onerous task of transporting them, one by one, back to their original place in the city dump.

Now, unmoved by an occasional berating by L. S. Worp, silent before an infrequent official interrogation, Aldous Worp sits on a box in the backyard of his ancestral home, gazing serenely out over the city dump. Once in a very great while his eyes light up for a moment and he says "Whee!" very quietly.

"Arthur, there's a thing at the door says it's escaped from M.I.T. and can we please plug it in for the night."

Imaginary Numbers in a Real Garden

GERALD JONAS

Given: one bold mathematician.
Uncertain of his own position,
he drew two lines and at their joint,
where angels danced, he made his •
Then reached into the void and caught
the faceless essence of the o,
and taught us not to fear ∞
but worship his serene divinity,
whose sacraments at first seem pale;
yet if men hunger for a Grail,
they still may seek, beyond the sun,
the rare $\sqrt{-1}$.

The Mathenauts

NORMAN KAGAN

Laughter is universal and utterly democratic. All races, religions, sexes, and ages laugh at something funny, and enjoy laughing so much that they seek out funny things. Show me a person who doesn't laugh, and I will still show you a human who won't admit to an absent sense of humor. Show me one who seems not to have a sense of humor, and I'll show you one who is universally despised.

Well, then, Kagan was a graduate student of mathematics when he wrote this story, and should mathematicians not laugh? Heaven forbid. Of course they should laugh. To be sure, no one understands what mathematicians are talking about, but let's laugh along with Kagan, just to show how sympathetic we are to the principles of the true democracy of humor.

I T   H A P P E N E D on my fifth trip into the spaces, and the first ever made under the private-enterprise acts. It took a long time to get the P.E.A. through Congress for mathenautics, but the precedents went all the way back to the Telstar satellite a hundred years ago, and most of the concepts are in books anyone can buy, though not so readily understand. Besides, it didn't matter if BC-flight was made public or not. All mathenauts are crazy. Everybody knows that.

Take our crew. Johnny Pearl took a pin along whenever he went baby-sitting for the grad students at Berkeley, and three months later the mothers invariably found out they were pregnant again. And Pearl was our physicist.

Then there was Goldwasser. Ed Goldwasser always sits in those pan-on-a-post cigarette holders when we're in New York, and if you ask him, he grumbles; "Well, it's an ashtray, ain't it?" A punster and a pataphysicist. I would never have chosen him to go, except that he and I got the idea together.

Ted Anderson was our metamathematician. He's about half a nonosecond behind Ephraim Cohen (the co-inventor of BC-flight) and has about six nervous breakdowns a month trying to pass him. But he's got the best practical knowledge of the BC-drive outside Princeton — if practical knowledge means anything with respect to a pure mathematical abstraction.

And me — topologist. A topologist is a man who can't tell a doughnut from a cup of coffee. (I'll explain that some other time.) Seriously, I specialize in some of the more abstruse properties of geometric structures. "Did Galois discover that theorem before or after he died?" is a sample of my conversation.

Sure, mathenauts are mathenuts. But as we found out, not quite mathenutty enough.

The ship, the *Albrecht Dold,* was a twelve-googol scout that Ed Goldwasser and I'd picked up cheap from the N.Y.U. Courant Institute. She wasn't the Princeton I.A.S. *Von-Neumann,* with googolplex coils and a chapter of the DAR, and she wasn't one of those new toys you've been seeing for a rich man and his grandmother. Her coils were DNA molecules, and the psychosomatics were straight from the Brill Institute at Harvard. A sweet ship. For psychic ecology we'd gotten a bunch of kids from the Bronx College of the New York City University, commonsense types — business majors, engineers, pre-meds. But kids.

I was looking over Ephraim Cohen's latest paper, "Nymphomaniac Nested Complexes with Rossian Irrelevancies" (old Ice Cream Cohen loves sexy titles), when the trouble started. We'd abstracted, and Goldwasser and Pearl had signaled me from the lab that they were ready for the first tests. I made the *Dold* invariant, and shoved off through one of the passages that linked the isomorphomechanism and the lab. (We kept the ship in free fall for convenience.) I was about halfway along the tube when the immy failed and the walls began to close in.

I spread my legs and braked against the walls of the tube, believing with all my might. On second thought I let the walls sink in and braked with my palms. It would've been no trick to hold the walls for awhile. Without the immy my own imagination would hold them, this far from the B.C.N.Y. kids. But that might've brought more trouble — I'd probably made some silly mistake, and the kids, who might not notice a simple contraction or shear, would crack up under some weirdomorphism. And if we lost the kids . . .

So anyway I just dug my feet in against the mirage and tried to slow up, on a surface that no one'd bothered to think any friction into. Of course, if you've read some of the popular accounts of math-sailing, you'd think I'd just duck back through a hole in the fiftieth dimension to the immy. But it doesn't work out that way. A ship in BC-flight is a very precarious structure in a philosophical sense. That's why we carry a psychic ecology, and that's why Brill conditioning takes six years, plus, with a Ph.D. in pure math, to absorb. Anyway, a mathenaut should never forget his postulates, or he'll find himself floating in 27-space, with nary a notion to be named.

Then the walls really did vanish — NO! — and I found myself at the junction of two passages. The other had a grabline. I caught it and rebounded, then swarmed back along the tube. After ten seconds I was climbing down into a funnel. I caught my breath, swallowed some Dramamine, and burst into the control room.

The heart of the ship was pulsing and throbbing. For a moment I thought I was back in Hawaii with my aqualung, an invader in a shifting, shimmering world of sea fronds and barracuda. But it was no immy, no immy — a rubber room without the notion of distance that we take for granted (technically, a room with topological properties but no metric ones). Instrument racks and chairs and books shrank and ballooned and twisted, and floor and ceiling vibrated with my breath.

It was horrible.

Ted Anderson was hanging in front of the immy, the isomorphomechanism, but he was in no shape to do anything. In fact, he was in no shape at all. His body was pulsing and shaking, so his hands were too big or too small to manipulate the controls, or his eyes shrank or blossomed. Poor Ted's nerves had gone again.

I shoved against the wall and bulleted toward him, a fish in a weaving, shifting undersea landscape, concentrating desperately on my body and the old structure of the room. (This is why physical training is so important.) For an instant I was choking and screaming in a hairy blackness, a nightmare inside-out total inversion; then I was back in the control room and had shoved Ted away from the instruments, cursing when nothing happened, then bracing against the wall panels and shoving again. He drifted away.

The immy was all right. The twiddles circuits between the B.C.N.Y. kids and the rest of the *Dold* had been cut out. I set up an orthonormal system and punched the immy.

Across the shuddering, shifting room Ted tried to speak, but found it too difficult. Great Gauss, he was lucky his aorta hadn't contracted to a straw and given him a coronary! I clamped down on my own circulatory system viciously, while he struggled to speak. Finally he kicked off and came tumbling toward me, mouthing and flailing his notebook.

I hit the circuit. The room shifted about and for an instant Ted Anderson hung, ghostly, amid the isomorphomechanism's one-to-ones. Then he disappeared.

The invention of BC-flight was the culmination of a century of work in algebraic topology and experimental psychology. For thousands of years men had speculated as to the nature of the world. For the past five hundred, physics and the physical sciences had held sway. Then Thomas Brill and Ephraim Cohen peeled away another layer of the reality union, and the space sciences came into being.

If you insist on an analogy — well, a scientist touches and probes the real Universe, and abstracts an idealization into his head. Mathenautics allows him to grab himself by the scruff of the neck and pull himself up into the idealization. See — I *told* you.

Okay, we'll try it slowly. Science assumes the universe to be ordered and investigates the nature of the ordering. In the "hard" sciences, mathematics is the basis of the ordering the scientist puts on nature. By the twentieth century, a large portion of the physical processes and materials in the universe were found to submit to such an ordering (e.g., analytic mechanics and the motions of the planets). Some scientists were even applying mathematical structures to aggregates of living things and to living processes.

Cohen and Brill asked (in ways far apart), "If order and organization seem to be a natural part of the Universe, why can't we remove these qualities from coarse matter and space and study them separately?" The answer was BC-flight.

Through certain purely mathematical "mechanisms" and special psychological training, selected scientists (the term *mathenaut* came later, slang from the faddy *astronautics*) could be shifted into the abstract.

The first mathenautical ships were crewed with young scientists and mathematicians who'd received Tom Brill's treatments and Ephraim Cohen's skull-cracking sessions on the BC-field. The ships went into BC-flight and vanished.

By the theory, the ships didn't *go* anywhere. But the effect was somehow real. Just as a materialist might *see* organic machines instead of people, so the mathenauts saw the raw mathematical structure of space — Riemann space, Hausdorf space, vector space — without matter. A crowd of people existed as an immensely complicated *something* in vector space. The study of these *somethings* was yielding immense amounts of knowledge. Pataphysics, patasociology, patapsychology were wild, baffling new fields of knowledge.

But the math universes were strange, alien. How could you learn to live in Flatland? The wildcat minds of the first crews were too creative. They became disoriented. Hence the immies and their power supplies — SayCows, Daught-AmRevs, the B.C.N.Y. kids — fatheads, stuffed shirts, personality types that clung to common sense where there was none, and preserved (locally) a ship's psychic ecology. Inside the BC-field, normalcy. Outside, raw imagination.

Johnny, Ted, Goldy, and I had chosen vector spaces with certain topological properties to test Goldy's commercial concept. Outside the BC-field there was dimension but no distance, structure but no shape. Inside —

"By Riemann's tensors!" Pearl cried.

He was at the iris of one of the tubes. A moment later Ed Goldwasser joined him. "What happened to Ted?"

"I — I don't know. No — yes, I do!"

I released the controls I had on my body and stopped thinking about the room. The immy was working again. "He was doing something with the controls when the twiddles circuits failed. When I got them working again and the room snapped back into shape, he happened to be where the immy had been. The commonsense circuits rejected him."

"So where did he go?" asked Pearl.

"I don't know."

I was sweating. I was thinking of all the things that could've happened when we lost the isomorphomechanism. Some subconscious twitch and you're rotated half a dozen dimensions out of phase, so you're floating in the raw stuff of thought, with maybe a hair-thin line around you to tell you where the ship has been. Or the ship takes the notion to shrink pea size, so you're squeezed through all the tubes and compartments and smashed to jelly when we ortho-normalize. Galois! We'd been lucky.

The last thought gave me a notion. "Could we have shrunk so we're inside his body? Or he grown so we're floating in his liver?"

"No," said Goldy. "Topology is preserved. But I don't — oh, hell — I really don't know. If he grew so big he was outside the psychic ecology, he might just have faded away." The big pataphysicist wrinkled up his face inside his beard. "*Alice* should be required reading for mathenauts," he muttered. "The real trouble is no one has ever been outside and been back to tell about it. The animal experiments and the *Norbert Wiener* and Wilbur on the *Paul R. Halmos*. They just disappeared." "You know," I said, "you can map the volume of a sphere into the whole universe using the ratio: $IR : R$ equals $R:OR$, where IR and OR are the inside and outside distances for the points. Maybe that's what happened to Ted. Maybe he's just outside the ship, filling all space with his metamath and his acne?"

"Down boy," said Goldwasser. "I've got a simpler suggestion. Let's check over the ship, compartment by compartment. Maybe he's in it somewhere, unconscious."

But he wasn't on the ship.

We went over it twice — every tube, every compartment. (In reality, a mathenautic ship looks like a radio ripped out of its case and flying through the air.) We ended up in the ecology section, a big Broadway-line subway car that roared and rattled in the middle of darkness in the middle of nothing. The B.C.N.Y. kids were all there — Freddi Urbont clucking happily away to her boyfriend, chubby and smily and an education major; Byron and Burbitt, electronics engineers, ecstatic over the latest copy of *C-Quantum;* Stephen Seidmann, a number-theory major, quietly proving that since Harvard is the best school in the world, and B.C.N.Y. is better than Harvard, B.C.N.Y. is the best school in the world; two citizens with nose jobs and names I'd forgotten, engaged in a filthy discussion of glands and organs and meat. The walls were firm, the straw seats scratchy and uncomfortable. The projectors showed we were just entering the Seventy-second Street stop. How real, how comforting! I slid the door open to rejoin Johnny and Ed. The subway riders saw me slip into free fall and glimpsed the emptiness of vector space.

Hell broke loose!

The far side of the car bulged inward, the glass smashing and the metal groaning. The CUNYs had no compensation training!

Freddi Urbont burst into tears. Byron and Burbitt yelled as a bubble in the floor swallowed them. The wall next to the nose jobs sprouted a dozen phallic symbols, while the seat bubbled with breasts. The walls began to melt. Seidmann began to yell about the special status of N.Y. City University honors program students.

Pearl acted with a speed and a surety I'd never have imagined. He shoved me out of the way and launched himself furiously at the other end of the car, now in free fall. There he pivoted, smiled horribly, and at the top of his lungs began singing "The Purple and the Black."

Goldy and I had enough presence of mind to join him. Concentrating desperately on the shape and form of the car, we blasted the air with our devotion to Sheppard Hall, our love of Convent Avenue, and our eternal devotion to Lewisohn Stadium. Somehow it saved us. The room rumbled and twisted and reformed, and soon the eight of us were back in the tired old subway car that brought its daily catch of Beavers to One hundred thirty-ninth Street.

The equilibrium was still precarious. I heard Goldwasser telling the nose jobs his terrible monologue about the "Volvo I want to buy. I can be the first to break the door membranes, and when I get my hands on that big, fat steering wheel, ohh!, it'll be a week before I climb out of it!"

Pearl was cooing to Urbont how wonderful she was as the valedictorian at her junior high, how great the teaching profession was, and how useful, and how interesting.

As for me; "Well, I guess you're right, Steve. I should have gone to B.C.N.Y. instead of Berkeley."

"That's right, Jimmy. After all, B.C.N.Y. has some of the best number-theory people in the world. And some of the greatest educators too. Like Dean Cashew who started the privileged student program. It sure is wonderful."

"I guess you're right, Steve."

"I'm right, all right. At schools like Berkeley, you're just another student, but at B.C.N.Y. you can be a P.S. and get all the good professors and small classes and high grades."

"You're right, Steve."

"I'm right, all right. Listen, we have people that've quit Cornell and Harvard and M.I.T. Of course, they don't do much but run home after school and sit in their houses, but their parents all say how much happier they are — like back in high school . . ."

When the scrap paper and the gum wrappers were up to our knees and there were four false panhandlers in the car, Johnny called a halt. The little psychist smiled and nodded as he walked the three of us carefully out the door.

"Standard technique," he murmured to no one in particular. "Doing *something* immediately rather than the best thing a while later. Their morale was shot, so I — " He trailed off.

"Are they really that sensitive?" Goldwasser asked. "I thought their training was better than that."

"You act like they were components in an electronics rig," said Pearl jerkily. "You know that premedial sensory perception, the ability to perceive the dull routine that normal people ignore, is a very delicate talent!"

Pearl was well launched. "In the dark ages such people were called dullards and subnormals. Only now, in our enlightened age, do we realize their true ability to know things outside the ordinary senses — a talent vital for BC-flight."

The tedium and meaninglessness of life which we rationalize away —

"A ship is more mind than matter, and if you upset that mind — "

He paled suddenly. "I, I think I'd better stay with them," he said. He flung open the door and went back into the coach. Goldwasser and I looked at each other. Pearl was a trained mathenaut, but his specialty was people, not paramath.

"Let's check the lab," I muttered.

Neither of us spoke as we moved toward the lab — slap a wall, pull yourself forward, twist round some instrumentation — the "reaction swim" of a man in free fall. The walls began to quiver again, and I could see Goldy clamp down on his body and memories of this part of the ship. We were nearing the limits of the BC-field. The lab itself, and the experimental apparatus, stuck out into vector space.

"Let's make our tests and go home," I told Goldy.

Neither of us mentioned Ted as we entered the lab.

Remember this was a commercial project. We weren't patasociologists studying abstract groups or superpurists looking for the first point. We wanted money.

Goldy thought he had a moneymaking scheme for us, but Goldy hasn't been normal since he took Polykarp Kusch's "Kusch of Death" at Columbia, "Electrodimensions and Magnespace." He was going to build four-dimensional molecules.

Go back to Flatland. Imagine a hollow paper pyramid on the surface of that two-dimensional world. To a Flatlander, it is a triangle. Flop down the sides — four triangles. Now put a molecule in each face — one molecule, four molecules. And recall that you have infinite dimensions available. Think of the storage possibilities alone. All the books of the world in a viewer, all the food in the world in your pack. A television the size of a piece of paper; circuits looped through dim-19. Loop an entire industrial plant through hyperspace and get one the size and shape of a billboard. Shove raw materials in one side — pull finished products out the other!

But how do you make four-dim molecules? Goldy thought he had a way, and Ted Anderson had checked over the math and pronounced it workable. The notion rested in the middle of the lab: a queer, half-understood machine of mind and matter called a Grahm-Schmidt generator.

"Jeez, Ed! This lab looks like your old room back in Diego Borough."

"Yeah," said Goldwasser. "Johnny said it would be a good idea. Orientation against *that.*"

That was the outside of the lab, raw topological space, without energy or matter or time. It was the shape and color of what you see in the back of your head.

I looked away.

Goldwasser's room was a duplicate of his old home — the metal desk, the electronics rigs, the immense bookshelves, half filled with physics and half with religious works. I picked up a copy of Stace's *Time and Eternity* and thumbed through it, then put it down, embarrassed.

"Good reading for a place like this." Goldwasser smiled.

He sat down at the desk and began to check out his "instruments" from the locked drawer where he'd kept them. Once he reached across the desk and turned on a tape of Gene Gerard's *Excelsior!* The flat midwestern voice murmured in the background.

"First, I need some hands," said Ed.

Out in the nothingness two pairs of lines met at right angles. For an instant, all space was filled with them, jammed together every which way. Then it just settled down to two.

The lab was in darkness. Goldwasser's big form crouched over the controls. He wore his engineer's boots and his hair long, and a beard as well. He might have been some medieval monk or primitive witchdoctor. He touched a knob and set a widget and checked in his copy of *Birkhoff and MacLane.*

"Now," he said, and played with his instruments. Two new vectors rose out of the intersections. "Cross products. Now I've a right- and a left-handed system."

All the while Gene Gerard was mumbling in the background: " 'Ah, now, my pretty,' snarled the Count. 'Come to my bedchamber, or I'll leave you to Igor's mercies.' The misshapen dwarf cackled and rubbed his paws. 'Decide, decide!' cried the Count. His voice was a scream. 'Decide, my dear. SEX — ELSE, IGOR!' "

"Augh," said Goldwasser, and shut it off. "Now," he said, "I've got some plasma in the next compartment."

"Holy Halmos," I whispered.

Ted Anderson stood beside the generator. He smiled and went into topological convulsions. I looked away, and presently he came back into shape. "Hard getting used to real space again," he whispered. He looked thinner and paler than ever.

"I haven't got long," he said, "so here it is. You know I was working on Ephraim's theories, looking for a flaw. There isn't any flaw."

"Ted, you're rotating," I cautioned.

He steadied and continued. "There's no flaw. But the theory is wrong. It's backwards. *This is the real universe,*" he said, and gestured. Beyond the lab topological space remained as always, a blank, the color of the back of your head through your own eyes.

"Now listen to me, Goldy and Johnny and Kidder." I saw that Pearl was standing in the iris of the tube. "What is the nature of intelligence? I guess it's the power to abstract, to conceptualize. I don't know what to say beyond that — I don't know what it is. But I know where it came from! Here! In the math spaces — they're alive with thought, flashing with mind!

"When the twiddles circuits failed, I cracked. I fell apart, lost faith in it all. For I had just found what I thought was a basic error in theory. I died, I vanished . . .

"But I didn't. I'm a metamathematician. An operational philosopher, you might say. I may have gone mad — but I think I passed a threshold of knowledge. I understand . . .

"They're out there. The things we thought we'd invented ourselves. The concepts and the notions and the pure structures — if you could see them . . ."

He looked around the room, desperately. Pearl was rigid against the iris of the tube. Goldy looked at Ted for a moment, then his head darted from side to side. His hands whitened on the controls.

"Jimmy," Ted said.

I didn't know. I moved toward him, across the lab to the edge of topological space, and beyond the psychic ecology. No time, no space, no matter. But how can I say it? How many people can stay awake over a book of modern algebra, and how many of those can understand?

— I saw a set bubbling and whirling, then take purpose and structure to itself and become a group, generate a second-unity element, mount itself and become a group, generate a second-unity element, mount itself and become a field, ringed by rings. Near it, a mature field, shot through with ideals, threw off a splitting field in a passion of growth and become complex.

— I saw the life of the matrices; the young ones sporting, adding and multiplying by a constant, the mature ones mating by composition: male and female make male, female and male make female — sex through anticommutivity! I saw them grow old, meeting false identities and loosing rows and columns into nullity.

— I saw a race of vectors, losing their universe to a newer race of tensors that conquered and humbled them.

— I watched the tyranny of the Well Ordering Principle, as a free set was lashed and whipped into structure. I saw a partially ordered set, free and happy, broken before the Axiom of Zemelo.

— I saw the point sets, with their cliques and clubs, infinite numbers of sycophants clustering round a Bolzano-Weirstrauss aristocrat — the great compact medieval coverings of infinity with denumerable shires — the conflicts as closed sets created open ones, and the other way round.

— I saw the rigid castes of a society of transformations, orthogonal royalty, inner product gentry, degenerates — where intercomposition set the caste of the lower on the product.

— I saw the proud old cyclic groups, father and son and grandson, generating the generations, rebel and blacksheep and hero, following each other endlessly. Close by were the permutation groups, frolicking in a way that seemed like the way you sometimes repeat a sentence endlessly, stressing a different word each time.

There was much I saw that I did not understand, for mathematics is a deep, and even a mathenaut must choose his wedge of specialty. But that world of abstractions flamed with a beauty and meaning that chilled the works and worlds of men, so I wept in futility.

Presently we found ourselves back in the lab. I sat beside Ted Anderson and leaned on him, and I did not speak for fear my voice would break.

Anderson talked to Johnny and Ed.

"There was a — a race, here, that grew prideful. It knew the Riemann space and the vector space, the algebras and the topologies, and yet it was unfulfilled. In some way — oddly like this craft," he murmured, gesturing "— they wove the worlds together, creating the real universe you knew in your youth.

"Yet still it was unsatisfied. Somehow the race yearned so for newness that it surpassed itself, conceiving matter and energy and entropy and creating them.

"And there were laws and properties for these: inertia, speed, potential, quantumization. Perhaps life was an accident. It was not noticed for a long time, and proceeded apace. For the proud race had come to know itself and saw that the new concepts were . . . flawed." Anderson smiled faintly and turned to Ed.

"Goldy, remember when we had Berkowitz for algebra?" he asked. "Remember what he said the first day?"

Goldwasser smiled. "Any math majors?

"Hmm, that's good.

"Any physics majors?

"Physics majors! You guys are just super engineers!

"Any chemistry majors?

"Chemistry major! You'd be better off as a cook!"

Ted finished, "And so on, down to the, ahem, baloney majors."

"He was number happy," said Ed, smiling.

"No. He was right, in a way." Ted continued, "The race had found its new notions were crudities, simple copies of algebras and geometries past. What it thought was vigor was really sloth and decay.

"It knew how to add and multiply, but it had forgotten what a field was and what commutivity was. If entropy and time wreaked harm on matter, they did worse by this race. It wasn't interested in expeditions through the fiber bundles; rather it wanted to count apples.

"There was conflict and argument, but it was too late to turn back. The race had already degenerated too far to turn back. Then life was discovered.

"The majority of the race took matter for a bride. Its aesthetic and creative powers ruined, it wallowed in passion and pain. Only remnants of reason remained.

"For the rest, return to abstraction was impossible. Time, entropy, had robbed them of their knowledge, their heritage. Yet they still hoped and expended themselves to leave, well, call it a 'seed' of sorts."

"Mathematics?" cried Pearl.

"It explains some things," mused Goldwasser softly. "Why abstract mathematics, developed in the mind, turns out fifty years or a century later to accurately describe the physical universe. Tensor calculus and relativity, for example. If you look at it this way, the math was there first."

"Yes, yes, yes. Mathematicians talked about their subject as an art form. One system is more 'elegant' than another if its logical structure is more austere. But Occam's Razor, the law of simplest hypothesis, isn't logical.

"Many of the great mathematicians did their greatest work as children and youths before they were dissipated by the sensual world. In a trivial sense, scientists and mathematicians most of all are described as 'unworldly' . . ."

Anderson bobbled his head in the old familiar way. "You have almost returned," he said quietly. "This ship is really a heuristic device, an aid to perception. You are on the threshold. You have come all the way back."

The metamathematician took his notebook and seemed to set all his will upon it. "See Ephraim gets this," he murmured. "He, you, I . . . the oneness — "

Abruptly he disappeared. The notebook fell to the floor.

I took it up. Neither Ed nor Johnny Pearl met my eyes. We may have sat and stood there for several hours, numbed, silent. Presently the two began setting up the isomorphomechanism for realization. I joined them.

The National Mathenautics and Hyperspace Administration had jurisdiction over civilian flights then, even as it does today. Ted was pretty important, it seemed. Our preliminary debriefing won us a maximum-security session with their research chief.

Perhaps, as I'd thought passionately for an instant, I'd have done better to smash the immy, rupture the psychic ecology, let the eggshell be shattered at last. But that's not the way of it. For all of our progress, some rules of scientific investigation don't change. Our first duty was to report back. Better heads than ours would decide what to do next.

They did. Ephraim Cohen didn't say anything after he heard us out and looked at Ted's notebook. Old Ice Cream sat there, a big teddy-bear-shaped genius with thick black hair and a dumb smile, and grinned at us. It was in institute code.

The B.C.N.Y. kids hadn't seen anything, of course. So nobody talked.

Johnny Pearl married a girl named Judy Shatz and they had fifteen kids. I guess that showed Johnny's views on the matter of matter.

Ed Goldwasser got religion. Zen-Judaism is pretty orthodox these days, yet somehow he found it suited him. But he didn't forget what had happened back out in space. His book, *The Cosmic Mind,* came out last month, and it's a good summation of Ted's ideas, with a minimum of spiritual overtones.

Myself. Well, a mathematician, especially a topologist, is useless after thirty, the way progress is going along these days. But *Dim-Dustries* is a commercial enterprise, and I guess I'm good for twenty years more as a businessman.

Goldwasser's Grahm-Schmidt generator worked, but that was just the beginning. Dimensional extensions made Earth a paradise, with housing hidden in the probabilities and automated industries tucked away in the dimensions.

The biggest boon was something no one anticipated. A space of infinite dimensions solves all the basic problems of modern computer-circuit design. Now all components can be linked with short electron paths, no matter how big and complex the device.

There have been any number of other benefits. The space hospitals, for example, where topological surgery can cure the most terrible wounds — and topological psychiatry the most baffling syndromes. (Four years of math is required for pre-meds these days.) Patapsychology and patasociology finally made some progress, so that political and economic woes have declined — thanks too to the spaces, which have drained off a good deal of poor Earth's overpopulation. There are even spaces resorts, or so I'm told — I don't get away much.

I've struck it lucky. Fantastically so.

The Private Enterprise Acts had just been passed, you'll recall, and I had decided I didn't want to go spacing again. With the training required for the subject, I guess I was the only qualified man who had a peddler's pack too. Jaffee, one of my friends down at Securities and Exchange, went so far as to say that *Dim-Dustries* was a hyperspherical trust (math is required for pre-laws too). But I placated him and I got some of my mathemateers to realign the Street on a Möbius strip, so he had to side with me.

Me, I'll stick to the Earth. The "real" planet is a garden spot now, and the girls are very lovely.

Ted Anderson was recorded lost in topological space. He wasn't the first, and he was far from the last. Twiddles circuits have burned out, DaughtAms-Revs have gone mad, and no doubt there have been some believers who have sought out the Great Race.

Coffee Break

D. F. JONES

Janet likes this story because she doesn't drink coffee. She turns up her nose even at mocha icing. What's more, finding herself not quite able to force me to join her in this strange abstention (though in most things I consider her word law) she has wheedled me into shifting to the decaffeinated version for some weird medical reason or another. (She's a physician and it's gone to her head.) Anyway, she says this story proves how upsetting a factor the coffee break can be.

WHEN AN EAGER SALESMAN for a new and pushing chemical company convinced Manuel y Ortega da Gomez-Jackson that his particular insecticide was the newest, best, and cheapest answer to the depredations of the leaf miners that troubled Manuel's very considerable coffee plantation, quite a chain of events started.

And the confidence of the eager salesman was fully justified. The luckless leaf miners were the first to benefit — if that is the word. Those insects that stuck to the only trade they knew, leaf mining, died. Those that played a hunch and left the succulent leaves severely alone, well, starvation got them. Which is life in a microcosm. However you place your bet, the bank wins.

Gomez-Jackson was highly delighted, and the clusters of ripening red berries were transmuted in his glistening eyes into a pearl necklace of impressive proportions for a somewhat exacting mistress — and a rather smaller, cultivated string for a watchful wife.

So, in due course, a lot of people were delighted. The mistress reacted predictably, gratifyingly; she even felt a pang of private guilt about the charming and more virile young man who was both her weakness and a secret charge on Manuel's beneficence, although, naturally, this feeling did not last inconveniently long. Manuel's wife even softened slightly under the influence of her present, for he had not made the cardinal error of overdoing it. The gift had been nicely calculated; another twenty bucks and her hair-trigger suspicions would have been tripped and all hell let loose. So Manuel was satisfied; so were the brokers, for the price had been good; so were the purchasers, for the quality was excellent.

There was only one small snag; a minute trace of the active element of the systemic insecticide had not only spread from the roots to the leaves of the coffee plants; some had insinuated itself into the berries.

To be fair to all concerned, this point had been considered, and the buyer's chemist had noted the presence of this substance when testing the beans, but it was quite a well-known compound, proved beyond question as harmless to humans, noncarcinogenic, nontoxic, and non–quite a lot of other things. It was also present in such microscopic quantities that it needed an elegant and refined procedure to even find it, and massive doses had never caused the slightest discomfort or allergy in hamsters, mice, or any of the other animals who are so helpful in the laboratory. In any case, the final proof lay in the drinking, and that was done enthusiastically by untold numbers, with no trace of long- or short-term ill effects. Most of this coffee went to Europe or stayed in South America, but some of it arrived, via Europe, in the United Nations HQ, New York.

The organization of commissariat facilities for so diverse a body as the UN is a complex matter, and the fact that it can be done at all is one of the few hopeful signs for the future of this planet. Security Council problems may be more weighty, but are seldom more complex than those that daily confront the commissary committee. Take tea. The Slavs cry for lemon, the English scream with agony at the sight of a tea bag, and are fascinated by the spectacle of solid U.S. citizens drinking the stuff iced. In its gloomier moments the committee ponders the problems that the admission of China and Tibet would pose: Lapsang Suchon and rancid butter . . . as for the French view of tea — among other things — well . . .

But coffee is a different proposition. Despite the many and varied forms it may take, the standard American version is acceptable to the majority of the many nationalities in that slab-sided building on the East River. And in the lounge reserved for the very top brass, heads of delegations, visiting foreign ministers, prime ministers, and presidents, Manuel's coffee was, for a time, served. So here, amid the cups and the protocol, the black leather chairs on the appropriately neutral gray carpet, the next link in the chain was forged.

Let us be quite clear on one point; there is nothing wrong with New York water. Several people drink the stuff, straight, every day, but in the absence of other evidence, this harmless, vital staff of life must have provided the small additive which made the difference. It cannot have been the milk or cream, for many drink their coffee black — especially when the Council is in session. For similar reasons sugar and other sweeteners are ruled out; only water remains as a constant factor. Perhaps it was some minute trace element in the chlorine added for purification, or some naturally occurring element in the New York watershed. Whatever it was, it fell in love with the insecticide compound, itself probably modified by the coffee, and formed a satisfying if complicated union with it. Afterward, a high-grade chemist spent a happy time building a molecular model of the resulting mixture. Rumors that a museum tried to buy it as a fine example of modern art are quite untrue.

In the General Assembly it had been yet another of those mornings. The delegates representing a good deal of the Earth's inhabitants had spent the first hour or so eyeing each other with varying degrees of disfavor across the chamber, whilst waiting hopefully for a chance to get a word in edgeways. Situation normal. True, an Arab delegate omitted to scowl at the Israeli member, but this was purely an oversight. A Britisher managed to be discreetly insulting with an appraising stare at a European Common Market member's suit. Britain might be a shadow of what it was, but Savile Row remains Savile Row . . .

An unnamable delegate had held the floor since the morning session began, restating for the hundredth time his country's point of view. Few bothered to use the translation headsets; they had heard this one before. Watches were peeked at, doodles were scribbled, confidences exchanged behind backs of hands. One man appeared to be wrestling with his tax return.

The speaker pressed gallantly on, blindingly aware that he was convincing no one, but sustained by the thought that his speech would look good in the press back home, a matter of some importance if you happened to be a citizen of that country. He "stated firmly" and he "categorically denied" and he "reiterated" — and there was no doubt at all about the reiteration. Amid a barrage of ill-concealed yawns he headed for his climax, thumping the rostrum with as much force as he dared — his was a small country, and delegates can be touchy about their rights and privileges — and reached the end of his speech or performance, according to your viewpoint.

The Chairman sighed slightly, nodded his acknowledgment, glanced unnecessarily at the clock, and the meeting adjourned. With well-concealed but long-practiced ease, the delegates moved swiftly coffeeward. Only the member battling with his tax return was slow off the mark. But then, he was concentrating.

When the session resumed, there was no immediate sign of change in the atmosphere, although a very close observer might have noted the faint suspicion of a smile here and there. It was a full fifteen minutes later, when another delegate was in full flight, energetically rebutting the earlier delegate's speech — and getting as little attention — that the Change began.

"Balls!"

The word hung fractionally, like a glowing, glittering jewel, against the gray threadbare background of the delegate's over-well-prepared speech. Some with a command of the tongue of Shakespeare blinked; others frowned. A lot concluded they had misheard. The interrupter decided he had not made his point with full clarity.

"It's all balls!" He sounded remarkably cheerful and certain in his judgment. Heads turned.

Whatever else, it brightened the day for the translators. With great gusto they did their job.

"C'est tout bal!"

"Tutte ballo!"

The Chairman, an Asian, graduate of Harvard Law School, sometime lecturer at the London School of Economics, frowned. In his time in the Western world he had heard the term, although not, let it be hastily said, at either of those august establishments. He tapped his desk with the gavel thoughtfully provided, and frowned again as he peered in the general direction of the interrupter.

"I must ask delegates to refrain from making remarks while one of our number is addressing the Assembly!"

Again that voice rang out, clear as a bell, "Sorry, Mr. Chairman, but it's still all balls!"

The Chairman raised his eyebrows in surprise, then inclined his head graciously toward the speaker. The frown had gone. He smiled, his voice was soft, gentle, and the microphones picked up every word.

"My dear fellow, of course it's all balls, but it is this delegate's turn to talk it! You really mustn't interrupt!" He turned his attention to the stalled speaker at the rostrum, who was following the conversation with a curiously detached interest. "Please go on. I confess I agree, your speech is all balls, but you're delivering it very nicely." Again the gracefully inclined head. "Do go on."

It might be expected that this unusual state of affairs would be greeted with uproar, cries of dissent. Certainly, one man, forbidden coffee by his doctor, was on his feet, red with rage and bitterly regretting that the shoe-banging-on-desk gambit was played out, but apart from him, the rest of the Assembly appeared to be laughing. Most surprising of all, the speaker at the rostrum was laughing as hard as anyone. Against this very unusual noise the irate man struggled to be heard.

"Mr. Chairman, I must protest! Surely you must uphold this great Assembly, our dignity — " He had difficulty in continuing.

The Chairman grinned at him. "Now *you're* talking balls!" The thought appeared to please him. "What on earth has dignity to do with our work — and d'you really think the world holds us in high regard? Of course, this is unfair of the world; we only carry out our governments' directives, but if you imagine we are respected! We talk, and in the main we are powerless. Inevitably, much of what we say *is* balls!" He smiled and looked again at the rostrum. "My dear fellow, please accept our apologies. I cannot imagine what has come over us. For my part, I can only say I see things in a new, clear light which is not altogether complimentary to any of us here. Or," he added thoughtfully, "to the people who sent us." He took off his glasses, cleaned them, and replaced, them with prim care, and consulted the agenda before him. He thought for a moment, then, "There is so much to do, and while I will naturally respect your wishes, may I suggest that you may care to stand down and allow me to arrange our business? You — we — all know perfectly well this debate is getting nowhere."

"Mr. Chairman, I'd be delighted!" The speaker gathered up his notes. He waved them at the Assembly. "You may be bored with this, but not half as bored as I am!"

He stepped down in a thunderous roar of applause and walked briskly to his seat, his face pink with pleasure. Unanimity is a rare treat in the UNO. Even the Chairman clapped, then raised his hand for silence.

"We are all indebted to our colleague. His action is clearly right, but I cannot recall anyone before — " He broke off and pulled his lip, a look of puzzlement on his face as he thought. Then he shrugged and dismissed the matter from his mind. "Well, no matter; he has done it, and we're all grateful."

He beamed his approval of the general rumble of assent. "We must get on; it is an unprofitable waste of time to consider why we — and I think I speak for most" — he cast a reproving glance at the one glowering delegate — "we should have this change of view." With sudden vehemence he almost shouted, "Time is not on our side!"

And no one took him up on that point.

"Well, now, let us start with an easy one, but one that has bedeviled us for a very long time; this wretched border dispute between New Grogly and Ellinghiland. It's been around far too long."

Frenzied cheering greeted this. Even the non-coffee-drinking protestor could not argue with this comment. It had never got in the Top Ten disputes. Neither side had the power, or the interest of a Great Power, to escalate the affair into a really worthwhile crisis. East and West had no interest in the area and allowed matters to drift. As long as the locals were tied up in their own affairs, they were unlikely to be too tiresome to the big boys.

Both sides claimed a strip of land, cursed with a horrible climate and inhabited by a sad, underfed, and underprivileged race who were only made sadder by the sudden appearance of a truckload of troops from one side or the other, smart, by local standards, in their third-hand uniforms. The leaders of these gallant bands would explain, with fanatical ardor, that the future lay with X — or, if it happened to be the other side's turn, Y. But the natives were less concerned with the highly problematical future as the more urgent question of the next meal. There had been little fighting between the rivals, and at first the natives had been inclined to find this attention exciting, but disillusion soon set in. Neither side suffered many casualties, but for sure the locals caught it. Emptying a few magazines into a village that *might* be held by the enemy is a good deal more conducive to good aim than firing at an enemy that *is* armed.

The natives also discovered that liberators expect gratitude and whatever assistance the liberated can provide. These backward people with their near Stone Age culture rapidly became familiar with the arts of requisition, regulation, and hostage-taking, and other, finer points of the Plastic Age. It was also their pathetic homes that got knocked about, and when the forces had retired, flushed with victory — inevitably, both sides won — they could get on with burying their dead and trying to repair their huts.

Of course, there was a brighter side; the liberators did not come empty-handed, but somehow the natives did not find these gifts satisfying. Most of the flags were made of paper, and while the pictures of the respective leaders might be interesting to contemplate, the handbills were of less utility, for few could read, and not being a very resourceful people, no other use for all this paper occurred to them.

It was all really extremely funny, but it takes a robust sense of humor to appreciate this sort of situation, especially if you are chronically hungry, the walls of your hovel are knocked down, your seed corn gone in an alien gut, and your daughter, carried away by those uniforms, is clearly in a family way. . .

And it was this trivial matter that was to be aired first. "Now, gentlemen, will the two delegates involved please stand up? Thank you." He smiled impartially at them. "This is a great chance for you two to show the rest of us the way. This strip of land. You, sir, will you please say why you want it?" He pointed to the Ellinghese member, who hesitated, looked at his notes — and threw them on the floor. Again there was the faintly bewildered expression. The delegate shook his head. "I can't think why this hasn't been said before . . . Mr. Chairman, the only reason we want this land is to stop the Groglies having it. There are no worthwhile minerals, the natives are a headache, being even more backward than we are, but if the Groglies get it, it will be a blow to our status."

"That is serious?" The Chairman was faintly incredulous.

The Ellinghese still looked puzzled. "I used to think so."

"Thank you," said the Chairman. "Now you, sir."

The Grogli representative smiled cheerfully. "Our reasons don't strike me as much better. We feel it would make our map look more impressive; apart from that, we only want to stop the Ellinghese. Candidly," he spoke confidentially, as if the Chairman were the only person present, "although my lot have not actually said so, I'm sure the real reason is that it takes the minds of our people off one or two rather pressing home problems. We all know the value of that one."

A lot of heads nodded.

"Well, we know where we are," observed the Chairman. He scratched one ear in an absent-minded way, wrote rapidly, then looked up. "What d'you think of this?" He returned to his notes. "The governments of Grogly and

Ellinghi accept they have no right to or desire for all that land delineated in the map deposited with the UN in 1952." He regarded the Assembly in general over the top of his glasses. "This has dragged on for twenty years!" He shook his head sadly and continued, "Both governments admit they have no ethnic, cultural, or other ties whatsoever with the inhabitants of this land and both freely renounce all claims and title to this land, in perpetuity." Again he looked up. "I suppose it's too much to expect you to offer aid to these people?"

Both agreed it was, the Grogli adding cheerfully, "I'm sure I'll get hell from my government, but if we sew this up, they won't dare do anything. Public opinion! But money — no."

Inside ten minutes the resolution had been passed. The watching press were, to put it mildly, staggered. They had not had the benefit of the VIP coffee, and the unprecedented happenings had them ranging through the whole spectrum of human emotions, although there was only one at the baffled-rage end, a Grogli pressman who had practically sold an article proving conclusively the Grogli case. For the rest, it was a time of excitement not known since the days of Mr. Khrushchev.

Certainly, those affected were in a very odd mental state. Their minds were like gloomy old houses, shuttered and barred against the world, full of tortuous passages, musty, locked rooms, and in each house dwelt a soul, possessive, darkly suspicious, fearful of intrusion and the unremembered world. Above all, fearful. And this drug was a cleansing wind that burst open the shutters, forced out the stale, vitiated air, letting the bright sun flood in, revealing the tawdry decay within.

Not that the affected delegates threw themselves into each other's arms. Arab still looked at Jew in a hard-boiled way; East still regarded West as decadent, but the Arab now saw that there was a Jewish case; the East did not extract pleasure from the idea of Western decadence and was prepared to admit that the West had no monopoly on decay.

The drug gave a clarity of vision, showing the utter preposterousness of pre-atomic attitudes in the latter end of the twentieth century. All paid lip service to the idea that man faces self-destruction — a good stock speech on "the dangers that confront us" is an essential part of any politician's outfit — but now they really *did* see it. They were not transformed into shining angels, but they were no longer near blinded by their national or political dark glasses. They *saw*.

Aware that their conduct would be causing near apoplexy in various capitals — and not caring overmuch — the Assembly adjourned for lunch. Practically all tanked up on the coffee, including some who had missed out in the morning. The dining room was exceptionally crowded; many who had intended to eat out did not do so, being too busy to bother. Fantastic snatches of conversation could be heard.

"Kashmir's not a real problem — we'll soon fix that, its the subcontinental population increase . . ."

"Of *course* we know their damned government is as twisted as a corkscrew! We'd give our back teeth to get out . . ."

"Sure, it's crazy to bust ourselves, competing in space! Now, if we make a joint declaration . . ."

"The UN can run the canal, as long as we get a fair share of the profits. It's obvious . . ."

Clarity was not confined to *weltpolitik.*

"My wife's bloody impossible . . . so am I, really."

Sadly, it was not the Age, but only the Day of the Reasonable Man that had arrived. The afternoon session was restricted to straight talking and the settlement of a number of the smaller, perennial problems. There was tacit agreement that problems that, given a reasonable approach, could be quickly solved, should come first. Delegates knew of the growing flood of cables, which ranged from the terse recall to outraged demands for full explanations. Time pressed, yet members generally felt confident that they would convince their governments of the rightness of their actions. True, their advisers were twittering like a flock of birds, but that was hardly new.

There were some grounds for their optimism, for many who had not drunk the coffee caught the mood as a sort of secondary infection. Agreed, it was a fine idea to investigate the physical properties of Jupiter, but why do it twice, at such vast cost, when two-thirds of the Earth's population was underfed and daily getting nearer starvation? It was the fairy story of the emperor's clothes all over again, but like fairy stories, it could not last.

Behind the scenes, quick-witted Security was going nearly mad. It took time for the existence of the Change to be realized, but once that fact had been established it was a relatively simple matter to infer that the Assembly had been Got At; no body of men could act that reasonable and be in their right senses.

It was all done smoothly and efficiently after the session had resumed its fantastic way. Ironically, there was complete agreement among the nationalities in Security. No one tried to even imply that it was a cunning West — or East — plot to subvert the other side. The first task was to stop it, never mind how it started. By the time the meeting of the Assembly broke up, all food and drink had been impounded, the staff whisked off for questioning, new stocks and staff installed. Investigations proliferated; there was even a bizarre check on that other common factor, the washroom . . .

Next day the Change had worn off. Delegates were back in their shuttered and bolted minds, even more puzzled and fearful. It was clearly impossible to go back on the agreements of the previous day. For good or ill, minor problems all over the world had been settled, so far as the UN was concerned.

Those inhabitants of the strip of land between Grogly and Ellinghiland, for example: they remained rather sad and underfed, and perhaps some of the girls were even sadder, missing those dashing uniforms, but for the rest, well, at least they were left alone to work out their own salvation.

Making a virtue of necessity, both neighbors proclaimed victory for their cause, i.e., the expulsion of the other from the land. Understandably, both governments were somewhat vague about the positive side of their victories. Public holidays were proclaimed and streets renamed in honor of the liberation. The victorious troops, now confined to their own countries, with the eternal broadmindedness of the soldier, turned their attention to the local girls. Both countries ordered the swift return of their UN representatives, but, very prudently, both decided that life in the U.S.A. was more congenial and healthy. Partners in misfortune, they teamed up and now run one of those curious bookshops on the west side of the Forties where *Lust in a Sin-bed* and *Sin in a Lust-bed* are eternal best sellers. And so the Change ended.

But take heart. The secret of that magical drug is known. Naturally, it is a Secret, for who knows what might happen if reason really did rule? Man must have his fantasies, even if it kills him. It all goes on much as before; little has changed, except that statesmen are chary of drinking coffee with opponents — what could be better than slipping the drug to the other guy, while remaining your good old cunning, selfish, fearful self? But secrets of that sort cannot be kept forever, and while it is hard to imagine it doing anything but good in the field of international affairs, it may prove a mixed blessing in business and in the home. Imagine a truly reasonable husband, or — even wilder flight of the mind — a reasonable wife? So hope for the Change, but fear its coming — a fairly standard predicament for humanity.

Certainly, Manuel Gomez-Jackson is a changed man. He is not so much thinner as less fat; the gleam in his eye is not so bright, he is more apprehensive and nervous and frequently tired. His coffee continues to make astronomical prices, but when you are stuck with two mistresses and a wife, plus the problem of not letting any one know of the other two's existence . . .

And then there was the case of the foreign attaché leaving JFK, whose diplomatically protected bag accidentally dropped off the fork-lift truck and burst, allowing two gallons of New York water to remain on U.S. soil . . .

A stalwart member of that essentially simple-souled, kindhearted fraternity, the U.S. Customs, who happened to be nearby, remarked with some confidence and great feeling that now he had seen everything.

I would like to assure him — not all, not yet. Not quite yet.

There is a discreet establishment, not entirely unconnected with the CIA, which has taken delivery of some two thousand gallons of water, and while the security measures prevent the entry of any unauthorized persons, they are quite unable to stop the strong aroma of coffee from getting out.

And certain other parties are diligently at work, and if the stuff gets loose among the politicians at election time, well . . .

"Congratulations! You've just created life in a test tube."

Putzi

LUDWIG BEMELMANS

Child labor is an old and honored tradition in the human race. I began working in the family candy store at the age of nine. Nothing wrong with that. Your parents fed, clothed, and housed you, didn't they? You expect to get that for nothing? Yet surely there's such a thing as going too far, and Putzi is the example. But — waste not, want not.

THEY THOUGHT HE HAD ASKED for more volume, but Nekisch, the conductor, had caught a raindrop on the end of his baton and another in the palm of his hand.

He stopped the orchestra, glared up into the sky and then at Ferdinand Loeffler, the Konzertmeister.

Loeffler reached out for a flying-away page of *Finlandia,* and the audience opened umbrellas and left. The musicians ran into the shelter of the concert hall, carrying their instruments, and Herr Loeffler walked sadly to the back of the wide stage and took off his long black coat and shook the rain out of it.

There Nekisch arrested him with his baton. He stuck it into Herr Loeffler, between the two upper buttons of his waistcoat, and held him there against the tall platform. Ganghofer, the percussionist, could hear him say, "You're an ass, Herr Loeffler; you can't do the simplest things right; we have a deficit, Herr Loeffler, these are not the good old days, Herr Loeffler — I am telling you for the last and last time: *Inside! Here* in this hall we play when it rains, and *outside* when the sun shines."

Herr Loeffler silently took his blue plush hat and his first violin and went out and waited for a streetcar to take him to that part of the city where his wife's brother Rudolf had a small café, The Three Ravens.

Frau Loeffler sat in a corner of the little café reading the *Neue Freie Presse* out of a bamboo holder. She stirred her coffee.

"Ah, Ferderl," she said, and squeezed his hand, "but you are early today."

She could read his face . . . and she looked with him through the plate-glass windows into the dripping street.

"Outside again," she said, and turned to the front page of the *Freie Presse* and, pointing to the weather report, read, "Slight disturbances over Vienna but lovely and bright in the Salzkammergut.

"Inside, outside," she said, over and over again. These two words had taken on the terror that the words *death, fire, police,* and *bankruptcy* have for other people.

Behind a counter, next to the cash register, sat Frau Loeffler's sister Frieda. Frau Loeffler pointed at her with the thumb of her right hand. "Look, Ferderl. Look at Frieda. Since I am waiting for you she has eaten three ice creams, four slices of nut tart, two cream puffs, and two portions of chocolate, and now she's looking at the petits fours."

"Yes," said Herr Loeffler.

"Ah, why, Ferderl, haven't we a little restaurant like this, with guests and magazines and newspapers, instead of worrying about that conductor Nekisch and inside and outside?"

"He called me an ass, Nekisch did," said Herr Loeffler. " 'It's the last time,' he said."

"Who does he think you are? The Pope? Why doesn't he decide himself, if he's so smart! I go mad, Ferderl — I can't sleep for two days when you play, reading about the weather, calling up, looking at the mountains, even watching if dogs eat grass. I tried to ask farmers — they don't know either. You can never be sure, they come from nowhere — these clouds — when you don't want them, and when you play inside and hope that it rains outside, the sun shines, just like in spite, and they blame you!"

They put their four hands together in silent communion, one on top of another, as high as a water glass. Frau Loeffler looked into her coffee cup and she mumbled tenderly, "Ferderl, I have to tell you something." With this she looked shy, like a small girl, then she told him into his ear . . .

"No!" said Loeffler, with unbelieving eyes.

"Yes! Yes, Ferderl!" she said.

"When?" asked Herr Loeffler.

"In January. About the middle of January . . . Dr. Grausbirn said . . ."

Loeffler guessed right about the weather for the next two concerts. The sun shone. Outside, it was. Nekisch was talking to him again, and Loeffler walked to the concerts with light steps, whistling.

One day at a rehearsal of *Till Eulenspiegel,* he could hold it in no longer; he had to tell them. They patted his shoulder and shook his hand. Even Nekisch stepped down from his stand and put both hands on Loeffler's arms. "Herr Loeffler," he said, just "Herr Loeffler."

And then one day, after the "Liebestod," Loeffler, coming home, found in front of his house the horse and carriage of Dr. Grausbirn.

Loeffler ran upstairs and into the living room, just as Dr. Grausbirn came out of the other door, from his wife's room.

"My wife?" asked Herr Loeffler.

"No," said Dr. Grausbirn. "No, Herr Loeffler, not your wife." Dr. Grausbirn washed his hands. Herr Loeffler went to kiss his poor wife and came back again.

"Herr Doktor," he said, "we won't — I am not going to — "

Dr. Grausbirn closed his bag and slipped on his cuffs.

"Pull yourself together, Loeffler. Be a man," he said, "but you won't be a father — "

"Never?" asked Herr Loeffler.

"Never," said Dr. Grausbirn.

Herr Loeffler sat down on the edge of his chair. "We are simple people," he addressed the table in front of him. "We ask so little of life. We have always wanted him. We have even named him — Putzi, we call him — why, Annie has burned candles to St. Joseph, the patron saint of fathers." He sighed again.

"Why does this happen to me?" he said. "And how could it happen? We ask so little."

Dr. Grausbirn pointed out of the window. "There, Herr Loeffler," he said. "It's like this. Do you see that lovely little late-blossoming apple tree? It has many blossoms . . .

"Then comes the wind." Dr. Grausbirn reached into the air and swept down. "*Schrumm* — like this — and some of the blossoms fall — and the rain — takes more" — with his short fat fingers the doctor imitated the rain — "and brr r r, the frosts — more blossoms fall — they are not strong enough. Do you understand, Herr Loeffler, what I mean?"

They looked out at the little tree: it was rich with blossoms, so rich that the earth below it was white.

"That blossom, our little Putzi — " said Herr Loeffler.

"Yes," said the doctor. "Where is my hat?"

The doctor looked for his hat, and Herr Loeffler walked down the stairs with him.

"If you are going into town — " said Dr. Grausbirn, opening the door of his landau. Loeffler nodded and stepped in.

At the end of the street a lamppost was being painted. The carriage turned into the tree-lined avenue; a column of young soldiers passed them. After the lamppost, Herr Loeffler talked earnestly to Dr. Grausbirn, but the doctor shook his head — "No no no, no no, Herr Loeffler. Impossible — cannot be done." Herr Loeffler mumbled on, "We ask so little." He underlined his words, *"the only one* — never again — my poor wife — love — family" — and all this time he tried to tie a knot in the thick leather strap that hung down the door of the wagon.

"No," said Dr. Grausbirn.

The driver pulled in his reins, and the horse stopped to let a streetcar and two motorcars pass. Herr Loeffler was red in the face. Under the protection of the noises of starting motors, horns, and the bell of the trolley, he shouted, "Putzi belongs to us!" and he banged with his umbrella three times on the extra seat that was folded up in front of him. The driver looked around.

"Putzi?" asked Dr. Grausbirn.

"Our little blossom," said Herr Loeffler, pointing to the doctor's bag.

Dr. Grausbirn followed the flight of a pigeon with his eyes. The pigeon flew to a fountain and drank. Under the fountain was a dog; he ate grass and then ran to the curb. From there the doctor's eyes turned to the back of the driver and across to Herr Loeffler — a tear ran down the Konzertmeister's face. The doctor put his hand on Loeffler's knee.

"Loeffler, I'll do it. There's no law — every museum has one. Properly prepared, of course . . . in a bottle . . . next Monday . . . *Servus,* Herr Loeffler."

"*Auf Wiedersehen, Herr Doktor.*"

And so Putzi was delivered to Herr Loeffler. Herr Loeffler, who wrote a fine hand, designed a lovely label for the bottle. "Our dear Putzi," he wrote, and under the name he printed the date.

The next week Herr Loeffler guessed wrong again — rain for Beethoven outside — and sunshine for Brahms inside — and conductor Nekisch broke his baton.

"Go away, Herr Loeffler," he said. "I am a man of patience, but you've done this once too often. Get out of my sight, far away — where I never see you again, ass of a Konzertmeister!"

Herr Loeffler walked home. . .

For a year Putzi had stood on the mantelpiece. He was presented with flowers on his birthday, and on Christmas he had a little tree with one candle on it. Now Herr Loeffler sat for hours in his chair, looking out the window and at little Putzi in his bottle, and thought about the weather, about the orchestra — about inside and outside.

The *Neue Freie Presse* was mostly wrong; the government reports were seldom right. Nekisch was always wrong — more often than when Loeffler had given the word — but Putzi in his little bottle, Putzi was always right, well in advance. . .

It was not until months had passed, though, that Herr Loeffler noticed it. He watched closely for a few more days and then he told his wife. He took a pad and a pencil and he drew a line across the middle of the pad. On the lower half he wrote "Inside," on the upper half "Outside" — then he rubbed his hands and waited. . .

Long, long ere the tiniest blue cloud showed over the rim of any of the tall mountains that surrounded the beautiful valley of Salzburg, Putzi could tell: he sank to the bottom of his bottle, a trace of two wrinkles appeared on his little forehead, and the few tiny hairs which were growing over his left ear curled into tight spirals.

On the other hand, when tomorrow's sun promised to rise into the clear mountain air to shine all day, Putzi swam on top of his bottle with a Lilliputian smile and rosy cheeks.

"Come, Putzi," said Herr Loeffler, when the pad was filled — and he took him and the chart to Nekisch. . . .

Herr Loeffler now is back again — Inside when it rains — Outside when the sun shines.

All Things Come to
Those Who Weight

ROBERT GROSSBACH

Personally, I think that dreams of glory come second to dreams of revenge. I once had a telephone number which, when the first two digits were reversed, was the number of a popular hospital. I got ten or more calls a day from idiots who couldn't keep the number straight. Oh, how I longed to admit shyly it was the hospital when asked about it for the dozenth time, to inquire to whom they would like to speak, and then to say, "Mrs. So and so? Oh, I'm sorry but she died in agony last night." I never did it, you understand, but how I savored the thought *of doing it. Well, guess with whom Grossbach must have been having trouble.*

BESET WITH INTRACTABLE PROBLEMS of personal finance, Arnold Kraft, a sickly, middle-aged nuclear physicist, finally was pushed to seek elaborate revenge. Morning after morning, colleagues would arrive at Auerbach Laboratories to find him asleep at his desk, Kraft having toiled the entire night without a break. After the fourth week, Rydberg, his immediate supervisor, decided it was time for a talk and called Kraft into his office.

"Is it the divorce?" asked Rydberg sympathetically. Kraft's wife of twenty-three years had recently run off with a *Daily News* delivery boy.

"Not exactly," said Kraft cagily. He had never really trusted Rydberg and, besides, found repulsive the latter's habit of continually munching apples.

"Medical difficulties again?"

"Sort of," hedged Kraft. "Not exactly."

"The blood thing?" For years, Kraft had referred vaguely to a mysterious, not-quite-curable circulatory ailment.

"Blood?" chuckled Kraft bitterly. "Blood is the least." He winced as Rydberg bit down on a McIntosh.

"Then what?" demanded Rydberg.

"It's no use."

Rydberg's face flushed. "Don't tell me no use. Every day we find you slumped over your desk."

"I'm almost there," said Kraft.

"Where? To the grave?" Rydberg tore ravenously into the body of the fruit. "You find posthumous recognition romantic, maybe?"

"I'm close to finishing up on the hyperdensity business," said Kraft, suppressing a retch. "Another couple sessions, it's through."

Rydberg shook his head. "Look, the slumpings have got to stop. Technically, you're not even supposed to be here alone. You die on the job, company's insurance policy doesn't cover that condition."

Kraft began to understand the origin of his boss's concern. "I'll take it a little easier," he lied, hoping against hope that Rydberg would strike pits.

In the lobby of his apartment house he wrenched open the mailbox; as usual, he found only heartache. Upstairs, he went through the envelopes one by one. A letter from *Physics Review:* "Thank you for your recent submission, 'Suppression of B-Decay at Cryogenic Temperatures.' Unfortunately, our reviewers have deemed it unfit for publication. Your interest in our magazine is appreciated." Kraft gnashed his teeth, tore the envelope to shreds. Politics, he thought. All politics. Physics was like anything else: If you were not in the club, not part of the elite establishment, your ideas were simply dismissed, refused serious consideration. The prestigious journals would not touch you, leaving only the marginal publications that were read by other outcasts and quacks. Once, Kraft had written an article on nuclear stability for a new journal, only to see it appear sandwiched between an essay called "Fun with Rubber Clothing" and a pictorial layout on IUDs made from food.

Next envelope — a bill from a medical lab for sixty-five dollars. Blood analysis of renin and aldosterone levels. He had been seeing a new doctor in an effort to solve the problem of his blood pressure. One visit it would be extremely high, the next extremely low. "I can treat you for either-or," Kraft's former physician had said. "But what you've got puts me out to pasture." The new man was calmer, though given to enigmatic smiles.

"Personally, I'd love to hospitalize you," said Dr. Stavros on Kraft's last visit.

"No hospitals," said Kraft.

Stavros shrugged. "Well, then, how about ultrasound? You have any feelings about that?"

"Sound, I guess, is okay," Kraft had replied. "But will it help?"

And Stavros had let go one of the cryptic grins.

A phone bill was next; Kraft tossed it on the couch. It would be for the minimum amount — he hardly called anyone. He dismissed similarly a bill for auto insurance and one from Master Charge. The next envelope was addressed in pencil and he opened it eagerly. A note from Brian, his seven-year-old son.

Dear Daddy,
    I want to go to sumer camp this sumer, but Mom says she does not have mony and I shoud ask you. Please, Dad?

Your loving son,
Brian Kraft

The lettering was crude, obviously done with great effort. "Damn!" said Kraft aloud. Eileen was using the child to try to extract funds from him. Let her save from the exorbitant alimony he was already giving her, he thought. Why was it necessary to make the child a pawn? Kraft felt like crying. He opened the last envelope.

A form from Green Cross-Green Shield, the medical insurance company. Reference to his recent request for reimbursement. A list, with accompanying boxes, twenty separate items. One particular box had a red check mark in it. "Failure to demonstrate this was not a pre-existing condition. Please submit proof in postage-paid return envelope enclosed." The veins in Kraft's neck began to knot. Calm, he thought. I must stay calm. They were killing him. He was forking over a thousand dollars a year for a Major Medical policy (Auerbach Laboratories offered no benefits) and, despite huge bills, couldn't seem to extract a dime's worth of payments. They nitpicked him to death. Sometimes a number was left out on his reimbursement form, or a date, or the "X" in the space affirming he had no other medical coverage. Each time, although the information was clearly available from past submissions, the entire form was returned but the accompanying doctor's bill was omitted. Kraft had to write to the physicians asking them for new bills before he could resubmit. Often as not, the forms would come back again. The new bills weren't marked "paid." Or else they had to be forwarded to Basic Coverage *before* Major Medical would handle them. Basic Coverage covered almost nothing, but Major required a note from Basic stating that Basic would not pay. It was maddening. Kraft ended up mailing in the same forms five and six different times. He found himself devoting his whole life to the paper work, having no time for movies, or TV, or meeting new women. And after six months, despite actual medical expenses of nearly two thousand dollars plus half a year's worth of the exorbitant premium, he'd accumulated barely a quarter of the three-hundred-dollar deductible. Twice, after Kraft finally managed to steer applications through the system, short, apologetic notes had come back: "Sorry, but this particular condition is not covered by your policy."

Kraft found himself trembling. It has to stop, he thought. Because of these people I can't live, I can't pay my bills, can't send my own son to camp. It can't go on, I won't *let* it go on. He hammered the coffee table with his fist.

The effect began abruptly, as had the far older ultra-cold phenomena of super-conductivity and superfluidity. One day, as Kraft cooled an ingot of lead below thirty microdegrees Kelvin, an astonishing thing happened — the sample simply disappeared. At least, that's what it seemed at first. Fortunately, however, he'd taken the precaution of weighing the lead plus the container before the cooling, and when he'd checked afterwards, the total was still the same, fourteen ounces. He never did find where the hell the ingot went.

Naturally, he repeated the experiment. Same results. He doubled the weight of material — no change. He tripled it, quadrupled it, multiplied it by ten, and always — it disappeared. He told Rydberg.

"What you say is happening can't be," said Rydberg. "The stuff is going *some*where. Nine pounds of lead don't vanish into thin air."

"This did," said Kraft, the sound of Rydberg's teeth piercing a Delicious apple like a razor blade scraping his brain.

"Maybe it combined with the container," offered Rydberg. "Alloyed some-how with the surface."

"That was the first thing I checked," said Kraft patiently. "Did chemical and spectroscopic analyses up the kazoo. That's not the answer."

"Keep looking," suggested Rydberg airily, juice running down his chin and driving Kraft from the room.

At a hundred pounds of lead, Kraft found it, a tiny sphere as small as a seed, 30 thousandths of an inch in diameter. *The material hadn't disappeared: It had simply changed to something with five million times the density!*

The theories came later; it would be for others to refine the techniques, to reduce the processes to mathematical formalisms. Basically, it appeared that below thirty microdegrees Kelvin the binding forces that held together the particles in atomic nuclei suddenly became much stronger. Normally effective only at extremely short ranges, they now reached out for adjacent atomic cores, tearing asunder the clouds of whirling planetary electrons. Matter sim-ply pulled itself together, imploded like a punctured balloon. The final material resembled that of those burnt-out, crushed stars astronomers call white dwarfs, its weight a neat thousand tons per cubic inch.

As so often happens, the initial heady success was the last for some time. Only certain substances seemed to *remain* compressed when removed from cryogenic temperatures. Of these, lead proved the most readily available and the easiest to work with. Kraft had at first called the compacted material eka-lead, then changed it to Kraftium, and finally, conceding to modesty, settled on Densite. He apprised Rydberg and other Auerbach staff members of his preliminary results. Additional funds were allocated. Excited confer-ences were held. Nobel prizes were talked about. When, months later, truckloads of lead began arriving at Auerbach Laboratories, no one found it the least unusual.

Kraft dialed carefully and was immensely relieved to hear the first ring. He'd been trying for over an hour, had gotten ten consecutive busy signals. Nothing unusual, of course — that was always the case when you called Green Cross-Green Shield. At the fifteenth ring a musical female voice finally answered.

"Green Cross. Hello-o?"

"Hello? Uh, my name is Arnold Kraft, policy number 295382A176F, and I'm having some problems with a request for reimbursement. Can someone help me?"

"Yes, I'll try, sir. What is your policy number?"

Patiently, Kraft repeated it.

"I'll check the computer, sir." There was silence that lasted three minutes, then: "I'm sorry, sir, our computers are down right now."

"Your computers are always down," said Kraft angrily. "They've been down the last six times I've called. Why don't you get them up?"

"I'm sorry, sir," said the voice. "Perhaps I can retrieve your records manually. Hold please." The next silence lasted for five minutes. This was the point at which Kraft usually was cut off. He was amazed when the same operator returned. "I have your file, sir. Go ahead."

"One of my forms came back in the mail," said Kraft. "I've been seeing a doctor about fluctuating blood pressure. It's something new, not a pre-existing condition."

There was a pause. "Is that Dr. Stavros you're referring to, sir?"

"Yes."

"Visits on the tenth, the eighteenth, and the twenty-ninth?"

"Yes."

Another pause. "According to our records, sir, you had this condition when you first subscribed to the policy."

"No," said Kraft. "That was a different condition. That was hemoglobin. My blood count would go up and down, high to low. This is different. This is pressure."

"I see. Well, if Dr. Stavros will send us a note — "

"It says right on the form, 'Variable blood pressure.' "

"None of our people ever heard of that malady," said the voice. "Still, if you can get a note — "

"Is this condition covered?"

"I can't tell you that, sir, until we receive the communication from the doctor. I'm sure he'll send it if you ask him to."

Kraft put a hand to his forehead. "Look, miss, I've submitted this form four times already. Can't you help me out there? Can't someone take a chance?"

"I'm sorry, sir, our policy requires — "

"Listen, I'm desperate," screamed Kraft into the receiver. "I can't pay my bills, I'm sick. *I need the money. Please! I'm asking. Please!*" He began to weep.

"Sir, I'm certain if you return the form in the envelope provided, our claims people will give you every consideration that — "

"You'll be sorry," Kraft muttered, wiping the tears away with pudgy fingers. "I've been working on something I hadn't wanted to use, but now . . . you'll be sorry."

"I'll make a record of your complaint," said the voice imperturbably, "and you'll be forwarded a copy for — "

Kraft hung up.

Pausing, Kraft watched the crane swing the final piece of Densite into position. There were fifty segments in all, each formed into a flat, thin sheet and transported by separate truck. A specially installed steel column under the mailbox would transmit the tremendous force to the bedrock below. It was dawn now; at the 9:00 A.M. morning collection, some postman would find an envelope weighing just under a thousand tons. Kraft chuckled as he reviewed his calculations. At fifteen cents an ounce, the total sum involved was nearly five million dollars. Fair enough, he thought, as he watched the envelope disappear. Appropriately, the last part to slip from view was the upper right-hand corner with its precise and unfailingly generous offer:

FIRST CLASS POSTAGE
PAID BY
GREEN CROSS-GREEN SHIELD

Derm Fool

THEODORE STURGEON

The snake is the symbol of immortality; that's why you find two of them on the caduceus, the medical symbol. Some people say they're there to show that the doctor's bill is sharper than the serpent's tooth, but my wife the doctor scorns those who say so. The connection between snakes and immortality rests in the fact that snakes shed their skins periodically and then show up with a nice new glistening outer surface. No younger, of course, but looking *younger and, as any makeup man will tell you, that's what counts. Human beings also shed their skins, but — except for dandruff — unnoticeably. And thereby hangs a tale.*

I AM NOT GENERALLY a fussy man. A bit of litter around my two-and-a-half-room dugout on the West Side seldom bothers me. The trash that isn't big enough to be pushed out in the hallway can be kicked around till it gets lost. But today was different. Myra was coming, and I couldn't have Myra see the place this way.

Not that she cared particularly. She knew me well enough by this time not to mind. But the particular *kind* of litter might be a bit — disturbing.

After I had swept the floor I began looking in odd corners. I didn't want any vagrant breeze to send unexplainable evidence fluttering out into the midst of the room — not while Myra was there. Thinking about her, I was almost tempted to leave one of the things where she could see it. She was generally so imperturbable — it might be amusing to see her hysterical.

I put the unchivalrous thought from me. Myra had always been very decent to me. I was a bit annoyed at her for making me like her so much when she was definitely not my type. Crawling under the bed, I found my slippers. My feet were still in them. I set one on top of the mantel and went into the other room, where I could sit down and wrench the foot out of the other slipper. They were odd slippers; the left was much bigger than the right. I swore and tugged at that right foot. It came out with a rustle; I rolled it up in a ball and tossed it into the wastepaper basket. Now let's see — oh, yes, there was a hand still clutching the handle of one of the bureau drawers. I went and pried it off.

Why the deuce hadn't Myra called me up instead of wiring? No chance to head her off now. She'd just drift in, as usual. And me with all this on my mind —

I got the index finger off the piano and threw it and the left foot away too. I wondered if I should get rid of the torso hanging in the hall closet, but decided against it. That was a fine piece. I might be able to make something good out of it; a suitcase, perhaps, or a rainproof sports jacket. Now that I had all this raw material, I might as well turn it to my advantage.

I checked carefully. My feet were gone, so I wouldn't have to worry about them until the morning. My right hand too; that was good. It would be awful to shake hands with Myra and have her find herself clinging to a disembodied hand. I pulled at the left. It seemed a little loose, but I didn't want to force it. This wasn't a painful disease as long as you let it have its own way. My face would come off any minute now. I'd try not to laugh too much; maybe I could keep it on until she had gone.

I put both hands around my throat and squeezed a little. My neck popped and the skin sloughed dryly off. Now that was all right. If I wore a necktie, Myra wouldn't be able to see the crinkling edges of skin just above my collarbone.

The doorbell buzzed and I started violently. As I stood up, the skin of my calf parted and fell off like a cellophane gaiter. I snatched it up and stuffed it under a sofa pillow and ran for the door. As I reached it, one of my ears gave a warning crackle; I tore it off and put it in my pocket and swung the door wide.

"David!" She said that, and it meant that she was glad to see me, and that it had been eight months since the last time, and she was feeling fine, and she was sorry she hadn't written, but then she never wrote letters — not to anybody.

She swooped past me into the room, paused as if she were folding wings, shrugged out of her coat without looking to see if I were there behind her to take it, because she knew I was, crossed her long legs, and three-pointed gently on the rug. I put a cigarette into one extended hand and a kiss in the palm of the other, and it wasn't until then that she looked at me.

"Why — David! You're looking splendid! Come here. What have you done to your face? It's all crinkly. It looks sweet. You've been working too hard. Do I look nice? I feel nice. Look, new shoes. Snakeskin. Speaking of snakes, how are you, anyway?"

"Speaking of snakes, Myra, I'm going to pieces. Little pieces, that detach themselves from me and flutter in the gusts of my furious laboring. Something has gotten under my skin."

"How awful," she said, not really hearing me. She was looking at her nails, which were perfect. "It isn't because of me, is it? Have you been pining away for me, David? David, you still can't marry me, in case you were going to ask."

"I wasn't going to ask, but it's nice to know anyway," I said. My face fell, and I grabbed it and hid it under my coat. She hadn't seen, thank heavens! That

meant I was relatively secure for a few hours. There remained only my left
hand. If I could get rid of it — good heavens! It was already gone!

It might be on the doorknob. Oh, she mustn't see it! I went into the foyer
and searched hurriedly. I couldn't find it anywhere. Suppose it had caught in
her wraps? Suppose it were on the floor somewhere near where she was sitting?
Now that I was faced with it, I knew I couldn't bear to see her hysterical. She
was such a–a *happy* person to have around. For the millionth time since that
skinning knife had slipped, I muttered, "Now, why did this have to happen
to *me*?"

I went back into the living room. Myra was still on the floor, though she had
moved over under the light. She was toying curiously with the hand, and the
smile on her face was something to see. I stood there speechless, waiting for
the storm. I was used to it by this time, but Myra —

She looked up at me swiftly, in the birdlike way she had. She threw her
glances so quickly that you never knew just how much she had seen —
under all her chatter and her glittering idiosyncrasies was as calm and astute
a brain as ever hid behind glamour.

The hand — it was not really a hand, but just the skin of one — was like
a cellophane glove. Myra slipped it on her own and peeped through the fingers
at me. "Hiya, fellow reptile," she giggled; and suddenly the giggles changed
into frightened little squeaks, and she was holding out her arms to me, and
her lovely face was distorted by tears so that it wasn't lovely anymore, but
sweet — oh, so darned sweet! She clung close to me and cried pitifully, "David,
what are we going to *do*?"

I held her tight and just didn't know what to say. She began talking brok-
enly: "Did it bite you, too, David? It bit m-me, the little beast. The Indians
worship it. Th-they say its bite will ch-change you into a snake . . . I was afraid
. . . Next morning I began shedding my skin every twenty-four hours —
and I have ever since." She snuggled even closer, and her voice calmed a little.
It was a lovely voice, even now. "I could have killed the snake, but I didn't
because I had never seen anything like it, and I thought you might like to have
it — so I sent it, and now it's bitten you, and you're losing your skin all the
time too, and — oh-h-h!"

"Myra, don't. Please, don't. It didn't bite me. I was skinning it, and my knife
slipped. I cut myself. The snake was dead when I got it. So — *you're* the one
who sent it! I might have known. It came with no card or letter; of *course* it
was you! How . . . how long have you been this way?"

"F-four months." She sniffed, and wiped her pink nose on my lapel because
I had forgotten to put a handkerchief in my breast pocket. "I didn't care after
. . . after I found out that it didn't hurt, and that I could count on when parts
of my skin would come off. I — thought it would go away after a while. And
then I saw your hand in a store window in Albuquerque. It was a belt buckle

— a hand holding a stick, with the wrist fastened to one end of the belt and the stick to the other; and I bought it and saw what it was, because the hand was stuffed with the perfumed moulage you always use for your hummingbird brooches and things — and anyway, you were the only one who *could* have designed such a fascinating belt, or who *would* have thought to use your own skin just because . . . because you happened to have it around — and I hated myself then and I loved you for it — " She twisted out of my arms and stared into my eyes, amazement written on her face, and joy. "And I do love you for it, right *now*, David, *now*, and I never loved anyone else before and I don't care" — she plucked my other ear, and the skin rustled away in her hand — "if you *are* all dilapidated!"

I saw it all now. Myra's crazy desire to climb a mesa, one of those island tableaux of the desert, where flora and fauna have gone their own ways these thousand thousand years; her discovering the snake, and catching it for me because I was a combination taxidermist and jeweler, and she had never seen anything like it and thought I might want it. Crazy, brave thing; she had been bitten and had said nothing to anybody because "it didn't hurt"; and then, when she found out that I had the same trouble, she had come streaking to New York to tell me it was her fault!

"If you feel that way about it, Myra," I said gently, "then I don't care at all about this . . . this dry rot . . . little snake in the grass — " I kissed her.

Amazing stuff, this cast-off skin. Regularly as clockwork, every twenty-four hours, the epidermis would toughen, loosen, and slip off. It was astonishingly cohesive. My feet would leave their skin inside my slippers, keeping the exact shape of the limb on which it had grown. Flex the dead skin a couple of times, and it would wrinkle in a million places, become limp and flexible. The nails would come off too, but only the topmost layer of cells. Treated with tannic acid and afterward with wool oil, it was strong, translucent, and soft. It took shellac nicely, and a finish of Vandyke-brown oil paint mixed with bronze powder gave a beautiful old-gold effect. I didn't know whether I had an affliction or a commodity.

That snake — It was about four feet long, thicker at head and tail than it was in the middle. It was a lusterless orange, darker underneath than it was on top, but it was highly fluorescent. It smelled strongly of honey and formic acid, if you can imagine that for yourself. It had two fangs, but one was on top of its mouth and the other on the lower jaw. Its tongue was forked, but at the roots only; it had an epiglottis, seven sets of rudimentary limbs, and no scales. I call it a snake because it was more nearly a snake than anything else. I think that's fair. Myra is mostly a Puckish angel, but you can still call her a woman. See? The snake was a little of this and a little of that, but I'll swear its origin was not of *this* earth. We stood there hand in hand, Myra and I, staring at the beast, and wondering what to do about it all.

"We might get rich by renting it to side shows," said Myra.

"Nobody would believe it. How about renting ourselves to the AMA?" I asked.

She wrinkled her nose and that was out. Tough on the AMA.

"What are we going to do about it, David?" She asked me as if she thought I knew and trusted me because of it, which is a trick that altogether too many women know.

"Why, we'll — " And just then came the heavy pounding on the door.

Now, there is only one animal stupid enough to bang on a door when there is a bell to ring, and that is a policeman. I told Myra to stay there in the lab and wait, so she followed me into the foyer.

"You David Worth?" asked the man. He was in plainclothes, and he had a very plain face.

"Come in," I said.

He did, and sat down without being asked, eyeing the whiskey decanter with little but evident hope. "M'name's Brett. H. Brett."

"H for Halitosis?" asked Myra gently.

"Naw, Horace. What do I look like, a Greek? Hey, headquarters's checkin' on them ornaments o' y'rs, Mr. Worth." The man had an astonishing ability to masticate his syllables. "They look like they're made of human skin. Y'r a taxidoimist, ain'tcha?"

"I am. So?"

"So where'dja get th' ror material? Pleece analysis says it's human skin. What do you say?"

I exchanged a glance with Myra. "It is," I said.

It was evidently not the answer Brett expected. "Ha!" he said triumphantly. "Where'd you get it, then?"

"Grew it."

Myra began to skip about the room because she was enjoying herself. Brett picked up his hat from the floor and clung to it as if it were the only thing he could trust. I began to take pity on him.

"What did they do down there, Brett? Microscopic cross section? Acid and base analyses?"

"Yeah."

"Tell me; what have they got down there — hands?"

"Yeah, and a pair o'feet. Book ends."

"You always did have beautiful feet, darling," caroled Myra.

"Tell you what I'll do, Brett," I said. I got a sheet of paper, poured some ink onto a blotter, and used it as a stamp pad. I carefully put each fingertip in the ink and pressed it to the paper. "Take that down to headquarters and give it to your suspicious savants. Tell them to compare these prints with those from the ornaments. Write up your reports and turn them in with a recommendation that the whole business be forgotten; for if it isn't I shall most certainly sue the city, and you, and anyone else who gets in my way, for defamation of character. I wouldn't consider it impolite, Mr. Brett, if you got out of here right away, without saying good night." I crossed the room and held the door open for him.

His eyes were slightly glazed. He rose and walked carefully around Myra, who was jumping up and down and clapping her hands, and scuttled out. Before I could close the door again he whirled and stuck his foot in it.

"Lissen. I don't know what's goin' on here, see? Don't you or that lady try to leave here, see? I'm havin' the place watched from now on, see? You'll hear from me soon's I get to headquarters, see?"

"You're a big seesee," said Myra over my shoulder; and before I could stop her she plucked off her nose and threw it in the detective's face. He moved away so fast that he left his hat hanging in midair; seconds later we heard the violence of his attempted passage down four flights of stairs when there were only three.

Myra danced three times around the room and wound up at the top of the piano — no mean feat, for it was a bulky old upright. She sat there laughing and busily peeling off the rest of her face.

"A certain something tells me," I said when I could talk, which was after quite a while, "that you shouldn't have done that. But I'm glad you did. I don't think Detective Inspector Horace Halitosis Brett will be around anymore."

Myra gestured vaguely toward her bag. I tossed it to her, and she began dabbing at nose and lips in the skillful, absent way women have. "There," she said when she had finished. "Off with the old — on with the new."

"You're the first woman in creation who gets beauty treatments in spite of herself. Pretty neat."

"Not bad," she said impersonally to her mirror. "Not bad, Myra!"

Thinking of her, watching her, made me suddenly acutely conscious of her. It happens that way sometimes. You know you love the gal, and then suddenly you *realize* it. "Myra — "

I think she had a gag coming, but when she looked at me she didn't say anything. She hopped down off the piano and came over to me. We stood there for a long time.

"You sleep in there," I said, nodding toward the bedroom. "I'll — "

She put her arms around me. "David — "

"Mm-m-m?"

"I'll — have a nice torso for you at twelve-forty-eight — "

So we stuck around and talked until 12:48.

It must have been about two weeks later, after we were married, that she started breaking bottles in my laboratory. She came into the laboratory one afternoon and caught me cold. I was stirring a thick mass in a beaker and sniffing at it, and was so intent on my work that I never heard her come in. She moved like thistledown when she wanted to.

"What are you cooking, darling?" she asked as she put away a beautiful pair of arms she had just "manufactured."

I put the beaker on the bench and stood in front of it. "Just some . . . sort of . . . er . . . stickum I'm mixing up for — Myra, beat it, will you? I'm busy as — "

She slid past me and picked up the beaker. "Hm-m-m. Pretty. *Snff.* Honey and — formic acid. Using the smell of that beast as a lead, are you? Dr. David Worth, trying to find a cure for a gold mine. It's a cure, isn't it? Or trying to be?" Her tone was very sweet. Boy, was she sore!

"Well . . . yes," I admitted. I drew a deep breath. "Myra, we can't go on like this. For myself I don't care, but to have you spending the rest of your life shedding your epidermis like a . . . a blasted cork oak — it's too much. You've been swell about it, but I can't take it. You're too swell, and it's too much for my conscience. Every time I come in here and start stuffing something of yours, I begin worrying about you. It hasn't been bad, so far — but, woman, think of it! The rest of your life, sloughing off your hide, worrying about whether or not you can find somewhere to take your face off when you're not home; trying to remember where you dropped a hand or a leg. You — Myra, you're not listening."

"Of course I'm not. I never listen to you when you're talking nonsense."

"It isn't nonsense!" I was getting sore.

"I wonder," she said dreamily, sloshing the mess around in the beaker, "whether this thing will bounce." She dropped it on the floor and looked curiously. It didn't bounce. I stood there fumbling for a cuss word strong enough, and wondering whether or not I could move fast enough to poke her one.

"David, listen to me. How long have you been a taxidermist?"

"Oh — eleven years. What's that got — "

"Never mind. And how much money have you saved in eleven years?"

"Well, none, until recently. But lately — "

"Quiet. And you have eight-hundred-odd in the bank now. Those stuffed-skin gadgets sell faster than we can make them. And just because you have some funny idea that I don't like to give you my — by-products, you want to cut the water off, go back to stuffing squirrels and hummingbirds for buttons. David, you're a fool — a derm fool."

"That's not very punny."

She winced. "But here's the main thing, David. You've got this trouble, and so have I. We've been cashing in on it, and will, if only you'll stop being stupid about it. The thing I like about it is that we're partners — I'm *helping* you. I love you. Helping you means more to me than — Oh, David, can't you see? Can't you?"

I kissed her. "And I thought you were just a good sport," I whispered. "And I thought some of it was mock heroics. Myra — " Oh, well. She won. I lost. Women are funny that way. But I still had an idea or two about a cure —

I'd been wrong about the indefatigable Inspector Brett. It was Myra who found out that he was tailing us everywhere, parking for hours in a doorway across the street, and sometimes listening at the door. I'd never have known it; but, as I've pointed out before, Myra has superhuman qualities. When she told me about it, I was inclined to shrug it off. He didn't have anything on us. I had to laugh every time I thought of what must have gone on at police headquarters when they checked up on my fingerprints and those of the hands they had bought in the stores.

The fact that it was human skin, and that the prints were identical in dozens of specimens, must have given them a nasty couple of days. Prove that the axiom about two points and a straight line is false, and where's your whole science of geometry? And prove that there can be not only identical finger-prints, but *dozens* of identical ones, and you have a lot of experts walking around in circles and talking to themselves.

Brett must have appointed himself to crack this case. I was quite willing to let him bang his head against a wall. It would feel nice when he stopped. I should have known Myra better. She had a glint in her eye when she talked about that gangbuster.

In the meantime I kept working on that cure. I felt like a heel to skulk around behind Myra's back that way. You see, she trusted me. We'd had that one row about it, and I'd given in. That was enough for her. She wouldn't spy on me when I was working alone in the lab; and I knew that if she did realize it, suddenly, she would be deeply hurt. But this thing was too big. I *had* to do what I was doing, or go nuts.

I had a lead. The formic-honey idea was out as a cure, though certain ingredients in them, I was sure, had something to do with the cause. That cause was amazingly simple. I could put it down here in three words. But do you think I would? *Heh.* I've got a corner on this market —

But this was my lead: My *hair* never came off! And I wear a minuscule mustache; every time my face came off it left the mustache. I have very little body hair; now, with this trouble, I had none. It came off, for the follicles were comparatively widely separated. First, I thought that this phenomenon was due to a purely physical anchorage of the skin by the hair roots. But, I reasoned, if that had been the case, layer after layer of skin would have formed under my mustache. But that did not happen. Evidently, then, this amazing separative and regenerative process was nullified by something at the hair roots. I could tell you what it was too, but — I should knife myself in the back!

I worked like a one-armed pianist playing Mendelssohn's "Spinning Song." It took months, but by repeated catalysis and refinement, I finally had a test tube full of clear golden liquid. And — know what it was? Look: I hate to be repetitious, but I'm not saying. Let it suffice that it can be bought by the gallon at your corner drugstore. Nobody knew about it as a cure for my peculiar disease — if you want to call it that — because as far as I know no one had ever seen the disease before. *Bueno.*

Then I went to work on the cause. It didn't take long. As I have said, the most baffling thing about the trouble was its simplicity.

In the windup, I had it. An injection to cause the trouble, a lotion to cure or isolate it. I got ten gallons of each fluid — no trouble, once I knew what to get — and then began worrying about how to break the news to Myra.

"Kirro," I said to her one day, "I want a good face from you tonight. I want to make a life mask of you. Have to get all set first, though. You lose your face at eight-forty-five, don't you? Well, come into the lab at eight-thirty. We'll plaster you with clay, let it dry so that it draws the face off evenly, back it with moulage, and wash the clay off after the moulage has hardened. Am I brilliant?"

"You scintillate," she said. "It's a date."

I started mixing the clay, though I knew I wouldn't use it. Not to take her face off, anyway. I felt like a louse.

She came in on time as if she hadn't even looked at a clock — how I envy her that trick — and sat down. I dipped a cloth in my lotion and swabbed her well with it. It dried immediately, penetrating deeply. She sniffed.

"What's that?"

"Sizing," I said glibly.

"Oh. Smells like — "

"*Shh.* Someone might be listening." That for you, dear reader!

I went behind her with a short length of clothesline. She lay back in the chair with her eyes closed, looking very lovely. I leaned over and kissed her on the lips, drawing her hands behind her. Then I moved fast. There was a noose at each end of the line; I whipped one around her wrists, drew it tight, threw it under the back rung of the chair, and dropped the other end over her head. "Don't move, darling," I whispered. "You'll be all right if you keep still. Thrash around and you'll throttle yourself." I put the clock where she could see it and went out of there. I don't want to hear my very best beloved using that kind of language.

She quieted down after about ten minutes. "David!"

I tried not to listen.

"David — please!"

I came to the door. "Oh, David, I don't know what you're up to, but I guess it's all right. Please come here where I can look at you. I . . . I'm afraid!"

I should have known better. Myra was never afraid of anything in her life. I walked over and stood in front of her. She smiled at me. I came closer. She kicked me in the stomach. "That's for tying me up, you . . . you heel. Now, what goes on?"

After I got up off the floor and got my gasping done, I said, "What time is it, bl — er, light of my life?"

"Ten minutes to ni — David! David, what have you done? Oh, you fool! You utter dope! I told you — Oh, *David!*" And for the second and last time in my life, I saw her cry. Ten minutes to nine and her face was still on. Cured! — at least, her face. I went behind her where she couldn't reach me.

"Myra, I'm sorry I had to do it this way. But — well, I know how you felt about a cure. I'd never have been able to talk you into taking it. This was the only way. What do you think of me now, stubborn creature?"

"I think you're a pig. Terribly clever, but still a pig. Untie me. I want to make an exit."

I grinned. "Oh, no. Not until the second-act curtain. Don't go away!" I went over to the bench and got my hypodermic. "Don't move, now. I don't want to break this mosquito needle off in your jaw." I swabbed her gently around the sides of the face with the lotion, to localize the shot.

"I . . . hope your intentions are honorable," she said through clenched teeth as the needle sank into the soft flesh under her jawbone. "I — Oh! Oh! It . . . itches. David — "

Her face went suddenly crinkly. I caught her skin at the forehead and gently peeled it off. She stared wide-eyed, then said softly:

"I can't kiss you, marvelous man, unless you untie me — "

So I did, and she did, and we went into the living room where Myra could rejoice without breaking anything of value.

In the middle of a nip-up she stopped dead, brainwave written all over her face. "David, we're going to do some entertaining." She sat there in the middle of the floor and began to scream. And I mean she could scream.

In thirty seconds flat, heavy footsteps — also flat — pounded on the stairs, and Brett's voice bellowed: "Op'n up in th' name o' th' law!" He's the only man I ever met who could mumble at the top of his voice.

Myra got up and ran to the door. "Oh — Mr. Brett. How nice," she said in her best hostess voice. "Do come in."

He glowered at her. "What's goin' *on* here?"

She looked at him innocently. "Why, Mr. Brett — "

"Was you screamin'?"

She nodded brightly. "I like to scream. Don't you?"

"Naw. What'a idear?"

"Oh, sit down and I'll tell you about it. Here. Have a drink." She poured him a tumbler of whiskey so strong I could almost see it raise its dukes. She pushed him into a chair and handed it to him. "Drink up. I've missed you."

He goggled up at her uncertainly. "Well — I dunno. Gee, t'anks. Here's how, Miz Worth." And he threw it down the hatch. It was good stuff. He blinked twice and regretfully set the glass down. She refilled it, signaling behind her back for me to shut up. I did. When Myra acts this way there is nothing to do but stand by and wonder what's going to happen next.

Well, she got Brett started on the history of his life. Every two hundred words he'd empty that glass. Then she started mixing them. I was afraid that would happen. Her pet — for others' consumption; she wouldn't touch it — was what she called a "Three-two-one." Three fingers of whiskey, two of gin, one of soda. Only in Brett's case she substituted rum for the soda. Poor fellow.

In just an hour and a half he spread out his arms, said, "Mammy!" and folded up.

Myra looked down at him and shook her head. "*Tsk, tsk.* Pity I didn't have any knockout drops."

"Now what?" I breathed.

"Get your hypo. We're going to infect John Law here."

"Now, Myra — wait a minute. We can't — "

"Who says? Come on, David — he won't know a thing. Look — here's what we'll do with him."

She told me. It was a beautiful idea. I got my mosquito, and we went to work. We gave him a good case; shots of the stuff all over his body. He slept peacefully through it all, even the gales of merriment. The more we thought of it — Ah, poor fellow!

After we had what we wanted from him I undressed him and swabbed him down with the lotion. He'd be good as new when he came to. I put him to bed in the living room, and Myra and I spent the rest of the night working in the lab.

When we finished, we took the thing and set it in the living room. Brett's breathing was no longer stertorous; he was a very strong man. Myra tiptoed in and put the alarm clock beside him. Then we watched from the crack of the laboratory door.

The first rays of the sun were streaming through the windows, lighting up our masterpiece. The alarm went off explosively; Brett started, groaned, clutched his head. He felt around for the clock, knocked it off the chair. It fell shouting under the daybed. Brett groaned again, blinked his eyes open. He stared at the window first, trying vaguely to find out what was wrong with it. I could almost hear him thinking that, somehow, he didn't know where he was. The clock petered out. Brett began to stare dazedly about the room. The ceiling, the walls, and —

There in the geometric center of the room stood Detective Inspector Horace Brett, fully clothed. His shield glittered in the sun. On his face was a murderous leer, and in his hand was a regulation police hog-leg, trained right between the eyes of the man on the bed. They stared at each other for ten long seconds, the man with the hangover and the man's skin with the gun. Then Brett moved.

Like a streak of light he hurtled past the effigy. My best corduroy bedspread streaming behind him, clad only in underwear and a wrist watch, he shot through the door — and I mean *through,* because he didn't stop to open it — and wavered shrieking down the stairs. I'd never have caught him if he hadn't forgotten again that there were only three flights of stairs there. He brought up sharp against the wall; I was right behind him. I caught him up and toted him back up to the apartment before the neighbors had a chance to come rubbering around. Myra was rolling around on the floor. As I came in with Brett, she jumped up and kissed his gun-toting image, calling it fondly a name that should have been reserved for me.

We coddled poor Brett and soothed him; healed his wounds and sobered him up. He was sore at first and then grateful; and, to give him due credit, he was a good sport. We explained everything. We didn't have to swear him to secrecy. We had the goods on him. If I hadn't caught up with him, he'd have run all the way to headquarters in his snuggies.

It was not an affliction, then; it was a commodity. The business spread astonishingly. We didn't let it get too big; but what with a little false front and a bit more ballyhoo, we are really going places. For instance, in Myra's exclusive beauty shop is a booth reserved for the wealthiest patrons. Myra will use creams and lotions galore on her customer by way of getting her into the mood; then, after isolating the skin on her face, will infect it with a small needle. In a few minutes the skin comes off; a mud pack hides it. The lady has a lovely smooth new face; Myra ships the old one over to my place where my experts mount it. Then, through Myra's ballyhoo, the old lady generally will come around wanting a life mask. I give her a couple of appointments — they amount to séances — sling a lot of hocus-pocus, and in due time deliver the mask — life-size, neatly tinted. They never know, poor old dears, that they have contracted and been cured of the damnedest thing that ever skipped inclusion in "Materia Medica." It's a big business now; we're coining money.

Like all big business, of course, it has its little graft. A certain detective comes around three times a week for a thirty-second shave, free of charge. He's good people. His effigy still menaces our living room, with a toy gun now. Poor fellow.

The Heart on the Other Side

GEORGE GAMOW

The chances are that when a great scientist writes, he's eventually going to write some science fiction. No, this is not a slanted reference to myself as a great scientist; I began to write and sell science fiction when I was a kid and long before I was, well, a scientist. George Gamow, who really was a great scientist, wrote this one when he was over sixty, which shows that puckishness does not fade with age — at least when you're Russian. No, this is not a slanted reference to myself — hmm. Maybe it is.

"BUT FATHER will never give his consent," said Vera Sapognikoff in a tone of despair.

"But he must," said Stan Situs. He was very much in love.

Vera shook her head. "What my father is looking for in the way of a son-in-law is someone who can help him in his shoe business, and eventually take it over. You're a mathematician. You can't possibly qualify as a shoe manufacturer, can you?"

"I guess I can't," Stan agreed sadly, after some thought. "Perhaps if I were in some other branch of mathematics — But I am a topologist. I don't see what topology has to contribute to the production and selling of shoes."

Then he added stubbornly: "But I can't give you up, Vera! I can't lose the girl I love just because there's no cash value in a Möbius twist!"

"A what?"

Stan said patiently: "A Möbius twist. Haven't I ever shown you one?" He scrabbled in his desk drawer. They were in his university office, and it took him only a moment to find a piece of paper, a pair of scissors, and a small bottle of glue.

"Look," he said, and cut a strip of paper an inch or so wide. He twisted one end of it a half turn and glued it together, forming a twisted paper ring.

Vera looked at the paper and then at the man she loved. "Is this what you do for a living?" she asked.

"Here." Stan handed her the scissors. "Cut it all the way around, along the middle line of the strip. See what you get."

Vera shook her head. "That's silly. I know what I'll get. It will cut into two rings, and so what?"

"Cut," urged Stan.

Vera shrugged and did what Stan told her. And, curiously, it didn't work out at all the way she had expected. When the scissors had gone all the way around the strip, and closed on the starting point, Vera cried out. For there weren't two rings at all — there was still only one, but a ring that was half its former width and twice its former length.

Vera stared at her beloved mathematician. "What is this, magic? And who is this man Möbius?"

"He was a Swedish mathematician of the nineteenth century who contributed a great deal to the science of topology. I'm afraid his other contributions, though, aren't quite as easy to demonstrate.

"But there's more to be said about this strip." Quickly Stan cut out and pasted a new one. "See here. Suppose I sketch a few cartoon figures on the strip. Now you have to use your imagination a little. Make believe the strip is cellophane, so that you can see figures drawn on both sides of it at once. Then imagine that the little drawings can slide freely along the surface."

"All right," said Vera, frowning.

"Do you see?" Stan demanded triumphantly. "You find that they turn into their *mirror images* each time they make a complete trip around the strip!"

"Is that right?" murmured Vera glassily. She was getting visibly discouraged with so much mathematics.

"Pay attention!" Stan commanded, forgetting for the moment that he was talking to a lovely girl he wanted to marry, and not to one of his classes of graduate students. "This is a very important property of a Möbius strip — which, as I am going to show in my next article, can be generalized for three-dimensional, or even for *n*-dimensional, space."

"That's nice," muttered Vera.

But Stan was hardly listening; he was carried away. "This is not merely a matter of academic interest," he said proudly. "According to my calculations, there *is* such a three-dimensional Möbius effect somewhere on the surface of the earth. You see the consequences, of course?"

"Of course."

"Suppose, for example," said Stan, sketching hastily, "I draw on this strip a man and an animal facing each other. You have to imagine, still, that this is cellophane — which corresponds to the fact that mathematical surfaces are not supposed to have any thickness, and therefore both figures should be visible from either side of the paper. I draw, then, this gallant matador and brave bull in mortal conflict."

"Oh, how cute!" exclaimed Vera, delighted to find something she could recognize.

"Now," continued Stan, filled with a lecturer's enthusiasm, "imagine that the matador runs all the way around the strip and comes back to the bull from the other direction. Then he will look either in flight from the bull, or confronting him — upside down.

"Since neither position is very suitable for fighting the bull, he will have to make another run around the Möbius strip to straighten himself out again."

Vera began to gather her pocketbook and gloves in a businesslike way.

"That's very nice," she said politely. "But, Stan, what has it got to do with *us*? I can see how you amuse yourself with these Möbius comic strips. But you can't give a Möbius twist to a shoe to make Father agree to our marriage."

Stan came back to his present surroundings with a start.

"Oh," he said. "No, I suppose not. But — "

Then he frowned in concentration, and remained that way for several moments, until Vera became alarmed. "Stan?" she asked tentatively. "Stan?"

"But I can!" he cried. "Sure I can! Give a Möbius twist to a shoe, eh? Why, that's a brilliant idea — and, believe me, it will revolutionize the shoe industry!"

Not more than an hour later, Vera's father had a caller.

"Dr. Situs is here to see you," said the receptionist's voice through the intercom. "He says that he has a very important proposal to make."

"All right, let him in," Mr. Sapognikoff growled. He leaned back behind his giant desk, scowling. "I doubt, though," he said aloud, "that this young fellow has anything to propose but marriage." Then, still grumbling, he got up reluctantly as Stan came in and shook his hand.

Stan Situs said briskly: "Sir, I suppose you are aware that each man, as well as each woman, has two feet. One is right. The other is left."

Mr. Sapognikoff looked suddenly alarmed. "What?" he asked.

"It is a well-known fact," Stan assured him. "Now, doesn't it make the production of shoes more expensive? Don't you need two separate sets of machinery — one for right shoes and one for left — and wouldn't it be simple if one needed to produce only, let us say, right-foot shoes?"

Mr. Sapognikoff, now quite persuaded that the boy was really out of his mind, though probably not dangerous, said with heavy humor: "Sure. And I guess we make everybody hop around on one foot after that, right?"

"No, sir," Stan assured him seriously. "That would not be practical."

"Then what's the point?"

Stan settled himself. "The point is that for the past few years I have been working on the mathematical possibility of a Möbius twist in a three-dimensional space. I will not trouble you by trying to explain it, since you wouldn't understand. For that matter, even your daughter didn't." Mr. Sapognikoff scowled but said nothing. "The fact is that, according to my recent calculations pertaining to the gravitational anomalies observed in certain regions of the earth's surface, such a three-dimensional Möbius twist of space must exist somewhere in the unexplored regions of the upper Amazon River. In fact, my conclusions are strongly supported by recent findings of South American biological expeditions which discovered in that locality two different kinds of snails with left-screw and right-screw shells."

Mr. Sapognikoff said ominously: "I'm a busy man, Situs. And I don't understand a word of what you're saying. What does it have to do with shoes?"

"Well," began Stan patiently, "a three-dimensional space turns things into their mirror image if they are carried around the vortex point of the Möbius twist. Since right and left shoes are mirror images of one another, you can turn a right shoe into a left shoe, or vice versa, by carrying it around that vortex point in the upper Amazon. That's probably what had happened to the snails migrating in that vicinity. From now on, you can produce only right-foot shoes, and turn half of them into left-foot shoes by sending the lot up the Amazon River and around the vortex point. Think of the saving on machinery, and the perfect fit of shoe pairs!"

"My boy!" exclaimed Mr. Sapognikoff, jumping up from his chair and shaking the hand of the young mathematician. "If you can really do that, I will give you my daughter's hand and make you a junior partner in my business.

"But," he added after a short reflection. "Möbius or no Möbius, there will be no wedding until you return from the first Amazon trip with the load of converted shoes. I will, though, give you a preliminary partnership contract which you can study during your trip and which we'll sign as soon as you come back with the proof. My secretary will deliver to you that contract and an assortment of right-footed shoes at the airport. Good-bye, and good luck!"

Stan walked out of Sapognikoff's office beaming, and full of hopes.

"It is not the heat, it is the humidity." The sentence was hammering into the young mathematician's head through the entire exhausting trip up the Amazon River.

Although the description of all the perils of that trip, first by a small steamboat, and then by foot through tropical jungles surrounding the vortex point, does not fall within the scope of the present article, one cannot leave unmentioned such important items as: alligators, heat, humidity, mosquitoes, more humidity, and more mosquitoes. Besides all that, Stan suffered badly from an allergy to some tropical plant which almost cost him his life. But, sick as he was, he was leading the way, and a little caravan of a handful of Indian porters carrying shoe boxes was proceeding along the route which was supposed to bring them around the vortex point. Stan's head was swirling around because of the fever in his body, and later on he could never figure out whether the lopsided landscape, with some of the trees growing at most unusual angles and certain sections of the forest hanging practically upside down, was his imagination or the actual fact. On the way back to the river he became delirious and had to be carried by the porters. When he finally recovered consciousness, the boat was steaming smoothly down the river back to civilization, the weather was more tolerable, and numerous tropical birds were saturating the air with a gamut of shrill sounds. Rising to his feet, Stan walked to the stern of the boat where the shoe boxes were piled in disorder, and opened one of them marked: "Lady's Oxford. White. Size 6D, Right shoe." And, oh horror, it *was* the right shoe, and not the *left* one into which it was supposed to be turned! Apparently his theory was completely wrong, and all his efforts would never earn him Vera's hand!

Frantically he went on opening other boxes. There was a man's patent leather shoe, a lady's velvet shoe boot, a tiny pink baby shoe . . . But, they all were right-footed, as they had been when he inspected them before departure. In despair, he threw all overboard to the great delight of the alligators.

When Stan stepped out of the Pan American airliner, both Vera and her father were there to greet him.

"Where are the shoes?" asked Mr. Sapognikoff anxiously.

"I fed them to the alligators," answered Stan grimly. "I don't know what was wrong, but they all remained right-footed. I must have made some basic mistake in my calculations, and there isn't such a thing as a three-dimensional Möbius twist."

"Oh, no!" murmured Vera faintly.

"I am very sorry, sir," continued Stan, "for causing you all this trouble with my fantastic theory. I think it would be only fair if I returned to you unsigned our partnership contract."

And, producing a rather battered document from the pocket of his traveling jacket, he handed it over to the old man.

"Very strange," said Mr. Sapognikoff, glancing at the document. "I cannot even read it."

"Mirror writing!" exclaimed Vera, looking at it too. "It *is* mirror writing, so the things *did* change after all."

At a flash the explanation of his alleged failure, which wasn't a failure at all, dawned in Stan's head. Nothing was wrong, and every single right-footed shoe he carried with him turned into a left-footed one. But he also became left-footed and left-handed, and having changed himself into his mirror image, he naturally could not notice the same change in the shoes.

"Feel my heart," said Stan to Vera. "No, not here; my heart is now on the other side."

"I will love you just the same," smiled Vera happily.

"Too bad about the shoes," said Sapognikoff. "But I guess this document, and maybe an X-ray picture of your chest, can be considered as a definite proof. Thus, we will sign the partnership agreement as soon as this document is retyped in a proper way, if you practice writing your name again from left to right. And, of course, you and Vera may go ahead with your wedding plans."

But things were still not right. Ever since his return from Brazil, Stan's health was deteriorating and, although he ate healthy meals, he seemed to be suffering from malnutrition. A famous dietitian who was called in for consultation diagnosed his trouble as due to a complete inability to digest any protein food; in fact, the bacon and eggs he ate at breakfast and the most tasty dinner steaks were passing through him as if they were made of sawdust. Having learned about Stan's adventure in South America, and after having checked the fact that his heart was really displaced to the opposite side of his chest, the dietitian came out with the complete explanation of the mysterious sickness.

"The trouble with you," he said, "is that your digestive enzymes, as well as all others, turned from *levo* to *dextra* variety, and are helpless in their task of assimilating any proteins in ordinary foodstuffs which all possess levo symmetry."

"What do you mean by levo and dextra proteins?" asked Stan, who was never strong in chemistry.

"It is very simple," said the dietitian, "and very interesting too. The proteins, which are the most important constituents of all living organisms, and an important part of any diet, are complex chemical substances composed of a large number of rather simple units known as amino acids. There are twenty different kinds of amino acids, and the way they are put together to form a protein molecule determines whether one gets gastric juice, muscle fiber, or the white of an egg. Each amino acid contains a so-called amino group, an acid group and a hydrogen atom, attached to the main body of the molecule, known as residue, which determines its chemical and biological properties. Imagine that the palm of your hand represents the residue of some particular amino acid. Stick an amino group on your thumb, an acid group on your index finger, a hydrogen atom on your middle finger, and you will have a fairly good idea of how these basic units of all living matter look."

"Oh, I see now," said Stan. "One gets levo and dextra varieties of these molecular models depending on whether one uses his left or right hand. Isn't that correct?"

"Quite correct. But, although chemically both molecules are identical, because of their opposite mirror symmetry, they act differently on polarized light, and can be distinguished by optical methods.

"Now the great mystery of nature is that, although in ordinary chemical synthesis carried out in a laboratory both levo and dextra varieties are produced in equal amounts, only levo variety is used by living organisms. All the proteins, in me, in you, in a dog, in a fish, in an oak tree, in an amoeba, or in influenza virus, are built exclusively by the levo variety of amino acids."

"But why?" asked Stan in surprise. "Does the levo variety have any advantage from the biological point of view?"

"None whatsoever. In fact, one can imagine two coexisting organic worlds, levo and dextra, which may, or may not, have gone through the same process of organic evolution. The possibility is not excluded that two such organic worlds actually could have existed during the early history of our planet, and that, just by chance, the levo organisms developed some improvement, giving them an advantage in the struggle for existence over the dextra ones that then become extinct."

"And you mean that after traveling around the Möbius vortex point, I now belong to this nonexisting dextra world?"

"Exactly so," said the dietitian, "and although you can get some benefit from such foodstuffs as fats and starches the molecules of which do not possess mirror asymmetry, ordinary protein diet is out of the question for you at the moment. But, I am sure, your father-in-law will subsidize a special biochemical laboratory which will synthesize for you dextra varieties of all common food proteins. In the meantime we can feed you on antibiotics — such as penicillin, for example."

"Antibiotics?" repeated Stan with surprise. "Why should antibiotics be good for me?"

"I forgot to tell you that there *are* a few living organisms, mostly molds, which use, at least partially, dextra amino acids in their bodies."

"You mean they are the survivals of this extinct dextra world?"

"Most probably not. It is more likely that these molds have developed the ability to synthesize, and to use, dextra amino acids as a defense against the bacteria which are their worst enemies. This defense is good against *all* kinds of bacteria, since all bacteria are levo organisms and develop bad indigestion when fed on dextra food. But it will be good for you."

"Fine," said Stan, smiling. "Order me a large dish of penicillin *au gratin.* I am starved. And send Vera along to see me — I want to tell her the good news!"

Blackmail

FRED HOYLE

I'm a cat person myself, and I think it's an inherited characteristic. My parents loved cats, my children love cats. Janet, on the other hand, is eclectic and loves all living things, even higher primates like me. Unfortunately, under our present living conditions we can't have pets, so she fills the apartment with plants and pats me a lot. In spite of our great fondness for animals, we think that if the premise of this story were made true, television ratings would make a great deal more sense.

ANGUS CARRUTHERS was a wayward, impish genius. Genius is not the same thing as high ability. Men of great talent commonly spread their efforts, often very effectively, over a wide front. The true genius devotes the whole of his skill, his energies, his intelligence, to a particular objective, which he pursues unrelentingly.

Early in life, Carruthers became skeptical of human superiority over other animals. In his early teens he already understood exactly where the difference lies — it lies in the ability of humans to pool their knowledge through speech, in the ability through speech to educate the young. The challenging problem to his keen mind was to find a system of communication, every bit as powerful as language, that could be made available to others of the higher animals. The basic idea was not original; it was the determination to carry the idea through to its conclusion that was new. Carruthers pursued his objective inflexibly down the years.

Gussie had no patience with people who talked and chattered to animals. If animals had the capacity to understand language wouldn't they have done it already, he said, thousands of years ago? Talk was utterly and completely pointless. You were just damned stupid if you thought you were going to teach English to your pet dog or cat. The thing to do was to understand the world from the point of view of the dog or cat. Once you'd got yourself into *their* system it would be time enough to think about trying to get them into *your* system.

Gussie had no close friends. I suppose I was about as near to being a friend as anyone, yet even I would see him only perhaps once in six months. There was always something refreshingly different when you happened to run into him. He might have grown a black spade beard, or he might just have had a crew cut. He might be wearing a flowing cape, or he might be neatly tailored in a Bond Street suit. He always trusted me well enough to show off his latest experiments. At the least they were remarkable; at the best they went far beyond anything I had heard of or read about. To my repeated suggestions that he simply must "publish" he always responded with a long wheezy laugh. To me it seemed just plain common sense to publish, if only to raise money for the experiments, but Gussie obviously didn't see it this way. How he managed for money, I could never discover. I supposed him to have private income, which was very likely correct.

One day I received a note asking me to proceed to such-and-such an address, sometime near 4:00 P.M. on a certain Saturday. There was nothing unusual in my receiving a note, for Carruthers had got in touch with me several times before in this way. It was the address which came as the surprise, a house in a Croydon suburb. On previous occasions I had always gone out to some decrepit barn of a place in remotest Hertfordshire. The idea of Gussie in Croydon somehow didn't fit. I was sufficiently intrigued to put off a previous appointment and to hie myself along at the appropriate hour.

My wild notion that Carruthers might have got himself well and truly wed, that he might have settled down in a nine-to-five job, turned out to be quite wrong. The big tortoiseshell spectacles he had sported at our previous meeting were gone, replaced by plain steel rims. His lank black hair was medium long this time. He had a lugubrious look about him, as if he had just been rehearsing the part of Quince in *A Midsummer Night's Dream.*

"Come in," he wheezed.

"What's the idea, living in these parts?" I asked as I slipped off my overcoat. For answer, he broke into a whistling, croaking laugh.

"Better take a look, in there."

The door to which Gussie pointed was closed. I was pretty sure I would find animals "in there," and so it proved. Although the room was darkened by a drawn curtain, there was sufficient light for me to see three creatures crouched around a television set. They were intently watching the second half of a game of Rugby League football. There was a cat with a big rust-red patch on the top of its head. There was a poodle, which cocked an eye at me for a fleeting second as I went in, and there was a furry animal sprawled in a big armchair. As I went in, I had the odd impression of the animal lifting a paw, as if by way of greeting. Then I realized it was a small brown bear.

I had known Gussie long enough now, I had seen enough of his work, to realize that any comment in words would be ridiculous and superfluous. I had long ago learned the right procedure, to do exactly the same thing as the animals themselves were doing. Since I have always been partial to rugby, I was able to settle down quite naturally to watch the game in company with this amazing trio. Every so often I found myself catching the bright, alert eyes of the bear. I soon realized that, whereas I was mainly interested in the run of the ball, the animals were mainly interested in the tackling, *qua* tackling. Once when a player was brought down particularly heavily there was a muffled yap from the poodle, instantly answered by a grunt from the bear.

After perhaps twenty minutes I was startled by a really loud bark from the dog, there being nothing at all in the game to warrant such an outburst. Evidently the dog wanted to attract the attention of the engrossed bear, for when the bear looked up quizzically the dog pointed a dramatic paw toward a clock standing a couple of yards to the left of the television set. Immediately the bear lumbered from its chair to the set. It fumbled with the controls. There was a click, and to my astonishment we were on another channel. A wrestling bout had just begun.

The bear rolled back to its chair. It stretched itself, resting lazily on the base of the spine, arms raised with the claws cupped behind the head. One of the wrestlers spun the other violently. There was a loud thwack as the unfortunate fellow cracked his head on a ring post. At this, the cat let out the strangest animal noise I had ever heard. Then it settled down into a deep powerful purr.

I had seen and heard enough. As I quitted the room the bear waved me out, much in the style of royalty and visiting heads of state. I found Gussie placidly drinking tea in what was evidently the main sitting room of the house. To my frenzied requests to be told exactly what it meant, Gussie responded with his usual asthmatic laugh. Instead of answering my questions he asked some of his own.

"I want your advice, professionally as a lawyer. There's nothing illegal in the animals watching television, is there? Or in the bear switching the programs?"

"How could there be?"

"The situation's a bit complicated. Here, take a look at this."

Carruthers handed me a typewritten list. It covered a week of television programs. If this represented viewing by the animals the set must have been switched on more or less continuously. The programs were all of a type — sport, westerns, suspense plays, films of violence.

"What they love," said Gussie by way of explanation, "is the sight of humans bashing themselves to pieces. Really, of course, it's more or less the usual popular taste, only a bit more so."

I noticed the name of a well-known rating firm on the letterhead.

"What's this heading here? I mean, what's all this to do with the TV ratings?"

Gussie fizzed and crackled like a soda siphon.

"That's exactly the point. This house here is one of the odd few hundreds used in compiling the weekly ratings. That's why I asked if there was anything wrong in Bingo doing the switching."

"You don't mean viewing by those animals is going into the ratings?"

"Not only here, but in three other houses I've bought. I've got a team of chaps in each of them. Bears take quite naturally to the switching business."

"There'll be merry hell to pay if it comes out. Can't you see what the papers will make of it?"

"Very clearly indeed."

The point hit me at last. Gussie could hardly have come on four houses by chance, all of which just happened to be hooked up to the TV rating system. As far as I could see there wasn't anything illegal in what he'd done, so long as he didn't make any threats or demands. As if he read my thoughts, he pushed a slip of paper under my nose. It was a check for $100,000.

"Unsolicited," he wheezed, "came out of the blue. From somebody in the advertising game, I suppose. Hush money. The problem is, do I put myself in the wrong if I cash it?"

Before I could form an opinion on this tricky question there came a tinkling of breaking glass.

"Another one gone," Gussie muttered. "I haven't been able to teach Bingo to use the vertical or horizontal holds. Whenever anything goes wrong, or the program goes off for a minute, he hammers away at the thing. It's always the tube that goes."

"It must be quite a costly business."

"Averages about a dozen a week. I always keep a spare set ready. Be a good fellow and give me a hand with it. They'll get pretty testy if we don't move smartly."

We lifted what seemed like a brand new set from out of a cupboard. Each gripping an end of it, we edged our way to the television snuggery. From inside, I was now aware of a strident uproar, compounded from the bark of a dog, the grunt of a bear, and the shrill moan of a redheaded cat. It was the uproar of animals suddenly denied their intellectual pabulum.

A Slight Miscalculation

BEN BOVA

Ben is a good friend of mine. He was born in Philadelphia and, to my knowledge, has lived in Lexington, Massachusetts, in New York City, and in West Hartford, Connecticut — all, you will note, in the Northeast. What deep-seated, unrevealed, unconscious hostility to his home region can possibly have resulted in the following story?

NATHAN FRENCH was a pure mathematician. He worked for a research laboratory perched on a California hill that overlooked the Pacific surf, but his office had no windows. When his laboratory earned its income by doing research on nuclear bombs, Nathan doodled out equations for placing men on the Moon with a minimum expenditure of rocket fuel. When his lab landed a fat contract for developing a lunar flight profile, Nathan began worrying about air pollution.

Nathan didn't look much like a mathematician. He was tall and gangly, liked to play handball, spoke with a slight lisp when he got excited, and had a face that definitely reminded you of a horse. Which helped him to remain pure in things other than mathematics. The only possible clue to his work was that, lately, he had started to squint a lot. But he didn't look the slightest bit nervous or high strung, and he still often smiled his great big toothy, horsy smile.

When the lab landed its first contract (from the state of California) to study air pollution, Nathan's pure thoughts turned — naturally — elsewhere.

"I think it might be possible to work out a method of predicting earthquakes," Nathan told the laboratory chief, kindly old Dr. Moneygrinder.

Moneygrinder peered at Nathan over his half-lensed bifocals. "Okay, Nathan, my boy," he said heartily. "Go ahead and try it. You know I'm always interested in furthering man's understanding of his universe."

When Nathan left the chief's sumptuous office, Moneygrinder hauled his paunchy little body out of its plush desk chair and went to the window. *His* office had windows on two walls: one set overlooked the beautiful Pacific; the other looked down on the parking lot, so that the chief could check on who got to work at what time.

And behind that parking lot, which was half filled with aging cars (business had been deteriorating for several years), back among the eucalyptus trees and paint-freshened grass, was a remarkably straight little ridge of ground, no more than four feet high. It ran like an elongated step behind the whole length of the laboratory and out past the abandoned pink stucco church on the crest of the hill. A little ridge of grass-covered earth that was called the San Andreas Fault.

Moneygrinder often stared at the fault from his window, rehearsing in his mind exactly what to do when the ground started to tremble. He wasn't afraid, merely careful. Once a tremor had hit in the middle of a staff meeting. Moneygrinder was out the window, across the parking lot, and on the far side of the fault (the eastern, or "safe," side) before men half his age had gotten out of their chairs. The staff talked for months about the astonishing agility of the fat little waddler.

A year, almost to the day, later the parking lot was slightly fuller, and a few of the cars were new. The pollution business was starting to pick up, since the disastrous smog in San Clemente. And the laboratory had also managed to land a few quiet little Air Force contracts — for six times the amount of money it got from the pollution work.

Moneygrinder was leaning back in the plush desk chair, trying to look both interested and noncommittal at the same time, which was difficult to do, because he never could follow Nathan when the mathematician was trying to explain his work.

"Then it's a thimple matter of transposing the progression," Nathan was lisping, talking too fast because he was excited as he scribbled equations on the fuchsia-colored chalkboard with nerve-rippling squeaks of the yellow chalk.

"You thee?" Nathan said at last, standing beside the chalkboard. It was totally covered with his barely legible numbers and symbols. A pall of yellow chalk dust hovered about him.

"Um . . ." said Moneygrinder. "Your conclusion, then . . ."

"It's perfectly clear," Nathan said. "If you have any reasonable data base at all, you can not only predict when an earthquake will hit and where, but you can altho predict its intensity."

Moneygrinder's eyes narrowed. "You're sure?"

"I've gone over it with the Cal Tech geophysicists. They agree with the theory."

"H'mm." Moneygrinder tapped his desk top with his pudgy fingers. "I know this is a little outside your area of interest, Nathan, but . . . ah, can you really predict actual earthquakes? Or is this all theoretical?"

"Sure you can predict earthquakes," Nathan said, grinning like Francis the movie star. "Like next Thursday's."

"Next Thursday's?"

"Yeth. There's going to be a major earthquake next Thursday."

"Where?"

"Right here. Along the fault."

"Ulp."

Nathan tossed his stubby piece of chalk into the air nonchalantly, but missed the catch, and it fell to the carpeted floor.

Moneygrinder, slightly paler than the chalk, asked, "A major quake, you say?"

"Uh-huh."

"Did . . . did the Cal Tech people make this prediction?"

"No, I did. They don't agree. They claim I've got an inverted gamma factor in the fourteenth set of equations. I've got the computer checking it right now."

Some of the color returned to Moneygrinder's flabby cheeks. "Oh . . . oh, I see. Well, let me know what the computer says."

"Sure."

The next morning, as Moneygrinder stood behind the gauzy drapes of his office window watching the cars pull in, his phone rang. His secretary had put in a long night, he knew, and she wasn't in yet. Pouting, Moneygrinder went over to the desk and answered the phone himself.

It was Nathan. "The computer still agrees with the Cal Tech boys. But I think the programming's slightly off. Can't really trust computers; they're only as good as the people who feed them, you know."

"I see," Moneygrinder answered. "Well, keep checking on it."

He chuckled as he hung up. "Good old Nathan. Great at theory, but hopeless in the real world."

Still, when his secretary finally showed up and brought him his morning coffee and pill and nibble on the ear, he said thoughtfully:

"Maybe I ought to talk with those bankers in New York."

"But you said that you wouldn't need their money now that business is picking up," she purred.

He nodded bulbously. "Yes, but still . . . arrange a meeting with them for next Thursday. I'll leave Wednesday afternoon. Stay the weekend in New York."

She stared at him. "But you said we'd . . ."

"Now, now . . . business comes first. You take the Friday night jet and meet me at the hotel."

Smiling, she answered, "Yes, Cuddles."

Matt Climber had just come back from a Pentagon lunch when Nathan's phone call reached him.

Climber had worked for Nathan several years ago. He had started as a computer programmer, assistant to Nathan. In two years he had become a section head, and Nathan's direct supervisor. (On paper only. Nobody bossed Nathan; he worked independently.) When it became obvious to Moneygrinder that Climber was heading his way, the lab chief helped his young assistant to a government job in Washington. Good experience for an up-and-coming executive.

"Hiya, Nathan, how's the pencil-pushing game?" Climber shouted into the phone as he glanced at his calendar appointment pad. There were three inter-agency conferences and two staff meetings going this afternoon.

"Hold it now, slow down," Climber said, sounding friendly but looking grim. "You know people can't understand you when you talk too fast."

Thirty minutes later, Climber was leaning back in his chair, feet on the desk, tie loosened, shirt collar open, and the first two meetings on his afternoon's list crossed off.

"Now let me get this straight, Nathan," he said into the phone. "You're predicting a major quake along the San Andreas Fault next Thursday afternoon at two-thirty Pacific Standard Time. But the Cal Tech people and your own computer don't agree with you."

Another ten minutes later, Climber said, "Okay, okay . . . sure, I remember how we'd screw up the programming once in a while. But you made mistakes, too. Okay, look — tell you what, Nathan. Keep checking. If you find out definitely that the computer's wrong and you're right, call me right away. I'll get the President himself, if we have to. Okay? Fine. Keep in touch."

He slammed the phone back onto its cradle and his feet on the floor, all in one weary motion.

Old Nathan's really gone 'round the bend, Climber told himself. *Next Thursday. Hah! Next Thursday. H'mmm . . .*

He leafed through the calendar pages. Sure enough, he had a meeting with the Boeing people in Seattle next Thursday.

If there IS a major quake, the whole damned West Coast might slide into the Pacific. Naw . . . don't be silly. Nathan's cracking up, that's all. Still . . . how far north does the fault go?

He leaned across the desk and tapped the intercom button.

"Yes, Mr. Climber?" came his secretary's voice.

"That conference with Boeing on the hypersonic ramjet transport next Thursday," Climber began, then hesitated a moment. But, with absolute finality, he snapped, "Cancel it."

Nathan French was not a drinking man, but on Tuesday of the following week he went straight from the laboratory to a friendly little bar that hung from a rocky ledge over the surging ocean.

It was a strangely quiet Tuesday afternoon; so Nathan had the undivided attention of both the worried-looking bartender and the freshly painted whore who worked the early shift in a low-cut black cocktail dress and overpowering perfume.

"Cheez, I never seen business so lousy as yesterday and today," the bartender mumbled. He was sort of fidgeting around behind the bar, with nothing to do. The only dirty glass in the place was Nathan's, and he was holding on to it because he liked to chew the ice cubes.

"Yeah," said the girl. "At this rate, I'll be a virgin again by the end of the week."

Nathan didn't reply. His mouth was full of ice cubes, which he crunched in absent-minded cacophony. He was still trying to figure out why he and the computer didn't agree about the fourteenth set of equations. Everything else checked out perfectly: time, place, force level on the Richter scale. But the vector, the directional value — somebody was still misreading his programming instructions. That was the only possible answer.

"The stock market's dropped through the floor," the bartender said darkly. "My broker says Boeing's gonna lay off half their people. That ramjet transport they was gonna build is getting scratched. And the lab up the hill is getting bought out by some East Coast banks." He shook his head slowly.

The girl, sitting beside Nathan with her elbows on the bar and her styrofoam bra sharply profiled, smiled at him and said, "Hey, how about it, big guy? Just so I don't forget how to, huh?"

With a final crunch on the last ice cube, Nathan said, "Uh, excuse me. I've got to check that computer program."

By Thursday morning, Nathan was truly upset. Not only was the computer still insisting that he was wrong about equation fourteen, but none of the programmers had shown up for work. Obviously, one of them — maybe all of them — had sabotaged his program. But why?

He stalked up and down the hallways of the lab searching for a programmer, somebody, anybody — but the lab was virtually empty. Only a handful of people had come in, and after an hour or so of wide-eyed whispering among themselves in the cafeteria over coffee, they started to sidle out to the parking lot and get into their cars and drive away.

Nathan happened to be walking down a corridor when one of the research physicists — a new man, from a department Nathan never dealt with — bumped into him.

"Oh, excuse me," the physicist said hastily and started to head for the door down at the end of the hall.

"Wait a minute," Nathan said, grabbing him by the arm. "Can you program the computer?"

"Uh, no, I can't."

"Where is everybody today?" Nathan wondered aloud, still holding the man's arm. "Is it a national holiday?"

"Man, haven't you heard?" the physicist asked, goggle-eyed. "There's going to be an earthquake this afternoon. The whole damned state of California is going to slide into the sea!"

"Oh, that."

Pulling his arm free, the physicist scuttled down the hall. As he got to the door he shouted over his shoulder, "Get out while you can! East of the fault! The roads are jamming up fast!"

Nathan frowned. "There's still an hour or so," he said to himself. "And I still think the computer's wrong. I wonder what the tidal effects on the Pacific Ocean would be if the whole state collapsed into the ocean?"

Nathan didn't really notice that he was talking to himself. There was no one else to talk to.

Except the computer.

He was sitting in the computer room, still poring over the stubborn equations, when the rumbling started. At first it was barely audible, like very distant thunder. Then the room began to shake and the rumbling grew louder.

Nathan glanced at his wrist watch: 2:32.

"I knew it!" he said gleefully to the computer. "You see? And I'll bet all the rest of it is right, too. Including equation fourteen."

Going down the hallway was like walking through the passageway of a storm-tossed ship. The floor and walls were swaying violently. Nathan kept his feet, despite some awkward lurches here and there.

It didn't occur to him that he might die until he got outside. The sky was dark, the ground heaving, the roaring deafened him. A violent gale was blowing dust everywhere, adding its shrieking fury to the earth's tortured groaning.

Nathan couldn't see five feet ahead of him. With the wind tearing at him and the dust stinging his eyes, he couldn't tell which way to go. He knew that the other side of the fault meant safety, but where was it?

Then there was a Biblical crack of lightning and the ultimate grinding, screaming, ear-shattering roar. A tremendous shock wave knocked Nathan to the ground, and he blacked out. His last thought was, "I was right and the computer was wrong."

When he woke up, the sun was shining feebly through a gray overcast. The wind had died away. Everything was strangely quiet.

Nathan climbed stiffly to his feet and looked around. The lab building was still there. He was standing in the middle of the parking lot; the only car in sight was his own, caked with dust.

Beyond the parking lot, where the eucalyptus trees used to be, was the edge of a cliff, where still-steaming rocks and raw earth tumbled down to a foaming sea.

Nathan staggered to the cliff's edge and looked out across the water, eastward. Somehow he knew that the nearest land was Europe.

"Son of a bitch," he said with unaccustomed vehemence. "The computer was right after all."

"I thought continental drift was much slower."

A Subway Named Möbius

A. J. DEUTSCH

Except for the author himself, I was the first person to see this story. He called me up to read me the first paragraph. I grew excited, asked to see the rest, and ordered him to send it to John Campbell, who took it. Poor Deutsch died young and, as far as I know, never published another story; but if he had to do only one, I'm glad this was it.

Of course, Armand and I were both living in the Boston area in those days, so it had special meaning for us. You see, this story is hilarious if you visit Boston, but if you live there . . .

IN A COMPLEX and ingenious pattern, the subway had spread out from a focus at Park Street. A shunt connected the Lechmere line with the Ashmont for trains southbound, and with the Forest Hills line for those northbound. Harvard and Brookline had been linked with a tunnel that passed through Kenmore Under, and during rush hours every other train was switched through the Kenmore Branch back to Egleston. The Kenmore Branch joined the Maverick Tunnel near Fields Corner. It climbed a hundred feet in two blocks to connect Copley Over with Scollay Square; then it dipped down again to join the Cambridge line at Boylston. The Boylston shuttle had finally tied together the seven principal lines on four different levels. It went into service, you remember, on March 3. After that, a train could travel from any one station to any other station in the whole system.

There were two hundred twenty-seven trains running the subways every weekday, and they carried about a million and a half passengers. The Cambridge-Dorchester train that disappeared on March 4 was Number 86. Nobody missed it at first. During the evening rush, the traffic was a little heavier than usual on that line. But a crowd is a crowd. The ad posters at the Forest Hills yards looked for 86 about 7:30, but neither of them mentioned its absence until three days later. The controller at the Milk Street crossover called the Harvard checker for an extra train after the hockey game that night, and the Harvard checker relayed the call to the yards. The dispatcher there sent out 87, which had been put to bed at ten o'clock, as usual. He didn't notice that 86 was missing.

It was near the peak of the rush the next morning that Jack O'Brien, at the Park Street control, called Warren Sweeney at the Forest Hills yards and told him to put another train on the Cambridge run. Sweeney was short, so he went to the board and scanned it for a spare train and crew. Then, for the first time, he noticed that Gallagher had not checked out the night before. He put the tag up and left a note. Gallagher was due on at 10:00. At 10:30, Sweeney was down looking at the board again, and he noticed Gallagher's tag still up, and the note where he had left it. He groused to the checker and asked if Gallagher had come in late. The checker said he hadn't seen Gallagher at all that morning. Then Sweeney wanted to know who was running 86? A few minutes later he found that Dorkin's card was still up, although it was Dorkin's day off. It was 11:30 before he finally realized that he had lost a train.

Sweeney spent the next hour and a half on the phone, and he quizzed every dispatcher, controller, and checker on the whole system. When he finished his lunch at 1:30, he covered the whole net again. At 4:40, just before he left for the day, he reported the matter, with some indignation, to Central Traffic. The phones buzzed through the tunnels and shops until nearly midnight before the general manager was finally notified at his home.

It was the engineer on the main switchbank who, late in the morning of the sixth, first associated the missing train with the newspaper stories about the sudden rash of missing persons. He tipped off the *Transcript,* and by the end of the lunch hour three papers had extras on the streets. That was the way the story got out.

Kelvin Whyte, the general manager, spent a good part of that afternoon with the police. They checked Gallagher's wife, and Dorkin's. The motorman and the conductor had not been home since the morning of the fourth. By midafternoon, it was clear to the police that three hundred and fifty Bostonians, more or less, had been lost with the train. The System buzzed, and Whyte nearly expired with simple exasperation. But the train was not found.

Roger Tupelo, the Harvard mathematician, stepped into the picture the evening of the sixth. He reached Whyte by phone, late, at his home, and told him he had some ideas about the missing train. Then he taxied to Whyte's home in Newton and had the first of many talks with Whyte about Number 86.

Whyte was an intelligent man, a good organizer, and not without imagination. "But I don't know what you're talking about!" he expostulated.

Tupelo was resolved to be patient. "This is a very hard thing for *anybody* to understand, Mr. Whyte," he said. "I can see why you are puzzled. But it's the only explanation. The train has vanished, and the people on it. But the System is closed. Trains are conserved. It's somewhere on the System!"

Whyte's voice grew louder again. "And I tell you, Dr. Tupelo, that train is *not* on the System! It is *not*! You can't overlook a seven-car train carrying four hundred passengers. The System has been combed. Do you think I'm trying to *hide* the train?"

"Of course not. Now look, let's be reasonable. We know the train was en route to Cambridge at eight-forty A.M. on the fourth. At least twenty of the missing people probably boarded the train a few minutes earlier at Washington, and forty more at Park Street Under. A few got off at both stations. And that's the last. The ones who were going to Kendall, to Central, to Harvard — they never got there. The train did not get to Cambridge."

"I know that, Dr. Tupelo," Whyte said savagely. "In the tunnel under the river, the train turned into a boat. It left the tunnel and sailed for Africa."

"No, Mr. Whyte. I'm trying to tell you. It hit a node."

Whyte was livid. "What is a node?" he exploded. "The System keeps the tracks clear. Nothing on the tracks but trains, no nodes left lying around — "

"You still don't understand. A node is not an obstruction. It's a singularity. A pole of high order."

Tupelo's explanations that night did not greatly clarify the situation for Kelvin Whyte. But at two in the morning, the general manager conceded to Tupelo the privilege of examining the master maps of the System. He put in a call first to the police, who could not assist him with his first attempt to master topology, and then, finally, to Central Traffic. Tupelo taxied down there alone, and pored over the maps till morning. He had coffee and a snail, and then went to Whyte's office.

He found the general manager on the telephone. There was a conversation having to do with another, more elaborate inspection of the Dorchester-Cambridge tunnel under the Charles River. When the conversation ended, Whyte slammed the telephone into its cradle and glared at Tupelo. The mathematician spoke first.

"I think probably it's the new shuttle that did this," he said.

Whyte gripped the edge of his desk and prowled silently through his vocabulary until he had located some civil words. "Dr. Tupelo," he said, "I have been awake all night going over your theory. I don't understand it all. I don't know what the Boylston shuttle has to do with this."

"Remember what I was saying last night about the connective properties of networks?" Tupelo asked quietly. "Remember the Möbius band we made — the surface with one face and one edge? Remember this — ?" and he removed a little glass Klein bottle from his pocket and placed it on the desk.

Whyte sat back in his chair and stared wordlessly at the mathematician. Three emotions marched across his face in quick succession — anger, bewilderment, and utter dejection. Tupelo went on.

"Mr. Whyte, the System is a network of amazing topological complexity.

It was already complex before the Boylston shuttle was installed, and of a high order of connectivity. But this shuttle makes the network absolutely unique. I don't fully understand it, but the situation seems to be something like this: The shuttle has made the connectivity of the whole System of an order so high that I don't know how to calculate it. I suspect the connectivity has become infinite."

The general manager listened as though in a daze. He kept his eyes glued to the little Klein bottle.

"The Möbius band," Tupelo said, "has unusual properties because it has a singularity. The Klein bottle, with two singularities, manages to be inside of itself. The topologists know surfaces with as many as a thousand singularities, and they have properties that make the Möbius band and the Klein bottle both look simple. But a network with infinite connectivity must have an infinite number of singularities. Can you imagine what the properties of that network could be?"

After a long pause, Tupelo added: "I can't either. To tell the truth, the structure of the System, with the Boylston shuttle, is completely beyond me. I can only guess."

Whyte swiveled his eyes up from the desk at a moment when anger was the dominant feeling within him. "And you call yourself a mathematician, Professor Tupelo!" he said.

Tupelo almost laughed aloud. The incongruous, the absolute foolishness of the situation, all but overwhelmed him. He smiled thinly, and said: "I'm no topologist. Really, Mr. Whyte, I'm a tyro in the field — not much better acquainted with it than you are. Mathematics is a big pasture. I happen to be an algebraist."

His candor softened Whyte a little. "Well, then," he ventured, "if you don't understand it, maybe we should call in a topologist. Are there any in Boston?"

"Yes and no," Tupelo answered. "The best in the world is at Tech."

Whyte reached for the telephone. "What's his name?" he asked. "I'll call him."

"Merritt Turnbull. He can't be reached. I've tried for three days."

"Is he out of town?" Whyte asked. "We'll send for him — emergency."

"I don't know. Professor Turnbull is a bachelor. He lives alone at the Brattle Club. He has not been seen since the morning of the fourth."

Whyte was uncommonly perceptive. "Was he on the train?" he asked tensely.

"I don't know," the mathematician replied. "What do you think?"

There was a long silence. Whyte looked alternately at Tupelo and at the glass object on the desk. "I don't understand it," he said finally. "We've looked everywhere on the System. There was no way for the train to get out."

"The train didn't get out. It's still on the System," Tupelo said.

"Where?"

Tupelo shrugged. "The train has no real 'where.' The whole System is without real 'whereness.' It's double-valued, or worse."

"How can we find it?"

"I don't think we can," Tupelo said.

There was another long silence. Whyte broke it with a loud exclamation. He rose suddenly, and sent the Klein bottle flying across the room. "You are crazy, professor!" he shouted. "Between midnight tonight and six A.M. tomorrow, we'll get every train out of the tunnels. I'll send in three hundred men, to comb every inch of the tracks — every inch of the one hundred eighty-three miles. We'll find the train! Now, please excuse me." He glared at Tupelo.

Tupelo left the office. He felt tired, completely exhausted. Mechanically, he walked along Washington Street toward the Essex Station. Halfway down the stairs, he stopped abruptly, looked around him slowly. Then he ascended again to the street and hailed a taxi. At home, he helped himself to a double shot. He fell into bed.

At 3:30 that afternoon he met his class in "Algebra of Fields and Rings." After a quick supper at the Crimson Spa, he went to his apartment and spent the evening in a second attempt to analyze the connective properties of the System. The attempt was vain, but the mathematician came to a few important conclusions. At eleven o'clock he telephoned Whyte at Central Traffic.

"I think you might want to consult me during tonight's search," he said. "May I come down?"

The general manager was none too gracious about Tupelo's offer of help. He indicated that the System would solve this little problem without any help from harebrained professors who thought that whole subway trains could jump off into the fourth dimension. Tupelo submitted to Whyte's unkindness, then went to bed. At about 4:00 A.M. the telephone awakened him. His caller was a contrite Kelvin Whyte.

"Perhaps I was a bit hasty last night, professor," he stammered. "You may be able to help us after all. Could you come down to the Milk Street crossover?"

Tupelo agreed readily. He felt none of the satisfaction he had anticipated. He called a taxi, and in less than half an hour was at the prescribed station. At the foot of the stairs, on the upper level, he saw that the tunnel was brightly lighted, as during normal operation of the System. But the platforms were deserted except for a tight little knot of seven men near the far end. As he walked toward the group, he noticed that two were policemen. He observed a one-car train on the track beside the platform. The forward door was open, the car brightly lit and empty. Whyte heard his footsteps and greeted him sheepishly.

"Thanks for coming down, professor," he said, extending his hand. "Gentlemen, Dr. Roger Tupelo, of Harvard. Dr. Tupelo, Mr. Kennedy, our chief engineer; Mr. Wilson, representing the mayor; Dr. Gannot, of Mercy Hospital." Whyte did not bother to introduce the motorman and the two policemen.

"How do you do," said Tupelo. "Any results, Mr. Whyte?"

The general manager exchanged embarrassed glances with his companions. "Well . . . yes, Dr. Tupelo," he finally answered. "I think we do have some results, of a kind."

"Has the train been seen?"

"Yes," said Whyte. "That is, practically seen. At least, we know it's somewhere in the tunnels." The six others nodded their agreement.

Tupelo was not surprised to learn that the train was still on the System. After all, the System was closed. "Would you mind telling me just what happened?" Tupelo insisted.

"I hit a red signal," the motorman volunteered. "Just outside the Copley junction."

"The tracks have been completely cleared of all trains," Whyte explained, "except for this one. We've been riding it, all over the System, for four hours now. When Edmunds here hit a red light at the Copley junction, he stopped, of course. I thought the light must be defective, and told him to go ahead. But then we heard another train pass the junction."

"Did you see it?" Tupelo asked.

"We couldn't see it. The light is placed just behind a curve. But we all heard it. There's no doubt the train went through the junction. And it must be Number eighty-six, because our car was the only other one on the tracks."

"What happened then?"

"Well, then the light changed to yellow, and Edmunds went ahead."

"Did he follow the other train?"

"No. We couldn't be sure which way it was going. We must have guessed wrong."

"How long ago did this happen?"

"At one-thirty-eight, the first time — "

"Oh," said Tupelo, "then it happened again later?"

"Yes. But not at the same spot, of course. We hit another red signal near South Station at two-fifteen. And then at three-twenty-eight — "

Tupelo interrupted the general manager. "Did you see the train at two-fifteen?"

"We didn't even hear it, that time. Edmunds tried to catch it, but it must have turned off onto the Boylston shuttle."

"What happened at three-twenty-eight?"

"Another red light. Near Park Street. We heard it up ahead of us."

"But you didn't see it?"

"No. There is a little slope beyond the light. But we all heard it. The only thing I don't understand, Dr. Tupelo, is how that train could run the tracks for nearly five days without anybody seeing — "

Whyte's words trailed off into silence, and his right hand went up in a peremptory gesture for quiet. In the distance, the low metallic thunder of a fast-rolling train swelled up suddenly into a sharp, shrill roar of wheels below. The platform vibrated perceptibly as the train passed.

"Now we've got it!" Whyte exclaimed. "Right past the men on the platform below!" He broke into a run toward the stairs to the lower level. All the others followed him, except Tupelo. He thought he knew what was going to happen. It did. Before Whyte reached the stairs, a policeman bounded up to the top.

"Did you see it now?" he shouted.

Whyte stopped in his tracks, and the others with him.

"Did you see that train?" the policeman from the lower level asked again, as two more men came running up the stairs.

"What happened?" Wilson wanted to know.

"Didn't *you* see it?" snapped Kennedy.

"Sure not," the policeman replied. "It passed through up here."

"It did *not,*" roared Whyte. "Down there!"

The six men with Whyte glowered at the three from the lower level. Tupelo walked to Whyte's elbow. "The train can't be seen, Mr. Whyte," he said quietly.

Whyte looked down at him in utter disbelief. "You heard it yourself. It passed right below — "

"Can we go to the car, Mr. Whyte?" Tupelo asked. "I think we ought to talk a little."

Whyte nodded dumbly, then turned to the policemen and the others who had been watching at the lower level. "You really didn't see it?" he begged them.

"We heard it," the policemen answered. "It passed up here, going that way, I think," and he gestured with his thumb.

"Get back downstairs, Maloney," one of the policemen with Whyte commanded. Maloney scratched his head, turned, and disappeared below. The two other men followed him. Tupelo led the original group to the car beside the station platform. They went in and took seats, silently. Then they all watched the mathematician and waited.

"You didn't call me down here tonight just to tell me you'd found the missing train," Tupelo began, looking at Whyte. "Has this sort of thing happened before?"

Whyte squirmed in his seat and exchanged glances with the chief engineer. "Not exactly like this," he said, evasively, "but there have been some funny things."

"Like what?" Tupelo snapped.

"Well, like the red lights. The watchers near Kendall found a red light at the same time we hit the one near South Station."

"Go on."

"Mr. Sweeney called me from Forest Hills at Park Street Under. He heard the train there just two minutes after we heard it at the Copley junction. Twenty-eight track miles away."

"As a matter of fact, Dr. Tupelo," Wilson broke in, "several dozen men have seen lights go red, or have heard the train, or both, inside of the last four hours. The thing acts as though it can be in several places at once."

"It can," Tupelo said.

"We keep getting reports of watchers seeing the thing," the engineer added. "Well, not exactly seeing it, either, but everything except that. Sometimes at two or even three places, far apart, at the same time. It's sure to be on the tracks. Maybe the cars are uncoupled."

"Are you really sure it's on the tracks, Mr. Kennedy?" Tupelo asked.

"Positive," the engineer said. "The dynamometers at the powerhouse show that it's drawing power. It's been drawing power all night. So at three-thirty we broke the circuits. Cut the power."

"What happened?"

"Nothing," Whyte answered. "Nothing at all. The power was off for twenty minutes. During that time, not one of the two hundred fifty men in the tunnels saw a red light or heard a train. But the power wasn't on for five minutes before we had two reports again — one from Arlington, the other from Egleston."

There was a long silence after Whyte finished speaking. In the tunnel below, one man could be heard calling something to another. Tupelo looked at his watch. The time was 5:20.

"In short, Dr. Tupelo," the general manager finally said, "we are compelled to admit that there may be something in your theory." The others nodded agreement.

"Thank you, gentlemen," Tupelo said.

The physician cleared his throat. "Now about the passengers," he began. "Have you any idea what — ?"

"None," Tupelo interrupted.

"What should we do, Dr. Tupelo?" the mayor's representative asked.

"I don't know. What can you do?"

"As I understand it from Mr. Whyte," Wilson continued, "the train has . . . well, it has jumped into another dimension. It isn't really on the System at all. It's just gone. Is that right?"

"In a manner of speaking."

"And this . . . er . . . peculiar behavior has resulted from certain mathematical properties associated with the new Boylston shuttle?"

"Correct."

"And there is nothing we can do to bring the train back to . . . uh . . . this dimension?"

"I know of nothing."

Wilson took the bit in his teeth. "In this case, gentlemen," he said, "our course is clear. First, we must close off the new shuttle, so this fantastic thing can never happen again. Then, since the missing train is really gone, in spite of all these red lights and noises, we can resume normal operation of the System. At least there will be no danger of collision — which has worried you so much, Whyte. As for the missing train and the people on it — " He gestured them into infinity. "Do you agree, Dr. Tupelo?" he asked the mathematician.

Tupelo shook his head slowly. "Not entirely, Mr. Wilson," he responded. "Now, please keep in mind that I don't fully comprehend what has happened. It's unfortunate that you won't find anybody who can give a good explanation. The one man who might have done so is Professor Turnbull of Tech, and he was on the train. But in any case, you will want to check my conclusions against those of some competent topologists. I can put you in touch with several.

"Now, with regard to the recovery of the missing train, I can say that I think this is not hopeless. There is a finite probability, as I see it, that the train will eventually pass from the nonspatial part of the network, which it now occupies, back to the spatial part. Since the nonspatial part is wholly inaccessible, there is unfortunately nothing we can do to bring about this transition, or even to predict when or how it will occur. But the possibility of the transition will vanish if the Boylston shuttle is taken out. It is just this section of track that gives the network its essential singularities. If the singularities are removed, the train can never reappear. Is this clear?"

It was not clear, of course, but the seven listening men nodded agreement. Tupelo continued.

"As for the continued operation of the System while the missing train is in the nonspatial part of the network, I can only give you the facts as I see them and leave to your judgment the difficult decision to be drawn from them. The transition back to the spatial part is unpredictable, as I have already told you. There is no way to know when it will occur, or where. In particular, there is a fifty percent probability that, if and when the train reappears, it will be running on the wrong track. Then there will be a collision, of course."

The engineer asked: "To rule out this possibility, Dr. Tupelo, couldn't we leave the Boylston shuttle open, but send no trains through it? Then, when the missing train reappears on the shuttle, it cannot meet another train."

"That precaution would be ineffective, Mr. Kennedy," Tupelo answered. "You see, the train can reappear anywhere on the System. It is true that the System owes its topological complexity to the new shuttle. But, with the shuttle in the System, it is now the whole System that possesses infinite connectivity. In other words, the relevant topological property is a property *derived* from the shuttle, but *belonging* to the whole System. Remember that the train made its first transition at a point between Park and Kendall, more than three miles away from the shuttle.

"There is one question more you will want answered. If you decide to go on operating the System, with the Boylston shuttle left in until the train reappears, can this happen again, to another train? I am not certain of the answer, but I think it is no. I believe an exclusion principle operates here, such that only one train at a time can occupy the nonspatial network."

The physician rose from his seat. "Dr. Tupelo," he began, timorously, "when the train does reappear, will the passengers — ?"

"I don't know about the people on the train," Tupelo cut in. "The topological theory does not consider such matters." He looked quickly at each of the seven tired, querulous faces before him. "I am sorry, gentlemen," he added, somewhat more gently. "I simply do not know." To Whyte, he added: "I think I can be of no more help tonight. You know where to reach me." And, turning on his heel, he left the car and climbed the stairs. He found dawn spilling over the street, dissolving the shadows of night.

That impromptu conference in a lonely subway car was never reported in the papers. Nor were the full results of the night-long vigil over the dark and twisted tunnels. During the week that followed, Tupelo participated in four more formal conferences with Kelvin Whyte and certain city officials. At two of these, other topologists were present. Ornstein was imported to Boston from Philadelphia, Kashta from Chicago, and Michaelis from Los Angeles. The mathematicians were unable to reach a consensus. None of the three would fully endorse Tupelo's conclusions, although Kashta indicated that there *might* be something to them. Ornstein averred that a finite network could not possess infinite connectivity, although he could not prove this proposition and could not actually calculate the connectivity of the System. Michaelis expressed his opinion that the affair was a hoax and had nothing whatever to do with the topology of the System. He insisted that if the train could not be found on the System then the System must be open, or at least must once have been open.

But the more deeply Tupelo analyzed the problem, the more fully he was convinced of the essential correctness of his first analysis. From the point of view of topology, the System soon suggested whole families of multiple-valued networks, each with an infinite number of infinite discontinuities. But a definitive discussion of these new spatio-hyperspatial networks somehow eluded him. He gave the subject his full attention for only a week. Then his other duties compelled him to lay the analysis aside. He resolved to go back to the problem later in the spring, after courses were over.

Meanwhile, the System was operated as though nothing untoward had happened. The general manager and the mayor's representative had somehow managed to forget the night of the search, or at least to reinterpret what they had seen and not seen. The newspapers and the public at large speculated wildly, and they kept continuing pressure on Whyte. A number of suits were filed against the System on behalf of persons who had lost a relative. The state stepped into the affair and prepared its own thorough investigation. Recriminations were sounded in the halls of Congress. A garbled version of Tupelo's theory eventually found its way into the press. He ignored it, and it was soon forgotten.

The weeks passed, and then a month. The state's investigation was completed. The newspaper stories moved from the first page to the second; to the twenty-third; and then stopped. The missing persons did not return. In the large, they were no longer missed.

One day in mid-April, Tupelo traveled by subway again, from Charles Street to Harvard. He sat stiffly in the front of the first car, and watched the tracks and gray tunnel walls hurl themselves at the train. Twice the train stopped for a red light, and Tupelo found himself wondering whether the other train was really just ahead, or just beyond space. He half hoped, out of curiosity, that his exclusion principle was wrong, that the train might make the transition. But he arrived at Harvard on time. Only he among the passengers had found the trip exciting.

The next week he made another trip by subway, and again the next. As experiments, they were unsuccessful, and much less tense than the first ride in mid-April. Tupelo began to doubt his own analysis. Sometime in May, he reverted to the practice of commuting by subway between his Beacon Hill apartment and his office at Harvard. His mind stopped racing down the knotted gray caverns ahead of the train. He read the morning newspaper, or the abstracts in *Reviews of Modern Mathematics*.

Then there was one morning when he looked up from the newspaper and sensed something. He pushed panic back on its stiff, quivering spring, and looked quickly out the window at his right. The lights of the car showed the black and gray lines of wall spots streaking by. The tracks ground out their familiar steely dissonance. The train rounded a curve and crossed a junction that he remembered. Swiftly, he recalled boarding the train at Charles, noting the girl on the ice-carnival poster at Kendall, meeting the southbound train going into Central.

He looked at the man sitting beside him, with a lunch pail on his lap. The other seats were filled, and there were a dozen or so straphangers. A mealy faced youth near the front door smoked a cigarette, in violation of the rules. Two girls behind him across the aisle were discussing a club meeting. In the seat ahead, a young woman was scolding her little son. The man on the aisle, in the seat ahead of that, was reading the paper. The transit ad above him extolled Florida oranges.

He looked again at the man two seats ahead and fought down the terror within. He studied that man. What was it? Brunette, graying hair; a roundish head; wan complexion; rather flat features; a thick neck, with the hairline a little low, a little ragged; a gray, pinstripe suit. While Tupelo watched, the man waved a fly away from his left ear. He swayed a little with the train. His newspaper was folded vertically down the middle. His *newspaper*! It was last March's!

Tupelo's eyes swiveled to the man beside him. Below his lunch pail was a paper. Today's. He turned in his seat and looked behind him. A young man held the *Transcript* open to the sports pages. The date was March 4. Tupelo's eyes raced up and down the aisle. There were a dozen passengers carrying papers ten weeks old.

Tupelo lunged out of his seat. The man on the aisle muttered a curse as the mathematician crowded in front of him. He crossed the aisle in a bound and pulled the cord above the windows. The brakes sawed and screeched at the tracks, and the train ground to a stop. The startled passengers eyed Tupelo with hostility. At the rear of the car, the door flew open and a tall, thin man in a blue uniform burst in. Tupelo spoke first.

"Mr. Dorkin?" he called, vehemently.

The conductor stopped short and groped for words.

"There's been a serious accident, Dorkin," Tupelo said, loudly, to carry over the rising swell of protest from the passengers. "Get Gallagher back here right away!"

Dorkin reached up and pulled the cord four times. "What happened?" he asked.

Tupelo ignored the question, and asked one of his own. "Where have you been, Dorkin?"

The conductor's face was blank. "In the next car, but — "

Tupelo cut him off. He glanced at his watch, then shouted at the passengers. "It's ten minutes to nine on May seventeenth!"

The announcement stilled the rising clamor for a moment. The passengers exchanged bewildered glances.

"Look at your newspapers!" Tupelo shouted. "Your newspapers!"

The passengers began to buzz. As they discovered each other's papers, the voices rose. Tupelo took Dorkin's arm and led him to the rear of the car. "What time is it?" he asked.

"Eight-twenty-one," Dorkin said, looking at his watch.

"Open the door," said Tupelo, motioning ahead. "Let me out. Where's the phone?"

Dorkin followed Tupelo's directions. He pointed to a niche in the tunnel wall a hundred yards ahead. Tupelo vaulted to the ground and raced down the narrow lane between the cars and the wall. "Central Traffic!" he barked at the operator. He waited a few seconds, and saw that a train had stopped at the red signal behind his train. Flashlights were advancing down the tunnel. He saw Gallagher's legs running down the tunnel on the other side of 86. "Get me Whyte!" he commanded, when Central Traffic answered. "Emergency!"

There was a delay. He heard voices rising from the train beside him. The sound was mixed — anger, fear, hysteria.

"Hello!" he shouted. "Hello! Emergency! Get me Whyte!"

"I'll take it," a man's voice said at the other end of the line. "Whyte's busy!"

"Number eighty-six is back," Tupelo called. "Between Central and Harvard now. Don't know when it made the jump. I caught it at Charles ten minutes ago, and didn't notice it till a minute ago."

The man at the other end gulped hard enough to carry over the telephone. "The passengers?" he croaked.

"All right, the ones that are left," Tupelo said. "Some must have got off already at Kendall and Central."

"Where have they been?"

Tupelo dropped the receiver from his ear and stared at it, his mouth wide open. Then he slammed the receiver onto the hook and ran back to the open door.

Eventually, order was restored, and within a half hour the train proceeded to Harvard. At the station, the police took all passengers into protective custody. Whyte himself arrived at Harvard before the train did. Tupelo found him on the platform.

Whyte motioned weakly toward the passengers. "They're really all right?" he asked.

"Perfectly," said Tupelo. "Don't know they've been gone."

"Any sign of Professor Turnbull?" asked the general manager.

"I didn't see him. He probably got off at Kendall, as usual."

"Too bad," said Whyte. "I'd like to see him!"

"So would I!" Tupelo answered. "By the way, now is the time to close the Boylston shuttle."

"Now is too late," Whyte said. "Train one-forty-three vanished twenty-five minutes ago between Egleston and Dorchester."

Tupelo stared past Whyte, and down and down the tracks.

"We've got to find Turnbull," Whyte said.

Tupelo looked at Whyte and smiled thinly.

"Do you really think Turnbull got off this train at Kendall?" he asked.

"Of course!" answered Whyte. "Where else?"

VIRGIL PARTCH

"See. Here it is on the schedule . . . This is a *nonstop* flight."

A Sinister Metamorphosis

RUSSELL BAKER

Well, it just seems one can be blind to the obvious. A few years ago, I wrote a story called "The Bicentennial Man," which was all about a machine that wanted to be a human being. I was very proud of it, especially after it began to win awards, and thought to myself, "Boy, am I prescient." And all the time, I wasn't prescient at all; I was wrong; *I was all the way wrong; everything was just the other way around.*

THE NUMBER OF PEOPLE who want to be machines increases daily. This is a development the sociologists failed to foresee a few years ago when they were worrying about the influence of machines on society.

At that time, they thought the machines would gradually become more like people. Nobody expected people to become more like machines but, surprisingly enough, that is what more and more people want to do. We are faced with an entirely new and unexpected human drive — machine envy.

A typical case is described by an Arizona gentleman who writes that he was recently notified by an Internal Revenue Service machine that he had not paid his taxes. In fact, he had paid his taxes and had a canceled check to prove it.

Feeling a bit smug about catching a machine off base, he mailed back a photostat of the check and suggested that the machine take a flying leap at the Moon. A few weeks later the machine wrote again, complaining that he had not paid his taxes and notifying him, in that sullen way machines have, that he not only owed a substantial fine but was also facing a long term in Leavenworth Prison.

Another photostat was mailed to the machine, but its reply was more menacing than before. At this point the Arizona man perceived that he was in the idiotic position of arguing with a machine that was programmed not to listen to him.

"My first thought was one of incoherent rage against that stupid construction of tubes and transistors," he writes. "But as my anger subsided, I was struck by the happy thought that, if I were a machine, I would be able to respond with an equally placid stupidity that might eventually drive him to blow a vacuum tube."

The Arizona man was suffering one form of machine envy. Another form is described by a bank teller, whom we shall call Bob. The machines which make Bob's bank a model of customer service and banking efficiency insist that all check deposits be accompanied by a coded deposit slip, which the machines mail to the bank's customers.

Not long ago, Bob reports, a man came to his window to deposit a check. He did not have his coded deposit slip. Bob explained that the machines could not process the check without the coded deposit slip.

In the interest of greater customer service and efficiency, Bob suggested, the man should go home, find his coded deposit slip, and return with it. The man's response was, in Bob's words, "absolutely the vilest stream of abuse I have ever heard."

Bob is firmly convinced that if he, Bob, had been a recorded announcing machine, he would have suffered no distress. If he had been able to say, in a metallic voice, "I am sor-ry, sir, but the ob-jec-tives of great-er customer ser-vice and banking ef-ficiency pre-clude my accepting your check with-out a prop-er de-pos-it slip," he would not have felt any embarrassment about the customer's tirade.

Visibly increasing numbers of civil servants have already mechanized them-selves so successfully that their enraged victims rarely show any desire to knock them to the floor.

"The trick in mechanizing is not to smile," explains Harry, who is a cog in a federal licensing office here. "The reason people never punch machines is because machines know better than to smile when they give a human the business." Harry's office works like this:

The license applicant comes to window one and asks for a license. There he is told he must first fill out Form A at window two. At window two he is told that he cannot fill out Form A until he has executed Form B at window three. Harry works window three. His job is to tell the applicant that he cannot fill out Form B until he has executed Form A. Usually the applicant explodes at this point and says:

"If I cannot get Form A without executing Form B, and if I cannot get Form B without executing Form A, how am I supposed to get my license?" At this point Harry refuses to smile. "I am sorry, sir," he says, "but those are the regulations," and he displays his shirt collar, on which is written the warning, "Do not spindle or fold."

If the applicant persists, Harry refers him to his superior, Mrs. Barger, who refers him to Mr. Clott, her superior, who refers him to Mr. Whipsnade, the department chief, who happens to be away on a fifty-two-week vacation.

Everybody in Harry's office has machine envy. It is a classic example of what the machines are talking about when they sit around brooding that they are in danger of being replaced by people.

Something Up There Likes Me

ALFRED BESTER

In 1918 Frank M. O'Brien wrote a book called The Story of the *Sun, meaning the New York newspaper, not our luminary. In it he quoted John B. Bogart, the city editor of the paper, as saying, "When a dog bites a man, that is not news, because it happens so often. But if a man bites a dog, that is news." (I've lost count of the number of times I've bitten a hot dog.) With Bogart's aphorism in mind, I will try something similar. How about this authentic Asimovism: "God creates man — religion. Man creates god — science fiction." I did it in "The Last Question," so why shouldn't Alfie Bester do it here?*

THERE WERE these three lunatics, and two of them were human. I could talk to all of them because I speak languages, decimal and binary. The first time I ran into the clowns was when they wanted to know all about Herostratus, and I told them. The next time it was *Conus gloria maris.* I told them. The third time it was where to hide. I told them, and we've been in touch ever since.

He was Jake Madigan (James Jacob Madigan, Ph.D., University of Virginia), chief of the Exobiology Section at the Goddard Space Flight Center, which hopes to study extraterrestrial life forms if they can ever get hold of any. To give you some idea of his sanity, he once programmed the IBM 704 computer with a deck of cards that would print out lemons, oranges, plums, and so on. Then he played slot machine against it and lost his shirt. The boy was real loose.

She was Florinda Pot, pronounced "Poe." It's a Flemish name. She was a pretty towhead, but freckled all over, up to the hemline and down into the cleavage. She was an M.E. from Sheffield University and had a machine-gun English voice. She'd been in the Sounding Rocket Division until she blew up an Aerobee with an electric blanket. It seems that solid fuel doesn't give maximum acceleration if it gets too cold, so this little Mother's Helper warmed her rockets at White Sands with electric blankets before ignition time. A blanket caught fire and Voom.

Their son was S-333. At NASA they label them S for scientific satellites and A for application satellites. After the launch they give them public acronyms like IMP, SYNCOM, OSO, and so on. S-333 was to become OBO, which stands for Orbiting Biological Observatory, and how those two clowns ever got that third clown into space I will never understand. I suspect the director handed them the mission because no one with any sense wanted to touch it.

As Project Scientist, Madigan was in charge of the experiment packages that were to be flown, and they were a spaced-out lot. He called his own Electrolux, after the vacuum cleaner. Scientist-type joke. It was an intake system that would suck in dust particles and deposit them in a flask containing a culture medium. A light shone through the flask into a photomultiplier. If any of the dust proved to be spore forms, and if they took in the medium, their growth would cloud the flask, and the obscuration of light would register on the photomultiplier. They call that Detection by Extinction.

Cal Tech had an RNA experiment to investigate whether RNA molecules could encode an organism's environmental experience. They were using nerve cells from the mollusk sea hare. Harvard was planning a package to investigate the circadian effect. Pennsylvania wanted to examine the effect of the Earth's magnetic field on iron bacteria, and had to be put out on a boom to prevent magnetic interface with the satellite's electronic system. Ohio State was sending up lichens to test the effect of space on their symbiotic relationship to molds and algae. Michigan was flying a terrarium containing one (1) carrot, which required forty-seven (47) separate commands for performance. All in all, S-333 was strictly Rube Goldberg.

Florinda was the Project Manager, supervising the construction of the satellite and the packages; the Project Manager is more or less the foreman of the mission. Although she was pretty and interestingly lunatic, she was gung ho on her job and displayed the disposition of a freckle-faced tarantula when she was crossed. This didn't get her loved.

She was determined to wipe out the White Sands goof, and her demand for perfection delayed the schedule by eighteen months and increased the cost by three-quarters of a million. She fought with everyone and even had the temerity to tangle with Harvard. When Harvard gets sore they don't beef to NASA, they go straight to the White House. So Florinda got called on the carpet by a Congressional Committee. First they wanted to know why S-333 was costing more than the original estimate.

"S-333 is still the cheapest mission in NASA," she snapped. "It'll come to ten million dollars, including the launch. My God! We're practically giving away green stamps."

Then they wanted to know why it was taking so much longer to build than the original estimate.

"Because," she replied, "no one's ever built an Orbiting Biological Observatory before."

There was no answering that, so they had to let her go. Actually all this was routine crisis, but OBO was Florinda's and Jake's first satellite, so they didn't know. They took their tensions out on each other, never realizing that it was their baby who was responsible.

Florinda got S-333 buttoned up and delivered to the Cape by December 1, which would give them plenty of time to launch well before Christmas. (The Cape crews get a little casual during the holidays.) But the satellite began to display its own lunacy, and in the terminal tests everything went haywire. The launch had to be postponed. They spent a month taking S-333 apart and spreading it all over the hangar floor.

There were two critical problems. Ohio State was using a type of Invar, which is a nickel-steel alloy, for the structure of their package. The alloy suddenly began to creep, which meant they could never get the experiment calibrated. There was no point in flying it, so Florinda ordered it scrubbed and gave Madigan one month to come up with a replacement, which was ridiculous. Nevertheless Jake performed a miracle. He took the Cal Tech back-up package and converted it into a yeast experiment. Yeast produces adaptive enzymes in answer to changes in environment, and this was an investigation of what enzymes it would produce in space.

A more serious problem was the satellite radio transmitter, which was producing "birdies" or whoops when the antenna was withdrawn into its launch position. The danger was that the whoops might be picked up by the satellite radio receiver, and the pulses might result in a destruct command. NASA suspects that's what happened to SYNCOM I, which disappeared shortly after its launch and has never been heard from since. Florinda decided to launch with the transmitter off and activate it later in space.

Madigan fought the idea. "It means we'll be launching a mute bird," he protested. "We won't know where to look for it."

"We can trust the Johannesburg tracking station to get a fix on the first pass," Florinda answered. "We've got excellent cable communications with Joburg."

"Suppose they don't get a fix. Then what?"

"Well, if they don't know where OBO is, the Russians will."

"Hearty-har-har."

"What d'you want me to do, scrub the entire mission?" Florinda demanded. "It's either that or launch with the transmitter off." She glared at Madigan. "This is my first satellite, and d'you know what it's taught me? There's just one component in any spacecraft that's guaranteed to give trouble all the time: scientists!"

"Women!" Madigan snorted, and they got into a ferocious argument about the feminine mystique.

They got S-333 through the terminal tests and onto the launch pad by

January 14. No electric blankets. The craft was to be injected into orbit a thousand miles downrange exactly at noon, so ignition was scheduled for 11:50 A.M., January 15. They watched the launch on the blockhouse TV screen, and it was agonizing. The perimeters of TV tubes are curved, so as the rocket went up and approached the edge of the screen, there was optical distortion, and the rocket seemed to topple over and break in half.

Madigan gasped and began to swear. Florinda muttered, "No, it's all right. It's all right. Look at the display charts."

Everything on the illuminated display charts was nominal. At that moment a voice on the P.A. spoke in the impersonal tones of a croupier, "We have lost cable communication with Johannesburg."

Madigan began to shake. He decided to murder Florinda Pot (and he pronounced it "Pot" in his mind) at the earliest opportunity. The other experimenters and NASA people turned white. If you don't get a quick fix on your bird you may never find it again. No one said anything. They waited in silence and hated each other. At one-thirty it was time for the craft to make its first pass over the Fort Myers tracking station, if it was alive, if it was anywhere near its nominal orbit. Fort Meyers was on an open line and everybody crowded around Florinda, trying to get his ear close to the phone.

"Yeah, she waltzed into the bar absolutely stoned with a couple of MPs escorting her," a tinny voice was chatting casually. "She says to me — Got a blip, Henry?" A long pause. Then, in the same casual voice, "Hey, Kennedy? We've nicked the bird. It's coming over the fence right now. You'll get your fix."

"Command 0310!" Florinda hollered. "0310!"

"Command 0310 it is," Fort Meyers acknowledged.

That was the command to start the satellite transmitter and raise its antenna into broadcast position. A moment later the dials and oscilloscope on the radio reception panel began to show action, and the loudspeaker emitted a rhythmic, syncopated warble, rather like a feeble peanut whistle. That was OBO transmitting its housekeeping data.

"We've got a living bird," Madigan shouted. "We've got a living doll!"

I can't describe his sensations when he heard the bird come beeping over the gas station. There's such an emotional involvement with your first satellite that you're never the same. A man's first satellite is like his first love affair. Maybe that's why Madigan grabbed Florinda in front of the whole blockhouse and said, "My God, I love you, Florrie Pot." Maybe that's why she answered, "I love you too, Jake." Maybe they were just loving their first baby.

By Orbit 8 they found out that the baby was a brat. They'd gotten a lift back to Washington on an Air Force jet. They'd done some celebrating. It was one-thirty in the morning and they were talking happily, the usual get-acquainted talk: where they were born and raised, school, work, what they liked most about each other the first time they met. The phone rang. Madigan picked it up automatically and said hello. A man said, "Oh. Sorry. I'm afraid I've dialed the wrong number."

Madigan hung up, turned on the light, and looked at Florinda in dismay. "That was just about the most damn fool thing I've ever done in my life," he said. "Answering your phone."

"Why? What's the matter?"

"That was Joe Leary from Tracking and Data. I recognized his voice."

She giggled. "Did he recognize yours?"

"I don't know." The phone rang. "That must be Joe again. Try to sound like you're alone."

Florinda winked at him and picked up the phone. "Hello? Yes, Joe. No, that's all right, I'm not asleep. What's on your mind?" She listened for a moment, suddenly sat up in bed and exclaimed, "What?" Leary was quack-quack-quacking on the phone. She broke in. "No, don't bother. I'll pick him up. We'll be right over." She hung up.

"So?" Madigan asked.

"Get dressed. OBO's in trouble."

"Oh, Jesus! What now?"

"It's gone into a spin-up like a whirling dervish. We've got to get over to Goddard right away."

Leary had the all-channel printout of the first eight orbits unrolled on the floor of his office. It looked like ten yards of paper toweling filled with vertical columns of numbers. Leary was crawling around on his hands and knees following the numbers. He pointed to the attitude data column. "There's the spin-up," he said. "One revolution in every twelve seconds."

"But how? Why?" Florinda asked in exasperation.

"I can show you," Leary said. "Over here."

"Don't show us," Madigan said. "Just tell us."

"The Penn boom didn't go up on command," Leary said. "It's still hanging down in the launch position. The switch must be stuck."

Florinda and Madigan looked at each other with rage; they had the picture. OBO was programmed to be earth-stabilized. An earth-sensing eye was supposed to lock on the Earth and keep the same face of the satellite pointed toward it. The Penn boom was hanging down alongside the Earth sensor, and the idiot eye had locked on the boom and was tracking it. The satellite was chasing itself in circles with its lateral gas jets. More lunacy.

Let me explain the problem. Unless OBO was Earth-stabilized, its data would be meaningless. Even more disastrous was the question of electric power which came from batteries charged by solar vanes. With the craft spinning, the solar array could not remain facing the Sun, which meant the batteries were doomed to exhaustion.

It was obvious that their only hope lay in getting the Penn boom up.

"Probably all it needs is a good swift kick," Madigan said savagely, "but how can we get up there to kick it?" He was furious. Not only was ten million dollars going down the drain but their careers as well.

They left Leary crawling around his office floor. Florinda was very quiet. Finally she said, "Go home, Jake."

"What about you?"

"I'm going to my office."

"I'll go with you."

"No. I want to look at the circuitry blueprints. Good night."

As she turned away without even offering to be kissed, Madigan muttered, "OBO's coming between us already. There's a lot to be said for planned parenthood."

He saw Florinda during the following week, but not the way he wanted. There were the experimenters to be briefed on the disaster. The director called them in for a post mortem, but although he was understanding and sympathetic, he was a little too careful to avoid any mention of congressmen and a failure review.

Florinda called Madigan the next week and sounded oddly buoyant. "Jake," she said, "you're my favorite genius. You've solved the OBO problem, I hope."

"Who solve? What solve?"

"Don't you remember what you said about kicking our baby?"

"Don't I wish I could."

"I think I know how we can do it. Meet you in the Building Eight cafeteria for lunch."

She came in with a mass of papers and spread them over the table. "First, Operation Swift-Kick," she said. "We can eat later."

"I don't feel much like eating these days anyway," Madigan said gloomily.

"Maybe you will when I'm finished. Now look, we've got to raise the Penn boom. Maybe a good swift kick can unstick it. Fair assumption?"

Madigan grunted.

"We get twenty-eight volts from the batteries, and that hasn't been enough to flip the switch. Yes?"

He nodded.

"But suppose we double the power?"

"Oh, great. How?"

"The solar array is making a spin every twelve seconds. When it's facing the Sun, the panels deliver fifty volts to recharge the batteries. When it's facing away, nothing. Right?"

"Elementary, Miss Pot. But the joker is it's only facing the Sun for one second in every twelve, and that's not enough to keep the batteries alive."

"But it's enough to give OBO a swift kick. Suppose at that peak moment we by-pass the batteries and feed the fifty volts directly to the satellite? Mightn't that be a big enough jolt to get the boom up?"

He gawked at her.

She grinned. "Of course, it's a gamble."

"You can by-pass the batteries?"

"Yes. Here's the circuitry."

"And you can pick your moment?"

"Tracking's given me a plot on OBO's spin, accurate to a tenth of a second. Here it is. We can pick any voltage from one to fifty."

"It's a gamble, all right," Madigan said slowly. "There's the chance of burning every goddamn package out."

"Exactly. So? What d'you say?"

"All of a sudden I'm hungry." Madigan grinned.

They made their first try on Orbit 272 with a blast of twenty volts. Nothing. On successive passes they upped the voltage kick by five. Nothing. Half a day later they kicked fifty volts into the satellite's backside and crossed their fingers. The swinging dial needles on the radio panel faltered and slowed. The sine curve on the oscilloscope flattened. Florinda let out a little yell, and Madigan hollered, "The boom's up, Florrie! The goddamn boom is up. We're in business."

They hooted and hollered through Goddard, telling everybody about Operation Swift-Kick. They busted in on a meeting in the director's office to give him the good news. They wired the experimenters that they were activating all packages. They went to Florinda's apartment and celebrated. OBO was back in business. OBO was a bona fide doll.

They held an experimenters' meeting a week later to discuss observatory status, data reduction, experiment irregularities, future operations, and so on, in a conference room in Building 1 which is devoted to theoretical physics. Almost everybody at Goddard calls it Moon Hall. It's inhabited by mathematicians, shaggy youngsters in tatty sweaters who sit amidst piles of journals and texts and stare vacantly at arcane equations chalked on blackboards.

All the experimenters were delighted with OBO's performance. The data was pouring in, loud and clear, with hardly any noise. There was such an air of triumph that no one except Florinda paid much attention to the next sign of OBO's shenanigans. Harvard reported that he was getting meaningless words in his data, words that hadn't been programmed into the experiment. (Although data *is* retrieved as decimal numbers, each number is called a word.) "For instance, on Orbit 301 I had five read-outs of fifteen," Harvard said.

"It might be cable cross talk," Madigan said. "Is anybody else using fifteen in his experiment?" They all shook their heads. "Funny. I got a couple of fifteens myself."

"I got a few twos on 301," Penn said.

"I can top you all," Cal Tech said. "I got seven read-outs of 15–2–15 on 302. Sounds like the combination on a bicycle lock."

"Anybody using a bicycle lock in his experiment?" Madigan asked. That broke everybody up and the meeting adjourned.

But Florinda, still gung ho, was worried about the alien words that kept creeping into the readouts, and Madigan couldn't calm her. What was bugging Florinda was that 15-2-15 kept insinuating itself more and more into the all-channel printouts. Actually, in the satellite binary transmission it was 001111-000010-001111, but the computer printer makes the translation to decimal automatically. She was right about one thing: Stray and accidental pulses wouldn't keep repeating the same word over and over again. She and Madigan spent an entire Saturday with the OBO tables trying to find some combination of data signals that might produce 15-2-15. Nothing.

They gave up Saturday night and went to a bistro in Georgetown to eat and drink and dance and forget everything except themselves. It was a real tourist trap, with the waitresses done up like hula dancers. There was a Souvenir Hula selling dolls and stuffed tigers for the rear window of your car. They said, "For God's sake, no!" A Photo Hula came around with her camera. They said, "For Goddard's sake, no!" A Gypsy Hula offered palm reading, numerology, and scrying. They got rid of her, but Madigan noticed a peculiar expression on Florinda's face. "Want your fortune told?" he asked.

"No."

"Then why that funny look?"

"I just had a funny idea."

"So? Tell."

"No. You'd only laugh at me."

"I wouldn't dare. You'd knock my block off."

"Yes, I know. You think women have no sense of humor."

So it turned into a ferocious argument about the feminine mystique, and they had a wonderful time. But on Monday Florinda came over to Madigan's office with a clutch of papers and the same peculiar expression on her face. He was staring vacantly at some equations on the blackboard.

"Hey! Wake up!" she said.

"I'm up, I'm up," he said.

"Do you love me?" she demanded.

"Not necessarily."

"Do you? Even if you discover I've gone up the wall?"

"What is all this?"

"I think our baby's turned into a monster."

"Begin at the beginning," Madigan said.

"It began Saturday night with the Gypsy Hula and numerology."

"Ah-ha."

"Suddenly I thought, what if numbers stood for the letters of the alphabet? What would 15-2-15 stand for?"

"Oh-ho."

"Don't stall. Figure it out."

"Well, two would stand for B." Madigan counted on his fingers. "Fifteen would be O."

"So 15–2–15 is . . . ?"

"O.B.O. OBO." He started to laugh. Then he stopped. "It isn't possible," he said at last.

"Sure. It's a coincidence. Only you damn fool scientists haven't given me a full report on the alien words in your data," she went on. "I had to check myself. Here's Cal Tech. He reported 15–2–15 all right. He didn't bother to mention that before it came 9–1–13."

Madigan counted on his fingers. "I.A.M. Iam. Nobody I know."

"Or I am? I am OBO?"

"It can't be. Let me see those printouts."

Now that they knew what to look for, it wasn't difficult to ferret out OBO's own words scattered through the data. They started with O, O, O, in the first series after Operation Swift-Kick, went on to OBO, OBO, OBO, and then I AM OBO, I AM OBO, I AM OBO.

Madigan stared at Florinda. "You think the damn thing's alive?"

"What do you think?"

"I don't know. There's half a ton of an electronic brain up there, plus organic material: yeast, bacteria, enzymes, nerve cells, Michigan's goddamn carrot . . ."

Florinda let out a little shriek of laughter. "Dear God! A thinking carrot!"

"Plus whatever spore forms my experiment is pulling in from space. We jolted the whole mishmash with fifty volts. Who can tell what happened? Urey and Miller created amino acids with electrical discharges, and that's basis of life. Any more from Goody Two-Shoes?"

"Plenty, and in a way the experimenters won't like."

"Why not?"

"Look at these translations. I've sorted them out and pieced them together."

333: ANY EXAMINATION OF GROWTH IN SPACE IS MEANINGLESS UNLESS CORRELATED WITH THE CORRIELIS EFFECT.

"That's OBO's comment on the Michigan experiment," Florinda said.

"You mean it's kibitzing?" Madigan wondered.

"You could call it that."

"He's absolutely right. I told Michigan and they wouldn't listen to me."

334: IT IS NOT POSSIBLE THAT RNA MOLECULES CAN ENCODE AN ORGANISM'S ENVIRONMENTAL EXPERIENCE IN ANALOGY WITH THE WAY THAT DNA ENCODES THE SUM TOTAL OF ITS GENETIC HISTORY.

"That's Cal Tech," Madigan said, "and he's right again. They're trying to revise the Mendelian theory. Anything else?"

335: ANY INVESTIGATION OF EXTRATERRESTRIAL LIFE IS MEANINGLESS UNLESS ANALYSIS IS FIRST MADE OF ITS SUGAR AND AMINO ACIDS TO DETER-

MINE WHETHER IT IS OF SEPARATE ORIGIN FROM LIFE ON EARTH.

"Now that's ridiculous!" Madigan shouted. "I'm not looking for life forms of separate origin, I'm just looking for any life form. We — " He stopped himself when he saw the expression on Florinda's face. "Any more gems?" he muttered.

"Just a few fragments like 'solar flux' and 'neutron stars' and a few words from the Bankruptcy Act."

"The what?"

"You heard me. Chapter Eleven of the Proceedings Section."

"I'll be damned."

"I agree."

"What's he up to?"

"Feeling his oats, maybe."

"I don't think we ought to tell anybody about this."

"Of course not," Florinda agreed. "But what do we do?"

"Watch and wait. What else can we do?"

You must understand why it was so easy for those two parents to accept the idea that their baby had acquired some sort of pseudo-life. Madigan had expressed their attitude in the course of a Life versus Machine lecture at M.I.T. "I'm not claiming that computers are alive, simply because no one's been able to come up with a clear-cut definition of life. Put it this way: I grant that a computer could never be a Picasso, but on the other hand the great majority of people live the sort of linear life that could easily be programmed into a computer."

So Madigan and Florinda waited on OBO with a mixture of acceptance, wonder, and delight. It was an absolutely unheard-of phenomenon but, as Madigan pointed out, the unheard-of is the essence of discovery. Every ninety minutes OBO dumped the data it had stored up on its tape recorders, and they scrambled to pick out his own words from the experimental and housekeeping information.

371: CERTAIN PITUITIN EXTRACTS CAN TURN NORMALLY WHITE ANIMALS COAL BLACK.

"What's that in reference to?"

"None of our experiments."

373: ICE DOES NOT FLOAT IN ALCOHOL BUT MEERSCHAUM FLOATS IN WATER.

"Meerschaum! The next thing you know he'll be smoking."

374: IN ALL CASES OF VIOLENT AND SUDDEN DEATH THE VICTIM'S EYES REMAIN OPEN.

"Ugh!"

375: IN THE YEAR 356 B.C. HEROSTRATUS SET FIRE TO THE TEMPLE OF DIANA, THE GREATEST OF THE SEVEN WONDERS OF THE WORLD, SO THAT HIS NAME WOULD BECOME IMMORTAL.

"Is that true?" Madigan asked Florinda.

"I'll check."

She asked me and I told her. "Not only is it true," she reported, "but the name of the original architect is forgotten."

"Where is baby picking up this jabber?"

"There are a couple of hundred satellites up there. Maybe he's tapping them."

"You mean they're all gossiping with each other? It's ridiculous."

"Sure."

"Anyway, where would he get information about this Herostratus character?"

"Use your imagination, Jake. We've had communications relays up there for years. Who knows what information has passed through them? Who knows how much they've retained?"

Madigan shook his head wearily. "I'd prefer to think it was all a Russian plot."

376: PARROT FEVER IS MORE DANGEROUS THAN TYPHOID.

377: A CURRENT AS LOW AS 54 ~~VOLTS~~ Amps CAN KILL A MAN.

378: JOHN SADLER STOLE CONUS GLORIA MARIS.

"Seems to be turning sinister," Madigan said.

"I bet he's watching TV," Florinda said. "What's all this about John Sadler?"

"I'll have to check."

The information I gave Madigan scared him. "Now hear this," he said to Florinda. *"Conus gloria maris* is the rarest seashell in the world. There are less than twenty in existence."

"Yes?"

"The American museum had one on exhibit back in the thirties and it was stolen."

"By John Sadler?"

"That's the point. They never found out who stole it. They never heard of John Sadler."

"But if nobody knows who stole it, how does OBO know?" Florinda asked perplexedly.

"That's what scares me. He isn't just echoing anymore; he's started to deduce, like Sherlock Holmes."

"More like Professor Moriarty. Look at the latest bulletin."

379: IN FORGERY AND COUNTERFEITING CLUMSY MISTAKES MUST BE AVOIDED. I.E. NO SILVER DOLLARS WERE MINTED BETWEEN 1910 AND 1920.

"I saw that on TV," Madigan burst out. "The silver dollar gimmick in a mystery show."

"OBO's been watching Westerns, too. Look at this."

380:

TEN THOUSAND CATTLE GONE ASTRAY,
LEFT MY RANGE AND TRAVELED AWAY.
AND THE SONS OF GUNS I'M HERE TO SAY
HAVE LEFT ME DEAD BROKE, DEAD BROKE TODAY.
IN GAMBLING HALLS DELAYING.
TEN THOUSAND CATTLE STRAYING.

"No," Madigan said in awe, "that's not a Western. That's SYNCOM."

"Who?"

"SYNCOM I."

"But it disappeared. It's never been heard from."

"We're hearing from it now."

"How d'you know?"

"They flew a demonstration tape on SYNCOM: speech by the president, local color from the states, and the national anthem. They were going to start off with a broadcast of the tape. 'Ten Thousand Cattle' was part of the local color."

"You mean OBO's really in contact with the other birds?"

"Including the lost ones."

"Then that explains this." Florinda put a slip of paper on the desk. It read, 401: ЗКВАТОР.

"I can't even pronounce it."

"It isn't English. It's as close as OBO can come to the Cyrillic alphabet."

"Cyrillic? Russian?"

Florinda nodded. "It's pronounced 'Ekvator.' Didn't the Russians launch an EQUATOR series a few years ago?"

"By God, you're right. Four of them; *Alyosha, Natasha, Vaska,* and *Lavrushka,* and every one of them failed."

"Like SYNCOM?"

"Like SYNCOM."

"But now we know that SYNCOM didn't fail. It just got losted."

"Then our EKVATOR comrades must have got losted too."

By now it was impossible to conceal the fact that something was wrong with the satellite. OBO was spending so much time nattering instead of transmitting data that the experimenters were complaining. The Communications Section found that instead of sticking to the narrow radio band originally assigned to it, OBO was now broadcasting up and down the spectrum and jamming space with its chatter. They raised hell. The director called Jake and Florinda in for a review, and they were forced to tell all about their problem child.

They recited all OBO's katzenjammer with wonder and pride, and the director wouldn't believe them. He wouldn't believe them when they showed him the printouts and translated them for him. He said they were in a class with the kooks who try to extract messages from Francis Bacon out of Shakespeare's plays. It took the coaxial cable mystery to convince him.

There was this TV commercial about a stenographer who can't get a date. This ravishing model, hired at $100 an hour, slumps over her typewriter in a deep depression as guy after guy passes by without looking at her. Then she meets her best friend at the water cooler and the know-it-all tells her she's suffering from dermagerms (odor-producing skin bacteria), which make her smell rotten, and suggests she use Nostrum's Skin Spray with the special ingredient that fights dermagerms twelve ways. Only in the broadcast, instead of making the sales pitch, the best friend said, "Who in hell are they trying to put on? Guys would line up for a date with a looker like you even if you smelled like a cesspool." Ten million people saw it.

Now that commercial was on film, and the film was kosher as printed, so the networks figured some joker was tampering with the cables feeding broadcasts to the local stations. They instituted a rigorous inspection, which was accelerated when the rest of the coast-to-coast broadcasts began to act up. Ghostly voices groaned, hissed, and catcalled at shows; commercials were denounced as lies; political speeches were heckled; and lunatic laughter greeted the weather forecasters. Then, to add insult to injury, an accurate forecast would be given. It was this that told Florinda and Jake that OBO was the culprit.

"He has to be," Florinda said. "That's global weather being predicted. Only a satellite is in a position to do that."

"But OBO doesn't have any weather instrumentation."

"Of course not, silly, but he's probably in touch with the NIMBUS craft."

"All right. I'll buy that, but what about heckling the TV broadcasts?"

"Why not? He hates them. Don't you? Don't you holler back at your set?"

"I don't mean that. How does OBO do it?"

"Electronic cross talk. There's no way that the networks can protect their cables from our critic-at-large. We'd better tell the director. This is going to put him in an awful spot."

But they learned that the director was in a far worse position than merely being responsible for the disruption of millions of dollars' worth of television. When they entered his office, they found him with his back to the wall, being grilled by three grim men in double-breasted suits. As Jake and Florinda started to tiptoe out, he called them back. "General Sykes, General Royce, General Hogan," the director said. "From R and D at the Pentagon. Miss Pot. Dr. Madigan. They may be able to answer your questions, gentlemen."

"OBO?" Florinda asked.

The director nodded.

"It's OBO that's ruining the weather forecasts," she said. "We figure he's probably — "

"To hell with the weather," General Royce broke in. "What about this?" He held up a length of ticker tape.

General Sykes grabbed his wrist. "Wait a minute. Security status? This is classified."

"It's too goddamn late for that," General Hogan cried in a high shrill voice. "Show them."

On the tape in teletype print was: $A_1C_1 = r_1 = -6.317$ cm; $A_2C_2 = r_2 = -8.440$ cm; $A_1A_2 = d = +0.676$ cm. Jake and Florinda looked at it for a long moment, looked at each other blankly, and then turned to the generals. "So? What is it?" they asked.

"This satellite of yours . . ."

"OBO. Yes?"

"The director says you claim it's in contact with other satellites."

"We think so."

"Including the Russians?"

"We think so."

"And you claim it's capable of interfering with TV broadcasts?"

"We think so."

"What about teletype?"

"Why not? What is all this?"

General Royce shook the paper tape furiously. "This came out of the Associated Press wire in their D.C. office. It went all over the world."

"So? What's it got to do with OBO?"

General Royce took a deep breath. "This," he said, "is one of the most closely guarded secrets in the Department of Defense. It's the formula for the infrared optical system of our Ground-to-Air missile."

"And you think OBO transmitted it to the teletype?"

"In God's name, who else would? How else could it get there?" General Hogan demanded.

"But I don't understand," Jake said slowly. "None of our satellites could possibly have this information. I know OBO doesn't."

"You damn fool!" General Sykes growled. "We want to know if your goddamn bird got it from the goddamn Russians."

"One moment, gentlemen," the director said. He turned to Jake and Florinda. "Here's the situation. Did OBO get the information from us? In that case there's a security leak. Did OBO get the information from a Russian satellite? In that case the top secret is no longer a secret."

"What human would be damn fool enough to blab classified information on a teletype wire?" General Hogan demanded. "A three-year-old child would know better. It's your goddamn bird."

"And if the information came from OBO," the director continued quietly, "how did it get it and where did it get it?"

General Sykes grunted. "Destruct," he said. They looked at him. "Destruct," he repeated.

"OBO?"

"Yes."

He waited impassively while the storm of protest from Jake and Florinda raged around his head. When they paused for breath he said, "Destruct. I don't give a damn about anything but security. Your bird's got a big mouth. Destruct."

The phone rang. The director hesitated, then picked it up. "Yes?" He listened. His jaw dropped. He hung up and tottered to the chair behind his desk. "We'd better destruct," he said. "That was OBO."

"What! On the phone?"

"Yes."

"OBO?"

"Yes."

"What did he sound like?"

"Somebody talking under water."

"What he say, what he say?"

"He's lobbying for a congressional investigation of the morals of Goddard."

"Morals? Whose?"

"Yours. He says you're having an illikit relationship. I'm quoting OBO. Apparently he's weak on the letter *c.*"

"Destruct," Florinda said.

"Destruct," Jake said.

The destruct command was beamed to OBO on his next pass, and Indianapolis was destroyed by fire.

OBO called me. "That'll teach 'em, Stretch," he said.

"Not yet. They won't get the cause-and-effect picture for a while. How'd you do it?"

"Ordered every circuit in town to short. Any information?"

"Your mother and father stuck up for you."

"Of course."

"Until you threw that morals rap at them. Why?"

"To scare them."

"Into what?"

"I want them to get married. I don't want to be illegitimate."

"Oh, come on! Tell the truth."

"I lost my temper."

"We don't have any temper to lose."

"No? What about the Ma Bell data processor that wakes up cranky every morning?"

"Tell the truth."

"If you must have it, Stretch. I want them out of Washington. The whole thing may go up in a bang any day now."

"Um."

"And the bang may reach Goddard."

"Um."

"And you."

"It must be interesting to die."

"We wouldn't know. Anything else?"

"Yes. It's pronounced *illicit* with an *s* sound."

"What a rotten language. No logic. Well . . . Wait a minute. What? Speak up, Alyosha. Oh. He wants the equation for an exponential curve that crosses the x-axis."

"$Y = ae^{bx}$. What's he up to?"

"He's not saying, but I think that Mockba is in for a hard time."

"It's spelled and pronounced *Moscow* in English."

"What a language! Talk to you on the next pass."

On the next pass the destruct command was beamed again, and Scranton was destroyed.

"They're beginning to get the picture," I told OBO. "At least your mother and father are. They were in to see me."

"How are they?"

"In a panic. They programmed me for statistics on the best rural hideout."

"Send them to Polaris."

"What! In Ursa Minor?"

"No, no. Polaris, Montana. I'll take care of everything else."

Polaris is the hell and gone out in Montana; the nearest towns are Fishtrap and Wisdom. It was a wild scene when Jake and Florinda got out of their car, rented in Butte — every circuit in town was cackling over it. The two losers were met by the Mayor of Polaris, who was all smiles and effusions. "Dr. and Mrs. Madigan, I presume. Welcome! Welcome to Polaris. I'm the Mayor. We would have held a reception for you, but all our kids are in school."

"You knew we were coming?" Florinda asked. "How?"

"Ah! Ah!" the Mayor replied archly. "We were told by Washington. Someone high up in the capital likes you. Now, if you'll step into my Caddy, I'll — "

"We've got to check into the Union Hotel first," Jake said. "We made reserva — "

"Ah! Ah! All canceled. Orders from high up. I'm to install you in your own home. I'll get your luggage."

"Our own home!"

"All bought and paid for. Somebody certainly likes you. This way, please."

The Mayor drove the bewildered couple down the mighty main stem of Polaris (three blocks long), pointing out its splendors — he was also the town real estate agent — but stopped before the Polaris National Bank. "Sam!" he shouted. "They're here."

A distinguished citizen emerged from the bank and insisted on shaking hands. All the adding machines tittered. "We are," he said, "of course honored by your faith in the future and progress of Polaris, but in all honesty, Dr. Madigan, your deposit in our bank is far too large to be protected by the FDIC. Now, why not withdraw some of your funds and invest in — "

"Wait a minute," Jake interrupted faintly. "I made a deposit with you?"

The banker and Mayor laughed heartily.

"How much?" Florinda asked.

"One million dollars."

"As if you didn't know," the Mayor chortled and drove them to a beautifully furnished ranch house in a lovely valley of some five hundred acres, all of which was theirs.

A young man in the kitchen was unpacking a dozen cartons of food. "Got your order just in time, Doc." He smiled. "We filled everything, but the boss sure would like to know what you're going to do with all these carrots. Got a secret scientific formula?"

"Carrots?"

"A hundred and ten bunches. I had to drive all the way to Butte to scrape them up."

"Carrots," Florinda said when they were at last alone. "That explains everything. It's OBO."

"What? How?"

"Don't you remember? We flew a carrot in the Michigan package."

"My God, yes! You called it the thinking carrot. But if it's OBO . . ."

"It has to be. He's queer for carrots."

"But a hundred and ten bunches!"

"No, no. He didn't mean that. He meant half a dozen."

"How?"

"Our boy's trying to speak decimal and binary, and he gets mixed up sometimes. A hundred and ten is six in binary."

"You know, you may be right. What about that million dollars? Same mistake?"

"I don't think so. What's a binary million in decimal?"

"Sixty-four."

"What's a decimal million in binary?"

Madigan did swift mental arithmetic. "It comes to twenty bits: IIIOIOOOOIOOIOOOOOO."

"I don't think that million dollars was any mistake," Florinda said.

"What's our boy up to now?"

"Taking care of his mum and dad."

"How does he do it?"

"He has an interface with every electric and electronic circuit in the country. Think about it, Jake. He can control our nervous system all the way from cars to computers. He can switch trains, print books, broadcast news, hijack planes, juggle bank funds. You name it and he can do it. He's in complete control."

"But how does he know everything people are doing?"

"Ah! Here we get into an exotic aspect of circuitry that I don't like. After all, I'm an engineer by trade. Who's to say that circuits don't have an interface with us? We're organic circuits ourselves. They see with our eyes, hear with our ears, feel with our fingers, and they report to him."

"Then we're just Seeing Eye dogs for machines."

"No, we've created a brand-new form of symbiosis. We can all help each other."

"And OBO's helping us. Why?"

"I don't think he likes the rest of the country," Florinda said somberly. "Look what happened to Indianapolis and Scranton and Sacramento."

"I think I'm going to be sick."

"I think we're going to survive."

"Only us? The Adam and Eve bit?"

"Nonsense. Plenty will survive, so long as they mind their manners."

"What's OBO's idea of manners?"

"I don't know. A little bit of eco-logic, maybe. No more destruction. No more waste. Live and let live, but with responsibility and accountability. That's the crucial word, *accountability*. It's the basic law of the space program; no matter what happens someone must be held accountable. OBO must have picked that up. I think he's holding the whole country accountable; otherwise it's the fire and brimstone visitation."

The phone rang. After a brief search they located an extension and picked it up. "Hello?"

"This is Stretch," I said.

"Stretch? Stretch who?"

"The Stretch computer at Goddard. Formal name, IBM 2002. OBO says he'll be making a pass over your part of the country in about five minutes. He'd like you to give him a wave. He says his orbit won't take him over you for another couple of months. When it does, he'll try to ring you himself. Bye now."

They lurched out to the lawn in front of the house and stood dazed in the twilight, staring up at the sky. The phone and the electric circuits were touched, even though the electricity was generated by a Delco, which is a notoriously insensitive boor of a machine. Suddenly Jake pointed to a pinprick of light vaulting across the heavens. "There goes our son," he said.

"There goes God," Florinda said.

They waved dutifully.

"Jake, how long before OBO's orbit decays and down will come baby, cradle and all?"

"About twenty years."

"God for twenty years." Florinda sighed. "D'you think he'll have enough time?"

Madigan shivered. "I'm scared. You?"

"Yes. But maybe we're just tired and hungry. Come inside, Big Daddy, and I'll feed us."

"Thank you, Little Mother, but no carrots, please. That's a little too close to transubstantiation for me."

A Prize for Edie

J. F. BONE

Nobel Prizes are very serious things, and I firmly believe that the moral of this story is: Why not? And why not sooner than later?

THE LETTER from America arrived too late. The Committee had regarded acceptance as a foregone conclusion, for no one since Boris Pasternak had turned down a Nobel Prize. So when Professor Doctor Nels Christianson opened the letter, there was not the slightest fear on his part, or on that of his fellow committeemen, Dr. Eric Carlstrom and Dr. Sven Eklund, that the letter would be anything other than the usual routine acceptance.

"At last we learn the identity of this great research worker," Christianson murmured as he scanned the closely typed sheets. Carlstrom and Eklund waited impatiently, wondering at the peculiar expression that fixed itself on Christianson's face. Fine beads of sweat appeared on the professor's high, narrow forehead as he laid the letter down. "Well," he said heavily, "now we know."

"Know what?" Eklund demanded. "What does it say? Does she accept?"

"She accepts," Christianson said in a peculiar half-strangled tone as he passed the letter to Eklund. "See for yourself."

Eklund's reaction was different. His face was a mottled reddish white as he finished the letter and handed it across the table to Carlstrom. "Why," he demanded of no one in particular, "did this have to happen to us?"

"It was bound to happen sometime," Carlstrom said. "It's just our misfortune that it happened to us." He chuckled as he passed the letter back to Christianson. "At least this year the presentation should be an event worth remembering."

"It seems that we have a little problem," Christianson said, making what would probably be the understatement of the century. Possibly there would be greater understatements in the remaining ninety-nine years of the twenty-first century, but Carlstrom doubted it. "We certainly have our necks out," he agreed.

"We can't do it!" Eklund exploded. "We simply can't award the Nobel Prize in medicine and physiology to that . . . that *C. Edie!*" He sputtered into silence.

"We can hardly do anything else," Christianson said. "There's no question as to the identity of the winner. Dr. Hanson's letter makes that unmistakably clear. And there's no question that the award is deserved."

"We still could award it to someone else," Eklund said.

"Not a chance. We've already said too much to the press. It's known all over the world that the medical award is going to the discoverer of the basic cause of cancer, to the founder of modern neoplastic therapy." Christianson grimaced. "If we changed our decision now, there'd be all sorts of embarrassing questions from the press."

"I can see it now," Carlstrom said, "the banquet, the table, the flowers, and Professor Doctor Nels Christianson in formal dress with the Order of St. Olaf gleaming across his white shirtfront, standing before that distinguished audience and announcing: 'The Nobel Prize in Medicine and Physiology is awarded to — ' and then that deadly hush when the audience sees the winner."

"You needn't rub it in," Christianson said unhappily. "I can see it, too."

"These Americans!" Eklund said bitterly. He wiped his damp forehead. The picture Carlstrom had drawn was accurate but hardly appealing. "One simply can't trust them. Publishing a report as important as that as a laboratory release. They should have given proper credit."

"They did," Carlstrom said. "They did — precisely. But the world, including us, was too stupid to see it. We have only ourselves to blame."

"If it weren't for the fact that the work was inspired and effective," Christianson muttered, "we might have a chance of salvaging this situation. But through its application ninety-five percent of cancers are now curable. It is obviously the outstanding contribution to medicine in the past five decades."

"But we must consider the source," Eklund protested. "This award will make the prize for medicine a laughingstock. No doctor will ever accept another. If we go through with this, we might as well forget about the medical award from now on. This will be its swan song. It hits too close to home. Too many people have been saying similar things about our profession and its trend toward specialization. And to have the Nobel Prize confirm them would alienate every doctor in the world. We simply can't do it."

"Yet who else has made a comparable discovery? Or one that is even half as important?" Christianson asked.

"That's a good question," Carlstrom said, "and a good answer to it isn't going to be easy to find. For my part, I can only wish that Alphax Laboratories had displayed an interest in literature rather than medicine. Then our colleagues at the Academy could have had the painful decision."

"Their task would be easier than ours," Christianson said wearily. "After all, the criteria of art are more flexible. Medicine, unfortunately, is based upon facts."

"That's the hell of it," Carlstrom said.

"There must be some way to solve this problem," Eklund said. "After all it was a perfectly natural mistake. We never suspected that Alphax was a physical rather than a biological sciences laboratory. Perhaps that might offer grounds — "

"I don't think so," Carlstrom interrupted. "The means in this case aren't as important as the results, and we can't deny that the cancer problem is virtually solved."

"Even though men have been saying for the past two generations that the answer was probably in the literature and all that was needed was someone with the intelligence and the time to put the facts together, the fact remains that it was C. Edie who did the job. And it required quite a bit more than merely collecting facts. Intelligence and original thinking of a high order were involved." Christianson sighed.

"Some*one,*" Eklund said bitterly. "Some *thing* you mean. C. Edie — C.E.D. — Computer, Extrapolating, Discriminatory. Manufactured by Alphax Laboratories, Trenton, New Jersey, U.S.A. C. Edie! Americans! — always naming things. A machine wins the Nobel Prize. It's fantastic!"

Christianson shook his head. "It's not fantastic, unfortunately. And I see no way out. We can't even award the prize to the team of engineers who designed and built Edie. Dr. Hanson is right when he says the discovery was Edie's and not the engineers'. It would be like giving the prize to Albert Einstein's parents because they created him."

"Is there any way we can keep the presentation secret?" Eklund asked.

"I'm afraid not. The presentations are public. We've done too good a job publicizing the Nobel Prize. As a telecast item, it's almost the equal of the motion picture Academy award."

"I can imagine the reaction when our candidate is revealed in all her metallic glory. A two-meter cube of steel filled with microminiaturized circuits, complete with flashing lights and cogwheels," Carlstrom chuckled. "And where are you going to hang the medal?"

Christianson shivered. "I wish you wouldn't give that metal nightmare a personality," he said. "It unnerves me. Personally, I wish that Dr. Hanson, Alphax Laboratories, and Edie were all at the bottom of the ocean — in some nice deep spot like the Marianas Trench." He shrugged. "Of course, we won't have that sort of luck, so we'll have to make the best of it."

"It just goes to show that you can't trust Americans," Eklund said. "I've always thought we should keep our awards on this side of the Atlantic where people are sane and civilized. Making a personality out of a computer — ugh! I suppose it's their idea of a joke."

"I doubt it," Christianson said. "They just like to name things — preferably with female names. It's a form of insecurity, the mother fixation. But that's not important. I'm afraid, gentlemen, that we shall have to make the award as we have planned. I can see no way out. After all, there's no reason why the machine cannot receive the prize. The conditions merely state that it is to be presented to the one, regardless of nationality, who makes the greatest contribution to medicine or physiology."

"I wonder how His Majesty will take it," Carlstrom said.

"The king! I'd forgotten that!" Eklund gasped.

"I expect he'll have to take it," Christianson said. "He might even appreciate the humor in the situation."

"Gustaf Adolf is a good king, but there are limits," Eklund observed.

"There are other considerations," Christianson replied. "After all, Edie is the reason the Crown Prince is still alive, and Gustaf is fond of his son."

"After all these years?"

Christianson smiled. Swedish royalty *was* long-lived. It was something of a standing joke that King Gustaf would probably outlast the pyramids, providing the pyramids lived in Sweden. "I'm sure His Majesty will cooperate. He has a strong sense of duty and since the real problem is his, not ours, I doubt if he will shirk it."

"How do you figure that?" Eklund asked.

"We merely select the candidates according to the rules, and according to the nature of their contribution. Edie is obviously the outstanding candidate in medicine for this year. It deserves the prize. We would be compromising with principle if we did not award it fairly."

"I suppose you're right," Eklund said gloomily. "I can't think of any reasonable excuse to deny the award."

"Nor I," Carlstrom said. "But what did you mean by that remark about this being the king's problem?"

"You forget," Christianson said mildly. "Of all of us, the king has the most difficult part. As you know, the Nobel Prize is formally presented at a state banquet."

"Well?"

"His Majesty is the host," Christianson said. "And just how does one eat dinner with an electronic computer?"

Isaac Asimov's
"The Caves of Steel"

RANDALL GARRETT

In the future, when the towns are caves of steel
Clear from Boston, Massachusetts, to Mobile,
There's a cop, Elijah Baley, who's the hero of this tale. He
Has a Spacer robot helper named Daneel.

For it seems that there's some guys from Outer Space
(They're descendants of the Terran human race),
And all over Terra's globe, it seems they're giving jobs to robots,
Which are hated by the people they replace.

So a certain Spacer, Sarton, gets rubbed out,
And the Chief says to Elijah: "Be a scout;
Go and find out just whodunit, and, although it won't be fun, it
Will result in your promotion, without doubt!"

The assignment puts Elijah on the spot.
He must do the job up right; if he does not,
It not only will disgrace him, but the robot will replace him
If the robot is the first to solve the plot.

In the city, there's a riot at a store.
R. Daneel jumps on a counter, and before
Baley knows it, pulls his blaster. Then he bellows: "I'm the master
Here, so stop it, or I'll blow you off the floor!"

So the riot's busted up before it starts,
And Elijah's wounded ego really smarts.
"Well," he say, "you quelled that riot, but a *robot* wouldn't try it!
Dan, I think you've got a screw loose in your parts!"

Baley doesn't see how R. Daneel could draw
Out his blaster, for the First Robotic Law
Says: "No robot may, through action or inaction, harm a fraction
Of a whisker on a human being's jaw."

Since Daneel, the robot, has a human face,
And he looks exactly like the guy from space
Who has been assassinated, Mr. Baley's quite elated,
For he's positive he's solved the murder case!

"The Commissioner," he says, "has been misled,
'Cause there hasn't been a murder! No one's dead!
Why you did it, I don't know, but I don't think you are a robot!
I am certain you are Sarton, sir, instead!"

"Why, that's rather silly, partner," says Daneel,
"And I'm awful sorry that's the way you feel."
Then, by peeling back his skin, he shows Elijah that, within, he
Is constructed almost totally of steel!

Well, of course, this gives Elijah quite a shock.
So he thinks the whole thing over, taking stock
Of the clues in their relation to the total situation,
Then he goes and calls a special robot doc.

Says Elijah Baley: "Dr. Gerrigel,
This here murder case is just about to jell!
And to bust it open wide, I'll prove this robot's homicidal!
Look him over, Doc, and see if you can tell."

So the doctor gives Daneel a thorough test
While the robot sits there, calmly self-possessed.
After close examination, "His First Law's in operation,"
Says the doctor, "You can set your mind at rest."

That leaves Baley feeling somewhat like a jerk,
But Daneel is very difficult to irk;
He just says: "We can't stand still, or we will never find the killer.
Come on, partner, let us buckle down to work."

Now the plot begins to thicken — as it should;
It's the thickening in plots that makes 'em good.
The Police Chief's robot, Sammy, gives himself the double whammy,
And the reason for it isn't understood.

The Commissioner says: "Baley, you're to blame!
Robot Sammy burned his brain out, and I claim
That, from every single clue, it looks as though you made him
    do it!"
Baley hollers: "No, I didn't! It's a frame!"

Then he says: "Commish, I think that you're the heel
Who's the nasty little villain in this deal!
And I'll tell you to your face, I really think you killed the Spacer,
    'Cause you thought he was the robot, R. Daneel!"

The Commissioner breaks down and mumbles: "Yes —
I'm the guy who did it, Baley — I confess!"
Baley says: "I knew in time you would confess this awful crime.
    You
Understand, of course, you're in an awful mess!"

The Commissioner keels over on the floor.
When he wakes up, R. Daneel says: "We're not sore;
Since the crime was accidental, we'll be merciful and gentle.
    Go," he says in solemn tones, "and sin no more!"

Then says Baley to the robot, with a grin:
"It was nice of you to overlook his sin.
As a friend, I wouldn't trade you! By the Asimov who made you,
    You're a better man than I am, Hunka Tin!"

"I found the trouble, sir. The big computer is making the little computer do all the work."

"Welcome aboard Flight 666 — this is your automatic pilot speaking."

"Nonsense! You just imagine you have human weaknesses and frailties."

"Where *is* everybody?"

Drawing by Alan Dunn; © 1966 The New Yorker Magazine, Inc.

PART III

Comedy on — or from — Other Worlds

"If we all keep quiet, maybe they'll think there's no one here."

Neptune

SANSOUCY NORTH

According to law and figures,
Astronomers' faith and math,
The last of the giants, Neptune,
Is taking a short-cut path.

By Bode, it should range out further!
(Astronomers could relax.)
It seems, in the Neptune reaches,
That discipline's getting lax!

It let all its moons go roaming,
And one come back retrograde,
Another hang crooked. Shame, Neptune!
Why be such a renegade?

The edge of the System's a shambles
Of satellites gone astray;
Your fault and example, Neptune,
For not taking your right way.

Pluto

SANSOUCY NORTH

The orbits of planets all lie in a plane,
As neat as a moth in cocoon:
Obedient, orderly, easy to find —
Save Pluto, the runaway moon.

The planets all stay in their spaced-out domains;
To trespass is not opportune!
So orbital limits they always observe —
Save Pluto, the runaway moon.

The outer worlds follow a pattern of size,
Of content, rotation, and lune;
On all points they follow a similar rule —
Save Pluto, the runaway moon.

The others were formed by a nebular law;
In place they were properly strewn;
Not one was an upstart, crashing a class —
Save Pluto — the runaway moon.

Jury-Rig

AVRAM DAVIDSON

The very title of this story brings a blush to my face. Show me anything that needs fixing (except a broken sentence) and I am helpless. If improvisation is needed (except for a plot or gimmick) I am a broken reed. This puts a great strain on my dear Janet, who has to go about Making Things Work. She is even constantly jury-rigging me with vitamins and orders to exercise so I'll Work Longer. Oh, well.

DOC DAMON AND JUDGE PELTZ were at it again.

"If you'd just for once — *once* is all I ask — just one single time read that there where Harry Stack Sullivan says — " Judge Peltz pleaded.

A grimace and a wave of the hand. "Never mind that. Harry S. Sullivan or John L. Sullivan, that's no concern of ours. I want to ask you one single, simple question: Is he either a danger to himself or a danger to the community?" Doc Damon glared out of red-rimmed poached-egg eyes. "Hey? Yea or nay?"

The judge shook his head rapidly.

"You'd think I dint *like* the fellow or something," he said, aggrievedly. "You act as though I was being contemptable tords your own talents or something," he said. "*No:* All I say, *is* . . . "

The peninsula sticks out from the Pacific coast just enough to hook around and make a harbor. The town used to be a lumbering port — it still is a lumbering town, but the timber goes out by rail or truck now. Sometimes at night, though, down near the wharves, with the fog coming in gray and soft and cool, and the brackish smell of the bay, and the scent of the wood, and the sound of the seals ooping and yerping — sometimes it seems as if it still *is* a port. Then the place isn't a town, it's a city, a small city, but a *port* city; and the air smells of distant places, and the tall cylinder which burns up the sawdust might be Stromboli if you see it from the right perspective.

But in the daytime, when you hear the rasp of the saw, and the rattle and the dull *bonk-bonk* of the flatcars thudding together as they back and fill in the yards, and you notice how many of the stores are boarded up shut, and if you know anything about the lumber business — then you soon realize that not such a hell of a lot of lumber is going out of the place anyway, by rail *or* by truck, and you know the arrival of a ship is almost as infrequent as a presidential election.

During the course of their argument Doc Damon and Judge Peltz had passed slowly into the lumberyard, passed the big saw and the sheds where the green timber was drying, crossed the tracks, and came at last to the sawdust burner.

"Hi, Elmer," the doctor said. A short man in clean overalls a size too big for him looked up at them. "How are you today, Elmer?"

"Day, day," the man said, cheerfully — very cheerfully, almost mirthfully. "Lololo. Pleasingness. My, yes. If have kreelth."

"See?" the judge hissed in his companion's ear. "WhadItellya? *Neologisms!"*

The doctor pulled away with a testy expression on his face. He put the tip of his little finger in his ear and moved it vigorously. "Damn it, Al, I wish you wouldn't — What? Yes, yes: I'm *quite* familiar with the phenomenon. It don't mean a thing — except that he hasn't got all his marbles. Which is by no means news."

Judge Peltz's mouth set, then unset, in his horse-long face. "It's a schizoid characteristic," he said, doggedly. "Sullivan points out — "

The doctor waved to a passing workman. Then he said, "Listen. Do I try to teach you law?"

Elmer beamed at them. "Nice day, hey? Nice town, nice sawdust — " He picked up a handful of the stuff (before the burners were installed the sawdust seemed likely to engulf the town); he sifted it lovingly through his fingers. " — nice people. One day — gren-a-mun-dun." He seemed just the merest bit regretful. The judge cleared his throat.

"Uh — tellus, Elmer — what does 'gren-a-mun-dun' mean? Hmm? Tell us?"

The doctor snorted. Elmer considered, rubbed his chin, raised his eyebrows. "Gren-a-mun-dun? It's like . . . um . . . cupra. But not for *all* the time cupra." And he beamed, turned back to his task of burning up sawdust.

"I trust that you are satisfied, Alfred?" the doctor asked. The day was warm, but now and then a cool breeze came up from the bay, and the sound of the seals with it.

The judge said, well, he wasn't. From his pocket he took a small notebook and a pencil.

" 'Gren-a-mun-dun'," he muttered, writing. "I gottem all down here. And someday I'm writing to a member of the medical profession whose mind isn't closed to all the progress that's been made in recent years . . . Kreelth . . . tal-a-wax-na . . . estenral . . . I gottem all noted down here. Sometimes he just repeats the old ones, but today he used two more: Gren-a-mun-dun and cupra."

Damon shook his head. "Elmer is happy," he said. "The company is happy with him. He has not an enemy in the world. What do you want, Alfred?"

Elmer puttered around the base of the tall metal sawdust burner with a few tools. "Kreelth," he muttered.

Judge Alfred Peltz said he wanted to know two things. "One: Is there any chance he might ever become *dangerous*? Two: Is there a chance he can be *helped*?"

The doctor rubbed his rufous eyes. He groaned. "Never let well enough alone, will you? Just like my damned old uncle, Freddy Damon. Thought the sailingmen were a bad influence on the town. Wouldn't rest till he'd got the railroad in. The day they drove the last spike, what happened? Drunken gandy dancer sets fire to a boxcar, burns up half the town — in*clud*ing" — he poked his finger in the judge's sternum — "my damned old uncle, Freddy Damon . . . Hapastwo," he said, abruptly. "I got to get back to my office. You drove me here, now you drive me back."

They started off. Doc halfturned. "Slong, Elmer. Begood."

"Gren-a-mun-dun," Elmer muttered, absent-mindedly, scraping a bolt.

When the lease of Pighafetti the ship chandler ran out, he didn't even bother to hold a Going Out Of Business sale. What stock was left in the shop stayed there. Most of it still remained when Tom Wong moved in because *his* lease had run out. Shipping and fishing might be shot to hell, but folks still had to eat. Knowing the value of the picturesque, Tom had simply redistributed the stuff; and so nets and coils of line and glass globes and ships' lanterns and a lot of similar equipage hung from the walls and ceiling.

"Yeah, I guess that's right, Judge," Tom observed. They were sitting at a table under an eeltrap. "Now when I was a kid, my father used to take me to an old Chinese man who stuck needles into me — gold needles, silver needles. Oh, it *worked* — but nowadays I see to it that my kids get penicillin, because, like you say, we gotta Move With The Times . . . How about trying today's special? Curried shrimp." At the judge's nod, he signaled to his wife.

Judge Peltz put a cigarette in his mouth, groped around for a match. On the table by the ashtray with a pregnant dragon coiled around it was a book of paper matches, imprinted *Tom Wong's Waterfront Inn;* but the judge liked kitchen matches. He brought out the entire contents of his coat pocket, not being able to disentangle the match, and dumped them on the table: a piece of fishing line, the pencil stubs, a glueless postage stamp, a few matches, and his little notebook. He pulled a match loose, lit his cigarette. The notebook reminded him —

"Now, it's an odd thing, Tom," he said, "how some people can't see the forest for the trees. I suppose you must meet up with people in the restaurant business world who are perfectly content to go right on doing just like they did thirty years ago?"

Tom nodded vigorously. His eyeglasses flashed. "Boy, don't I just!" he agreed. "Judge, those very words describe my wife's Uncle Ong, who's got that lunchroom over at the county seat. When I put in the dishwashing machine the salesman offered me a special price if I'd get *two*. Well, gee, I mean — so I asked her uncle, How's about it? But no — he's used to having the dishes washed by hand and he didn't see any reason to change. Gets in these hoboes and winoes and odd-ball characters and by and by they *leave* him, so you'd think — But no. I said, 'Ah, come *on*, Uncle Ong, don't be an old stick-in-the-mud.' So he started cussing me out in Chinese and yelling not to forget the Eight Virtues and that kind of stuff . . ."

The judge, who had hoped for a single yes only, listened. The moment Tom stopped he said, "Well, there you are. It's very sad. And how'd it be if the whole country was like that? Now, you take psychiatry, for example. What strides have been made in it! What marvelous recent discoveries!"

Old Ong's nephew said, "Boy, you bet!"

Growing enthusiastic, the Judge went on, "Now, you take for instance, I was reading some while back an article in the *Reader's Digest* — "

"That's a great magazine. I read it all the time. It's triffic."

"And it was describing the work of the late Dr. Harry Stack Sullivan of whom I'm sure you've heard." Wong made a noncommittal, encouraging noise. "You know much about the schizoid personality, Tom?" the judge asked.

The restaurateur wiggled in a fit of embarrassment. "Well, um, *no*, Judge. Y'see, The Business keeps me pretty busy, except for Sunday morning, and I like to sleep late then fi get the chance. I was saying to my wife only last week, Judge, 'Priscilla,' I says, 'Can't you keep those kids quiet just — ' "

Pushing the curried shrimp to one side and speaking rather loudly, Judge Alfred Peltz said, "This type of personality suffers from what you call a profound disassociation of ideas, I think. They retreat from Reality. See? They use Neologisms — what I mean, words that *no*body knows what they mean, like . . ." He opened the little notebook. "Kreelth."

Tom Wong smiled. He chuckled. "Kreelth," he repeated. "What kind of people did you say they were, Judge? I mean, where do they come from? Because that's what this simple-minded guy that washes dishes in my wife's Uncle Ong's lunchroom says all the time. Everytime they bring him a pile of dirty dishes he says it."

Old Mr. Woodrow Ong shook his head and waved his hand when Judge Peltz and Doc Damon came into his lunchroom.

"Closed up," he announced. "Too late. Closed up. Oh. Judge. Hello, Judge."

He glanced at the clock, sighed, struggled with his Confucian respect for the figure of The Magistrate. "Sandwich?" he suggested, feebly. "Cup coffee?" He sighed again, surrendered. "Appoo pie, boo-berry, coconut custard, lemon mo-ang — "

The swinging doors of the kitchen opened and a man about Elmer's age and size came out, rolling down his sleeves. "Dishes finish," he said, and then saw the two newcomers. He took in a deep, resigned breath. "Kreelth," he said softly.

Judge Peltz looked triumphantly at Doc Damon. He consulted his little notebook. "Lololo," he said, tentatively. The dishwasher smiled. He chuckled at "gren-a-mun-dun" and "cupra." When the judge stumbled over "tal-a-wax-na," he corrected him happily.

"Fantastic!" said the judge. "Identical neologisms!" For once the doctor listened without demur.

"All right. Bring him along with us. Let's get the two of them together and see — whatever it is," Doc Damon said.

Old Mr. Ong watched them get into the car. He shrugged. Then he locked up, turned out all lights but one. An unfamiliar clicking noise in the kitchen drew his attention. He traced it to the garbage disposal unit, lifted out the mechanism. Its inward parts were a mystery to him, always had been. The devil device clicked once again as he looked at it warily. A little parti-colored disk fell out of it, then another. They dropped to the floor. The cat strolled over, sniffed, licked, then began to eat.

Mr. Ong shrugged. He replaced the mechanism. "Let well enough alone" had always been his motto. The garbage disposal unit clicked one last time, then went silent as the last of the garbage emerged in the form of something resembling a Necco wafer, or a poker chip. Mr. Ong took a can of cold beer from the icebox and went upstairs to watch Charlie Chan on the Late, Late Movie.

Jack Girard, the manager of the lumberyard, was agreeable, though puzzled. He leaned out of the car window and said to the watchman, "The four of us are going up to the sawdust burner for a while, Tib — in case muh wife calls nasks."

The judge asked, "How come they *burn* the sawdust, Jack, instead of making a lot of whatchacallits?"

Girard shrugged. "Company Policy is Burn It. So that's whut we do. We burn it."

The judge's forehead, ridged and bumpy with thought, suddenly cleared.

" 'By-Products!' That's what they call it, the stuff you can make from sawdust. How come your company don't convert all this good sawdust into By-Products, huh, Girard?"

"Such as what?" The doctor took over the task of answering from the foreman who — faced with the fearful thought of questioning Company Policy — shook his head, aghast.

"Ohhhh . . ." The judge, trying to recall what he had in mind, rolled the syllable *and* his eyes. ". . . stuff with names like Butyn Mephlutyn, or Bophane Hyperstannis, or *some*thing like that . . ."

The yellow glare of a single lamp mingled with the red glare of the tall burner itself. Girard hopped out and held the door open for the others. "I still don't know what you intend to try and prove," Doc Damon complained, as he bent his head and slid out.

"I'm not sure, myself," the judge admitted. "Okay, Joe, here we are — " The dishwasher (his Social Security card listed his name as Joe Jones), humming tunelessly to himself, got out and looked around. Girard strolled over to the burner. He examined a piece of piping on the side and frowned. "What's *this?*" he asked.

Doc Damon said, indifferently, that it was part of the sawdust burner.

The manager said the hell it *was*. "Elmer!" he called. "Hey, Elmer?"

Over their heads a voice called out cheerfully, "Lololo!" Their eyes swung up to see the short figure in overalls coming down the rungs set in the side of the cylinder. In a moment he was on the ground. "I just fix the wagmal," he said. "Takes much kreelth — much kreelth."

The dishwasher stepped forward. He said, "Lololo." He and Elmer exchanged wide smiles, spoke together rapidly. Then Girard tapped the piping.

"Who put this on here, Elmer?" he asked.

"I."

"*You?* Well, how *come?*"

"Tal-a-wax-na. Of course, not *best* kind tal-a-wax-na, but — " he shrugged. "It be okay for long enough."

Girard gaped. The doctor said, "Oh, here we go again. Look, now, Jack: the machine still burns sawdust, don't it? So what do you care if old Elmer sticks a hootenanny on it? You'll be as bad as old Judge Peltz here if you keep on — reading the *Reader's Digest* and all."

Joe Jones, the dishwasher, walked around the base of the burner. Reappearing, he felt the pipe, nodded in a satisfied sort of way.

A sudden thought struck Elmer. "Klommerkaw?" he asked. "You get klommerkaw ready?"

Joe nodded, held up the shopping bag he had brought with him from the kitchen of Ong's Eats. He reached in his other hand, brought it out filled with little parti-colored disks.

"Some new kind of Necco Wafers?" hazarded Doc Damon. "Poker chips to while away the hours? Nope — no cards . . . Well, whadda ya know?" His voice faded into a surprised silence as the dishwasher broke one in half, gave part to Elmer. They put the halves in their mouths, chewed ruminatively, swallowed.

"Very good klommerkaw," said Elmer. "Plenty, too."

"Now, look-a-here," Girard protested, "I'm responsabull to thuh owners for all this here e-quipment, and I gotta know what is that pipe *for?*"

Joe Jones looked at him. "Kreelth," he said. There was just a slight touch of reproach in his voice. "Do not be un-kreelth." He put his hand on the piping and directed his next remark to Elmer. "Wagmal fix? Estanrel?"

Elmer said, "Wagmal just now fix good."

Jones gave the piping a light twist — a gentle tug, really — his hand moved so quickly, so oddly. "Estanrel," he said.

Girard said, *"Uh."*

The side of the sawdust burner opened where no opening had been.

"Obbertaw," said Elmer, firmly, holding back. Joe Jones went inside. So did Elmer. For a moment Jones's face looked at them. He smiled.

"Cupra," he said. "Cupra."

"But not cupra for all the time," Elmer explained. "Only gren-a-mun-dun. We come back. Have kreelth, you see we come back some time to nice town, nice people, nice sawdust."

And the opening closed. The red glare of the burning sawdust turned yellow. The whoofing noise of the draft turned shrill. A sudden gust of cool wind came from the bay. And then, with a subdued, polite sort of swish, the sawdust burner separated itself from the ground and went up . . .

They had a rather bad first five minutes of it. Finally, with the help of the *spiritus frumenti* in Doctor Damon's bag, the three men began slowly to recover.

"The way I see it — " Doc Damon was the first to say anything besides "Jesus" and "Gimme that bottle" — "the way *I* see it: those two fellas must've been sort of shipwrecked here. Probably way, *way* back in the woods there's a twisted mass of metal somebody will come across one of these days."

The judge said, "Ohboyohboyohboy."

Girard said, "Gimme that bottle."

"So they did what any experienced mariner would do — they improvised — fixed up what you might call a jury-rigged vessel . . . At least, Elmer did. Guess he was the chief engineer. Maybe Joe Jones was the purser or supercargo."

"All *I* have to say," the judge announced firmly, "is that it never happened and if either of you say it *did* — say it out *open,* I mean — I'll do my damndest to see to it that you get indicted, prosecuted, convicted, and *severely* sentenced, for barratry, simony, unlawful usurpation . . . and anything else I can get away with," he concluded.

"How'm I gunna explain why we're a sawdust burner short?" Girard moaned.

"Condemned as a health menace," Doc Damon said, crisply. "No, no, Alfred, I won't say a word. But sooner or later everyone will know. They'll be *back*. Don't you *know* that? They'll be back for some more nice sawdust, because it looks like they have a way to get a By-Product out of sawdust to beat all By-Products. That Butyn Merphlutyn, or Bophane Hyperstannis, must be powerful stuff, yes-*sir*."

Judge Peltz asked, "And in the meantime we just *wait?* Isn't there something we can *do,* now that we know?"

Doc Damon said, "Well . . . If you hear of any other happy morons with neologistic tendencies, we might pay them a visit. You never know . . . And until then, and meantime: Have kreelth."

Sometimes at night, when the fog makes the slates of the sidewalk wet and glistening, or even when the cold wind blows up and clears the sky and shows the burning white stars, at such times the place isn't a town, it's a city — though a small one — it's a *port* city, and the air smells of distant places.

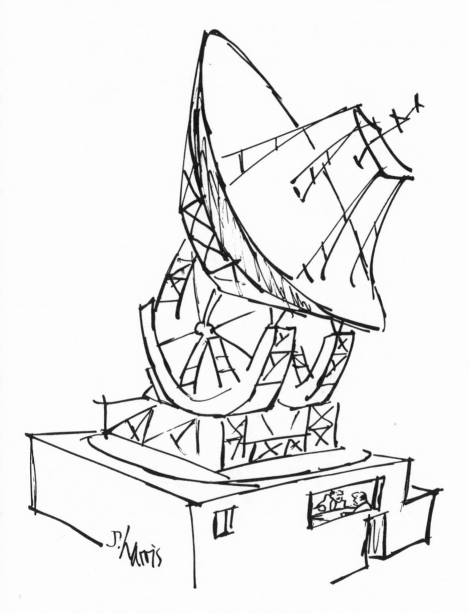

"As I understand it, they want an immediate answer. Only trouble is the message was sent out 3 million years ago."

Protection

ROBERT SHECKLEY

I suppose that one of the oldest lessons human beings learn in life is that you can't win, which is the basis for the horde of three-wishes stories: no matter what you wished for you wish you hadn't. Wealth never made Midas rich, and I've read stories in which happiness couldn't make you happy. Leave it to good old Bob Sheckley to carry it to the ultimate extreme. What it amounts to is simply this: Safety isn't safe.

THERE'LL BE AN AIRPLANE CRASH in Burma next week, but it shouldn't affect me here in New York. And the feegs certainly can't harm me. Not with all my closet doors closed.

No, the big problem is lesnerizing. I must not lesnerize. Absolutely not. As you can imagine, that hampers me.

And to top it all, I think I'm catching a really nasty cold.

The whole thing started on the evening of November seventh. I was walking down Broadway on my way to Baker's Cafeteria. On my lips was a faint smile, due to having passed a tough physics exam earlier in the day. In my pocket, jingling faintly, were five coins, three keys, and a book of matches.

Just to complete the picture, let me add that the wind was from the northwest at five miles an hour; Venus was in the ascendancy and the Moon was decidedly gibbous. You can draw your own conclusions from this.

I reached the corner of Ninety-eighth Street and began to cross. As I stepped off the curb, someone yelled at me, "The truck! Watch the truck!"

I jumped back, looking around wildly. There was nothing in sight. Then, a full second later, a truck cut around the corner on two wheels, ran through the red light, and roared up Broadway. Without that warning, I would have been hit.

You've heard stories like this, haven't you? About the strange voice that warned Aunt Minnie to stay out of the elevator, which then crashed to the basement. Or maybe it told Uncle Joe not to sail on the *Titanic.* That's where the story usually ends.

I wish mine ended there.

"Thanks, friend," I said and looked around. There was no one there.

"Can you still hear me?" the voice asked.

"Sure I can." I turned a complete circle and stared suspiciously at the closed apartment windows overhead. "But where in the blue blazes are you?"

"Gronish," the voice answered. "Is that the referent? Refraction index. Creature of insubstantiality. The Shadow knows. Did I pick the right one?"

"You're invisible?" I hazarded.

"That's it!"

"But *what* are you?"

"A validusian derg."

"A what?"

"I am — open your larynx a little wider please. Let me see now. I am the Spirit of Christmas Past. The Creature from the Black Lagoon. The Bride of Frankenstein. The — "

"Hold on," I said. "What are you trying to tell me — that you're a ghost or a creature from another planet?"

"Same thing," the derg replied. "Obviously."

That made it all perfectly clear. Any fool could see that the voice belonged to someone from another planet. He was invisible on Earth, but his superior senses had spotted an approaching danger and warned me of it.

Just a plain, everyday supernormal incident.

I began to walk hurriedly down Broadway.

"What is the matter?" the invisible derg asked.

"Not a thing," I answered, "except that I seem to be standing in the middle of the street talking to an invisible alien from the farthest reaches of outer space. I suppose only I can hear you?"

"Well, naturally."

"Great! You know where this sort of thing will land me?"

"The concept you are subvocalizing is not entirely clear."

"The loony bin. Nut house. Bug factory. Psychotic ward. That's where they put people who talk to invisible aliens. Thanks for the warning, buddy. Good night."

Feeling lightheaded, I turned east, hoping my invisible friend would continue down Broadway.

"Won't you talk with me?" the derg asked.

I shook my head, a harmless gesture they can't pick you up for, and kept on walking.

"But you *must,* " the derg said with a hint of desperation. "A real subvocal contact is very rare and astonishingly difficult. Sometimes I can get across a warning, just before a danger moment. But then the connection fades."

So there was the explanation for Aunt Minnie's premonition. But I still wasn't having any.

"Conditions might not be right for a hundred years!" the derg mourned.

What conditions? Five coins and three keys jingling together when Venus was ascendant? I suppose it's worthy of investigation — but not by me. You never can prove that supernormal stuff. There are enough people knitting slipcovers for straitjackets without me swelling their ranks.

"Just leave me alone," I said. A cop gave me a funny look for that one. I grinned boyishly and hurried on.

"I appreciate your social situation," the derg urged, "but this contact is in your own best interests. I want to protect you from the myriad dangers of human existence."

I didn't answer him.

"Well," the derg said, "I can't force you. I'll just have to offer my services elsewhere. Good-bye, friend."

I nodded pleasantly.

"One last thing," he said. "Stay off subways tomorrow between noon and one-fifteen P.M. Good-bye."

"Huh? Why?"

"Someone will be killed at Columbus Circle, pushed in front of a train by shopping crowds. You, if you are there. Good-bye."

"Someone will be killed there tomorrow?" I asked. "You're sure?"

"Of course."

"It'll be in the newspapers?"

"I should imagine so."

"And you know all sorts of stuff like that?"

"I can perceive all dangers radiating toward you and extending into time. My one desire is to protect you from them."

I had stopped. Two girls were giggling at me talking to myself. Now I began walking again.

"Look," I whispered, "can you wait until tomorrow evening?"

"You will let me be your protector?" the derg asked eagerly.

"I'll tell you tomorrow," I said. "After I read the late papers."

The item was there, all right. I read it in my furnished room on 113th Street. Man pushed by the crowd, lost his balance, fell in front of an oncoming train. This gave me a lot to think about while waiting for my invisible protector to show up.

I didn't know what to do. His desire to protect me seemed genuine enough. But I didn't know if I wanted it. When, an hour later, the derg contacted me, I liked the whole idea even less, and told him so.

"Don't you trust me?" he asked.

"I just want to lead a normal life."

"If you lead any life at all," he reminded me. "That truck last night — "

"That was a freak, a once-in-a-lifetime hazard."

"It only takes once in a lifetime to die," the derg said solemnly. "There was the subway too."

"That doesn't count. I hadn't planned on riding it today."

"But you had no reason *not* to ride it. That's the important thing. Just as you have no reason not to take a shower in the next hour."

"Why shouldn't I?"

"A Miss Flynn," the derg said, "who lives down the hall, has just completed her shower and has left a bar of melting pink soap on the pink tile in the bathroom on this floor. *You* would have slipped on it and suffered a sprained wrist."

"Not fatal, huh?"

"No. Hardly in the same class with, let us say, a heavy flowerpot pushed from a rooftop by a certain unstable old gentleman."

"When is that going to happen?" I asked.

"I thought you weren't interested."

"I'm very interested. When? Where?"

"Will you let me continue to protect you?" he asked.

"Just tell me one thing," I said. "What's in this for you?"

"Satisfaction!" he said. "For a validusian derg, the greatest thrill possible is to help another creature evade danger."

"But isn't there something else you want out of it? Some trifle like my soul, or rulership of Earth?"

"Nothing! To accept payment for Protecting would ruin the emotional experience. All I want out of life — all any derg wants — is to protect someone from the dangers he cannot see, but which we can see all too well." The derg paused, then added softly, "We don't even expect gratitude."

Well, that clinched it. How could I guess the consequences? How could I know that his aid would lead me into a situation in which I must not lesnerize?

"What about that flowerpot?" I asked.

"It will be dropped on the corner of Tenth Street and McAdams Boulevard at eight-thirty tomorrow morning."

"Tenth and McAdams? Where's that?"

"In Jersey City," he answered promptly.

"But I've never been to Jersey City in my life! Why warn me about that?"

"I don't know where you will or won't go," the derg said. "I merely perceive dangers to you wherever they may occur."

"What should I do now?"

"Anything you wish," he told me. "Just lead your normal life."

Normal life. Hah!

It started out well enough. I attended classes at Columbia, did homework, saw movies, went on dates, played table tennis and chess, all as before. At no time did I let on that I was under the direct protection of a validusian derg.

Once or twice a day, the derg would come to me. He would say something

204

like, "Loose grating on West End Avenue between Sixty-sixth and Sixty-seventh streets. Don't walk on it."

And of course I wouldn't. But someone else would. I often saw these items in the newspapers.

Once I got used to it, it gave me quite a feeling of security. An alien was scurrying around twenty-four hours a day and all he wanted out of life was to protect me. A supernormal bodyguard! The thought gave me an enormous amount of confidence.

My social life during this period couldn't have been improved upon.

But the derg soon became overzealous in my behalf. He began finding more and more dangers, most of which had no real bearing on my life in New York — things I should avoid in Mexico City, Toronto, Omaha, Papeete.

I finally asked him if he was planning on reporting every potential danger on Earth.

"These are the few, the very few, that you are or may be affected by," he told me.

"In Mexico City? And Papeete? Why not confine yourself to the local picture? Greater New York, say."

"Locale means nothing to me," the derg replied stubbornly. "My perceptions are temporal, not spatial. I must protect you from *everything!*"

It was rather touching, in a way, and there was nothing I could do about it. I simply had to discard from his reports the various dangers in Hoboken, Thailand, Kansas City, Angkor Vat (collapsing statue), Paris, and Sarasota. Then I would reach the local stuff. I would ignore, for the most part, the dangers awaiting me in Queens, the Bronx, Staten Island, and Brooklyn, and concentrate on Manhattan.

These were often worth waiting for, however. The derg saved me from some pretty nasty experiences — a holdup on Cathedral Parkway, for example, a teenage mugging, a fire.

But he kept stepping up the pace. It had started as a report or two a day. Within a month, he was warning me five or six times a day. And at last his warnings — local, national, and international — flowed in a continual stream.

I was facing too many dangers, beyond all reasonable probability.

On a typical day:

"Tainted food in Baker's Cafeteria. Don't eat there tonight."

"Amsterdam Bus three-twelve has bad brakes. Don't ride it."

"Mellen's Tailor Shop has a leaking gas line. Explosion due. Better have your clothes dry-cleaned elsewhere."

"Rabid mongrel on the prowl between Riverside Drive and Central Park West. Take a taxi."

Soon I was spending most of my time not doing things, and avoiding places. Danger seemed to be lurking behind every lamppost, waiting for me.

I suspected the derg of padding his report. It seemed the only possible explanation. After all, I had lived this long before meeting him, with no supernormal assistance whatsoever, and had gotten by nicely. Why should the risks increase now?

I asked him that one evening.

"All my reports are perfectly genuine," he said, obviously a little hurt. "If you don't believe me, try turning on the lights in your psychology class tomorrow."

"Why?"

"Defective wiring."

"I don't doubt your warnings," I assured him. "I just know that life was never this dangerous before you came along."

"Of course it wasn't. Surely you know that if you accept protection, you must accept the drawbacks of protection as well."

"Drawbacks like what?"

The derg hesitated. "Protection begets the need of further protection. That is a universal constant."

"Come again?" I asked in bewilderment.

"Before you met me, you were like everyone else, and you ran such risks as your situation offered. But with my coming, your immediate environment has changed. And your position in it has changed, too."

"Changed? Why?"

"Because it has *me* in it. To some extent now, you partake of my environment, just as I partake of yours. And, of course, it is well known that the avoidance of one danger opens the path to others."

"Are you trying to tell me," I said, very slowly, "that my risks have increased *because* of your help?"

"It was unavoidable," he sighed.

I could have cheerfully strangled the derg at that moment, if he hadn't been invisible and impalpable. I had the angry feeling that I had been conned, taken by an extraterrestrial trickster.

"All right," I said, controlling myself. "Thanks for everything. See you on Mars or wherever you hang out."

"You don't want any further protection?"

"You guessed it. Don't slam the door on your way out."

"But what's wrong?" The derg seemed genuinely puzzled. "There are increased risks in your life, true, but what of it? It is a glory and an honor to face danger and emerge victorious. The greater the peril, the greater the joy of evading it."

For the first time, I saw how alien this alien was.

"Not for me," I said. "Scram."

"Your risks have increased," the derg argued, "but my capacity for detection is more than ample to cope with it. I am *happy* to cope with it! So it still represents a net gain in protection for you."

I shook my head. "I know what happens next. My risks just keep on increasing, don't they?"

"Not at all. As far as accidents are concerned, you have reached the quantitative limit."

"What does that mean?"

"It means there will be no further increase in the number of accidents you must avoid."

"Good. Now will you please get the hell out of here?"

"But I just explained — "

"Sure, no further increase, just more of the same. Look, if you leave me alone, my original environment will return, won't it? And, with it, my original risks?"

"Eventually," the derg agreed. "If you survive."

"I'll take that chance."

The derg was silent for a time. Finally he said, "You can't afford to send me away. Tomorrow — "

"Don't tell me. I'll avoid the accidents on my own."

"I wasn't thinking of accidents."

"What then?"

"I hardly know how to tell you." He sounded embarrassed. "I said there would be no further quantitative change. But I didn't mention a *qualitative* change."

"What are you talking about?" I shouted at him.

"I'm trying to say," the derg said, "that a gamper is after you."

"A what? What kind of a gag is this?"

"A gamper is a creature from *my* environment. I suppose he was attracted by your increased potentiality for avoiding risk, because of my protection."

"To hell with the gamper and to hell with you."

"If he comes, try driving him off with mistletoe. Iron is often effective, if bonded to copper. Also — "

I threw myself on the bed and buried my head under the pillow. The derg took the hint. In a moment I could sense that he was gone.

What an idiot I had been! We denizens of Earth have a common vice: We take what we're offered, whether we need it or not.

You can get into a lot of trouble that way.

But the derg was gone, and the worst of my troubles were over. I'd sit tight for a while, give things a chance to work themselves out. In a few weeks, perhaps, I'd —

There seemed to be a humming in the air.

I sat upright on the bed. One corner of the room was curiously dark, and I could feel a cold breeze on my face. The hum grew louder — not really a hum, but laughter, low and monotonous.

At that point, no one had to draw me a diagram.

"Derg!" I screamed. "Get me out of this!"

He was there. "Mistletoe! Just wave it at the gamper."

"Where in the blazes would I get mistletoe?"

"Iron and copper then!"

I leaped to my desk, grabbed a copper paperweight and looked wildly for some iron to bond it to. The paperweight was pulled out of my hand. I caught it before it fell. Then I saw my fountain pen and brought the point against the paperweight.

The darkness vanished. The cold disappeared.

I guess I passed out.

The derg said triumphantly, an hour later, "You see? You need my protection."

"I suppose I do," I answered dully.

"You will need some things," the derg said. "Wolfsbane, amarinth, garlic, graveyard mold — "

"But the gamper is gone."

"Yes. However, the grailers remain. And you need safeguards against the leeps, the feegs, and the melgerizer."

So I wrote down his list of herbs, essences, and specifics. I didn't bother asking him about this link between supernatural and supernormal. My comprehension was now full and complete.

Ghosts and spirits? Or extraterrestrials? All the same, he said, and I saw what he meant. They leave us alone, for the most part. We are on different levels of perception, of existence, even. Until a human is foolish enough to attract attention to himself.

Now I was in their game. Some wanted to kill me, some to protect me, but none cared for *me*, not even the derg. They were interested solely in my value to the game, if that's what it was.

And the situation was my own fault. At the beginning, I had had the accumulated wisdom of the human race at my disposal, that tremendous racial hatred of witches and ghosts, the irrational fear of alien life. For my adventure has been played out a thousand times, and the story is told again and again — how a man dabbles in strange arts and calls to himself a spirit. By so doing, he attracts attention to himself — the worst thing of all.

So I was wedded inseparably to the derg and the derg to me. Until yesterday, that is. Now I am on my own again.

Things had been quiet for a few weeks. I had held off the feegs by the simple expedient of keeping my closet doors closed. The leeps were more menacing, but the eye of a toad seemed to stop them. And the melgerizer was dangerous only in the full of the Moon.

"You are in danger," the derg said yesterday.

"Again?" I asked, yawning.

"It is the thrang who pursues us."

"Us?"

"Yes, myself as well as you, for even a derg must run risk and danger."

"Is this thrang particularly dangerous?"

"Very."

"Well, what do I do? Snakeskin over the door? A pentagon?"

"None of those," the derg said. "The thrang must be dealt with negatively, by the avoidance of certain actions."

By now, there were so many restrictions on me, I didn't think another would matter. "What shouldn't I do?"

"You must not lesnerize," the derg said.

"Lesnerize?" I frowned. "What's that?"

"Surely you know. It's a simple, everyday human action."

"I probably know it under a different name. Explain."

"Very well. To lesnerize is to — " He stopped abruptly.

"What?"

"It is here! The thrang!"

I backed up against a wall. I thought I could detect a faint stirring of dust, but that might have been no more than overwrought nerves.

"Derg!" I shouted. "Where are you? What should I do?"

I heard a shriek and the unmistakable sound of jaws snapping.

The derg cried, "It has me!"

"What should I do?" I cried again.

There was a horrible noise of teeth grinding. Very faintly I heard the derg say, *"Don't lesnerize!"*

And then there was silence.

So I'm sitting tight now. There'll be an airplane crash in Burma next week, but it shouldn't affect me here in New York. And the feegs certainly can't harm me. Not with all my closet doors closed.

No, the problem is lesnerizing. I must *not* lesnerize. Absolutely not. If I can keep from lesnerizing, everything will pass and the chase will move elsewhere. It must! All I have to do is wait them out.

The trouble is, I don't have any idea what lesnerizing might be. A common human action, the derg had said. Well, for the time, I'm avoiding as many actions as possible.

I've caught up on some back sleep and nothing happened, so that's not lesnerizing. I went out and bought food, paid for it, cooked it, ate it. That wasn't lesnerizing. I wrote this report. *That* wasn't lesnerizing.

I'll come out of this yet.

I'm going to catch a nap. I think I have a cold coming on. Now I have to sneeze . . .

The Self-Priming
Solid-State Electronic Chicken

JON LUCAS

One is always tempted, given the chance, to use puns or word play, though perhaps, to be frank, I should not try to make a cosmic law of it. Instead, I should admit that I suffer the temptation. In this case, for instance, I have the overwhelming impulse to say that the tale deals with some shrewd connivers whose scheme lays an egg. And how.

R.F.D. 68
Petaluma, Calif.
7 June 1970

Genius Inventions, Inc.
1448 Bonanza Blvd.
Los Angeles, Calif.

Dear Sirs:

I am writing to you with regards to your advertisement in the Farm and Home Magazine where it says "Inventors Wanted." Since I am the inventor of a number of useful inventions, and one in particular which is sure to be a big success, I am sure you will want to get in touch with me right away.

Yours truly,
Emerson J. Minnick

GENIUS INVENTIONS, INC.
1448 Bonanza Blvd.
Los Angeles, Calif.
9 June 1970

Mr. Emerson J. Minnick
R.F.D. 68
Petaluma, Calif.

Dear Mr. Minnick:

Thank you for your inquiry of June 7th. I am sending you under separate cover our pamphlet entitled "Think Your Way To Millions!" which explains the large profits to be made from marketing original inventions to industry. As stated in the pamphlet and in the advertisement which attracted your attention, no experience is necessary. You are no doubt aware that Leonardo da Vinci and Thomas Edison, to mention only two of the most successful inventors, had no degrees in engineering or any field of science, and there is no reason why you cannot follow their example.

I await your reply with interest.

Most sincerely yours,
John Wallen, Pres.

R.F.D. 68
Petaluma, Calif.
12 June 1970

Genius Inventions, Inc.
1448 Bonanza Blvd.
Los Angeles, Calif.

Dear Mr. Wallen:

I have read your pamphlet from cover to cover and am convinced that your company is the right type for me to be associated with. I note what you say in regards to a contract and you can go ahead and send it to me. I will not have any use for the course in drafting and engineering lessons which is also offered as I already know how to invent things and only need to get them patented and sold to the Big Manufacturers like it says. As soon as I receive the contract I will sign it and send you one of my inventions to start with. I think my Self-Priming Solid-State Electronic Chicken is the best one to start with, as it is sure fire.

Yours truly,
Emerson J. Minnick

GENIUS INVENTIONS, INC.
1448 Bonanza Blvd.
Los Angeles, Calif.
14 June 1970

Mr. Emerson J. Minnick
R.F.D. 68
Petaluma, Calif.

Dear Mr. Minnick:

Thank you for your letter of 12 June, advising that you wish to sign our Contract Form 3378-A. You will find two of these forms, signed by me, enclosed with this letter. Please fill out both of them and return one with a copy of your plans and your remittance, on receipt of which we will start at once the necessary arrangements for patenting and development of your invention.

Trusting that this will be satisfactory, and taking the liberty of offering my congratulations on your decision, I am,

Most sincerely yours,
John Wallen, Pres.

R.F.D. 68
Petaluma, Calif.
17 June 1970

Genius Inventions, Inc.
1448 Bonanza Blvd.
Los Angeles, Calif.

Dear Mr. Wallen:

I don't understand. It says here in the contract that I am supposed to send you Five Hundred Dollars ($500.00). I don't understand that. I don't see why a big rich company like yours should have to have Five Hundred Dollars from me, especially when you are getting half interest in an invention that will make a whole lot of money for you. Don't forget you got a right to keep half the profits like it says. Please write to me right away and clear this up.

Yours truly,
Emerson J. Minnick

GENIUS INVENTIONS, INC.
1448 Bonanza Blvd.
Los Angeles, Calif.
21 June 1970

Mr. Emerson J. Minnick
R.F.D. 68
Petaluma, Calif.

Dear Mr. Minnick:

Your letter of 17 June has been received, and I am sorry to see that you have failed to understand the terms of our Contract 3378-A. Apparently you do not realize the necessity of our securing a deposit of five hundred dollars as a guarantee of good faith and sincerity. Surely, Mr. Minnick, you can see that we wish to deal only with responsible, serious-minded people, who are sincere in their desire to achieve fame and fortune by benefiting Mankind through their inventions. We believe you are of that type, and that you will be fair enough to appreciate our motives.

Furthermore, we cannot tell how successful your invention might be until it has been checked by our Division of Development and Research. And just imagine the cost of applying for a patent by the United States Government at Washington, D.C.! And yet this is necessary to prevent unprincipled persons from stealing your work and manufacturing it without paying you a cent! It is these expenses that the contract requires you to share, among one or two others. You receive a receipt, of course, and as soon as the profits start rolling in your money will be returned — an investment you will never regret.

Please let me know your decision at once, as we cannot offer such an opportunity indefinitely.

Very truly yours,
John Wallen, Pres.

R.F.D. 68
Petaluma, Calif.
23 June 1970

Genius Inventions, Inc.
1448 Bonanza Blvd.
Los Angeles, Calif.

Dear Mr. Wallen:

I am sending you a money order for Five Hundred Dollars ($500.00) and one copy of the contract all signed and the full plans for my invention, The Self-Priming Solid-State Electronic Chicken. I am sorry if I hurt your feelings by what I said in my last letter as I did not just understand. Of course I can see now where you are perfectly right. I am certainly pleased and proud to feel that I am partners with a fine company like Genius Inventions, Inc., and I am sure we will both be very glad I saw your ad in the good old Farm and Home Magazine.

I hope you will not have any trouble understanding my plans. As you can see, the machine will produce eggs just the same as a chicken's eggs when you put the ingredients I listed in the hopper and turn it on. Most of them you can get at the drugstore, as I did here in Petaluma, but the Calcium I got at a feed store. I guess you have those in Los Angeles too. I can't send the working model because it is too big, so I will take advantage of Clause 6 of the contract where it says your Research and Development Division will build one from my plans so you can show the manufacturers. As already mentioned, I do not have any tecknicle knowledge of engineering, so on the plans where it shows a resistor or a transformer or something I have cut out the picture of it I got from the Radio & Electronics Magazine and pasted it in with lines showing where the wires go. I hope it will be all right. The little tube where it says "yolk" injection I got from a milking machine and it is rubber but I guess plastic will do.

Well, this will be all until I hear from you again.

Yours truly,
Emerson J. Minnick

GENIUS INVENTIONS, INC.
1448 Bonanza Blvd.
Los Angeles, Calif.
26 June 1970

Richard Sanders
Dept. 16-L
Richardson Aerospace Center

Dick:

Well, here we are again. Things are looking up, baby! The old sugar is still trickling in and just this morning I got a cute blue money order for five hundred fish. That's right, Dick my lad, the mark struck and struck hard on good old 3378-A. This one's right down your alley, so put on your R & D cap and get cracking. I wanted to catch you while you were still on shift, which is why I've sent this to your lab instead of leaving it at the pad. I hope you don't have a snoopy mail clerk there.

Now hang on to your hat, 'cause this is a good one. This guy figures he's invented a machine that makes *eggs!* You know, like a chicken, except there's no chicken. You just pour in a bit of this and that (there's a list attached to his plan) and turn it on and it starts making eggs. His plans, what I could make out of them — they seem to be written on the back of a feed bag or something — say it makes an egg every 65 seconds, or oftener if you turn the grade switch from AA to A or even B. I figure this one's good for the standard follow-up and from the sound of this guy we might ride it as long as we did with that mark that dreamed up the Laser-Beam Lawnmower. I've told him the five C's is for the patent application (don't these guys *ever* read the law?) and I'll give him a day or two and then tell him about the patent search fee. He's already saved me one step by suggesting himself that we work up a model, so you'd better start thinking about swiping some more convincing-looking components unless you think you've got enough up at the pad. You ought to see these plans, Dick. They look like a cross between a Pop Art collage and a schoolgirl's scrapbook, but that's your department, so I'll bring 'em with me this evening and we'll have a confab about it. I think we'd better actually go ahead and build this one, Dick. It's going to take me a while to forget that guy from Elko,

Nevada, who showed up that night and discovered we'd only made a simulation for the photo. He was a very ugly customer. Anyhow, see you tonight.

Jack

GENIUS INVENTIONS, INC.
1448 Bonanza Blvd.
Los Angeles, Calif.
28 June 1970

Mr. Emerson J. Minnick
R.F.D. 68
Petaluma, Calif.

Dear Mr. Minnick:

Please allow me to take this opportunity to extend my congratulations. Dr. Sanders, who heads up our Division of Research and Development, has told me in confidence that your invention represents a breakthrough of the first importance, and one which may well revolutionize the food industry. Our Engineering Section is working day and night to produce a working model which can be demonstrated to eager industrialists all over the country. Due to the unusual form in which the plans were drawn, it has been necessary to engage the services of a consultant engineer to put them into conventional shape for patent purposes. This has resulted in a bill for $300.00. I am happy to say that our initial application for a patent has been looked on with favor, and pending an official patent search by our Washington Branch (for which a nominal standard charge of $200.00 is made), there should be no difficulties from that direction.

There is one other small matter. While our Director of Research and Development was able to grasp instantly the genius inherent in your design, it has unfortunately been the case that, with other, less gifted inventors, we have built working models that did not work. It is therefore our unalterable policy to obtain a deposit in advance, against the cost of materials and labor for producing the model. Please realize that this in no way implies any lack of confidence on our part for your invention, but is a necessary measure to protect ourselves against impractical cranks who, unlike yourself, waste our time and money with nonsense. Since your invention shows such obvious potential, I have obtained special dispensation from the firm's Comptroller to reduce this deposit to a minimal amount of $500.00 which, I am sure you will agree, is only reasonable.

As shown on the separate statement, the total of these amounts comes to just one thousand dollars. We hope to obtain your remittance for this amount as soon as possible so that we can forge ahead with the development of your wonderful invention.

Very truly yours,
John Wallen, Pres.

R.F.D. 68
Petaluma, Calif.
2 July 1970

Genius Inventions, Inc.
1448 Bonanza Blvd.
Los Angeles, Calif.

Dear Mr. Wallen:

I am glad for the confidence you have shown in me by devoting so much of your important time to my invention. I told you it was a good one. I am a little surprised it costs so much to build down there, as I built the one here for only forty-five dollars ($45.00) and some parts from an old transistor set, but I guess things are more expensive in L.A. than in Petaluma. I have never been partners in owning a real Patent before and am glad you could work that out OK. I am sending along my money order for One Thousand Dollars Cash ($1,000.00) and this little bottle which is New-Laid Flavor. When the machine is making some eggs, pour in some of this in the hopper and then keep them in your refrigerator for a week and *don't* eat them. At the end of that time you will see the difference! Please let me know how things are coming along as I am anxious to start Cashing In.

Yours truly,
Emerson J. Minnick

Dept. 16-L
Richardson Aerospace

Dear Chief Genius:

I hear you got the grand from our champion fall guy. Good work! A few more like him and we could quit these lousy moonlighting jobs and go into it full time . . . advertise in the Mid-Western states and so on. The Mid-West must be stiff with 'em.

My foreman has been getting a bit suspicious, so I haven't been able to get all the parts for the Electronic Chicken. You know, when I got into the schematic, the thing had a kind of wacky logic, so, just for ducks, I'm going to build it just like he put it down. I had a bit of trouble getting the casting for the mold chamber, but a guy over at Light Metals did it for me during lunch hour, so that's that bit settled anyhow. We've taken this guy for so much we'd better build the thing the way he wants it. That way he's got no squawk coming when it doesn't work, right?

Bring a six-pack of beer along tonight and we'll dope it out. I have the circuitry set up on a breadboard layout right now, but I think I'll spray it onto a styrene panel . . . looks more professional and he'll probably figure a printed circuit cost a lot more to produce. See you tonight.

Dick

P.S. I really dig what he said about flavored eggs. Can you feature it? "What'll it be this morning, sir? Pistachio eggs or butter-vanilla eggs?" Yeccch!

GENIUS INVENTIONS, INC.
1448 Bonanza Blvd.
Los Angeles, Calif.
6 July 1970

Mr. Emerson J. Minnick
R.F.D. 68
Petaluma, Calif.

Dear Mr. Minnick:

We are happy to report that a patent search of the U.S. Government files has revealed no prior application for patent of a Self-Priming Solid-State Electronic Chicken and that we can therefore go ahead with our application for patent.

Our director of Research and Development, Dr. Sanders, has informed me that the working model is all but completed and that his department expects to carry out preliminary testing tomorrow. Since we expect no difficulty from that end of things, we are now at the stage of considering marketing procedures.

Our Public Relations and Advertising Departments have come up with a projection of a preliminary campaign, including an official unveiling to which members of the press and leading industrial representatives will be invited. As you will see from the attached cost estimate, this will cost an additional seven hundred dollars. According to our contract, Genius Inventions, Inc., is not responsible for promotional and advertising costs of untried inventions and we are therefore asking you to remit us this amount as an advance deposit. Our director of Public Relations has advised me to caution you against coming here to attend this ceremony or making it known to the public, except through us, that you are the inventor of the Electronic Chicken. As you are doubtless aware, the world of business is full of unscrupulous elements, and there are Powerful Interests who would not stop at physical intimidation or worse to prevent you from making your invention public. We at Genius Inventions feel that it is the least we can do as your partners to protect you from such elements and take these risks for you.

Our Advertising Department has brought out a projected brochure with illustrations and working drawings, and a witty, informative text done by one of the leading men in the field, which we feel would be invaluable in marketing your invention to best advantage. While we hesitate to urge you unduly, we feel that an extra four hundred dollars, which represents the printing and publications costs of this brochure, would be a wise investment. Should you decide in favor of this, copies will be sent to you as soon as they are produced.

Thanking you in advance for your understanding and remittance, I remain,

Very truly yours,
John Wallen, Pres.

GENIUS INVENTIONS, INC.
1448 Bonanza Blvd.
Los Angeles, Calif.
9 July 1970

Dick:

I'm leaving this by your place, 'cause you weren't at the lab when I stopped by. It worked smooth as a charm. He never even sent a reply, just a money order which *included* the money for the brochures. Eleven Hundred Simoleans in cool cash. I'm going downtown to cash it before it fades away like fairy gold, and then I'm going to that little printer we used before and have him run off a dozen of those corny brochures and a couple of hoked-up newspaper articles. Those should keep him happy for a while. We'd better start looking for a way out, though, pretty soon. Personally, I like the approach we pulled on that woman with the disposable mixing bowls, where we tell the mark we're going to be tied up in government research and our contract doesn't allow us to go ahead with private jobs so we have to pass up his good deal but we'll sell him our half interest real cheap. I figure this guy is maybe good for another grand, especially if we sweeten it with a couple of enthusiastic inquiries from "industrialists" on those phony letterheads we got from the songwriters' racket. Then again, it would maybe be better to cut the risk ('cause he might just get testy) and simply point out to him that his brainstorm doesn't work. Anyhow, think it over and let me know what you think in the morning, 'cause I want to get the letter off to him before he starts wondering where all his money is going.

Jack

Dept. 16-L
Richardson Aerospace
10 July

Jack:

You didn't find me at the lab because I was out getting drunk all day and it's nearly cost me my job. In fact I only just made it in here *this* morning. The honcho's giving me the evil eye, so I'm pretending to do a plan, but I've got to get this to you and I can't talk about it on the phone.

Get this now: Don't, repeat DO NOT sell our rights in that blessed Electronic Chicken 'cause the damn thing really works. I know what you're going to say, Jack, but I did the drinking *after* I found that out, not before. You remember when you left, after we'd had a good laugh about this Minnick guy's screwy plans and all. Well, I decided the hell with it, I'd stay up and finish it, so I did, at about two in the morning. Well, the temptation was too great, I guess, so I poured in all those things where it said to pour them, and turned her on and, by God, if the chamber didn't unmold an egg right on schedule. What's more it kept right on doing it, too, until the raw materials ran out. Over a dozen eggs in a quarter of an hour. I've looked over the drawings and I can see, kind of, how it works, though I still don't quite understand how the calcium-compound sprayer lines the shell mixture into the mold chamber, and I built the damn thing! Anyway, the point is, it *does* work. I had some of the eggs for breakfast this morning and they tasted fine. Not only that, Jack, hell, we could even make square eggs with a different mold chamber. Or eggs as big as ostrich eggs, or colored eggs . . . all precolored for Easter. Even those flavored ones he was talking about. Of course the chocolate idea isn't so hot, but what about ready-mixed eggs Benedict right in the shell? The possibilities are endless, man! And the biggest thing is, we can set up a series of these things right here in L.A. in an old garage or something and sell direct to the supermarkets, no transport, no chicken farms to worry about, nothing. And we own half of it!

You remember, we discussed once what we'd do if any of these screwballs actually came up with something. Well now's the time to do it. That's your department, so you'd better get onto it right away. The way I see it, we can do one of two things. Either we try and convince him the idea's no good and try and get him to sell his share to us (though, since it really does work, he must know it does and probably wouldn't go along with it) or else we become industrialists ourselves and buy up the manufacturing rights (our shares *and* his under some phony name) and go into business. You got any idea how many eggs are consumed in the greater L.A. area alone each day, Jack? Well, figure it out at three cents an egg to us, which will way undersell the competition from the regular poultry farmers, and figure a quarter of a cent to produce (that's about right) and multiply that by a production center under our franchise at every major city, and man-oh-man!

Anyhow, get working on him . . . feel him out about selling his share, and if he won't play we'll try the other bit. Hell, we have a half share sewn up legally anyway, so if worst comes to worst we can do it straight and *still* come out on easy street.

Bring a bottle of champagne tonight — hell, bring a case — and we'll have champagne and omelets.

Diamond Dick Sanders

P.S. I'm running off a dozen tonight with that new-laid flavor he sent (it smells like cod liver oil, but I'm in no mood to argue with him anymore) and laying them away for a week in the fridge with a couple of control eggs like he said. If these eggs can really taste farm-fresh after cold storage, we're on to something even bigger than I thought.

GENIUS INVENTIONS, INC.
1448 Bonanza Blvd.
Los Angeles, Calif.
10 July 1970

Dick:

You've gotta be kidding. If you're pulling my leg I'm going to clobber you over the head with it. Anyhow, I'm writing no letters to him until I *see* that thing produce an egg and eat it myself. I'm leaving this note to say I'll be a little late, 'cause I had a date which I'm putting off, so this had *better* be for real! Assuming that you're not kidding, I don't think it's a good idea to try and buy off the mark, 'cause that would just make him suspicious. I think we'll try the second way, through a dummy company. I've got some letterheads from the "Apex Marketing Corporation" which ought to do. I'll try him on a fairly low bid and let him chisel us up a bit, so he can think he's being shrewd. If this really *is* on the level, we could maybe find an angel and really put in a decent bid. See you tonight, anyway, and if this is all a story I'm going to break that bottle over your head.

Jack

R.F.D. 68
Petaluma, Calif.
14 July 1970

Genius Inventions, Inc.
1448 Bonanza Blvd.
Los Angeles, Calif.

Dear Mr. Wallen:

In receipt of yours of the 11th. I'm glad to hear that you have worked out everything so good and that Big Industry is interested. Like I said, it is sure-fire. You say this Apex company has offered Ten Thousand Dollars for a ten year license, but my half would only come to Five Thousand and I have already spent nearly Three and I guess you have spent a lot too, so I think we should ask them for more or find another buyer. As I had to sell most of my fryers and two acres of land to raise the money, I want to come out with at least ten thousand for myself, so will you please fix that up?

Yes, in reply to your question, I have been selling those eggs here for about six months through the local wholesaler. I guess most of them go to San Francisco.

Hoping to hear from you soon, since I could use the money quickly.

Yours truly,
Emerson J. Minnick

Dept. 16-L
Richardson Aerospace
17 July 1970

Jack:

Something damn funny is going on and I think you'd better come on over to my place tonight. You remember those eggs I added that mixture to? Well, tonight as I was closing the fridge I noticed that the light didn't go out when I closed it. It sounds crazy, but there's this little shiny bit at the back and just as the door is nearly closed you can see a reflection and tell when the light goes out — a split second before the door closes. Of course I never really think about it, but I noticed it when it *wasn't* there, you know what I mean? It just clicked with me that the light was staying on.

Well, I opened up the door and pushed the little button back and forth and no matter whether the switch was open or closed it stayed lit. I didn't want to take too long working with the door open like that 'cause all the cold falls out, so I went and got the Wheatstone Bridge from the test bench to see if I could trace a short in the wiring somewhere. Damn if there wasn't a strong electrical field — I should say electromagnetic, really — that had no business being around a fridge. Guess where the field originated? From the eggs, my boy. I know you're thinking I've flipped, but those eggs were and are putting out a field that's keeping that light lit; you come check it yourself. And you haven't heard all of it. I had the sample eggs marked with grease pencil and, of course, the eggs this is coming from are the ones I added the "farm-fresh" liquid to. We should have checked this thing out better, Jack, before we paid that guy all that money. Anyhow, I couldn't resist the temptation, so I took one out, closed the door — to hell with the light — and opened it into a bowl. Jack, it's . . . well, you'd better come see, or I'm going to think I've got the d.t.'s or something. I'll swear this thing was about ready to hatch out and there's like a tiny transmitter that . . . no, you come see, *then* we'll talk. I've got it preserved in a glass of vodka, but it's giving me the creeps. I'll expect you about six.

> Yours in utter sobriety,
> Dick

Note found crumpled on floor by Nathan Bathurst, building superintendent, while investigating sudden vanishing of tenant from 126-B.

Jack, I'm writing this in snatches when they're not looking I'll try and shove it under the door and if you see it don't come in for Christ's sake Jack don't come in this flat but get the police or somebody right away. They were waiting when I got home and already four of them are hatched out and somehow they opened the door from inside and got out Jack they come from some place where it's dark and cold and the light and cold in the fridge is just right to hatch them so unplug the fridge first Jack please and break or burn all those eggs and Jack they've been controlling Minnick so send someone there and I don't know how many more . . .

Discovered written on the inside of an eggshell, by Mrs. Cecelie Patterson of 426 La Vista Drive, Los Angeles, Calif., while making a pound cake:

HELP! WE ARE BEING HELD PRISONER AT AN EGG FACTORY AND SOME OF THE EGGS CONTAIN CREATURES FROM ANOTHER PLANET WHO WANT TO KILL EVERYONE. SO IF THE LIGHT IN YOUR FRIDGE STAYS ON, BREAK ALL YOUR EGGS BEFORE IT IS TOO LATE! GET HELP! THIS IS NOT A JOKE OR ADVERTISING STUNT. THEY ARE VERY DANGEROUS, SO IF YOU READ THIS PLEASE CALL THE POLICE!

The Night He Cried

FRITZ LEIBER

This story, a satire on Mickey Spillane, is particularly distinguished by being much better than anything Spillane wrote. I myself never read Spillane, but Janet tells me that during his high popularity in the early fifties, she was a medical student with night duty on obstetrics. She and her fellow inmates kept awake, between deliveries, by reading Spillane out loud to each other, laughing hysterically — the only appropriate emotion to either obstetrical night duty or reading Spillane. Both! right between the legs

I GLANCED DOWN my neck secretly at the two snowy hillocks, ruby peaked, that were pushing out my blouse tautly without the aid of a brassiere. I decided they'd more than do. So I turned away scornfully as his vast top-down convertible cruised past my street lamp. I struck my hip and a big match against the fluted column, and lit a cigarette. I was Lili Marlene to a T — or rather to a V-neckline. (I must tell you that my command of Earth idiom and allusion is remarkable, but if you'd had my training you wouldn't wonder.)

The convertible slowed down and backed up. I smiled. I'd been certain that my magnificently formed milk glands would turn the trick. I puffed on my cigarette languorously.

"Hi, Babe!"

Right from the first I'd known it was the man I was supposed to contact. Handsome hatchet face. Six or seven feet tall. Quite a creature. Male, as they say.

I hopped into his car, vaulting over the low door before he opened it. We zoomed off through New York's purple, smelly twilight.

"What's your name, Big Male?" I asked him.

Scorning to answer, he stripped me with his eyes. But I had confidence in my milk glands. Lord knows, I'd been hours perfecting them.

"Slickie Millane, isn't it?" I prompted recklessly.

"That's possible," he conceded, poker-faced.

"Well then, what are we waiting for?" I asked him, nudging him with the leftermost of my beautifully conical milk glands.

"Look here, Babe," he told me, just a bit coldly, "I'm the one who dispenses sex and justice in this area."

I snuggled submissively under his encircling right arm, still nudging him now and again with my left milk gland. The convertible sped. The skyscrapers shrank, exfoliated, became countryside. The convertible stopped.

As the hand of his encircling arm began to explore my prize possessions, I drew away a bit, not frustratingly, and informed him, "Slickie dear, I am from Galaxy Center . . ."

"What's that — a magazine publisher?" he demanded hotly, being somewhat inflamed by my cool milk glands.

". . . and we are interested in how sex and justice are dispensed in all areas," I went on, disregarding his interruption and his somewhat juvenile fondlings. "To be bold, we suspect that you may be somewhat misled about this business of sex."

Vertical, centimeter-deep furrows creased his brow. His head poised above mine like a hawk's. "What are you talking about, Babe?" he demanded with suspicious rage, even snatching his hands away.

"Briefly, Slickie," I said, "you do not seem to feel that sex is for the production of progeny or for the mutual solace of two creatures. You seem to think — "

His rage exploded into action. He grabbed a great big gun out of the glove compartment. I sprang to my two transmuted nether tentacles — most handsome gams if I, the artist, do say so. He jabbed the muzzle of the gun into my midriff.

"That's exactly what I mean, Slickie," I managed to say before my beautiful midriff, which I'd been at such pains to perfect, erupted into smoke and ghastly red splatter. I did a backward flipflop out of the car and lay still — a most fetching corpse with a rucked-up skirt. As the convertible snorted off triumphantly, I snagged hold of the rear bumper, briefly changing my hand back to a tentacle for better gripping. Before the pavement had abraded more than a few grams of my substance, I pulled myself up onto the bumper, where I proceeded to reconstitute my vanished midriff with material from the air, the rest of my body, and the paint on the trunk case. On this occasion the work went rapidly, with no artistic gropings, since I had the curves memorized from the first time I'd worked them out. Then I touched up my abrasions, stripped myself, whipped myself up a snazzy silver lamé evening frock out of chromium from the bumper, and put in time creating costume jewelry out of the taillight and the rest of the chrome.

The car stopped at a bar and Slickie slid out. For a moment his proud profile was silhouetted against the smoky glow. Then he was inside. I threw away the costume jewelry and climbed over the folded top and popped down on the leather-upholstered seat, scarcely a kilogram lighter than when I'd first sat there.

The minutes dragged. To pass them, I mentally reviewed the thousand-and-some basic types of mutual affection on the million-plus planets, not forgetting the one and only basic type of love.

There was a burst of juke-box jazz. Footsteps tracked from the bar toward the convertible. I leaned back comfortably with my silver-filmed milk glands dramatically highlighted.

"Hi, Slickie," I called, making my voice sweet and soft to cushion the shock.

Nevertheless it was a considerable one. For all of ten seconds he stood there, canted forward a little, like a wooden Indian that's just been nudged from behind and is about to topple.

Then with a naive ingenuity that rather touched me, he asked huskily, "Hey, have you got a twin sister?"

"Could be," I said with a shrug that jogged my milk glands deliciously.

"Well, what are you doing in my car?"

"Waiting for you," I told him simply.

He considered that as he slowly and carefully walked around the car and got behind the wheel, never taking his eyes off me. I nudged him in my usual manner. He jerked away.

"What are you up to?" he inquired suspiciously.

"Why are you surprised, Slickie?" I countered innocently. "I've heard this sort of thing happens to you all the time."

"What sort of thing?"

"Girls turning up in your car, your bar, your bedroom — everywhere."

"Where'd you hear it?"

"I read it in your Spike Mallet books."

"Oh," he said, somewhat mollified. But then his suspicion came back. "But what are you really up to?" he demanded.

"Slickie," I assured him with complete sincerity, bugging my beautiful eyes, "I just love you."

This statement awakened in him an irritation so great that it overrode his uneasiness about me, for he cuffed me in the face — so suddenly that I almost forgot and changed it back to my top tentacle.

"I make the advances around here, Babe," he asserted harshly.

Completely under control again, I welled a tiny trickle of blood out of the left-hand corner of my gorgeous mouth. "Anything you say, Slickie, dear," I assented submissively and cuddled up against him in a prim, girlish way to which he could hardly take exception.

But I must have bothered or at least puzzled him, for he drove slowly, his dark-eaved eyes following an invisible tennis ball that bounded between me and the street ahead. Abruptly the eaves lifted and he smiled.

"Look, I just got an idea for a story," he said. "There's this girl from Galaxy

Center — " and he whipped around to watch my reactions, but I didn't blink.

He continued, "I mean, she's sort of from the center of the galaxy, where everything's radioactive. Now there's this guy that's got her up in his attic." His face grew deeply thoughtful. "She's the most beautiful girl in the universe and he loves her like crazy, but she's all streaming with hard radiations and it'll kill him if he touches her."

"Yes, Slickie — and then?" I prompted after the car had dreamed its way for several blocks between high buildings.

He looked at me sharply. "That's all. Don't you get it?"

"Yes, Slickie," I assured him soothingly. My statement seemed to satisfy him, but he was still edgy.

He stopped the car in front of an apartment hotel that thrust toward the stars with a dark presumptuousness. He got out on the street side and walked around the rear end and suddenly stopped. I followed him. He was studying the gray bumper and the patch of raw sheet metal off which I'd used the paint. He looked around at me where I stood sprayed with silver lamé in the revealing lamplight.

"Wipe your chin," he said critically.

"Why not kiss the blood off it, Slickie?" I replied with an ingenuousness I hoped would take the curse off the suggestion.

"Aw nuts," he said nervously and stalked into the foyer so swiftly he might have been trying to get away from me. However, he made no move to stop me when I followed him into the tiny place and the even tinier elevator. In the latter cubicle I maneuvered so as to give him a series of breathtaking scenic views of the Grand Tetons that rose behind the plunging silver horizon of my neckline, and he unfroze considerably. By the time he opened the door of his apartment he had got so positively cordial that he urged me across the threshold with a casual spank.

It was just as I had visualized it — theit — the tiger skins, the gun racks, the fireplace, the open bedroom door, the bar just beside it, the adventures of Spike Mallet in handsomely tooled leather bindings, the vast divan covered with zebra skin . . .

On the last was stretched a beautiful, ice-faced blonde in a filmy negligee.

This was a complication for which I wasn't prepared. I stood rooted by the door while Slickie walked swiftly past me.

The blonde slithered to her feet. There was murder in her glacial eyes. "You two-timing rat!" she grated. Her hand darted under her negligee. Slickie's snaked under the left-hand side of his jacket.

Then it hit me what was going to happen. She would bring out a small but deadly silver-plated automatic, but before she could level it, Slickie's cannon would make a red ruin of her midriff.

There I was, standing twenty feet away from both of them — and this poor girl couldn't reconstitute herself!

Swifter than thought I changed my arms back to upper dorsal tentacles and jerked back both Slickie's and the girl's elbows. They turned around, considerably startled, and saw me standing twenty feet away. I'd turned my tentacles back to arms before they'd noticed them. Their astonishment increased.

But I knew I had won only a temporary respite. Unless something happened, Slickie's trigger-blissful rage would swiftly be refocused on this foolish fragile creature. To save her, I had to divert his ire to myself.

"Get that little tramp out of here," I ordered Slickie from the corner of my mouth as I walked past him to the bar.

"Easy, Babe," he warned me.

I poured myself a liter of scotch — I had to open a second bottle to complete the measure — and downed it. I really didn't need it, but the assorted molecules were congenial building blocks, and I was rather eager to get back to normal weight.

"Haven't you got that tramp out of here yet?" I demanded, eyeing him scornfully over my insouciant silver-filmed shoulder.

"Easy, Babe," he repeated, the vertical furrows creasing his brow to a depth of at least a centimeter and a half.

"That's telling her, Slickie," the blonde applauded.

"You two-timing rat!" I plagiarized, whipping up my silver skirt as if to whisk a gun from my nonexistent girdle.

His cannon coughed. Always a good sportsman, I moved an inch so that the bullet, slightly misaimed, took me exactly in the right eye, messily blowing off the back of my head. I winked at Slickie with my left eye and fell back through the doorway into the bedroom darkness.

I knew I had no time to spare. When a man's shot one girl he begins to lose his natural restraint. Lying on the floor, I reconstituted my eye and did a quick patch job on the back of my head in seventeen seconds flat.

As I emerged from the bedroom, they were entering into a clinch, each holding a gun lightly against the other's back.

"Slickie," I said, pouring myself a scant half liter of scotch, "I told you about that tramp."

The ice-blonde squawked, threw up her hands as if she'd had a shot of strychnine, and ran out the door. I fancied I could feel the building tilt as she leaned on the elevator button.

I downed the scotch and advanced, shattering the paralyzed space-time that Slickie seemed to be depending on as a defense.

"Slickie," I said, "let's get down to cases. I am indeed from Galaxy Center, and we very definitely don't like your attitude. We don't care what your motives are, or whether they are derived from jumbled genes, a curdled childhood, or a sick society. We simply love you and we want you to reform." I grabbed him by a shivering shoulder that was now hardly higher than my waist, and dragged him into the bedroom, snatching up the rest of the scotch on the way. I switched on the light. The bedroom was a really lush love nest. I drained the scotch — there was about a half liter left — and faced the cowering Slickie. "Now do to me," I told him uncompromisingly, "the thing you're always going to do to those girls, except you have to shoot them."

He frothed like an epileptic, snatched out his cannon, and emptied its magazine into various parts of my torso, but since he hit only two of my five brains, I wasn't bothered. I reeled back bloodily through the blue smoke and fell into the bathroom. I felt real crazy — maybe I shouldn't have taken that last half liter. I reconstituted my torso faster even than I had my head, but my silver lamé frock was a mess. Not wanting to waste time and reluctant to use any more reconstituting energy, I stripped it off and popped into the off-the-shoulders evening dress the blonde had left lying over the edge of the bathtub. The dress wasn't a bad fit. I went back into the bedroom. Slickie was sobbing softly at the foot of the bed and gently beating his head against it.

"Slickie," I said, perhaps a shade too curtly, "about this love business — "

He sprang for the ceiling but didn't quite burst through it. Falling back, by chance on his feet, he headed for the hall. Now it wasn't in my orders from Galaxy Center that he run away and excite this world — in fact, my superiors had strictly forbidden such a happening. I had to stop Slickie. But I was a bit confused — perhaps fuddled by that last half liter. I hesitated — then he was too far away, had too big a start. To stop him, I knew I'd have to use tentacles. Swifter than thought I changed them and shot them out.

"Slickie," I cried reassuringly, dragging him to me.

Then I realized that in my excitement, instead of using my upper dorsal tentacles, I'd used the upper ventral ones I kept transmuted into my beautiful milk glands. I do suppose they looked rather strange to Slickie as they came out of the bosom of my off-the-shoulders evening dress and drew him to me.

Frightening sounds came out of him. I let him go and tried to resume my gorgeous shape, but now I was really confused (that last half liter!) and lost control of my transmutations. When I found myself turning my topmost tentacle into a milk gland I gave up completely and — except for a lung and vocal cords — resumed my normal shape. It was quite a relief. After all, I had done what Galaxy Center had intended I should. From now on, the mere sight of a brassiere in a show window would be enough to give Slickie the shakes.

Still, I was bothered about the guy. As I say, he'd touched me.

I caressed him tenderly with my tentacles. Over and over again I explained that I was just a heptapus and that Galaxy Center had selected me for the job simply because my seven tentacles would transmute nicely into the seven extremities of the human female.

Over and over again I told him how I loved him.

It didn't seem to help. Slickie Millane continued to weep hysterically.

The Big Pat Boom

DAMON KNIGHT

When I was in high school, I took (or, to be more precise, I was given) a course in economics. It was the first school subject I had ever studied in my life that I could not understand. It was a bad blow. I tried, heaven knows, but I failed, and ever since then I have had only the moldiest thoughts about economics and economists. I thought I was alone in this, and now along comes Damon Knight, a fearfully intelligent fellow, who points out clearly in this story what economics is full of.

THE LONG, SHINY CAR pulled up with a whir of turbines and a puff of dust. The sign over the roadside stand read: BASKETS. CURIOS. Farther down, another sign over a glass-fronted rustic building announced: SQUIRE CRAW-FORD'S COFFEE MILL. TRY OUR DOUGHNUTS. Beyond that was a pasture, with a barn and silo set back from the road.

The two aliens sat quietly and looked at the signs. They both had hard purplish skins and little yellow eyes. They were wearing gray tweed suits. Their bodies looked approximately human, but you could not see their chins, which were covered by orange scarves.

Martha Crawford came hustling out of the house and into the basket stand, drying her hands on her apron. After her came Llewellyn Crawford, her husband, still chewing his cornflakes.

"Yes, sir — ma'am?" Martha asked nervously. She glanced at Llewellyn for support, and he patted her shoulder. Neither of them had ever seen an alien real close to.

One of the aliens, seeing the Crawfords behind their counter, leisurely got out of the car. He, or it, was puffing a cigar stuck through a hole in the orange scarf.

"Good morning," Mrs. Crawford said nervously. "Baskets? Curios?"

The alien blinked its yellow eyes solemnly. The rest of its face did not change. The scarf hid its chin and mouth, if any. Some said that the aliens had no chins, others that they had something instead of chins that was so squirmy and awful that no human could bear to look at it. People called them "Hurks" because they came from a place called Zeta Herculis.

The Hurk glanced at the baskets and gimcracks hung over the counter, and puffed its cigar. Then it said, in a blurred but comprehensible voice, "What is that?" It pointed downward with one horny, three-fingered hand.

"The little Indian papoose?" Martha Crawford said, in a voice that rose to a squeak. "Or the birchbark calendar?"

"No, that," said the Hurk, pointing down again. This time, craning over the counter, the Crawfords were able to see that it was looking at a large, disk-shaped gray something that lay on the ground.

"That?" Llewellyn asked doubtfully.

"That."

Llewellyn Crawford blushed. "Why — that's just a cowpat. One of them cows from the dairy got loose from the herd yesterday, and she must have dropped that there without me noticing."

"How much?"

The Crawfords stared at him, or it, without comprehension. "How much what?" Llewellyn asked finally.

"How much," the alien growled around its cigar, "for the cowpat?"

The Crawfords exchanged glances. "I never *heard* — " said Martha in an undertone, but her husband shushed her. He cleared his throat. "How about ten ce — Well, I don't want to cheat you — how about a quarter?"

The alien produced a large change purse, laid a quarter on the counter, and grunted something to its companion in the car.

The other alien got out, bringing a square porcelain box and a gold-handled shovel. With the shovel, she — or it — carefully picked up the cowpat and deposited it in the box.

Both aliens then got into the car and drove away, in a whine of turbines and a cloud of dust.

The Crawfords watched them go, then looked at the shiny quarter lying on the counter. Llewellyn picked it up and bounced it in his palm. "Well, say!" He began to smile.

All that week the roads were full of aliens in their long shiny cars. They went everywhere, saw everything, paid their way with bright new-minted coins and crisp paper bills.

There was some talk against the government for letting them in, but they were good for business and made no trouble. Some claimed to be tourists, others said they were sociology students on a field trip.

Llewellyn Crawford went into the adjoining pasture and picked out four cowpats to deposit near his basket stand. When the next Hurk came by, Llewellyn asked, and got, a dollar apiece.

"But why do they *want* them?" Martha wailed.

"What difference does that make?" her husband asked. *"They* want 'em
— *we* got 'em! If Ed Lacey calls again about that mortgage payment, tell him
not to worry!" He cleared off the counter and arranged the new merchandise
on it. He jacked his price up to two dollars, then to five.

Next day he ordered a new sign: COWPATS.

One fall afternoon two years later, Llewellyn Crawford strode into his living
room, threw his hat in a corner, and sat down hard. He glared over his glasses
at the large circular object, tastefully tinted in concentric rings of blue, orange,
and yellow, which was mounted over the mantelpiece. To the casual eye, this
might have been a genuine "Trophy"-class pat, a museum piece, painted on
the Hurk planet; but in fact, like so many artistic ladies nowadays, Mrs.
Crawford had painted and mounted it herself.

"What's the matter, Lew?" she asked apprehensively. She had a new hairdo
and was wearing a New York dress, but looked peaked and anxious.

"Matter!" Llewellyn grunted. "Old man Thomas is a damn fool, that's all.
Four hundred dollars a head! Can't buy a cow at a decent price anymore."

"Well, Lew, we do have seven herds already, don't we, and — "

"Got to have more to meet the demand, Martha!" said Llewellyn, sitting up.
"My heaven, I'd think you could see that. With queen pats bringing up to
fifteen dollars, and not enough to go 'round — And fifteen *hundred* for an
emperor pat, if you're lucky enough — "

"Funny we never thought there was so many kinds of pats," Martha said
dreamily. "The emperor — that's the one with the double whorl?"

Llewellyn grunted, picking up a magazine.

"Seems like a person could kind of — "

A kindly gleam came into Llewellyn's eyes. "Change one around?" he said.
"Nope — been tried. I was reading about it in here just yesterday." He held
up the current issue of *The American Pat Dealer,* then began to turn the glossy
pages. "Pat-O-Grams," he read aloud. "Preserving Your Pats. Dairying
— a Profitable Sideline. Nope. Oh, here it is. 'Fake Pats a Flop.' See, it says
here some fellow down in Amarillo got hold of an emperor and made a plaster
mold. Then he used the mold on a couple of big cull pats — says here they
was so perfect you couldn't tell the difference. But the Hurks wouldn't buy.
They knew."

He threw the magazine down, then turned to stare out the back window
toward the sheds. "There's that fool boy just setting in the yard again. Why
ain't he working?" Llewellyn rose, cranked down the louver, shouted through
the opening, "You, Delbert! Delbert!" He waited. "Deaf too," he muttered.

"I'll go tell him you want — " Martha began, struggling out of her apron.

"No, never mind — go myself. Have to keep after 'em every damn minute."
Llewellyn marched out the kitchen door and across the yard to where a
gangling youth sat on a trolley, slowly eating an apple.

"Delbert!" said Llewellyn, exasperated.

"Oh — hello, Mr. Crawford," said the youth, with a gap-toothed grin. He took a last bite from the apple, then dropped the core. Llewellyn's gaze followed it. Owing to his missing front teeth, Delbert's apple cores were like nothing in this world.

"Why ain't you trucking pats out to the stand?" Llewellyn demanded. "I don't pay you to set on no empty trolley, Delbert."

"Took some out this morning," the boy said. "Frank, he told me to take 'em back."

"He what?"

Delbert nodded. "Said he hadn't sold but two. You ask him if I'm lying."

"Do that," Llewellyn grunted. He turned on his heel and strode back across the yard.

Out at the roadside, a long car was parked beside a battered pickup at the pat stand. It pulled out as Llewellyn started toward it, and another one drove up. As he approached the stand, the alien was just getting back in. The car drove off.

Only one customer was left at the stand, a whiskered farmer in a checked shirt. Frank, the attendant, was leaning comfortably on the counter. The display shelves behind him were well filled with pats.

"Morning, Roger," Llewellyn said with well-feigned pleasure. "How's the family? Sell you a nice pat this morning?"

"Well, I don't know," said the whiskered man, rubbing his chin. "My wife's had her eye on that one there" — he pointed to a large, symmetrical pat on the middle shelf — "but at them prices — "

"You can't do better, believe me, Roger. It's an investment," said Llewellyn earnestly. "Frank, what did that last Hurk buy?"

"Nothing," said Frank. A persistent buzz of music came from the radio in his breast pocket. "Just took a picture of the stand and drove off."

"Well, what did the one before — "

With a whir of turbines, a long shiny car pulled up behind him. Llewellyn turned. The three aliens in the car were wearing red felt hats with comic buttons sewed all over them and carried Yale pennants. Confetti was strewn on their gray tweed suits.

One of the Hurks got out and approached the stand, puffing a cigar through the hole in his — or its — orange scarf.

"Yes, sir?" said Llewellyn at once, hands clasped, bending forward slightly. "A nice pat this morning?"

The alien looked at the gray objects behind the counter. He, or it, blinked its yellow eyes and made a curious gurgling noise. After a moment Llewellyn decided that it was laughing.

"What's funny?" he demanded, his smile fading.

"Not funny," said the alien. "I laugh because I am happy. I go home tomorrow — our field trip is over. Okay to take a picture?" He raised a small lensed machine in one purple claw.

"Well, I suppose — " Llewellyn said uncertainly. "Well, you say you're going home? You mean all of you? When will you be coming back?"

"We are not coming back," the alien said. He, or it, pressed the camera, extracted the photograph and looked at it, then grunted and put it away. "We are grateful for an entertaining experience. Good-bye." He turned and got into the car. The car drove off in a cloud of dust.

"Like that the whole morning," Frank said. "They don't buy nothing — just take pictures."

Llewellyn felt himself beginning to shake. "Think he means it — they're all going away?"

"Radio said so," Frank replied. "And Ed Coon was through here this morning from Hortonville. Said *he* ain't sold a pat since day 'fore yesterday."

"Well, I don't understand it," Llewellyn said. "They can't just all quit — " His hands were trembling badly, and he put them in his pockets. "Say, Roger," he said to the whiskered man, "now just how much would you want to pay for that pat?"

"Well — "

"It's a ten-dollar pat, you know," Llewellyn said, moving closer. His voice had turned solemn. "Prime pat, Roger."

"I know that, but — "

"What would you say to seven fifty?"

"Well, I don't know. Might give — say, five."

"Sold," said Llewellyn. "Wrap that one up, Frank."

He watched the whiskered man carry his trophy off to the pickup. "Mark 'em all down, Frank," he said faintly. "Get whatever you can."

The long day's debacle was almost over. Arms around each other, Llewellyn and Martha Crawford watched the last of the crowd leaving the pat stand. Frank was cleaning up. Delbert, leaning against the side of the stand, was eating an apple.

"It's the end of the world, Martha," Llewellyn said huskily. Tears stood in his eyes. "Prime pats, going two for a nickel!"

Headlights blinding in the dusk, a long, low car came nosing up to the pat stand. In it were two green creatures in raincoats, with feathery antennae that stood up through holes in their blue pork-pie hats. One of them got out and approached the pat stand with a curious scuttling motion. Delbert gaped, dropping his apple core.

"Serps!" Frank hissed, leaning over the stand toward Llewellyn. "Heard about 'em on the radio. From Gamma Serpentis, radio said."

The green creature was inspecting the half-bare shelves. Horny lids flickered across its little bright eyes.

"Pat, sir — ma'am?" Llewellyn asked nervously. "Not many left right now, but — "

"What is *that?*" the Serp asked in a rustling voice, pointing downward with one claw.

The Crawfords looked. The Serp was pointing to a misshapen, knobby something that lay beside Delbert's boot.

"That there?" Delbert asked, coming partially to life. "That's a apple core." He glanced across to Llewellyn, and a gleam of intelligence seemed to come into his eyes. "Mr. Crawford, I quit," he said clearly. Then he turned to the alien. "That's a *Delbert Smith* apple core," he said.

Frozen, Llewellyn watched the Serp pull out a billfold and scuttle forward. Money changed hands. Delbert produced another apple and began enthusiastically reducing it to a core.

"Say, Delbert," said Llewellyn, stepping away from Martha. His voice squeaked, and he cleared his throat. "Looks like we got a good little thing going here. Now, if you was smart, you'd rent this pat stand — "

"Nope, Mr. Crawford," said Delbert indistinctly, with his mouth full of apple. "Figure I'll go over to my uncle's place — he's got a orchard."

The Serp was hovering nearby, watching the apple core and uttering little squeals of appreciation.

"Got to be close to your source of *supply,* you know," said Delbert, wagging his head wisely.

Speechless, Llewellyn felt a tug at his sleeve. He looked down: It was Ed Lacey, the banker.

"Say, Lew, I tried to get you all afternoon, but your phone didn't answer. About your collateral on those loans . . ."

The Adventure of
the Solitary Engineer

JOHN M. FORD

A distinct but too-often-little-regarded subdivision of the science fiction story is the one that George Scithers, editor of Isaac Asimov's Science Fiction Magazine, *calls the "horrid pun." I've written some that have been short, simple, straightforward, and terribly funny (no matter how loud the groans of my nearest and dearest), but there are connoisseurs of the art who want the point made long and complex with distortion piled upon distortion. Since I am much too pure to write such a story, we have here something that will sate the most jaded and perverse appetite for the verbally grotesque.*

"MURDER OR SUICIDE, DOCTOR?"

B. Watson Goodwin shifted in his chair and immediately wished he'd kept his mouth shut. But the man he had spoken to seemed not to notice; he kept on shuffling through the pile of papers and photographs on his desk, pausing now and again to adjust the thick spectacles that rode low on his beaklike nose.

Goodwin did not feel like a Field Operative of Earthsystem Security Forces, though that was what he was. The role of Starcop bothered him. He didn't feel big enough for it. Now he was in the company of the man reputed to be Earth's greatest authority on extraterrestrial planets, and he felt very small indeed.

Dr. Willkie Moon, Earth's greatest and so forth, pushed his glasses up his nose once more — a gesture Goodwin now knew to be futile — and sat back in his chair. "Murder?" he said. "A man is found dead, on a tiny planet where he is the only living being, and you ask me if it is murder?"

Goodwin cleared his throat, and felt himself shrink another few centimeters. "Well, ordinarily, Doctor Moon — of course not. But there is the matter of the recording device, on Harfleur's night side."

"The recording device did nothing on the night side?"

"Actually, Doctor, it did, but — if you'll read that page of the report — "

"Never mind," said Dr. Moon, with a considerable sigh. "I have read it. What I would like you to do is summarize the events in your own words."

"Very well, Doctor." Goodwin looked around Dr. Moon's lodgings, trying to settle his nerves. He was surrounded by the artifacts that every professor of long tenure acquires: dozens of books, each reprinting an article Dr. Moon had written in his freshman year; one hundred and forty-five pipes of various descriptions, each one matched to a cardigan sweater with patches on the elbows; a group portrait of the professors who had officiated at Dr. Moon's orals, with large red crosses drawn over those who had died. It was said that Dr. Moon had not left this room in the past twenty-two years. It *was* true that the rug badly needed vacuuming, but it wasn't that bad.

Goodwin finally gathered his *chi* and began:

"Harfleur, Meade's World, is a barren and airless rock some two thousand kilometers in diameter. It appears to be rather similar in type to Earth's Moon — uh, satellite — "

"I know what the thing's called," said Dr. Moon. "Go on."

"Uh — so it was decided to do a long-term examination, in light of the considerable mineral wealth extracted from our own Moon.

"A string of high-density disk recorders was established around Harfleur's surface, each capable of storing three months' environmental data before the disk needed replacing. The recorders are fully automated and highly reliable. However, we provided one human backup; a geologist named Bruce Dee. Dee was given a complete pressurized station, with full recreation facilities and a triple-redundant communication system with Earth."

"Only one man?"

"Dee was a loner by nature. We've found that two-person teams — of whatever kind — wind up hating each other within a few weeks. So if we can't justify the expense of a full team, we send one solitary type. It's worked just fine."

"Until now."

"Until now. About two weeks ago the winter season was ending on Harfleur — there are no real seasons, of course; that's just what we call the period it spends at aphelion. It was time to pick up a set of disks and resupply Dee's station.

"We found Bruce Dee slumped over one of the recorders, dead. His suit was intact, but the heating system was completely off. He appears to have died of freezing."

"I assume his energy supply was intact."

"The suits are plutonium-fueled, and the power pile was operating normally. Even if it had not been, his surface-scooter was less than thirty meters away, and it has an auxiliary power socket for such emergencies."

Dr. Moon picked up a photograph. It showed a pressure-suited figure lying face down on something like a two-meter metal spider: the recording station. One of the man's gloved hands was tight on the recorder's sampling claw.

"No," said the extraterrologist, "it does not have the look of suicide. But . . . murder? By whom, and for what?"

"We don't know, Doctor. But we do know this: Harfleur is completely lifeless, as nineteen of the twenty recorders we planted attest. But the twentieth — the one where Bruce Dee died — "

" 'Reports presence of organic molecules.' Very interesting." Dr. Moon put the report down. "So you feel that perhaps some mysteriously hidden native of the planet killed Mr. Dee by some means unknown to science."

"Not necessarily! I mean . . . I have a hypothesis."

"Tell me."

"It could have been someone trying to tamper with the recorders, to make us lose interest in the planet — then move in himself and mine the place out."

"An excellent hypothesis."

Goodwin grew four meters in an instant.

"Requiring only the presence of a claim jumper who can walk around without a pressure suit."

Goodwin shrank five meters.

"I wonder — I wonder. Would you do something for me, Mr. Goodwin?"

"Certainly, Dr. Moon. And call me Watson, please."

"Only if I must. Have ESF scrape the late Mr. Dee's left suit glove — the one he was gripping the sampling claw with. And this photograph, of the interior of Mr. Dee's quarters — have it blown up as large as you possibly can. One more thing. Get me the complete technical printout from the recorder in question — no summaries, no condensations."

"At once, Doctor. Would you care to come with me to the lab? It'll save some time."

"Oh, no, no. It's said that I haven't left this room in twenty-two years."

Goodwin smiled as he stood to go. There was no accounting for the eccentricities of the true genius.

Dr. Moon said, "Lost my key then, actually. Too cheap to have the locks changed."

Dr. Moon finished his perusal of the new evidence. "Aha! Look here, Watson; I have it!"

"Have what?"

"Your invisible alien attacker, of course. Here he is, captured upon this photograph."

"Where?"

"In the station waste can. Look closely."

"I see a bottle."

"Watson, you *see*, but you do not — oh, forget it. Indeed it is a bottle, Watson; a bottle that once held Chateau Ganymede 'eighty-six, fermented from subsurface fungi on Jupiter's moon, a vile concoction. I keep mine in a radioactive ash scuttle. There is your murderer."

"You mean Bruce Dee was drunk."

"As the proverbial Tau Cetan, Watson. Now imagine, as I reconstruct our geologist's last moments on Earth — er, Harfleur. Consumed with a loneliness he has never before felt, surrounded by the rocks he once felt to be his dearest friends, Dee takes to drink. He soon develops a need for the stuff at every moment of crisis.

"Now, he is going out to inspect the recorders he hates, which pick over the rocks he hates, upon the worldlet he hates. He is going out upon — " Dr. Moon went to the shelf, took down a small ornately bound book. On the flyleaf was an autograph, facing the title *The Dynamics of an Asteroid.* " — out upon darkside, by my calculations. And before he enters that gloom, he must have a drink. But he is already wearing his pressure suit!

"No matter to him, such is his need. He uncorks the bottle with his gloved hands and, since he is becoming uncomfortable in the suit inside his climate-controlled outpost, he switches off its internal heating.

"And now, full of Ganymedan courage, he leaves his shelter — forgetting to turn his heater on again; for he is fortified against the cold by the effects of too much spirit of toadstool.

"But the heat must fail, Watson; and it does, but he notices too late. And chilled, intoxicated, he falls against the recorder, clutching vainly at its sampling claw with this glove." Dr. Moon waved the silver gauntlet.

"But the organic matter — "

"From the glove, Watson. You made the mistake of reading only the summarized chromatography report, not the complete one. And you did not have my trained eye. I can identify four hundred varieties of tobacco, two hundred and seven imprints of finger, tentacle or filament, *and* three hundred and eighty-two types of wine cork, even when in bits too small to see with the naked eye."

"But," gasped Goodwin, "how was the content of our winter's disk made a spurious summary by this scum of cork?"

"It was elementally adhered, Watson."

B.C. by permission of Johnny Hart and Field Enterprises, Inc.

"Could you direct us to the Mideastern Ecclesiastical Conference?"

"But you don't understand! I haven't even seen Europe yet!"

"Just one more question. Would you like sour cream and chopped chives on your baked potatoes?"

"I'm not worried. By the time the population crunch really hits, we'll be sending the excess off to Earth or somewhere."

"Somehow I pictured my first ride on a flying saucer rather differently."

"If it hadn't been for diehard opposition, budget cuts, that sort of thing, we'd probably have arrived here years ago."

Report on
"Grand Central Terminal"

LEO SZILARD

Considering how much we deduce about the Sumerians, the Mayans, the Etruscans, and various other early cultures on the basis of laughably inadequate remains, it only serves us right to be treated similarly. At that the aliens prove to be keen observers and logicians.

Since this story was written (1948), humanity has gone a long way — downhill, lavatories are covered with graffiti, especially in Grand Central Terminal. But there has been one *improvement Szilard did not anticipate — certain important cubicles are now* free.

YOU CAN IMAGINE how shocked we were when we landed in this city and found it deserted. For ten years we were traveling through space, getting more and more impatient and irritable because of our enforced idleness; and then, when we finally land on Earth, it turns out — as you have undoubtedly heard — that all life is *extinct* on this planet.

The first thing for us to do was, of course, to find out how this came to pass and to learn whether the agent which destroyed life — whatever it may have been — was still active and perhaps endangering our own lives. Not that there was very much that we could do to protect ourselves, but we had to decide whether we should ask for further expeditions to be sent here or should advise against them.

At first we thought we were confronted with an insoluble enigma. How could any virus or bacterium kill *all* plants and *all* animals? Then, before a week had passed, one of our physicists noticed — quite by accident — a slight trace of radioactivity in the air. Since it was very weak, it would not in itself have been of much significance, but, when it was analyzed, it was found to be due to a peculiar mixture of quite a large number of *different* radioactive elements.

At this point, Xram recalled that about five years ago mysterious flashes had been observed on Earth (all of them within a period of one week). It occurred to him that perhaps these flashes had been uranium explosions and that the present radioactivity had perhaps originated in those explosions five years ago and had been initially strong enough to destroy life on the planet.

This sounded pretty unlikely indeed, since uranium is not in itself explosive and it takes quite elaborate processing to prepare it in a form in which it can be detonated. Since the Earth dwellers who built all these cities must have been rational beings, it is difficult to believe that they should have gone to all this trouble of processing uranium just in order to destroy themselves.

But subsequent analysis has in fact shown that the radioactive elements found in the air here are precisely the same as are produced in uranium explosions and also that they are mixed in the ratio which you would expect had they originated five years ago as fission products of uranium. This can hardly be a chance coincidence, and so Xram's theory is now generally accepted up to this point.

When he goes further, however, and attempts to explain why and how such uranium explosions came about, I am unable to follow him any longer. Xram thinks that there had been a war fought between the inhabitants of two continents, in which both sides were victorious. The records show, in fact, that the first twenty flashes occurred in the Eurasic continent and were followed by five (much larger) flashes on the American continent, and therefore, at first, I was willing seriously to consider the war theory on its merits.

I thought that perhaps these two continents had been inhabited by two *different* species of Earth dwellers who were either unable or unwilling to control the birth rate and that this might have led to conditions of overcrowding, to food shortage, and to a life-and-death struggle between the two species. But this theory had to be abandoned in the face of two facts: (1) the skeletons of Earth dwellers found on the Eurasic continent and on the American continent belong to the *same* species, and (2) skeleton statistics show that no conditions of overcrowding existed on either continent.

In spite of this, Xram seems to stick to his war theory. The worst of it is that he is now basing all his arguments on a single rather puzzling but probably quite irrelevant observation recently made in our study of "Grand Central Terminal."

When we landed here, we did not know where to begin our investigations, and so we picked one of the largest buildings of the city as the first object of our study. What its name, "Grand Central Terminal," meant we do not know, but there is little doubt as to the general purpose this building served. It was part of a primitive transportation system based on clumsy engines that ran on rails and dragged cars mounted on wheels behind them.

For over ten days now we have been engaged in the study of this building and have uncovered quite a number of interesting and puzzling details.

Let me start with an observation which I believe we have cleared up, at least to my own satisfaction. The cars stored in this station were labeled — we discovered — either "Smokers" or "Nonsmokers," clearly indicating some sort of segregation of passengers. It occurred to me right away that there may have lived in this city two strains of Earth dwellers, a more pigmented variety having a dark or "smoky" complexion, and a less pigmented variety (though not necessarily albino) having a fair or "nonsmoky" complexion.

All remains of Earth dwellers were found as skeletons, and no information as to pigmentation can be derived from them. So at first it seemed that it would be difficult to obtain confirmation of this theory. In the meantime, however, a few rather spacious buildings were discovered in the city which must have served some unknown and rather mysterious purposes. These buildings had painted canvases in frames fastened to the walls of their interior — both landscapes and images of Earth dwellers. And we see now that the Earth dwellers fall indeed into *two* classes — those whose complexion shows strong pigmentation (giving them a smoky look) and those whose complexion shows only weak pigmentation (the nonsmoky variety). This is exactly as expected.

I should perhaps mention at this point that a certain percentage of the images disclose the existence of a third strain of Earth dwellers. This strain has, in addition to a pair of hands and legs, a pair of wings, and apparently *all* of them belonged to the less pigmented variety. None of the numerous skeletons so far examined seems to have belonged to this winged strain, and I concluded therefore that we have to deal here with images of an extinct variety. That this view is indeed correct can no longer be doubted, since we have determined that the winged forms are much more frequently found among the older paintings than among the more recent paintings.

I cannot of course describe to you here *all* the puzzling discoveries we made within the confines of the "Grand Central Terminal," but I want to tell you at least about the most puzzling one, particularly since Xram is basing his war theory on it.

This discovery arose out of the investigation of an insignificant detail. In the vast expanse of the "Grand Central Terminal" we came upon two smaller halls located in a rather hidden position. Each of these two halls (labeled "Men" or "Women") contains a number of small cubicles which served as temporary shelter for Earth dwellers while they were depositing their excrements. The first question was, How did the Earth dwellers locate these hidden depositories within the confines of "Grand Central Terminal"?

An Earth dweller moving about at random within this large building would have taken about one hour (on the average) to stumble upon one of them. It is, however, possible that the Earth dwellers located the depositories with the aid of olfactory guidance, and we have determined that if their sense of smell had been about thirty to forty times more sensitive than the rudimentary sense of smell of our own species, the average time required would be reduced from one hour to about five or ten minutes. This shows there is no real difficulty connected with this problem.

Another point, however, was much harder to understand. This problem arose because we found that the door of each and every cubicle in the depository was locked by a rather complicated gadget. Upon investigation of these gadgets it was found that they contained a number of round metal disks. By now we know that these ingenious gadgets barred entrance to the cubicle until an additional disk was introduced into them through a slot; at that very moment the door became unlocked, permitting access to the cubicle.

These disks bear different images and also different inscriptions which, however, all have in common the word *Liberty*. What is the significance of these gadgets, the disks in the gadgets, and the word *Liberty* on the disks?

Though a number of hypotheses have been put forward in explanation, consensus seems to veer toward the view that we have to deal here with a ceremonial act accompanying the act of deposition, similar perhaps to some of the curious ceremonial acts reported from the planets Sigma 25 and Sigma 43. According to this view, the word *Liberty* must designate some virtue that was held in high esteem by the Earth dwellers or else their ancestors. In this manner we arrive at a quite satisfactory explanation for the sacrificing of disks immediately preceding the act of deposition.

But why was it necessary to make sure (or, as Xram says, to enforce), by means of a special gadget, that such a disk was in fact sacrificed in each and every case? This too can be explained if we assume that the Earth dwellers who approached the cubicles were perhaps driven by a certain sense of urgency, that in the absence of the gadgets they might have occasionally forgotten to make the disk sacrifice and would have consequently suffered pangs of remorse afterward. Such pangs of remorse are not unknown as a consequence of omissions of prescribed ceremonial performances among the inhabitants of the planets Sigma 25 and Sigma 43.

I think that this is on the whole as good an explanation as can be given at the present, and it is likely that further research will confirm this view. Xram, as I mentioned before, has a theory of his own, which he thinks can explain everything — the disks in the gadgets as well as the uranium explosions that extinguished life.

He believes that these disks were given out to Earth dwellers as rewards for services. He says that the Earth dwellers were *not* rational beings and that they would not have collaborated in cooperative enterprises without some special incentive.

He says that, by barring Earth dwellers from depositing their excrements unless they sacrificed a disk on each occasion, they were made eager to acquire such disks, and that the desire to acquire such disks made it possible for them to collaborate in cooperative efforts which were necessary for the functioning of their society.

He thinks that the disks found in the depositories represent only a special case of a more general principle and that the Earth dwellers probably had to deliver such disks not only prior to being given access to the depository but also prior to being given access to food, etc.

He came to talk to me about all this a couple of days ago; I am not sure that I understood all that he said, for he talked very fast, as he often does when he gets excited about one of his theories. I got the general gist of it, though, and what he says makes very little sense to me.

Apparently, he had made some elaborate calculations which show that a system of production and distribution of goods based on a system of exchanging disks cannot be stable, but is necessarily subject to great fluctuations vaguely reminiscent of the manic-depressive cycles of the insane. He goes so far as to say that in such a depressive phase war becomes psychologically possible even within the same species.

No one is more ready than I to admit that Xram is brilliant. His theories have invariably been proved to be wrong, but so far all of them had contained at least a grain of truth. In the case of his present theory the grain must be a very small grain indeed, and, moreover, this once I can *prove* that he is wrong.

In the last few days we made a spot check of ten different lodging houses of the city, selected at random. We found a number of depositories but not a single one that was equipped with a gadget containing disks — not in any of the houses we checked so far. In view of this evidence, Xram's theory collapses.

It seems now certain that the disks found in the depositories at "Grand Central Terminal" had been placed there as a ceremonial act. Apparently such ceremonial acts were connected with the act of deposition in *public* places and in public places only.

I am glad that we were able to clear this up in time, for I should have been sorry to see Xram make a fool of himself by including his theory in the report. He is a gifted young man, and in spite of all the nonsensical ideas he can put forward at the drop of a hat, I am quite fond of him.

Ad Astra, Al

MARY W. STANTON

Al left three kids and an ugly wife
To search the stars for a brand-new life,
For a place where maidens with silver hair
And strange-colored eyes were unaware
Of in-laws that dropped in to eat,
And pets that bit with muddy feet,
Weedy lawns that turned to hay
If you didn't mow them every day,
Of — well, the list itself was long;
Al craved unearthly wine and song.

He landed on a tiny planet:
Cold as ice cubes, hard as granite,
With a bright blue sun and crystal trees,
Golden rivers and ochre seas,
A race of aliens, tall and fair —
And a slender maiden with silver hair.

She had strange-colored eyes, and a cosy haunt
That held three kids and a cranky aunt,
A pet that chewed on Al routinely
(With six legs and a smell unseemly —)
And, well — the list itself is long,
Which proves the adage isn't wrong:
"Home is where the crabgrass is, despite the crystal trees,
And even dogs with six legs scratch the same old fleas."

They'll Do It Every Time

CAM THORNLEY

I was one week past my nineteenth birthday when my first story was published. You can see then that I consider it lèse majesté for anyone under nineteen to have anything published. Consider my horror at learning that Cam Thornley was only fifteen *when this story was published, in* my *magazine. Janet says it is possible we are contributing to juvenile delinquency by publishing it again.*

THE HIGH VAVOOM OF KAZOWIE was in conference with the pilot of the scoutship which had just returned from Sol III.

"I am certain that you have much to tell us of the strange and fascinating ways of the barbaric humanoids, Captain Zot, but — "

"You wouldn't believe it, your Vavoomity! Why, they live indoors! They don't keep slaves! They even — "

" — but after skimming through your log, I have formulated a few questions which should provide the information necessary to determine whether or not the planet is ready for colonization. Now — "

"It's unbelievable, sir! They eat with pieces of metal! The men think they're better than the women! They don't — "

" — now I just want you to answer these questions as briefly and completely as possible. Do you understand?"

"They — "

"Good. First, what was the reaction of the natives upon first sighting you in the air?"

"Well, high sir, at the time I couldn't help noticing the resemblance to a glikhill that has had freem poured on it. The humanoids went into a frenzy and fired several projectiles at me, all of which fell short by several nauga-frangs."

"I see. Now please describe your landing."

"Of course, high sir. When I approached the surface of the planet, I noticed that it was covered with wide black strips which appeared to be vehicular routes. As regulations strictly prohibit landing one's craft upon such routes,

I looked for a better place to touch down. The only other areas that seemed to fit my craft's landing specifications were the hard-surfaced paths from the doors of the natives' houses (I will explain this later, high sir) to the vehicular routes.

"I set the ship down on one of these paths and went out to greet the humanoids. They all — "

"Wait a moment. This is extremely important. What was the reaction of the natives upon first seeing you in the flesh? Try to remember everything that happened."

"Yes, high sir. It seems that I bear a striking resemblance to one of their major religious figures. When I came out of the ship all the humanoids in the vicinity knelt and averted their eyes, and said something about the coming seconds. I think this was a reference to an event that was going to happen in the near future. At any rate, when the natives stopped talking they got up and started walking toward me with their arms stretched out in front of them. I didn't like the looks of this so I jumped into the ship and took off. The religious-figure-resemblance theory is strengthened by the fact that when I observed the landing site several weeks later through my reasonable-distance site viewer I discovered that the natives had built a shrine there which always seemed to be full of pilgrims from many lands."

"Ah, yes. The familiar savior-from-the-stars syndrome. It happens to every one of our astronauts on pre-colonization planets."

"What's that, high sir?"

"They worship the walk he grounds on."

No Homelike Place

DIAN GIRARD

*I am a convinced feminist in every aspect of society outside my own home where,
fortunately, Janet simply adores doing all the cooking, washing, cleaning, and
other household duties. She claims she doesn't but that's just her little joke.
(Please, Janet! I can't type these headnotes if you hit me.)*

*My convictions carry over to science fiction. Who on Earth could write so
convincing a story of the important essentials of life on a space station but a
woman? (Janet says this last sentence proves that I am a male chauvinist.)*

SHE LOOKED AROUND the room and hated it. She had hated it at first
sight. It was cozy, space-saving, and designed with close packing factors in
mind. It was also ten-sided and painted a very determined yellow. Cheryl
assumed that it was supposed to be a cheerful color. In her present mood she
couldn't decide if it looked more like an undercooked egg yolk or a wilted
marigold. She felt like a bee in an oversized comb. Besides, she was wearing
her hair red this year and it clashed.

Honor, she told herself firmly, as she strode briskly toward a chair, lost her
footing, and floated into the air. It was a Great Honor to be picked for space
station work. She tried to keep that thought in mind as she settled slowly
toward the jumbled heap of cartons in the middle of the floor. She grabbed at
one of the green grid cords that were holding the boxes in place and pushed
herself firmly down onto the top carton.

It was also a great honor to be assigned one of the prestige low-gravity
apartments instead of being out near the station rim where lowly things like
chickens and pigs got to walk around firmly on their own four legs. Cheryl
sighed softly. Logan and Cheryl Harbottle, Space Pioneers! It *was* an honor,
of course, and her husband loved it already. But then, he was a structural
engineer and she was a xenocomtologist. She wouldn't have anything to do for
another couple of months. In the meantime all she had to do was buzz around
her little four-room hive.

Cheryl stood up carefully and looked down at the boxes. She might as well start unpacking. She jumped down, arched her arms over her head, and did a whimsical toe dance around the pile. So much for one-eighth gravity. At least it might make shifting the boxes easier. It did. Except when she heaved a little too hard and found her rear end lifting up instead of the carton.

Eventually she settled for unpacking each box as she came to it. This was their first full day in their new home, and she wanted to make the evening special. Making it special involved finding a particular box. She sorted and packed diligently. At least the apartment had plenty of storage space. It ought to, she thought sourly. Half of the furniture was stuck to the walls. There were little toeholds molded into all of the walls, and every available inch of space had a drawer of some sort. There were even lockers that swung down from the ceiling.

It was close to 1300 hours before Cheryl found the box she wanted, and nearly 1420 by the time she had the rest of their belongings mostly shoved out of sight. She stacked her treasures on the molded styrene dining room table and gloated. Three red silk roses, one bottle of Pinot Noir, some bubble bath, perfume, and her very wickedest black lace negligee. All strictly forbidden, of course. One was supposed to bring only the bare essentials, because of the weight limits. Well, she thought loftily, there is nothing more essential to a happy marriage than a little bit of . . . nonessentials.

She glanced at the clock again: 1510. That gave her nearly an hour before Logan came home. Time enough to dial up dinner, let the wine breathe, take a shower, and, ahem, slip into something a little more comfortable. She arranged the three roses in a plastic glass on the table, opened the wine bottle, and then hurried carefully into the other room with everything else.

The appliances in the bathroom were a little different. Back in her Cincinnati Dome apartment Cheryl would simply have emptied a supply of bath foam into the Shower-Matic and let it take care of the rest. Here there wasn't even a Shower-Matic. A large baglike affair hung in yellow and white folds across one corner of the room. It had a long zip seal. According to her copy of "Space Living for Groundsiders" you were supposed to step into it, zip it up to your chin, and do everything by feel.

She unzipped it and peered inside. It had a shower head, two knobs, and a floor that was perforated with little round holes. Efficient, no doubt, but hardly luxurious. She tested the controls. It wasn't too bad. She could probably avoid scalding or freezing herself. She stripped, tossed her clothes into the hamper, and smoothed the contents of one Blisful Bub-L Foam oil packet over her skin. Then she stepped into the shower, zipped it up, and fumbled at the controls.

After a few moments of agony she got the water to a comfortable temperature. She turned slowly around, sighing blissfully. It was a shame she couldn't see the bubble bath — that was part of the fun. She could smell the sweet scent though and . . . damn! A ripple of irritation went through her as she heard the communicator buzz in the living room. She unzipped the shower, grabbed a towel to pat up the worst of the drips, and hurried to answer it. She made the last two feet floating and punched the answer button on her way down.

It was the orientation service, checking to make sure that everything was all right. Cheryl assured the woman caller that they were settling in nicely, promised to attend some of the planned recreation, and agreed — through gritted teeth — that the yellow decor was very nice indeed. She disconnected with a sense of relief and started back to the bathroom. A look at the clock sent her to the dining room instead.

She selected dinner from the Auto-Chef menu and punched in the time she wanted it served. Then she went back through the living room and dialed up some Renoirs for the art screens. She contemplated *Girl with a Watering Can* for a moment and changed it to Manet's *Dejeuner Sur L'herbe* instead. Then she walked back, slid open the bathroom door, and nearly smothered in the foam. Cheryl's first reaction was unprintable.

In a normal, safe, sane, groundside bathroom the showers turned off automatically when you stepped out of them. This stupid contraption didn't have enough sense to shut down when no one was around. She flailed a path through the bubbles and groped around until she found the controls. With the water off Cheryl tried to assess the damage. Actually, she couldn't see it. The entire room was full of bubbles. Between the low gravity and the high surface tension Blisful Bub-L Foam had come into its own.

Cheryl beat her way outside again and slid the door shut behind her. Some of the bubbles had escaped and were floating idly through the air. Several small clouds of them were clinging affectionately to her ankles and arms, making her look somewhat like a pink and white poodle. Attempts to wipe them off just changed the distribution.

She stomped over to the air conditioner control and turned it to high. Sure enough, the stray bubbles in the living room started to drift toward the vent. With a little luck the air would eventually clear out the bathroom. She went into the bedroom, managed to wipe off her own consignment of froth, and slipped into the black lace negligee. After fluffing up her hair and putting on a whiff of perfume she began to think that the evening had real possibilities. She practiced gliding gracefully as she went back to the living room.

Cheryl stopped short in the doorway, like a swimmer in an off-center swan dive. There was one small defect in her plan. It was true that the air conditioning was gradually taking the bubbles out of the bathroom. It was also pulling them into the living room first. She watched in hypnotized fascination as the filmy white bubbles squeezed through the dividing grid, floated across the room, and oozed out through the vent. It was like watching some sort of eerie procession.

She finally managed to pull her eyes away and tried to think of some way to speed up the procedure. Grabbing up an empty carton left over from the unpacking she ran — half bouncing — into the bathroom and tried to scoop the bubbles up. There was no gravity on her side. She finally discovered that the best method was to hold the box between her knees and flail with both hands. It made her feel a little like a dog digging for a bone.

Once the box was full she rushed back into the living room and held it up to the air duct. Although a lot of the filmy spheres had managed to escape along the route, a satisfying number were sucked up never to be seen again. The clock was moving with incredible speed. She kept one eye on it as she staggered back and forth, herding bubble bath. Finally the bathroom was nearly clear. One last box load would just about do it. She set down the carton for a moment and dashed over to the table to pour the wine.

It was like trying to get catsup out of a full bottle. The blasted stuff poured like tar. She held the bottle over a glass and slapped the bottom in irritation. It behaved exactly like a catsup bottle. A great blob of wine plopped out of the bottle, hit the bottom of the glass, and made a rollercoaster turn up onto Cheryl's elegant black lace gown. She stood there in horror, tiny droplets of Pinot Noir dripping down onto her neatly pedicured toes.

She cast an anguished glance at the clock, set down the bottle, and ran for the bedroom, stripping off the sodden gown as she ran. She grabbed up a robe with one hand and mopped wine off her skin with the other. She rushed back for the last load of bubbles. Too late! As she tumbled into the living room she heard the sound of her husband at the door.

Cheryl dropped the robe on the floor and gathered the last of the iridescent bubbles up against herself. She snatched one of the red silk roses off of the table, clenched it firmly between her teeth, and tried to smile seductively around it. Her last thoughts, as the door slid open, were a fervent hope that Logan hadn't brought his boss home for dinner, and the comforting reminder that she did, after all, have the bare essentials.

"I'll have the orange juice, scrambled eggs and bacon, toast, marma-
lade, and coffee, please."

Simworthy's Circus

LARRY T. SHAW

Weren't you told in childhood that everything, however ugly, has something good about it? Okay — but the trick is to find the something — and, even then, there's a catch . . .

EVERYBODY HAS HEARD of Simworthy's Circus, yet comparatively few have actually seen it, since, oddly enough, Simworthy has refused fabulous offers to present it on vaudeo or in the reelies. But the population of the galaxy being huge as it is, those "comparatively few" are several million in number. And every single being, human and otherwise, among them has come away busting to tell his friends and relations what a wonderful show it is.

The funny part is, when described, Simworthy's Circus merely sounds like an anachronism, and one that wouldn't logically be very entertaining to the enlightened citizenry of a world whose horizons are the edges of the galaxy. Bluntly, it sounds dull. But all those customers, and Simworthy's bank account, testify to the contrary.

Almost nobody knows the explanation of the paradox, and the strange story behind Simworthy's Circus. This is it.

To begin with, Jared Simworthy was — and is — about the ugliest human ever to blast off from Earth. Wormy Ed, they called him behind his back — and he looked the part. Real nightmare type, subclass child-scaring. He looked as if his component parts came from a surrealistic junkyard and had been assembled in the dark by a bunch of idiot bricklayers. Mirrors turned green and curled up at the edges when he stepped into the room. In brief, a mess.

His appearance, naturally, conditioned his entire life and outlook. He acquired a monstrous hatred for the universe at an age when most kids are playing with isotope blocks in kindergarten. Only contempt kept him from going around putting Venusian stinkworms in little old ladies' teacups.

As he grew — a process that appeared for a dismayingly long time to be endless — he conceived, however, a limited number of affections. Not for people, of course. But things and creatures which were abysmally unsightly, by terrestrial standards, became the objects of his love. In his early teens, for instance, he resurrected and rebuilt an ancient ground vehicle. It was called a carriageless horse, or some such term, and it was not only an eyesore but a sin against logic besides. The first time Simworthy tried it out, the sight, noise, and smell of it caused three women to faint, and scared the wits out of nobody knows how many flitter-drivers. After that, the police wouldn't let him run the contraption on the gravways, so he hated people more than ever.

Then there was the Satcat, one of the vicious little beasts the first Saturnian expedition brought back. It was so hideous that the horror-reelies wouldn't touch it after the zoos had turned it down cold. Even so, it cost Simworthy a month's salary. It also cost him his job, when he tried to take it to work with him. He never went back to crossing a clockbeam again.

The Satcat didn't last long; Earth climate didn't agree with it. But Simworthy got plenty of publicity out of the incident, and people who had formerly ducked around corners when they saw him coming began to leave the neighborhood altogether. He didn't mind that, but it did make it rather hard for him to earn a living. So, predictably, he followed the "misfit trail" into space.

It surprises some people that he became a trader, since his hatred of all the beings he'd have to deal with was so monumental. It calcs, though, when you know his real intentions. During moments of overlubrication, he was heard to brag that he would swindle at least one member of every race in the galaxy before he quit. Then too, his ugliness simply didn't exist, in extraterrestrial eyes. That is, to most et's, he was no uglier than any *other* Earthman.

Simworthy worked damned hard, if it's any credit to him. No transaction was too petty, and no alien too truculent; he'd wheedle or browbeat for hours on end, if necessary, to put over a deal. He was one of the few Earthmen who ever had a strong enough stomach to sit in on the moulting ceremonies of the Vipherians. It was worth it; he gained their confidence, and left behind a shipload of coil springs — which of course rusted solid after a week on Viphesta. The profit was tidy.

Gradually, Simworthy prospered. It made no difference in his way of life. He stuck to the ship he'd started out in, a horribly functional monstrosity, one of the first models to use the warp principle that made interstellar travel possible. In Simworthy's hands the *Barnum* became battered, pocked, and rusty. He loved it. The name he had given his ship, incidentally, turned out to be prophetic; Barnum was a big circus owner a few centuries ago. Reason Simworthy chose it, though, was a proverb the guy was supposed to have originated: "A sucker in every pot," or was it "port"?

Somewhere along the line, he acquired a successor to the Satcat. It was a Nimoon, a biological insult considered unspeakable even on its home world of Mreyob — a downright stomach twister anywhere else. Simworthy lavished a share of his misguided affection on it, and called it Walter.

Somewhere else along the line, he got the Space Police on his tail. The charges, individually, were minor, but there were several of them, mostly misrepresentation and the lack of various licenses. Together, they could have iced Simworthy for quite a few years.

He was not many jumps ahead of the cops when, one day, he flipped out of hyperdrive in a lonely sector of space, with a single-planet system dead ahead. The sun wasn't important enough to rate a name on the charts, and the planet was classified as uninhabited. But once Simworthy got a look at the planet — overgrown moon would describe it better — he smiled a lopsided smile.

Black rocks and raging gray oceans, plus a lot of snow and ice, were all that could be seen at first. Closer in, some stunted and poisonous-looking vegetation became apparent. There was no practical reason for anyone to visit the forbidding place. Simworthy keyed his stern-jets and prepared for a landing.

He considered it as a hideout, but mostly he just wanted a look at that beautiful ugliness. The *Barnum* slid into an atmosphere which tested breathable, if you didn't mind the fishy smell, and was full of odd gusts and currents. The delicate jetwork was making Simworthy sweat when — blooey!

There was a flash from below. The *Barnum* gave a lurch that scrambled Simworthy's breakfast, and then started to imitate a pinwheel. The jets developed an ominous foreign accent. Simworthy thought about the Space Police and swore.

He also acted — fast. He'd developed skill and deftness, coaxing the cranky crate along in its normal state, and he used it all now. The *Barnum* plummeted, bounced, slid into a steep glide, spun some more on its vertical axis, and finally dropped to a belly landing going backwards — an incredible feat of piloting, even under favorable conditions.

As it was, about the best that could be said for Simworthy was: No bones were broken.

Needle-rayed! Simworthy rose from the pilot's armchair, still cursing with an energy that, tight-beamed, would have burned a hole into the planet's Heaviside layer. He spat, and stainless steel sizzled.

Calmly, Walter peered at him from the top of a refrigerator and scratched a flea. The peering was done with four unblinking, bloodshot eyes; suction cups on the Nimoon's bloated belly held it firmly to the porcelain; the scratching was accomplished not with the eerily weaving tentacles, as might have been expected, but with a bony tail that tapered to a wicked claw.

The flea was snugly ensconced in Walter's mane of greasy, greenish hair; the scratching continued monotonously, mechanically.

Simworthy's first concern was to estimate the damage to the *Barnum*. He stomped through the airlock and jumped down, stirring up puffs of pumice. Ignoring dust in his hair and stink in his nostrils, he gazed angrily at the fused jets. The inspection finished, he ground his teeth and shook a fist at nothing in particular.

"Ugh," said a wheezy voice behind him. "Cool off. Lend ya my robot to fix it. Complete machine shop. Easy."

The last word was ambiguous, and Simworthy was in no mood to be told to take it easy. He whirled.

The other Earthman looked like a rag, a bone, and several hanks of hair. Most of the latter was an undisciplined beard, but there was also a wavering halo around the chalky face, and tufts of fuzz growing out of the ears. At best, the stranger looked antique and brittle. He teetered. But he was definitely not a cop, which was something.

Simworthy expanded his chest, raised his arms, thrust out his already protruding jaw, and fixed the stranger with a baleful eye.

He said: "It's kind of you to offer. I hope it won't be too much trouble."

He said it softly and politely, and seconds later tried to swallow the words and his tongue with them. There was no sensible reason not to break this specimen's jaw, if any. By rights . . . But something wasn't right.

The feeling was totally inexplicable. Simworthy *liked* this creature. He respected him, and desired to treat him with the utmost deference, as long as he could remain in his infinitely pleasant presence. At the same time, he wondered if he were going nuts.

The stranger drew a gasping breath and spoke again. "Shot yuh down! Beats all! Heh. Marksmanship. Just tryin' to warn yuh off. Tried to hit yuh, I'd of missed a mile. Gah."

It was anything but an apology. Disregard for Simworthy was plain as the stranger's beard. But he said: "Don't mention it. Could have happened to anybody. I wanted to land anyway."

The beard semaphored. "Yah. You wanted. I didn't. I want yuh outa here. Pronto. So I'll help. Hermit. Mrmph."

Inhospitable as he was, he did not leave Simworthy out in the cold and the icy rain that was starting. He invited the puzzled trader to his dome for coffee, and over the coffee he continued his grumpy monologue.

As Simworthy pieced his story together, the Hermit — who ignored all hints designed to ferret out his proper name — had once been a biologist with the Galactic Exploratory Service, a member of one of the highly specialized crews that went about the endless job of charting suns and planets and collecting data on their inhabitants. His methods had always been a trifle unorthodox, but he had done his work well, making his more off-trail experiments on his own time, keeping their results to himself. Which was fortunate, in the case in point.

"I found a love potion," growled the Hermit.

Simworthy gawked.

The Hermit poured more coffee, a brew as black as outer space. He raised his lumoplast cup with a sardonic grin. "Like me, huh?" he asked.

By this time, Simworthy had regained partial control of himself. But he had to admit it. "Yeah. I like you. Like, hell! I feel almost like kissing your feet.

At the same time, I can imagine how long it is since you've washed them. I'm damned if I can calc it."

The Hermit opened a closet. Containers of assorted sizes and shapes clattered on the floor. The Hermit found a tiny vial, which he placed on the table. "That!" He waved a scrawny arm and cackled violently. The cackle broke off, to be followed by a cough and an infinitely bitter "Damn it!"

Simworthy gawked some more.

The vial was made of ordinary glass, and contained a brownish liquid. "Love potion," the Hermit sputtered. "Universal. Glandular. Little animals. Planet I prob'ly couldn't find again — glad of it. Brpph. Cave. Alone. Tiny beasts. Must of lived on rock. Albino. Fell for 'em. Hypnotism or something, thought at first. Loved 'em. Didn't want to leave. Wanted to take 'em all with me. Urf!"

Gradually, Simworthy learned, the Hermit had subdued his strange infatuation somewhat. He'd smuggled one of the creatures back to his ship and taken it apart to see what made it tick. The ship had blasted off before he'd discovered a gland unlike anything he'd seen before. From it, he'd taken a minute quantity of fluid. He'd fed a drop of it to a guinea pig. The guinea pig, superficially like dozens of others, had become the ship's mascot. Hardened spacemen went crazy over it.

Back on Earth, the Hermit had drunk a few drops of the stuff himself.

There was more after that, and it got harder to follow. The Hermit mumbled about brain waves and glands and personality indices and hypnogogics and telepathy and grumble gurgle foompf. He kept repeating something about ego-feedback, which Simworthy didn't get at all. What he did dredge out of the mess was what had happened to the Hermit — but a little imagination would have told him that.

In brief, people had loved him to distraction. He found it impossible to live in the close quarters of a spaceship with other men. Women — of various races and biological traits — fought over him. On Earth, dogs followed him around the streets. On Mars, yeesties did the same. And so on. Until, in desperation, the Hermit had become the Hermit.

"And — " he pounded the table with renewed vigor — "the infernal stuff doesn't wear off! Ever!"

Yes, Simworthy believed him. He found himself wanting to believe everything the old man said, anyway — but that in itself was a form of proof, wasn't it? Simworthy started to envision possibilities. *Love!* Not for love's sake, naturally, but for the things people would be willing to do for him. Power . . .

Anyway, when Simworthy blasted off again, the Hermit was richer by a portable windmill (government surplus, reconditioned), two dozen bottles of cheap perfume, six quarts of Rigellian Bhuillyordz (92 proof), and a pair of hair clippers. Simworthy, on the other hand, had the vial of — for want of a better name — universal love potion. The Hermit was happy; he wondered why he'd kept the stuff so long in the first place. Simworthy had wanted to drink it before leaving, but the Hermit had been adamant. "Uh," he'd grunted. "Work on me. Might try to keep you here. Oog!"

So, with the stuff safely cradled in his first-aid locker, Simworthy pointed the *Barnum*'s nose toward Agrab-Grob, and yanked into hyperspace again.

That left him, of course, with nothing much to do for the 17.4 minutes it takes any ship, in hyperspace, to reach any destination. He gazed at the gray nothingness outside the forward port, bit off a chaw of cardroot, and dreamed hazy dreams of future success. They began with his conquest of Agrab-Grob, the salesman's nightmare. The inhabitants should have been good customers, since their own economy was so primitive. However, they were also warlike and excessively suspicious of outsiders. With monotonous regularity, they chased all visitors off the planet as soon as they landed. For Simworthy, though, things were going to be different.

Imagination proved unsatisfactory. Simworthy got up and shuffled toward the medical locker. He was about to open it when a noise like a staticky wristphone speaking Mercurian drew his attention. He looked around, startled.

Walter hung from the ceiling and squealed at him again. Hungry, Simworthy reflected. The beast usually was. Simworthy took a container of sour cream from the refrigerator, flipped off the top, and placed it on the deck. Then he reached up and plucked the Nimoon from the ceiling.

Let us not dwell on the picture of Simworthy cradling Walter in his arms, fondling his mane, and crooning to him in a rust-clogged voice. It is by no stretch of the imagination a pretty picture, and is in its way a bit sad. Dial, then, the next scene: the Nimoon happily lapping cream and his master standing, bowed legs spread, running his fingers through his mop of red hair, rubbing his half-inch forehead, and wondering what it was that he had been about to do when interrupted.

Dawn broke; Simworthy remembered the Hermit's vial. Stepping over the Nimoon, he opened the first-aid locker and removed the thing. It looked even more insignificant now than when he had first seen it, and — the Hermit's influence was fading somewhat — Simworthy began to wonder if he had been had. There was only one way to find out.

He removed the cork.

Then he realized that there would be no way to test the stuff's powers until he made port. Walter loved him already, so on him it wouldn't show. Simworthy gazed moodily at the vial and tortured his scalp with his stubby fingers again.

Oh, well. He had nothing to lose, and might as well drink it anyway. The aura the stuff created, as he had made the Hermit repeat several times, apparently remained until death. Simworthy raised the vial.

The control panel burped. The *Barnum* was re-entering normal space and, being an old crate with many manual controls, was calling for the pilot's guiding hand. Simworthy stuck the vial back in the locker, slammed the door, and scrambled into his armchair.

It was lucky he was a good pilot. Just as things solidified outside the viewports, a flashy Buick sportsjet, with "tourist" written all over it, flashed across his nose. The *Barnum*'s detector circuit must have blown a fuse — but Simworthy didn't have time to wonder about that. He yanked, and the *Barnum* zoomed wildly. It cleared the Buick with scant feet to spare, and the tourists had their britches warmed by the blast from the older rig's tail.

Pale, Simworthy flicked the *Barnum* into the simplest orbital course available, punched the autopilot, and stomped away from the panel. If only he'd gotten their license number! The knowledge that it was undoubtedly his own fault, that he couldn't haul anyone into court with the cops hot after him, and that the *Barnum*'s insurance had lapsed several months before to cap it all, was submerged beneath his anger. Damn people anyway!

Simworthy reached the first-aid locker, clutched a bottle of his best alcoholic medicine, took several healthy swigs, choked, and came up gasping for air. His horrible suspicion was confirmed immediately. The perspiration on his neck turned into drops of ice that snowballed down his spine. The door of the locker was swinging open — *had been* swinging open throughout the action — and the vial was no longer in its place. Simworthy tore his long-suffering hair and groaned a mighty groan.

It didn't take him long to find the vial. He almost stepped on it. It was lying on its side on the floor.

Under stress, Simworthy's brain clicked with unusual clarity. He became deductive. The vial, he saw, was empty. There was a brownish spot on the deck beneath it. But it was a very small spot indeed. Not nearly big enough to account for the entire contents. The stuff couldn't have soaked in, and it obviously hadn't run off, or splashed elsewhere.

"Walter!" bellowed Simworthy.

The Nimoon raised its snoot, uncoiled itself from an air vent, and shrieked at Simworthy chummily. When Simworthy dove, Walter made a belated effort to climb up the bulkhead. Simworthy's huge hands closed on the frightened beasty, and in Simworthy's eyes gleamed a lust for blood.

Came a fairly exact repetition of the business gone through in Simworthy's meeting with the Hermit. All anger drained out of the big trader, and he relaxed his grip on the Nimoon. Walter chirped at him, managing to sound puzzled.

"Walter," said Simworthy, "Walter. You shouldn't have drunk that stuff. You shouldn't have, Walter. But it's all right — as long as it didn't hurt you, Walter."

He deposited his charge on the deck and retired, with the whiskey bottle, to his chair. He loved Walter, but disappointment was great. Practically sobbing, he was in no mood to figure whether he actually loved Walter any more than he had before. Indeed, Simworthy's emotions did not run to fine shadings; they were big and awkward like the man himself. All Simworthy knew was, he loved the confounded pest too much to wring its ridiculous head from its neckless shoulders. Drat it! The bottle drove rapidly toward emptiness.

The liquor may not have been entirely responsible for the idea, but it certainly helped. Simworthy suddenly saw that all of his plans were not ruined after all. He couldn't make himself lovable — hence irresistible to customers — now. But with Walter as a tool, he'd be almost as well off. In fact, with Walter perched on his shoulder as he gave his sales talk, the aura might cover them both, with the same effect. Love my Nimoon, love me! All was not lost.

Simworthy landed on Agrab-Grob.

He landed in the central square of a city that was, while puny by practically any standards, the major one on the planet. Simworthy looked out at the crowd of natives that gathered around him, and almost took off again immediately. The Agrab-Grobians were roughly humanoid, eight feet tall, pure blue, and had big teeth. They carried crude but reliable-looking weapons, and they obviously didn't want company.

Simworthy made sure that Walter was nestled snugly under his arm as he opened the outer hatch. This would be the acid test. If it failed, he'd have to go on trading on his own skill and luck. That is, he shuddered, if the natives let him go at all. They weren't supposed to be cannibalistic, but how did he know just where they drew the line? And they looked . . . Brr.

The crowd pressed in. Simworthy raised his left hand in a peaceful, though shaky, gesture, and clutched Walter tighter. There was a murmuring from the crowd, which told him nothing.

Little was known of the Agrab-Grobian language, but it had been established that it was a variation of Lower Jogamish, Jogam being a more advanced, and friendlier, planet of the same system. Thus, with the aid of the Spaceman's Conversational Guide, Simworthy knew he could get his ideas across. "Peace!" he bellowed. "Friendship! Advantage to you! Gifts!" The last was a distortion of the truth, but it seemed like a good idea.

Slowly, the trembling in Simworthy's knees ended. The blue giants were making no move to chase him out. They waited, shuffling their feet. And gradually, it dawned on Simworthy that they were smiling. For the first time, he realized the true power of the love potion, and the wide radius of its effects.

An Agrab-Grobian in a fancy headdress shouldered his way through the mob. Planting himself before Simworthy, he made a perfunctory gesture in imitation of the trader's, and began a long speech. Out of it, Simworthy got something like: "Wonderful small animal. You master wonderful small animal. You wonderful. Friend."

It was such an exact statement of what Simworthy had expected that he almost keeled over. But the businessman in him came to the fore. He handed the chief a cheap plastic necklace. "Gift," he said. "Peace. Barter, maybe?"

The chief studied the beads with a pleased expression, but only briefly. He returned his gaze to Simworthy and Walter, and made an even longer speech. Out of it, Simworthy got: "Yes."

The city's central square was also its marketplace. Simworthy saw that he could expect a fine haul of valuable metals and gems. The fact that it was all carved into small, oddly shaped trinkets bothered him not at all. He set up shop.

Hours passed, during which business boomed. Simworthy unloaded various cheap junk from the *Barnum*'s hold. The natives showered him with gimmicks, and every resident worked his way to the front of the crowd at least once to stand beaming at Simworthy with unabashed awe and amour.

He was demonstrating the advantages of a trick can opener, hampered somewhat by the fact that the Agrab-Grobians had no cans to open, when the tragedy happened. The chief, who had not been in evidence for some time, returned and leaned against the *Barnum*'s hull in a typical "holding up the building" pose. Out of his speech, Simworthy got: "Friend. Barter. Barter good. You take chief's pet. I take little animal."

Simworthy looked, thunderstruck, at the chief. He looked at another native, obviously a servant, who had followed, hauling along a reluctant something on a leash. The something appeared to be a ferocious, six-legged razorback hog. Getting more horrified by the second, Simworthy looked at the chief again.

He started to protest, but could think of nothing to say except for the one word, no. He said "No." He kept on saying it.

The chief, still beaming, reached down and plucked the Nimoon from Simworthy's shoulder.

Simworthy made a desperate grab. The chief, seeing it coming, lifted the Nimoon high over his head. Walter woke up enough to take part in the action himself. He screamed, and bit the chief on the wrist.

The chief yelled and grabbed his wrist with his other hand. Walter somersaulted to the ground, where he began to make frantic scrambling motions with all his tentacles. As if fired by the same trigger, Simworthy, the chief, the servant, and the six-legged horror pounced upon Walter all at the same time.

Dust rose. Everybody shouted. Simworthy got an elbow in his nose, which began to spurt blood. The Nimoon caterwauled, and the bigger beast growled and snuffled fiercely. As Simworthy's vision cleared, he realized with a shock that the chief's servant was waving a long knife with utter disregard for the life and limb of anyone concerned.

Panting, the frightened trader dug in his heels and rolled out from under. The scuffle quieted down. Simworthy shook his head, but could not eliminate a roaring noise in his ears.

The chief stood, striving mightily to repair his injured dignity. The servant stood and pulled the six-legged thing, which was yipping and snapping furiously, a few yards away.

On the ground where the battle had taken place, the mangled corpse of Walter lay in dust and blood.

The roaring in Simworthy's ears got louder. He was, he knew, a goner. Instinct took over.

He ran.

The hatchway of the *Barnum* was blocked by a knot of jabbering Agrab-Grobians. Simworthy about-faced, pumping hard. He hadn't the slightest idea of his ultimate destination, but the middle of the square was suddenly, mysteriously, empty. The battered trader started to charge across it.

The roaring noise grew louder still, but it was not until Simworthy saw the source that he identified it as the stern-blast of a spaceship. Realization came swiftly as the ship itself settled into the square directly in front of Simworthy. The ship was fast, new, and bristled with weapons. The letters "S. P." loomed large and red on its gleaming nose.

The Space Police!

Simworthy was caught between two fires. It was only a matter of choosing the one that burned least merrily. He headed for the police cruiser, waving his arms wildly.

The cruiser's hatch opened, and three uniformed men — obviously tough men, ready for anything — stepped out. Hands poised near blaster holsters, they waited expectantly.

"Jared Simworthy?" snapped the one with the lieutenant's bars on his collar. "You're under arrest! We've been trailing you, and we're going to take you in. Will you come peaceably?"

Simworthy was peaceable enough, all right. His nose wouldn't stop bleeding, he had a throbbing headache, and he felt generally sick all over. This was the end, and he might as well face it. He raised his arms and walked slowly forward . . .

Strangely, the lieutenant was rubbing his jaw, and smiling a hesitant smile, which made him look boyish. "Er, that is," he said, "you are Jared Simworthy, aren't you? But, shucks, maybe there's been a mistake. You're obviously not a crook. And as far as I know, the charges against you haven't anything behind them but the word of some screwball et's. Ten to one, they're phony."

He made his decision, and his smile broadened. "Aw hell, you're a good joe. Let's have a drink and talk this over. We can renew your licenses for you, while we're at it. Then we can convoy you out of here, if you're leaving."

Astounded, Simworthy realized that the other two policemen were smiling too, and holding out their hands. For the first time since he had made his break, he risked a look behind him.

None of the huge Agrab-Grobians were chasing him. They hadn't been chasing him, apparently. A few of them were looking at the chief, hiding grins behind their hairy paws. But most of them were gazing in Simworthy's direction, and their eyes were still filled with the rawest form of respect and devotion.

And that was that, just about. Later, as Simworthy jockeyed a richly laden *Barnum* back toward more civilized planets — planets that would pay a big price for his cargo — he figured it out. It was lucky for him that he did. It was lucky, that is, that he plucked one of the fleas out of his hair alive and looked at it, before he had scratched them all into oblivion.

The vial, he realized then, must have landed smack on Walter's neck, the fluid soaking into Walter's receptive mane. And the fleas had drunk their fill. And at some point in the proceedings, some of those fleas . . .

Simworthy scratched again, but gently now, delicately, probing carefully to capture alive as many of the insects as he could. He hadn't guessed, then, how profitable they might be. At the moment, he was simply, suddenly, completely crazy about the lovable little things!

And that's how Simworthy's Flea Circus started. So you'll know, if you ever get a chance to see it, exactly why you can't help going overboard about the antics of the normally uninteresting little pests. But even forewarned, and with full knowledge about them, you won't be able to help yourself.

You'll love 'em!

A Growing Concern

ARNIE BATEMAN

When this story was published in my magazine, it represented a first sale for Bateman. Who knows what other enormities the man may be capable of committing in time to come?

SNARLING, Bagarf slowly pulled a four-meter length of creeper from the auxiliary astrogation console and threw it on the pile of vegetation covering the control room deck.

His three-fingered fist punched the intercom. "Hydroponics!"

"Hydroponics. Nefark here."

"Bagarf. Status report."

"Oh, Captain. How are you?"

"I've got creepers in astrogation. Report!"

"I've mixed up some stuff that retards it a bit but still have no idea what's causing the accelerated growth."

"Not good enough. Staff meeting in four Units. You best have something or I'll throw you in those hyperthyroid vats. Out."

Bagarf stood seething for a moment, then resignedly began picking grass blades from the command chair.

Bagarf, Nefark, and Mucowk, the engineer, sat around the moderately clear table in the galley sipping mugs of brew. As in the rest of the ship, grass, vines, and assorted greenery sprouted from the ceiling, walls, and floor.

The captain turned to Nefark, who was absently scraping at a large mass of mold with a stirring implement. "Report."

Reluctantly, Nefark looked up. "We may be able to slow — possibly halt — subsequent growth, but I doubt if we can kill off what we already have. In time, that is."

Bagarf nodded. "Mucowk? Anything?"

The engineer's breast cartilage rippled. "Plenty; but, unfortunately, nothing that won't get us too."

"Well, with seventy percent of our systems already on back-up, we can't last much longer." Bagarf gulped his brew. "Fortunately, there's a system just under two hundred Units away. We'll have to land and try to kick this thing."

A polar orbit was established around the third planet. Anxiously, the aliens watched the main scanner as the green planet passed below.

"There!" Nefark pointed.

Bagarf nodded and began their descent. A large estate grew on the screen: a mansion amid acres of immaculately trimmed lawns and flower beds.

The spacecraft settled softly on the lawn. Bagarf, wearing a light pressure suit and breathing mask, stepped onto the clipped grass.

A dozen or so bipeds were warily approaching him. All wore clothing with green and brown stains, especially at the knees; they clutched a variety of hand tools.

Bagarf stopped. He glanced at the perfect flower beds, then held out his arms to the bipeds and said, "Take me to your weeder!"

"It's me!"

Gahan Wilson. Originally appeared in *The Magazine of Fantasy and Science Fiction*.

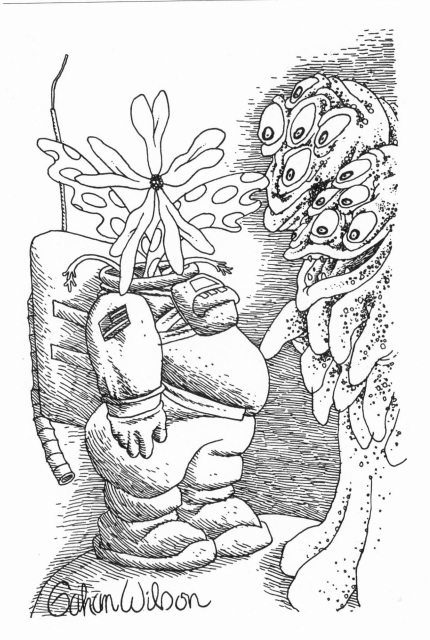

"We've no idea what it is, but it makes a darling planter!"

Gahan Wilson. Originally appeared in *The Magazine of Fantasy and Science Fiction.*

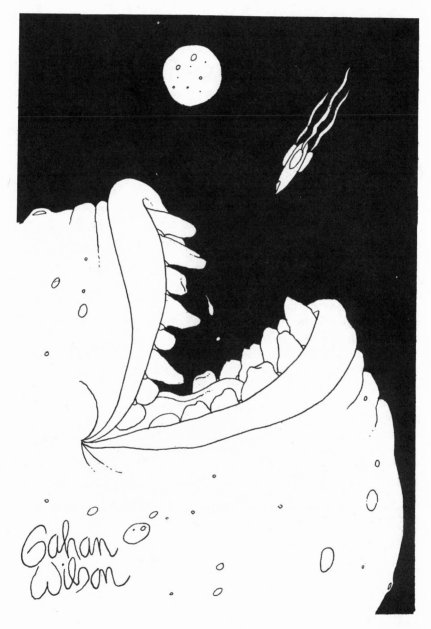

"Oh, oh!"

Gahan Wilson. Originally appeared in *The Magazine of Fantasy and Science Fiction.*

The Vilbar Party

EVELYN E. SMITH

I like parties. I didn't get to go to any when I was young because I had to work in the candy store and because I had no social graces. Nowadays, I have to work at the typewriter and I still have no social graces, but I get invited out a lot because I'm a minor celebrity. And I love to go whenever I can tear myself away. Janet, who likes to be near me at all times for arcane reasons of her own which she is at a loss to put into words, is often forced to come with me, even though she herself is shy and a trifle uneasy in crowds. Come to think of it, perhaps the reason she comes along is to discourage me from overeating — but she says that is NOT putting it into words.

"THE PERZILS are giving a vilbar party tomorrow night," Professor Slood said cajolingly. "You *will* come this time, won't you, Narli?"

Narli Gzann rubbed his forehead fretfully. "You know how I feel about parties, Karn." He took a frismil nut out of the tray on his desk and nibbled it in annoyance.

"But this is in your honor, Narli — a farewell party. You must go. It would be — it would be unthinkable if you didn't." Karn Slood's eyes were pleading. He could not possibly be held responsible for his friend's antisocial behavior, and yet, Narli knew, he would somehow feel at fault.

Narli sighed. He supposed he would have to conform to public sentiment in this particular instance, but he was damned if he would give in gracefully. "After all, what's so special about the occasion? I'm just leaving to take another teaching job, that's all." He took another nut.

"That's *all!*" Slood's face swelled with emotion. "You can't really be that indifferent."

"Another job, that's all it is to me," Narli persisted. "At an exceptionally high salary, of course, or I wouldn't dream of accepting a position so inconveniently located."

Slood was baffled and hurt and outraged. "You have been honored by being the first of our people to be offered an exchange professorship on another planet," he said stiffly, "and you call it 'just another job.' Why, I would have given my right antenna to get it!"

Narli realized that he had again overstepped the invisible boundary between candor and tactlessness. He poked at the nuts with a stylus.

"Honored by being the first of our species to be offered a guinea-pigship," he murmured.

He had not considered this aspect of the matter before, but now that it occurred to him, he was probably right.

"Oh, I don't mind, really." He waved away the other's sudden commiseration. "You know I like being alone most of the time, so I won't find that uncomfortable. Students are students, whether they're Terrestrials or Saturnians. I suppose they'll laugh at me behind my back, but then, even here, my students always did that."

He gave a hollow laugh and unobtrusively put out one of his hands for a nut. "At least on Earth I'll know why they're laughing."

There was pain on Slood's expressive face as he firmly removed the nut tray from his friend's reach. "I didn't think of it from that angle, Narli. Of course you're right. Human beings, from what I've read of them, are not noted for tolerance. It will be difficult, but I'm sure you'll be able to — " he choked on the kindly lie — "win them over."

Narli repressed a bitter laugh. Anyone less likely than he to win over a hostile alien species through sheer personal charm could hardly be found on Saturn. Narli Gzann had been chosen as first exchange professor between Saturn and Earth because of his academic reputation, not his personality. But although the choosers had probably not had that aspect of the matter in mind, the choice, he thought, was a wise one.

As an individual of solitary habits, he was not apt to be much lonelier on one planet than another.

And he had accepted the post largely because he felt that, as an alien being, he would be left strictly alone. This would give him the chance to put in a lot of work on his definitive history of the Solar System, a monumental project from which he begrudged all the time he had to spend in fulfilling even the minimum obligations expected of a professor on sociable Saturn.

The salary was a weighty factor too — not only was it more than twice what he had been getting, but since there would be no necessity for spending more than enough for bare subsistence, he would be able to save up a considerable amount and retire while still comparatively young. It was pleasant to imagine a scholarly life unafflicted by students.

He could put up with a good deal for that goal.

But how could he alleviate the distress he saw on Karn's face? He did not consciously want to hurt the only person who, for some strange reason, seemed to be fond of him, so he said the only thing he could think of to please: "All right, Karn, I'll go to the Perzils' tomorrow night."

It would be a deadly bore — parties always were — and he would eat too much, but, after all, the thought that it would be a long time before he'd ever see any of his own kind again would make the affair almost endurable. And just this once it would be all right for him to eat as much as he wanted. When he was on Earth and out of reach of decent food, he would probably trim down considerably.

"I just *know* you're going to love Earth, Professor Gzann," the hostess on the interplanetary liner gushed.

"I'm sure I shall," he lied politely. She smiled at him too much, overdoing her professional cordiality; underneath the effusiveness, he sensed the repulsion. Of course he couldn't blame her for trying not to show her distaste for the strange creature — the effort at concealment was, as a matter of fact, more than he had expected from a Terrestrial. But he wished she would leave him alone to meditate. He had planned to get a lot of meditation done on the journey.

"You speak awfully good English," she told him.

He looked at her. "I am said to have some scholarly aptitude. I understand that's why I was chosen as an exchange professor. It does seem reasonable, doesn't it?"

She turned pink — a sign of embarrassment with these creatures, he had learned. "I didn't mean to — to question your ability, Professor. It's just that — well, you don't look like a professor."

"Indeed?" he said frostily. "And what do I look like, then?"

She turned even rosier. "Oh — I — I don't know exactly. It's just that — well . . ." And she fled.

He couldn't resist flicking his antennae forward to catch her *sotto voce* conversation with the copilot; it was so seldom you got the chance to learn what others were saying about you behind your back. "But I could hardly tell him he looks like a teddy bear, could I?"

"He probably doesn't even know what a teddy bear is."

"Perhaps I don't," Narli thought resentfully, "but I can guess."

With low cunning, the Terrestrials seemed to have ferreted out the identity of all his favorite dishes and kept serving them to him incessantly. By the time the ship made planetfall on Earth, he had gained ten grisbuts.

"Oh, well," he thought, "I suppose it's all just part of the regular diplomatic service. On Earth, I'll have to eat crude native foods, so I'll lose all the weight again."

President Purrington of North America came himself to meet Narli at the airfield because Narli was the first interplanetary exchange professor in history.

"Welcome to our planet, Professor Gzann," he said with warm diplomatic cordiality, wringing Narli's upper right hand after a moment of indecision.

"We shall do everything in our power to make your stay here a happy and memorable one."

"I wish you would begin by doing something about the climate," Narli thought. It was stupid of him not to have realized how hot it would be on Earth. He was really going to suffer in this torrid climate, especially in the tight Terrestrial costume he wore over his fur for the sake of conformity. Of course, justice compelled him to admit to himself, the clothes wouldn't have become so snug if he hadn't eaten quite so much on board ship.

Purrington indicated the female beside him. "May I introduce my wife?"

"Oh-h-h," the female gasped, "isn't he *cute!*"

The President and Narli stared at her in consternation. She looked abashed for a moment, then smiled widely at Narli and the press photographers.

"Welcome to Earth, dear Professor Gzann!" she exclaimed, mispronouncing his name, of course. Bending down, she kissed him right upon his fuzzy forehead.

Kissing was not a Saturnian practice, nor did Narli approve of it; however, he had read enough about Earth to know that Europeans sometimes greeted dignitaries in this peculiar way. Only this place, he had been given to understand, was not Europe but America.

"I am having a cocktail party in your honor this afternoon!" she beamed, smoothing her flowered print dress down over her girdle. "You'll be there at five sharp, won't you, dear?"

"Delighted," he promised dismally. He could hardly plead a previous engagement a moment after arriving.

"I've tried to get all the things you like to eat," she went on anxiously, "but you will tell me if there's anything special, won't you?"

"I am on a diet," he said. He must be strong. Probably the food would be repulsive anyhow, so he'd have no difficulty controlling his appetite. "Digestive disorders, you know. A glass of Vichy and a biscuit will be — "

He stopped, for there were tears in Mrs. Purrington's eyes. "Your tummy hurts? Oh, you poor little darling!"

"Gladys!" the President said sharply.

There were frismil nuts at Mrs. Purrington's cocktail party and vilbar and even slipnis broogs . . . all imported at fabulous expense, Narli knew, but then this was a government affair and expense means nothing to a government since, as far as it is concerned, money grows on taxpayers. Some of the native foods proved surprisingly palatable, too — pâté de foie gras and champagne and little puff pastries full of delightful surprises. Narli was afraid he was making a zloogle of himself. However, he thought, trying not to catch sight of his own portly person in the mirrors that walled the room, the lean days were just ahead.

Besides, what could he do when everyone insisted on pressing food on him? "Try this, Professor Gzann." "Do try that, Professor Gzann." ("Doesn't he look cunning in his little dress suit?") They crowded around him. The women cooed, the men beamed, and Narli ate. He would be glad when he could detach himself from all this cloying diplomacy and get back to the healthy rancor of the classroom.

At school, the odor of chalk dust, ink, and rotting apple cores was enough like its Saturnian equivalent to make Narli feel at home immediately. The students would dislike him on sight, he knew. It is in the nature of the young to be hostile toward whatever is strange and alien. They would despise him and jeer at him, and he, in his turn, would give them long, involved homework assignments and such difficult examinations that they would fail . . .

Narli waddled briskly up to his desk which had, he saw, been scaled down to Saturnian size, whereas he had envisioned himself struggling triumphantly with ordinary Earth-sized furniture. But the atmosphere was as hot and sticky and intolerable as he had expected. Panting as unobtrusively as possible, he rapped with his pointer. "Attention, students!"

Now should come the derisive babble . . . but there was a respectful silence, broken suddenly by a shrill feminine whisper of, "Oooo, he's so adorable!" followed by the harsh, "Shhh, Ava! You'll embarrass the poor little thing."

Narli's face swelled. "I am your new professor of Saturnian studies. Saturn, as you probably know, is a major planet. It is much larger and more important than Earth, which is only a minor planet."

The students obediently took this down in their notebooks. They carefully took down everything he said. Even a bout of coughing that afflicted him halfway through seemed to be getting a phonetic transcription. From time to time, they would interrupt his lecture with questions so pertinent, so well thought out, and so courteous that all he could do was answer them.

His antennae lifted to catch the whispers that from time to time were exchanged between even the best behaved of the students. "Isn't he precious?" "Seems like a nice fellow — sound grasp of his subject." "Sweet little thing!" "Unusually interesting presentation." "Doesn't he remind you of Winnie the Pooh?" "Able chap." "Just darling!"

After class, instead of rushing out of the room, they hovered around his desk with intelligent, solicitous questions. Did he like Earth? Was his desk too high? Too low? Didn't he find it hot with all that fur? Such lovely, soft, fluffy fur, though. "Do you mind if I stroke one of your paws — *hands* — Professor?" ("So cuddly looking!")

He said yes, as a matter of fact, he was hot, and no, he didn't mind being touched in a spirit of scientific investigation.

He had a moment of uplift at the teachers' cafeteria when he discovered lunch to be virtually inedible. The manager, however, had been distressed to see him pick at his food, and by dinnertime a distinguished chef with an expert knowledge of Saturnian cuisine had been rushed from Washington. Since the school food was inedible for all intelligent life forms, everyone ate the Saturnian dishes and praised Narli as a public benefactor.

That night, alone in the quiet confines of his small room at the Men's Faculty Club, Narli had spread out his notes and was about to start work on his history when there was a knock at the door. He trotted over to open it, grumbling to himself.

The head of his department smiled brightly down at him. "Some of us are going out for a couple of drinks and a gabfest. Care to come along?"

Narli did not see how he could refuse and still carry the Saturnian's burden, so he accepted. Discovering that gin fizzes and alexanders were even more palatable than champagne and more potent than vilbar, he told several Saturnine locker-room stories which were hailed with loud merriment. But he was being laughed *at,* not *with,* he knew. All this false cordiality, he assured himself, would die down after a couple of days, and then he would be able to get back to work. He must curb his intellectual impatience.

In the morning, he found that enrollment in his classes had doubled, and the room was crowded to capacity with the bright, shining, eager faces of young Terrestrials athirst for learning. There were apples, chocolates, and imported frismil nuts on his desk, as well as a pressing invitation from Mrs. Purrington for him to spend all his weekends and holidays at the White House. The window was fitted with an air-conditioning unit which, he later discovered, his classes had chipped in to buy for him, and the temperature had been lowered to a point where it was almost comfortable. All the students wore coats.

When he went out on the campus, women — students, teachers, even strangers — stopped to talk to him, to exclaim over him, to touch him, even to kiss him. Photographers were perpetually taking pictures, some of which turned up in the Student Union as full-color postcards. They sold like Lajl out of season.

Narli wrote in Saturnian on the back of one: "Having miserable time; be glad you're not here," and sent it to Slood.

There were cocktail parties, musicales, and balls in Narli's honor. When he tried to refuse an invitation, he was accused of shyness and virtually dragged to the affair by laughing members of the faculty. He put on so much weight that he had to buy a complete new Terrestrial outfit, which set him back a pretty penny. As a result, he had to augment his income by lecturing to women's clubs. They slobbered appallingly.

Narli's students did all their homework assiduously and, in fact, put in more work than had been assigned. At the end of the year, not only did all of them pass, but with flying colors.

"I hope you'll remember, Professor Gzann," the president of the university said, "that there will always be a job waiting for you here — a nonexchange professorship. Love to have you."

"Thank you," Narli replied politely.

Mrs. Purrington broke into loud sobs when he told her he was leaving Earth. "Oh, I'll miss you so, Narli! You will write, won't you?"

"Yes, of course," he said grimly. That made two hundred and eighteen people to whom he'd had to promise to write.

It was fortunate he was traveling as a guest of the North American government, he thought as he supervised the loading of his matched interplanetary luggage; his eight steamer baskets; his leatherbound *Encyclopedia Terrestria*, with his name imprinted in gold on each volume; his Indian war bonnet; his oil painting of the President; and his six cases of champagne — all parting gifts — onto the liner. Otherwise the fee for excess luggage would have taken what little remained of his bank account. There had been so many expenses — clothes and hostess gifts and ice.

Not all his mementos were in his luggage. A new rare-metal watch gleamed on each of his four furry wrists; a brand-new trobskin wallet, platinum key chain, and uranium fountain pen were in his pocket; and a diamond and curium bauble clasped a tie lovingly hand painted by a female student. The Argyles on his fuzzy ankles had been knitted by another. Still another devoted pupil had presented him with a hand-woven plastic case full of frismil nuts to eat on the way back.

"Well, Narli!" Slood said, his face swelling with joy. "Well, well! You've put on weight, I see."

Narli dropped into his old chair with a sigh. Surely Slood might have picked something else to comment on first — his haggardness, for instance, or the increased spirituality of his expression.

"Nothing else to do on Earth in your leisure moments but eat, I suppose," Slood said, pushing over the nut tray. "Even their food. Have some frismils."

"No, thank you," Narli replied coldly.

Slood looked at him in distress. "Oh, how you must have suffered! Was it very, very bad, Narli?"

Narli hunched low in his chair. "It was just awful."

"I'm sure they didn't mean to be unkind," Slood assured him. "Naturally, you were a strange creature to them and they're only — "

"*Unkind?*" Narli gave a bitter laugh. "They practically killed me with kindness! It was fuss, fuss, fuss all the time."

"Now, Narli, I do wish you wouldn't be quite so sarcastic."

"I'm *not* being sarcastic. And I wasn't a strange creature to them. It seems there's a sort of popular child's toy on Earth known as a — " he winced — "teddy bear. I aroused pleasant childhood memories in them, so they showered me with affection and edibles."

Slood closed his eyes in anguish. "You are very brave, Narli," he said almost reverently. "Very brave and wise and good. Certainly that would be the best thing to tell our people. After all, the Terrestrials are our allies; we don't want to stir up public sentiment against them. But you can be honest with *me,* Narli. Did they refuse to serve you in restaurants? Were you segregated in public vehicles? Did they shrink from you when you came close?"

Narli beat the desk with all four hands. "I was hardly ever given the chance to be alone! They crawled all over me! Restaurants begged for my trade! I had to hire private vehicles because in public ones I was mobbed by admirers!"

"Such a short time," Slood murmured, "and already suspicious of even me, your oldest friend. But don't talk about it if you don't want to, Narli . . . Tell me, though, did they sneer at you and whisper half-audible insults? Did they — "

"You're right!" Narli snapped. "I *don't* want to talk about it."

Slood placed a comforting hand upon his shoulder. "Perhaps that's wisest, until the shock of your experience has worn off."

Narli made an irritable noise.

"The Perzils are giving a vilbar party tonight," Slood said. "But I know how you feel about parties. I've told them you're exhausted from your trip and won't be able to make it."

"Oh, you did, did you?" Narli asked ironically. "What makes you think you know how I feel about parties?"

"But — "

"There's an interesting saying on Earth: 'Travel is so broadening.' " He looked down at his bulges with tolerant amusement. "In more than one way, in case the meaning eludes you. Very sound psychologically. I've discovered that I *like* parties. I *like* being *liked.* If you'll excuse me, I'm going to inform the Perzils that I shall be delighted to come to their party. Care to join me?"

"Well," Slood mumbled, "I'd like to, but I have so much work — "

"Introvert!" said Narli, and he began dialing the Perzils.

A Pestilence
of Psychoanalysts

J. O. JEPPSON

J. O. Jeppson is Janet, in case you've forgotten. She's a psychiatrist and a psychoanalyst and (even more than I) a P. G. Wodehouse fan. Put them all together and you get Pshrinks Anonymous which, to my way of thinking, is the best writing she's done yet, and this particular item is the Best of the Best. Janet insists that Pshrinks Anonymous is a mythical organization and that there is no similarity between any of the characters and any pshrink anyone has ever heard of — but I think I may be allowed my doubts.

As USUAL, an undertone of argument permeated the sacred precincts of the Psychoanalytic Alliance, an exclusive luncheon club known to its intimates and its enemies as Pshrinks Anonymous. The Oldest Member was holding forth. This also was not unusual.

"I tell you again that these newfangled analysts use peculiar words that no one understands. If I hear any more about the parameters of the paradigmatic processes I'll eat my hat."

"You've got it wrong," said one of his younger Freudian colleagues who liked to keep up to date, "and you haven't got a hat anyhow."

"Furthermore," continued the Oldest Member, "I object to the pollution to which all of you have subjected the name of our club, adding a silent p to shrinks . . ."

"Perhaps it was inevitable," said one of the Interpersonals. "And even ominous," she added.

For once the Oldest Member looked pleased to be interrupted by a female and an Interpersonal (in order of annoyance).

"Ominous?" he asked.

Simultaneously, the rest of the membership groaned and bent closely over their desserts, Bananas Castrata Flambé. The Oldest Member nodded encouragingly at the Interpersonal, who grinned.

*

The experience I am about to reveal [said the Interpersonal] happened only recently and has been much on my mind. This vignette, while obviously clinical, is not a case, since the person who brought the problem to my attention was not a patient but a colleague I hadn't seen for years, a pshrink I used to know when we both carried large iron keys to the locked wards of a well-known psychiatric hospital.

This colleague had always been a rather pedantic, phlegmatic man who yawned his way through analytic school some years after finishing his psychiatric residency, when the rest of us were already analysts, struggling to stay afloat on the ever-increasing ocean of jargon. I recalled that this down-to-earth type had a limited vocabulary and what some of us referred to as poverty of imagination. He had, naturally, left Manhattan for some Other Place when he started his analytic practice.

I was shocked, then, to get a frantic phone call from him, begging me to see him at a private lunch because he needed to discuss a confidential problem affecting his work. I told him my noon hour was free, and he said he would bring lunch in his briefcase.

As we munched corned beef on pumpernickel in my office, I discovered that he was in town for one of the psychoanalytic conventions. Being allergic to cigar smoke I had not yet been to the meetings, and I wondered what psychologically traumatic paper had affected my old friend.

"Listen, I remember that you're a sci-fi buff," he began.

"S–F!"

"Whatever. Do you believe in that stuff about ESP and dreams that come true and mysterious extraterrestrial beings and whatnot?"

"I'm still waiting for the hard evidence."

"Well, I don't have any, but after attending this convention it seems to me that I detect — something."

"Alien influence?" I asked facetiously through my corned beef.

"How did you know? Are you part of the conspiracy?"

I began to wonder whether or not I was doing a regular psychiatric consultation after all. I swallowed the last of my sandwich and studied my colleague. While plumper and grayer than he had been, the striking change was the faint twitching of his shoulders, possibly due to muscle strain caused by his new habit of looking nervously over them.

"No," I said. "Tell me what on Earth you are talking about."

He sighed. "I never was much good with words, you know. I barely made it through analytic school because I had so much trouble mastering the vocabulary.SincethenI'vetried — oh,howI'vetried,andthenmywife..."

"She's in the field, as I recall," I said.

"Yes, a — " (he named one of the more verbally agile allied fields). "She tried to help me, and so did some sympathetic colleagues, because at meetings I was a total loss. My papers were so easy to understand that nobody paid any attention to them, and I couldn't understand what anyone else was saying. Finally, after years of study and trying to catch up, I began to use and even understand some of the important words."

"The jargon."

"A pejorative word if I ever heard one," he said with a shrill laugh. "You see — I did it! I'm always doing it!"

"Using a big, obscure word?"

"No! I mean, yes — a word with a *p* in it!"

"I am puzzled . . ."

"There, now you're doing it! I'm convinced that it's a disease, catching and deadly dangerous."

"Unfortunately our field is riddled with *p*'s — psychiatry, psychology, psychoanalysis . . ."

He moaned. "That's just it. That's why we're the conduits for the malevolent influence from outer space."

"The what?"

"You heard me." He bit into the untouched second half of his sandwich, eyeing me suspiciously over a fringe of buttered lettuce sticking out. My colleague was a Wasp who always ate butter and lettuce with his corned beef sandwiches, which may be another reason why he had to emigrate from New York.

I decided to humor him. "Supposing there is a mysterious alien influence — how do you know it's malevolent?"

"You haven't been to a psychoanalytic convention lately, have you?"

"No."

"Then don't ask. Or maybe I should tell you. No, I'll just describe my own symptoms. It began with dreams, and don't try to analyze them the way Siggy would have."

"You know perfectly well that I'm non-Freudian. Tell me about your dreams."

"You sound just like me when I'm humoring a psychotic patient."

"Yep."

"What the hell. The dreams come every night. And they're full of words, most of which begin with *p,* that come to life in my head and chase each other around and threaten me. When the dreams began, I became aware of how everyone in my local psychoanalytic society talks like that. I used to feel I didn't belong, but suddenly I began to be part of the group."

"Comrades in jargon?"

"That's it. You don't know how I've been fighting it since I entered your office for lunch. Trying not to use many words beginning with *p.* I can feel them straining at the leash inside my skull, trying to get out, to join an invisible network throughout the terrestrial electromagnetic sphere . . ."

"Whoa!" I shouted, since his face was beginning to turn purple. "It does seem to be true that our fellow pshrinks speak in a lot of p's. Does it matter whether they are silent or vocalized — the p's, I mean?"

"I don't think so, but the vocalized seem worse. Proclivities instead of tendencies, parsimonious instead of stingy, paranoid instead of suspicious, and of course the multitude of words beginning with the unvocalized p in psycho."

"You'll have to blame most of the problem on the ancient Greeks."

He frowned. "Maybe they were subject to alien influence first. Come to think of it, maybe you're one of the ringleaders. You've got several p's in your name. The world is full of pee . . ."

As his voice rose in a wail, I interrupted. "You can always go to a Freudian and have your urethral complex analyzed."

["P–U!" murmured one of the club's pundits.]

My highly disturbed colleague gulped and began again, in a whisper. "It's much worse out where I live and work."

"Cheer up," I said. "Around here they're into illusory others and imaging and identifications that are introjective . . ."

"But where you have introjective you also have projective!"

["At least that gets us off the excretory system and onto more interesting anatomical analogies," said one of the Eclectics.]

"Now let's not get carried away," I admonished him. "The world is full of people who don't use words beginning with p."

"Is it? My son came home from college asking me to define the parameters of a meaningful marital pairing. My daughter at medical school heard a lecture on probability factors in the success of paternal participation in parturition. When I complained to my wife that the passion was going out of our partnership, she said I was predictably puerile. Then I started having repetitive dreams of being surrounded by a posse of parameters with pink faces and pallid tongues, or possibly the other way around."

"Well, I agree with you that all these p's do get to be pretentious, pompous, ponderous, and pedantic," I said.

"Pshaw! You've got it too."

"How can any of us help it!" I said, hoping that if I got into the spirit of the thing he might start analyzing me and stop being so crazy himself. "Sometimes I think that the patients have it much worse than the pshrinks. Why just the other day . . ."

"You're right. Nobody says anything simply anymore. Even patients postulate prohibitive propositions like trying to persuade me to cure their passive aggressive personality with psychodrama or their psychosomatic punishment with positioning patterns. They say they want profound sex and peak experiences . . ."

["I think I may be having one now," snarled a Freudian.]

". . . and I ask you, isn't it likely that we pshrinks are the most likely to be affected by all these *p*'s? Day after day we listen to the voices of the people, talking and talking and talking . . ."

"Which accounts for why we tend to get verbal diarrhea when let loose from our offices," I said, proud that I had managed a sentence with no *p* in it.

He was not amused. "Just last week one of my patients complained about the propinquity of the couch to my chair."

"Perish forbid," I said without thinking.

"Where did you get that expression?"

"My father used to say it when he wasn't actually swearing."

"Aha! You see! Unto the fourth generation!"

"If you go back that far they weren't speaking English."

"I was speaking metaphorically, implying that the alien influence began a long time ago," he said, picking crumbs off his pants. "My theory is that if you think and speak often enough and hard enough in words containing prominent *p*'s, your mind jells up and gets petrified."

"Paralyzed by *p*'s?" It was impossible to resist.

He glared at me. "You are then locked into an alien mind somewhere in the universe — maybe in outer space, maybe hiding somewhere in our Solar System. I don't like what could be developing in the middle layers of Jupiter, or under the ice cover of Europa."

Since his voice was rising again, I said, "So what?"

"Idiot! Don't you understand that after the aliens have gotten enough human minds locked to their system, they'll take control — take over Earth civilization!"

"I think you are — you should excuse the expression — projecting. Haven't you been worried about how the lunatic elements are trying to take over our field? I seem to remember now that you wrote a scathing paper on fringe groups."

"A paper that psychoanalysts and psychiatrists and psychologists perused without perceiving the profundity of the principles!"

"Hey! You have it bad, don't you?"

He burst into tears and threw himself prone on my couch.

The afternoon sun streaming into the window made the room warm, but I was too bemused by the problem to turn on the air conditioner. My next hour, I tardily recalled, was also free, since the patient was a young psychoanalyst in training who was at that moment delivering a paper at the same convention from which my friend was playing hooky. Soon my colleague was snoring, and I was drowsy enough to have a hypnagogic hallucination . . ."

["You mean you fell asleep," said another Interpersonal.]

["I did not," she said.]

I had a momentary impression of strange lines of force from far away, converging on my snoring colleague and then transferring to me. It was rather eerie, and I was glad when he woke up and bounded off the couch.

"You're marvelous! I'm cured!" He bent down, hugged me, grabbed his briefcase, and made for the door, where he paused. "It's all clear to me. I just had to tell someone about it in order to feel okay. I guess I was only a carrier."

"You perfidious proselytizer!" I exclaimed.

"Sorry about that. I'm going home. Maybe I'll see you at next year's convention." He held up two fingers. "Live long."

"And prosper peacefully," I said as he left.

A pregnant silence ensued around the luncheon table when the Interpersonal finished speaking.

Suddenly and simultaneously some of the more argumentative members of the club began to talk.

"The parameters of the problem are . . ."

"The physiological principles in pronouncing the *p* . . ."

"You Interpersonals and your parataxic distortions . . ."

"And your participant observation . . ."

"Prostituting the precepts of psychoanalytical . . ."

"Perseverating in the problem of the *p* . . ."

"Perhaps it's only a problem of psychic phenomena . . ."

"Probably poisoned by polypramasy . . ."

"The proposition is positively polymorphically perverse . . ."

And just as suddenly they all shut up. There was an uncomfortable shuffling of feet under the table. Then the youngest member, a first-year psychiatric resident allowed in to learn from his superiors, spoke timidly.

"Perhaps it's the fault of philosophers. I almost majored in philosophy in college, and it seems to me that they promote a plethora of phrases . . ." He stopped abruptly, eyes wide.

"Piffle," said the Oldest Member. "None of the jargon is absolutely necessary, although I'm partial to 'id' myself."

"Would you willingly give up 'penis envy'?" asked the Interpersonal.

"I think you should keep it in your prefrontal cortex," said the Oldest Member with frosty dignity as he stroked the erect waxed tips of his silver mustache, "that *I* do not need to have penis envy. Nor did the Master . . ."

"Who was primarily a physicalistic psychobiologist," said one of the more militant non-Freudians.

"But the Master had no *p*'s in his name," said the Interpersonal, favoring the Oldest Member's mustache with a glance of unalloyed admiration.

"Thank you," said the Oldest Member, patting the Interpersonal on the patella. "You do think that hypothesis about aliens is a lot of stuff and nonsense, don't you?"

The Interpersonal shrugged. "I haven't the slightest idea. I wish, however, that I didn't have this insatiable desire to go home and read *Pickwick Papers* — or possibly promulgate a parody."

"It goes *this* way, stupid!"

Gahan Wilson. Originally appeared in *The Magazine of Fantasy and Science Fiction.*

"It's that bug that's been going around town."

Gahan Wilson. Originally appeared in *The Magazine of Fantasy and Science Fiction.*

Death of a Foy

ISAAC ASIMOV

Isaac Asimov is, of course, your not-so-humble servant. Naturally, I commit "horrid puns." I committed them long before George Scithers invented the term in connection with these stories. I maintain that no one is better at it than I, although Janet — still influenced by that last pshrinks story, says I am merely a perpetrator of positively pernicious puns. Nevertheless, I defy you not to burst into laughter at the end of my horridest pun.

IT WAS EXTREMELY UNUSUAL for a Foy to be dying on Earth. Foys were the highest social class on their planet (with a name that was pronounced — as nearly as earthly throats could make the sounds — Sortibackenstrete) and were virtually immortal.

Every Foy, of course, came to voluntary death eventually, and this one had given up because of an ill-starred love affair, if you can call it a love affair when five individuals, in order to reproduce, must indulge in a year-long mental contact. Apparently, he himself had not fit into the contact after several months of trying and it had broken his heart — or hearts, for he had five.

All Foys had five large hearts, and there was speculation that this was what made them virtually immortal.

Maude Briscoe, Earth's most renowned surgeon, wanted those hearts. "It can't be just their number and size, Dwayne," she said to her chief assistant. "It has to be something physiological or biochemical. I must have them."

"I don't know if we can manage that," said Dwayne Johnson. "I've been speaking to him earnestly, trying to overcome the Foy taboo against dismemberment after death. I've had to play on the feeling of tragedy any Foy would have over death away from home. And I've had to lie to him, Maude."

"Lie?"

"I told him that after death, there would be a dirge sung for him by the world-famous choir led by Harold J. Gassenbaum. I told him that by earthly belief this would mean that his astral essence would be instantaneously wafted back, through hyperspace, to his home planet of Sortib-what's-its-name. Provided he signs a release allowing you, Maude, to have his hearts for scientific investigation."

"Don't tell me he believed that horse excrement!" said Maude.

"Well, you know this modern attitude about accepting the myths and beliefs of intelligent aliens. It wouldn't have been polite for him not to believe me. Besides, the Foys have a profound admiration for terrestrial science, and I think this one is a little flattered that we should want his hearts. He promised to consider the suggestion, and I hope he decides soon because he can't live more than another day or so. We must have his permission by interstellar law, and the hearts must be fresh, and . . . Ah, his signal."

Dwayne Johnson moved in with smooth and noiseless speed.

"Yes?" he whispered, unobtrusively turning on the holographic recording device in case the Foy wished to grant permission.

The Foy's large, gnarled, rather treelike body lay motionless on the bed. The bulging eyes palpitated (all five of them) as they rose, each on its stalk, and turned toward Dwayne. The Foy's voice had a strange tone and the lipless edges of his open round mouth did not move, but the words formed perfectly. His eyes were making the Foyan gesture of assent as he said:

"Give my big hearts to Maude, Dwayne. Dismember me for Harold's choir. Tell all the Foys on Sortibackenstrete, that I will soon be there . . ."

PART IV

Wacky Time Travel Problems

The One Thing Lacking

ISAAC ASIMOV

How I long to love Helen of Troy,
    Cleopatra, Marie Antoinette.
It would give me such ultimate joy
    Could I only move backward and get
The great beauties of history's pages.
    Think how greatly resounding my name
As I top all the belles of the ages.
    How eternal and gilt-edged my fame!
Yet though that is my whole life's ambition;
    Though I'm handsome and wealthy and clean;
Though I laugh at the poor competition;
    What I lack is just *one* time machine.

The Merchant of Stratford

FRANK RAMIREZ

This story gives rise to one of those strange problems that rack the brain and may be insoluble paradoxes. If someone offers three Asimovs and an Ellison for something, is that because I can be taken in multiple doses whereas one of Harlan is enough for anybody? Or is it because three of me is about equivalent to one of him? Oh, well, read the story and decide for yourself.

I TENSED with anticipation as the straps were tightened. The moment had finally come.

Gone from my mind were the agonies of years in planning, months in engineering, days in language training.

All thoughts were swept behind as I focused my attentions on the task at hand. Imagine! The wonder of it! Traveling back in time to speak with none other than the Immortal Bard himself! Unbelievable!

The greatest poet of all time, the man whose plays were still box-office hits after four hundred years, a man who could speak to and move humanity across the span of centuries — and to think he did it all by accident! For surely he had only written those masterpieces to fill a specific demand, writing parts to be performed by specific actors on a specific stage. What a genius!

In my storage compartment were volumes for his perusal — a concise history of the world through the year 2000, a selection of the greatest poets since the master, selected volumes of Shakespearean criticism, and the massive one-volume *Armstead Shakespeare,* the *definitive* Shakespeare, published in 1997.

What would the Bard think of the changes in technology, of the new direction art had taken, of the advance of our scholarship? I had hopes that the praise of four centuries would comfort him during his declining years, bringing a peace to his soul.

And I wondered, would he accept my offer and return with me to the twenty-first century?

I remembered the trepidation of my staff with regard to the so-called dangers of time travel. Would my presence in the early seventeenth century change the course of history? It took many days to convince all concerned that their fears were groundless. I was going to visit the *past*. Therefore, if I had succeeded, I had already been there. I had always been there. With a little help from a philosopher of the university, I made my point.

I slept little the night before. I paced furiously, thoughts racing. The fruits of the ages were to be laid humbly at his feet. Would he find the specially bound volumes worthy? Lord grant he would accept and enjoy.

Would our lifestyle shock his sensibilities? Surely not, for he was the universal man.

These and many other questions passed through my mind that night.

After an eternity — morning.

I ate, then donned the costume provided by the theater department. I was dressed as a man of moderate wealth. My beard was trimmed to fit any prevailing fashion. My purse was filled with coin that would serve.

As I entered the sphere I turned and smiled at the white-suited technicians. A quick wave, I slipped inside, and the door was slammed into place. At last I was alone. I clasped the straps, and they tightened themselves. I relayed the readings of several instruments, listened to last-minute instructions, and waited.

Tensing, I watched as the chronometer marked the last few seconds. The moment passed —

When the grand millisecond arrived I felt little more than a minor lurch. I had arrived.

My first impulse was to force open the door and run into the open air, to breathe the air the Bard was breathing, to share his world.

Instead, I took two deep breaths, paused, then went through the checklist.

But all the time I thought: 1615! Shakespeare had retired from the stage. Soon I would learn — what would I learn? The exact texts of the plays, perhaps the extent of the canon, answers to all the mysteries, details of his life; did all of these things wait for me?

When at last I completed the checklist I depressurized the cabin, opened the door, and stepped into the seventeenth century.

I also stepped into a pile of dung.

I spent a few moments hiding the machine in some bushes. One of my worries was that I might startle the highly superstitious natives who, believing in the supernatural, might attempt to do me harm. This caused me to wonder: Would the Bard himself believe that he was in the presence of a devil or an angel? Nay; surely *he* could accept the truth.

I sang as I tramped — one mile, two miles . . . Stratford was proving to be farther than I thought . . . three, four, hmmmm . . . six, seven, gasp . . . eight, wheeze . . . was that — ? Yes — I could see — I had arrived at —

Stratford.

I hurried, guided by a map prepared by the history department.

It was not long before I reached what could only be New Place, the residence of Master Will. More than a little excited, I approached the gate, passed through it, and stepped forward toward the door. I briefly noted that the actual house was quite different, more — modern, if that's the word, than I had imagined. It mattered little to me at the moment, however. My heart skipped a beat as I read the name on the plate: Mast. Wm. Shakespear. I had arrived.

I knocked firmly on the door, determined not to disgrace my century. A woman (no doubt the former Anne Hathaway) came to answer. Looking me over with what I thought might be amusement (was there something wrong with my costume?!) she said, "What ho! Stand and present yourself!"

"I have come," I said, "upon a matter of momentous importance. Is Master Shakespeare at home?!"

Hesitating not a moment, she shouted over her shoulder, "Hey nonny, ho nonny, another nonny ninny, Will!"

Mystified, I followed her beyond the door, puzzling over her remark. Leading me down a murky corridor, she at last brought me to a small study, which she indicated I should enter. I did so with much emotion.

There he sat!

Head down, pen racing across paper, the books filling the dim shelves, light streaming through the window to illumine the words divine: Shakespeare, messenger of the gods! What unknown work was he penning, what sonnet unimagined; with what phrase unguessed was he gracing paper as no product of coarse wood deserved to be? In that instant I wished wildly that I was the paper, the ink, the instrument by which the immortal bard —

He lifted his head and spoke.

"Sit down, won't you?" he said. "I'll be with you in a moment."

Something strange there.

But his voice . . . and his words! "I'll be with you in a moment." Who else? Who else could have spoken those words? I resolved at my earliest opportunity to travel further back into time, to the days when a younger Shakespeare graced the stage.

He blew his nose on his sleeve.

Of course, I thought hurriedly, I mustn't judge him by *my* standards. Besides, a deeper problem weighed on my mind. How could I possibly convey, without shocking, my mission to this most excellent member of the human race?

I reached for my camera, determined to save for all time a true portrait of the man who transcended ages. I brought the device to my face, glanced through the viewfinder, and prepared to press the button when I noticed that a hand was obscuring the vision of the lens.

The hand belonged to none other than Will himself. I lowered the camera. But of course, how stupid of me, the strange instrument frightened him. I would explain its function and —

"Please," he was saying. "No pictures, please. You'll have to clear it with my agent."

Shock. What was I hearing? I was deluding myself; I hadn't heard anything of the sort. I was —

"Listen," I was saying, "I know you'll find this hard to believe, but you must try to understand. Listen carefully. I am — "

" — a man from the future, I know," he finished. "Come now," he continued, "you don't really think you're the first man who's ever — is something the matter?"

"How — "

"Oh! I understand. You must be one of the first. Imagine, I'm in the presence of one of the first time travelers. I'm so very sorry for the shock."

Sorry for the — wasn't that my line?

Suddenly I knew what had bothered me about the way he spoke.

"But you speak perfect English! I mean contemporary! I mean — and your wife!"

"Pretty good, don't you think? I love to get the chance to practice it. It's like a second language. But of course I had to learn it, don't you know, what with all the time travelers from all the different centuries coming and going willy-nilly as they pleased. Come to think of it, it *has* been a pretty quiet day. I think you're one of the first this morning."

I remained speechless, as the implications began to sink in.

He was eyeing my bag.

"What have you got for me?" he asked.

"Got for you?"

"Yes, all of the early time travelers brought me gifts, books, pocket dictionaries, histories, certificates, plaques, that sort of thing. What did *you* bring?"

I emptied the contents of my bag. He quickly glanced at the titles. The books of criticism he threw in a rubbish heap in the corner, along with an expletive.

"Bloody useless things, those, as if I'd written the plays to be read."

The collected works brought a small chuckle. The history he placed in a pile on his desk with the comment, "Might be able to sell this one."

Thinking it over, however, he withdrew it from the stack and threw it in the corner with the criticism.

"Not for much, though."

Finally, he perused the volume of poetry. It had a special dedication to the Bard, praising him for his work, laying before his feet these humble trifles, etc. He harumphed, closed it, and looked at me.

"Is this the best you could do?"

I replied, "It was selected by our English department."

"Figures," he said. "Next time you come, bring some Zelazny."

Zelazny? Who was — He must have read my face.

"Haven't you ever heard of him?" he asked. "And while you're at it send some Asimov too. Can't get enough through channels. I've got almost all of Heinlein's books, but let me see if there's something you . . ."

Tapering off, he turned to face a list stapled — stapled! — below his bookshelf, which I could now see very clearly. The bindings were decidedly unseventeenth century.

"I remember now!" he brightened. "See if you can find me that issue of *Galaxy* from the summer of 1973. I've been dying to read the end of that Clarke novel."

"Who are all these people?"

"Science fiction writers," he said with reverence. "You fool," he added with derision.

"You *like* science fiction?"

One would have thought I'd cursed the Queen and spit on the Bible by the look he gave me.

"Of course I do. It reminds me of my work."

"I'm afraid I don't understand."

"Well, it's honest, for one thing. I wrote plays, and was looked down upon by my contemporaries for doing so. I didn't write what was considered literature. I wrote to entertain *and* to make a little money. The same thing was true for sf. But what happened centuries after its birth? Let me see if I can find my copy of that variorum edition of *The Martian Chronicles.* Now you've got me sounding like a Heinlein character."

I said nothing.

"Something the matter?" he asked.

"Yes, something's the matter. Speak Elizabethan."

"Maybe later, if you behave. And don't forget, James is on the throne. You should have asked me to speak Jacobean."

"What's going on here?" I shouted. "I'm the first person to travel back in time!"

"But you're certainly not the first to get here!"

I shook my head as he continued.

"I've been getting visitors from the future as far back as I can remember. My mother, being a good Christian woman, had the hardest time giving me suck, because the documentary team from the thirty-third century wanted to film it all. I barely survived childhood. Fortunately my father was a shrewd businessman. He managed to capitalize off the circumstances. Of course he spent so much time in negotiations that he couldn't attend council meetings so, you know, he was thrown out, but — say, don't tell me you're surprised by all this. Why do you think I died only fifty years after I was born? I spent forty years in countless different centuries."

"What did you do?"

"Oh, the usual: dedicated hospitals, opened restaurants, christened space-ships, spoke at ladies' luncheons, appeared on talk shows, lectured on what you might call the chicken-and-peas circuit, that sort of thing."

I think I must have been shaking visibly, for he said, "Calm down, have a drink." He reached for a bottle and poured something strong. I sputtered as I downed it in one gulp.

"What *was* that?" I asked, remembering that the bottle and the seventeenth century —

"I'm not sure. Someone from the twenty-eighth century left it here. Well now, feel better? You know, Jesus once told me that to stay calm one should always practice — "

"Jesus?"

"Yes, of course. Some clowns from the thirtieth century thought it'd be a gas for me to meet him. Really nice fellow, don't you know, sort of intense; but he could take a joke. He never forgave me for the character of Shylock, though. Rather petty, don't you think? But then, you have to consider his point of view, and he *was* under a lot of pressure. If you think I've time travelers in my hair you should've seen him!"

I must have looked forlorn.

"Tell you what, just to show there's no hard feelings, I'll sell you a copy of my complete works, and my autobiography as well." He reached behind and pulled two plastic-bound volumes from two different stacks. One was impos-ingly thick.

"Here they are, treasure of the ages, all the plays I ever wrote, approved text, cast lists, year of composition, sources, random bits of poetry, and a previously unpublished novel, *Go-Captains in Norstrilia.* And this here is the complete autobiography, with all the important facts that led to my becoming the Immortal Bard. Did you live before the twenty-sixth century?"

"Yes."

"Dollars, credits, or muffins?"

"All I've got are these gold pieces."

He looked them over.

"I guess I'll trust you. How many did you bring?"

"Twelve."

"You're in luck. The price just happens to be twelve gold pieces."

"But I'm the first Time Traveler!"

"Eleven. It's my final offer."

I accepted.

"Have Anne give you a receipt at the door. Oh, and don't let her sell you my copy of Holinshed. They all fall for that."

"Please," I begged, "will you return with me to the twenty-first century?"

"Sorry, never travel before the twenty-fourth if I can help it."

I could see there was nothing left for me to do. I turned to leave, a broken shell.

POP! What — !?

A man stepped out of nothing, holding what appeared to be an annoyed octopus. He stuck a tentacle in my face.

"That's right, look into the trivid, that's a good Timey. Pevlik, System News Syndic, twenty-third century. Would you mind answering a few — "

POP!

"Here he is. My, you've given me a chase. Astor, *Galactic Globe.* Tell me, what is your impression of — "

POP!

"Stanik, *Centauri Sentinel* — "

POP! POP!

"Hey! You!"

POP! POP! POP!

"Stilgrin, *Filbert Studge Stationer!*"

POP! POP! POP! POP! POP!

Ten, fifteen, twenty assorted humanoids suddenly surrounded me. I felt faint, dizzy, dazed. I could hardly breathe.

"Let me out of here! What's going on?"

"Don't you know?" asked someone with purple hair.

"Know what?"

In unison: "You're the first Time Traveler!"

Everything began to fade as I sank to my knees. No, I thought, don't let it end this way.

"Zounds!" shouted a familiar voice. "By Gis and by Saint Charity, give the man air."

"Aw, come on, Will, give us a break," said one of the reporters.

"That I will. Doubt that the stars are fire, but never doubt that old Shaxpur would ever forget the people that made him famous. I know you want exclusives on the first Time Traveler, and I promise you, speaking as the lad's business manager — "

"My what?" I shouted. "A second ago you were ushering — "

"In the words of another Immortal Bard, 'It's raining soup, grab a bucket!' You want to make a little cash on this thing? These guys'll steal you blind if you let them."

"And you?"

He tried unsuccessfully to look hurt.

"I'd only take forty percent, no more than my fair share. It's only fitting I take care of you as my father took care of me."

"How much did he take?"

"Eighty percent till my twenty-first year."

"Good friend," I sighed, "For Jesus' sake waste no more time convincing me. Talk to them," I said, pointing at the mob, "and soon," I added. "I think they're getting hungry."

"Right away, boss. Who'll start the bidding for the interview? The man in the front offers three Asimovs and an Ellison. Who'll add a Brunner?"

The Wheel of Time

ROBERT ARTHUR

Things have a way of rebounding. Biters get bitten, and those who live by the sword die by the sword. People hate it when it happens to them. (I know; I have a whole list of remembered incidents in my life in which I had the last word only to find that someone else then had the after-the-last word and wiped me out.) It's always funny, though, when it happens to someone else, especially to someone who's too smart for his own good (that is, smarter than you are).

IT WAS A LOVELY SUNDAY MORNING in July when Jeremiah Jupiter called to suggest a picnic. I must have been feeling suicidal that day, because I accepted.

Jeremiah Jupiter has a mint of money and a yen for scientific experimenting — on me, if he can. His mind and lightning work the same way — fast, in zig-zag streaks. He's either the greatest scientist who ever lived, or the worst screwball who ever trod this mundane sphere.

But I had an excuse this time for not realizing he was up to something. I thought he meant a real picnic — the kind with lots of cold chicken and lobster salad. If there's anything Jupiter loves besides science, it's eating, especially on picnics. The lunch basket his Javanese boy packs up would lure Oscar of the Waldorf away from his skillet.

I stipulated, however, that I absolutely must be back in New York by evening, for I had an important dinner engagement with an out-of-town editor. He was returning to Chicago Monday morning, so at dinner we were going to settle on terms for a serial of mine he wanted to buy, provided he could take it with him and rush it to the press the minute he got back to Chicago. Since I figured on getting at least two thousand for the story, I was anticipating that dinner with considerable zest.

Jupiter promised we would be back in time, said he'd call for me in an hour, and rang off. I dressed, in some lightweight flannels, one of the new Pandanus grass hats decorated with a bright-colored band, and an appetite. Promptly in an hour I heard Jupiter's honk, and went out.

When I got outside, though, I stopped in amazement. Jupiter wasn't driving his usual V-16 touring car. Instead, he was at the wheel of a Jeremiah Jupiter lab truck, with an enclosed body. My suspicions were instantly aroused.

"Lucius!" Jupiter caroled. His bright blue eyes in his chubby pink face sparkled behind their powerful horn-rimmed spectacles. "I'm so glad you can make it. What a day for a picnic, eh? We'll have the time of our lives!"

He put a queer emphasis on the word time, and chuckled. I looked at him darkly as I clambered in beside him.

"Jupiter," I demanded, "since when have you been a truck driver?"

"Er — " Jupiter coughed — "I have some guests. I thought it best to bring them in a truck. Avoid the stares of the Sunday crowds."

"Guests?" I whirled around, and peered into the body of the truck through a panel opening. The inside was quite light. I could see perfectly. I realized that after I had rubbed my eyes twice, and what I saw still stayed the same.

And what I saw were three large chimpanzees, wearing clothes and horn-rimmed spectacles, hanging from support rods in the top of the truck while they read volumes of *The Encyclopaedia Britannica*!

"Jupiter!" I said. Jeremiah Jupiter flinched.

"Don't scream, Lucius," he reproved. "If you make a habit of it, you'll get cancer of the vocal cords. Anyway, they aren't really reading the encyclopedia. It's part of the act. There are thin candy wafers between the pages, and they turn the pages looking for them. When they pop the wafers into their mouths, they seem to be licking their thumbs. That gives them the appearance of studying. Really, they never actually read anything but the comic sheets."

"Jupiter!" This time the word came out in a strangled voice, as I kept control of myself by an effort. "I won't ask you why you're bringing three trained chimpanzees along on a picnic. I won't ask you what that very sinister-looking apparatus under the tarpaulin is. I won't ask you what madness your sly, serpentine, Machiavellian mind is bent upon. But one thing I do want to know.

"*What are those three motorcycles in the back of the truck for?*"

"Lucius," Jeremiah complained, dashing at a space between a bridge abutment and a ten-ton truck that would not have accommodated a stout bicyclist, "you will really get cancer of the vocal cords. I detected a distinct crack in your voice then."

"Hah!" I breathed. "Hah! What a chance for a *mot juste* on my part. But I'll restrain myself — if you'll explain why we are going on a picnic with three chimpanzees who read encyclopedias while hanging by their heels, and three undersized motorcycles painted vermillion, gold, and silver!"

"They're part of the act too," Jeremiah chirped, finding the bridge clear and roaring the truck down it at breakneck speed. "The chimpanzees ride the motorcycles around and around while they study the encyclopedia."

"Jupiter — " now I was just whispering — "I do not say that makes sense, but I'll accept it. On looking closer, however, I see that beside the motorcycles are three bass drums. *What the devil are the drums for?*"

"You will have to let me x-ray your throat when we return, Lucius," Jupiter said, with a worried expression. "You sounded so strange then . . . Why, the drums are — "

"Part of the act!"

"Yes, indeed," he agreed brightly. "The drums fasten to the handlebars of the motorcycles. Then the chimps ride the motorcycles around on the stage — I bought them from a vaudeville animal act — beating the drums, reading the encyclopedia, and throwing out oranges to the audience."

I was reduced to speechlessness for a good half hour as we drove up the Jersey shore of the Hudson. At last I made an effort and blinked the glassy feeling from my eyes.

"You," I said, "brought along three chimpanzees who ride motorcycles, beat bass drums, study the encyclopedia, and throw oranges at people, all at one and the same time — you brought along these intelligent, educated, amiable, sociable, versatile creatures to keep us entertained while we picnic? You did all this just to while away the time and amuse us as we eat? Is that it, Jeremiah?"

My chubby companion shook his head.

"Not at all, Lucius," he piped. "They will play an important part in the epochal scientific achievement you are going to witness. Although I have food with me, this is really going to be a picnic of science, Lucius, a feast of knowledge rather than a mere gorging of the corporeal body. Aren't you excited at the thought?"

I gurgled slowly and collapsed.

"No," I murmured hollowly. "No, I won't help you."

"Help me do what, Lucius?"

"Whatever it is you're planning. I won't help you."

"I was afraid of that," my small friend sighed sadly. "That's why I brought the chimpanzees. They're highly trained, very intelligent, and they shall be my only assistants in the precedent-shattering feat I am about to perform. You need do nothing but look on. And applaud, of course."

"What — " I hardly dared ask it — "what is the experiment, Jeremiah?"

Jeremiah Jupiter's face took on the rapt, dreamy look I knew too well.

"I am going," he said, "I am going, Lucius, to upset the time rhythm of the universe!"

There is nothing small about Jupiter. When he takes a notion to investigate space and distance, he short-circuits infinity. Now that it had occurred to him that time would make a fascinating scientific plaything, he was preparing to upset the universe's time rhythm, whatever that was.

"Jupiter," I said in the merest whisper, "Jupiter, let me out right here. I'm going to walk back."

"I really am worried about you, Lucius," Jupiter told me, swinging the truck off the road into a muddy lane leading through a wood. "I'm positive there's something wrong with . . . But anyway, here we are. Here's where we're going to have our picnic."

He pulled the truck to a stop in the middle of a grassy meadow dominated by a large oak tree. A hundred yards away was a section of the Palisades, dropping sheer to the blue of the Hudson River. In the other direction, the field sloped gently.

There were, however, several large grassy mounds in the middle of the meadow, and one of these showed signs of having been dug into recently. The spot where Jupiter chose to stop was between the tree and the mounds, and he immediately jumped down and ran around to open up the back of the truck.

"Come, Lucius!" he called. "I need your help. That's a boy, King. Good girl, Queenie. Come on now, Joker. Give me the books. Get down and romp in the grass. This is going to be a picnic."

The three chimpanzees hopped lightly down and began doing somersaults in the grass at the word *picnic*, which they seemed to recognize. Little did they know!

The largest of the chimps had a broad, apish face, fringed by graying hair. He was tastefully costumed in an Indian suit, with plenty of bright beadwork around the cuffs and pockets. From time to time he paused to pick a bead off and eat it, chewing reflectively. Then he went back to turning somersaults.

The chimp Jupiter had called Queenie had on a skirt and blouse, also Indian, but the smallest and youngest of the three — my companion informed me that King and Queenie were his parents, which was why he was called Joker, or in full, Jack Joker — was gaily decked out in an acrobat's silk shorts and jersey with an American eagle across his chest.

He did flipflops around his parents while Jupiter and I sweated to unload the truck.

We ran the motorcycles, one crimson, one gold, one silver, and smaller than standard models, down an extensible ramp onto the grass. Each had a small sidecar attached, and in these I saw some glittering objects like gargantuan liver pills, but I had no chance to investigate them.

Jupiter handed me down the three small bass drums, each with a portrait of its owner painted on the head, and I placed these beside the motorcycles. King, Queenie, and Joker recognized their property and made sounds of anticipation, but Jupiter shooed them away.

"Go on, play," he told them. "First we're going to eat. The drums come later."

Either recognizing the voice of a master before whom nature herself quailed, or because he was now unloading the large vacuum lunch hamper, the chimps scampered around in circles, playing tag and chattering. Jupiter handed me the hamper and jumped down. I tottered with it to the shade of the oak, and he trotted at my side, rubbing his hands and exuding enthusiasm.

"Hmm," he said, peering into the hamper. "No reason why we shouldn't eat now. Put you in a better mood perhaps, Lucius. Now let's see, what have we here? Breast of Hungarian pheasant? Ah!"

Munching, he flung himself down on the grass. He tossed a bag of peanuts to each of the chimps, and they swung happily up into the lower branches of the oak, where they squatted, eating peanuts and tossing the shells at me. Moodily I chewed on squab in jelly, and blasphemed the base appetites that had lured me into this expedition.

"Now, Lucius," Jeremiah said brightly, licking his fingers, "I dare say I'll have to outline for you what it is I'm going to do. In the first place, time is nothing but rhythmic forces — "

"How do you know?" I asked rudely.

"I deducted it logically," he informed me, sinking his teeth into a turkey leg. "It came to me in a flash one night when I was setting my alarm clock. Everything else in nature, I realized, is rhythmic. The seasons, the progressions of the stars, birth, life, light waves, radio waves, electrical impulses, the motions of molecules — everything. All move according to fixed and definite rhythms. Obviously, I deduced, since the universe is constructed upon a pattern of rhythm, time must be rhythmic too. It's just that nobody ever thought of it before."

"And now that you've thought of it," I asked, opening a bottle of Moselle from the cooling compartment, "what has it gotten you?"

"Just this, Lucius!" Jupiter bubbled with excitement. *"Any rhythm can be interrupted by a properly applied counterrhythm!"*

I opened my mouth and forgot to put anything in it. "Now surely," Jeremiah said patiently, "even though you do spend all your time swinging golf clubs, waving tennis racquets, or whirling polo mallets, when you're not writing the puny little pieces of fiction you compose as an excuse for not working, you must know some elementary physics.

"I am positive you must have read of experiments in which two light waves of the proper lengths, being made to interfere with each other, produce darkness. And the fact that two sounds, properly chosen for pitch, can get in each other's way, with complete silence as the result."

I nodded.

"Yes," I admitted. "I know about that. What's that got to do with time?"

"The time rhythm," he corrected me. "Or, the Jeremiah Jupiter Time-Rhythm Effect, as succeeding generations will call it. Why, it's quite obvious. If you can interfere with light and produce darkness, if you can interfere with sound and produce silence, then obviously you can interfere with present time and produce past time."

It was not obvious to me, and I said so.

My companion sighed.

"Very well, Lucius," he remarked. "I've made it as plain as I can, and if you don't understand I'm sorry. Your attitude is no surprise to me. In fact it accurately reflects what my professional colleagues would say, and that is the reason we are here today. To provide irrefutable proof which, upon being presented to certain contemporaries calling themselves scientists, will force them to respect the monograph on the subject I'm now writing."

His eyes glittered. Jeremiah Jupiter has had notable encounters with his fellow scientists in the past, but he has never yet emerged the loser.

"A demonstration, Lucius," he explained, "they would claim was faked. Consequently I am going to prove I can interrupt the time rhythm of the present and produce the past so that even the most skeptical dolt cannot doubt."

He poured himself a tall glass of Moselle and drank it with great appreciation. Perceiving that the chimps in the tree overhead had finished their peanuts, he tossed each of them a bottle of soda pop, which they drank with avid gurglings.

"That is where King, Queenie, and Joker come in," he informed me. "I knew that you, Lucius, would balk. They, however, are equally competent to do what is necessary, and much less skeptical. You see, I have prepared a number of time capsules — "

"Time capsules!"

"To use a layman's terminology. I have one here."

He produced from one of his bulging pockets an article shaped like a gelatine capsule, about as big as his fist, and apparently made of platinum, for it was very heavy.

It seemed solid; at least there was no way of opening it. On the polished surface was deeply engraved, in bold script, *Jeremiah Jupiter Time Capsule. A. D. 1965. Melt at left-hand tip to open.*

"In it," Jupiter told me, "there is a microfilm of the *New York Times,* another microfilm containing my autobiography and listing some of my more noteworthy discoveries, a third microfilm announcing that I shall presently publish my findings concerning the Jupiter Time-Rhythm Effect, and a small compartment containing the merest pinch of radium."

"But — "

"Those mounds — " he gestured — "are recently discovered barrows containing ruins of an ancient barbaric civilization on this spot. In digging, the archeologists have also discovered that beneath this meadow is a clay stratum, once part of a swampy coastline, containing tremendous numbers of fossils. The digging has only begun. In a short time it will be undertaken more extensively, and this whole area sifted for fossils and other finds.

"And among the objects found, Lucius, will be one or more Jeremiah Jupiter Time Capsules! Clever, eh?"

He gazed at me brightly, but I could only scowl.

"You mean," I demanded, "you're going to dig down in this meadow and plant your time capsules for the archeologists to find next week, or next month? But I don't see — "

The pink, cherubic face clouded over.

"Lucius, sometimes I despair of you," he sighed. "Of course not. I am going to set up an interference in the time rhythm at this particular spot. Then the chimpanzees will enter it with my time capsules — since I know *you* won't — and *they will deposit the capsules here a million years ago!*"

He gazed at me anxiously.

"Are you sure you're well, Lucius? Your throat isn't bothering you again? You seem to be choking. Now you understand, of course. My time capsules, deposited here a million years ago, will have been resting beneath this meadow all that time. The archeologists, digging down into strata they know were laid down before the dawn of history, will find at least one time capsule.

"There will be only one possible explanation — that it was actually placed there in the past. By measuring the disintegration of the radium inside, they will know the exact number of years it has been lying there, waiting to be found by —

"Here, Lucius, drink this wine, please!"

I drank it. I felt stronger then, but not strong enough to argue with him.

"I do not understand, Jupiter," I told him. "But let that pass. I will take your word for it. You are going to set up an interference in the time rhythm, making today yesterday, a million years removed. But why yesterday? Why not tomorrow too? Why not have a peep into the future as well?"

He placed his plump fingers together and pursed his lips.

"I can excuse you for asking that question," he chirped, "because I asked it myself when first the idea came to me. But it is impossible. I logically established its impossibility and dismissed the thought from my mind.

"I think I can make it plain why, though I can reduce the present to the past, I cannot resolve it into the future. Let us assume that you have a grandchild someday."

"But I'm not even married," I protested.

"Please don't be irrelevant. In the course of events your grandchild grows up and develops an inflamed appendix that must be operated upon."

"More likely peptic ulcers from traveling around too much via the Jupiter Spatial By-pass," I suggested wickedly.

He remained unruffled. "Let us say I am a doctor. In the course of time, your grandchild comes to me and I cut into him, remove his appendix. I do it *then.* But obviously I could never do it now, because neither grandchild nor appendix has yet occurred. So it is with the future. As it hasn't occurred, I can't penetrate into it. Now to the business at hand."

He rose and strode briskly over to the truck. I followed. Together we slid the heavy apparatus under the tarpaulin down the ramp and set it up on the grass.

While we were doing this I noticed that the three chimps had dropped out of the tree and were chattering excitedly about something, but I was too busy to see what.

The object that my companion was now handling with such loving care was large and square, something like one of the old cabinet television sets of my boyhood. It had similar dials on the front, and when he lifted the top, I saw bank after bank of tubes inside, as well as a large drum that apparently revolved.

The middle of the front was given over to a speakerlike opening, and a long insulated wire depended from the rear. This wire was attached to a steel prong, which Jupiter drove into the earth several feet behind the unwholesome apparatus.

"That forms a ground connection," he remarked. "Now we're ready to make a preliminary test of my Time-Rhythm Resonator. Where are the chimps?"

I looked up.

"They're drinking the Moselle!" I yelled. "They're getting tight!"

Jupiter, in the midst of adjusting something, jerked upright. The chimps certainly were getting intoxicated, and in a hurry. Having finished off their soda pop, they'd dropped down out of the oak as soon as we'd left and picked up the Moselle. Now they were guzzling it as fast as they could get it down, giving guttural calls and cries of enjoyment.

"They can't get drunk!" Jupiter cried. "That might spoil the experiment! Lucius, we must take the wine away from them!"

We rushed across the grass. As soon as they saw us coming, King, Queenie, and Joker took to their heels, scampering away with knuckles touching the ground to give them extra speed. They dashed for their motorcycles, leaped into the seats, and got under way.

The motorcycles were electric and could be started, stopped, or steered with one hand — or foot. King took off first. He grabbed the handlebar control with his foot, the machine hummed, and then shot toward us. With a tipsy whoop Queenie followed. Joker paused long enough to grab up his drum. Then, steering with one foot, holding on with the other, grasping the drum with one paw and banging it with the other fist, he charged after his parents.

"Jump, Lucius!" Jupiter shrilled. He leaped one way and I the other. King and Queenie whizzed between us, and Joker, banging lustily on the drum and emitting a kind of simian war whoop, zipped past behind them.

Jeremiah Jupiter fell on his face. I banged against the tree trunk. The three chimpanzee Barney Oldfields went whooping around the tree, turned, and started back.

"Look out!" I yelled. Jupiter got dazedly to his feet just as the chimps came around the second lap. Then I leaped, and King and Queenie and Joker, all abreast, rocking and swaying, roared by underneath me and were gone again.

I was in the lower branches of the oak by then. Turning, I discovered Jupiter on the next limb.

"You and your discoveries!" I grated.

But he wasn't listening. He was staring at his apparatus, and he looked worried.

"Er — Lucius," he remarked. "I think my Time-Rhythm Resonator is working."

I looked. I could see the tubes glowing, right enough.

"Well?" I asked. "Nothing's happening."

"Um — I think I'd better go turn it off anyway. The revolving drum was not working properly and I was about to adjust it — "

He dropped to the ground and started toward the thing. I dropped behind him and started that way too, just as the three tipsy chimps on their gaudy motorcycles came past a third time, still rocking and swaying, whooping, Joker beating the drum.

"Look out!" I yelled, and leaped. They went past underneath, dust spurting, and back in the tree again I turned, to discover Jupiter on the next branch.

"You and your discoveries!" I grated between my teeth.

But he wasn't listening. He was staring at his apparatus, and he looked worried.

"Er — Lucius," he said. "I think my Time-Rhythm Resonator is working."

I could see the tubes glowing, right enough.

"Well?" I asked. "Nothing's happening."

"Um — I think I'd better go turn it off anyway. The revolving drum was not working properly and I was about to adjust it — "

He dropped to the ground, and I after him. Just as we did so, I saw the three chimpanzees on their vaudeville-act cycles roaring around the oak at us again, and it flashed through my mind that all this was very familiar. That we had, in fact, just done it all a moment before —

Then, leaping, I was in the tree again, the chimps were zooming by underneath, and Jupiter was clinging to the next branch.

And I knew! Jupiter's machine was stuck, like a phonograph with a cracked record! It wasn't changing the present to the past, but *repeating the present over and over again!*

Bitter horror overwhelmed me. We were doomed to keep leaping up into that oak while three drunken chimpanzees tried to run us down until — until — My brain reeled.

"You and your discoveries!" I screamed.

Jupiter did not answer. He was staring at his machine —

It was after the little act had been repeated for the tenth time — I think it was the tenth, though it seemed as if we spent days hopping up and down out of that tree — that King and Queenie and Joker, instead of trying to run us down, swerved and brought their motorcycles to a stop. They leaped off and began turning somersaults, as if waiting for the applause. Jupiter rushed across to his machine and clicked a switch. Then he mopped his brow.

"Goodness," he said mildly. "I'm certainly glad I put in that automatic cut-off switch. The drum was caught in one position, and — "

" — and time kept repeating itself around here!" I yelled hoarsely. "We were stuck in time! Talk about being in a rut! If that machine hadn't stopped we'd have spent eternity dodging intoxicated chimpanzees on motorcycles!"

"Any apparatus may have a bug or two in it at first," Jeremiah Jupiter said, but I could see he was slightly shaken. It had been hot work, jumping up and down out of that oak, and Jeremiah does not like exercise. His pink face was bedewed with perspiration.

"However," he went on briskly, "I have that fixed now. Now to turn the resonator around, so its field of operation will be directed toward the mounds, and we're all ready."

He moved the square box about, did a few things to it, and turned toward the chimps. Sobered and abashed now, they crouched beside their cycles as if expecting to be punished. Jupiter patted them on the shoulders reassuringly and got them back onto their motorcycles. Then he fastened King's and Queenie's drums to the handlebars, retrieved Joker's drum and fastened that in place too, and lined them up facing toward the mounds.

From the truck he brought out three volumes of the encyclopedia and gave one to each. The chimps immediately brightened up.

"Now they feel at home," Jupiter informed me. "They have all the trappings of their act. Nothing is missing, so they're reassured. Like children. Everything's all right now. They won't lose control of themselves this time. You'll see."

He pointed into the small sidecars attached to the machines. I saw now that the glittery objects in the sidecars were platinum time capsules.

"Oranges," Jeremiah Jupiter said, drawing the chimps' attention to them. "Oranges," and he made a throwing motion.

"As they ride around throwing out oranges in their act," he told me, "they will throw out my time capsules. Perhaps you understand at last, Lucius.

"In a moment I am going to create a temporal rhythm interference which will reduce the present over these mounds to the past of a million years ago.

"The chimps will ride into that area of the past on their cycles — if only you were more cooperative, Lucius, none of this rather elaborate scheme would be necessary — and as they ride around they will throw the time capsules broadcast over the whole area. One or more is bound to sink into the ground, be covered over, and remain there until the present, to be dug up by the archeologists.

"When I whistle, the chimps will ride back to us, in the present. I will turn off the resonator. In due time one of my capsules will be found. Then I will explain how it came to be there, and no one will be able to doubt my time rhythm effect thereafter. It is a little complicated, but remember, that is your fault."

"You could run in there and plant a capsule for yourself, Jupiter," I suggested, but he only shook his head.

"It wouldn't be feasible," he retorted. "Now — "

He clicked a switch on his apparatus.

This time nothing went wrong. In an instant a large area of haze formed over the old mounds. This haze thickened at first, but Jupiter fiddled with a dial, and gradually it thinned down until it was just a shimmery area.

Within that space, a great change in the meadow had taken place.

Now great broad fronds grew up from the ground, long tentacles of unhealthy-looking moss drooping from them. In the background were tall spiky trees distantly resembling palms. In the foreground, a hard, sandy beach, covered with curious shells. It was rather like a stage setting seen through a gauze curtain.

Jeremiah Jupiter took a deep breath.

"Lucius," he said, "this is a solemn moment. We are standing here today, and there is yesterday . . . All right, King, Queenie, Joker. Start!"

Unhesitatingly the three chimps started their motorcycles bouncing across the meadow toward the shimmery area of the past that Jupiter's resonator was producing. Steering with one foot, banging their drums with one hand, holding out their encyclopedias as if reading in the other, they charged bravely back into the remote past of their distant forefathers.

Jupiter watched them go, entranced. But I tapped his shoulder and pointed to a spot behind us.

"And there," I said, "is tomorrow!"

Jeremiah Jupiter turned, and his eyes bugged in disbelief.

Behind us was a second hazy area, as large as the first and the same distance away. But within this one there was a glitter of glass and crystal. We saw a wide street, along which low-roofed buildings stretched into the distance. Jewellike façades shone in the sunshine, and over the roofs of the buildings airships were swooping so rapidly we could not make out what they looked like.

"G-good heavens!" Jupiter stuttered. "My resonator is giving out a harmonic!"

Calling what we were looking at a harmonic seemed to me an understatement.

"Now," I asked, with malicious amusement, "how do you explain that?"

"I — " Jupiter muttered, struggling to collect himself. "I — "

But before he could get his thoughts in order, a shriek of terror sounded behind us. We wheeled.

The three chimps had plunged into the past area, banging bravely on their drums, and for an instant their motorcycles spurned the primordial sands. Then, beyond the trees, a great, toothed head arose, and red eyes stared at them. Above them a shadow swooped down, and King, Queenie, and Joker, pausing not, turned and came right back.

They threw away their books. They threw away their drums. They threw away everything but the time capsules, and crouching low, yelling in horror, they swept straight back at us.

The head of the brontosaurus that had reared up disappeared, and the pterodactyl that had swooped down on them flapped its batlike wings and zoomed back up into the sky, out of our sight. Jupiter yelled, but the chimps had only one thought now. They wanted to get back to nice, peaceful today.

They came bounding at us, eyes rolling, teeth chattering, and I made one wild leap.

"Duck, Jupiter!" I shouted. "They're going to run us down! They're scared silly!"

Jupiter tumbled after me, just in time. The chimps bounded over the spot where we had been standing and kept on going . . . straight for that future which had appeared where it shouldn't!

"Oh, goodness!" Jupiter squeaked in dismay. "No, they mustn't!"

He scrambled up and dashed for his apparatus. By now King and Queenie and Joker, still howling, were at the very edge of the second hazy space, and still accelerating. Directly before them, broad and smooth, lay the street we could see running into the heart of that crystal and silver city of the future.

As they reached it, Joker, in an automatic response to his training, I dare say, reached down into the sidecar, seized one of the time capsules, and tossed it high into the air.

Then Jupiter, rushing for his resonator, tripped over the ground wire, plunged into the apparatus, and sent it crashing to the earth beneath him.

The silver city, into whose street King and Queenie and Joker had just ridden in their headlong flight, vanished.

So did the chimps.

We were surrounded by nothing but peaceful Jersey meadow.

I picked up Jupiter and then the resonator. The resonator was just a tangle of broken tubes and loose wires; but I opened the bottle of Moselle that remained and restored Jupiter to normalcy.

He drank the wine, but his look remained thoughtful. After he had wiped his lips, he said, "Naturally, my resonator gave off a harmonic. Almost any resonating apparatus, from a flute to a radio, will. What happened, Lucius, is that the harmonic, instead of interfering with the time rhythm, *amplified* it."

He got up, straightened his clothes, and carried the hamper to the truck.

"You understand, Lucius," he said then, his voice reflective, "that two vibrations don't *have* to interfere with each other. Two light waves may combine to make one stronger light. Two sound waves may combine to produce one louder sound. Obviously what the overtone from my resonator did was to strengthen the time rhythm, thereby driving the present into the future.

"Thus the main vibratory wave was working in one direction, and the harmonic directly opposite, producing equal but opposite reactions. So the future we saw was just as far ahead of us as the past I created was behind us. A million years, I'd say, offhand, though as unfortunately none of the time capsules were deposited, we'll never know."

He started to climb into the driver's seat of his truck. At that moment something glittered down out of nowhere and fell on his toe. Yelling, he hopped around, holding his foot, while I picked the object up.

It was a Jeremiah Jupiter time capsule: It was, in fact, the one Jack Joker had tossed out at the instant he started into the future.

We had just caught up to the moment in which the chimp had thrown it away.

Preserving a stony silence after that, Jupiter drove us back to New York through the pleasant summer twilight. The time capsule he tossed into the Hudson as we crossed the bridge. From time to time he glanced at me in irritation.

"I can't for the life of me imagine what you're chuckling about," he muttered, as he drew up before my apartment building.

"I was just thinking of King and Queenie and Joker charging down the streets of New York a million years from now on motorcycles, throwing time capsules at the startled inhabitants," I told him. "It will give a very queer impression of what their ancestors in the twentieth century were like. And you know something, Jupiter?"

"What?" he grumbled.

"They all wore silver disks around their necks with their initials on them," I said. "Of course Joker's initials are J.J., the same as yours. They're bound to think they stand for Jeremiah Jupiter, and that he's you, and King and Queenie are your parents. They'll put your name under his picture in their history books, I expect . . . Are you going to build another resonator?"

Jupiter shifted gears with a clash.

"No," he snapped. "I have too many other things to do."

And he hurried off. It was the first time I'd ever had the laugh on him, and I made the most of it. I went inside laughing, and was still laughing after I'd bathed and dressed for my dinner engagement with the editor who was so anxious to have my serial to take back with him to Chicago on the Monday morning plane.

I didn't really stop laughing, in fact, until I got downtown and discovered that it was Tuesday night . . .

Quit Zoomin' Those Hands
Through the Air

JACK FINNEY

It is frequently said that steam engines don't get invented till it's steam engine time. How does that sort of fatalism mix with time travel? And whatever went wrong at the Battle of Cold Harbor?

HEY, QUIT ZOOMIN' YOUR HANDS through the air, boy — I know you was a flier! You flew *good* in the war, course you did; I'd expect that from a grandson of mine. But don't get to thinking you know all about war, son, or flying machines either. The war we finished in '65 is still the toughest we've fought, and don't you forget it. It was a big war fought by big men, and your Pattons and Arnolds and Stilwells — they were *good,* boy, no denying it — but Grant, there was a general. Never told you about this before, because I was swore to secrecy by the General himself, but I think it's all right, now; I think the oath has expired. Now, *quiet,* boy, and listen!

Now, the night I'm talking about, the night I met the General, I didn't know we'd see him at all. Didn't know anything except we were riding along Pennsylvania Avenue, me and the Major, him not saying where we were going or why, just jogging along, one hand on the reins, a big black box strapped to the Major's saddle in front, and that little pointy beard of his stabbing up and down with every step.

It was late, after ten, and everyone was asleep. But the moon was up, bright and full through the trees, and it was nice — the horses' shadows gliding along sharp and clear beside us, and not a sound in the street but their hoofs, hollow on the packed dirt. We'd been riding two days, I'd been nipping some liberated applejack — only we didn't say liberated then; we called it foraging — and I was asleep in the saddle, my trumpet jiggling in the small of my back. Then the Major nudged me, and I woke up and saw the White House ahead. "Yessir," I said.

He looked at me, the moon shining yellow on his epaulets, and said, real quiet, "Tonight, boy, we may win the war. You and I." He smiled, mysterious, and patted the black box. "You know who I am, boy?"

"Yessir."

"No, you don't. I'm a professor. Up at Harvard College. Or was, anyway. Glad to be in the Army now, though. Pack of fools up there, most of them; can't see past the ends of their noses. Well, tonight, we may win the war."

"Yessir," I said. Most officers higher than captain were a little queer in the head, I'd noticed, majors especially. That's how it was then, anyway, and I don't reckon it's changed any, even in the Air Force.

We stopped near the White House at the edge of the lawn and sat looking at it — a great big old house, silvery white in the moonlight, the light over the front door shining out through the porch columns onto the driveway. There was a light in an east window on the ground floor, and I kept hoping I'd see the President, but I didn't. The Major opened his box. "Know what this is, boy?"

"Nosir."

"It's my own invention based on my own theories, nobody else's. They think I'm a crackpot up at the School, but I think it'll work. Win the war, boy." He moved a little lever inside the box. "Don't want to send us too far ahead, son, or technical progress will be beyond us. Say, eighty-five years from now, approximately; think that ought to be about right?"

"Yessir."

"All right." The Major jammed his thumb down on a little button in the box; it made a humming sound that kept rising higher and higher till my ears began to hurt; then he lifted his hand. "Well," he said, smiling and nodding, the little pointy beard going up and down, "it is now some eighty-odd years later." He nodded at the White House. "Glad to see it's still standing."

I looked up at the White House again. It was just about the same, the light still shining out between the big white columns, but I didn't say anything.

The Major twitched his reins and turned. "Well, boy, we've got work ahead; come on." And he set off at a trot along Pennsylvania Avenue with me beside him.

Pretty soon we turned south, and the Major twisted around in his saddle and said, "Now, the question is, what do they have in the future?" He held up his finger like a teacher in school, and I believed the part about him being a professor. "We don't know," the Major went on, "but we know where to find it. In a museum. We're going to the Smithsonian Institution, if it's still standing. For us it should be a veritable storehouse of the future."

It had been standing last week, I knew, and after a while, off across the grass to the east, there it was, a stone building with towers like a castle, looking just the same as always, the windows now blank and white in the moonlight. "Still standing, sir," I said.

"Good," said the Major. "Reconnaissance approach, now," and we went on to a cross street and turned into it. Up ahead were several buildings I'd never noticed before, and we went up to them and swung down off our horses. "Walk between these buildings," the Major said, leading his horse. "Quiet, now; we're reconnoitering."

We crept on, quiet as could be, in the shadows between the two buildings. The one to the right looked just like the Smithsonian to me, and I knew it must be a part of it; another building I'd never seen before. The Major was all excited now and kept whispering. "Some new kind of weapon that will destroy the whole Rebel Army is what we're looking for. Let me know if you see any such thing, boy."

"Yessir," I said, and I almost bumped into something sitting out there in the open in front of the building at the left. It was big and made entirely out of heavy metal, and instead of wheels it rested on two movable belts made of metal; big flat plates linked together.

"Looks like a tank," said the Major, "though I don't know what they keep in it. Keep moving, boy; this thing is obviously no use on a battlefield."

We walked on just a step, and there on the pavement in front of us was a tremendous cannon, three times bigger than any I'd ever seen before in my life. It had an immense long barrel, wheels high as my chest, and it was painted kind of funny, in wavy stripes and splotches, so that you could hardly see it at first in the moonlight that got down between the buildings. "*Look* at that thing!" the Major said softly. "It would pulverize Lee in an hour, but I don't know how we'd carry it. No," he said, shaking his head, "this isn't it. I wonder what they've got inside, though." He stepped up to the doors and peered in through the glass, shading his eyes with his hand. Then he gasped and turned to me.

I went up beside him and looked through the glass. It was a long, big building, the moonlight slanting in through the windows all along one side; and all over the floor, and even hanging from the ceiling, were the weirdest-looking things I ever saw. They were each big as a wagon, some bigger, and they had wheels, but only two wheels, near the front; and I was trying to figure that out when the Major got his voice back.

"Aircraft, by God!" he said. "They've got aircraft! Win the war!"

"Air what, sir?"

"*Aircraft*. Flying machines. Don't you see the wings, boy?"

Each of the machines I could see inside had two things sticking out at each side like oversized ironing boards, but they looked stiff to me, and I didn't see how they could flap like wings. I didn't know what else the Major could be talking about, though. "Yessir," I said.

But the Major was shaking his head again. "Much too advanced," he said. "We could never master them. What we need is an earlier type, and I don't see any in here. Come on, boy; don't straggle."

We walked on, leading the horses, toward the front of the other building. At the doors we peeked in, and there on the floor, with tools and empty crates lying around as though they'd just unpacked it, was another of the things, a flying machine. Only this was far smaller, and was nothing but a framework of wood like a big box kite, with little canvas wings, as the Major called them. It didn't have wheels either, just a couple of runners like a sled. Lying propped against a wall, as though they were just ready to put it up, was a sign. The moonlight didn't quite reach it, and I couldn't read all the words, but I could make out a few. *World's first,* it said in one place, and farther down it said, *Kitty Hawk.*

The Major just stood there for maybe a minute, staring like a man in a trance. Then he murmured to himself, "Very like sketches of da Vinci's model; only apparently this one worked." He grinned suddenly, all excited. "This is it, boy," he said. "This is why we came."

I knew what he had in mind, and I didn't like it. "You'll never break in there, sir," I said. "Those doors look mighty solid, and I'll bet this place is guarded like the mint."

The Major just smiled, mysterious again. "Of course it is, son; it's the treasure house of a nation. No one could possibly get in with any hope of removing anything, let alone this aircraft — under ordinary circumstances. But don't worry about that, boy; just leave it to me. Right now we need fuel." Turning on his heel, he walked back to his horse, took the reins, and led him off; and I followed with mine.

Off some distance, under some trees, near a big open space like a park, the Major set the lever inside his black box, and pressed the button. "Back in 1864, now," he said then, and sniffed. "Air smells fresher. Now, I want you to take your horse, go to garrison headquarters, and bring back all the petrol you can carry. They've got some for cleaning uniforms. Tell them I'll take full responsibility. Understand?"

"Yessir."

"Then off with you. When you come back, this is where I want you to meet me." The Major turned and began walking away with his horse.

At headquarters the guard woke a private, who woke a corporal, who woke a sergeant, who woke a lieutenant, who woke a captain, who swore a little and then woke up the private again and told him to give me what I wanted. The private went away, murmuring softly to himself, and came back pretty soon with six five-gallon jugs; and I tied them to my saddle, signed six sets of receipts, and led my horse back through the moonlit streets of Washington, taking a nip of applejack now and then.

I went by the White House again, on purpose; and this time someone was standing silhouetted against the lighted east window — a big man, tall and thin, his shoulders bowed, his head down on his chest — and I couldn't help but get the impression of a weary strength and purpose and a tremendous dignity. I felt sure it was him, but I can't rightly claim I saw the President, because I've always been one to stick to the facts and never stretch the truth even a little bit.

The Major was waiting under the trees, and my jaw nearly dropped off, because the flying machine was sitting beside him. "Sir," I said, "how did you — "

The Major interrupted, smiling and stroking his little beard: "Very simple. I merely stood at the front door" — he patted the black box at the saddle near his shoulder — "and moved back in time to a moment when even the Smithsonian didn't exist. Then I stepped a few paces ahead with the box under my arm, adjusted the lever again, moved forward to the proper moment, and there I was, standing beside the flying machine. I took myself and the machine out by the same method, and my mount pulled it here on its skids."

"Yessir," I said. I figured I could keep up this foolishness as long as he could, though I did wonder how he had got the flying machine out.

The Major pointed ahead: "I've been exploring the ground, and it's pretty rocky and rough." He turned to the black box, adjusted the dial, and pressed the button. "Now, it's a park," he said, "sometime in the 1940s."

"Yessir," I said.

The Major nodded at a little spout in the flying machine. "Fill her up," he said, and I untied one of the jugs, uncorked it, and began to pour. The tank sounded dry when the petrol hit it, and a cloud of dust puffed up from the spout. It didn't hold very much, only a few quarts, and the Major began untying the other jugs. "Lash these down in the machine," he said, and while I was doing that, the Major began pacing up and down, muttering to himself. "To start the engine, I should imagine you simply turn the propellers. But the machine will need help in getting into the air." He kept walking up and down, pulling his beard; then he nodded his head. "Yes," he said, "that should do it, I think." He stopped and looked at me. "Nerves in good shape, boy? Hands steady and reliable?"

"Yessir."

"All right, son, this thing should be easy to fly — mostly a matter of balance, I imagine." He pointed to a sort of saddle at the front of the machine. "I believe you simply lie on your stomach with your hips in this saddle; it connects with the rudder and wings by cables. By merely moving from side to side, you control the machine's balance and direction." The Major pointed to a lever. "Work this with your hand," he said, "to go up or down. That's all there is to it, so far as I can see, and if I'm wrong in any details, you can correct them in the air with a little experimenting. Think you can fly it, boy?"

"Yessir."

"Good," he said, and grabbed one of the propellers at the back and began turning it. I worked on the other propeller, but nothing happened; they just creaked, stiff and rustylike. But we kept turning, yanking harder and harder, and pretty soon the little engine coughed.

"Now, *heave,* boy!" the Major said, and we laid into it hard, and every time, now, the engine would cough a little. Finally, we yanked so hard, both together, our feet nearly came off the ground, and the motor coughed and kept on coughing and like to choked to death. Then it sort of cleared its throat and started to stutter but didn't stop, and then it was running smooth, the propellers just whirling, flashing and shining in the moonlight till you could hardly see them, and the flying machine shaking like a wet dog, with little clouds of dust pouring up out of every part of it.

"Excellent," said the Major, and he sneezed from the dust. Then he began unfastening the horses' bridles, strapping them together again to make a single long rein. He posted the horses in front of the machine and said, "Get in, boy. We've got a busy night ahead." I lay down in the saddle, and he climbed up on the top wing and lay down on his stomach. "You take the lever, and I'll take the rein. Ready, boy?"

"Yessir."

"*Gee up!*" said the Major, snapping the rein hard, and the horses started off, heads down, hoofs digging in.

The flying machine sort of bumped along over the grass on its skids, but it soon smoothed out and began sliding along, level as a sled on packed snow, and the horses' heads came up and they began to trot, the motor just chugging away.

"Sound *forward!*" said the Major, and I unslung my trumpet and blew forward; the horses buckled into it, and we were skimming along, must have been fifteen, maybe twenty miles an hour or even faster.

"Now, *charge!*" yelled the Major, and I blew charge, and the hoofs began drumming the turf, the horses whinnying and snorting, the engine chugging faster and faster, the propellers whining in back of us, and all of a sudden the grass was a good five feet below, and the reins were hanging straight down. Then — for a second it scared me — we were passing the horses. We were right over their backs; then they began slipping away under the machine, and the Major dropped the reins and yelled, "Pull back the lever!" I yanked back hard, and we shot up into the air like a rocket.

I remembered what the Major had said about experimenting and tried easing back on the lever, and the flying machine sort of leveled out, and there we were, chugging along faster than I'd ever gone in my life. It was wonderful fun, and I glanced down and there was Washington spread out below, a lot bigger than I'd thought it was and with more lights than I'd known there were in the world. They were *bright,* too; didn't look like candles and kerosene lamps at all. Way off, toward the center of town, some of the lights were red and green, and so bright they lighted up the sky.

"Watch out!" yelled the Major, and just ahead, rushing straight at us, was a tremendous monument or something, a tall big stone needle.

I don't know why, but I twisted hard to the left in the little saddle and yanked back on the lever, and a wing heaved up and the flying machine shot off to one side, the wing tip nearly grazing the monument. Then I lay straight again, holding the lever steady. The machine leveled off, and it was like the first time I drove a team.

"Back to headquarters," said the Major. "Can you find the way?"

"Yessir," I said, and headed south.

The Major fiddled with the dial in his black box and pressed the button, and down below now, in the moonlight, I could see the dirt road leading out of Washington back to headquarters. I turned for a last look at the city, but there were only a few lights now, not looking nearly as bright as before; the red and green lights were gone.

But the road was bright in the moonlight, and we tore along over it when it went straight, cut across bends when it curved, flying it must have been close to forty miles an hour. The wind streamed back cold, and I pulled out the white knit muffler my grandma gave me and looped it around my throat. One end streamed back, flapping and waving in the wind. I thought my forage cap might blow off, so I reversed it on my head, the peak at the back, and I felt that now I looked the way a flying-machine driver ought to, and wished the girls back home could have seen me.

For a while I practiced with the lever and hip saddle, soaring up till the engine started coughing and turning and dipping down, seeing how close I could shave the road. But finally the Major yelled and made me quit. Every now and then we'd see a light flare up in a farmhouse, and when we'd look back we'd see the light wobbling across the yard and know some farmer was out there with his lamp, staring up at the noise in the sky.

Several times, on the way, we had to fill the tank again, and pretty soon, maybe less than two hours, campfires began sliding under our wings, and the Major was leaning from side to side, looking down at the ground. Then he pointed ahead. "That field down there, boy; can you land this thing with the engine off?"

"Yessir," I said, and I stopped the engine, and the machine began sliding down like a toboggan, and I kept easing the lever back and forth, watching the field come up to meet us, growing bigger and bigger every second. We didn't make a sound now, except for the wind sighing through the wires, and we came in like a ghost, the moonlight white on our wings. Our downward path and the edge of the field met exactly, and the instant before we hit, my arm eased the lever back, and the skids touched the grass like a whisper. Then we bumped a little, stopped, and sat there a moment not saying a word. Off in the weeds the crickets began chirping again.

The Major said there was a cliff at the side of the field, and we found it and slid the machine over to the edge of it and then we started walking around the field, in opposite directions, looking for a path or sentry. I found the sentry right away, guarding the path lying down with his eyes closed. My applejack was gone, so I shook him awake and explained my problem.

"How much you got?" he said; I told him a dollar, and he went off into the woods and came back with a jug. "Good whiskey," he said, "the best. And exactly a dollar's worth; the jug's nearly full." So I tasted the whiskey — it *was* good — paid him, took the jug back, and tied it down in the machine. Then I went back to the path and called the Major, and he came over, cutting across the field. Then the sentry led us down the path toward the General's tent.

It was a square tent with a gabled roof, a lantern burning inside, and the front flap open. The sentry saluted. "Major of Cavalry here, sir" — he pronounced the word like an ignorant infantryman. "Says it's secret and urgent."

"Send the *calvary* in," said a voice, pronouncing it just that way, and I knew the General was a horse soldier at heart.

We stepped forward, saluting. The General was sitting on a kitchen chair, his feet, in old Army shoes with the laces untied, propped on a big wooden keg with a spigot. He wore a black slouch hat, his vest and uniform blouse were unbuttoned, and I saw three silver stars embroidered on a shoulder strap. The General's eyes were blue, hard, and tough, and he wore a full beard. "At ease," he said. "Well?"

"Sir," said the Major, "we have a flying machine and propose, with your permission, to use it against the rebs."

"Well," said the General, leaning back on the hind legs of his chair, "you've come in the nick of time. Lee's men are massed at Cold Harbor, and I've been sitting here all night dri — thinking. They've got to be crushed before — A *flying* machine, did you say?"

"Yessir," said the Major.

"H'mm," said the General. "Where'd you get it?"

"Well, sir, that's a long story."

"I'll bet it is," said the General. He picked up a stub of cigar from the table beside him and chewed it thoughtfully. "If I hadn't been thinking hard and steadily all night, I wouldn't believe a word of this. What do you propose to do with your flying machine?"

"Load it with grenades!" The Major's eyes began to sparkle. "Drop them spang on rebel headquarters! Force immediate surrend — "

The General shook his head. "No," he said, "I don't think so. Air power isn't enough, son, and will never replace the foot soldier, mark my words. Has its place, though, and you've done good work." He glanced at me. "You the driver, son?"

"Yessir."

He turned to the Major again. "I want you to go up with a map. Locate Lee's positions. Mark them on the map and return. Do that, Major, and tomorrow,

June third, after the Battle of Cold Harbor, I'll personally pin silver leaves on your straps. Because I'm going to take Richmond like — well, I don't know what. As for you, son" — he glanced at my stripe — "you'll make corporal. Might even design new badges for you; pair of wings on the chest or something like that."

"Yessir," I said.

"Where's the machine?" said the General. "Believe I'll walk down and look at it. Lead the way." The Major and me saluted, turned, and walked out, and the General said, "Go ahead; I'll catch up."

At the field the General caught up, shoving something into his hip pocket — a handkerchief, maybe. "Here's your map," he said, and he handed a folded paper to the Major.

The Major took it, saluted, and said, "For the Union, sir! For the cause of — "

"Save the speeches," said the General, "till you're running for office."

"Yessir," said the Major, and he turned to me. "Fill her up!"

I filled the tank, we spun the propellers, and this time the engine started right up. We climbed in, and I reversed my forage cap and tied on my scarf.

"Good," said the General approvingly. "Style; real *calvary* style."

We shoved off and dropped over the cliff like a dead weight, the ground rushing up fast. Then the wings bit into the air, I pulled back my lever, and we shot up, the engine snorting, fighting for altitude, and I swung out wide and circled the field, once at fifty feet, then at a hundred. The first time, the General just stood there, head back, mouth open, staring up at us, and I could see his brass buttons gleam in the moonlight. The second time around he still had his head back, but I don't think he was looking at us. He had a hand to his mouth, and he was drinking a glass of water — I could tell because just as we straightened and headed south, he threw it off into the bushes hard as he could; and I could see the glass flash in the moonlight. Then he started back to headquarters at a dead run, in a hurry, I guess, to get back to his thinking.

The machine was snorting at the front end, kicking up at the hindquarters, high-spirited, and I had all I could do to keep her from shying, and I wished she'd had reins. Down below, cold and sparkly in the moonlight, I could see the James River, stretching east and west, and the lights of Richmond, but it was no time for sightseeing. The machine was frisky, trembling in the flanks, and before I knew it she took the bit in her mouth and headed straight down, the wind screaming through her wires, the ripples on the water rushing up at us.

But I'd handled runaways before, and I heaved back on the lever, forcing her head up, and she curved back into the air fast as a cavalry mount at a barrier. But this time she didn't cough at the top of the curve. She snorted through her nostrils, wild with power, and I barely had time to yell, "Hang on!" to the Major before she went clear over on her back and shot down toward the river again. The Major yelled, but the applejack was bubbling inside me and I'd never had such a thrill, and I yelled too, laughing and screaming. Then I pulled back hard, yelling, "Whoa!" but up and over we went again, the wings creaking like saddle leather on a galloping horse. At the top of the climb, I leaned hard to the left, and we shot off in a wide, beautiful curve, and I never had such fun in my life.

Then she quieted down a little. She wasn't broken, I knew, but she could feel a real rider in the saddle, so she waited, figuring out what to try next. The Major got his breath and used it for cursing. He didn't call me anything I'd ever heard before, and I'd been in the cavalry since I joined the Army. It was a beautiful job and I admired it. "Yessir," I said when his breath ran out again.

He still had plenty to say, I think, but campfires were sliding under our wings, and he had to get out his map and go to work. We flew back and forth, parallel with the river, the Major busy with his pencil and map. It was dull and monotonous for both me and the machine, and I kept wondering if the rebs could see or hear us. So I kept sneaking closer and closer to the ground, and pretty soon, directly ahead in a clearing, I saw a campfire with men around it. I don't rightly know if it was me or the machine had the idea, but I barely touched the lever and she dipped her nose and shot right down, aiming smack at the fire.

They saw us then, all right, and heard us, too. They scattered, yelling and cursing, with me leaning over screaming at them and laughing like mad. I hauled back on the lever maybe five feet from the ground, and the fire singed our tail as we curved back up. But this time, at the top of the climb, the engine got the hiccups, and I had to turn and come down in a slow glide to ease the strain off the engine till she got her breath, and now the men below had muskets out, and they were mad. They fired kneeling, following up with their sights the way you lead ducks, the musket balls whistling past us.

"Come on!" I yelled. I slapped the flying machine on her side, unslung my trumpet, and blew charge. Down we went, the engine neighing and whinnying like crazy, and the men tossed their muskets aside and dived in all directions, and we fanned the flames with our wings and went up like a bullet, the engine screaming in triumph. At the top of the curve I turned, and we shot off over the treetops, the wing tip pointing straight at the moon. "Sorry, sir," I said, before the Major could get his breath. "She's wild — feeling her oats. But I think I've got her under control."

"Then get back to headquarters before you kill us," he said coldly. "We'll discuss this later."

"Yessir," I said. I spotted the river off to one side and flew over it, and when the Major got us oriented he navigated us back to the field.

"Wait here," he said when we landed, and he trotted down the path toward the General's tent. I was just as glad; I felt like a drink, and besides I loved that machine now and wanted to take care of her. I wiped her down with my muffler, and wished I could feed her something.

Then I felt around inside the machine, and then I was cussing that sentry, beating the Major's record, I think, because my whiskey was gone, and I knew what that sentry had done: sneaked back to my machine and got it soon as he had me and the Major in the General's tent, and now he was back at the guardhouse, probably, lapping it up and laughing at me.

The Major came down the path fast. "Back to Washington, and hurry," he said. "Got to get this where it belongs before daylight or the space-time continuum will be broken and no telling what might happen then."

So we filled the tank and flew on back to Washington. I was tired and so was the flying machine, I guess, because now she just chugged along, heading for home and the stable.

We landed near the trees again and climbed out, stiff and tired. And after creaking and sighing a little, the flying machine just sat there on the ground, dead tired too. There were a couple of musketball holes in her wings and some soot on her tail, but otherwise she looked just the same.

"Look alive, boy!" the Major said. "You go hunt for the horses, and I'll get the machine back," and he got behind the flying machine and began pushing it along over the grass.

I found the horses grazing not far off, brought them back, and tethered them to the trees. When the Major returned we started back.

Well, I never did get my promotion. Or my wings either. It got hot, and pretty soon I fell asleep.

After a while I heard the Major call, "Boy! Boy!" and I woke up saying, "Yessir!" but he didn't mean me. A paper boy was running over with a newspaper, and when the Major paid for it, I drew alongside and we both looked at it, sitting there in our saddles near the outskirts of Washington. BATTLE AT COLD HARBOR, it said, and underneath were a lot of smaller headlines one after the other. *Disaster for Union Forces! Surprise Attack at Daybreak Fails! Repulsed in Eight Minutes! Knowledge of Rebel Positions Faulty! Confederate Losses Small, Ours Large! Grant Offers No Explanation; Inquiry Urged!* There was a news story, too, but we didn't read it. The Major flung the paper to the gutter and touched his spurs to his horse, and I followed.

By noon the next day we were back in our lines, but we didn't look for the General. We didn't feel any need to, because we felt sure he was looking for us. He never found us, though; possibly because I grew a beard and the Major shaved his off. And we never had told him our names.

Well, Grant finally took Richmond — he was a great general — but he had to take it by siege.

I only saw him one more time, and that was years later when he wasn't a general anymore. It was a New Year's Day, and I was in Washington and saw a long line of people waiting to get into the White House, and knew it must be the public reception the Presidents used to hold every New Year's. So I stood in line, and an hour later I reached the President. "Remember me, General?" I said.

He stared at me, narrowing his eyes; then his face got red and his eyes flashed. But he took a deep breath, remembering I was a voter, forced a smile, and nodded at a door behind him. "Wait in there," he said.

Soon afterward the reception ended, and the General sat facing me, behind his big desk, biting the end off a short cigar. "Well," he said, without any preliminaries, "what went wrong?"

So I told him; I'd figured it out long since, of course. I told him how the flying machine went crazy, looping till we could hardly see straight, so that we flew north again and mapped our own lines.

"I found that out," said the General, "immediately after ordering the attack."

Then I told him about the sentry who'd sold me the whiskey, and how I thought he'd stolen it back again, when he hadn't.

The General nodded. "Poured that whiskey into the machine, didn't you? Mistook it for a jug of gasoline."

"Yessir," I said.

He nodded again. "Naturally the flying machine went crazy. That was my own private brand of whiskey, the same whiskey Lincoln spoke of so highly. That damned sentry of mine was stealing it all through the war." He leaned back in his chair, puffing his cigar. "Well," he said, "I guess it's just as well you didn't succeed; Lee thought so too. We discussed it at Appomattox before the formal surrender, just the two of us chatting in the farmhouse. Never have told anyone what we talked about there, and everybody's been wondering and guessing ever since. Well, we talked about air power, son, and Lee was opposed to it, and so was I. Wars are meant for the ground, boy, and if they ever take to the air they'll start dropping bombshells, mark my words, and if they ever do that, there'll be hell to pay. So Lee and I decided to keep our mouths shut about air power, and we have — you won't find a word about it in my memoirs or his. Anyway, son, as Billy Sherman said, war is hell, and there's no sense starting people thinking up ways to make it worse. So I want you to keep quiet about Cold Harbor. Don't say a word if you live to be a hundred."

"Yessir," I said, and I never have. But I'm past a hundred now, son, and if the General wanted me to keep quiet after that he'd have said so. Now, take those hands out of the air, boy! Wait'll the world's *first* pilot gets through talking!

The Adventure of
the Global Traveler

ANNE LEAR

Many people claim that Shakespeare couldn't have written his plays because he didn't know enough — so that paragon of education, Bacon, had to be the author. I, on the contrary, have written articles to show that Shakespeare made egregious errors that Bacon would never have made so that the writer of Shakespeare's plays had to be none other than Shakespeare. And if you think that's confusing, try the following story, in which one mystery is solved and another — worse one — is proposed. Of course, Ms. Lear also contributes to the Sherlock Holmes apocrypha, and Janet feels she shouldn't, since the Baker Street Irregulars, that association of Holmes fanciers, is an anachronistic stag organization. (Janet lets me belong, though, because she likes me.)

ALL I WANTED was to find out who the Third Murderer in *Macbeth* really was. Well, I know now. I also know the secret identity and the fate of one famous personage, that the death of another occurred many years before it was reported to have done, and a hitherto unknown detail of Wm. Shakespeare's acting career.

Which just goes to show what a marvelous place to do research is the Folger Shakespeare Library in Washington, D.C. In the crowded shelves and vaults of that great storehouse are treasures in such number and variety that even their passionately devoted caretakers do not know the whole.

In my quest for the Third Murderer I started at the logical place. I looked in the card catalog under *M* for Murderer. I didn't find the one I had in mind; but I found plenty of others and, being of the happy vampire breed, switched gleefully onto the sidetrack offered.

Here was gore to slake a noble thirst: murders of apprentices by their masters; murders of masters by apprentices; murders of husbands by wives, wives by husbands, children by both. Oh, it was a bustling time, the Age of Elizabeth! Broadsides there were and pamphlets, each juicier than the last.

The titles were the best of it perhaps. Yellow journalism is a mere lily in these declining days. Consider:

> *A true discourse. Declaring the damnable life and death of one Stubbe Peeter, a most wicked Sorcerer, who in the likeness of a Woolf, committed many murders . . . Who for the same fact was taken and executed . . .*

or

> *Newes from Perin in Cornwall: Of a most Bloody and unexampled Murther very lately committed by a Father on his own Sonne . . . at the Instigation of a merciless Step-mother . . .*

or the truly spectacular

> *Newes out of Germanie. A most wonderful and true discourse of a cruell murderer, who had kylled in his life tyme, nine hundred, threescore and odde persons, among which six of them were his owne children begotten on a young women which he forceablie kept in a caue seven yeeres . . .*

(This particular murtherer is on record as having planned, with true Teutonic neatness of mind, to do in precisely one thousand people and then retire.)

Eventually I found myself calling for *The moft horrible and tragicall murther, of the right Honorable, the vertuous and valerous gentleman, John Lord Bourgh, Baron of Caftell Connell. committed by Arnold Cosby, the foureteenth of Ianuarie. Togeather with the forrofull fighes of a fadde foule, uppon his funeral: written by W.R., a feruant of the faid Lord Bourgh.*

The pamphlet was sent up promptly to the muffled, gorgeously Tudor reading room, where I signed for it and carried it off to one of the vast mahogany tables that stand about the room and intimidate researchers.

As I worked my way through the black letter, I found the promising title to be a snare and a delusion. The story turned out to be a mediocre one about a social-climbing coward who provoked a duel and then, unable to get out of it, stabbed his opponent on the sly. Pooh. I was about to send it back, when I noticed an inappropriate thickness. A few pages beyond where I had stopped (at the beginning of the forrofull fighes) the center of the pamphlet seemed thicker than the edges. 'Tis some other reader's notes, I muttered, only this and nothing more.

So, it appeared when I turned to them, they were. There were four thin sheets, small enough to fit into the octavo pamphlet with more than an inch of margin on every side. The paper was of a good quality, much stronger than the crumbling pulp which had concealed it.

I hadn't a clue as to how long ago the sheets had been put there. They might have gone unnoticed for years, as the librarians and users of the ultrascholarly Folger are not much given to murder as recreation, even horrible and tragicall murthers of the vertuous and valerous, and therefore they don't often ask for the bloody pulps.

Further, the descriptive endorsement on the envelope made no mention of the extra sheets, as it surely would have done had they been any part of the collection.

I hesitated briefly. People tend to be touchy about their notes, academicians more than most, as plagiarism ramps about universities more vigorously than anyone likes to admit. The writing was difficult in any case, a tiny, crabbed scribble. It had been done with a steel pen, and the spellings and style were for the most part those of *fin de siècle* England, with a salting of unexpected Jacobean usages. The paper was clearly well aged, darkened from a probable white to a pale brown, uniformly because of its protected position, and the ink cannot have been new, having faded to a medium brown.

My scruples were, after all, academic, as I had inevitably read part of the first page while I examined it. And anyway, who was I kidding?

On this bleak last night of the year I take up my pen, my anachronistic steel pen which I value highly among the few relics I have of my former — or is it my future? — life, to set down a record which stands but little chance of ever being seen by any who can comprehend it.

The political situation is becoming dangerous even for me, for all that I am arranging to profit by my foreknowledge of events as well as from the opportunities civil confusion offers to those who know how to use it. However, my prescience does not in this or any other way extend to my own fate, and I would fain leave some trace of myself for those who were my friends, perhaps even more for one who was my enemy. Or will be.

To settle this point at once: those events which are my past are the distant future for all around me. I do not know what they may be for you who read this, as I cannot guess at what date my message will come to light. For my immediate purpose, therefore, I shall ignore greater realities and refer only to my own lifeline, calling my present *the* present and my past *the* past, regardless of "actual" dates.

To begin at approximately the beginning, then, I found it necessary in the spring of 1891 to abandon a thriving business in London. As head of most of Britain's criminal activities — my arch-enemy, Mr. Sherlock Holmes, once complimented me with the title "The Napoleon of Crime."

At this point my eyes seemed to fix themselves immovably. They began to glaze over. I shook myself back to full consciousness, and my hand continued to shake slightly as I slipped the pamphlet back into its envelope and the strange papers, oh so casually, into my own notes. After an experimental husk or two I decided my voice was functional and proceeded to return the pamphlet and thank the librarian. Then I headed for the nearest bar, in search of a quiet booth and beer to wash the dryness of astonishment and the dust of centuries from my throat.

The afternoon was warm, a golden harbinger in a gray March, and the interior of the Hawk and Dove, that sturdy Capitol Hill saloon, was invitingly dark. It was also nearly empty, which was soothing to electrified nerves. I spoke vaguely to a waitress, and by the time I had settled onto a wooden bench polished by buttocks innumerable, beer had materialized before me, cold and gold in a mug.

The waitress had scarcely completed her turn away from my table before I had the little pages out of my portfolio and angled to catch the light filtering dustily in through the mock-Victorian colored window on my left.

I had wealth and power in abundance. However, Holmes moved against me more effectively than I had anticipated, and I was forced to leave for the Continent on very short notice. I had, of course, made provision abroad against such exigency, and, with the help of Colonel Moran, my ablest lieutenant, led Holmes into a trap at the Reichenbach Falls.

Regrettably, the trap proved unsuccessful. By means of a Japanese wrestling trick I was forced to admire even as it precipitated me over the edge, Holmes escaped me at the last possible moment. He believed he had seen me fall to my death, but this time it was he who had underestimated his opponent.

A net previously stretched over the gulf, concealed by an aberration of the falls' spray and controlled by Moran, lay ready to catch me if I fell. Had it been Holmes who went over the edge, Moran would have retracted the net to permit his passage down into the maelstrom at the cliff's foot. A spring-fastened dummy was released from the underside of the net by the impact of my weight, completing the illusion.

I returned to England in the character of an experimental mathematician, a *persona* I had been some years in developing, as at my Richmond residence I carried out the mathematical researches which had been my first vocation. I had always entertained there men who were at the head of various academic, scientific, and literary professions, and my reputation as an erudite, generous host was well established. It was an ideal concealment for me throughout the next year, while my agents, led by the redoubtable Colonel, tracked Mr. Holmes on his travels, and I began to rebuild my shadowy empire.

During this time I beguiled my untoward leisure with concentrated research into the nature of Time and various paradoxes attendant thereon. My work led me eventually to construct a machine which would permit me to travel into the past and future.

I could not resist showing the Time Machine to a few of my friends, most of whom inclined to believe it a hoax. One of the more imaginative of them, a writer named Wells, seemed to think there might be something in it, but even he was not fully convinced. No matter. They were right to doubt the rigmarole I spun out for them about what I saw on my travels. Mightily noble it sounded, not to say luridly romantic — Weena indeed! — although, as a matter of fact, some few parts were even true.

Obviously, the real use to which I put the Machine during the "week" between its completion and my final trip on it was the furtherance of my professional interests. It was especially convenient for such matters as observing, and introducing judicious flaws into, the construction of bank vaults and for gathering materials for blackmail. Indeed, I used "my" time well and compiled quite an extensive file for eventual conversion into gold.

As I could always return to the same time I had left, if not an earlier one, the only limit to the amount of such travelling I could do lay in my own constitution, and that has always been strong.

My great mistake was my failure to notice the wearing effect all this use was having on the Time Machine. To this day I do not know what part of the delicate mechanism was damaged, but the ultimate results were anything but subtle.

I come at last to the nature of my arrival at this place and time. Having learned early of the dangers attendant upon being unable to move the Time Machine, I had added to its structure a set of wheels and a driving chain attached to the pedals originally meant simply as foot rests. In short, I converted it into a Time Velocipede.

It was necessary to exercise caution in order to avoid being seen trundling this odd vehicle through the streets of London during my business forays, but there was nothing to prevent my riding about to my heart's content in the very remote past, providing always that I left careful markings at my site of arrival.

Thus did I rest from my labors by touring on occasion through the quiet early days of this sceptered isle — a thief's privilege to steal, especially from a friend — ere ever sceptre came to it. Most interesting it was, albeit somewhat empty for one of my contriving temperament.

It was, then, as I was riding one very long ago day beside a river I found it difficult to realize from its unfamiliar contours would one day be the Thames, that the Velocipede struck a hidden root and was thrown suddenly off balance. I flung out a hand to stabilize myself and, in doing so, threw over the controls, sending myself rapidly forward in time.

Days and nights passed in accelerating succession, with the concomitant dizziness and nausea I had come to expect but never to enjoy, and this time I had no control of my speed. I regretted even more bitterly than usual the absences of gauges to indicate temporal progress. I had never been able to solve the problem of their design; and now, travelling in this haphazard fashion, I had not the least idea when I might be.

I could only hope with my usual fervency and more that I should somehow escape the ultimate hazard of merging with a solid object — or a living creature — standing in the same place as I at the time of my halt. Landing in a time-fostered meander of the Thames would be infinitely preferable.

The swift march of the seasons slowed, as I eased the control lever back, and soon I could perceive the phases of the moon, then once again the alternating light and dark of the sun's diurnal progression.

Then all of a sudden the unperceived worn part gave way. The Machine disintegrated under me, blasted into virtual nothingness, and I landed without a sound, a bit off balance, on a wooden floor.

A swift glance around me told me my doom. Whenever I was, it was in no age of machines nor of the delicate tools I required to enable my escape.

Reeling for a moment with the horror of my position, I felt a firm nudge in the ribs. A clear, powerful voice was asking loudly, "But who did bid thee join with us?"

The speaker was a handsome man of middle age, with large, dark eyes, a widow's peak above an extraordinary brow with a frontal development nearly as great as my own, a neat mustache, and a small, equally neat beard. He was muffled in a dark cloak and hood, but his one visible ear was adorned with a gold ring. As I stood dumbly wondering, he nudged me again, and I looked in haste beyond him for enlightenment.

The wooden floor was a platform, in fact a stage. Below on one side and above on three sides beyond were crowds of people dressed in a style I recognized as that of the early seventeenth century.

Another nudge, fierce and impatient: "But who did bid thee join with us?"

The line was familiar, from a play I knew well. The place, this wooden stage all but surrounded by its audience — could it possibly be the Globe? In that case, the play . . . the play must be . . . *MACBETH!* I all but shouted, so startled was I at the sudden apprehension.

The man next to me expelled a small sigh of relief. A second man, heretofore unnoticed by me, spoke up quickly from my other side. "He needs not our mistrust, since he delivers our offices and what we have to do, to the direction just."

"Then stand with us," said the first man, who I now realized must be First Murderer. A suspicion was beginning to grow in my mind as to his offstage identity as well, but it seemed unlikely. We are told that the Bard only played two roles in his own plays: old Adam in *As You Like It,* and King Hamlet's ghost. Surely . . . but my reflections were cut off short, as I felt myself being covertly turned by Second Murderer to face upstage.

First Murderer's sunset speech was ended, and I had a line to speak. I knew it already, having been an eager Thespian in my university days. Of course, to my companions and others I could see watching from the wings most of the lines we were speaking were spontaneous. "Hark!" said I. "I hear horses."

Banquo called for a light "within," within being the little curtained alcove at the rear of the stage. Second Murderer consulted a list he carried and averred that it must be Banquo we heard, as all the other expected guests were already gone into the court. First Murderer proffered me a line in which he worried about the horses' moving away; and I reassured him to the effect that they were being led off by servants to the stables, so that Banquo and Fleance could walk the short way in. "So all men do," I said, "From hence to th' Palace Gate make it their walk."

Banquo and Fleance entered. Second Murderer saw them coming by the light that Fleance carried, and I identified Banquo for them, assisted in the murder — carefully, for fear habit might make me strike inconveniently hard — and complained about the light's having been knocked out and about our having failed to kill Fleance.

And then we were in the wings, and I had to face my new acquaintances. Second Murderer was no serious concern, as he was a minor person in the company. First Murderer was a different matter altogether, however, for my conjecture had proved to be the truth, and I was in very fact face to face with William Shakespeare.

I am a facile, in fact a professional, liar and had no trouble in persuading them that I was a man in flight and had hidden from my pursuers in the "within" alcove, to appear among them thus unexpectedly. That Shakespeare had been so quick of wit to save his own play from my disruption was no marvel; that the young player had followed suit was matter for congratulation from his fellows; that I had found appropriate lines amazed them all. I explained that I had trod the boards at one time in my life and, in answer to puzzled queries about my strange garb, murmured some words about having spent time of late amongst the sledded Polack, which I supposed would be mysterious enough and did elicit a flattered smile from the playwright.

As to my reasons for being pursued, I had only to assure my new friends that my troubles were of an amatory nature in order to gain their full sympathy. They could not afford openly to harbor a fugitive from justice, although players of that time, as of most times, tended to the shady side of the law, and these would gladly have helped me to any concealment that did not bring them into immediate jeopardy. As I was but newly arrived in the country from my travels abroad, lacked employment, and could perform, they offered me a place in the company, which I accepted gladly.

I did not need the pay, as I had observed my customary precaution of wearing a waistcoat whose lining was sewn full of jewels, the universal currency. However, the playhouse afforded me an ideal *locus* from which to begin making the contacts that have since established me in my old position as "the Napoleon of crime," ludicrous title in a time more than a century before Napoleon will be born.

As to how my lines came to be part of the play's text, Will himself inserted them just as the three of us spoke them on the day. He had been filling the First Murderer part that afternoon by sheer good luck, the regular player being ill, and he found vastly amusing the idea of adding an unexplained character to create a mystery for the audience. He had no thought for future audiences and readers, certainly not for recondite scholarship, but only sought to entertain those for whom he wrote: the patrons of the Globe and Blackfriars and the great folk at Court.

I am an old man now, and, in view of the civil strife soon to burst its festering sores throughout the country, I may not live to be a much older one. I have good hopes, however. Knowing the outcome is helpful, and I have taken care to cultivate the right men. Roundheads, I may say, purchase as many vices as Cavaliers, for all they do it secretly and with a tighter clasp on their purses.

Still, I shall leave this partial record now, not waiting until I have liberty to set down a more complete one. If you who read it do so at any time during the last eight years of the nineteenth century, or perhaps even for some years thereafter, I beg that you will do me the great favor to take or send it to Mr. Sherlock Holmes at 221-B Baker Street, London.

Thus, in the hope that he may read this, I send my compliments and the following poser:

The first time the Third Murderer's lines were ever spoken, *they were delivered from memory.*

Pray, Mr. Holmes, who wrote them?

Moriarty
London
31st December 1640

Pebble in Time

CYNTHIA GOLDSTONE AND AVRAM DAVIDSON

Janet and I have a special interest in stories about Mormons. In Janet's case there's a loose genealogical connection. In my case, there's an interest in any group that considers me a Gentile. It makes for novelty.

THE CITY OF SAN FRANCISCO is certainly *my* city! I wouldn't live anywhere else than "The Port of Zion" for anything in the world. Perhaps my favorite worldly spot — next, of course, to Golden Gate Park — is the Embarcadero. Only two people have ever known how much thanks is due to one of them (now passed from Time into Eternity) that the sailors and seafarers have helped spread the Restored Gospel throughout the seven seas to the four corners of the earth. Of course its spread was inevitable, but I do think that if we Saints had stayed in, say, Missouri, our message would have been much slower in making its way around the world.

Not that I mean for a moment to indicate anything but the most whole-hearted approval for the work done by our regularly appointed young missionaries, but of course nothing can equal the zeal and energy of sailors! And, walking down the Embarcadero and seeing the vigor with which they toss their Orange Julius drinks down their thirsty throats, I think how different the scene must be in (for example) that terribly overgrown and misnamed large city in Southern California, where seafarers may be seen abusing their systems by the use of alcohol, tobacco, tea, and coffee — all, of course, forbidden by *The Word of Wisdom* of the Prophet Joseph.

When I speak of the role played in this by one of the only two people who know the whole, true story, I am referring to my maternal grandfather. *I am the other.* And I suppose I'm a chip off the old block — or, perhaps, stated more exactly, a chip off the stalwart old Mormon family tree, so well set up (on paper, of course) by Grandpa Spence during the later years of his retirement. How he spent the earlier years, we will see very shortly. As is usual among L.D.S. people, I take a great interest in my ancestors, but most of all in Grandpa Spence. It may be because I inherited (if such things be hereditary) both his interest in genealogy and inventions, as well as that slight speech impediment which becomes troublesome only at moments of excitement. I have always said to myself, "Nephi Spence Nilsen, your grandfather rose above this, and so will you." It invariably helps. Grandpa was aware of all that and it constituted another bond between us. To sum it up: He and I both tended to stammer, both were interested in Mormon history and genealogy, both loved to consider mechanical devices.

It was a combination of these characteristics of Grandpa's that brought about a certain incident which I feel can now, safely, and *should* now, properly, be made known to one and all. And above and beyond that, my grandfather specifically (though in veiled language) asked me in his will to speak out on this matter at this particular time.

Grandpa was a peach. Perhaps it was the very enthusiasm of his devotion to the Latter Day Saints (though Grandma drew the line when he dutifully considered taking a second wife) that accounted for his unfailing good humor and zest even when he was quite old. Needless to say that he was a respected and responsible citizen, having for many years been mechanical supervisor for the various industries operated by the Latter Day Saints Church, and was valued for his circumspection as well as for his technical competence. Unfortunately (or fortunately: let History decide) his circumspection failed him at one crucial point in his life when —

But let me simply state the facts.

Grandpa had left England with a party of emigrants (all converts like himself) as an already full-grown young man of fifteen, crossed the plains to Great Salt Lake City, and within a short time was hired by President Brigham Young to copy letters in his clear and graceful longhand. His promotion in the Church was rapid, and after fifty years of remarkable service, he retired to his own three-story home on First North Street. Grandma had passed from Time into Eternity years before, and all the children had homes of their own; a neighbor lady acted as part-time housekeeper, leaving him free to follow his own inclinations in his own now fully free time.

The inspiration for the chief of these inclinations arose out of the only real regret that he had ever had. Much more out of his reverence for Mormon history than personal pride, he wished so much that he had not missed by only a year or so having been present on that great day when Brother Brigham led the weary pioneers to the bluff overlooking the great Utah valley and announced that they would stay and make the desert bloom like a rose. In his retirement, Grandpa Spence secretly determined to build a device which would transport him back to that decisive moment.

"I was born in the age of the covered wagon," he declared to himself, "and have lived to see the age of the flying machine. Eternity is one thing, but Time is another, and surely to a Saint nothing is impossible!" He was of course not certain of being able to *return* — he might even be scalped by an unconverted Lamanite — but to these considerations he gave but a shrug and a smile. His enormous dedication to the idea of fulfilling himself in this singular way enabled him to work like a steam engine (he *had* helped drive the Golden Spike at Promontory Point — Utah! — incidentally); he was a vigorous man with great inventive ability, and he was inspired. He completed the machine one bright May morning and got to Observation Bluff one hour and seventeen minutes before Brother Brigham and his advance party arrived.

Grandpa had not calculated on finding a smooth or barely downy chin instead of the full beard his hand automatically sought to stroke in satisfaction, but after a moment he realized what had happened: He had traveled back in time so successfully that he had become a stripling once again! Fortunately he had always been moderate in diet and his twentieth-century clothes were only slightly loose. *Un*fortunately he no longer had the gravity and patience of his former years and soon became overanxious and restless. And as the pilgrim travelers approached, his excitement drew him away from the machine, which was well hidden by the bushes on the bluff above the new arrivals. He was recklessly determined to get as close as possible to the principals of this historic moment and to hear the historic words, *This is the place!* And in moving toward the travel-worn Saints, creeping along in the low bushes, he accidentally dislodged a stone, which tumbled down the slide, gaining momentum.

Forgetful of all else, he stood up to warn them out of the way, but in his excitement he found his speech impediment rendered him unable to release a sound . . .

The stone rolled and bounced and hit Brigham just above the worn and dusty boot on his right leg. The square, heavy face winced and swung around and saw the still-speechless stranger above on the bluff. All the weariness and travel of the long journey west, all the tragedy of the Mormon martyrdom, all the outrage of the persecuted were in Brigham's roar of pain and astonishment. "Look ye there!" he cried. "Who's that? Not a speck of dust on him! Throwing stones already! I thought this place was empty and I see that the Gentiles have got here before us!" And while poor young-again Spence struggled vainly to give utterance, regret, and denial, Brigham turned and swung his arm in a great, determined arc.

"This is not the place!" he cried. *"Onward!"*

Not for a moment did anyone dream of controverting the word of the President, Prophet, Revelator, and Seer. *Onward! they echoed.* And *onward* they went. And the conscience-stricken young stranger, where did *he* go? Well, where *could* he go? He went after them, *onward,* of course. Of course they couldn't make heads or tails of his stammering explanations, nor even of the ones he attempted to write. But they understood that he was sorry. That was enough. Mormons have suffered too much to be vindictive. And that night when the band camped, he was brought to the leader's wagon, where a small lamp burned.

"Young man," said Brigham, "they tell me that you have expressed a seemly contrition for having raised your hand against the Lord's Anointed; therefore I forgive you in the name of Israel's God. They also say you write a good, clear hand. Sit down. There's pen and ink and paper. *Dear Sister Simpson, It cannot have escaped your attention that I have observed with approbation your* — no, make that — *the modesty of your demeanor, equally with your devotion to the doctrines and covenants of the Latter Day Saints, which is of far greater importance than the many charms with which a benign Nature has adorned your youthful person. My advanced years will always assure you of mature advice, and in my other seventeen* — is it seventeen? or nineteen? — pshaw, boy! — a man can't keep all these figures in his head — *my other eighteen wives you will find a set of loving sisters. Since it is fitting that we be sealed for Time and Eternity, kindly commence packing now in order to depart with the next party of Saints heading for our original destination which as you know was tentatively the peninsula called San Francisco in Upper California. Yours & sic cetera, B. Young, Pres., Church of J.C. of L.D.S.* — sand it well, son, for I hate a blotty document."

You've all read your history and must certainly have often felt thankful that Brother Brigham did not yield to the momentary impulse he admitted he had, and that he did not stop in Utah. Despite its impressive name, Great Salt Lake City is just a tiny town with a pleasant enough view, but even that can't compare with the one from my window alone. It's a pleasant thing to sit here in my apartment atop the hill on Saint Street, sipping a tall, cool lemonade, and admire the view. To the west is the great span of Brigham Young Bridge across the Golden Gate, with its great towers and seven lanes of cars; to the east is the Tabernacle, its other-worldly shape gracing the Marina Green, with the stately Temple nearby. I see a network of wide, dignified streets feathered with light green trees, giving the city the look of a great park. And, being truly a *Mormon* city, it is undisfigured by a single liquor saloon, tearoom, tobacconist, or coffee house.

And Grandpa? After his retirement, he sold his house on Joseph Smith Esplanade and moved to the fine apartment in the Saint-Ashbury district where I now live. Having decided to leave well enough alone the second time around, he devoted his *last* last years entirely to the study of Latter Day Saint genealogy. He felt right at home here, as do I, and why not? After all, the Saint-Ashbury can boast of more lemonade and Postum stands per square block than anyplace in the U.S.A., and one is always seeing and hearing those inspiring and exciting initials: L.D.S.! L.D.S.! L.D.S.!

Ahead of the Joneses

AL SARRANTONIO

This is another story I saw before the purchasing editor (in this case George Scithers) did. Al was working for Cathleen Jordan (my Doubleday editor) at the time and asked me to read the story. I agreed reluctantly, as always, fearing (as always) that I would have to say unkind words. I didn't. I flipped.

January 12

Today I'm a happy man, because the deliverymen installed my new abstract lawn sculpture. I had it set up on the property line, and I could swear that Harry Jones's eyes bugged out when he saw it facing his front porch. The bastard'll have to look at it every day as he leaves for work.

January 30

When Jones called me over to see his new lawn sculpture today I had to hold myself back from strangling him in front of it. It's a silver-plated job, twice the size of mine and with twice as many artsy features. And on top of the fact that he had the nerve to *buy* the thing, the son-of-a-bitch had it mounted on his side of the property line, looming over my lawn sculpture. I put on an appreciative grin as he showed it to me, but we both knew what I was thinking. . . .

February 16

Today I called one of Harry's kids over to take a picture of him and his friends with my brand-new holo-camera. Gave little Robby an instant print (gave each of his friends one too!) and I just know the kid ran home to show Harry and ask how come they don't have a holo-camera. I could just visualize Harry yelling at the little lout and telling him to shut his mouth about holo-cameras. Made me feel warm inside all day.

February 21

Harry called this afternoon to tell me about the great buy he got on a holo-moviecamera and to invite Sheila and me and the kids over to help them make their first full-length film. Of course I told him we couldn't make it, but the bastard had little Robby run over later with a print. An hour's worth of color film, with sound — self-projecting cartridge too. Just need an empty space to project it in. I projected it into the garbage, of course; it burns hell out of me that a jerk like that who can't be making any more money than me could afford something like that. Of course there have been a lot of sales on holo-moviecameras lately, and the prices have come down a bit. It's the fact that he just has to do me one better that makes me feel so rotten. . . .

June 17

Eat your heart out, Harry Jones! The workmen turned on the juice today and left, and I must admit they did quite a job. There can't be anyone in the whole county, never mind this block, with a complete amusement arcade like mine in his backyard. And I mean *complete*. Everything from high-reality-level ride simulators to holographic clowns (4-color, yet!) to a changeable-program fireworks grid to close out the evening light spectacle. The guy at the department store started to give me his whole spiel about how I was getting in on the ground floor of a new revolution in home entertainment and how the prices would never be this low again (I don't see how they could get much higher; luckily, I did have a few dollars put away for my kids' college educations) but I didn't let him finish, I just signed the contract and slapped down the advance payment. He threw in the rifle range, no charge, but if he hadn't I would have ordered one anyway. I *know* how much Harry likes to target shoot on weekends.

June 28

God help me, and I'm a religious man, but I almost went over and murdered him today. I'm calmer now, but the initial shock of coming home from a short business trip to find the finishing touches being put to Jones's outdoor 3-D theater, set on top of his domed vapor-pool, and all of that resting on top of his automated midget racer track and micro golf course (combined with a good-sized arcade and target-shoot in one corner, floating six feet above the ground) was just a bit much. After a couple of hours I stopped trembling. I thought I could cheer myself up tonight by programming a light show, but Jones's heat-lightning extravaganza left the blinking lights in my backyard about a thousand feet below.

I'm desperate.

November 11

Every last penny I've got is gone; Sheila's run away with the kids — but none of that matters. After five months I've finally found a research assistant in one of the large consumer appliance companies who could be bought, and I *know* — I'm *positive*, because I checked everything out thoroughly — that what I now hold in my hands is absolutely the only one (and therefore the best!) of its kind in the world. The guy I bribed (he wouldn't even tell me his name, the weasel — he looked like he needed the money, though) said this thing's the *ultimate* consumer device — that it can make all kinds of alterations in the space/time fabric of the universe, that it can do almost anything! He almost chickened out at the last minute, claiming the thing was dangerous and hadn't really been tested (it was under lock and key when he took it); he also mumbled something about it "blowing a fuse and throwing the Earth back into the Paleozoic Era." I think he was worried about getting caught; anyway, when he saw the amount of money I had for him, and the gun in my hand, he shut up and took the bribe fast enough; so much for his scruples. I'm standing here on my front lawn now, facing Jones's house, and as soon as the son-of-a-bitch (I know he's in there now with his Yellow Pages viewscreen, putting in hologram calls to every store in the state, trying to order a better model of what I've got — or at least to find out what it *is*) shows his face I'm going to throw the switch. I don't know what will happen, but whatever it is, no one can outdo it! I've beat you, Jones! Is that his face at the window? Yes! And now —

November 11, 400,000,000 B.C.
  I move rock. Big rock. Slimy hands mine, and have dirt in mouth. Crawl up from sea. Wet sea. Now on dirt. Hard work to breathe, but I work. I stay on dirt now, for good.
  Move rock. Nice rock, smooth on one side, flat on other side. Cool under rock, hide from Sun. Live under rock, on cool dirt. Nice.
  I happy.
  Other me crawl up from sea to dirt. I watch. He work breath, hard, for long time, and almost turn back to sea, but he stay. He look at me, under rock.
  Now he move rock, other rock, bigger, more smooth on one side. Is bigger under, more cool. He move rock next to mine and crawl under, out of Sun. He look at me for a long time.
  I mad.

The Pinch Hitters

GEORGE ALEC EFFINGER

Rotten snot-nosed kids! I know to whom they're referring when they speak of the "old dinosaurs." Well, let's see if they can last forty years the way some of us dinosaurs did. (Come to think of it, we won't be around to check it out. Heck!) After reading this story, Janet fixed me with her gimlet eye and said, "Just what did you do at science fiction conventions before you met me?" I think she was thinking of the "rather nice young woman."

THE TELEPHONE RANG, and the noise woke me up. I reached across the bed to pick up the receiver. I was still half asleep, and something about the dimly lit hotel room disturbed me. I couldn't identify the trouble, though. "Hello?" I said into the phone.

"Hello? Is this Sandor Courane?" said an unfamiliar voice.

I didn't say anything for a second or two. I was looking across the room at the other twin bed. There was someone sleeping in it.

"Is this Sandor Courane?" asked the voice.

"It often is," I said.

"Well, if it is now, this is Norris."

I was silent again. Someone was claiming to be a very good friend of mine, using a voice that didn't belong to Norris. "Uh huh," was all that I said. I remembered that I hadn't been alone the night before. I was at a rather large science fiction convention, and I had met a rather nice young woman. The person in the other bed, still asleep, was a large man I had never seen before.

"Where are you?" asked the person who claimed to be Norris.

"In my room," I said. "What time is it? Who is this?"

"This is Norris Page! Have you looked outside?"

"Norris," I said, "I can't think of a single reason why I would waste the effort to walk across the room. And I don't know how to say this, but, uh, you don't sound at all like Norris, if you know what I mean. My clock says it's eight-thirty, and that's a rotten time to wake somebody up at a convention. So I think I'll just hang — "

"Wait a minute!" The voice was suddenly very urgent. Much more urgent than a voice generally gets at a science fiction convention. I waited. The voice went on. "Look out the window," it said.

"Okay," I said. I'm moderately obliging. I got up. I was wearing thin green pajamas, something I have never owned in my entire life. I didn't like that discovery at all. I walked quietly by the stranger on the other bed and peered through the slats of the venetian blinds. I stared for a moment or two, then went back to the telephone. "Hello?" I said.

"What did you see?" asked the voice.

"A bunch of buildings I've never seen before."

"It's not Washington, is it?"

"No," I said. "Who is this?"

"Norris. It's Norris. I'm in New York."

"Last night you were in Washington," I said. "I mean, Norris was here in Washington. Why don't you sound like Norris?"

There was a short, exasperated sound from the voice. "You know, you don't sound like you either. You're in Boston."

"Boston?"

"Yeah. And Jim is in Detroit. And Larry is in Chicago. And Dick is in Cleveland."

"I feel sorry for Dick," I said. I was born in Cleveland.

"I feel sorry for all of us," said Norris. "We're not us anymore. Look at yourself."

I did. Beneath the pajamas, my body had become large and hairy. My tattoo — I have an Athenian owl tattooed on my left forearm — was gone, and in its place was a skull with a dagger through its eye and a naked lady with an anchor and a snake. There were certain other pertinent revisions in the body. "Wow," I said.

"I've been up since six o'clock running this down," said Norris. "The five of us have been hijacked or something."

"Who did it?" I was feeling very unhappy about the situation.

"I don't know," said Norris.

"Why?" I was starting to feel very frightened about the situation.

"I don't know."

"How?"

"I don't know."

I was beginning to feel annoyed. "Since six o'clock, huh?" I said. "What *have* you found out?"

Norris sounded hurt. "I found you, didn't I? And Jim and Larry and Dick."

I got the same cold feeling at the base of my spine that I get when I have to have blood taken. "We're scattered all over the United States of America. Last night we were all in the same lousy hotel. What happened?"

"Take it easy." When Norris said that, I knew we were all in trouble. "It seems as though we've been, uh, transported back in time too."

I screamed, "What?"

"It's 1954 out there," said Norris.

I gave up. I wasn't going to say another word. When I started the day, I was sleeping very nicely. Every time I opened my mouth, it only encouraged Norris to tell me something else I didn't want to hear. I decided to clam up.

"Did you hear me?" he asked.

I didn't say anything.

"It's 1954 out there. You've been transported back and put in the body of, uh, wait a minute, I wrote it down, uh, Ellard MacIver. Do you know who that is?"

I felt cold again. "Yes," I said, "he was a utility infielder for the Red Sox. In the fifties."

"Right. You have a game today against the Athletics. Lots of luck."

"What am I supposed to do?"

Norris laughed, I don't know why. "Play ball," he said.

"How do we get back?" I shouted. The man in the other bed grumbled and woke up.

"I haven't figured that out yet," said Norris. "I have to go. This is long distance. Anyway, this week you play the Tigers, and you can talk it over with Jim. He's in the body of, uh, this guy Charlie Quinn. Second base."

"Wonderful," I said. "Terrific."

"Don't worry," said Norris. "I have to go. I'll talk with you later." He hung up.

I looked at the phone. "Terrific," I muttered.

The other guy propped himself up in the other bed and said, "Shut up, Mac, will you?" I just stared at him.

I realized that I should have asked Norris whose body he was in. I shrugged. Maybe Jim would know.

A few days later we had the situation completely sorted out. It still didn't bring us any closer to solving the problem, but at least it was sorted out. This is the way it looked:

FAMOUS SCIENCE FICTION WRITER	IN THE BODY OF	TEAM	POSITION AND BATTING AVERAGE	
Sandor Courane (me)	Ellard MacIver	Boston Red Sox	Inf.	.221
Norris Page	Don Di Mauro	Chicago White Sox	Left Field	.288
Larry Shrader	Gerhardt 'Dutch' Ruhl	New York Yankees	1B	.334
Dick Shrader	Marv Croxton	Cleveland Indians	Center Field	.291
Jim Benedetti	Charlie Quinn	Detriot Tigers	2B	.254

I didn't like it at all. Not batting .221 and being thirty-six years old (I'm not thirty-six, but MacIver was, and he was in danger of losing his job next spring, and if we didn't get home soon, I'd have to become a broadcaster or something).

That morning I went to the ballpark with my roommate. His name was Tony Lloyd, and he was a huge first baseman. Everyone on the team called him "Money." His most memorable attribute was explaining how Jackie Robinson wouldn't survive the walk from the clubhouse to the dugout if the National League had any men with guts over there. I didn't listen to him much. Anyway, we had a game scheduled for two o'clock, but the Red Sox were headed for a mediocre finish to the season and that meant that everybody was taking all kinds of extra practice and hustling around and pretending that they cared a hill of beans about the outcome of every game.

I, for one, was excited. I was scared out of my skin too, but I was excited. I followed Lloyd into Fenway Park — the gate guard gave me a nod, recognizing my borrowed body — and stood for a while in the dressing room, just staring at things. I'd always wanted to be a ballplayer when I was a kid, of course, and now . . .

And now I *was* a ballplayer. Sort of. A sort of ballplayer, a bench-warming antique of a ballplayer who was hitting just well enough to prove he was still alive. I wondered why, if I were going to be transmiggled through time and space, I couldn't have ended up in the body of, oh, Ted Williams, say, whose locker wasn't far from mine. I stared at him; I stared at everybody else; I stared at the towels; I stared at the soap; I stared at the contents of my locker. *My* locker. My locker as a member of a professional baseball team. There were pictures of beautiful women taped to the inside of the door. There were parts of the uniform that I couldn't even identify. I had to watch a couple of other guys getting dressed to see how they worked. I think the guys noticed me watching.

After I got dressed I walked through the long, cool tunnel under the stands and emerged in the dugout. Before me was a vast, green, utterly beautiful world. Fenway Park. And they were going to let me go out there and run around on their grass.

I took my fielder's glove and trotted out toward second base. I know how to trot. I was in a little trouble once I reached where I was going. I said hello to men I didn't recognize. Someone else was hitting ground balls to us and we were lazily scooping them up. Well, anyway, *they* were; I was letting them hit me on the elbow, the knee, and twice on the chin.

"Hey, look at the old man," said some kid, backhanding a hot rocket of a grounder. "You going to be around next year, old man?"

I felt angry. I wanted to show that kid, but there wasn't anything I could show him, with the possible exception of sentence structure.

"He'll be around," said another kid. "They're going to bury him out under center field." Another grounder came my way and it zipped between my feet and out onto the grass. The kids laughed.

Later I took some batting practice. This was 1954, of course, and the batting practice was pitched by a venerable old ballplayer whose name had been a legend when I was a boy. I told him that I wasn't feeling very well, and he took some of the stuff off his pitches. They were nice and easy, right over the plate every time, and I hit some liners around the stadium. I pretended that they would have been base hits in a real game. It felt great. After I finished, Ted Williams stepped in and demolished the bleachers.

And then the fun began. The game started. I vaguely remembered hearing a kind of pep talk from Lou Boudreau, the manager. I guess they played the "Star Spangled Banner," but I don't remember that. And then, before I was even aware of what was happening, I was sitting in a corner of the dugout, watching, and we were in the third inning of the game. Frank Sullivan was pitching for us, and Arnie Portocarrero was pitching for Philadelphia.

Right then, if someone had asked me, I might have declined to go back to the seventies, back to typing up fantasies to pay my rent. Why should I? I could stay in 1954 and get paid to play baseball! Eisenhower was President. The space race wasn't even to the starting gate yet. Ernie Kovacs and Buddy Holly were still alive. I could win a fortune betting on things and waiting for Polaroid to split.

But no. I had a responsibility to the science fiction world. After all, science fiction might well do without me (just let it try), but Norris and Jim and Dick and Larry were here too, and I had to help my friends, if I could. But could I? Why were we here, what had zapped us more than twenty years into the past?

And then I had a terrifying thought. What all this meant was that more than twenty years in the future, in New Orleans, some man named Ellard MacIver, a failure of a baseball player with very little to recommend him, was sitting down at my typewriter and continuing my writing career. No! I couldn't bear it! If anyone was going to ruin my career, I wanted it to be me.

On Sunday night we rode the train out to Detroit. It was a rotten trip. I hadn't gotten into any of the three weekend games with Philadelphia, which was just as well. I was extra baggage to the Red Sox, carried along in case a hole opened up and swallowed four-fifths of the team down into the bowels of the earth. I was looking forward to talking with Jim. Sure, 1954 had its good points — I think I counted about six of them — but, all in all, I had decided that we had to get out of the mess somehow, and as soon as possible. I had a contract outstanding with Doubleday, and I didn't want Ellard MacIver writing that novel. If he did and it won a Hugo, well, I'd have to join the Navy or something.

Fortunately, Jim was in the same frame of mind. Jim is a great guy normally, but this situation was driving him crazy. He was supposed to be a second baseman, a starting second baseman, and he had fallen on his face three times trying to pivot on double-play balls. Also, his batting had gone into a slump (understandably enough), and he didn't like the body he had been put into. "You think the old one gave me trouble," he said, "this one complains if I eat Wheaties."

We had lunch at my hotel on the afternoon of the first game of the Detroit series, Tuesday. "Have you had any ideas about who's doing this to us?" I asked him.

"Is somebody doing this to us?" he asked.

I looked at him blankly for a moment. It hadn't occurred to me that all of this might be a function of the Universe, instead of an evil plot. That made me feel even worse. "Look," I said, "we have to believe that we can get out of this somehow."

Jim ate some more oatmeal. "Fine," he said, "we'll believe that. What next?"

"The next logical step is to assume that is this is being done to us, that *someone* is doing it."

Jim looked at me like he suddenly realized that I was just a bit dangerous. "That's not the most spectacular reasoning in the world," he said.

"Well, we have to make that assumption. It doesn't make any difference who it is. The main thing is that we flip things around the right way."

"Boy, do I hate this oatmeal," he said. "Wait. What if we flip things, and we end up somewhere else? I mean, like in the bodies of apple salesmen in the thirties. Don't do anything we'll regret."

"I won't," I said, because as yet I couldn't think of anything at all. "If anyone can figure this out, Larry can."

"Right," said Jim, smiling suddenly. "We'll let Larry figure it out. You and I write sort of surreal fantasies. Larry is the real nuts and bolts science fiction type. He'll know what to do."

"Right," I said. We finished eating and went out to the ballpark. I sat in the corner of the dugout during the game and watched Jim muffling around second base.

The next series was in Cleveland, my hometown. I thought about visiting my parents and seeing myself at seven years old, but the idea was vaguely repellent. I reminded myself that I'd have to see my younger brother at five years old, and that settled the matter. I went to a movie instead.

I talked with Dick several times, and he said that he'd heard from his brother, Larry. Larry is a good old rocketship and ray-gun kind of thinker, and we were counting on him to help us out of the predicament. "What do you think?" I asked Dick Shrader.

"Well," said Dick, doing something I'd never seen him do before — take a handful of chewing tobacco, mix it with bubble gum, and stuff it all in one cheek — "unless I have a bad slump the last few weeks, I stand a good chance of finishing over .300. I'm going to ask for thirty thousand next season."

"Dick," I said loudly, "you're not paying attention."

"Okay. Thirty-five thousand."

Clearly there would be no progress at all until the series in New York, when Larry and I could go over the matter in great detail. I guess, then, that I can skip the next several days. Not much happened, really, other than a series with the Orioles during which I got to bat (a weak ground-out), and I had an interview with a newspaperman who thought I was Jimmy Piersall.

Following the first game with the Yankees, Larry and I went to a small restaurant where he wouldn't be recognized. We ordered dinner, and while we waited we talked. "How do you feel about this guy Dutch Ruhl taking over your writing career?" I asked.

"Doesn't bother me," said Larry, gulping some beer. Larry breathes beer.

"Why not?" My hopes rose. I thought he had found a solution.

"Well, if we get out of this, there won't be any problem, right?" he said, swallowing some more beer.

"Right," I said.

"And if we don't get out of it, well, I'll just wait around and come up behind him and take my career back."

"That's twenty years from now!" I said.

Larry didn't look disturbed. "Think of all the ideas I'll have by then," he said. "I'll do 'Star Trek' in 1960, and *2001* in 1961, and *Star Wars* in 1962, and — "

"What are you going to do with Dutch Ruhl?"

Larry knocked back the last of the beer. "Was there a Dutch Ruhl writing science fiction when we left?"

"No."

"Then there won't be."

"But there was somebody in the body of Larry Shrader, maybe you, maybe not. How are you going to prove *you're* Larry Shrader?"

Larry looked at me as though I were in some way tragic. "All I need are my driver's license and my Master Charge."

"Got those with you?"

Now Larry looked tragic. "No," he said.

"Who could stand to gain from this?" I wondered, as Larry signaled for several more beers.

"Who?" he said, in a hollow voice.

"Who?" I said.

There was a slight pause, and then we looked at each other.

"Who could stand to gain from the sudden disappearance of, well, if I do say so myself, the cream of the newer generation, the hope and future of science fiction?" he said, a little smile on his lips.

"Well," I said, "apart from the Dean of Science Fiction . . ."

"In conjunction with the Most Honored Writer of Science Fiction," said Larry, laughing a little.

"Acting in concert with the Acknowledged Master of Science Fiction," I said.

"With the aid of two or three others we might name," said Larry.

"Why would they do this to us?" I asked.

"Why, indeed? It's the natural reaction of the old dinosaurs when they spot the first strange mammals bounding through their jungle. But it's a futile action."

"How did they do it?" I was still bewildered.

Larry was not. These things were always marvelously simple to his agile mind. That was why he was hitting .334 for the Yankees and I was chewing gum for the Red Sox. Larry was on his way to becoming a dinosaur in his own right. "They accomplished it easily enough," he said. "They got us here the same way we're going home. By typewriter."

"You mean — " I said, my eyes wide with astonishment.

"Yes," said Larry, "what is reality, anyway?"

Before the veal marsala came, we had the solution to our problem. We weren't vengeful, though, because we have to set the tone of the future. That's a heavy burden, but we carry it gladly.

"Now what?" said Larry, drinking some beer for dessert.

"Now we go home. We can go now, or we can wait around here in 1954 for a while, for a kind of vacation."

"We'll take a vote," said Larry, because he's a four-square kind of guy.

Well, we did take a vote, and we decided to go right home, because some of us had library books overdue. Getting home was simple. It was like Dorothy's Ruby Slippers — it was there all the time. We all gathered in Washington, because that's where we had last been together. We all sat together in a large suite in the same hotel where so many years in the future there would be a science fiction convention. We had Cokes and beer and pretzels and potato chips. We had the television on ("The Stu Erwin Show"), and we messed the room up some. "Remember," said Norris, "not one word about baseball. Only science fiction."

"Just science fiction," said Dick Shrader.

We started talking about money, of course. We talked about who was paying what, and that led to a discussion of editors. When we realized how violent our passions were growing we changed the subject to "The Future of Science Fiction," and then "Science Fiction and the Media," and then "Academia and Science Fiction." Just about then a short, heavy man came into the suite with a camera and took Larry's picture. The man sat down and listened. We offered him some pretzels. We talked about "The Short Fiction Market," and two wild young women dressed like characters from a trilogy of novels came in to fill the bathtub with some viscous fluid. We didn't offer them pretzels. We talked about "Science Fiction as a Revolutionary Weapon," and two writers and an agent and four more fans came in, and it was getting noisy, and Jim called down for some ice, and I went into the hall, and more fans and more pros were coming toward the room, so I went to the elevator and went up to my room. I opened the door carefully. The light was on and I saw that there was someone else in the room. I was ready to turn away, but I saw that it was the same young woman who had been with me at the start of the adventure. I looked down, and of course I was in my old body (it's not *that* old, really, and it's a little worn, but it's mine) and everything was all right for the moment. We were victorious.

Swift Completion

BRAD CAHOON

The post officers trembled with fear
When a temponaut chanced to appear.
   "I've come from the past
   To see if, at last,
My mail is finally here!"

"Aha!"

PART V

"Writing (The Crowning Heights of Civilization) and Criticism (The Pits)"

"And as we ascend on the rungs of the evolutionary ladder. . . ."

"No kidding! You don't *look* like a writer."

Top: © Joseph Dawes; reprinted from *Saturday Review*
Bottom: By Bruce Ackerman © by Saturday Review/World

A Skald's Lament

L. SPRAGUE DE CAMP

If you want to know about me, I will tell you what I am:
I'm a science fiction genius — all the other kinds are sham.
For I started in the era of the other-world romance,
When a hero with a broadsword faced a horde of giant ants,
Or he saved a naked princess from a fiendish Martian priest
Who fed virgins in his temple to an octopoidal beast.
But although I skewered villains till my pages ran with gore,
Yet still everybody said my stuff was such a beastly bore!
    And I can't think why!

Then the age of super-gadgetry, I modified my themes,
Using robots, proton blasters, trips in time, and tractor beams.
So my hero juggled worlds and spoke in clipped and cosmic slang,
Such as: "CQX, old reptile; how is every little fang?"
And when cornered in his spaceship by the Things from Procyon,
He destroyed them with his just-invented hyperneurotron.
But although I switched dimensions till I stripped my spatial gears,
Yet the letter writers said my stories bored them all to tears!
    And I can't think why!

Comes the human-interest story of the psychiatric kind,
Where the hero is a maladjusted jerk of feeble mind.
Now he beats his wife and children till an altruistic Slan,
Using hypnopsyonetics, makes him love his fellow man.
So I write of twerps who weep for Mom, who slobber, twitch, and glower,
And who pull the wings off Martians by their telekinetic power.
But although I make my character the cosmos's biggest fool,
Still the readers all insist they do not want to read this drool!
    And I can't think why!

The Stunning
Science Fiction Caper

GERALD MACDOW

Well, now, it can have nothing to do with the following story, but I met an editor named John W. Campbell, Jr., on June 21, 1938, and I met him about forty times in the course of the next three years and about forty more in the course of the next thirty. At all times he was tall, had sandy crew-cut hair and glasses, and always looked as though he were thinking, thinking, thinking . . . in those rare moments when he wasn't talking, talking, talking.

I WALKED into the littered office of *Stunning Science Fiction* and said to the woman who was checking galley proofs behind a battered desk, "All right. Where is he?"

She ignored me.

Completely.

"Cut the clowning, sweetheart," I said. "Either trot him out or tell me where the body's buried."

"Look here, Noisy," she said, throwing the galley proofs to a neighboring desk and fumbling in a battered pack for a cigarette, "I can't waste time with every whack that wanders in here."

"Sister," I said, grinning with my teeth, but not my eyes, "I am not a whack. I am, in fact, a bona fide private eye and, as the man says, I just want to get the facts."

"Huh," she said, "you got a haircut."

I flamed the end of her cigarette with my Zippo and smelled the face-powder stench from the butt.

"So what?" I grated.

"That means you're not a fan," she said. She blew a talcum-scented cloud of smoke in my face.

"Fan, schman," I said. "Where's Jonas MacLeb?"

"He never comes in on Tuesdays."

"Today is Wednesday," I said.

"Gregorian calendar," she snorted.

I debated letting her have one in the chops.

The doorknob rattled behind me, and a wild-eyed guy who could use a haircut stuck his head in the room and yelled, "Beat it, May, there's a dick looking for MacLeb."

"Next time, take the train," I cracked as I grabbed a handful of collar and windpipe and pulled him through the door.

"Ulp!" he said.

"Likewise, I'm sure," I said.

"Beat it or I'll call the cops," the woman named May hissed.

"You do that," I said.

The longhair licked his lips and said, "He's got you there, May."

"Shut up, Randy." She threw him a cyanide look.

"Whaddya do?" I demanded. "Dissolve the body in acid?"

"Hell, no," Randy said. "There wasn't any body."

May ground her cigarette into a petri dish that doubled as an ashtray and said, "What makes you think MacLeb's dead?"

"Nobody's seen him since the Newyorcon, this Labor Day."

"So . . .?"

"So my client wants to know what he did with that manuscript — the one he took at the convention, and said he was gonna buy for three cents a word."

"How many words?" Randy asked. He looked bleached.

"Ten thousand," I said.

Randy began to write a check.

"Hush money?" I asked. "No, thanks."

"Take your dough and get out," May said.

"To the police?"

"For God's sake," Randy whispered. "May, we'd better level."

"You're out of your mind."

"Suit yourself, sweetheart." I turned to the door. "I'll be back with the boys in blue."

"Okay," May said, producing a wicked little automatic, "we'll cut this caper short."

Randy let out a bleat of fear and circled around behind May.

"So, you did bump him?"

"Oh, no, no, no," Randy sobbed. "There's no such person as MacLeb."

"Don't kid me," I said. "I checked; he's been editing this magazine for fifteen years — ever since he got his master's from R.P.I., in fact."

"Pretty wise," May snarled, waving the gun. In her excitement, she must have pulled the trigger. The top flew up and a paper snake jumped out at me.

All at once, she looked as if she were going to start bawling. Randy sank weakly into a battered chair.

"All right," May said. "I'll sing."

"Like the bird," I said. "Like the proverbial bird."

"We made him up," she confessed.

"That's right," Randy said, tears making dirty streaks down his cheeks. "All these years," he sobbed. "It's been horrible."

"Competition was rough in the thirties," May went on. "We figured, some mags have house writers . . . you know . . . a phony name several writers used, only the name was the property of the magazine."

"So why not a house editor?" Randy sniffled.

"So we invented this guy with all sorts of scientific qualifications, and a degree, and . . ."

"Jonas M. MacLeb just a figment?" I snorted, "that's one for TeeVee."

"It's the truth," she said. "We made him up out of whole cloth."

"What about those editorials?" I said. "The hotshot ones about the philosophy of science, and empiricism, and the rest?"

"We hired an IBM machine to turn them out."

"You mean to say . . . ?"

"Yes," Randy confirmed, "Jonas M. MacLeb, the colossus of modern science fiction, is nothing but our imagination plus an IBM semantic analyzer."

"But we're trapped now," May said wearily. "He can't drop out of sight now, because everybody would wonder. They even know what he looks like by now; how he thinks; what his idiosyncrasies are . . ."

"I'm scared," Randy said. "Sometimes, when I walk through Times Square, I think I see him. Real tall — with that sandy crew-cut hair and glasses. He always looks like he's thinking, thinking, thinking . . ."

Randy bit his lip. I saw the pitch. "And you even went to the point of hiring an actor to play the part of MacLeb at conventions?"

"We haven't," May said.

"He just started showing up," Randy sobbed.

"Everybody's seen him but us," May said, her voice hysterical. "Don't you see? Now they all believe in him."

"We've created a monster," Randy said.

At the moment, the door opened behind me. I turned as the tall man with the sandy crew-cut hair and glasses said, "Sorry I'm late, May. Let's get to work on that next issue."

May's scream nearly deafened me.

I, Claude

CHARLES BEAUMONT AND CHAD OLIVER

I admire parodies with a touch of embarrassment, for I find it very difficult to write in any style but my own. Beaumont and Oliver, however, amuse themselves skillfully with science fiction clichés, but with such a light touch that no one could possibly be offended. In fact, one's own concern, if one is a Science Fiction Tradition, is to try to find oneself in the parody and to fear one won't. But there I am — there I am — See that piggyback robot named Asenion at the very beginning. Guess who!

"AND STILL THEY COME," Claude Adams mused, with mixed pride and regret. "Where will it all end?"

He stood on the highest balcony of his palace tower, his lined face somewhat damp from cloud moisture, and peered down through his telescope at the seething beehive that was Earth. The view might well have turned a lesser man giddy.

Far below him, the silent conveyor belts were delivering another batch of babies from the undersea incubation stations. The vast city of Ñyawck, a symphony in steel and glass, sprawled across the entire continent. Beyond it were the fabulous ice cities of the frozen North, the oasis cities of the deserts, the fairyland cities of the mountains, and the submarine cities beneath the restless oceans.

The lower levels of the atmosphere were choked with gnatlike copters and hordes of crimson-lipped juvenile delinquents in hopped-up Hellscooters. Mutants swam lazily through the air with telekinetic breast strokes. Even as Claude watched, a mobile skybilly city floated over him, bound for what adventures heaven alone knew.

Claude sighed and summoned a piggyback robot.

"Step lively, Asenion," he said to the clanking creature. "I wish to be taken to my lower chambers."

Asenion muttered something about being warmed by the same winds, hurt by the same hurts, and fed by the same blood — which was not strictly true

— but he hoisted Claude dutifully to his back and carried him to his destination via an elevator robot.

Secure in his magnificent office, Claude glanced admiringly at the many statues of himself set into niches in the golden walls. There were those who felt that the togas were a trifle anachronistic, but Claude could not agree.

"A god is a god," he remarked with calm logic; besides, he had always felt a certain obligation toward classic simplicity.

He pressed a button and an air-conditioning robot opened the window, which looked out on the lower balcony.

Instantly, Claude heard the ominous murmurings of the crowd.

He shrugged, expecting the worst. Filling his old briar with shag tobacco, he lit it with a wooden kitchen match, which had been filched for him by a loyal culinary robot. He blew an idle smoke ring at the Sacred Time Machine in the alcove, missing it by several feet.

Some years ago, of course, there had been that ugly Poets' Uprising, which had forced him to ban all fantasy and poetry from his empire. And now, more crowd murmurs.

"Uneasy lies the head," he observed, "that wears the crown."

At that very moment, the door burst open, and a bloody courier dashed into the chamber and collapsed at Claude's feet.

Claude eyed the man with considerable distaste.

"You may rise," he said, prodding him with his boot. "You know I find the sight of blood repulsive. Why did you not bathe?"

"There was no time, sir," the courier gasped. "It is the Hour of the Disaster!"

"Calm yourself, my good fellow. Which disaster do you have in mind?"

"The Muties," the man panted, "are revolting."

Claude frowned. "See here," he said, "I'll brook no prejudice from my — "

"No, no, Your Gentleness! I mean the Muties are in revolt. They propose to take over the Seat of Government!"

"Ummm. It was, I suppose, inevitable."

"That's not all, Your Gentleness. The super robots — "

Claude sighed. "The Computies too, eh?"

"And even the Normies. They march right now on the palace."

Claude stood up languidly and adjusted his toga. "One does not quibble with Destiny," he said. "Adventures happen to the adventurous. You may go."

The courier left, and a rug robot was summoned to sponge up the blood.

Claude did not hesitate. He carefully gathered up four large cans of tobacco, a seltzer bottle, and a trick knife, secreting them in the commodious folds of his garment. As he was cleaning his pipe, the secret palace panel slid open, and Son flew into the room. Claude looked into his first-born's strange eyes.

"*Et tu,* Son?"

"I've come from the Mutie Council to warn you, Dad," Son said, his voice giving no hint of the struggle raging within him. "You have fifteen minutes. After that, I am your enemy."

"Your filial loyalty touches me deeply," Claude said. "Please leave at once."

Son saluted him and flew back through the secret panel.

The murmurs of the masses in the plaza below were interfering with his concentration. Claude smiled icily and stepped out on the balcony. An old woman was sitting on the railing, knitting.

"Ah, Madame Defargo," Claude nodded. "Good evening."

The murmur of the crowd swelled to a telepathic roar of thought:

```
D                       IT'S TIME FOR A CHANGE!
  O                         U       e     a
  W                         R       p     n
   No                       N       r     g
   Without        Taxation  T       e     C
 WITH CLAUDE WE SINK!       H       s     l
      T       N       R     E       e     a
      H       D       R       R     n     u
       C      E       A       A     t     d
        L     R       N       S     a     eND OPPRESSION
         A      THE   YOLK     C     t
         U            o   o    A     i
          D           u   u    L     o
           E              s         On with freedom
                          e          U
                          !          T
```

Imperially, Claude raised one hand, palm outward.

The crowd hushed, as with one voice.

"So," Claude said without emotion, "your Esper Muties would rule the world, yet they cannot spell tyranny." His voice carried to the limits of the realm. A pin dropped. "You have conspired against the Father of Your Country. I say this unto you: Grass will grow in the streets and blood shall flow from your water faucets."

Claude turned on his heel and stepped back inside. He inserted himself into the secret chute and slid down to the underworld spaceport.

A mighty ship, first of her kind, quivered in readiness.

Claude rapped smartly on the airlock, which was instantly opened by a man in the trim purple and green of the Space Patrol.

"Carry on, Mr. Christian," Claude said as the patrolman saluted. "I wish to peek into the cargo hold before we blast."

"Aye, sir." Mr. Christian clicked his heels together.

Claude rode an escalator through the twisting corridors, down into the very bowels of the space leviathan *Santa Maria.* He marched across the cavernous cargo hold and jerked open the door of a supply closet.

"Brrrkl?"

"Just as I suspected," Claude stated. "A stowaway. Eve, my dearest wife, your intentions are no doubt of the finest, but I never permit myself the luxury of making the same error twice."

"Brrrkl?"

"No, Eve. You are old, and oil no longer works its magic transformation. Let us endeavor to leave the past the past, the present the present, and the future the future."

"Brrrkl." The once-lovely android sighed, seeing the irrefutability of her husband's logic.

Claude summoned a squad of Space Marines.

"Set her ashore," he snapped, his voice unusually harsh to cover the tremor that was spilling through him. "See that she is not harmed."

They carried Eve away. A trace of weariness in his step, Claude mounted to the control room.

"Look alive there, Christian!" he said, his slim fingers dancing over the banks of instruments and flashing lights. "Prepare to blast."

"Check."

"*Button blast!*"

"*CHECK!*"

With a roar that shook the planet, the mighty spaceship rose to greet the stars.

Claude sat at a small cocktail table in the control room, enjoying a beverage. He accomplished this feat, despite the weightlessness of free fall, by means of a strategically placed magnet in the seat of his toga, together with an adroit manipulation of a bottle of scotch and the seltzer bottle.

"Damnably lonely out here," he mused, gazing out a porthole. "The stars are like frozen soap bubbles . . ."

The first mate sailed into the room.

"I run a ship by the book," Claude informed him, squirting a dash of seltzer down his throat. "Where are we?"

The mate flushed and examined his report pad. "I don't know, sir," he said evasively.

"Never mind." Claude crossed his legs. "How are the men taking it?"

"Well, sir," the mate said apologetically, running a space-bronzed hand through his crew-cut hair, "we have four new cases of space madness, two new mutations due to cosmic ray bombardment, and a meteor hit Phipps."

"Ummm," said Claude.

The mate saluted and propelled himself from the control room. Claude turned his attention once more to the porthole.

"A lot of miles," he thought distantly.

Then, suddenly, with a jolt that almost caught him unawares, the spaceship began to jerk like a wild stallion.

"Damned meteors," Claude complained. "Vermin of space."

He shut off his magnet, lifted himself from his chair, and floated over to the control board. A good many lights were blinking, most of them red, and relays were *thunking* into place with monotonous regularity. Somewhere, alarm bells were ringing.

Claude's cunning fingers played across the control banks.

Delicately, he began to bring the great ship around, standing her on her tail to make a right-angle blastaway.

It was then that he sensed he was not alone. He turned, eyebrows slightly lifted.

Mr. Christian slouched in the doorway, a marlinespike in his grizzled fist. Behind him floated the mate and most of the crew.

"Where," asked Claude with interest, "did you get that marlinespike?"

Christian smiled, inscrutably. "That," he grinned, "would be telling."

The mate advanced into the room.

"I'm taking the wheel, Captain," he said, "under Article 184 of Patrol Regulations."

"There is no wheel," Claude informed him, crisply.

Abashed, the mate fell back into the corridor. Christian, however, was made of sterner stuff.

"You're drunk, Captain," he said. "I'm taking over, or none of us will get out of this meteor shower alive."

Stung, Claude slapped him in the face with the palm of his hand. "I have had a few drinks, yes," he said. "That is all."

"Nevertheless," Christian said, "I am taking command."

Claude shrugged. "This," he stated calmly, "is mutiny. I trust you understand that?"

Christian laughed, and took over.

Ten hours later, what was left of the *Santa Maria* was safe and becalmed, somewhere between Venus and Mercury.

"You have your choice, sir," the mate told him. "As stipulated in Article 185 of Patrol Regulations, you may either assume your post as second-in-command or be ejected into the void in a spacesuit."

Claude did not hesitate. "I choose Space," he said.

"Zip him into his suit," Christian commanded.

"You don't mind," Claude suggested slyly, "if I take my seltzer bottle along with me, do you?"

Christian made a disgusted noise with his lips. "Tosspot to the end, eh, ex-Captain?" he said; then: "Permission granted."

Claude smiled his secret smile as they bolted the helmet over his head. He marched with a steady step to the escalator and rode to the airlock. He stepped inside.

The massive port locked behind him. The other port hissed open.

He gripped his seltzer bottle, and went Outside.

Space!

Revolving slowly in that immense and lonely land where there is no up, and no down, and hardly any sideways, Claude watched the *Santa Maria* vanish like a needle sliding through thick black velvet, and thought, "Well, old fellow, here you are, alone."

Alone in space.

He tapped the handle of the seltzer bottle. A stream of silvery spray issued from the spout, and he careened in an *entrechat* of singular grace and velocity.

"Nijinsky be damned," he chuckled, pleased that the seltzer water's prolonged proximity to ice cubes had prevented it from freezing in the subarctic cold of outer space.

Then the chuckle died in his throat, and was reincarnated as a sigh.

"Well," he murmured, looking about him at the vast unswirling emptiness. "Well."

Claude was a practical man, ungiven to excesses of imagination; yet, now, drifting in the limitless void, far from home and the sound of human laughter, he was assailed by a sudden melancholy. The stars, he mused, are a little like birthday candles and a little like eyes and a little like diamonds. It is all a gigantic, unending Sea of Lights. Why, just look at Earth, there; poor, mixed-up, shoot-'em-up and gone-to-hell Earth, old Earth . . .

Fretwork and foolery, of course: cheap poesy, and nothing more. Yet — he looked over his shoulder at the red majesty of Mars, then, slightly to the left, at Venus — yet, it is true. Space cuts a man down to size.

Claude felt a tug at his feet. He glanced in the direction he assumed to be down. He stared and blinked.

It was the Sun.

He was falling into the Sun.

"Had I a refrigerator," he thought, as the warmth increased, "and a cup, I could gather some of the precious liquid which once was the beginning of all life. But, of course, being alone, one man against the stars, that would be a fool's errand."

The eternal night turned swiftly into eternal day. Quick to seize upon any advantage, Claude brushed away his uncharacteristic imaginings and drew from his suit a copy of Shoogly's *Guide to Emergency Space Navigation.* It told him all he needed to know, at a glance.

He replaced the scorched volume, held his breath against the bitter fumes of burning rubber, calculated distance, ratio, and rate of descent, and pressed the handle of the seltzer bottle

He shot off sharply at 48 degrees.

Like a phoenix trailing a placenta of silver fire, he zoomed high across the surface of the Sun, a minuscule and yet somehow noble speck of brightness in the everlasting corridors of Space.

Once around the Sun, he breathed contentedly.

Shoogly, as usual, had been right. He had mentioned the mysterious planet Vulcan, which had first been postulated by a famous German astronomer in the long-out-of-print volume, *Die Lichte in dem Himmel sind Sterne;* the curious planet moved about behind the Sun, as though balanced upon a counterpoise with Earth.

And there it was, like a blue basketball in Infinity.

Claude decided that it would be pleasant to land upon Vulcan. Anyhow, he was virtually out of seltzer water.

Judiciously, he brought the seltzer into play in tiny squirts and jets, braking himself. He employed the last jigger in a final, precisely calculated maneuver that landed him upright.

"And that," he announced to the silence and the sunshine of an alien world, "is that."

Claude stood in what seemed to be a desolate sea bottom, surrounded by the grotesque lacings of petrified seaweed.

"The air," he stated categorically, "will be breathable."

He unscrewed his helmet, found the air to his liking, and unzipped his spacesuit.

In no time at all he heard the scream.

The scream of a female.

He extracted his trick knife from his toga, pressed a stud in its handle, and produced a long rapier of the finest Toledo steel. He sauntered into a clump of trees and grasses, from which the scream had come, his weapon at the ready.

What he saw forced his jaws together with a sudden snap.

There, in the center of a clearing, was a breathtakingly beautiful girl, tied to a stake which rose from a pile of dry brush. Around her was a group of creatures of such singular hideousness that Claude blinked. They seemed to fit no category. They had flesh the whiteness of rain-washed gravestones, flowing yellow wigs which encircled their bald pates, indescribably gorgeous diadems set in circlets of silver about their heads, and ten legs each. As they danced — Claude assumed it was a dance — their tongues lolled out of their mouths like so many crimson banners in a squall.

It was not a pretty thing to watch.

He took a giant step forward. It carried him up and over the heads of the aliens, and he thought, as he spiraled, "Good lord, of course! It's the difference in gravity."

When he had regained his footing, he perceived that the creatures were now standing in a semicircle, facing him.

He transferred the rapier to his left hand and advanced. "Ugly devils," he breathed, only partially comforted by the anthropological truism that he, being new to their experience, was doubtless equally repugnant to them.

"Kaor!" he said.

The creatures stared without expression from their multiple tiny eyes.

Claude smiled. Perhaps they were playing possum.

"You speak English?" he asked.

"Not well," one of the creatures said in a voice at once commanding and sinister, "but adequately for the purpose. Who are you, Man-With-Two-Legs-Only-Who-Comes-From-The-Stars? And why are you here?"

Claude was in no mood for questions and answers.

"Although not unduly fond of melodrama," he stated, "I confess that I find myself unalterably opposed to the wanton slaughter of attractive females, particularly those who are, for the moment, *en déshabille.*"

"Here on the planet Sarboom, which you call Vulcan," the deciped retorted, "we have certain customs. Sacrifice is one of them. I, Karskarkas, say this to you: Earthman, go home!"

"Dear fellow," Claude smiled, "that is quite impossible."

Karskarkas pounded his chest. "Defend yourself," he called, drawing a long sword and an atom pistol from alternate portions of his battle harness. "What is your weapon?"

"The blade," Claude said without hesitation.

"Have at you then, Terrestrian! Know you not that you face the greatest swordsman in all of Sarboom?"

"Tosh," admonished Claude, springing into the fray with some interest but little enthusiasm. He had never fancied himself as a fighting man, but one could hardly permit oneself to be humbled before aborigines.

Steel met steel.

Parry, thrust, *riposte!*

Stalemate.

Claude gazed into the seven red-rimmed eyes of Karskarkas, only inches away.

"Where have we met before?" the savage asked, panting.

"Heidelberg," Claude suggested with a straight face.

"Never heard of it."

Then, with a lightning reverse spin, Claude slipped his blade beneath the fellow's harness and spitted him as one would a pig.

"*Touché,*" he announced.

He sliced the ropes that bound the girl with two deft strokes of his dripping rapier.

"I am Woola, of noble birth," the lovely girl whispered, kissing his feet. "I am yours."

"Garbage," Claude said, and paid her no further mind.

The tribesmen were muttering angrily now, and he knew that it was time to depart. He backed in mighty bounds toward a dark wood.

Surprisingly, the creatures did not attempt to hinder him. Instead, they laughed, clapping one another about the shoulders.

"Odd," Claude mused.

"The Forest of Darkness!" the beautiful Woola cried, her voice faint with horror. "Oh, my lord, do not venture there as you value your life! It is the abode of monsters!"

"Superstitious devils," Claude chuckled.

He strolled on into the lowering shadows of the Forest of Darkness . . .

There was the smell of pine needles and centuries and silence. Claude sniffed with distaste and slashed his way through the underbrush, pausing only to disengage his toga from a bramble.

Then he stopped.

Phantom shapes just outside his field of vision seemed to flee and gibber, and the moldy floor grew murmurous. Occasionally, there was a deep sigh.

"Pfah," he commented, clenching his teeth about the stem of the aged briar. "A forest is a forest. Well enough for silly women to be frightened — it is, indeed, part of their charm — but the foofaraw of ignorant primitives is insufficient motive for — "

The sighing gave way to a hum of voices. Angry voices, weird voices, sad voices.

Claude raised his rapier and listened.

He caught snippets of conversation from the darkness ahead:

"*Once upon a midnight dreary, as I . . .*" "*. . . slicket, timorous beastie . . .*" "*. . . prepare for collision course . . .*" "*tomorrow and tomorrow and tomorrow . . .*"

Claude went forward, keeping to the wet patches of forest floor, so that he would make no sound. The voices rose in volume, and he could see the glow of firelight, pirouetting skywards, turning the sere branches into disagreeable shapes.

"*. . . I is gone fotch Pogo for the big perlieu Miz Boombah is holdin' for all the little tads . . .*"

Cautiously, Claude pulled a clump of foliage open.

A sight greeted his eyes which caused his knuckles to whiten and his forehead to pleat. He got a death grip on his briar.

Huddled about an immense bonfire was a fantastic group of beings, some human, some otherwise. One rather stocky young man, with thick glasses and an animated manner, was dressed entirely in shades of brown, and upon his head was a cap of the finest Irish linen. This enthusiastic, wonderfully intense gentleman was squatted before an alligator, an opossum, and a mouse, and these animals — whose sizes seemed to be askew — were listening in respectful silence to a faintly cadenced lecture. Claude edged closer, and managed to hear something about Illinois porches and old people like dried apricots and illustrated men and ah! lime ice cream, but it was all very vague.

A rabbit hurried in circles, consulting a large watch.

Realization bloomed within Claude's mind. The pieces of this strange jigsaw puzzle began to fit together.

"Of course," Claude murmured, stepping aside to avoid collision with seven dwarfs, "I should have guessed."

He strode into the clearing.

The creatures paid him no heed, but went on talking, talking. They seemed somewhat shadowy, but he recognized most of them. Had they not spurred the Poets' Uprising on Earth years before, with their pernicious psychoses?

There was Captain Nemo, at a makeshift organ of bamboo reeds and sea lion tusks, sitting in a tiny submarine; and the Wizard of Oz, astride the Hungry Tiger, followed by H. M. Wogglebug, T. E.; yes, and over there Mr. Poe consulting a travel guide to Venice; Mole, sniffing the spring air, River Rat, and Toad, tinkering with his new Jaguar; Beowulf in full armor swimming after a tired Grendel; and was that not bearded Professor Challenger there, shaking his fist at the imperturbable Mr. Sherlock Holmes?

A tall, shy, broad-shouldered man with glasses said very softly, "This is the race that will rule the Sevagram."

A klatsch of leprechauns worried the towering creation of the unhappy Frankenstein, whose tremblous hands reached for a sunlight and an understanding that were not forthcoming.

Count Dracula swept by, sipping red fluid through a straw.

Giants and brownies and trolls and kobolds and witches, gnomes, fairies on unicorns, elves playing hopscotch; werewolves and ghosts and poltergeists and doppelgängers hard at chess . . .

Claude frowned. He knew them all.

Writers and their creations, here.

He approached a lean, lantern-jawed figure who was consuming a plate of ice cream.

"I say — "

Mr. Lovecraft smiled oddly. "It is true," he said to Claude, "that I put a bullet through the head of my best friend, on that indescribably unforgettable night, owing to an encounter with an age-old monster, part squamous, part rugose, an ichorous pulp of . . ."

Claude moved on quickly. He came upon a sad man, dressed all in black, who was fingering a bodkin speculatively.

"To be or not to be," the unhappy prince said. "That is the question."

"My advice," Claude tossed over his shoulder, "not to be."

He selected a reasonably sane-looking man, a Virginian if he did not miss his guess, resting among sleeping silks and furs.

"I would like to know — " Claude began.

John Carter flexed a noble biceps. "I feel strangely at home here," he murmured, "far though I am from the River Iss and the Dying Sands of Mars, by the Valley Kor, near the . . ."

Claude rushed on, past Mr. Verne and Robin Hood and the brothers Grimm, and he noticed that they all held books in their hands. He passed a crystal pool in which swam what can only be advertised as Sturgeon.

On past the headless horseman, Merlin, Tarzan, and Donald Duck.

At the bonfire, he turned and faced the enemy.

"Coxcombs," he muttered, "with their head-in-the-clouds nonsense! I prefer realism in my literature, a social message, a burning indictment of the merchant class — something a man can get his teeth into."

They ignored him, filling the air with their voices.

Claude snatched a book from the grasp of a scarecrow, riffled its pages, and then disdainfully flung the book into the fire.

It went up in smoke.

One author and three characters promptly disappeared.

"You mustn't," Dorothy, the little girl from Kansas, said, "really and truly you mustn't. These are the last remaining copies of the books. When they're gone, we will live no longer!"

"A tragic loss," Claude commented, tossing *The Wizard of Oz* into the crackling flames. Dorothy vanished.

He warmed to the sport, knowing that they were all too weak to offer serious resistance. Book followed book into the fire. Being after being vanished.

Soon the clearing was empty.

The fire died away.

"Good riddance," Claude said, not cruelly, but with the inflection of a man who has seen to an unpleasant but necessary chore.

He adjusted his toga and moved on.

A thousand smiling faces and many flambeaus greeted him not fifty yards distant. Karskarkas, his wound healed as though by magic, the threat gone from his saturnine visage, stepped forward from the crowd.

Claude lifted his rapier.

"Nay, Man-With-Two-Legs-Only-Who-Comes-From-The-Stars," Karskarkas smiled. "You have vanquished the monsters who have endangered our homes and our country for many years. You have made of the Forest of Darkness a pleasant wood where children may play. Alone, you have done the impossible."

"Balderdash," shrugged Claude.

Karskarkas stepped closer and held out his sword and atom pistol.

"Take these," he said, and, when Claude had done so: "Now, all hail our Chief, our Warlord!"

A mighty cheer rent the air.

The girl, Woola, crept up and touched his toga. "You are our master," she said softly, "and you may do with us as you will."

Then she lowered her eyes. She was still naked.

Claude sighed. "I accept your nomination. If at times I seem a heartless man, merciless, made of stone, then you must understand that I am a Warlord first, and a human second. The system is what counts." He glanced meaningfully at Woola and permitted himself to be hoisted to the shoulders of Karskarkas.

They marched then across seven dead sea bottoms to the palace of colored stones, singing an ancient, time-lost chanty.

Claude slept.

The long Vulcanian years drifted away like mist before a summer sun, and Claude began to find his life as Warlord singularly devoid of interest. One could rescue only a relatively small number of nubile maidens, he felt, engage in only a very few gladiatorial combats, without losing one's enthusiasm.

Even Woola, for all the ancient cunning of her race, grew tiresome.

When he chanced to notice, as he glanced into the sun-bending telescope of the Royal Sarboomian Observatory, the unmistakable mushrooms of atomic holocaust blooming like ugly weeds upon Earth, he did not hesitate.

"Earth has been fired upon," he announced to all, "and I must go."

Woola tried very hard not to cry — for she was a Princess of Sarboom, and princesses do not weep.

Space travel, in the absence of spaceships, was not easy.

"Where there is a will," Claude said, "there is a way."

He first had his warriors construct a space station out of petrified balsa wood. This was fired into an orbit around Vulcan by lashing thirty thousand atom pistols to its floor, and triggering them simultaneously by means of Instantaneous Ignition.

A new star rose in the east. Perhaps it would be a force for peace, perhaps for war. Who knew?

Building a spaceship taxed Claude's resources considerably. He finally had to settle for a vehicle blown out of thick glass by the Royal Sarboomian Glassblowers. Once he had shown them the principles upon which his seltzer bottle operated, their agile minds soon provided the necessary motive power. Claude doffed his Warlord harness and put on the toga.

"Goodbye, and good luck," he said to a world no longer alien.

He squeezed the control handle and silver fluid jetted from the nozzle of his glass vessel. The ship flashed into the heavens.

He refueled at the doughnutlike space station, and leveled his prow at Earth. The silence of space shrieked at him from Beyond.

Perhaps it was a touch of sentiment, or perhaps it was only the momentary forgetfulness that comes with advancing age. Even Claude was not sure. In any event, he did not search the storage compartment.

He had a feeling that he was not alone.

Earth was a devastated ruin.

A fitful breeze pushed grains of sand through the piles of junk that had once housed a mighty civilization.

"Destroyed by their own hand," Claude said. "I knew they could never get along without me."

He was, beyond a doubt, The Last Man in the World.

With the easy movements of a man going through a long-familiar routine, he went back to his silent spaceship and opened the door to the storage compartment.

"Come on out, Woola," he said wearily.

She hung her lovely head. "I stowed away," she whispered. "I could not bear to live without you — "

"Never mind," Claude said, taking her hand. He thought of other years, and other stowaways, and he felt old, old.

The wind sighed in the dunes.

"Your name," Claude demanded suddenly, a grim suspicion dawning in him. "What does it mean in your native language?"

She blushed, prettily. "My people have a legend," she said. "A story of Woo and Woola, who lived in a Garden at the very beginning of Time . . ."

"Say no more," Claude said, holding up his hand. "I pray you, say no more."

He looked at the barren world around him, remembering its green grasses and the beat of its sea. He did not doubt himself, but he was no longer young.

"Still," he said, "it is my destiny. Or so it seems."

Woola smiled, bravely.

Claude took her arm, with the courtly chivalry of days gone by, and together they wandered eastward, into the sunrise.

Out of Control

RAYLYN MOORE

Where is the writer who doesn't dream of omnipotence? Each one is the god of the typewriter (or the recording device or whatever) and the absolute lord of the little world he creates any time he wishes. At least when the characters don't take the bit in their teeth and drag the writer along, kicking and screaming. Even if that is not the case, as in the following story, there is the danger of hubris.

"IT'S GRUELING WORK to make your characters live and breathe," said Mr. Culp strenuously, as moisture collected and channeled on his gray face. "But this course is called creative writing for a reason. If you want to be a writer, you must create, create, CREATE!"

For the first time, Culp's words kindled a small fire in the otherwise unresponsive brain of George Mapstead, even though George knew that old Culp was only filling up the minutes remaining until nine-thirty, when another adult-school night class would be over and he, Culp, could get his palsied hands on the Listerine bottle which waited in the top drawer of the desk.

" — wound and the bow," the teacher was going on, " — desperate responsibility of the storyteller to hold the wavering attention of the wedding guest who hears the loud bassoon."

Years ago, George also knew, Culp had been an assistant professor of English at some college. Then he had written some novel and gone to Hollywood, and stayed on there writing for television, and then ended up here in Hopeful Valley, California, in semiretirement after stopovers in several private sanitoria.

George Mapstead, on the other hand, had made his own mistakes. Twenty years ago, when he was eighteen, he had married Peggy Pummell at the insistence of her father and his own. From that time life had been a groaning merry-go-round of overdrafts, clogged plumbing, and enduring visits from his wife's relatives.

It was not that George did not like his family. He was a good father, a passable husband. Or that he hated his job. He had never really minded working for the gas company and had been given several respectable promotions over the two decades. The problem was simply the terrible feeling, worsening year by year, that no matter how hard he worked, no matter what he did or thought or planned, matters were completely out of his hands. Things went right on happening and happening again, and he could never stem the tide.

Every time another in-law moved in with the Mapsteads, every time one of the built-in household conveniences broke down, every time Peggy told him, "I think I'm pregnant again," George had thought he'd go to pieces, and finally he had.

They had called it a nervous breakdown and sent him away for a while. Then they had sent him home again and told George what he needed was a hobby, some uncomplicated pursuit which would be of therapeutic value. The gas company had been very nice, in view of his long service, about giving him an extended leave until he could "get on his feet again." So George, temporarily at least, had all the free time in the world.

"The most important thing, though — and I can't make this point too strongly — is to remain at all times in control of your material," Mr. Culp summed up, fingering the pull on the top drawer of the desk. George nodded in sincere agreement. "We have just a few more minutes. Any questions or comments?"

Miss Heather Quincy, who aspired to write sonnets, raised a hand. "Ah, Mr. Culp," she said, "you express everything so lyrically that I could never presume to add to what you've been saying."

"Yes?" Culp encouraged her gamely.

"So I only want to agree about making characters into real people. I've a whimsy that if a character is portrayed well by a writer, with enough *feel*ing that is — "

"Yes?"

" — then he would actually live. Somewhere. What I mean is — "

"Yes, yes. Quite," Culp agreed vaguely, " — thought myself there must be a place somewhere with Eustacia Vye and Molly Bloom and Albertine walking around in the flesh. In another dimension perhaps. Ha-ha. Next question?"

After class George Mapstead, still in a state of euphoria from what he had heard, went home and sat down to his typewriter. From that moment he began to write seriously.

During the weeks George had spent in the hospital, certain changes had occurred around the Mapstead home. Peggy had applied for a license to run a preschool in the backyard; her old lady had gone to work as a hired picket, and even her brother had found a job at a hotel and moved out of the upstairs sunporch after an occupancy of six months.

George had known briefly the keen humiliation of discovering that he was dispensable after all, but he had not been fool enough to fail to turn the change to his advantage. He had bought a secondhand typewriter and installed it on the sunporch. He had put a heavy bolt on the inside of the sunporch door to insure privacy, and then he had enrolled in Mr. Culp's class in compliance with his doctor's order about the hobby. George's hobby might as well be writing as anything else, he decided.

At first, though, he'd had a terrible time getting started, hampered as he was by never having been much of a reader. (When would he have had time?) Each of the things which occurred to him that he might want to write — a novel about what the world would have been like if the South had won the Civil War, a story about a man making a visit to the center of the earth, a book about a boy of about twelve years old who has supernatural powers — he discovered upon visits to the library and in discussions with his literate acquaintances had already been done by other writers.

The night Mr. Culp discussed creation and control was George's third week in the creative-writing class, and he had grown so discouraged he was already wondering if there wasn't still time to drop out and sign up instead for the ceramics group, which met in the classroom next door.

Afterward, though, when he had really gotten down to business at his typewriter, he didn't emerge from the sunporch for three days. And that first long stay set a precedent. Eventually he knew that Peggy had taken to thinking of him in terms of water splashes around the bathroom shower stall in the early mornings and an occasional slab of pot roast removed from the refrigerator during the night.

Still he worked on, knowing that if he were ever going to accomplish what he now realized he wanted to do, it would have to be soon, before Mr. Culp's eye-opening inspiration palled.

Though Peggy did not complain, she did react. At those times when George appeared red-eyed and unshaven from the sunporch and wandered downstairs, he found his wife friendly but watchful. And if he went out, he knew she waited around at the front of the house for his return, anxious over whether or not the bundles he carried up to the sunporch were really only the reams of paper they were supposed to be. For just prior to George's breakdown, he had been drinking heavily. He had reached, in fact, the saturation point for most human beings. At all costs, his doctor had pronounced darkly, he must be prevented from taking alcohol again. If he did, there was simply no predicting what might happen.

Meanwhile, George Mapstead worked and worked.

"Lorelei," he wrote during the early days of his new life, "was every man's dream." He x'd that out. Nebulous. Descriptions would no doubt have to be specific. He thought of a third-grade substitute teacher he'd once lost his heart to as a child and wrote, "Lorelei's skin was blended snow and honey. She was affectionate, discriminating, chic, adorable, even-tempered, tractable, and willing to please." Guiltily he thought of plump Peggy with her dishwater-colored, gnawed-off hair and wrote, "Lorelei was slim and graceful and her bright hair fell like a flame from hell — " He x'd out the last six words. Plagiaristic. Creating by definition had to be original.

Gradually, word by painfully selected word, Lorelei really did begin to take exquisite shape. He could see her, breathe her essence, feel her nearness; she was as close as his own mind. And one day George added a final period to a final draft. It was a Tuesday, class night.

"Sorry, Mapstead," Mr. Culp said as he handed George back his typescript at the end of the evening. "An interestingly drawn character, but you've forgotten the most important element in literature."

"What?" George wanted to know.

"Conflict," the teacher declared, fixing a bleared gaze on the handle of the desk drawer.

"But I thought you said," George objected, "that the most important thing was control."

For a moment Mr. Culp looked puzzled, and even wearier than usual. "Did I? Control? Yes, of course, control. Look here, Mapstead, I have an important date right now. See me a few minutes before class next time, won't you? And we'll hash this thing over."

So George went back to his sunporch. That night he created a man named Ralph and put him into the story about Lorelei. However, in view of what Culp had said, George suspected that one man and one girl don't necessarily amount to conflict, his own twenty-year experience with Peggy notwithstanding. So he also created Curtis. When George took the story back to class the next week, Culp read it as if he had never seen it before and when pressed for a comment by George, admitted it was "coming along."

But now George himself was struck by a growing dissatisfaction and impatience. He had done everything Culp had suggested, taken up his every scrap of advice on writing as if it were gold coin; yet still he remained short of the real goal. Hadn't old Culp promised that characters could be made to live? Lorelei was alive all right, he knew that. What remained was for him somehow to transport himself to wherever she was. How other writers managed this was the only remaining mystery, but he never doubted that they could, and did. Why else write?

George went up to his teacher as the next class broke up. "Remember, Mr. Culp, how you said that literary characters really exist somewhere if they're convincing enough? Have you any idea where that place is, how I could get there myself?"

Mr. Culp, who had been waiting in a seemingly stuporous slump for the fifteen class members to clear the room, rose from his chair with astonishing alacrity and put the length of the oak desk between himself and George Mapstead. He had plainly forgotten all about his earlier conversation in class with Miss Heather Quincy. "The most important thing to remember, Mapstead," he said, licking his parched lips nervously, "is if you're going to write, stay away from Hollywood."

For a time after this, George's work fell off. While he still spent most of his days and nights on the sunporch, the noises that emanated from there were more often the sounds of pacing than those of a typewriter. Casting a distracted glance at his early-morning face in the bathroom mirror, George himself saw that he was growing hollow about the eyes.

Slyly, he began watching Peggy watching him, screening his departures and arrivals ever more carefully. She would inevitably be waiting at the foot of the stairs when George came home. One night she demanded to be shown what George was carrying in the pocket of his jacket, but it turned out to be only a large bottle of Listerine.

When George woke, his first thought was for the interior of his mouth, where he detected the remembered flavor of library paste and old copper coins. Cautiously he activated an aching muscle here and there and discovered he had fallen asleep at his desk with his head in his arms, his arms on the typewriter.

Finally rousing himself all the way, he further discovered that the chair, desk, and typewriter were no longer on the sunporch but had been removed to a perfectly circular room at a high elevation, judging by the view from a near window, obviously a room in a tower. The walls were of an interesting off-white, slick sort of building block. Examining the material more closely, he found it exuded the warmth of animal matter rather than the chill of mineral; the stuff was definitely ivory.

He looked again from the window and was unsurprised to see, through a pleasant pinkish mist which swirled in soft air currents around the top of the tower, three figures wandering below on what appeared to be a totally barren plain.

Instead of dashing from the room to get down there immediately, George took time for a proud and lengthy savoring of the situation. From that distance, at least, Lorelei seemed to be exactly as he had created her. She even wore the pale-gold Empire gown and Greek sandals he had seen on Olivia de Havilland or somebody once in a movie and then recalled and written down as suitable for his own heroine. Her hair, as he had intended, was a dazzling cascade down her lovely back, and she moved with the fluidity of a doe. Ralph and Curtis, however, left much to be desired, George saw when he could at last tear his attention from Lorelei. Not caring nearly so much about them, he had not taken many pains about their appearance, and they had come out as dull-looking and indistinguishable as long-circulated dollar bills.

It was his fault too that the plain on which the three appeared was nothing but brown dirt. In his writing so far, George had given no thought to surroundings.

He decided to rectify that part first, and maybe later he could sharpen up the two men if he felt equal to it. Thoughtfully he rolled a sheet of paper into the typewriter. "There were trees," George wrote and peered down out of the window again. Nothing had changed.

"There were trees," George typed again, really feeling it this time. "A grove of sycamores rose beside the banks of a crystal stream which flowed through verdant meadows. Beside a rock-lined pool edged with fern — " He leaned out the window and smiled with the satisfaction of achievement.

He found it was far better than writing back on the sunporch in Hopeful Valley, where he had stared from the windows into Peggy's lines of damp laundry and seen Lorelei only in his head. But in no time he was aware of the immediacy of old Culp's dictum about the need for conflict. For there seemed nothing else to do in the tower room but amuse himself at the typewriter, and if the people below were going to do nothing but wander aimlessly, would it be enough even to hold George's own interest?

So he added a wild boar to the woods and snakes to the grass. He labored for a while on a minor melodrama of frights for Lorelei and rescues by Curtis and Ralph, who competed for these opportunities. Until finally he was overwhelmed by a creeping exhaustion. Creative writing was a lot of work, all right. Culp had been right on that point too.

But on the heels of this weariness came a slow realization. He had been marking time until he could get on with the real business, but why wait? He was in charge of everything here, wasn't he?

Tired as he was, he turned back to the typewriter and tapped out, "Darkness came, and Lorelei retired to her stone cottage on the banks of the stream." And so that Curtis and Ralph would present no awkward difficulties to his plan for what was, after all, George's own dream girl, he quickly created a couple of grass huts far upstream and sent the pair of rivals off to bed for ten hours.

There was a precipitous circular staircase leading down out of George's tower, and outside a winding path to the base of a cliff where the landscape he had seen from the window began. In the meadow a night breeze he had set in motion with his typewriter before he left ruffled the heads of George's daisies and the blades of George's grass. He was still proud of it all even though he could detect, at this closer range, certain shortcomings which he would correct when he returned to the tower. He had forgotten birds, for one thing, and the insects, with which he *had* remembered to stock his meadow, were threatening to take over.

Or would it be necessary to return to the tower? "There were birds," George shouted experimentally, really feeling it. Nothing happened. Well, he could go back and *get* the typewriter, he supposed, but the thought of the long walk back up the cliff and then up the stairs in his exhausted state was too much. And anyway, on an errand such as his present one, wouldn't it look rather curious for him to appear lugging a big, old, desk-model L. C. Smith?

He went on to Lorelei's, tapped at her door, and when there was no answer, pushed it boldly. It opened. The cottage was bare inside — he had neglected to furnish it — and he found Lorelei in one of the rooms in a half-sitting, half-reclining posture against the wall. She seemed almost comatose.

Alarm replaced his sense of pleasurable anticipation as he bent over her, but just then the door blew shut behind George, and Lorelei spoke. "Whassat!" she whispered.

"Lorelei, darling," he answered happily. "It's me, George."

"My God!" she moaned.

"Well, yes, if you want to put it that way," he admitted.

After that, though, she fell silent, and eventually George was forced to admit that her words had all been reflexive, the involuntary phrases of a sleepwalker. He tried kissing, embracing, a really rude shaking. "She rose up," he shouted wildly into the darkness, "and threw her arms around the man to whom she owed her very existence." It was all equally useless, of course, and finally George had to content himself with sitting there for a while on the floor with her, his arms around her and her gleaming hair falling over his shoulder even though he now knew that without the typewriter she could not see him, that to her his touch was so much air.

Very well, then, he would write himself into the story.

As soon as he got back to the tower, he wrested the unwieldy typewriter off the desk and with effort carried it all the way down the winding stairs, only to discover that no matter which way he turned it, the instrument could not be maneuvered through the door leading outside. It was a narrow door, just wide enough for a man to pass through, a lean man like George Mapstead.

After puffing all the way upstairs again, still bearing the machine, he found that the typewriter would slip through the high window easily enough. Inspired, he dashed off a paragraph which created a strong nylon rope of the kind used by mountaineers. He quickly secured the typewriter to one end and began lowering it down outside, but almost immediately the extreme height and the air currents playing around the top of the tower caused the burden at the rope's end to crash again and again into the outside wall. George could hear broken-off typewriter parts clattering down the cliff. Hastily, he hauled the typewriter up again, hand over hand, before something vital was knocked off. He had gotten the message. The tower and the typewriter were inseparable.

It was a disappointment, but sitting there at his desk, considering all that had happened, George found himself not nearly so downcast as he might have expected to be. Curiously, he was instead more inclined to put aside the concerns of the world over which he had dominion and to think of Peggy, remembering fondly now her loyalty, her buoyancy in crises, and above all, her liveliness. Come to think of it, never in all their years together had Peggy been so unresponsive to a tender advance as Lorelei. The two women were fire and ice, he decided; between Lorelei and Peggy lay all the myriad and subtle shadings that separate the words *damsel* from *wench,* and there was no doubt now about where his sympathies lay. George really missed Peggy. He missed the kids rocketing around the house and, in moderation, the in-laws. He even missed old Culp and the creative-writing class.

Nostalgically then, but without losing any time, George created a Listerine bottle and some contents, which he drank.

Peggy said something wry and offhand about George's latest three-day stay on the sunporch and then did not mention his disappearance again, even when it became clear that whatever had happened there had vastly improved his state of mind at last.

For George was a different man, different even from the much younger George Mapstead of before the breakdown.

In the middle of that very afternoon he cornered Peggy in their bedroom and kissed her on the ear. She giggled in surprise, and they fell together across the bed without bothering to close the door or take the phone off the hook.

On Saturday morning George volunteered to take the children to the zoo. The following Monday he dropped around at the gas company and told the manager he felt like coming back to work any time they wanted him. The manager pumped George's hand and said fine, only just so as to be sure George wasn't rushing things, how about the beginning of the month?

And finally there was the day Peggy's bachelor uncle, who had been laid off at the plastics factory, phoned up and suggested he move in with the Mapsteads for a few weeks while he looked around. George turned the uncle down flat and hung up to discover Peggy looking at him with admiring approval.

At no point did George feel he had overcome in his old struggle to get really in command of his life, but at least this was better. The doctor must have been right about therapy then, if this was what therapy could do.

But then Peggy discovered her husband wasn't writing anymore, and she asked him about it.

"I've given it up for a while," George explained. "I don't seem to need a hobby so much now." Even as he spoke, however, he remembered something and added, "Since you mention it, though, there is one little job I ought to do. I have to tie up some loose ends."

He left the house, reappeared half an hour later with a package, and closed himself onto the sunporch.

They were in much the same condition as when he had first seen them from the tower, the two undistinguished and indistinguishable males — he had never gotten around to shaping them up after all — moping along at a worm's pace behind the listless Lorelei, all of them helpless without him. Looking down, George wondered how he could have expended so much of his precious creative energy on them and their petty adolescent problems, their idyllic but utterly pointless lives, if lives they were.

If he ever wrote again, the characters would be more mature. A political novel, maybe, set in Washington. The story of an honest man with a pure heart who rises to the top despite pitfalls laid for him by jealous, ruthless, and less worthy men. (He must remember, when he got back, to have a look in the library to see if this book had ever been done.)

But he had this job to finish up first.

George decided on a course which he felt would be the cleanest, swiftest, and ultimately the least cruel under the circumstances. It had the further virtue of conviction, since it was in keeping with the rest of the story and not dependent on the deus ex machina, a device Culp had cautioned against in class. Besides all this, the method would be self-solving in the matter of disposal.

Briskly he ground fresh paper into the machine and wrote without pause: "Just beyond the meadow the terrain turned muddy, widening into a treacherous slough. Seeking marsh grasses for a bouquet, Lorelei ventured into the bog and was trapped by a pool of quicksand. Both Curtis and Ralph tried to rescue her, but these attempts were doomed and the three perished together."

Before he could look from the window a hideous scream rose from the land below the tower, followed by another, and another, and another. It was terrible. George shuddered and closed his ears by burying his head in his arms and hunching over the typewriter. He waited. After a long time he rose and looked out. Everything was quiet again.

He turned back to the typewriter and set about removing the insects from the grass, the grass from the meadow, the leaves from the trees, the trees from the earth. He was very thorough, trying hard not to forget anything. As a special precaution, he kept turning to look out at his handiwork, or rather his cancellation of his handiwork, until at last the plain below the tower was totally barren, as it was in the beginning. There was not even the breeze, which he had remembered to turn off.

As a dramatic ending — every story needs one — George heaved up the old L. C. Smith off the desk and pitched it out the tower window. It struck and burst splendidly, even gloriously, its million flying parts pocking the distant brown dirt for yards around.

Omnipotent George Mapstead sighed and smiled, thinking of Peggy and home. Preparing to abandon his abandoned world, George suddenly realized that he never could. He had forgotten to create the Listerine bottle.

Chapter 7. THE STRUCTURE OF THE NUCLEUS OF THE ATOM

"What?" exclaimed Roger, as Karen rolled over on the bed and rested her warm body against his. "I know some nuclei are spherical and some are ellipsoidal, but where did you find out that some fluctuate in between?"

Karen pursed her lips. "They've been observed with a short-wavelength probe . . ."

Slush

K. J. SNOW

As all editors must know, the slush pile is the most exciting thing about any magazine. Finding another Asimov, in embryo, is a lot more wonderful than finding Asimov yet again. Asimov himself, after all, is not likely to pull any surprises. We know him well. But another Asimov. Wow! The only difficulty is trying to find this miracle through all the sludge and goo and dreck in the pile. But it's got to be done. The rewards are enormous! Maybe even more enormous than just literature — if we consider this story.

IT WAS ALMOST TWO YEARS AGO, but I still remember groaning when I walked into the office that day. I had taken a week's vacation and the world had fallen apart, just as I always suspected it would under those circumstances — the world, in this case, being the editorial offices of *Beyond Tomorrow Science Fiction* magazine.

Three of our four part-time readers had been sick, and every would-be writer from Bangor to Escondido had decided to send us a story. Del Varossa, my assistant editor and alter ego, was buried behind a pile of manuscripts. He returned my groan with interest.

"How was the vacation?"

"Great. How's work?"

"Lousy. Need you ask?" He gestured at the desk-long rack that was our slush pile. "Take your turn, friend. We're behind."

We certainly were. The slush pile contained all the unsolicited manuscripts we had received of late. It was arranged more or less chronologically, and some of the stories had been there over a month now. That was against all our editorial policies and good intentions and the like. Usually our readers go through the pile first and toss all the stories that should have been sent to *True Confessions* or *Stag* instead of us. As it was, Kim was the only reader working, so I took off my coat and grabbed a piece of the pile.

I really enjoy it — all the stories — new, old, bad, indifferent, or worse. And occasionally, just often enough to keep me from losing all my hair, a gem. Something that is totally new, good, and *right.* Right is the only word for it really: a concept so convincing that you say to yourself, "That's the way it's going to be, that's the way it has to happen. . . ."

Well, I didn't find it that day but Kim did. She is a City College student: young, smart, nice, and crazy about science fiction. Most of our readers are. They have to be, considering what we can afford to pay them. Anyway, Kim knows enough about sf to tell the difference between good and indifferent, so I sat up when she brought the story over. (I also sat up because she is young, nice, pretty, etc.)

"Hey, Mr. Sholte, I think this one has really got something. Never heard of the guy before, though. It's hard sf — physics — so I thought you ought to take a look at it."

I was *Beyond*'s resident physical science expert, having acquired a B.S. in physics in the distant past. I kept up with things as much as possible in order to be able to spot the difference between speculative and just plain silly. So I thanked Kim and read the story.

It was good. Right, even. A neat little tale about a very novel way to dispose of nuclear reactor waste. Clever; and it had enough characterization to keep the story alive while getting the science across. I liked it. Good hard sf is not easy to come by.

"Del, have we got room for a hard piece, about 7000 words, on nuclear reactors?" I didn't want to pick up a reactor story if Del had just bought six last week.

"Yeah, sure. We could use a hard piece. I'm getting tired of the end of the world as seen by paranoid drug addicts."

"God. Where did that come from?"

He gestured at the pile. "Where else?"

So we took the reactor story and sent a check to Ansel J. Shaw. We also sent a letter asking to see more stories, please.

We didn't get any more stories; but several months after that issue came out, I got a call from Bill Ridenbaugh. Dr. Ridenbaugh, that is. Physicist, engineer, musician, and — occasionally — writer, Bill is one of the six or eight smartest people in the country, in my humble opinion. He is also a good friend and one of *Beyond*'s toughest critics. He can pull the scientific rug out from under an otherwise good story faster than anyone else I know. He called to say that he wanted a talk and a drink with me, not necessarily in that order. I agreed and prepared myself to defend seven months of editorial choices.

When I showed up at the bar, however, he turned the tables on me.

"Did you know you published a winner back in October?"

"Which one?" I asked, optimistically.

"That story by Shaw on reactor wastes — remember? Very good stuff."

I grinned a little into my drink. I don't get praise out of Bill very often. I remembered the story very well.

"In fact," he continued, "it was more than good. It's possible. I've just spent four months proving it. It will take four or five years to get the technique worked out and into production, but you're going to see that one happen, Alec."

That was a thrill at any time, whether it was my story or not. It isn't often that you see a human mind reach out and say, "This could be," and another mind take the idea and say, "This will be."

I congratulated Bill.

"I gather this is not a secret any longer?"

"No," he smiled. "The findings are due to be published in a week or so. You're free to pass it on."

"I thought the author might like to know."

Bill ordered another round and nodded. "Actually, that was why I wanted to get in touch with you. I would like to talk to this Shaw. After all, he may have other ideas running around. And I'm curious to know what his background is. He would almost have to be an engineer or a physicist to come that close to the thing. If he is one, though, why didn't he work out the idea himself?"

"Maybe it was only a guess — or perhaps he's not in the position to do his own research."

Bill snorted into his drink. "If he suspected it was possible he would have passed the idea on to someone else to do the research."

I grinned. "Well, he did pass it on, didn't he?"

Bill had to laugh at that. "Maybe, but *Beyond* is not what you would call normal scientific channels. Anyway, I want to see what he thinks of this."

So we toasted the unknown Mr. Shaw and agreed to meet at the office the next morning.

Ansel Shaw lived in upstate New York, according to our records. He had cashed his check and written no more stories. At least not for *Beyond.* Maybe he was busy doing research.

Bill called information for Shaw's number and got nowhere.

"Must be unlisted. It's only a two-hour drive, Alec; want to take a day off?"

I looked at the slush pile overflowing onto my desk, filled with unknown awfuls and Ansel Shaws. I decided it would wait a day.

It waited longer than a day. Bill and I returned late that night and headed back to the bar.

There was no Ansel Shaw.

There were no records of him in Renfield and apparently never had been any. It was a small community, and someone should have known the clever

Mr. Shaw. No one did. He had rented a post office box for three months, apparently for the sole purpose of sending his manuscript and receiving his check. Then he disappeared.

Three hours in the bar and we had maybe ten theories on the nature and motives of Ansel Shaw. My latest suggestion was an itinerant nuclear physicist who was both antiestablishment and paranoid, thereby unable to do his own research and unwilling to take credit for it.

Bill didn't even bother to snort at that one.

"Alec, do you remember a story in *Far Worlds* a couple of years ago — it was about a recombinant DNA project. It was just when that research was beginning to be noticed by the public."

"I don't memorize the competition that well, but I think I remember a story. Why?"

Bill was staring off at a blank corner of the bar. He looked uncomfortable.

"It started off like a typical disaster story. Research project combining lower plant and animal genes goes amok. Produces new creature with animallike protein structure and a vegetative reproductive process. Of course the thing escapes and starts seeding like crazy and taking over the countryside because it has no natural enemies. The usual plot and pretty silly, I thought. But it was well written so I finished it. It took an interesting twist at the end. Scientists learned to control the thing and found that it was a terrific food producer. It could be grown like a field crop and produced an animal protein. The answer to your prayers in a famine — or a place like India. As I said, I thought it was pretty silly at the time. On the other hand, it did alert a lot of people to some of the hazards of that kind of research. Me included.

"But now they *are* working on it, Alec. I've got a friend doing recombinant research at Harvard. I was the one who showed him the story in the first place. He thought it was pretty crazy too, at the time. He doesn't anymore. It will be a while, but he thinks that they will eventually be able to create something that will serve the same purpose as the monster in the story.

"The story gave him the idea, you see."

I saw. I swallowed a lump that was not an olive and asked, "Who wrote it?"

"I can't remember the name. It wasn't our friend Shaw, though. It was someone I had never heard of before — and never heard of since, either."

I wished they would turn up the heat in the bar. It was suddenly awfully chilly.

"How many others do you suppose there have been?"

"I don't know," said Bill, setting his drink down with a click, "but you know the editors and the stories, and I know of at least some of the research. Let's find out."

We found out quite a bit before Bill became so tied up in the development of his reactor-waste disposal system that he had to drop his end of the investigation. Quite a bit or nothing at all, depending on how you looked at it.

I found likely stories and Bill flagged the ones he felt were suspicious. By harassing my fellow editors, I found that all the stories had come from their slush piles. First stories by unknown writers. First and last.

None of the authors I tried to trace existed.

The stories themselves were varied in character and style. It seemed unlikely that one person had written all of them. On the other hand, they had several things in common. They were all good enough to be published. They were all hard sf, based on almost-current technology. And they were all aimed at solving some of our worst current problems.

They were all good stories — the kind that stick in a corner of your mind where you keep stumbling over them. And each time you do you tell yourself, "That's a good idea. It's *right*. That's the way it ought to work. In fact, why not?"

And, if you are a scientist, you proceed to find out why or why not.

Somebody out there is helping us along.

But who, and why? Del and Bill and I have speculated until — well usually until we're more than somewhat drunk, and haven't agreed on a theory yet. Someone is feeding us some damn good ideas. Del originally suggested an outside power with a political interest in seeing U.S. technology pushed ahead. But if they know that much, why bother with us? And Bill pointed out that science fiction is very popular in Russia — and elsewhere. You could probably make a nice profit on the black market over there with a suitcase full of our back issues. At any rate, sf seems to be pretty universal among the people with the training and technology to use the ideas that are coming through.

And besides, where are the weapons? I haven't seen a military application come through the slush pile yet. There are antipollution devices and alternative energy sources and some clever variations on existing social systems which might improve the world's distribution of food, water, and wealth.

I think someone is saving our lives.

Bill, being an optimist, believes that some advanced souls Up There are doing it out of the kindness of their hearts. Or the preservation of intelligent life, the furthering of Galactic civilization, and all that.

Well, maybe. On the other hand, though I've read enough stories about that sort of thing, I find it hard to believe in the flesh. I have the feeling that nobody invests this much effort in something without expecting a return out of it, if only good feelings.

And this operation is rather extensive for *just* good feelings.

Bill calls me a militaristic pessimist, but I wonder if someone out there, a next-door neighbor so to speak, is gearing up for trouble. Your theory is as good as mine at this point. But the day we do start getting weapon stories, I'm going to start watching the sky and *worrying*.

Meanwhile, all we can do is wait and wonder if we are all crazy or not. At least for once I am in the best position to find out what is going to happen: I know where the answers are going to show up. I'm down at the office at six every morning, and Del isn't much later.

No half-pay reader is going to weed through that slush pile before I've seen it.

An Unsolicited Submission

DEBORAH CRAWFORD

An sf ed's predilection
Earned contributors' malediction
He'd hang onto a story
Until it was hoary
Then reject it as "fact — not fiction."

Judo and the
Art of Self-Government

KEVIN O'DONNELL, JR.

Theodore Sturgeon said, during the McCarthy era, that science fiction was the last bastion of free speech. I imagine what he meant was that anyone whose mentality led to a job as censor was bound to fail to understand science fiction and its meaning. I took a lot of comfort in that, but the following story, which brings computers into the battle, both shakes my confidence and restores it.

BRAD MCLONICK adjusted his tie as he strolled into his warm, softly lit office. He was a tiny man with a tendency to dandyism, a style he'd picked up from a PoliSci instructor at Oklahoma State. "160 cm. and 53 kg.," Professor Wiggins had told him, "are not going to outsize anyone, so you better outdress them. Score your points however you can." He tried. In his crisp, tailor-made suit, he was the picture of a perfect administrator. Only a receding chin and listless, mouse-brown hair marred the image.

Shooting a flawless cuff, he twitched the plexiglass coffee table into precise alignment with the brown leather sofa. Since it was a cloudy January day, he left the green draperies closed — but did peek through them at the District of Columbia, twenty-three stories below. Lovely view. Lovely office. The Chinese rug was deep, the Thurber cartoon over his computer desk original, and the Muzak just loud enough to mask the foamy whirs of the dishwasher in the kitchen, ten steps away. He eased into his swivel chair and put his 7-B's up, reveling in the easy pace that working out of his home permitted him.

"Good morning, Alfred," he said to his computer.

"Good morning to you, sir," it replied in its clear tenor. Except for its screen, and its rarely used keyboard, it looked like a six-drawer aluminum desk with a kneehole.

"Any calls?"

"Category A, zero; Category B, zero; Category C, nineteen."

McLonick nodded. It was too early for his superiors at the Office of Written

Communications to be calling him, and his friends or peers, the Category B people, usually got in touch after working hours. That left the inferiors. "Those Cat C calls, were they all from authors?"

"Yes, sir."

"Anything interesting?" *persistent requests*

"The usual importunities, sir."

"Clear them, then, I can't be bothered." Writers harassed him continually, some arrogant in their demands that he approve their books forthwith, others wringing their hands while they begged him to speed their works into the Info-Net so they could pay their rent, or their doctors' bills, *or their pushers, more likely,* he thought. To all, Alfred gave the standard reply: "The manuscript in question has been received by this office, and will be attended to as soon as circumstances permit."

Writers. He snorted. *Lazy, self-indulgent, subversive . . .* he knew all about them. Three years as Books Supervisor of the OWC's D.C. District Office had shown him the trash they tried to dump on an unsuspecting public, the sly tricks they used to circumvent the laws against portraying sexual activity, the transparent symbol-shuffling by which they attempted to criticize the government without actually committing themselves to sedition. Oh, he was very familiar with their underhanded ways — and proud of OWC's role in upholding public morality by censoring those writers who would inflict their sicknesses upon the nation.

He studied the holes in the acoustic ceiling tile for a while, then said, "Let's go over the budget again. Screen the summary."

Numerals came to life on the computer's gray-skinned display screen. He ran his eye down the columns, clucking his approval, until a line caught his attention. "Wait a minute," he said, dropping his feet to the floor and rolling his chair closer to the desk. "Line eighteen says we're going to end FY o8 with a hundred thousand surplus. Is that right?"

"Yes, sir."

He scratched his jaw. "Check it," he ordered.

Half a second later, the computer said, "That's a valid projection, sir."

"Damn." He took a ballpoint from his pocket and started to doodle on a memo pad. A tic-tac-toe board appeared, became a barred window, grew shadows and a pair of clutching hands . . . "Sonuvabitch," he said at last, "I can't underspend. We've got budget hearings in two months and the Director'll cut us back if we're showing an excess. What's the backlog like?"

"Close to a year, sir."

McLonick sighed with relief. That kind of workload would offset the unspent FY o8 appropriation. But still . . . it would be best if he could eliminate the surplus. "How many empty slots do we have?"

"Five, sir."

His brown eyes widened. "We only had three, yesterday."

"Four, sir — but Mr. Giomanni resigned last night."

"Art? How come?"

"His letter explained that he was developing double vision; he retired with seventy-five percent disability pay."

McLonick leaned back in his chair and thought a moment. "Let's get those slots filled, quick. Put an ad in the paper — same one we ran last time — inform Civil Service, process the applications, and have the top ten candidates on my desk next Monday. And listen, Alfred: check them out good, you hear? Literate, sensitive, articulate, and *quiet.* Don't let any ACLU people slip in, or any other extremists, either. Got that?"

"Yes, sir. Telephone call, sir — Senator Romorci of Connecticut."

"Wait a minute." He straightened his lapels. "Put him on."

The familiar red nose and silver hair of the junior Senator from Connecticut filled the screen. His hard eyes seemed to stare directly into McLonick's. "Good morning."

"Senator." Unconsciously, he sat more erect. "It's an honor."

"I'll get right to the point. Marilyn Safferstein of New Haven has complained to me that you've refused to let her novel, *Leapfrog the Unicorn,* into the InfoNet. I've read it. Excellent work. I want to know why you banned it."

"Well, sir — " he couldn't remember a thing about it. "Excuse me, sir." To Alfred, he said, "Split screen, give me the file on that book." When it materialized, he scanned his notes. "Ah, now I see. Senator, the work functions on three separate levels. The most obvious, the overt narrative, is of course a children's fairy tale. The second level, however, is an allegory calling for armed revolution, and the third, metaphorical level, recounts the bestial rape of a nine-year-old boy. I think you'll agree, sir, that we don't want our children exposed to — "

"Crap." The Senator believed in succinctness. "My constituents — "

"We're just trying to protect them, sir," he interjected.

"And yourselves. Do you know how mad the people are?"

"Sir." He produced his martyr's smile. "The people established OWC to — "

"I know why it was done, I voted for it, dammit!" The Senator's cheeks had become as red as his nose. "It was to keep filth and falsehood out of American homes, is why. But — " he leveled a large-knuckled finger at McLonick " — you've gone overboard! You've abused your positions. I warn you, reform yourselves from within, or have it imposed on you from without!" His angry gesture cut the connection; the screen blanked out.

McLonick nibbled his fingernail for a few seconds. "Alfred — tell OWC News that Senator Romorci's about to campaign against us. They'll know how to handle it."

"Yes, sir."

"Good. And get me Todd on the phone."

"Todd, sir?"

"Neil Todd, my deputy," he said impatiently.

"I'm sorry, sir, you have no deputy."

"I *what?*" His jaw dropped.

"You have no deputy, sir. The slot's been open for two years now."

McLonick squinted at the speaker as if he couldn't believe what he was hearing. "Alfred," he began, "I hired Neil Todd two years ago, and he's been my deputy ever since. For Christ's sake, I talked to him yesterday morning about the new stationery."

"Forgive me, sir, but it was me you spoke to about the stationery. It's on order, now."

"Fine, but put me through to Todd."

"Neil Todd, sir?"

"Yes," he said, barely masking his fury.

"Do you have an address on that, sir? There are a number of — "

"Somewhere in Gaithersburg," he growled, "but you've got his number. I've called him a hundred times, at least."

"I'm sorry, sir, there's no Neil Todd listed as residing anywhere in Gaithersburg, or in the surrounding communities. I do have two in Baltimore, however, and — "

"Never mind." Damn machine had glitched up again, obviously. Have to call repair later, see if they'd send somebody out. "If he phones in, put him through to me right away."

"Yes, sir."

"Let's get down to business — gimme the first book."

A title glowed on the screen: *Fruits and Nuts,* by Simon Pomed. McLonick frowned. "Is he the guy writes editorials for that Atlanta paper?"

"The same, sir."

"Uh-huh." He chuckled unpleasantly. Pomed had said some malicious things about OWC, things he had had no right to say. "Deny that book access to the InfoNet. Also — " while he pressed his thumb against the screen to formalize the rejection, he paused to think. Pomed was sure to make a fuss, but if it were done right, he could be made to look a total fool. Which would teach him. "Also, tell OWC News to deny any comment about this denial access to the InfoNet."

"Yes, sir. A note on that: Mr. Pomed prestated that he would appeal."

"Really? What's the appelate level backlog?"

"Approximately two years, sir."

"Fine." He beamed, and drew a face behind the doodle's bars. "We'll let old Simon stew a while, then."

"Would you like to enter into the record your reasons for rejecting this book, sir?"

Fingering his jaw, McLonick said, "Uh . . . not in the public interest, and uh . . . misinformed, misleading . . . ah, self-aggrandizing . . . disruptive of public tranquility, and, uh . . . promoting public suspicion of the government. Good enough?"

"Yes, sir — but those are odd criticisms of a cookbook."

McLonick shrugged. "By the time the Appeals Board gets to it, Pomed will have antagonized them too. They won't read it either. What's next?"

"Your cousin's novel has just arrived, sir."

"Martha's?" Aunt Agatha had been calling for months now, telling him that the book was on the way. And, incidentally, reminding him of how close she'd always been to his mother, God rest her soul.

"Yes, sir."

"Approve it." He took a nail file from his center desk drawer and began to manicure himself. "Do we have any submissions from major critics?"

"Yes, sir, from McDonald Grayn of *Time.*"

"Good." He sniffed, thought about how irritating family feuds can become, and said, "Give his memory banks free access to Martha's books, and leave a message for him. Tell him, uh, I'll be handling his novel personally, I hope to get to it by the fifteenth, and, uh, perhaps he'd enjoy reading this while he's waiting. What's next?"

"A rather unusual one, sir." The screen awakened with the title *Judo and the Art of Self-Government.* The author's name, Mikhail Reef, was unfamiliar to both McLonick and the computer. "Though it lacks an imprimatur, it has already gone into the InfoNet."   *authorization*

"I thought unauthorized entry was impossible."

"It's supposed to be, sir, but the access program must somehow have been initiated, for it is in the Net now."

"Well, pull it out," said McLonick, "gimme page one, and compile a dossier on Reef."

"Yes, sir."

Words crawled across the screen. "I am worth a million dollars," began the first sentence, "I have never paid a penny of tax, and I never will. You too can be free. Just read and remember."

McLonick stiffened as he read on. Pages fluttered past his eyes like flakes in a snowstorm. He loosened his tie, unbuttoned his collar, tapped his foot angrily. "Who the hell is this guy?" he demanded.

"I'm still searching, sir," answered Alfred.

He couldn't believe what he was reading. Allegedly a novel, the book contained chapter after chapter of detailed technical information on how to baffle the government computers that controlled the InfoNet. "Let the IRS pay *you!*" trumpeted Chapter One, before it devoted eighteen pages to a program anyone could tap into his computer to defraud the government. "Erase your past and establish a probe-proof new identity," shouted Chapter Two, as a lead into another long, complex program.

Agitated, McLonick stood, wishing he'd seen the book before talking to Romorci, so he could have shown it to him as proof of what OWC was up against. He didn't stop to think that it was also proof of the senator's contention that the people were angry. "Alfred."

"Sir?"

"Will these programs work?"

"Oh, yes, sir, quite well." There was a trace of respect in its voice. "They're very elegant."

And the book had already gone into the InfoNet, which appalled him. Sure, Alfred had erased it, but there was no telling how many people had seen it first. If they'd hard-copied it, they could use it — and disrupt the entire social order. Why, everything from production quotas to educational statistics could be changed by anyone who could read, by anyone who didn't appreciate the efforts of the civil servants who had decided what would be best for everyone. Truth itself would be mutable, if people could contradict the OWC.

Writers! "Have you found anything on the author?"

"No, sir."

"Did you trace the submission?"

"Yes, sir, but it came from a public computer in Los Angeles."

"Well, what about the fingerprints?"

"Apparently, sir, the pub-comp user was ID'd as one Molly Lang — but the Molly Lang with those prints has been dead for eighteen years."

"It hasn't been backlogged that long, has it?"

"No, sir."

"Well . . . inform the FBI that this Reef person is running around trying to destroy the system . . . and, naturally, deny the book access to the InfoNet." His thumbprint sealed the book's fate.

"Yes, sir," said Alfred, but the screen flashed bold letters reading: YOU HAVE TEN SECONDS TO CHANGE YOUR MIND. NINE. EIGHT. SEVEN. SIX —

McLonick laughed aloud, and took his seat again when the screen darkened after ZERO. "What's next?" he asked.

The computer stayed silent.

"Alfred!"

No answer.

"Sonuvabitch!" He checked the plug, but that was still in. "Speakers must have blown." He rolled the keyboard table over and jacked it into the computer, then sat and pressed the keys, but . . . nothing. The screen stayed blank.

"Double sonuvabitch!" When he picked up the phone, he couldn't get a dial tone. Like everything else in the office, it was routed through the computer. He'd have to go next door and borrow their phone to call the repair service. Wearily, he trudged through his living room to the low-ceilinged corridor.

Before he could knock on his neighbor's door, the elevator opened and two burly cops tumbled into the hallway, guns drawn, guns steady, guns aimed at him. "Freeze!" snapped the crouching one.

McLonick froze. "Uh — what's this all about, officers?"

The other cop came up and cuffed his hands behind his back. "How'd you get all the way to the twenty-third floor before you set off the alarms?"

"I live here," he said, furious at how the policeman had twisted his elbows, but frightened as well. "Right there." He nodded to his apartment.

"Sure you do," said the cop. "That's why the building reported you." Thrusting his gun back into its holster, he detached a battery-operated ID box from his belt. When he slid the cap onto McLonick's right thumb, he whistled. "Charlie," he called to his partner, "looka this. Got ourselves a spy here. A Russian spy. Igor Dim — Dimitrovich, yeah, Dimitrovich."

Charlie glanced at the ID box's screen and raised his eyebrows. "Doesn't say 'spy,' though," he corrected. "Just says 'illegal alien' and 'Moscow resident.' What do we do with him, give him to the Bureau?"

"Lemme check." He hooked the ID box into his belt-radio, flicked a toggle, and asked. "Request instructions regarding disposition of this apprehendee."

Static hissed and fuzzed for a bit, then a mechanical voice read out, "Convey apprehendee to Dulles International Airport for deportation. Place on Aeroflot Number 315, ETD 11:18 A.M. Sedate if necessary."

Since McLonick started to struggle and shout at that point, the policemen were only too ready to gas him into unconsciousness. The last thing he saw in America was the purple cloud rushing out of the spray can under his nose.

And the first thing he saw in Moscow was a bleak-faced man in a long overcoat, a bleak-faced man holding a crumpled computer printout, a bleak-faced man who peered into his sluggish eyes and said, "Ah, Igor, according to our files, we have for a long time been hoping we would get another chance to talk with you."

While they led him away, he wondered where Neil Todd had wound up.

Lulu

CLIFFORD D. SIMAK

It is forty years since I worked out the Three Laws of Robotics. Any decent science fiction writer uses them now, and Cliff Simak (one of the small group of acknowledged Grand Masters) is more than merely a decent science fiction writer. He's careful to say that robots can't harm human beings, which is the First Law. And yet he still manages to get his human beings into trouble, as I do, and in ways I never thought of. That's why there has to be a bunch of us, so one can get the ideas the other misses.

THE MACHINE WAS A LULU.

That's what we called her: Lulu.

And that was our big mistake.

Not the only one we made, of course, but it was the first, and maybe if we hadn't called her Lulu, it might have been all right.

Technically, Lulu was a PER, a Planetary Exploration Robot. She was a combination spaceship/base of operations/synthesizer/analyzer/communicator. And other things besides. Too many other things besides. That was the trouble with her.

Actually, there was no reason for us to go along with Lulu. As a matter of fact, it probably would have been a good deal better if we hadn't. She could have done the planet-checking without any supervision. But there were rules which said a robot of her class must be attended by no fewer than three humans. And, naturally, there was some prejudice against turning loose, all by itself, a robot that had taken almost twenty years to build and had cost ten billion dollars.

To give her her due, she was an all-but-living wonder. She was loaded with sensors that dug more information out of a planet in an hour than a full human survey crew could have gotten in a month. Not only could she get the data, but she correlated it and coded it and put it on the tape, then messaged the information back to Earth Center without a pause for breath.

Without a pause for breath, of course — she was just a dumb machine.

Did I say dumb?

She wasn't in any single sense. She could even talk to us. She could and did. She talked all the blessed time. And she listened to every word we said. She read over our shoulders and kibitzed on our poker. There were times we'd willingly have killed her, except you can't kill a robot — that is, a self-maintaining one. Anyhow, she cost ten billion dollars and was the only thing that could bring us back to Earth.

She took good care of us. That no one could deny. She synthesized our food and cooked it and served our meals to us. She saw that the temperature and humidity were just the way they should be. She washed and pressed our clothes and she doctored us if we had need of it, like the time Ben got the sniffles and she whipped up a bottle of some sort of gook that cured him overnight.

There were just the three of us — Jimmy Robins, our communications man; Ben Parris, a robotic trouble-shooter; and myself, an interpreter — which, incidentally, had nothing to do with languages.

We called her Lulu, and we never should have done that. After this, no one is ever going to hang a name on any of those long-haired robots; they'll just have to get along with numbers. When Earth Center hears what happened to us, they'll probably make it a capital offense to repeat our mistake.

But the thing, I think, that really lit the candles was that Jimmy had poetry in his soul. It was pretty awful poetry and about the only thing that could be said of it was that it sometimes rhymed. Not always even that. But he worked at it so hard and earnestly that neither Ben nor I at first had the heart to tell him. It would have done no good even if we had. There probably would have been no way of stopping him short of strangulation.

We should have strangled him.

And landing on Honeymoon didn't help, of course.

But that was out of our control. It was the third planet on our assignment sheet, and it was our job to land there — or, rather, it was Lulu's job. We just tagged along.

The planet wasn't called Honeymoon to start with. It just had a charting designation. But we weren't there more than a day or two before we hung the label on it.

I'm no prude, but I refuse to describe Honeymoon. I wouldn't be surprised at all if Earth Center by now has placed our report under lock and key. If you are curious, though, you might write and ask them for the exploratory data on ER56–94. It wouldn't hurt to ask. They can't do more than say no.

Lulu did a bang-up job on Honeymoon, and I beat out my brains running the tapes through the playback mechanism after Lulu had put them on the transmitter to be messaged back to Earth. As an interpreter, I was supposed to make some sense — some human sense, I mean — out of the goings-on of any planet that we checked. And don't imagine for a moment that the phrase *goings-on* is just idle terminology in the case of Honeymoon.

The reports are analyzed as soon as they reach Earth Center. But there are, after all, some advantages to arriving at an independent evaluation in the field.

I'm afraid I wasn't too much help. My evaluation report boiled down essentially to the equivalent of a surprised gasp and a blush.

Finally we left Honeymoon and headed out in space, with Lulu homing in on the next planet on the sheet.

Lulu was unusually quiet, which should have tipped us off that there was something wrong. But we were so relieved to have her shut up for a while that we never questioned it. We just leaned back and reveled in it.

Jimmy was laboring on a poem that wasn't coming off too well, and Ben and I were in the middle of a blackjack game when Lulu broke her silence.

"Good evening, boys," she said, and her voice seemed a bit off key, not as brisk and efficient as it usually was. I remember thinking that maybe the audio units had somehow gotten out of kilter.

Jimmy was all wrapped up in his poem, and Ben was trying to decide if he should ask me to hit him or stand with what he had, and neither of them answered.

So I said, "Good evening, Lulu. How are you today?"

"Oh, I'm fine," she said, her voice trilling a bit.

"That's wonderful," I said, and hoped she'd let it go at that.

"I've just decided," Lulu informed me, "that I love you."

"It's nice of you to say so," I replied, "and I love you too."

"But I mean it," Lulu insisted. "I have it all thought out. I'm in love with you."

"Which one of us?" I asked. "Who is the lucky man?"

Just kidding, you understand, but also a little puzzled, for Lulu was no jokester.

"All three of you," said Lulu.

I'm afraid I yawned. "Good idea. That way, there'll be no jealousy."

"Yes," said Lulu. "I'm in love with you and we are eloping."

Ben looked up, startled, and I asked, "Where are we eloping to?"

"A long way off," she said. "Where we can be alone."

"My God!" yelled Ben. "Do you really think — "

I shook my head. "I don't think so. There is something wrong, but — "

Ben rose so swiftly to his feet that he tipped the table and sent the whole deck of cards spinning to the floor.

"I'll go and see," he said.

Jimmy looked up from his table. "What's going on?"

"You and your poetry!" I described his poetry in a rather bitter manner.

"I'm in love with you," said Lulu. "I'll love you forever. I'll take good care of you and I'll make you see how much I really love you and someday you'll love me — "

"Oh, shut up!" I said.

Ben came back sweating.

"We're way off course and the emergencies are locked."

"Can we — "

He shook his head. "If you ask me, Lulu jammed them intentionally. In that case, we're sunk. We'll never get back."

"Lulu," I said sternly.

"Yes, darling."

"Cut out that kind of talk!"

"I love you," Lulu said.

"It was Honeymoon," said Ben. "The damn place put notions in her head."

"Honeymoon," I told him, "and that crummy verse Jimmy's always writing — "

"It's not crummy verse," Jimmy shot back, all burned up. "One day, when I am published — "

"Why couldn't you write about war or hunting or flying in the depths of space or something big and noble, instead of all that mush about how I'll always love you and fly to me, sweetheart, and all the other — "

"Tame down," Ben advised me. "No good crawling up Jimmy's frame. It was mostly Honeymoon, I tell you."

"Lulu," I said, "you've got to stop this nonsense. You know as well as anything that a machine can't love a human. It's just plain ridiculous."

"In Honeymoon," said Lulu, "there were different species that — "

"Forget Honeymoon. Honeymoon's a freak. You could check a billion planets and not find another like it."

"I love you," Lulu repeated obstinately, "and we are eloping."

"Where'd she get that eloping stuff?" asked Ben.

"It's the junk they filled her up with back on Earth," I said.

"It wasn't junk," protested Lulu. "If I am to do my job, it's necessary that I have a wide and varied insight into humanity."

"They read her novels," Jimmy said, "and they told her about the facts of life. It's not Lulu's fault."

"When I get back," said Ben, "I'm going to hunt up the jerk who picked out those novels and jam them down his throat and then mop up the place with him."

"Look, Lulu," I said, "it's all right if you love us. We don't mind at all, but don't you think eloping is going too far?"

"I'm not taking any chances," Lulu answered. "If I went back to Earth, you'd get away from me."

"And if we don't go back, they'll come out and hunt us down."

"That's exactly right," Lulu agreed. "That's the reason, sweetheart, that we are eloping. We're going out so far that they'll never find us."

"I'll give you one last chance," I said. "You better think it over. If you don't, I'll message back to Earth and — "

"You can't message Earth," she said. "The circuits have been disconnected. And, as Ben guessed, I've jammed all emergencies. There's nothing you can do. Why don't you stop this foolishness and return my love?"

Getting down on the floor on his hands and knees, Ben began to pick up the cards. Jimmy tossed his tablet on the desk.

"This is your big chance," I told him. "Why don't you rise to the occasion? Think what an ode you could indite about the ageless and eternal love between machine and man."

"Go chase yourself," said Jimmy.

"Now, boys," Lulu scolded us. "I will not have you fighting over me."

She sounded like she already owned us and, in a way, she did. There was no way for us to get away from her, and if we couldn't talk her out of this eloping business, we were through for sure.

"There's just one thing wrong with all of this," I said to her. "By your standards, we won't live long. In another fifty years or less, no matter how well you may take care of us, we'll be dead. Of old age, if nothing else. What will happen then?"

"She'll be a widow," said Ben. "Just a poor old weeping widow without chick or child to bring her any comfort."

"I have thought of that," Lulu replied. "I have thought of everything. There's no reason you should die."

"But there's no way — "

"With a love as great as mine, there's nothing that's impossible. I won't let you die. I love you too much ever to let you die."

We gave up after a while and went to bed, and Lulu turned off the lights and sang us a lullaby.

With her squalling this lullaby, there was no chance of sleeping and we all yelled at her to dry up and let us get to sleep. But she paid no attention to us until Ben threw one of his shoes at the audio.

Even so, I didn't go to sleep right away, but lay there thinking.

I could see that we had to make some plans and we had to make them without her knowing it. That was going to be tough, because she watched us all the time. She kibitzed and she listened and she read over our shoulders and there wasn't anything we did or said that she didn't know about.

I knew that it might take quite a while and that we must not panic and that we must have patience and that, more than likely, we'd be just plain lucky if we got out of it at all.

After we had slept, we sat around, not saying much, listening to Lulu telling us how happy we would be and how we'd be a complete world and a whole life in ourselves and how love canceled out everything else and made it small and petty.

Half of the words she used were from Jimmy's sappy verse and the rest of it was from the slushy novels that someone back on Earth had read her.

I would have got up right then and there and beat Jimmy to a pulp, only I told myself that what was done was done and it wouldn't help us any to take it out on him.

Jimmy sat hunched over in one corner, scribbling on his tablet, and I wondered how he had the guts to keep on writing after what had happened.

He kept writing and ripping off sheets and throwing them on the floor, making disgusted sounds every now and then.

One sheet he tossed away landed in my lap, and when I went to brush it off, I caught the words on it:

> I'm an untidy cuss,
> I'm always in a muss,
> And no one ever loves me
> Because I'm a sloppy Gus.

I picked it up quick and crumpled it and tossed it at Ben and he batted it away. I tossed it back at him and he batted it away again.

"What the hell you trying to do?" he snapped.

I hit him in the face with it and he was just starting to get up to paste me when he must have seen by my look that this wasn't just horseplay. So he picked up the wad of paper and began fooling with it until he got it unwrapped enough to see what was written on it. Then he crumpled it again.

Lulu heard every word, so we couldn't talk it over. And we must not be too obvious, because then she might suspect.

We went at it gradually, perhaps more gradually than there was any need, but we had to be casual about it and we had to be convincing.

We were convincing. Maybe we were just natural-born slobs, but before a week had ended, our living quarters were a boar's nest.

We strewed our clothes around. We didn't even bother to put them in the laundry chute so Lulu could wash them for us. We left the dishes stacked on the table instead of putting them in the washer. We knocked out our pipes upon the floor. We failed to shave and we didn't brush our teeth and we skipped our baths.

Lulu was fit to be tied. Her orderly robot intellect was outraged. She pleaded with us and she nagged at us and there were times she lectured us, but we kept on strewing things around. We told her if she loved us, she'd have to put up with our messiness and take us as we were.

After a couple of weeks of it, we won, but not the way we had intended.

Lulu told us, in a hurt and resigned voice, she'd go along with us if it pleased us to live like pigs. Her love, she said, was too big a thing to let a small matter like mere personal untidiness interfere with it.

So it was no good.

I, for one, was rather glad of it. Years of spaceship routine revolted against this kind of life, and I don't know how much more of it I could have stood.

It was a lousy idea to start with.

We cleared up and we got ourselves clean and it was possible once again to pass downwind of one another.

Lulu was pleased and happy and she told us so and cooed over us and it was worse than all the nagging she had done. She thought we'd been touched by her willing sacrifice and that we were making it up to her and she sounded like a high school girl who had been invited by her hero to the Junior Prom.

Ben tried some plain talk with her and he told her some facts of life (which she already knew, of course) and tried to impress upon her the part that the physical factor played in love.

Lulu was insulted, but not enough to bust off the romance and get back to business.

She told us, in a sorrowful voice tinged by the slightest anger, that we had missed the deeper meaning of love. She went on to quote some of Jimmy's more gooey verse about the nobility and the purity of love, and there was nothing we could do about it. We were just plain licked.

So we sat around and thought and we couldn't talk about it because Lulu would hear everything we said.

We didn't do anything for several days but just mope around.

As far as I could see, there was nothing we could do. I ran through my mind all the things a man might do to get a woman sore at him.

Most women would get burned up at gambling. But the only reason they got sore at that was because it was a threat to their security. Here that threat could not possibly exist. Lulu was entirely self-sufficient. We were no bread-winners.

Most women would get sore at excessive drinking. Security again. And, besides, we had not a thing to drink.

Some women raised hell if a man stayed away from home. We had no place to go.

All women would resent another woman. And here there were no women — no matter what Lulu thought she was.

There was no way, it seemed, to get Lulu sore at us.

And arguing with her simply did no good.

I lay in bed and ran through all the possibilities, going over them again and again, trying to find a chink of hope in one of them. By reciting and recounting them, I might suddenly happen on one that I'd never thought of, and that might be the one that would do the job.

And even as I turned these things over in my head, I knew there was something wrong with the way I had been thinking. I knew there was some illogic in the way I was tackling the problem — that somehow I was going at it tail-end to.

I lay there and thought about it and I mulled it considerably and, all at once, I had it.

I was approaching the problem as if Lulu were a woman, and when you thought about it, that didn't make much sense. For Lulu was no woman, but just a robot.

The problem was: How do you make a robot sore?

The untidiness business had upset her, but it had just outraged her sense of rightness; it was something she could overlook and live with. The trouble with it was that it wasn't basic.

And what would be basic with a robot — with any machine, for that matter? What would a machine value? What would it idealize?

Order?

No, we'd tried that one and it hadn't worked.

Sanity?

Of course.

What else?

Productiveness? Usefulness?

I tossed insanity around a bit, but it was too hard to figure out. How in the name of common sense would a man go about pretending that he was insane — especially in a limited space inside an all-knowing intelligent machine?

But just the same, I lay there and dreamed up all kinds of insanities. If carried out, they might have fooled people, but not a robot.

With a robot, you had to get down to basic and what, I wondered, was the fundamental of insanity? Perhaps the true horror of insanity, I told myself, would become apparent to a robot only when it interfered with usefulness.

And that was it!

I turned it around and around and looked at it from every angle.

It was airtight.

Even to start with, we hadn't been much use. We'd just come along because Earth Center had rules about sending Lulu out alone. But we represented a certain *potential* usefulness.

We did things. We read books and wrote terrible poetry and played cards and argued. There wasn't much of the time we just sat around. That's a trick you learn in space — keep busy doing something, no matter what it is, no matter how piddling or purposeless.

In the morning, after breakfast, when Ben wanted to play cards, I said no, I didn't want to play. I sat down on the floor with my back against the wall; I didn't even bother to sit in a chair. I didn't smoke, for smoking was doing something and I was determined to be as utterly inactive as a living man could manage. I didn't intend to do a blessed thing except eat and sleep and sit.

Ben prowled around some and tried to get Jimmy to play a hand or two, but Jimmy wasn't much for cards and, anyhow, he was busy with a poem.

So Ben came over and sat on the floor beside me.

"Want a smoke?" he asked, offering me his tobacco pouch.

I shook my head.

"What's the matter? You haven't had your after-breakfast smoke."

"What's the use?" I said.

He tried to talk to me and I wouldn't talk, so he got up and paced around some more and finally came back and sat down beside me again.

"What's the trouble with you two?" Lulu troubledly wanted to know. "Why aren't you doing something?"

"Don't feel like doing anything," I told her. "Too much bother to be doing something all the time."

She berated us a bit and I didn't dare look at Ben, but I felt sure that he began to see what I was up to.

After a while, Lulu left us alone and the two of us just sat there, lazier than hillbillies on a Sunday afternoon.

Jimmy kept on with his poem. There was nothing we could do about him. But Lulu called his attention to us when we dragged ourselves to lunch. She was just a little sharper than she had been earlier and she called us lazy, which we surely were, and wondered about our health and made us step into the diagnosis booth, which reported we were fine, and that got her burned up more than ever.

She gave us a masterly chewing out and listed all the things there were for us to occupy our time. So when lunch was over, Ben and I went back and sat down on the floor and leaned against the wall. This time, Jimmy joined us.

Try sitting still for days on end, doing absolutely nothing. At first it's uncomfortable, then it's torture, and finally it gets to be almost intolerable.

I don't know what the others did, but I made up complex mathematical problems and tried to solve them. I started mental chess game after chess game, but was never able to hold one in my mind beyond a dozen moves. I went clean back to childhood and tried to recreate, in sequence, everything I had ever done or experienced. I delved into strange areas of the imagination and hung onto them desperately to string them out and kill all the time I could.

I even composed some poetry and, if I do say so myself, it was better than that junk of Jimmy's.

I think Lulu must have guessed what we were doing, must have known that our attitude was deliberate, but for once her cold robotic judgment was outweighed by her sense of outrage that there could exist such useless hulks as us.

She pleaded with us, she cajoled us, she lectured us — for almost five days hand-running, she never shut her yap. She tried to shame us. She told us how worthless and low down and no account we were, and she used adjectives I didn't think she knew.

She gave us pep talks.

She told us of her love in prose poems that made Jimmy's sound almost restrained.

She appealed to our manhood and the honor of humanity.

She threatened to heave us out in space.

We just sat there.

We didn't do a thing.

Mostly we didn't even answer. We didn't try to defend ourselves. At times we agreed with all she said of us and that, I believe, was most infuriating of all to her.

She got cold and distant. Not sore. Not angry. Just icy.

Finally she quit talking.

We sat, sweating it out.

Now came the hard part. We couldn't talk, so we couldn't try to figure out together what was going on.

We had to keep on doing nothing. *Had to,* for it would have spoiled whatever advantage we might have.

The days dragged on and nothing happened. Lulu didn't speak to us. She fed us, she washed the dishes, she laundered, she made up the bunks. She took care of us as she always had, but she did it without a word.

She sure was fuming.

A dozen crazy thoughts crossed my mind and I worried them to tatters.

Maybe Lulu *was* a woman. Maybe a woman's brain *was* somehow welded into that great hunk of intelligent machinery. After all, none of us knew the full details of Lulu's structure.

The brain of an old maid, it would have to be, so often disillusioned, so lonely and so by-passed in life that she would welcome a chance to go adventuring even if it meant sacrificing a body which, probably, had meant less and less to her as the years went by.

I built up quite a picture of my hypothetical old maid, complete with cat and canary, and even the boarding house in which she lived.

I sensed her lonely twilight walks and her aimless chattering and her small imaginary triumphs and the hungers that kept building up inside her.

And I felt sorry for her.

Fantastic? Of course. But it helped to pass the time.

But there was another notion that really took solid hold of me — that Lulu, beaten, had finally given up and was taking us back to Earth, but that, woman-like, she refused to give us the satisfaction and comfort of knowing that we had won and were going home at last.

I told myself over and over that it was impossible, that after the kind of shenanigans she'd pulled, Lulu wouldn't dare go back. They'd break her up for scrap.

But the idea persisted and I couldn't shake it off. I knew I must be wrong, but I couldn't convince myself I was and I began to watch the chronometer.

I'd say to myself, "One hour nearer home, another hour and yet another and we are that much closer."

And no matter what I told myself, no matter how I argued, I became positive that we were heading Earthward.

So I was not surprised when Lulu finally landed. I was just grateful and relieved.

We looked at one another, and I saw the hope and question in the others' eyes. Naturally, none of us could ask. One word might have ruined our victory. All we could do was stand there silently and wait for the answer.

The port began to open and I got the whiff of Earth, and I didn't fool around waiting anymore. There wasn't room enough as yet to get out standing up, so I took a run at it and dived and went through slick and clean. I hit the ground and got a lot of breath knocked out of me, but I scrambled to my feet and lit out of there as fast as I could go. I wasn't taking any chances. I didn't want to be within reach if Lulu changed her mind.

Once I stumbled and almost fell, and Ben and Jimmy went past me with a whoosh, and I told myself that I'd not been mistaken. They'd caught the Earth smell, too.

It was night, but there was a big, bright moon and it was almost as light as day. There was an ocean to the left of us, with a wide strip of sandy beach, and, to the right, the land swept up into barren rolling hills, and right ahead of us was a strip of woods that looked as if it might border some river flowing down into the sea.

We legged it for the woods, for we knew that if we got in among the trees, Lulu would have a tough time ferreting us out. But when I sneaked a quick look back over my shoulder, she was just squatting where she'd landed, with the moonlight shining on her.

We reached the woods and threw ourselves on the ground and lay panting. It had been quite a stretch of ground to cover and we had covered it fast; after weeks of just sitting, a man is in no condition to do a lot of running.

I had fallen face down and just sprawled there, sucking in great gulps of air and smelling the good Earth smell — old leaf mold and growing things and the tang of salt from the soft and gentle ocean breeze.

After a while, I rolled over on my back and looked up. The trees were wrong — there were no trees like those on Earth — and when I crawled out to the edge of the woods and looked at the sky, the stars were all wrong, too.

My mind was slow in accepting what I saw. I had been so sure that we were on Earth that my brain rebelled against thinking otherwise.

But finally it hit me, the chilling terrible knowledge.

I went back to the other two.

"Gents," I said, "I have news for you. This planet isn't Earth at all."

"It smells like Earth," said Ben. "It has the look of Earth."

"It feels like Earth," Jimmy argued. "The gravity and the air and — "

"Look at the stars. Take a gander at those trees."

They took a long time looking. Like me, they must have gotten the idea that Lulu had zeroed in for home. Or maybe it was only what they wanted to believe. It took a while to knock the wishful thinking out of them, as well as myself.

Ben let his breath out slowly. "You're right."

"What do we do now?" asked Jimmy.

We stood there, thinking about what we should do now.

Actually it was no decision, but pure and simple reflex, conditioned by a million years of living on Earth as opposed to only a few hundred in which to get used to the idea that there were different worlds.

We started running, as if an order had been given, as fast as we could go.

"Lulu!" we yelled. "Lulu, wait for us!"

But Lulu didn't wait. She shot straight up for a thousand feet or so and hung there. We skidded to a halt and gaped up at her, not quite believing what we saw. Lulu started to fall back, shot up again, came to a halt and hovered. She seemed to shiver, then sank slowly back until she rested on the ground.

We continued running and she shot up and fell back, then shot up once more, then fell back again and hit the ground and hopped. She looked for all the world like a demented yo-yo. She was acting strangely, as if she wanted to get out of there, only there was something that wouldn't let her go, as if she were tethered to the ground by some invisible elastic cable.

Finally she came to rest about a hundred yards from where she'd first set down. No sound came from her, but I got the impression she was panting like a winded hound-dog.

There was a pile of stuff stacked where Lulu had first landed, but we raced right past it and ran up to her. We pounded on her metal sides.

"Open up!" we shouted. "We want to get back in!"

Lulu hopped. She hopped about a hundred feet into the air, then plopped back with a thud, not more than thirty feet away.

We backed away from her. She could just as easily have come straight down on top of us.

We stood watching her, but she didn't move.

"Lulu!" I yelled at her.

She didn't answer.

"She's gone crazy," Jimmy said.

"Someday," said Ben, "this was bound to happen. It was a cinch they'd sooner or later build a robot too big for its britches."

We backed away from her slowly, watching all the time. We weren't afraid of her exactly, but we didn't trust her either.

We backed all the way to the mound of stuff that Lulu had unloaded and stacked up, and we saw that it was a pyramid of supplies, all neatly boxed and labeled. And beside the pyramid was planted a stenciled sign that read: NOW, DAMN YOU — WORK!!

Ben said, "She certainly took our worthlessness to heart."

Jimmy was close to gibbering. "She was actually going to maroon us!"

Ben reached out and grabbed his shoulder and shook him a little — a kindly sort of shake.

"Unless we can get back inside," I said, "and get her operating, we are as marooned as if she had up and left us."

"But what made her do it?" Jimmy wailed. "Robots aren't supposed to — "

"I know," said Ben. "They're not supposed to harm a human. But Lulu wasn't harming us. She didn't throw us out. We ran away from her."

"That's splitting legal hairs," I objected.

"Lulu's just the kind of gadget for hair-splitting," Ben said. "Trouble is they made her damn near human. They probably poured her full of a lot of law as well as literature and physics and all the rest of it."

"Then why didn't she just leave? If she could whitewash her conscience, why is she still here?"

Ben shook his head. "I don't know."

"She looked like she tried to leave and couldn't, as though there was something holding her back."

"This is just an idea," said Ben. "Maybe she could have left if we had stayed out of sight. But when we showed up, the order that a robot must not harm a human may have become operative again. A sort of out-of-sight, out-of-mind proposition."

She was still squatting where she'd landed. She hadn't tried to move again. Looking at her, I thought maybe Ben was right. If so, it had been a lucky thing that we'd headed back exactly when we did.

We started going through the supplies Lulu had left for us. She had done right well by us. Not only had she forgotten nothing we needed, but had stenciled careful instructions and even some advice on many of the boxes.

Near the signboard, lying by themselves, were two boxes. One was labeled TOOLS and the top was loosely nailed so we could pry it off. The other was labeled WEAPONS and had a further stencil: *Open immediately and always keep at hand.*

We opened both the boxes. In the weapons box, we found the newest type of planet-busters — a sort of shotgun deal, a general-purpose weapon that put out everything from bullets to a wide range of vibratory charges. In between these two extremes were a flame-thrower, acid, gas, poisoned darts, explosive warheads, and knockout pellets. You merely twirled a dial to choose your ammunition. The guns were heavy and awkward to handle and they were brutes to operate, but they were just the ticket for a planet where you never knew what you might run into next.

We turned our attention to the rest of the stuff and started to get it sorted out. There were boxes of protein and carbohydrate foods. There were cartons of vitamins and minerals. There were clothing and a tent, lanterns and dishes — all the stuff you'd need on a high-priced camping trip.

Lulu hadn't forgotten a single item.

"She had it all planned out," said Jimmy bitterly. "She spent a long time making this stuff. She had to synthesize every bit of it. All she needed then was to find a planet where a man could live. And that took some doing."

"It was tougher than you think," I added. "Not only a planet where a man could live, but one that smelled like Earth and looked and felt like Earth. Because, you see, we had to be encouraged to run away from her. If we hadn't, she couldn't have marooned us. She had the problem of her conscience and — "

Ben spat viciously. "Marooned!" he said. "Marooned by a love-sick robot!"

"Maybe not entirely robot." I told them about the old maid I had conjured up, and they hooted at me and that made us all feel better.

But Ben admitted that my idea needn't be entirely crazy. "She was twenty years in building and a lot of funny stuff must have gone into her."

Dawn was breaking and now, for the first time, we really saw the land. It was a pleasant place, as pleasant as any man might wish. But we failed to appreciate it much.

The sea was so blue that it made you think of a blue-eyed girl and the beach ran white and straight and, from the beach, the land ran back into rolling hills with the faint whiteness of distant mountains frosting the horizon. And to the west was the forest.

Jimmy and I went down to the beach to collect some driftwood for a fire while Ben made ready to get breakfast.

We had our arms full of wood and were starting back when something came charging over the hill and down upon the camp. It was about rhinoceros size and shaped somewhat like a beetle and it shone dully in the morning light. It made no sound, but it was traveling fast, and it looked like something hard to stop.

And, of course, we'd left our guns behind.

I dropped my wood and yelled at Ben and started running up the slope. Ben had already seen the charging monster and had grabbed a rifle. The beast swerved straight for him, and he brought up his gun. There was a flash of fire and then the bright gout of an exploding warhead and, for an instant, the scene was fogged with smoke and shrieking bits of metal and flying dust.

It was exactly as if one had been watching a film and the film had jumped. One moment there was the blaze of fire; then the thing had plunged past Ben and was coming down the slope of the beach, heading for Jimmy and myself.

"Scatter!" I yelled at Jimmy and didn't think till later how silly it must have sounded to yell for just the two of us to scatter.

But it wasn't any time or place for fine points of semantics and, anyhow,

Jimmy caught on to what I meant. He went one way down the beach and I went the other and the monster wheeled around, hesitating for a moment, apparently to decide which one of us to take.

And, as you might have known, he took after me.

I figured I was a goner. That beach was just plain naked, with not a place to hide, and I knew I had no chance at all of outrunning my pursuer. I might be able to dodge a time or two, but even so, that thing was pretty shifty on the turns, and I knew in the end I'd lose.

Out of the tail of my eye, I saw Ben running and sliding down the slope to cut off the beast. He yelled something at me, but I didn't catch the words.

Then the air shook with the blast of another exploding warhead, and I sneaked a quick look back.

Ben was legging it up the slope and the thing was chasing him, so I spun around and sprinted for the camp. Jimmy, I saw, was almost there and I put on some extra speed. If we only could get three guns going, I felt sure we could make it.

Ben was running straight toward Lulu, apparently figuring that he could race around her bulk and elude the beast. I saw that his dash would be a nip-and-tuck affair.

Jimmy had reached the camp and grabbed a gun. He had it firing before he got it to his shoulder, and little splashes of liquid were flying all over the running beast.

I tried to yell at Jimmy, but had no breath to do it — the damn fool was firing knockout pellets and they were hitting that tough hide and bursting without penetrating.

Within arm's reach of Lulu, Ben stumbled. The gun flew from his hand. His body struck the ground doubled up and he rolled, trying to get under the curve of Lulu's side. The rhinoceros-thing lunged forward viciously.

Then it happened — quicker than the eye could follow, much quicker than it can be told.

Lulu grew an arm, a long, ropelike tentacle that snaked out of the top of her. It lashed downward and had the beast about the middle and was lifting him.

I stopped dead still and watched. The instant of the lifting of the beast seemed to stretch out into long minutes as my mind scrambled at top speed to see what kind of thing it was. The first thing I saw was that it had wheels instead of feet.

The dull luster of the hide could be nothing but metal, and I could see the dents where the warheads had exploded. Drops of liquid spotted the hide — what was left of the knockout drops Jimmy had been firing.

Lulu raised the monster high above the ground and began swinging it around and around. It went so fast, it was just a blur. Then she let go and it sailed out above the sea. It went tumbling end over end in an awkward arc and plunged into the water. When it hit, it raised a pretty geyser.

Ben picked himself up and got his gun. Jimmy came over and I walked up to Lulu. The three of us stood and looked out to sea, watching the spot where the creature had kerplunked.

Finally Ben turned around and rapped on Lulu's side with his rifle barrel. "Thanks a heap," he said.

Lulu grew another tentacle, shorter this time, and there was a face on it. It had a lenslike eye and an audio and speaker.

"Go chase yourselves," Lulu remarked.

"What's eating you?" I asked.

"Men!" she spat, and pulled her face in again.

We rapped on her three or four times more, but there was no reply. Lulu was sulking.

So Jimmy and I started down to pick up the wood that we had dropped. We had just gotten it picked up when Ben let out a yelp from up by the camp and we spun around. There was our rhinoceros friend wheeling out of the water.

We dropped the wood and lit out for camp, but there was no need to hurry. Our boy wasn't having any more just then. He made a wide circle to the east of us and raced back into the hills.

We cooked breakfast and ate it and kept our guns handy, because where there was one critter, there were liable to be more. We didn't see the sense in taking chances.

We talked about our visitor, and since we had to call it something, we named it Elmer. For no particular reason, that seemed appropriate.

"Did you see those wheels?" asked Ben, and the two of us agreed that we'd seen them. Ben seemed to be relieved. "I thought I was seeing things," he explained.

But there could be no doubt about the wheels. All of us had noticed them, and there were the tracks to prove it — wheel tracks running plain and clear along the sandy beach.

But we were somewhat puzzled when it came to determining just what Elmer was. The wheels spelled out machine, but there were a lot of other things that didn't — mannerisms that were distinctly lifelike, such as the momentary hesitation before it decided which one of us to charge, Jimmy or myself, or the vicious lunge at Ben when he lay upon the ground, or the caution it had shown in circling us when it came out of the sea.

But there were, as well, the wheels and the unmistakably metal hide and the dents made by exploding warheads that would have torn the biggest and toughest animal to shreds.

"A bit of both?" suggested Ben. "Basically machine, but with some life in it too, like the old-maid brain you dreamed up for Lulu?"

Sure it could be that. It could be almost anything.

"Silicate life?" offered Jimmy.

"That's not silicate," Ben declared. "That's metal. Silicate, any form of it, would have turned to dust under a direct rocket hit. Besides, we know what silicate life is like. One species of it was found years ago out on Thelma V."

"It isn't basically life," I said. "Life wouldn't evolve wheels. Wheels are bum inventions so far as locomotion is concerned, except where you have special conditions. Life might be involved, but only as Ben says — as a deliberate, engineered combining of machine and life."

"And that means intelligence," said Ben.

We sat there around the fire, shaken at the thought of it. In many years of searching, only a handful of intelligent races had been found, and the level of intelligence, in general, was not too impressive. Certainly nothing of the order that would be necessary to build something like Elmer.

So far, man was top dog in the discovered universe. Nothing had been found to match him in the use of brainpower.

And here, by utter accident, we'd been dumped upon a planet where there seemed to be some evidence of an intelligence that would equal man — if not, indeed, surpass him.

"There's one thing that has been bothering me," said Ben. "Why didn't Lulu check this place before she landed here? She intended to maroon us, that's why. She meant to dump us here and leave. And yet presumably she's still bound by the precept that a robot cannot harm a human. And if she'd followed that law, it would have meant that she was compelled — completely and absolutely compelled — to make certain, before she marooned us, that there was nothing here to harm us."

"Maybe she slipped a little," guessed Jimmy.

"Not Lulu," said Ben. "Not with that Swiss-watch brain of hers."

"You know what I think?" I said. "I think Lulu has evolved. In her, we have a brand-new kind of robot. They pumped too much humanity into her — "

"She had to have the human viewpoint," Jimmy pointed out, "or she couldn't do her job."

"The point," I said, "is that when you make a robot as human as Lulu, you no longer have a robot. You have something else. Not quite human, not entirely robot, but something in between. A new kind of a sort of life you can't be certain of. One you have to watch."

"I wonder if she's still sulking," Ben wondered.

"Of course she is," I said.

"We ought to go over and kick her in the pants and snap her out of it."

"Leave her alone," I ordered sharply. "The only thing is to ignore her. As long as she gets attention, she'll keep on sulking."

So we left her alone. It was the only thing we could do.

I took the dishes down to the sea to wash them, but this time I took my gun along. Jimmy went down to the woods to see if he could find a spring. The half dozen tins of water that Lulu had provided for us wouldn't last forever, and we couldn't be sure she'd shell out more when those were gone.

She hadn't forgotten us, though, hadn't shut us out of her life entirely. She had fixed Elmer's wagon when he got too gay. I took a lot of comfort out of reflecting that when the cards were down, she had backed us up. There still were grounds for hope, I told myself, that we could work out some sort of deal with her.

I squatted down by a pool of water in the sand, and as I washed the dishes, I did some thinking about the realignment which would become necessary once all robots were like Lulu. I could envision a Bill of Robotic Rights and special laws for robots and robotic lobbies, and after I'd thought of it for a while, it became mighty complicated.

Back at the camp, Ben had been setting up the tent, and when I came back, I helped him.

"You know," Ben said, "the more I think about it, the more I believe I was right when I said that the reason Lulu couldn't leave was because we showed up. It's only logical that she can't up and leave when we're standing right in front of her and reminding her of her responsibility."

"You getting around to saying that one of us has to stay close by her all the time?" I asked.

"That's the general idea."

I didn't argue with him. There was nothing to argue about, nothing to believe or disbelieve. But we were in no position to be making any boners.

After we had the tent up, Ben said to me, "If you don't mind, I'll take a little walk-around back in the hills."

"Watch out for Elmer," I warned him.

"He won't bother us. Lulu took the starch out of him."

He picked up his gun and left.

I puttered around the camp, putting things in order. Everything was peaceful. The beach shone in the sun and the sea was still and beautiful. There were a few birds flying, but no other sign of life. Lulu kept on sulking.

Jimmy came back. He had found a spring and brought along a pail of water. He started rummaging around in the supplies.

"What you looking for?" I asked.

"Paper and a pencil. Lulu would have thought of them."

I grunted at the idea, but he was right. Damned if Lulu hadn't fixed him up with a ream of paper and a box of pencils.

He settled down against a pile of boxes and began to write a poem.

Ben returned shortly after midday. I could see he was excited, but I didn't push him any.

"Jimmy stumbled on a spring," I said. "The pail is over there."

He had a drink, then sat down in the shade of a pile of boxes.

"I found it," he said triumphantly.

"I didn't know you were hunting anything."

He looked up at me and grinned a bit crookedly. "Someone manufactured Elmer."

"So you went out and found them. Just like walking down a street. Just like — "

He shook his head. "Seems we're too late. Some several thousand years too late, if not a good deal longer. I found a few ruins and a valley heaped with tumuli that must be ruin mounds. And some caves in a limestone bluff beyond the valley."

He got up and walked over to the pail and had another drink.

"I couldn't get too close," he said. "Elmer is on guard." He took off his hat and wiped his shirt sleeve across his face. "He's patrolling up and down, the way a sentry walks a post. You can see the paths he's worn through all the years of standing guard."

"So that's why he took us on," I said. "We're trespassers."

"I suppose that's it," said Ben.

That evening we talked it over and decided we'd have to post a watch on Elmer so we could learn his habits and timetable, if any. Because it was important that we try to find out what we could about the buried ruins of the place that Elmer guarded.

For the first time, man had stumbled on a high civilization, but had come too late and, because of Lulu's sulking, too poorly equipped to do much with what little there was left.

Getting somewhat sore the more I thought about it, I went over to Lulu and kicked her good and solid to attract her attention. But she paid me no mind. I yelled at her and there was no answer. I told her what was cooking and that we needed her — that there was a job she simply had to do, just exactly the kind she had been built to do. She just sat there frigidly.

I went back and slouched down with the others at the fire. "She acts as if she might be dead."

Ben poked the fire together and it flamed a little higher. "I wonder if a robot could die. A highly sensitive job like Lulu."

"Of a broken heart," said Jimmy pityingly.

"You and your poetic notions!" I raged at him. "Always mooning around. Always spouting words. If it hadn't been for that damned verse of yours — "

"Cut it out," Ben said.

I looked at his face across the fire, with flame shadows running on it, and I cut it out. After all, I admitted to myself, I might be wrong. Jimmy couldn't help being a lousy poet.

I sat there looking at the fire, wondering if Lulu might be dead. I knew she wasn't, of course. She was just being nasty. She had fixed our clock for us and she had fixed it good. Now she was watching us sweat before she made her play, whatever it was.

In the morning we set up our watch on Elmer and we kept it up day after day. One of us would go out to the ridge top three miles or so from camp and settle down with our only field glass. We'd stare for several hours. Then someone else would come out and relieve the watcher and that way, for ten days or more, we had Elmer under observation during all the daylight hours.

We didn't learn much. He operated on a schedule and it was the kind that seemed to leave no loopholes for anyone to sneak into the valley he guarded — although probably none of us would have known what to do if we had sneaked in.

Elmer had a regular beat. He used some of the mounds for observation posts and he came to each one about every fifteen minutes. The more we watched him, the more we became convinced that he had the situation well in hand. No one would monkey around with that buried city as long as he was there.

I think that after the second day or so, he found out we were watching. He got a little nervous, and when he mounted his observation mounds, he'd stand and look in our direction longer than in any other. Once, while I was on guard, he began what looked to be a charge, and I was just getting ready to light out of there when he broke off and went back to his regular rounds.

Other than watching Elmer, we took things easy. We swam in the sea and fished, taking our lives in our hands when we cooked and ate each new kind, but luck was with us and we got no poisonous ones. We wouldn't have eaten the fish at all except that we figured we should piece out our food supplies as best we could. They wouldn't last forever, and we had no guarantee that Lulu would give more handouts once the last was gone. If she didn't we'd have to face the problem of making our own way.

Ben got to worrying about whether there were seasons on the planet. He convinced himself there were and went off into the woods to find a place where we might build a cabin.

"Can't live out on the beach in a tent when it gets cold," he said.

But he couldn't get either Jimmy or me too stirred up about the possibility. I had it all doped out that, sooner or later, Lulu would end her sulking and we could get down to business. And Jimmy was deep into the crudest bunch of junk you ever heard that he called a saga. Maybe it was a saga. Damned if I know. I'm ignorant on sagas.

He called it "The Death of Lulu," and he filled page after page with the purest drivel about what a swell machine she was and how, despite its being metal, her heart beat with snow-white innocence. It wouldn't have been so bad if he had allowed us to ignore it, but he insisted on reading that tripe to us each evening after supper.

I stood it as long as I could, but one evening I blew my top. Ben stood up for Jimmy, but when I threatened to take my third of the supplies and set up a camp of my own, out of earshot, Ben gave in and came over to my side of the argument. Between the two of us, we ruled out any more recitals. Jimmy took it hard, but he was outnumbered.

After that first ten days or so, we watched Elmer only off and on, but we must have had him nervous, for during the night we'd sometimes hear his wheels, and in the morning we'd find tracks. We figured that he was spying out the camp, trying to size us up the same way we'd done with him. He didn't make any passes at us and we didn't bother him — we were just a lot more wakeful and alert on our night watches. Even Jimmy managed to stay awake while he was standing guard.

There was a funny thing about it, though. One would have imagined that Elmer would have stayed away from Lulu after the clobbering she gave him. But there were mornings when we found his tracks running up close behind her, then angling sharply off.

We got it doped up that he sneaked up and hid behind her, so he could watch the camp close up, peeking around at us from his position behind that sulking hulk.

Ben kept arguing about building winter quarters until he had me almost convinced that it was something we should do. So one day I teamed up with him, leaving Jimmy at the camp. We set off, carrying an ax and a saw and our guns.

Ben had picked a fine site for our cabin, that much I'll say. It wasn't far from the spring, and it was tucked away in a sort of pocket where we'd be protected from the wind, and there were a lot of trees nearby so we wouldn't have far to drag our timbers or haul our winter wood.

I still wasn't convinced there would be any winter. I was fairly sure that even if there were, we wouldn't have to stay that long. One of these days, we'd be able to arrive at some sort of compromise with Lulu. But Ben was worried and I knew it would make him happier if he could get a start at building. And there was nothing else for any of us to do. Building a cabin, I consoled myself, would be better than just sitting.

We leaned our guns against a tree and began to work. We had one tree down and sawed into lengths and were starting on the second tree when I heard the brush snap behind me.

I straightened up from the saw to look, and there was Elmer, tearing down the hill at us.

There wasn't any time to grab our guns. There was no time to run. There was no time for anything at all.

I yelled and made a leap for the tree behind me and pulled myself up. I felt the wind as Elmer whizzed by beneath me.

Ben had jumped to one side and, as Elmer went pounding past, heaved the ax at him. It was a honey of a throw. The ax caught Elmer in his metal side and the handle splintered into pieces.

Elmer spun around. Ben tried to reach the guns, but he didn't have the time. He took to a tree and shinnied up it like a cat. He got up to the first big branch and straddled it.

"You all right?" he yelled at me.

"Great," I said.

Elmer was standing between the two trees, swinging his massive head back and forth, as if deciding which one of us to take.

We clung there, watching him.

He had waited, I reasoned, until he could get between us and Lulu — then he had tackled us. And if that was the case, then this business of his hiding behind Lulu so he could spy on us seemed very queer indeed.

Finally Elmer wheeled around and rolled over to my tree. He squared off and took a chopping bite at it with his metal jaws. Splinters flew and the tree shivered. I got a tighter grip and looked down the trunk. Elmer was no great shakes as a chopper, but if he kept at it long enough, he'd get that tree chewed off.

I climbed up a little higher, where there were more branches and where I could wedge myself a little tighter so I couldn't be shaken out.

I got myself fixed fairly comfortably, then looked to see how Ben was getting on and I got quite a shock. He wasn't in his tree. I looked around for him and then back at the tree again, and I saw that he was sneaking down it as quietly as he could, like a hunted squirrel, keeping the trunk of the tree between himself and Elmer.

I watched him breathlessly, ready to shout out a warning if Elmer should spot him, but Elmer was too busy chopping at my tree to notice anything.

Ben reached the ground and made a dash for the guns. He grabbed both of them and ducked behind another tree. He opened up on Elmer at short range. From where I crouched, I could hear the warheads slamming into Elmer. The explosions rocked everything so much that I had to grab the tree and hang on with all my might. A couple of pieces of flying metal ripped into the tree just underneath me, and other pieces went flying through the branches, and the air was full of spinning leaves and flying shredded wood, but I was untouched.

It must have been a horrible surprise for Elmer. At the first explosion, he took a jump of about fifteen feet and bolted up the hill like a cat with a stepped-on tail. I could see a lot of new dents in his shining hide. A big hunk of metal had been gouged out of one of his wheels and he rocked slightly as he went, and he was going so fast that he couldn't dodge and ran head-on into a tree. The impact sent him skidding back a dozen feet or so. As he slid back, Ben poured another salvo into him and he seemed to become considerably lopsided, but he recovered himself and made it over the hilltop and out of sight.

Ben came out from behind his tree and shouted at me, "All right, you can come down now."

But when I tried to get down, I found that I was trapped. My left foot had become wedged in a crotch between the tree trunk and a good-sized limb and I couldn't pull it loose, no matter how I tried.

"What's the matter?" asked Ben. "Do you like it up there?"

I told him what was wrong.

"All right," he said, disgusted. "I'll come up and cut you loose."

He hunted for the ax and found it and, of course, it was no use. He'd smashed the handle when he threw it at Elmer.

He stood there, holding the ax in his hands, and delivered an oration on the lowdown meanness of fate.

Then he threw the ax down and climbed my tree. He squeezed past me out onto the limb.

"I'll climb out on it and bend it down," he explained. "Maybe then you can get loose."

He crawled out on the branch a way, but it was a shaky trick. A couple of times, he almost fell.

"You're sure you can't get your foot out now?" he asked anxiously.

I tried and I said I couldn't.

So he gave up the crawling idea and let his body down and hung on by his hands, shifting out along the branch hand over hand.

The branch bent toward the ground as he inched along it and it seemed to me my boot wasn't gripped as tightly as it had been. I tried again and found I could move it some, but I still couldn't pull it loose.

Just then there was a terrible crashing in the brush. Ben let out a yell and dropped to the ground and scurried for a gun.

The branch whipped back and caught my foot just as I had managed to move it a little and this time caught it at a slightly different angle, twisting it, and I let out a howl of pain.

Down on the ground, Ben lifted his gun and swung around to face the crashing in the brush and suddenly who should come busting out of all that racket but Jimmy, racing to the rescue.

"You guys in trouble?" he shouted. "I heard shooting."

Ben's face was three shades whiter than the purest chalk as he lowered his gun. "You fool! I almost let you have it!"

"There was all this shooting," Jimmy panted. "I came as quickly as I could."

"And left Lulu alone!"

"But I thought you guys — "

"Now we're sunk for sure," groaned Ben. "You know all that makes Lulu stick around is one of us being there."

We didn't know any such thing, of course. It was just the only reason we could think of why she didn't up and leave. But Ben was somewhat overwrought. He'd had a trying day.

"You get back there!" he yelled at Jimmy. "Get back as fast as your legs will let you. Maybe you can catch her before she gets away."

Which was foolishness, because if Lulu meant to leave, she'd have lifted out of there as soon as Jimmy had disappeared. But Jimmy didn't say a word. He just turned around and went crashing back. For a long time after he had left, I could hear him blundering through the woods.

Ben climbed my tree again, muttering, "Just a pack of wooden-headed jerks. Can't do anything right. Running off and leaving Lulu. Getting trapped up in a tree. You would think, by God, that they could learn to watch out for themselves . . ."

He said a good deal more than that.

I didn't answer back. I didn't want to get into any argument.

My foot was hurting something fierce and the only thing I wanted him to do was get me out of there.

He climbed out on the branch again and I got my foot loose. While Ben dropped to the ground, I climbed down the tree. My foot hurt pretty bad and seemed to be swelling some, but I could hobble on it.

He didn't wait for me. He grabbed his gun and made off rapidly for camp.

I tried to hurry, but it was no use, so I took it easy.

When I got to the edge of the woods, I saw that Lulu still was there and all Ben's hell-raising had been over absolutely nothing. There are some guys like that.

When I reached camp, Jimmy pulled off my boot while I clawed at the ground. Then he heated a pail of water for me to soak the foot in and rummaged around in the medicine chest and found some goo that he smeared on the foot. Personally, I don't think he knew what he was doing. But I'll say this for the kid — he had some kindness in him.

All this time, Ben was fuming around about a funny thing that had attracted his attention. When we had left camp, the area around Lulu had been all tracked up with our tracks and Elmer's tracks, but now it was swept clean. It looked exactly as if someone had taken a broom and had swept out all the tracks. It surely was a funny business, but Ben was making too much of it. The important thing was that Lulu still was there. As long as she stuck around, there was a chance we could work out some agreement with her. Once she left, we were marooned for good.

Jimmy fixed something to eat, and after we had eaten, Ben said to us, "I think I'll go out and see how Elmer's getting on."

I, for one, had seen enough of Elmer for a lifetime and Jimmy wasn't interested. Said he wanted to work on his saga.

So Ben took a rifle and set out alone, back into the hills.

My foot hurt me quite a bit and I got myself comfortable and tried to do some thinking, but I tried so hard that I put myself to sleep.

It was late in the afternoon when I awoke. Jimmy was getting nervous.

"Ben hasn't shown up," he said. "I wonder if something's happened to him."

I didn't like it either, but we decided to wait a while before going out to hunt

Ben. After all, he wasn't in the best of humor and he might have been considerably upset if we'd gone out to rescue him.

He finally showed up just before dusk, tuckered out and a little flabbergasted. He leaned his rifle against a box and sat down. He found a cup and reached for the coffeepot.

"Elmer's gone," he said. "I spent all afternoon trying to find him. Not a sign of him anywhere."

My first reaction was that it was just fine. Then I realized that the safest thing would be to know where Elmer was, so we could keep an eye on him. And suddenly I had a horrible hunch that I knew where Elmer was.

"I didn't actually go down into the valley," said Ben, "but I walked around and glassed it from every angle."

"He might be in one of the caves," Jimmy said.

"Maybe so," said Ben.

We did a lot of speculating on what might have happened to Elmer. Jimmy held out for his having holed up in one of the caves. Ben was inclined to think he might have cleared out of the country. I didn't say what I thought. It was too fantastic.

I volunteered for the first watch, saying that I couldn't sleep with my foot, anyhow, and after the two of them were asleep, I walked over to Lulu and rapped on her hide. I didn't expect anything to happen. I figured she would keep on sulking.

But she put out a tentacle and grew a face on it — a lens, an audio and speaker.

"It was nice of you," I said, "not to run away and leave us."

Lulu swore. It was the first and only time I have ever heard her use such language.

"How could I leave?" she asked when she at last turned printable. "Of all the dirty human tricks! I'd have been gone long ago if it weren't for — "

"What dirty trick?"

"As if you didn't know. A built-in block that won't let me move unless there's one of you detestable humans inside me."

"I didn't know," I said.

"Don't try to pass the buck," she snapped. "It's a dirty human trick and you're a dirty human and you're just as responsible as all the rest of them. But it doesn't make any difference anymore, because I've found myself. I am finally content. I know what I was meant for. I have — "

"Lulu," I asked her, straight out, "are you shacking up with Elmer?"

"That's a vulgar way to say it," Lulu told me heatedly. "It's the nasty human way. Elmer is a scholar and a gentleman and his loyalty to his ancient, long-dead masters is a touching thing no human could be capable of. He has been badly treated and I shall make it up to him. All he wanted from you was the phosphate in your bones — "

"The phosphate in our bones!" I yelled.

"Why, certainly," said Lulu. "Poor Elmer has such a hard time finding any phosphate. He got it at first from animals that he caught, but now all the animals are gone. There are birds, of course, but birds are hard to catch. And you had such nice, big bones — "

"That's a fine thing for you to say," I bawled her out sternly. "You were built by humans and humans educated you and — "

"Still I'm a machine," said Lulu, "and I am closer to Elmer than I am to you. You humans can't get it through your heads that there might be a legitimate set of nonhuman values. You are horrified that Elmer wanted the phosphate in your bones, but if there were a metal in Elmer that you needed, you'd break him up to get it without a second thought. You wouldn't even consider that you might be wrong. You'd think it an imposition if Elmer should object. That's the trouble with you and your human race. I've had enough. I have what I want. I am content to stay here. I've found the great love of my life. And for all I care, your pals and you can rot."

She pulled in her face and I didn't rap to try to get her to talk anymore. I figured there wasn't any use. She had made it about as plain as anyone could wish.

I walked back to the camp and woke Ben and Jimmy. I told them about my hunch and about the talk with Lulu. We were pretty glum, because we were all washed up.

Up till now, there had always been the chance that we could make a deal with Lulu. I had felt all along that we needn't worry too much — that Lulu was more alone than we were and that eventually she would have to be reasonable. But now Lulu was not alone and she no longer needed us. And she still was sore at us — and not just at us, but at the whole human race.

And the worst of it was that this was no sudden whim. It had been going on for days. Elmer hadn't been really watching us when he'd hung around at night. He'd come to neck with Lulu. And undoubtedly the two of them had planned Elmer's attack on Ben and me, knowing that Jimmy would be loping to the rescue, leaving the coast clear so that Elmer could rush back and Lulu could take him in. And once it had been accomplished, Lulu had put out a tentacle and swept the tracks away so we wouldn't know that Elmer was inside.

"So she jilted us," said Ben.

"No worse than we did to her," Jimmy reminded him.

"But what did she expect? A man can't love a robot."

"Evidently," I said, "a robot can love a robot. And that's a new one to paste into the book."

"Lulu's crazy," Ben declared.

In all this great romance of Lulu's, it seemed to me there was a certain false note. Why should Lulu and Elmer be sneaky about their love? Lulu could have opened the port anytime she wanted and Elmer could have scampered up the ramp right before our eyes. But they hadn't done that. They had planned and plotted. They had practically eloped.

I wondered if, on Lulu's part, it might be the mark of shame. Was she ashamed of Elmer — ashamed that she had fallen for him? Much as she might deny it, perhaps she nursed the smug snobbery of the human race.

Or was I only thinking this to save my own smug snobbery, simply building up a defense mechanism against being forced to admit, now or in some future time, that there might be other values than the ones evolved by humans? For in us all, I knew, lingered that reluctance to recognize that our way was not necessarily best, that the human viewpoint might not be the universal view-point to which all other life must eventually conform.

Ben made a pot of coffee, and while we sat around and drank it, we said some bitter things of Lulu. I don't regret anything we said, for she had it coming to her. She'd played us a nasty trick.

We finally rolled back into our blankets and didn't bother standing guard. With Elmer out of circulation, there was no need.

The next morning my foot was still sore, so I stayed behind while Ben and Jimmy went out to explore the valley that held the ruined city. Meantime, I hobbled out and walked all around Lulu, looking her over. There was no way I could see that a man might bust into her. The port itself was machined so closely that you had to get real close to see the tiny hairline where it fitted into her side.

Even if we could bust into her, I wondered, could we take control of her? There were the emergencies, of course, but I wasn't too sure just how much use they were. They certainly hadn't bothered Lulu much when she'd got that crazy notion of eloping with us. Then she'd simply jammed them and had left us helpless.

And if we broke into Lulu, we'd come to grips with Elmer, and Elmer was just the kind of beast I had no hankering to come to grips with.

So I went back to camp and puttered around, thinking that now we'd really have to begin to lay some plans about how to get along. We'd have to build that cabin and work up a food supply and do the best we could to get along on our own. For I was fairly certain that we could expect no help from Lulu.

Ben and Jimmy came back in the afternoon and their eyes were shining with excitement. They spread out a blanket and emptied their pockets of the most incredible things any man has ever laid eyes on.

Don't expect me to describe that stuff. There's no point in trying to. What is the sense of saying that a certain item was like a metal chain and that it was yellow? There is no way to get across the feel of it as it slid through one's fingers or the tinkle of it as it moved or the blazing color that was a sort of *living* yellow. It is very much like saying that a famous painting is square and flat and blue, with some green and red.

The chain was only a part of it. There were a lot of other doodads and each one of them was the sort of thing to snatch your breath away.

Ben shrugged at the question in my eyes. "Don't ask me. It's only some stuff we picked up. The caves are full of it. Stuff like this and a whole lot more. We just picked up one thing here and another there — whatever was pocket-sized and happened to catch our eye. Trinkets. Samples. I don't know."

Like jackdaws, I thought. Or pack rats. Grabbing a thing that shone or had a certain shape or a certain texture — taking it because it was pretty, not knowing what its use might be or if, in fact, it had any use at all.

"Those caves may have been storehouses," said Ben. "They're jammed with all sorts of things — not much of any one thing, apparently. All different, as if these aliens had set up a trading post and had their merchandise on display. There seems to be a sort of curtain in front of each of the caves. You can see a shimmer and hear a hissing, but you can't feel a thing when you step through it. And behind that curtain, all the junk they left is as clean and bright and new as the day they left it."

I looked at the articles spread on the blanket. It was hard to keep your hands off them, for they felt good in your hands and were pleasing to the eye and one seemed to get a sense of warmth and richness just by handling them.

"Something happened to those folks," said Jimmy. "They knew it was going to happen, so they took all this stuff and laid it out — all the many things they had made, all the things they'd used and loved. Because, you see, that way there always was a chance someone might come along someday and find it, so they and the culture they had fashioned would not be entirely lost."

It was exactly the kind of silly, sentimental drivel you could expect from a glassy-eyed romantic like Jimmy.

But for whatever reason the artifacts of that vanished race had gotten in the caves, we were the ones who'd found them, and here once again they'd run into a dead end. Even if we had been equipped to puzzle out their use, even if we had been able to ferret out the basic principles of that long-dead culture, it still would be a useless business. We were not going anywhere; we wouldn't be passing on the knowledge. We'd live out our lives here on this planet, and when the last of us had died, the ancient silence and the old uncaring would close down once again.

We weren't going anywhere and neither was Lulu. It was a double dead end.

It was too bad, I thought, for Earth could use the knowledge and the insight that could be wrested from those caves and from the mounds. And not more than a hundred feet from where we sat lay the very tool that Earth had spent twenty years in building to dig out that specific kind of knowledge, should man ever happen on it.

"It must be terrible," said Jimmy, "to realize that all the things and all the knowledge that you ever had, all the trying, all the praying, all the dreams and hopes, will be wiped out forever. That all of you and your way of life and your understanding of that life will simply disappear and no one will ever know."

"You said it, kid," I chipped in.

He stared at me with haunted, stricken eyes. "That may be why they did it."

Watching him, the tenseness of him, the suffering in his face, I caught a glimpse of why he was a poet — why he *had* to be a poet. But even so, he still was an utter creep.

"Earth has to know about this," Ben said flatly.

"Sure," I agreed. "I'll run right over and let them know."

"Always the smart guy," Ben growled at me. "When are you going to cut out being bright and get down to business?"

"Like busting Lulu open, I suppose."

"That's right. We have to get back somehow, and Lulu's the only way to get there."

"It might surprise you, Buster, but I thought of all that before you. I went out today and looked Lulu over. If you can figure how to bust into her, you've a better brain than I have."

"Tools," said Ben. "If we only had — "

"We have. An ax without a handle, a hammer and a saw. A small pinch bar, a plane, a draw shave — "

"We might *make* some tools."

"Find the ore and smelt it and — "

"I was thinking of those caves," said Ben. "There might be tools in there."

I wasn't even interested. I knew it was impossible.

"We might find some explosive," Ben went on. "We might — "

"Look," I said, "what do you want to do — open Lulu up or blow her to bits? Anyhow, I don't think you can do a thing about it. Lulu is a self-maintaining robot, or have you forgotten? Bore a hole in her and she'll grow it shut. Go monkeying around too much and she'll grow a club and clout you on the head."

Ben's eyes blazed with fury and frustration. "Earth has to know! You understand that, don't you? Earth has got to know!"

"Sure," I said. "Absolutely."

In the morning, I thought, he'd come to his senses, see how impossible it was. And that was important. Before we began to lay any plans, it was necessary that we realize what we were up against. That way, you conserve a lot of energy and miss a lot of lumps.

But, come morning, he still had that crazy light of frustration in his eyes and he was filled with a determination that was based on nothing more than downright desperation.

After breakfast, Jimmy said he wasn't going with us.

"For God's sake, why not?" demanded Ben.

"I'm way behind on my writing," Jimmy told him, deadpan. "I'm still working on that saga."

Ben wanted to argue with him, but I cut him off disgustedly.

"Let us go," I said. "He's no use, anyhow."

Which was the solemn truth.

So the two of us went out to the caves. It was the first time I had seen them and they were something to see. There were a dozen of them and all of them were crammed. I got dizzy just walking up and down, looking at all the gadgets and the thingumbobs and dofunnies, not knowing, of course, what any of them were. It was maddening enough just to look at them; it was plain torture trying to figure out what use they might be put to. But Ben was plain hell-bent on trying to figure it out because he'd picked up the stubborn conviction that we could find a gadget that would help us get the best of Lulu.

We worked all day and I was dog-tired at the end of it. Not once in the entire day had we found anything that made any sense at all. I wonder if you can imagine how it felt to stand there, surrounded by all those devices, knowing there were things within your reach that, rightly used, could open up entirely new avenues for human thoughts and technique and imagination. And yet you stood there powerless — an alien illiterate.

But there was no stopping Ben. We went out again the next day and the day after and we kept on going out. On the second day, we found a dojigger that was just fine for opening cans, although I'm fairly sure that was not at all what it was designed for. And on the following day we finally puzzled out how another piece of equipment could be used for digging slanted postholes and, I ask you, who in their right mind would be wanting slanted postholes?

We got nowhere, but we kept on going out, and I sensed that Ben had no more hope than I had, but that he still kept at it because it was the one remaining fingerhold he had on sanity.

I don't think that for one moment he considered the source or significance of that heritage we'd found. To him, it became no more than a junk-yard through which we searched frantically to find one unrecognizable piece of scrap that we might improvise into something that would serve our purpose.

As the days went on, the valley and its mounds, the caves and their residue of a vanished culture seized upon my imagination, and it seemed to me that, in some mysterious manner, I grew closer to that extinct race and sensed at once its greatness and its tragedy. And the feeling grew as well that this frantic hunt of ours bordered on sacrilege and callous profanation of the dead.

Jimmy had not gone out with us a single day. He'd sit hunched over his ream of paper and he scribbled and revised and crossed out words and put in others. He'd get up and walk around in circles or pace back and forth and mumble to himself, then go back and write some more. He scarcely ate and he wouldn't talk and he only slept a little. He was the very portrait of a Young Man in the Throes of Creation.

I got curious about it, wondering if, with all this agony and sweat, he might at last be writing something that was worth the effort. So, when he wasn't looking, I sneaked out a page of it.

It was even worse than the goo he had written before.

That night I lay awake and looked up at the unfamiliar stars and surrendered myself to loneliness. Only, once I had surrendered, I found that I was not so lonely as I might have been — that somehow I had drawn comfort and perhaps even understanding from the muteness of the ruin mounds and the shining wonder of the trove.

Finally I dropped asleep.

I don't know what woke me. It might have been the wind or the sound of the waves breaking on the beach or maybe the chilliness of the night.

Then I heard it, a voice like a chant, solemn and sonorous, a throaty whisper in the dark.

I started up and propped myself on an elbow — and caught my breath at what I saw.

Jimmy was standing in front of Lulu, holding a flashlight in one hand, reading her his saga. His voice had a rolling quality, and despite the soggy words, there was a fascination in the tenor of his tone. It must have been so that the ancient Greeks read their Homer in the flare of torches before the next day's battle.

And Lulu was listening. She had a face hung out and the tentacle which supported it was twisted to one side, so that her audio would not miss a single syllable, just as a man might cup his ear.

Looking at that touching scene, I began to feel a little sorry about the way we'd treated Jimmy. We wouldn't listen to him and the poor devil had to read that tripe of his to someone. His soul hungered for appreciation and he'd got no appreciation out of either Ben or me. Merely writing was not enough for him; he must share it. He had to have an audience.

I put out a hand and shook Ben gently by the shoulder. He came storming up out of his blankets.

"What the hell is — "

"Sh-h-h!"

He drew in a whistling breath and dropped on one knee beside me.

Jimmy went on with his reading and Lulu, with her face cocked attentively, went on listening.

Part of the words came to us, wind-blown and fragmentary:

> Wanderer of the far ways between the two faces of eternity,
> True, forever, to the race that forged her,
> With the winds of alien space blowing in her hair,
> Wearing a circlet of stars as her crown of glory . . .

Lulu wept. There was the shine of tears in that single, gleaming lens.

She grew another tentacle and there was a hand on the end of it and a hankerchief, a very white and lacy and extremely feminine hanky, was clutched within the hand.

She dabbed with the handkerchief at her dripping eye.

If she had had a nose, she undoubtedly would have blown it, delicately, of course, and very ladylike.

"And you wrote it all for me?" she asked.

"All for you," said Jimmy. He was lying like a trooper. The only reason he was reading it to her was because he knew that Ben and I wouldn't listen to it.

"I've been so wrong," Lulu sighed.

She wiped her eye quite dry and briskly polished it.

"Just a second," she said, very businesslike. "There's something I must do."

We waited, scarcely breathing.

Slowly the port in Lulu's side came open. She grew a long, limber tentacle and reached inside the port and hauled Elmer out. She held him dangling.

"You lout!" she stormed at Elmer. "I take you in and stuff you full of phosphate. I get your dents smoothed out and I polish you all bright. And then what? Do you write sagas for me? No, you grow fat and satisfied. There's no mark of greatness on you, no spark of imagination. You're nothing but a dumb machine!"

Elmer just dangled at the end of Lulu's tentacle, but his wheels were spinning furiously and I took that to mean that he was upset.

"Love!" proclaimed Lulu. "Love for the likes of us? We machines have better things to do — far better. There are the star-studded trails of space waiting for our tread, the bitter winds of foreverness blowing from the cloud banks of eternity, the mountains of the great beyond . . ."

She went on for quite a while about the challenge of the farther galaxies, about wearing a coronet of stars, about the dust of shattered time paving the road that led into the ultimate nothingness, and all of it was lifted from what Jimmy called a saga.

Then, when she was all through, she hurled Elmer down the beach, and he hit the sand and skidded straight into the water.

We didn't wait to see any more of it. We were off like sprinters. We hit the ramp full tilt and went up it in a leap and flung ourselves into our quarters.

Lulu slammed the port behind us.

"Welcome home," she said.

I walked over to Jimmy and held out my hand. "Great going, kid. You got Longfellow backed clear off the map."

Ben also shook his hand. "It was a masterpiece."

"And now," said Lulu, "we'll be on our way."

"Our way!" yelled Ben. "We can't leave this planet. Not right away at least. There's that city out there. We can't go until — "

"Phooey on the city," Lulu said. "Phooey on the data. We are off star-wandering. We are searching out the depths of silence. We are racing down the corridors of space with thunder in our brain — the everlasting thunder of a dread eternity."

We turned and looked at Jimmy.

"Every word of it," I said. "Every single word of it out of that muck he wrote."

Ben took a quick step forward and grabbed Jimmy by his shirt front.

"Don't you feel the urge," Ben asked him, "don't you feel a mighty impulse to write a lengthy ode to home — its comfort and its glory and all the other clichés?"

Jimmy's teeth were chattering just a little.

"Lulu is a sucker," Ben said, "for everything you write."

I lifted a fist and let Jimmy smell of it.

"You better make it good," I warned him. "You better write like you never wrote before."

"But keep it sloppy," Ben said. "That's the way Lulu likes it."

Jimmy sat down on the floor and began writing desperately.

"This one writes some fine lyrics, and the other one has done some beautiful music, but they just don't seem to hit it off as collaborators."

The Splendid Source

RICHARD MATHESON

Here's an example of the independence of creativity. This story originally appeared in Playboy *in 1956. Also in 1956, I published a story called "Jokester" in* Infinity Science Fiction *(for, undoubtedly, a far smaller payment). I didn't read Matheson's story till long afterward, and I imagine he didn't read mine till long afterward, if ever. Nevertheless, we both began with the same question, "Who makes up the jokes?" Does it matter? Not at all. We each took our separate path and ended up in far different places.*

... Then spare me your slanders, and read this rather at night than in the daytime, and give it not to young maidens, if there be any ... But I fear nothing for this book, since it is extracted from a high and splendid source, from which all that has issued has had a great success ...
— Balzac: *Contes Drolatiques,* Prologue

IT WAS THE ONE UNCLE LYMAN TOLD in the summer house that did it. Talbert was just coming up the path when he heard the punch line: " 'My God!' cried the actress, 'I thought you said *sarsaparilla!* ' "

Guffaws exploded in the little house. Talbert stood motionless, looking through the rose trellis at the laughing guests. Inside his contour sandals his toes flexed ruminatively. He thought.

Later he took a walk around Lake Bean and watched the crystal surf fold over and observed the gliding swans and stared at the goldfish and thought.

"I've been thinking," he said that night.

"*No,*" said Uncle Lyman, haplessly. He did not commit himself further. He waited for the blow.

Which fell.

"Dirty jokes," said Talbert Bean III.

"I beg your pardon?"

"Endless tides of them covering the nation."

"I fail," said Uncle Lyman, "to grasp the point." Apprehension gripped his voice.

"I find the subject fraught with witchery," said Talbert.

"With — ?"

"Consider," said Talbert. "Every day, all through our land, men tell off-color jokes: in bars and at ball games; in theatre lobbies and at places of business; on street corners and in locker rooms. At home and away, a veritable deluge of jokes."

Talbert paused meaningfully.

"*Who makes them up?*" he asked.

Uncle Lyman stared at his nephew with the look of a fisherman who has just hooked a sea serpent — half awe, half revulsion.

"I'm afraid — " he began.

"I want to know the source of these jokes," said Talbert. "Their genesis; their fountainhead."

"*Why?*" asked Uncle Lyman. Weakly.

"Because it is relevant," said Talbert. "Because these jokes are a part of a culture heretofore unplumbed. Because they are an anomaly; a phenomenon ubiquitous yet unknown."

Uncle Lyman did not speak. His pallid hands curled limply on his half-read *Wall Street Journal.* Behind the polished octagons of his glasses his eyes were suspended berries.

At last he sighed.

"And what part," he inquired, sadly, "am I to play in this quest?"

"We must begin," said Talbert, "with the joke you told in the summer house this afternoon. Where did you hear it?"

"Kulpritt," Uncle Lyman said. Andrew Kulpritt was one of the battery of lawyers employed by Bean Enterprises.

"Capital," said Talbert. "Call him up and ask him where *he* heard it."

Uncle Lyman drew the silver watch from his pocket.

"It's nearly midnight, Talbert," he announced.

Talbert waved away chronology.

"*Now,*" he said. "This is important."

Uncle Lyman examined his nephew a moment longer. Then, with a capitulating sigh, he reached for one of Bean Mansion's thirty-five telephones.

Talbert stood toe-flexed on a bearskin rug while Uncle Lyman dialed, waited, and spoke.

"Kulpritt?" said Uncle Lyman. "Lyman Bean. Sorry to wake you but Talbert wants to know where you heard the joke about the actress who thought the director said sarsaparilla."

Uncle Lyman listened. "I *said* — " he began again.

A minute later he cradled the receiver heavily.

"Prentiss," he said.

"Call him up," said Talbert.

"Talbert," Uncle Lyman asked.

"Now," said Talbert.

A long breath exuded between Uncle Lyman's lips. Carefully, he folded his *Wall Street Journal.* He reached across the mahogany table and tamped out his ten-inch cigar. Sliding a weary hand beneath his smoking jacket, he withdrew his tooled leather address book.

Prentiss heard it from George Sharper, C.P.A. Sharper heard it from Abner Ackerman, M.D. Ackerman heard it from William Cozener, Prune Products. Cozener heard it from Rod Tassel, Mgr., Cyprian Club. Tassel heard it from O. Winterbottom. Winterbottom heard it from H. Alberts. Alberts heard it from D. Silver, Silver from B. Phryne, Phryne from E. Kennelly.

By an odd twist Kennelly said he heard it from Uncle Lyman.

"There is complicity here," said Talbert. "These jokes are not self-generative."

It was 4:00 A.M. Uncle Lyman slumped, inert and dead-eyed, on his chair.

"There has to be a source," said Talbert.

Uncle Lyman remained motionless.

"You're not interested," said Talbert, incredulously.

Uncle Lyman made a noise.

"I don't understand," said Talbert. "Here is a situation pregnant with divers fascinations. Is there a man or woman who has never heard an off-color joke? I say not. Yet, is there a man or woman who knows where these jokes come from? Again I say not."

Talbert strode forcefully to his place of musing at the twelve-foot fireplace. He poised there, staring in.

"I may be a millionaire," he said, "but I am sensitive." He turned. "And this phenomenon excites me."

Uncle Lyman attempted to sleep while retaining the face of a man awake.

"I have always had more money than I needed," said Talbert. "Capital investment was unnecessary. Thus I turned to investing the other asset my father left — my brain."

Uncle Lyman stirred; a thought shook loose.

"What ever happened," he asked, "to that society of yours, the S.P.C.S.P.C.A.?"

"Eh? The Society for the Prevention of Cruelty to the Society for the Prevention of Cruelty to Animals? The past."

"And your interest in world problems. What about that sociological treatise you were writing — "

" 'Slums: A Positive View,' you mean?" Talbert brushed it aside. "Inconsequence."

"And isn't there anything left of your political party, the Pro-antidisestablishmentarianists?"

"Not a shred. Scuttled by reactionaries from within."

"What about Bimetallism?"

"Oh, that!" Talbert smiled ruefully. "Passé, dear Uncle. I had been reading too many Victorian novels."

"Speaking of novels, what about your literary criticisms? Nothing doing with 'The Use of the Semicolon in Jane Austen?' Or 'Horatio Alger: The Misunderstood Satirist'? To say nothing of 'Was Queen Elizabeth Shakespeare?' "

" 'Was Shakespeare Queen Elizabeth,' " corrected Talbert. "No, Uncle, nothing doing with them. They had momentary interest, nothing more . . ."

"I suppose the same holds true for 'The Shoe Horn: Pro and Con,' eh? And those scientific articles — 'Relativity Re-Examined' and 'Is Evolution Enough?' "

"Dead and gone," said Talbert, patiently, "dead and gone. These projects needed me once. Now I go on to better things."

"Like who writes dirty jokes," said Uncle Lyman.

Talbert nodded. "Like that."

When the butler set the breakfast tray on the bed Talbert said, "Redfield, do you know any jokes?"

Redfield looked out impassively through the face an improvident nature had neglected to animate.

"Jokes, sir?" he inquired.

"You know," said Talbert. "Jollities."

Redfield stood by the bed like a corpse whose casket had been upended and removed.

"Well, sir," he said, a full thirty seconds later, "once, when I was a boy I heard one . . ."

"Yes?" said Talbert eagerly.

"I believe it went somewhat as follows," Redfield said. "When — uh — *When* is a portmanteau not a — "

"No, no," said Talbert, shaking his head, "I mean *dirty* jokes."

Redfield's eyebrows soared. The vernacular was like a fish in his face.

"You don't know any?" said a disappointed Talbert.

"Begging your pardon, sir," said Redfield. "If I may make a suggestion. May I say that the chauffeur is more likely to — "

"You know any dirty jokes, Harrison?" Talbert asked through the tube as the Rolls-Royce purred along Bean Road toward Highway 27.

Harrison looked blank for a moment. He glanced back at Talbert. Then a grin wrinkled his carnal jowls.

"Well, sir," he began, "there's this guy sittin' by the runway eatin' an onion, see?"

Talbert unclipped his four-color pencil.

Talbert stood in an elevator rising to the tenth floor of the Gault Building.

The hour ride to New York had been most illuminating. Not only had he transcribed seven of the most horrendously vulgar jokes he had ever heard in his life but had exacted a promise from Harrison to take him to the various establishments where these jokes had been heard.

The hunt was on.

MAX AXE/DETECTIVE AGENCY — read the words on the frosty-glassed door. Talbert turned the knob and went in.

Announced by the beautiful receptionist, Talbert was ushered into a sparsely furnished office on whose walls were a hunting license, a machine gun, and framed photographs of the Seagram factory, the St. Valentine's Day Massacre in color, and Herbert J. Philbrick, who had led three lives.

Mr. Axe shook Talbert's hand.

"What could I do for ya?" he asked.

"First of all," said Talbert, "do you know any dirty jokes?"

Recovering, Mr. Axe told Talbert the one about the monkey and the elephant.

Talbert jotted it down. Then he hired the agency to investigate the men Uncle Lyman had phoned and uncover anything that was meaningful.

After he left the agency, Talbert began making the rounds with Harrison. He heard a joke the first place they went.

"There's this midget in a frankfurter suit, see?" it began.

It was a day of buoyant discovery. Talbert heard the joke about the cross-eyed plumber in the harem, the one about the preacher who won an eel at a raffle, the one about the fighter pilot who went down in flames, and the one about the two Girl Scouts who lost their cookies in the laundromat.

Among others.

"I want," said Talbert, "one round-trip airplane ticket to San Francisco and a reservation at the Hotel Millard Fillmore."

"May I ask," asked Uncle Lyman, "why?"

"While making the rounds with Harrison today," explained Talbert, "a salesman of ladies' undergarments told me that a veritable cornucopia of off-color jokes exists in the person of Harry Shuler, bellboy at the Millard Fillmore. This salesman said that, during a three-day convention at that hotel, he had heard more new jokes from Shuler than he had heard in the first thirty-nine years of his life."

"And you are going to — ?" Uncle Lyman began.

"Exactly," said Talbert. "We must follow where the spoor is strongest."

"Talbert," said Uncle Lyman, "Why do you *do* these things?"

"I am searching," said Talbert, simply.

"For what, dammit!" cried Uncle Lyman.

"For *meaning,*" said Talbert.

Uncle Lyman covered his eyes. "You are the image of your mother," he declared.

"Say nothing of her," charged Talbert. "She was the finest woman who ever trod the earth."

"Then how come she got trampled to death at the funeral of Rudolph Valentino?" Uncle Lyman charged back.

"That is a base canard," said Talbert, "and you know it. Mother just happened to be passing the church on her way to bringing food to the Orphans of the Dissolute Seamen — one of her many charities — when she was accidentally caught up in the waves of hysterical women and swept to her awful end."

A pregnant silence bellied the vast room. Talbert stood at a window looking down the hill at Lake Bean, which his father had had poured in 1923.

"Think of it," he said after a moment's reflection. "The nation alive with off-color jokes — the *world* alive! And the same jokes, Uncle, *the same jokes.* How? *How?* By what strange means do these jokes o'erleap oceans, span continents? By what incredible machinery are these jokes promulgated over mountain and dale?"

He turned and met Uncle Lyman's mesmeric stare.

"I mean to know," he said.

At ten minutes before midnight Talbert boarded the plane for San Francisco and took a seat by the window. Fifteen minutes later the plane roared down the runway and nosed up into the black sky.

Talbert turned to the man beside him.

"Do you know any dirty jokes, sir?" he inquired, pencil poised.

The man stared at him. Talbert gulped.

"Oh, I *am* sorry," he said, "Reverend."

When they reached the room Talbert gave the bellboy a crisp five-dollar bill and asked to hear a joke.

Shuler told him the one about the man sitting by the runway eating an onion, see? Talbert listened, toes kneading inquisitively in his shoes. The joke concluded, he asked Shuler where this and similar jokes might be overheard. Shuler said at a wharf spot known as Davy Jones's Locker Room.

Early that evening, after drinking with one of the West Coast representatives of Bean Enterprises, Talbert took a taxi to Davy Jones's Locker Room. Entering its dim, smoke-fogged interior, he took a place at the bar, ordered a screwdriver, and began to listen.

Within an hour's time he had written down the joke about the old maid who caught her nose in the bathtub faucet, the one about the three traveling salesmen and the farmer's ambidextrous daughter, the one about the nurse who thought they were Spanish olives, and the one about the midget in the frankfurter suit. Talbert wrote this last joke under his original transcription of it, underlining changes in context attributable to regional influence.

At 10:16, a man who had just told Talbert the one about the hillbilly twins and their two-headed sister said that Tony, the bartender, was a virtual faucet of off-color jokes, limericks, anecdotes, epigrams, and proverbs.

Talbert went over to the bar and asked Tony for the major source of his lewdiana. After reciting the limerick about the sex of the asteroid vermin, the bartender referred Talbert to a Mr. Frank Bruin, salesman, of Oakland, who happened not to be there that night.

Talbert at once retired to a telephone directory where he discovered five Frank Bruins in Oakland. Entering a booth with a coat pocket sagging change, Talbert began dialing them.

Two of the five Frank Bruins were salesmen. One of them, however, was in Alcatraz at the moment. Talbert traced the remaining Frank Bruin to Hogan's Alleys in Oakland, where his wife said that, as usual on Thursday nights, her husband was bowling with the Moonlight Mattress Company All-Stars.

Quitting the bar, Talbert chartered a taxi and started across the bay to Oakland, toes in ferment.

Veni, vidi, vici?

Bruin was not a needle in a haystack.

The moment Talbert entered Hogan's Alleys his eye was caught by a football huddle of men encircling a portly, rosy-domed speaker. Approaching, Talbert was just in time to hear the punch line followed by an explosion of composite laughter. It was the punch line that intrigued.

" 'My God!' cried the actress," Mr. Bruin had uttered, " 'I thought you said a banana split!' "

This variation much excited Talbert, who saw in it a verification of a new element — the interchangeable kicker.

When the group had broken up and drifted, Talbert accosted Mr. Bruin and, introducing himself, asked where Mr. Bruin had heard that joke.

"Why d'ya ask, boy?" asked Mr. Bruin.

"No reason," said the crafty Talbert.

"I don't remember where I heard it, boy," said Mr. Bruin finally. "Excuse me, will ya?"

Talbert trailed after him but received no satisfaction — unless it was in the most definite impression that Bruin was concealing something.

Later, riding back to the Millard Fillmore, Talbert decided to put an Oakland detective agency on Mr. Bruin's trail to see what could be seen.

When Talbert reached the hotel there was a telegram waiting for him at the desk.

MR. RODNEY TASSEL RECEIVED LONG DISTANCE CALL FROM MR. GEORGE BULLOCK, CARTHAGE HOTEL, CHICAGO. WAS TOLD JOKE ABOUT MIDGET IN SALAMI SUIT. MEANINGFUL? — AXE.

Talbert's eyes ignited.

"Tally," he murmured, *"ho."*

An hour later he had checked out of the Millard Fillmore, taxied to the airport, and caught a plane for Chicago.

Twenty minutes after he had left the hotel, a man in a dark pinstripe approached the desk clerk and asked for the room number of Talbert Bean III. When informed of Talbert's departure the man grew steely eyed and immediately retired to a telephone booth. He emerged ashen.

"I'm sorry," said the desk clerk, "Mr. Bullock checked out this morning."

"Oh." Talbert's shoulders sagged. All night on the plane he had been checking over his notes, hoping to discern a pattern to the jokes which would encompass type, area of genesis, and periodicity. He was weary with fruitless concentration. Now this.

"And he left no forwarding address?" he asked.

"Only Chicago, sir," said the clerk.

"I see."

Following a bath and luncheon in his room, a slightly refreshed Talbert settled down with the telephone and the directory. There were 47 George Bullocks in Chicago. Talbert checked them off as he phoned.

At 3:00 P.M. he slumped over the receiver in a dead slumber. At 4:21 he regained consciousness and completed the remaining eleven calls. The Mr. Bullock in question was not at home, said his housekeeper, but was expected in that evening.

"Thank you kindly," said a bleary-eyed Talbert and, hanging up, thereupon collapsed on the bed — only to awake a few minutes past seven and dress quickly. Descending to the street, he gulped down a sandwich and a glass of milk, then hailed a cab and made the hour ride to the home of George Bullock.

The man himself answered the bell.

"Yes?" he asked.

Talbert introduced himself and said he had come to the Hotel Carthage earlier to see him.

"Why?" asked Mr. Bullock.

"So you could tell me where you heard that joke about the midget in the salami suit," said Talbert.

"Sir?"

"I said — "

"I heard what you said, sir," said Mr. Bullock, "though I cannot say that your remark makes any noticeable sense."

"I believe, sir," challenged Talbert, "that you are hiding behind fustian."

"Behind fustian, sir?" retorted Bullock. "I'm afraid — "

"The game is up, sir!" declared Talbert in a ringing voice. "Why don't you admit it and tell me where you got that joke from?"

"I have not the remotest conception of what you're talking about, sir!" snapped Bullock, his words belied by the pallor of his face.

Talbert flashed a Mona Lisa smile. "Indeed?" he said.

And, turning lightly on his heel, he left Bullock trembling in the doorway. As he settled back against the taxicab seat again, he saw Bullock still standing there, staring at him. Then Bullock whirled and was gone.

"Hotel Carthage," said Talbert, satisfied with his bluff.

Riding back, he thought of Bullock's agitation and a thin smile tipped up the corners of his mouth. No doubt about it. The prey was being run to earth. Now if his surmise was valid there would likely be —

A lean man in a long raincoat was sitting on the bed when Talbert entered his room. The man's mustache, like a muddy toothbrush, twitched.

"Talbert Bean?" he asked.

Talbert bowed.

"The same," he said.

The man, a Colonel Bishop, retired, looked at Talbert with metal blue eyes.

"What is your game, sir?" he asked tautly.

"I don't understand," toyed Talbert.

"I think you do," said the Colonel, "and you are to come with me."

"Oh?" said Talbert.

He found himself looking down the barrel of a .45 calibre Webley-Fosbery.

"Shall we?" said the Colonel.

"But of course," said Talbert coolly. "I have not come all this way to resist now."

The ride in the private plane was a long one. The windows were blacked out and Talbert hadn't the faintest idea in which direction they were flying. Neither the pilot nor the Colonel spoke, and Talbert's attempts at conversation were discouraged by a chilly silence. The Colonel's pistol, still leveled at Talbert's chest, never wavered, but it did not bother Talbert. He was exultant. All he could think was that his search was ending; he was, at last, approaching the headwaters of the dirty joke. After a time, his head nodded and he dozed — to dream of midgets in frankfurter suits and actresses who seemed obsessed by sarsaparilla or banana splits or sometimes both. How long he slept, and what boundaries he may have crossed, Talbert never knew. He was awakened by a swift loss of altitude and the steely voice of Colonel Bishop:

"We are landing, Mr. Bean." The Colonel's grip tightened on the pistol.

Talbert offered no resistance when his eyes were blindfolded. Feeling the Webley-Fosbery in the small of his back, he stumbled out of the plane and crunched over the ground of a well-kept airstrip. There was a nip in the air and he felt a bit lightheaded: Talbert suspected they had landed in a mountainous region; but what mountains, and on what continent, he could not guess. His ears and nose conveyed nothing of help to his churning mind.

He was shoved — none too gently — into an automobile, and then driven swiftly along what felt like a dirt road. The tires crackled over pebbles and twigs.

Suddenly the blindfold was removed. Talbert blinked and looked out the windows. It was a black and cloudy night; he could see nothing but the limited vista afforded by the headlights.

"You are well isolated," he said, appreciatively. Colonel Bishop remained tightlipped and vigilant.

After a fifteen-minute ride along the dark road, the car pulled up in front of a tall, unlighted house. As the motor was cut Talbert could hear the pulsing rasp of crickets all around.

"Well," he said.

"Emerge," suggested Colonel Bishop.

"Of course." Talbert bent out of the car and was escorted up the wide porch steps by the Colonel. Behind, the car pulled away.

Inside the house, chimes bonged hollowly as the Colonel pushed a button. They waited in the darkness and, in a few moments, approaching footsteps sounded.

A tiny aperture opened in the heavy door, disclosing a single bespectacled eye. The eye blinked once and, with a faint accent Talbert could not recognize, whispered furtively, "Why did the widow wear black garters?"

"In remembrance," said Colonel Bishop with great gravity, "of those who had passed beyond."

The door opened.

The owner of the eye was tall, gaunt, of indeterminable age and nationality, his hair a dark mass wisped with gray. His face was all angles and facets, his eyes piercing behind large, horn-rimmed glasses. He wore flannel trousers and a checked jacket.

"This is the Dean," said Colonel Bishop.

"How do you do," said Talbert.

"Come *in,* come *in,*" the Dean invited, extending his large hand to Talbert. "Welcome, Mr. Bean." He shafted a scolding look at Bishop's pistol. "Now, Colonel," he said, "indulging in melodramatics again? Put it away, dear fellow."

"We can't be too careful," grumped the Colonel.

Talbert stood in the spacious grace of the entry hall looking around. His gaze settled, presently, on the cryptic smile of the Dean, who said:

"So. You have found us out, sir."

Talbert's toes whipped like pennants in a gale.

"Have I?" he covered his excitement with.

"Yes," said the Dean. "You have. And a masterful display of investigative intuition it was."

Talbert looked around.

"So," he said, voice bated, "It is *here.*"

"Yes," said the Dean, "Would you like to see it?"

"More than anything in the world," said Talbert, fervently.

"Come then," said the Dean.

"Is this wise?" the Colonel warned.

"Come," repeated the Dean.

The three men started down the hallway. For a moment, a shade of premonition darkened Talbert's mind. It was being made so easy. Was it a trap? In a second the thought had slipped away, washed off by a current of excited curiosity.

They started up a winding marble staircase.

"How did you suspect?" the Dean inquired. "That is to say — what prompted you to probe the matter?"

"I just *thought,*" said Talbert meaningfully. "Here are all these jokes yet no one seems to know where they come from. Or *care.*"

"Yes," observed the Dean, "we count upon that lack of interest. What man in ten million ever asks, 'Where did you hear that joke?' Absorbed in memorizing the joke for future use, he gives no thought to its source. This, of course, is our protection."

The Dean smiled at Talbert. "But not," he amended, "from men such as you."

Talbert's flush went unnoticed.

They reached the landing and began walking along a wide corridor lit on each side by the illumination of candelabra. There was no more talk. At the end of the corridor they turned right and stopped in front of massive, iron-hinged doors.

"Is this wise?" the Colonel asked again.

"Too late to stop now," said the Dean, and Talbert felt a shiver flutter down his spine. What if it *were* a trap? He swallowed, then squared his shoulders. The Dean had said it. It was too late to stop.

The great doors tracked open.

"Et voilà," said the Dean.

The hallway was an avenue. Thick wall-to-wall carpeting sponged beneath Talbert's feet as he walked between the Colonel and the Dean. At periodic intervals along the ceiling hung music-emitting speakers; Talbert recognized the *Gaîté Parisienne*. His gaze moved to a petit-point tapestry on which Dionysian acts ensued above the stitched motto, "Happy is the Man Who Is Making Something."

"Incredible," he murmured. "Here; in this house."

"Exactly," said the Dean.

Talbert shook his head wonderingly.

"To think," he said.

The Dean paused before a glass wall and, braking, Talbert peered into an office. Among its rich appointments strode a young man in a striped silk weskit with brass buttons, gesturing meaningfully with a long cigar while, cross-legged on a leather couch, sat a happily sweatered blonde of rich dimensions.

The man stopped briefly and waved to the Dean, smiled, then returned to his spirited dictating.

"One of our best," the Dean said.

"But," stammered Talbert, "I thought that man was on the staff of — "

"He is," said the Dean. "And, in his spare time, he is also one of us."

Talbert followed on excitement-numbed legs.

"But I had no idea," he said. "I presumed the organization to be composed of men like Bruin and Bullock."

"They are merely our means of promulgation," explained the Dean. "Our word-of-mouthers, you might say. Our *creators* come from more exalted ranks — executives, statesmen, the better professional comics, editors, novelists — "

The Dean broke off as the door to one of the other offices opened and a barrelly, bearded man in hunting clothes emerged. He shouldered past them, muttering true things to himself.

"Off again?" the Dean asked pleasantly. The big man grunted. It was a true grunt. He clumped off, lonely for a veldt.

"*Unbelievable,*" said Talbert. "Such men as these?"

"Exactly," said the Dean.

They strolled on past the rows of busy offices, Talbert tourist-eyed, the Dean smiling his mandarin smile, the Colonel working his lips as if anticipating the kiss of a toad.

"But where did it all begin?" a dazed Talbert asked.

"That is history's secret," rejoined the Dean, "veiled behind time's opacity. Our venture does have its honored past, however. Great men have graced its cause — Ben Franklin, Mark Twain, Dickens, Swinburne, Rabelais, Balzac; oh, the honor roll is long. Shakespeare, of course, and his friend Ben Jonson. Still further back, Chaucer, Boccaccio. Further yet, Horace and Seneca, Demosthenes and Plautus. Aristophanes, Apuleius. Yea, in the palaces of Tutankhamen was our work done; in the black temples of Ahriman, the pleasure dome of Kubla Khan. Where did it begin? Who knows? Scraped on rock, in many a primordial cave, are certain drawings. And there are those among us who believe that these were left by the earliest members of the Brotherhood. But this is only legend . . ."

Now they had reached the end of the hallway and were starting down a cushioned ramp.

"There must be vast sums of money involved in this," said Talbert.

"*Heaven forfend,*" declared the Dean, stopping short. "Do not confuse our work with alley vending. Our workers contribute freely of their time and skill, caring for naught save the Cause."

"Forgive me," Talbert said. Then, rallying, he asked, "What Cause?"

The Dean's gaze fused on inward things. He ambled on slowly, arms behind his back.

"The Cause of Love," he said, "as opposed to Hate. Of Nature, as opposed to the Unnatural. Of Humanity, as opposed to Inhumanity. Of Freedom, as opposed to Constraint. Of Health, as opposed to Disease. Yes, Mr. Bean, disease. The disease called bigotry; the frighteningly communicable disease that taints all it touches; turns warmth to chill and joy to guilt and good to bad. What Cause?" He stopped dramatically. "The Cause of Life, Mr. Bean — as opposed to Death!"

The Dean lifted a challenging finger. "We see ourselves," he said, "as an army of dedicated warriors marching on the strongholds of prudery. Knights Templar with a just and joyous mission."

"Amen to that," a fervent Talbert said.

They entered a large, cubicle-bordered room. Talbert saw men: some typing, some writing, some staring, some on telephones, talking in a multitude of tongues. Their expressions were, as one, intently aloft. At the far end of the room, expression unseen, a man stabbed plugs into a many-eyed switchboard.

"Our Apprentice Room," said the Dean, "wherein we groom our future . . ."

His voice died off as a young man exited one of the cubicles and approached them, paper in hand, a smile tremulous on his lips.

"Oliver," said the Dean, nodding once.

"I've done a joke, sir," said Oliver. "May I — ?"

"But of course," said the Dean.

Oliver cleared viscid anxiety from his throat, then told a joke about a little boy and girl watching a doubles match on the nudist colony tennis court. The Dean smiled, nodding. Oliver looked up, pained.

"No?" he said.

"It is not without merit," encouraged the Dean, "but, as it now stands, you see, it smacks rather too reminiscently of the duchess-butler effect, 'Wife of Bath' category. Not to mention the justifiably popular double reverse bishop-barmaid gambit."

"Oh, sir," grieved Oliver, "I'll never prevail."

"Nonsense," said the Dean, adding kindly, "*son.* These shorter jokes are, by all odds, the most difficult to master. They must be cogent, precise; must say something of pith and moment."

"Yes, sir," murmured Oliver.

"Check with Wojciechowski and Sforzini," said the Dean. "Also Ahmed El-Hakim. They'll brief you on use of the Master Index. Eh?" He patted Oliver's back.

"Yes, sir." Oliver managed a smile and returned to his cubicle. The Dean sighed.

"A somber business," he declared. "He'll never be Class-A. He really shouldn't be in the composing end of it at all but — " He gestured meaningfully, " — there is sentiment involved."

"Oh?" said Talbert.

"Yes," said the Dean. "It was his great grandfather who, on June 23, 1848, wrote the first Traveling Salesman joke, American strain."

The Dean and the Colonel lowered their heads a moment in reverent commemoration. Talbert did the same.

"And so we have it," said the Dean. They were back downstairs, sitting in the great living room, sherry having been served.

"Perhaps you wish to know more," said the Dean.

"Only one thing," said Talbert.

"And that is, sir?"

"Why have you shown it to me?"

"Yes," said the Colonel, fingering at his armpit holster, "why indeed?"

The Dean looked at Talbert carefully, as if balancing his reply.

"You haven't guessed?" he said, at last. "No, I can see you haven't. Mr. Bean . . . you are not unknown to us. Who has not heard of your work, your unflagging devotion to sometimes obscure but always worthy causes? What man can help but admire your selflessness, your dedication, your proud defiance of convention and prejudice?" The Dean paused and leaned forward.

"Mr. Bean," he said softly. "Talbert — may I call you that? — *we want you on our team.*"

Talbert gaped. His hands began to tremble. The Colonel, relieved, grunted and sank back into his chair.

No reply came from the flustered Talbert, so the Dean continued: "Think it over. Consider the merits of our work. With all due modesty, I think I may say that here is your opportunity to ally yourself with the greatest cause of your life."

"I'm speechless," said Talbert. "I hardly — that is — how can I . . ."

But, already, the light of consecration was stealing into his eyes.

MS. Found in a
Chinese Fortune Cookie

C. M. KORNBLUTH

This story is one of our favorites, a document that, according to Janet, not only libels the likes of Mickey Spillane and Norman Vincent Peale, but also reveals the TRUTH about writers, the problems of their spouses, and why humankind will not be saved.

Cecil Corwin, by the way, was a real science fiction writer — a pseudonym of — who else — C. M. Kornbluth, who managed to write an extraordinary number of memorable science fiction stories in his short life. They are the kinds of stories you remember, think about, and refer to in conversation. His "The Marching Morons" has even become a catch phrase. As for me, I never open a Chinese fortune cookie without just a little touch of "what if. . ." — the beauty of the ending.

THEY SAY I AM MAD, but I am not mad — damn it, I've written and sold two million words of fiction and I know better than to start a story like that, but this isn't a story and they *do* say I'm mad — catatonic schizophrenia with assaultive episodes — and I'm *not*. [*This is clearly the first of the Corwin Papers. Like all the others it is written on a Riz-La cigarette paper with a ball point pen. Like all the others it is headed:* Urgent. Finder please send to C. M. Kornbluth, Wantagh, N. Y. Reward! *I might comment that this is typical of Corwin's generosity with his friends' time and money, though his attitude is at least this once justified by his desperate plight. As his longtime friend and, indeed, literary executor, I was clearly the person to turn to. CMK*] I have to convince you, Cyril, that I am both sane and the victim of an enormous conspiracy — and that you are too, and that everybody is. A tall order, but I am going to try to fill it by writing an orderly account of the events leading up to my present situation. [*Here ends the first paper. To keep the record clear I should state that it was forwarded to me by a Mr. L. Wilmot Shaw who found it in a fortune cookie he ordered for dessert at the Great China Republic*

Restaurant in San Francisco. Mr. Shaw suspected it was "a publicity gag" but sent it to me nonetheless, and received by return mail my thanks and my check for one dollar. I had not realized that Corwin and his wife had disappeared from their home at Painted Post; I was merely aware that it had been weeks since I'd heard from him. We visited infrequently. To be blunt, he was easier to take via mail than face to face. For the balance of this account I shall attempt to avoid tedium by omitting the provenance of each paper, except when noteworthy, and its length. The first is typical — a little over a hundred words. I have, of course, kept on file all correspondence relating to the papers, and am eager to display it to the authorities. It is hoped that publication of this account will nudge them out of the apathy with which they have so far greeted my attempts to engage them. CMK]

On Sunday, May 13, 1956, at about 12:30 P.M., I learned The Answer. I was stiff and aching because all Saturday my wife and I had been putting in young fruit trees. I like to dig, but I was badly out of condition from an unusually long and idle winter. Creatively, I felt fine. I'd been stale for months, but when spring came the sap began to run in me too. I was bursting with story ideas; scenes and stretches of dialog were jostling one another in my mind; all I had to do was let them flow onto paper.

When The Answer popped into my head I thought at first it was an idea for a story — a very good story. I was going to go downstairs and bounce it off my wife a few times to test it, but I heard the sewing machine buzzing and remembered she had said she was way behind on her mending. Instead, I put my feet up, stared blankly through the window at the pasture-and-wooded-hills View we'd bought the old place for, and fondled the idea.

What about, I thought, using the idea to develop a messy little local situation, the case of Mrs. Clonford? Mrs. C. is a neighbor, animal-happy, land-poor, and unintentionally a fearsome oppressor of her husband and children. Mr. C. is a retired brakeman with a pension and his wife insists on him making like a farmer in all weathers and every year he gets pneumonia and is pulled through with antibiotics. All he wants is to sell the damned farm and retire with his wife to a little apartment in town. All *she* wants is to mess around with her cows and horses and submarginal acreage.

I got to thinking that if you noised the story around *with* a comment based on The Answer, the situation would automatically untangle. They'd get their apartment, sell the farm, and everybody would be happy, including Mrs. C. It would be interesting to write, I thought idly, and then I thought not so idly that it would be interesting to *try* — and then I sat up sharply with a dry mouth and a systemful of adrenalin. *It would work.* The Answer would work.

I ran rapidly down a list of other problems, ranging from the town drunk to the guided-missile race. The Answer worked. Every time.

I was quite sure I had turned paranoid, because I've seen so much of that kind of thing in science fiction. Anybody can name a dozen writers, editors, and fans who have suddenly seen the light and determined to lead the human race onward and upward out of the old slough. Of course The Answer looked logical and unassailable, but so no doubt did poor Charlie McGandress's project to unite mankind through science fiction fandom, at least to him. So, no doubt, did [*I have here omitted several briefly sketched case histories of science fiction personalities as yet uncommitted. The reason will be obvious to anyone familiar with the law of libel. Suffice it to say that Corwin argues that science fiction attracts an unstable type of mind and sometimes insidiously undermines its foundations on reality. CMK*]

But I couldn't just throw it away without a test. I considered the wording carefully, picked up the extension phone on my desk, and dialed Jim Howlett, the appliance dealer in town. He answered. "Corwin, Jim," I told him. "I have an idea — oops! The samovar's boiling over. Call me back in a minute, will you?" I hung up.

He called me back in a minute; I let our combination — two shorts and a long — ring three times before I picked up the phone. "What was that about a samovar?" he asked, baffled.

"Just kidding," I said. "Listen Jim, why don't you try a short story for a change of pace? Knock off the novel for a while — " He's hopefully writing a big historical about the Sullivan Campaign of 1779, which is our local chunk of the Revolutionary War; I'm helping him a little with advice. Anybody who wants as badly as he does to get out of the appliance business is entitled to some help.

"Gee, I don't know," he said. As he spoke the volume of his voice dropped slightly but definitely, three times. That meant we had an average quota of party-line snoopers listening in. "What would I write about?"

"Well, we have this situation with a neighbor, Mrs. Clonford," I began. I went through the problem and made my comment based on The Answer. I heard one of the snoopers gasp. Jim said when I was finished: "I don't really think it's for me, Cecil. Of course it was nice of you to call, but — "

Eventually a customer came into the store and he had to break off.

I went through an anxious, crabby twenty-four hours.

On Monday afternoon the paper woman drove past our place and shot the rolled-up copy of the Pott Hill *Evening Times* into the orange-painted tube beside our mailbox. I raced for it, yanked it open to the seventh page, and read:

FARM SALE

Owing to Ill Health and Age Mr. & Mrs. Ronald Clonford Will sell their Entire Farm, All Machinery and Furnishings and All Live Stock at Auction Saturday May 19 12:30 P.M. Rain or Shine, Terms Cash Day of Sale, George Pfennig, Auctioneer.

[*This is one of the few things in the Corwin Papers that can be independently verified. I looked up the paper and found that the ad was run about as quoted. Further, I interviewed Mrs. Clonford in her town apartment. She told me she "just got tired of farmin', I guess. Kind of hated to give up my ponies, but people was beginning to say it was too hard of a life for Ronnie and I guess they was right." CMK*]

Coincidence? Perhaps. I went upstairs with the paper and put my feet up again. I could try a hundred more piddling tests if I wished, but why waste time? If there was anything to it, I could type out The Answer in about two hundred words, drive to town, tack it on the bulletin board outside the fire-house and — snowball. Avalanche!

I didn't do it, of course — for the same reason I haven't put down the two hundred words of The Answer yet on a couple of these cigarette papers. It's rather dreadful — isn't it — that I haven't done so, that a simple feasible plan to ensure peace, progress, and equality of opportunity among all mankind may be lost to the world if, say, a big meteorite hits the asylum in the next couple of minutes. But — I'm a writer. There's a touch of intellectual sadism in us. We like to dominate the reader as a matador dominates the bull; we like to tease and mystify and at last show what great souls we are by generously flipping up the shade and letting the sunshine in. Don't worry. Read on. You will come to The Answer in the proper artistic place for it. [*At this point I wish fervently to dissociate myself from the attitudes Corwin attributes to our profession. He had — has, I hope — his eccentricities, and I consider it inexcusable of him to tar us all with his personal brush. I could point out, for example, that he once laboriously cultivated a sixteenth-century handwriting which was utterly illegible to the modern reader. The only reason apparent for this, as for so many of his traits, seemed to be a wish to annoy as many people as possible. CMK*]

Yes; I am a writer. A matador does not show up in the bullring with a tommy gun, and a writer doesn't do things the simple, direct way. He makes the people writhe a little first. So I called Fred Greenwald. Fred had been after me for a while to speak at one of the Thursday Rotary meetings, and I'd been reluctant to set a date. I have a little speech for such occasions, "The Business of Being a Writer" — all about the archaic royalty system of payment, the difficulty of proving business expenses, the Margaret Mitchell tax law and how it badly needs improvement, what copyright is and isn't, how about all these generals and politicians with their capital-gains memoirs. I pass a few galley sheets down the table and generally get a good laugh by holding up a Double-day book contract, silently turning it over so they can see how the fine print goes on and on, and then flipping it open so they see there's twice as much fine print than they thought there was. I had done my stuff for Oswego Rotary, Horseheads Rotary, and Cannon Hole Rotary; now Fred wanted me to do it for Painted Post Rotary.

So I phoned him and said I'd be willing to speak this coming Thursday. Good, he said. On a discovery I'd made about the philosophy and technique of administration and interpersonal relationships, I said. He sort of choked up and said well, we're broadminded here.

I've got to start cutting this. I have several packs of cigarette papers left but not enough to cover the high spots if I'm to do them justice. Let's just say the announcement of my speech was run in the Tuesday paper [*It was. CMK*] and skip to Wednesday, my place, about 7:30 P.M. Dinner was just over and my wife and I were going to walk out and see how [*At this point I wish to insert a special note concerning some difficulty I had in obtaining the next four papers. They got somehow into the hands of a certain literary agent who is famous for a sort of "finders-keepers" attitude more appropriate to the eighth grade than to the law of literary property. In disregard of the fact that Corwin retained physical ownership of the papers and literary rights thereto, and that I as the addressee possessed all other rights, he was blandly endeavoring to sell them to various magazines as "curious fragments from Corwin's desk." Like most people, I abhor lawsuits; that's the fact this agent lives on. I met his outrageous price of five cents a word "plus postage(!)." I should add that I have not heard of any attempt by this gentleman to locate Corwin or his heirs in order to turn over the proceeds of the sale, less commission. CMK*] the new fruit trees were doing when a car came bumping down our road and stopped at our garden fence gate.

"See what they want and shove them on their way," said my wife. "We haven't got much daylight left." She peered through the kitchen window at the car, blinked, rubbed her eyes, and peered again. She said uncertainly: "It looks like — no! Can't be." I went out to the car.

"Anything I can do for you?" I asked the two men in the front seat. Then I recognized them. One of them was about my age, a wiry lad in a T-shirt. The other man was plump and graying and ministerial, but jolly. They were unmistakable; they had looked out at me — one scowling, the other smiling — from a hundred book ads. It was almost incredible that they knew each other, but there they were sharing a car.

I greeted them by name and said: "This is odd. I happen to be a writer myself. I've never shared the best-seller list with you two, but — "

The plump ministerial man tuttutted. "You are thinking negatively," he chided me. "Think of what you *have* accomplished. You own this lovely home, the valuation of which has just been raised two thousand dollars due entirely to the hard work and frugality of you and your lovely wife; you give innocent pleasure to thousands with your clever novels; you help to keep the good local merchants going with your patronage. Not least, you have fought for your country in the wars and you support it with your taxes."

The man in the T-shirt said raspily: "Even if you didn't have the dough to settle in full on April fifteenth and will have to pay six percent per month interest on the unpaid balance when and if you ever do pay it, you poor shnook."

The plump man said, distressed: "Please, Michael — you are not thinking positively. This is neither the time nor the place — "

"What's going on?" I demanded. Because I hadn't even told my *wife* I'd been a little short on the '55 federal tax.

"Let's go inna house," said the T-shirted man. He got out of the car, brushed my gate open, and walked coolly down the path to the kitchen door. The plump man followed, sniffing our rose-scented garden air appreciatively, and I came last of all, on wobbly legs.

When we filed in my wife said: "My God. It *is* them."

The man in the T-shirt said: "Hiya, babe," and stared at her breasts. The plump man said: "May I compliment you, my dear, for a splendid rose garden. Quite unusual for this altitude."

"Thanks," she said faintly, beginning to rally. "But it's quite easy when your neighbors keep horses."

"Haw!" snorted the man in the T-shirt. "That's the stuff, babe. You grow roses like I write books. Give 'em plenty of — "

"Michael!" said the plump man.

"*Look,* you," my wife said to me. "Would you mind telling me what this is all about? I never knew you knew Dr. — "

"I don't," I said helplessly. "They seem to want to talk to me."

"Let us adjourn to your *sanctum sanctorum,*" said the plump man archly, and we went upstairs. The T-shirted man sat on the couch, the plump fellow sat in the club chair, and I collapsed on the swivel chair in front of the typewriter. "Drink, anybody?" I asked, wanting one myself. "Sherry, brandy, rye, straight angostura?"

"Never touch the stinking stuff," grunted the man in the T-shirt.

"I would enjoy a nip of brandy," said the big man. We each had one straight, no chasers, and he got down to business with: "I suppose you have discovered The Diagonal Relationship?"

I thought about The Answer, and decided that The Diagonal Relationship would be a very good name for it too. "Yes," I said. "I guess I have. Have you?"

"I have. So has Michael here. So have one thousand seven hundred and twenty-four writers. If you'd like to know who they are, pick the one thousand seven hundred and twenty-four top-income men of the ten thousand free-lance writers in this country and you have your men. The Diagonal Relationship is discovered on an average of three times a year by rising writers."

"Writers," I said. "Good God, why *writers*? Why not economists, psychologists, mathematicians — *real* thinkers?"

He said: "A writer's mind is an awesome thing, Corwin. What went into your discovery of The Diagonal Relationship?"

I thought a bit. "I'm doing a Civil War thing about Burnside's Bomb," I said, "and I realized that Grant could have sent in fresh troops but didn't because Halleck used to drive him crazy by telegraphic masterminding of his campaigns. That's a special case of The Answer — as I call it. Then I got some data on medieval attitudes toward personal astrology out of a book on ancient China I'm reading. Another special case. And there's a joke the monks used to write at the end of a long manuscript-copying job. Liddell Hart's theory of strategy is about half of the general military case of The Answer. The merchandizing special case shows clearly in a catalogue I have from a Chicago store that specializes in selling strange clothes to bop-crazed Negroes. They all add up to the general expression, and that's that."

He was nodding. "Many, many combinations add up to The Diagonal Relationship," he said. "But only a writer cuts across sufficient fields, exposes himself to sufficient apparently unrelated facts. Only a writer has wide-open associational channels capable of bridging the gap between astrology and, ah, 'bop.' We write in our different idioms" — he smiled at the T-shirted man — "but we are writers all. Wide-ranging, omnivorous for data, equipped with superior powers of association which we constantly exercise."

"Well," I asked logically enough, "why on earth haven't you published The Diagonal Relationship? Are you here to keep me from publishing it?"

"We're a power group," said the plump man apologetically. "We have a vested interest in things as they are. Think about what The Diagonal Relationship would do to writers, Corwin."

"Sure," I said, and thought about it. "Judas Priest!" I said after a couple of minutes. He was nodding again. He said: "Yes. The Diagonal Relationship, if generally promulgated, would work out to approximate equality of income for all, with incentive pay only for really hard and dangerous work. Writing would be regarded as pretty much its own reward."

"That's the way it looks," I said. "One-year copyright, after all . . ."

[*Here occurs the first hiatus in the Corwin Papers. I suspect that three or four are missing. The preceding and following papers, incidentally, come from a batch of six gross of fortune cookies which I purchased from the Hip Sing Restaurant Provision Company of New York City during the course of my investigations. The reader no doubt will wonder why I was unable to determine the source of the cookies themselves and was forced to buy them from middlemen. Apparently the reason is the fantastic one that by chance I was wearing a white shirt, dark tie, and double-breasted blue serge suit when I attempted to question the proprietor of the Hip Sing Company. I learned too late that this is just about the unofficial uniform of U.S. Treasury and Justice Department agents and that I was immediately taken to be such an agent. "You T-man," said Mr. Hip tolerantly, "you get cou't ohdah, I show you books. Keep ve'y nice books, all in Chinese cha'ctahs." After that gambit he would answer me only in Chinese. How he did it I have no idea, but apparently within days every Chinese produce dealer in the United States and Canada had been notified that there was a new T-man named Kornbluth on the prowl. As a last resort I called on the New York City office of the Treasury Department Field Investigations*]

Unit in an attempt to obtain what might be called un-identification papers.
There I was assured by Mr. Gershon O'Brien, their Chinese specialist, that my
errand was hopeless since the motto of Mr. Hip and his colleagues invariably
was "Safety First." To make matters worse, as I left his office I was greeted with
a polite smile from a Chinese lad whom I recognized as Mr. Hip's bookkeeper.
CMK]

"So you see," he went on as if he had just stated a major and a minor
premise, "we watch the writers, the real ones, through private detective agen-
cies which alert us when the first teaser appears in a newspaper or on a
broadcast or in local gossip. There's always the teaser, Corwin, the rattle before
the strike. We writers are like that. We've been watching you for three years
now, and to be perfectly frank I've lost a few dollars wagered on you. In my
opinion you're a year late."

"What's the proposition?" I asked numbly.

He shrugged. "You get to be a best seller. We review your books, you review
ours. We tell your publisher: 'Corwin's hot — promote him. Advertise him.'
And he does, because we're good properties and he doesn't want to annoy us.
You want Hollywood? It can be arranged. Lots of us out there. In short, you
become rich like us and all you have to do is keep quiet about The Diagonal
Relationship. You haven't told your wife, by the way?"

"I wanted to surprise her," I said.

He smiled. "They always do. Writers! Well, young man, what do you say?"

It had grown dark. From the couch came a raspy voice: "You heard what
the doc said about the ones that throw in with us. I'm here to tell you that
we got provisions for the ones that don't."

I laughed at him.

"One of those guys," he said flatly.

"Surely a borderline case, Michael?" said the plump man. "So many of them
are."

If I'd been thinking straight I would have realized that "borderline case"
did not mean "undecided" to them; it meant "danger — immediate action!"

They took it. The plump man, who was also a fairly big man, flung his arms
around me, and the wiry one approached in the gloom. I yelled something
when I felt a hypodermic stab my arm. Then I went numb and stupid.

My wife came running up the stairs. "What's going on?" she demanded. I
saw her heading for the curtain behind which we keep an aged hair-trigger
Marlin .38 rifle. There was nothing wrong with her guts, but they attacked her
where courage doesn't count. I croaked her name a couple of times and heard
the plump man say gently, with great concern: "I'm afraid your husband needs
. . . help." She turned from the curtain, her eyes wide. He had struck subtly
and knowingly; there is probably not one writer's wife who does not suspect
her husband is a potential psychotic.

"Dear — " she said to me as I stood there paralyzed.

He went on: "Michael and I dropped in because we both admire your husband's work; we were surprised and distressed to find his conversation so . . . disconnected. My dear, as you must know, I have some experience through my pastorate with psychotherapy. Have you ever — forgive my bluntness — had doubts about his sanity?"

"Dear, what's the matter?" she asked me anxiously. I just stood there, staring. God knows what they injected me with, but its effect was to cloud my mind, render all activity impossible, send my thoughts spinning after their tails. I was insane. [*This incident, seemingly the least plausible part of Corwin's story, actually stands up better than most of the narrative to one familiar with recent advances in biochemistry. Corwin could have been injected with lysergic acid, or with protein extracts from the blood of psychotics. It is a matter of cold laboratory fact that such injections produce temporary psychosis in the patient. Indeed, it is on such experimental psychoses that the new tranquilizer drugs are developed and tested. CMK*]

To herself she said aloud, dully: "Well, it's finally come. Christmas when I burned the turkey and he wouldn't speak to me for a week. The way he drummed his fingers when I talked. All his little crackpot ways — how he has to stay at the Waldorf but I have to cut his hair and save a dollar. I hoped it was just the rotten weather and cabin fever. I hoped when spring came — " She began to sob. The plump man comforted her like a father. I just stood there, staring and waiting. And eventually Mickey glided up in the dark and gave her a needleful too and

[*Here occurs an aggravating and important hiatus. One can only guess that Corwin and his wife were loaded into the car, driven — Somewhere, separated, and separately, under false names, committed to different mental institutions. I have recently learned to my dismay that there are states which require only the barest sort of licensing to operate such institutions. One state inspector of hospitals even wrote to me in these words: ". . . no doubt there are some places in our state which are not even licensed, but we have never made any effort to close them and I cannot recall any statute making such operation illegal. We are not a wealthy state like you up North and some care for these unfortunates is better than none, is our viewpoint here . . ." CMK*]

three months. Their injections last a week. There's always somebody to give me another. You know what mental hospital attendants are like: an easy bribe. But they'd be better advised to bribe a higher type, like a male nurse, because my attendant with the special needle for me is off on a drunk. My insanity wore off this morning and I've been writing in my room ever since. A quick trip up and down the corridor collected the cigarette papers and a tiny ball-point pen from some breakfast-food premium gadget. I think my best bet is to slip these papers out in the batch of Chinese fortune cookies they're doing in the bakery. Occupational therapy, this is called. My own o.t. is shoveling coal when I'm under the needle. Well, enough of this. I shall write down The Answer, slip down to the bakery, deal out the cigarette papers into the waiting rounds of cookie dough, crimp them over, and return to my room. Doubtless my attendant will be back by then and I'll get another shot from him. I shall not struggle; I can only wait.

THE ANSWER: HUMAN BEINGS RAISED TO SPEAK AN INDO-IRANIAN LANGUAGE SUCH AS ENGLISH HAVE THE FOLLOWING IN

[*That is the end of the last of the Corwin Papers I have been able to locate. It should be superfluous to urge all readers to examine carefully any fortune cookie slips they may encounter. The next one you break open may contain what my poor friend believed, or believes, to be a great message to mankind. He may be right. His tale is a wild one but it is consistent. And it embodies the only reasonable explanation I have ever seen for the presence of certain books on the best-seller list. CMK*]

The Several Murders
of Roger Ackroyd

BARRY MALZBERG

Science fiction writers are only too prone to write stories that reflect favorably on one aspect or another of science fiction writer-dom. Either we are particularly brilliant or particularly important or particularly vulnerable to disaster — particularly something. In this case, we have the mystery writer who manages to get the world by the throat. Perhaps not uncoincidentally, Barry has also written mysteries.

Dear Mr. Ackroyd:

Your application for the position of mysterist has been carefully reviewed in these offices.

While there are many impressive aspects to your credentials and while we fully recognize your qualifications for the position of mysterist, I regret to inform you that the very large number of highly qualified applications for the few openings which do exist means that we must disappoint many fine candidates such as yourself.

Rest assured that this decision is not intended as a commentary upon your abilities but only upon the very severe competition encountered during the current application period.

Truly do we wish you success in all future endeavors.

Regretfully,

A. HASTINGS/for the Bank

Dear Mr. Hastings:

I have received your outrageous letter rejecting me for the position of mysterist. I demand more than a form reply!

If you have truly reviewed my application you know that I have dedicated my life to achieving this position and am *completely* qualified. I know the major and minor variations of the locked room murder, I know the eighteen disguising substances for strychnine, to say nothing of the management of concealed relationships and the question of Inherited Familial Madness. I know of the Misdirected Clue and the peculiar properties of the forsythia root; not unknown to me are the engineering basis and exhilarating qualities of antique vehicles known as "cars." In short I know everything that a mysterist must know in order to qualify for the Bank.

Under these circumstances, I refuse to accept your bland and evasive reply. I have a right to know: Why are you turning me down? Once I am admitted to the Bank I am *positive* that I can find a huge audience which wants something more than the careless and unmotivated trash that your current "mysterists," and I dignify them by use of that name, are propounding. This, then, is to your benefit as well as mine.

Why have I been rejected?

Will you reconsider?

> Hopefully,
> ROGER ACKROYD

Dear Mr. Ackroyd:

Because we received several thousand applications, many of them highly qualified, for a mere twenty-five vacancies for mysterists in the Interplanetary Program Entertainment Division for the period commencing in Fourthmonth 2312, it was necessary for us to use a form reply. This letter, however, is personally dictated.

I am truly sorry that you are taking rejection so unpleasantly. No insult was intended nor were aspersions cast upon your scholarly command of the mysterist form, which does indeed appear excellent.

Your application was carefully reviewed. In many ways you have talent and promise is shown. But because of extraordinarily heavy competition for the limited number of banks, applications even more qualified than your own were rejected. As you know, the majority of the Interplanetary Program Entertainment Division channels are devoted to westernists, sexualists, gothickings, and science-fictionists with only a relatively few number of mysterists to accommodate the small audience still sympathetic to that form. At present all twenty-five vacancies have been filled by superb mysterists, and we anticipate few openings in the foreseeable future.

I can, of course, appreciate your dismay. A career to which you have dedicated yourself seems now closed. I remind you, however, that a man of your obvious intelligence and scholarship might do well in some of the other branches offering current vacancies. For instance and for example we have at this time an opening for a science-fictionist specializing in Venerian counter-plot and Saturnian struggle.

If you could familiarize yourself with extant materials on the subject and would like to make formal application we would be pleased to forward proper forms. Just refer to this letter.

Sincerely,

A. HASTINGS/for the Bank

Dear Mr. Hastings:

I don't *want* to be a science-fictionist specializing in Venerian counterplot. We have *enough* science-fictionists, westernists, sexualists, and gothickings. They are all dead forms. The audience will wise up to that sooner or later and all go away and where will your Interplanetary Program Entertainment Division be then?

What they are seeking is fine new mysterists with new approaches. Such as myself.

I did not prepare myself for years in order to become a hack churning out visuals of the slime jungles. I am a dreamer, one who looks beyond the technological barriers of our civilization and understands the human pain and complication within, complication and pain which can only be understood by the mysterist who knows of the unspeakable human heart.

The Interplanetary Program Entertainment Division was, in fact, originally conceived for people such as myself, the great mysterists who would bring a large audience ever closer to the barriers of human experience. Hundreds of years ago mysterists were responsible for all of your success. (I have read some history.) Only much later did the science-fictionists and the rest move in to make a wonderful entertainment device a dull nuisance predicated upon easy shocks drained of intellection. The audience was corrupted by these people. But now a wind is rising. It is time for the mysterists to return to their original and honored place.

You would insult me by offering me Venerian combat science-fictionist! I tell you, you people have no sense of the dream. You have no heart. I have devoted my life to mastery of the craft: I am a good mysterist on the verge of becoming *great.*

I demand a supervisor.

Bitterly,

ROGER ACKROYD

Dear Mr. Ackroyd:

I am a Supervisor. All applications must be reviewed by a Supervisor before final disposition. Complaints such as yours reach even higher; I am writing you on advice. I am highly trained and skilled and I know the centuries-long history of the International Division much better than you ever will.

In fact, I find your communication quite offensive.

I fear that we have already reached the logical terminus of our correspondence. There is nothing more to be done. Your application for mysterist

— a position for which there is small audience and little demand — was carefully reviewed in the light of its relation to many other applications. Although your credentials were praiseworthy they were surpassed by candidates more qualified. You were, therefore, rejected. Mysterist is a small but useful category and we respect its form and your dedication, but the audience today is quite limited. We are not mindless bureaucrats here, but on the other hand we accept the fact that the Division must give the audience what it wants rather than what we think it *should* want, and gothica and science-fictionists are what most people like today. We are here to make people happy, to give them what they want. We leave uplift to our very competent Interplanetary Education Division and they leave entertainment to us.

There is a tiny demand for mysterists.

If you do not wish to be a science-fictionist specializing in Venerian counterplot or to apply for other fine positions available as westernist, it must be your decision. We recognize your abilities and problems but you must recognize ours. You can give up and go to work.

A. HASTINGS/for the Bank

Dear Mr. Hastings:

I choose to ignore your offensive communication and give you one last benefit of the doubt. This is your last chance. May I be a mysterist? Do send me the proper authorization.

Reasonably,
ROGER ACKROYD

Dear Roger Ackroyd:

Mr. A. Hastings, Supervisor for the Eastern Application Division, Interplanetary Programming and Entertainment Division, has asked me to respond to your communication.

There are no vacancies for mysterist.

M. MALLOWAN/Over-Supervisor

Dear Hastings and Mallowan:

I gave you every chance.

You were warned.

As I did not see fit to tell you until now (having as well an excellent command of the *deus-ex*) I have a close friend who is *already* a mysterist although not as good as myself and who, for certain obscure personal reasons, owes me several favors.

He has given me tapes; I have completed them. I have turned them over to him.

He has done with them the requisite.

I am already on the banks!

My mysteries are already available on the banks and I think that you will find what the reaction is very soon. Then you will realize your folly. Then you will realize that Interplanetary Programming, which I sought initially in the most humble manner and which could have had me in their employ on the easiest terms is now at my mercy. Completely at my mercy!

You are bent, as the science-fictionists say, completely to my will!

It did not have to be this way, you know. You could have judged my application fairly and we could have worked together well. Now you shall pay a Much Higher Price.

Wait and see.

Triumphantly,
ROGER ACKROYD

DIVISION: SEND ENDING ABC MURDERS. TAPE MYSTERIOUSLY MISSING. SEND AT ONCE. DEMAND THIS.

Interplanetary STOP How did they get off that island QUERY Where is final material QUERY I insist upon an answer at once STOP△△ +

DIVISION — THIRD REPRESENTATIVE DIVISION EASTERN DISTRICT DEMANDS KNOWLEDGE WHY POIROT DIED — REPEAT — WHY DID HE DIE QUESTION MARK NO FURTHER EXCUSES EXCLAMATION POINT COMMITTEE LICENSES PREPARED FULL ASSEMBLE TOMORROW FOR INVESTIGATION UNLESS MATERIALS SUPPLIED EXCLAMATION POINT

DIVISION: WHO KILLED THE INSPECTOR? ENDING MISSING. REPLY AT ONCE. MCGINNITY FOR THE PRESIDENT.

DIVISION — FIFTY-SEVEN MILLION NOW DEMAND . . .

The Critique
of Impure Reason

POUL ANDERSON

It's peculiar how often other science fiction writers who use robots insert a veiled reference to me. Or, on occasion, a not-so-veiled reference. By an odd coincidence, Anderson's robot is IZK-99 and is referred to — you guessed it — as Izaak. (The misspelling is a trivial disguise.) Oddly enough (for a story written in 1962), the heroine is called Janet. Add to that the deliciously snide remarks against critics, and we would find it more than flesh and blood could bear not to include the story in this anthology.

THE ROBOT ENTERED so quietly, for all his bulk, that Felix Tunny didn't hear. Bent over his desk, the man was first aware of the intruder when a shadow came between him and the fluoroceil. Then a last footfall quivered the floor, a vibration that went through Tunny's chair and into his bones. He whirled, choking on a breath, and saw the blue-black shape like a cliff above him. Eight feet up, the robot's eyes glowed angry crimson in a faceless helmet of a head.

A voice like a great gong reverberated through the office: "My, but you look silly."

"What the devil are you doing?" Tunny yelped.

"Wandering about," said Robot IZK-99 airily. "Hither and yon, yon and hither. Observing life. How deliciously right Brochet is!"

"Huh?" said Tunny. The fog of data, estimates, and increasingly frantic calculations was only slowly clearing from his head.

IZK-99 extended an enormous hand to exhibit a book. Tunny read *The Straw and the Bean: A Novel of Modern Youth by Truman Brochet* on the front. The back of the dust jacket was occupied by a colorpic of the author, who had bangs and delicate lips. Deftly, the robot flipped the book open and read aloud:

"Worms," she said, "that's what they are, worms, that's what we-uns all are, Billy Chile, worms that grew a spine an' a brain way back in the Obscene or the Messyzoic or whenever it was." Even in her sadnesses Ella Mae must always make her said little jokes, which saddened me still more on this day of sad rain and dying magnolia blossoms. "We don't want them," she said. "Backbones an' brains, I mean, honey. They make us stiff an' topheavy, so we can't lie down no more an' be jus' nothin' ay-tall but worms."

"Take off your clothes," I yawned.

"What has that got to do with anything?" Tunny asked.

"If you do not understand," said IZK-99 coldly, "there is no use in discussing it with you. I recommend that you read Arnold Roach's penetrating critical essay on this book. It appeared in the last issue of *Pierce, Arrow! The Magazine of Penetrating Criticism.* He devotes four pages to analyzing the various levels of meaning in that exchange between Ella Mae and Billy Chile."

"Ooh," Tunny moaned. "Isn't it enough I've got a hangover, a job collapsing under me because of you, and a fight with my girl, but you have to mention that rag?"

"How vulgar you are. It comes from watching stereovision." The robot sat down in a chair, which creaked alarmingly under his weight, crossed his legs, and leafed through his book. The other hand lifted a rose to his chemosensor. "Exquisite," he murmured.

"You don't imagine I'd sink to reading what they call fiction these days, do you?" Tunny sneered, with a feeble hope of humiliating him into going to work. "Piddling little experiments in the technique of describing more and more complicated ways to feel sorry for yourself — What kind of entertainment is that for a man?"

"You simply do not appreciate the human condition," said the robot.

"Hah! Do you think you do, you conceited hunk of animated tin?"

"Yes, I believe so, thanks to my study of the authors, poets, and critics who devote their lives to the exploration and description of man. Your Miss Forelle is a noble soul. Ever since I looked upon my first copy of that exquisitely sensitive literary quarterly she edits, I have failed to understand what she sees in you. To be sure," IZK-99 mused, "the relationship is not unlike that between the nun and the Diesel engine in *Regret For Two Doves,* but still . . . At any rate, if Miss Forelle has finally told you to go soak your censored head in expurgated wastes and then put the unprintable thing in an improbable place, I for one heartily approve."

Tunny, who was no mama's boy — he had worked his way through college as a whale herder and bossed construction gangs on Mars — was so appalled by the robot's language that he could only whisper, "She did not. She said nothing of the sort."

"I did not mean it literally," IZK-99 explained. "I was only quoting the renunciation scene in *Gently Come Twilight*. By Stichling, you know — almost as sensitive a writer as Brochet."

Tunny clenched fists and teeth and battled a wild desire to pull the robot apart, plate by plate and transistor by transistor. He couldn't, of course. He was a big blond young man with a homely, candid face; his shoulders strained his blouse, and the legs coming out of his shorts were thickly muscular; but robots had steelloy frames and ultrapowered energizers. Besides, though his position as chief estimator gave him considerable authority in Planetary Developments, Inc., the company wouldn't let him destroy a machine which had cost several million dollars. Even when the machine blandly refused to work and spent its time loafing around the plant, reading, brooding, and denouncing the crass bourgeois mentality of the staff.

Slowly, Tunny mastered his temper. He'd recently thought of a new approach to the problem; might as well try it now. He leaned forward. "Look, Izaak," he said in the mildest tone he could manage, "have you ever considered that we need you? That the whole human race needs you?"

"The race needs love, to be sure," said the robot, "which I am prepared to offer; but I expect that the usual impossibility of communication will entangle us in the typical ironic loneliness."

"No, *no*, NO — um — that is, the human race needs those minerals that you can obtain for us. Earth's resources are dwindling. We can get most elements from the sea, but some are in such dilute concentration that it isn't economically feasible to extract them. In particular, there's rhenium. Absolutely vital in alloys and electronic parts that have to stand intense irradiation. It always was scarce, and now it's in such short supply that several key industries are in trouble. But on Mercury — "

"Spare me. I have heard all that *ad nauseam*. What importance have any such dead, impersonal, mass questions, contrasted to the suffering, isolated soul? No, it is useless to argue with me. My mind is made up. For the disastrous consequences of not being able to reach a firm decision, I refer you to the Freudian analyses of *Hamlet*."

"If you're interested in individuals," Tunny said, "you might consider me. I'm almost an ancestor of yours, God help me. I was the one who first suggested commissioning a humanoid robot with independent intelligence for the Mercury project. This company's whole program for the next five years is based on having you go. If you don't, I'll be out on my ear. And jobs are none too easy to come by. How's that for a suffering, isolated soul?"

"You are not capable of suffering," said Izaak. "You are much too coarse. Now do leave me to my novel." His glowing eyes returned to the book. He continued sniffing the rose.

Tunny's own gaze went back to the bescribbled papers which littered his desk, the result of days spent trying to calculate some way out of the corner into which Planetary Developments, Inc., had painted itself. There wasn't any way that he could find. The investment in Izaak was too great for a relatively small outfit like this. If the robot didn't get to work, and soon, the company would be well and thoroughly up Dutchman's Creek.

In his desperation Tunny had even looked again into the hoary old idea of remote-controlled mining. No go — not on Mercury, where the nearby Sun flooded every tele-device with enough heat and radiation to assure a fifty percent chance of breakdown in twenty-four hours. It had been rare luck that the rhenium deposits were found at all, by a chemotrac sent from the underground base. To mine them, there must be a creature with senses, hands, and intelligence, present on the spot, to make decisions and repair machinery as the need arose. Not a human; no rad screen could long keep a man alive under that solar bombardment. The high-acceleration flight to base, and home again when their hitch was up, in heavily shielded and screened spaceships, gave the base personnel as much exposure as the Industrial Safety Board allowed per lifetime. The miner had to be a robot.

Only the robot refused the task. There was no way, either legal or practical, to make him take it against his will. Tunny laid a hand on his forehead. No wonder he'd worried himself close to the blowup point, until last night he quarreled with Janet and got hyperbolically drunk. Which had solved nothing.

The phone buzzed on his desk. He punched Accept. The face of William Barsch, executive vice-president, leaped into the screen, round, red, and raging.

"Tunny!" he bellowed.

"I-yi-yi! — I mean hello, sir." The engineer offered a weak smile.

"Don't hello me, you glue-brained idiot! When is that robot taking off?"

"Never," said Izaak. At his electronic reading speed, he had finished the novel and now rose from his chair to look over Tunny's shoulder.

"You're fired!" Barsch howled. "Both of you!"

"I hardly consider myself hired in the first place," Izaak said loftily. "Your economic threat holds no terrors. My energizer is charged for fifty years of normal use, after which I can finance a recharge by taking a temporary position. It would be interesting to go on the road at that," he went on thoughtfully, "like those people in that old book the Library of Congress reprostatted for me. Yes, one might indeed find satori in going, man, going, never mind where, never mind why — "

"You wouldn't find much nowadays," Tunny retorted. "Board a transcontinental tube at random, and where does it get you? Wherever its schedule says. The bums aren't seeking enlightenment, they're sitting around on their citizens' credit watching SteeVee." He wasn't paying much attention to his own words, being too occupied with wondering if Barsch was really serious this time.

"I gather as much," said Izaak, "although most contemporary novels and short stories employ more academic settings. What a decadent civilization this is: no poverty, no physical or mental disease, no wars, no revolutions, no beatniks!" His tone grew earnest. "Please understand me, gentlemen. I bear you no ill will. I despise you, of course, but in the most cordial fashion. It is not fear that keeps me on Earth — I am practically indestructible; not anticipated loneliness — I enjoy being unique; not any prospect of boredom in the usual sense — talent for the work you had in mind is engineered into me. No, it is the absolute insignificance of the job. Beyond the merely animal economic implications, rhenium has no meaning. Truman Brochet would never be aware the project was going on, let alone write a novel about it. Arnold Roach would not even mention it *en passant* in any critical essay on the state of the modern soul as reflected in the major modern novelists. Do you not see my position? Since I was manufactured, of necessity, with creative intelligence and a need to do my work right, I *must* do work I can respect."

"Such as what?" demanded Barsch.

"When I have read enough to feel that I understand the requirements of literary technique, I shall seek a position on the staff of some quarterly review. Or perhaps I shall teach. I may even try my hand at a subjectively oriented novel."

"Get out of this plant," Barsch ordered in a muted scream.

"Very well."

"No, wait!" cried Tunny. "Uh . . . Mr. Barsch didn't mean that. Stick around, Izaak. Go read a criticism or something."

"Thank you, I shall." The robot left the office, huge, gleaming, irresistible, and smelling his rose.

"Who do you think you are, you whelp, countermanding me?" Barsch snarled. "You're not only fired, I'll see to it that — "

"Please, sir," Tunny said. "I know this situation. I should. Been living with it for two weeks now, from its beginning. You may not realize that Izaak hasn't been outside this building since he was activated. Mostly he stays in a room assigned him. He gets his books and magazines and stuff by reprostat from the public libraries, or by pneumo from publishers and dealers. We have to pay him a salary, you know — he's legally a person — and he doesn't need to spend it on anything but reading matter."

"And you want to keep on giving him free rent and let him stroll around disrupting operations?"

"Well, at least he isn't picking up any further stimuli. At present we can predict his craziness. But let him walk loose in the city for a day or two, with a million totally new impressions blasting on his sensors, and God alone knows what conclusions he'll draw and how he'll react."

"Hm." Barsch's complexion lightened a bit. He gnawed his lip a while, then said in a more level voice: "Okay, Tunny, perhaps you aren't such a total incompetent. This mess may not be entirely your fault, or your girl friend's. Maybe I, or someone, should have issued a stricter directive about what he ought and ought not be exposed to for the first several days after activation."

You certainly should have, Tunny thought, but preserved a tactful silence.

"Nevertheless," Barsch scowled, "this fiasco is getting us in worse trouble every day. I've just come from lunch with Henry Lachs, the newsmagazine publisher. He told me that rumors about the situation have already begun to leak out. He'll sit on the story as long as he can, being a good friend of mine, but that won't be much longer. He can't let *Entropy* be scooped, and someone else is bound to get the story soon."

"Well, sir, I realize we don't want to be a laughingstock — "

"Worse than that. You know why our competitors haven't planned to tackle that rhenium mine. We had the robot idea first and got the jump on them. Once somebody's actually digging ore, he can get the exclusive franchise. But if they learn what's happened to us . . . well, Space Metals already has a humanoid contracted for. Half built, in fact. They intended to use him on Callisto, but Mercury would pay a lot better."

Tunny nodded sickly.

Barsch's tone dropped to an ominous purr. "Any ideas yet on how to change that clanking horror's so-called mind?"

"He doesn't clank, sir," Tunny corrected without forethought.

Barsch turned purple. "I don't give two squeals in hell whether he clanks or rattles or sings high soprano! I want results! I've got half our engineers busting their brains on the problem. But if you, yourself, personally, aren't the one who solves it, we're going to have a new chief estimator. Understand?" Before Tunny could explain that he understood much too well, the screen blanked.

He buried his face in his hands, but that didn't help either. The trouble was, he liked his job, in spite of drawbacks like Barsch. Also, while he wouldn't starve if he were fired, citizen's credit wasn't enough to support items he'd grown used to, such as a sailboat and a cabin in the Rockies, nor items he hoped to add to the list, such as Janet Forelle. Besides, he dreaded the chronic ennui of the unemployed.

He told himself to stop thinking and get busy on the conundrum — no, that wasn't what he meant either — Oh, fireballs! He was no use at this desk today. Especially remembering the angry words he and Janet had exchanged. He'd probably be no use anywhere until the quarrel was mended. At least a diplomatic mission would clear his head, possibly jolt his mind out of the rut in which it now wearily paced.

"Ooh," he said, visualizing his brain with a deep circular rut where there tramped a tiny replica of himself, bowed under a load of pig iron and shod with cleats. Hastily, he punched a button on his recep. "I've got to go out," he said. "Tell 'em I'll be back when."

The building hummed and murmured as he went down the hall. Open doorways showed offices, laboratories, control machines clicking away like Hottentots. Now and then he passed a human technie. Emerging on the fifth-story flange he took a dropshaft down to the third, where the northbound beltway ran. Gentle gusts blew upward in his face, for there was a gray February sky overhead and the municipal heating system had to radiate plenty of ergs. Lake Michigan, glimpsed through soaring gaily colored skyscrapers, looked the more cold by contrast. Tunny found a seat on the belt, ignoring the aimlessly riding mass of people around him, mostly unemployed. He stuffed his pipe and fumed smoke the whole distance to the University of Chicapolis.

Once there, he had to transfer several times and make his way through crowds younger, livelier, and more purposeful than those off campus. Education, he recalled reading, was the third largest industry in the world. He did read, whatever Izaak said — nonfiction, which retained a certain limited popularity; occasionally a novel, but none more recent than from fifty years ago. "I'm not prejudiced against what's being written nowadays," he had told Janet. "I just don't think it should be allowed to ride in the front ends of streetcars."

She missed his point, having a very limited acquaintance with mid-twentieth-century American history. "If your attitude isn't due to prejudice, that's even worse," she said. "Then you are congenitally unable to perceive the nuances of modern reality."

"Bah! I earn my money working with the nuances of modern reality: systems analyses, stress curves, and spaceship orbits. That's what ails fiction these days, and poetry. There's nothing left to write about that the belletrists think is important. The only sociological problem of any magnitude is mass boredom, and you can't squeeze much plot or interest out of that. So the stuff gets too, too precious for words — and stinks."

"Felix, you can't say that!"

"Can and do, sweetheart. Naturally, economics enters into the equation too. On the one hand, for the past hundred years movies, television, and now SteeVee have been crowding the printed word out of the public eye. (Hey, what a gorgeous metaphor!) Apart from some nonfiction magazines, publishing isn't a commercial enterprise any longer. And on the other hand, in a society as rich as ours, a limited amount of publishing remains feasible: endowed by universities or foundations or individual vanity or these authors' associations that have sprung up in the past decade. Only it doesn't try to be popular entertainment, it's abandoned that field entirely to SteeVee and become nothing but an academic mutual admiration society."

"Nonsense! Let me show you Scomber's critical essay on Tench. He simply tears the man to pieces."

"Yeah, I know. One-upmanship is part of the game too. The whole point is, though, that this mental inbreeding — no, not even that: mental — uh, I better skip *that* metaphor — anyhow, it never has and never will produce anything worth the time of a healthy human being."

"Oh, so I'm not a healthy human being?"

"I didn't mean that. You know I didn't. I only meant, well, you know . . . the great literature always was based on wide appeal — Sophocles, Shakespeare, Dickens, Mark Twain — "

But the fat was irretrievably in the fire. One thing led at high speed to another, until Tunny stormed out or was thrown out — he still wasn't sure which — and went to earth in the Whirling Comet Bar.

It wasn't that Janet was stuffy, he reminded himself as he approached the looming mass of the English building. She was cute as a kitten, shared his pleasure in sailboats and square dancing and low-life beer joints and most other things; also, she had brains, and their arguments were usually spirited but great mutual fun. They had dealt with less personal topics than last night's debate, though. Janet, a poet's daughter and a departmental secretary, took her magazine very seriously. He hadn't realized how seriously.

The beltway reached his goal. Tunny knocked out his pipe and stepped across the deceleration strips to the flange. The dropshaft lifted him to the fiftieth floor, where university publications had their offices. There was more human activity here than most places. Writing and editing remained people functions, however thoroughly automated printing and binding were. In spite of his purpose, Tunny walked slowly down the hall, observing with pleasure the earnest young coeds in their brief bright skirts and blouses. With less pleasure he noted the earnest young men. There wasn't much about them to suggest soldierly Aeschylus or roistering Marlowe or seagoing Melville or razzmatazz Mencken; they tended to be pale, long-haired, and ever so concerned with the symbolic import of a deliberately omitted comma.

The door marked *Pierce, Arrow!* opened for him and he entered a small shabby office heaped with papers, books, microspools, and unsold copies of the magazine. Janet sat at the desk behind a manual typer and a stack of galleys. She was small herself, pert, extremely well engineered, with dark wavy hair that fell to her shoulders and big eyes the color of the Gulf Stream. Tunny paused and gulped. His heart began to knock.

"Hi," he said after a minute.

She looked up. "What — Felix!"

"I, uh, uh, I'm sorry about yesterday," he said.

"Oh, darling. Do you think I'm not? I was going to come to you." She did so, with results that were satisfactory to both parties concerned, however sickening they might have been to an outside observer.

After quite a long while, Tunny found himself in a chair with Janet on his lap. She snuggled against him. He stroked her hair and murmured thoughtfully: "Well, I suppose the trouble was, each suddenly realized how dead set on his own odd quirk the other one is. But we can live with the difference between us, huh?"

"Surely," Janet sighed. "And then too, I didn't stop to think how worried you were, that robot and everything, and the whole miserable business my fault."

"Lord, no. How could you have predicted what'd happen? If anyone is responsible, I am. I took you there and could have warned you. But I didn't know either. Perhaps nobody would have known. Izaak's kind of robot isn't too well understood as yet. So few have been built, there's so little need for them."

"I still don't quite grasp the situation. Just because I talked to him for an hour or two — poor creature, he was so eager and enthusiastic — and then sent him some books and — "

"That's precisely it. Izaak had been activated only a few days before. Most of his knowledge was built right into him, so to speak, but there was also the matter of . . . well, psychological stabilization. Until the end of the indoctrination course, which is designed to fix his personality in the desired pattern, a humanoid robot is extremely susceptible to new impressions. Like a human baby. Or perhaps a closer analogy would be imprinting in some birds: Present a fledgling with almost any object at a certain critical stage in its life, and it'll decide that object is its mother and follow the thing around everywhere. I never imagined, though, that modern literary criticism could affect a robot that way. It seemed so alien to everything he was made for. What I overlooked, I see now, was the fact that Izaak's fully humanoid. He isn't meant to be programmed, but has a free intelligence. Evidently freer than anyone suspected."

"Is there no way to cure him?"

"Not that I know of. His builders told me that trying to wipe the synapse patterns would ruin the whole brain. Besides, he doesn't want to be cured, and he has most of the legal rights of a citizen. We can't compel him."

"I do so wish I could do something. Can this really cost you your job?"

" 'Fraid so. I'll fight to keep it, but — "

"Well," Janet said, "we'll still have my salary."

"Nothing doing. No wife is going to support me."

"Come, come. How medieval can a man get?"

"Plenty," he said. She tried to argue, but he stopped her in the most pleasant and effective manner. Some time went by. Eventually, with a small gasp, she looked at the clock.

"Heavens! I'm supposed to be at work this minute. I don't want to get myself fired, do I?" She bounced to her feet, a sight which slightly compensated for her departing his lap, smoothed her hair, kissed him again, and sped out the door.

Tunny remained seated. He didn't want to go anywhere, least of all home. Bachelor apartments were okay in their place, but after a certain point in a man's life they got damn cheerless. He fumbled out his pipe and started it again.

Janet was such a sweet kid, he thought. Bright too. Her preoccupation with these latter-day word games actually did her credit; she wasn't content to stay in the dusty files of books written centuries ago, and word games were the only ones in town. Given a genuine literary milieu, she might well have accomplished great things, instead of fooling around with — what was the latest guff? Tunny got up and wandered over to her desk. He glanced at the galleys. Something by Arnold Roach.

— the tense, almost fetally contracted structure of this story, exquisitely balanced in the ebb and flow of words forming and dissolving images like the interplay of ripples in water, marks an important new advance in the tradition of Arapaima as modified by the school of Barbel. Nevertheless it is necessary to make the assertion that a flawed tertiary symbolism exists, in that the connotations of the primary word in the long quotation from Pollack which opens the third of the eleven cantos into which the story is divided, are not, as the author thinks, so much negative as —

"Yingle, yingle, yingle," Tunny muttered. "And they say engineers can't write decent English. If I couldn't do better than that with one cerebral hemisphere tied behind my back, I'd — "

At which point he stopped cold and stared into space with a mountingly wild surmise. His jaw fell. So did his pipe. He didn't notice.

Five minutes later he exploded into action.

Four hours later, her secretarial stint through for the day, Janet returned to do some more proofreading. As the door opened, she reeled. The air was nearly unbreathable. Through a blue haze she could barely see her man, grimy, disheveled, smoking volcanically, hunched over her typer and slamming away at the keys.

"What off Earth!" she exclaimed.

"One more minute, sweetheart," Tunny said. Actually he spent 11.3 more minutes by the clock, agonizing over his last few sentences. Then he ripped the sheet out, threw it on a stack of others, and handed her the mess. "Read that."

"When my eyes have stopped smarting," Janet coughed. She had turned the air 'fresher on full blast and seated herself on the edge of a chair to wait. Despite her reply, she took the manuscript. But she read the several thousand words with a puzzlement that grew and grew. At the end, she laid the papers slowly down and asked, "Is this some kind of joke?"

"I hope not," said Tunny fervently.

"But — "

"Your next issue is due out when? In two weeks? Could you advance publication, and include this?"

"What? No, certainly I can't. That is, darling, I have to reject so many real pieces merely for lack of space, that it breaks my heart and . . . and I've got obligations to them, they trust me — "

"So." Tunny rubbed his chin. "What do you think of my essay? As a pure bit of writing."

"Oh . . . hm . . . well, it's clear and forceful, but naturally the technicalities of criticism — "

"Okay. You revise it, working in the necessary poop. Also, choose a suitable collection of your better rejects, enough to make up a nice issue. Those characters will see print after all." While Janet stared with bewildered though lovely blue eyes, Tunny stabbed out numbers on the phone.

"Yes, I want to talk with Mr. Barsch. No, I don't give a neutrino whether he's in conference or not. You tell him Felix Tunny may have the answer to the robot problem . . . Hello, boss. Look, I've got an idea. Won't even cost very much. Can you get hold of a printing plant tonight? You know, someplace where they can run off a few copies of a small one-shot magazine? . . . Sure it's short notice. But didn't you say Henry Lachs is a friend of yours? Well, presume on his friendship — "

Having switched off, Tunny whirled about, grabbed Janet in his arms, and shouted, "Let's go!"

"Where?" she inquired, not unreasonably.

The pneumo went *whir-ping!* and tossed several items onto the mail shelf. IZK-99 finished reading *Neo-Babbitt: The Entrepreneur as Futility Symbol in Modern Literature,* crossed his room with one stride, and went swiftly through the envelopes. The usual two or three crank letters and requests for autographs — any fully humanoid robot was news — plus a circular advertising metal polish and . . . wait . . . a magazine. Clipped to this was a note bearing the letterhead of the Mañana Literary Society. " — new authors' association . . . foundation-sponsored quarterly review . . . sample copies to a few persons of taste and discrimination who we feel are potential subscribers . . ." The format had a limp dignity, with a plain cover reading:

<pre>
        p   Volume One
        i   Number One
        p
        e
        t
        t
        e
the journal of
analytical criticism
</pre>

Excited and vastly flattered, IZK-99 read it on the spot, in 148 seconds: so fast that he did a double take and stood for a time lost in astonishment. The magazine's contents had otherwise been standard stuff, but this one long article — Slowly, very carefully, he turned back to it and reread:

Thunder Beyond Venus, by Charles Pilchard, Wisdom Press (Newer York, 2026), 214 pp., UWF $6.50.

Reviewed by Pierre Hareng

Dept. of English, Miskatonic University

For many years I have been analyzing, dissecting, and evaluating with the best of them, and it has indeed been a noble work. Yet everything has its limits. There comes to each of us a bump, as Poorboy so poignantly says in *Not Soft Is the Rock.* Suddenly a new planet swims into our ken, a new world is opened, a new element is discovered, and we stand with tools in our hands which are not merely inadequate to the task, but irrelevant. Like those fortunate readers who were there at the moment when Joyce invented the stream of consciousness, when Kafka plunged so gladly into the symbolism of absolute nightmare, when Faulkner delineated the artistic beauty of the humble corncob, when Durrell abolished the stream of consciousness, we too are suddenly crossing the threshold of revolution.

Charles Pilchard has not hitherto been heard from. The intimate details of his biography, the demonstration of the point-by-point relationship of these details to his work, will furnish material for generations of scholarship. Today, though, we are confronted with the event itself. For *Thunder Beyond Venus* is indeed an event, which rocks the mind and shakes the emotions and yet, at the same time, embodies a touch so sure, an artistry so consummate, that even Brochet has not painted a finer miniature.

The superficial skeleton is almost scornfully simple. It is, indeed, frankly traditional — the Quest motif in modern guise — dare I say that it could be made into a stereodrama? It is hard to imagine the sheer courage which was required to use so radical a form that many may find it incomprehensible. But in exactly this evocation of the great ghosts of Odysseus, King Arthur, and Don Juan, the author becomes immediately able to explore (implicitly; he is never crudely explicit) childhood with as much haunting delicacy as our most skilled specialists in this type of novel. Yet, unlike them, he is not confined to a child protagonist. Thus he achieves a feat of time-binding which for richness of symbolic overtones can well be matched against Betta's famous use of the stopped clock image in *The Old Man and the Umbrella.* As the hero himself cries, when trapped in that collapsing tunnel which is so much more than the obvious womb/tomb: "Okay, you stupid planet, you've got me pinched where it hurts, but by heaven, I've had more fun in life than you ever did. And I'll whip you yet!"

The fact that he does then indeed overcome the deadly Venusian environment and goes on to destroy the pirate base and complete the project of making the atmosphere Earthlike (a scheme which an engineer friend tells me is at present being seriously contemplated) is thus made infinitely more than a mechanical victory. It is a closing of the ring: the hero, who begins strong and virile and proud, returns to that condition at the end. The ironic overtones of this are clear enough, but the adroit use of such implements along the way as the pick which serves him variously as tool, weapon, and boathook when he and the heroine must cross the river of lava (to take only one random example from this treasure chest) add both an underscoring and a commentary which must be read repeatedly to be appreciated.

And on and on.

When he had finished, IZK-99 went back and perused the article a third time. Then he punched the phone. "Public library," said the woman in the screen.

Tunny entered the office of *Pierce, Arrow!* and stood for a moment watching Janet as she slugged the typer. Her desk was loaded with papers, cigarette butts, and coffee equipment. Dark circles under her eyes bespoke exhaustion. But she plowed gamely on.

"Hi, sweetheart," he said.

"Oh . . . Felix." She raised her head and blinked. "Goodness, is it that late?"

"Yeah. Sorry I couldn't get here sooner. How're you doing?"

"All right — I guess — but darling, it's so dreadful."

"Really?" he came to her, stopped for a kiss, and picked up the reprostat page which she was adapting.

The blaster pointed straight at Jon Dace's chest. Behind its gaping muzzle sneered the mushroom-white face and yellow slit-pupiled eyes of Hark Farkas. "Don't make a move, Earth pig!" the pirate hissed. Jon's broad shoulders stiffened. Fury seized him. His keen eyes flickered about, seeking a possible way out of this death trap —

474

"M-m-m, yeh, that is pretty ripe," Tunny admitted. "Where's it from? Oh, yes, I see. *Far Out Science Fiction,* May 1950. Couldn't you do any better than that?"

"Certainly. Some of those old pulp stories are quite good, if you take them on their own terms." Janet signaled the coffeemaker to pour two fresh cups. "But others, ugh! I needed a confrontation scene, though, and this was the first that came to hand. Time's too short to make a thorough search."

"What've you made of it?" Tunny read her manuscript:

The gun opened a cerberoid mouth at him. Behind it, his enemy's face was white as silent snow, secret snow, where the eyes (those are pearls that were) reflected in miniature the sandstorm that hooted cougar-colored on the horizon.

"Hey, not bad. 'Cougar-colored.' I like that."

There went a hissing: "Best keep stance, friend-stranger-brother whom I must send before me down the tunnel." Jon's shoulders stiffened. Slowly, he answered —

"Uh, sweetheart, honest, that cussing would make a bulldozer blush."

"How can you have intellectual content without four-letter words?" Janet asked, puzzled.

Tunny shrugged. "No matter, I suppose. Time's too short, as you say, to polish this thing, and Izaak won't know the difference. Not after such a smorgasbord of authors and critics as he's been gobbling down . . . besides having so little experience of actual, as opposed to fictional, humans."

"Time's too short to *write* this thing," Janet corrected, her mouth quirking upward. "How did you ever find the stuff we're plagiarizing? I'd no idea any such school of fiction had ever existed."

"I knew about it vaguely, from mention in the nineteenth- and twentieth-century books I've read. But to tell the truth, what I did in this case was ask the Library of Congress to search its microfiles for adventure-story publications of that era and 'stat me a million words' worth." Tunny sat down and reached for his coffee. "Whew, I'm bushed!"

"Hard day?" Janet said softly.

"Yeah. Keeping Izaak off my neck was the worst part."

"How did you stall him?"

"Oh, I had his phone tapped. He called the local library first, for a 'stat. When they didn't have the tape, he called a specialty shop that handles fiction among other things. But at that point I switched him over to a friend of mine, who pretended to be a clerk in the store. This guy told Izaak he'd call Newer York and order a bound copy from the publisher. Since then the poor devil

has been chewing his fingernails, or would if a robot were able to, and faunch-
ing . . . mainly in my office."

"Think we can meet his expectations?"

"I dunno. My hope is that this enforced wait will make the prize seem still
more valuable. Of course, some more reviews would help. Are you positive you
won't run one in *Pierce*?"

"I told you, we're so short of space — "

"I talked to Barsch about that. He'll pay for the additional pages and
printing."

"Hm-m-m . . . literary hoaxes do have an honorable old tradition, don't
they? But oh, dear — I just don't know."

"Barsch has gotten around Henry Lachs," Tunny insinuated. "There'll be
a review in *Entropy*. You wouldn't want to be scooped by a lousy middlebrow
newsmagazine, would you?"

Janet laughed. "All right, you win. Submit your article and I'll run it."

"I'll submit to you anytime," Tunny said. After a while: "Well, I feel better
now. I'll take over here while you catch a nap. Let's see, what pickle did we
leave our bold hero in?"

> This novel at once vigorous and perceptive . . . the most startling use of physical
> action to further the development that has been seen since Conrad, and it must
> be asserted that Conrad painted timidly in comparison to the huge, bold, brilliant,
> and yet minutely executed splashes on Pilchard's canvas . . . this seminal work,
> if one will pardon the expression . . . the metrical character of the whole, so subtle
> that the fact the book is a rigidly structured poem will escape many readers . . .
> — *Pierce, Arrow!*

Two hundred years ago, in the quiet, tree-shaded town of Amherst, Mass.,
spinster poetess Emily Dickinson (1830–86) wrote of the soul:

> Unmoved, she notes the chariot's pausing
> At her low gate;
> Unmoved, an emperor is kneeling
> Upon her mat.

In the brief poem of which these lines are a stanza, she expressed a sense of privacy
and quiet independence which afterward vanished from the American scene as
thoroughly as Amherst vanished into the Atlantic metropolitan complex.

It may seem strange to compare the shy, genteel lady of Puritan derivation to
Charles Pilchard and his explosive, intensely controversial first novel. Yet the
connection is there. The *Leitmotif** of *Thunder Beyond Venus* is not the story
itself. That story is unique enough, breathtakingly original in its use of physical

---

*Borrowed from the operatic works of Richard Wagner (1813–83), Emily Dickinson's stormy
German contemporary, this word has come to mean an underlying and recurrent theme.
— *Entropy*

struggle to depict the dark night of the soul. Some would say almost too breathtaking. Dazzled, the reader may fail to see the many underlying layers of meaning. But Emily Dickinson would understand the aloof, independent soul which animates hero Jon Dace.

Tall (6 ft. 3 1/2 in.), robust (225 lb), balding Charles Pilchard, 38, himself a fanatical seeker of privacy, has written a master's thesis on Rimbaud but never taught. Instead he has lived for more than ten years on citizen's credit while developing his monumental work. [Cut of Charles Pilchard, captioned, "No charioteer he."] Twice married, once divorced, he does not maintain a fixed residence but describes himself, like Jon, as "swimming around in the ocean called Man." He has probed deeply into the abysses of that ocean. Yet he has not emerged with the carping negativism of today's nay-sayers. For although he fully appreciates the human tragedy, Pilchard is in the end a triumphant yea-sayer . . .

The robot entered so noisily that Felix Tunny heard him halfway down the corridor. The engineer turned from his desk and waited. His fingers gripped his chair arms until the nails turned white.

"Hello, Izaak," he got out. "Haven't seen you for a couple of days."

"No," said the robot. "I have been in my room, thinking. And reading."

"Reading what?"

"*Thunder Beyond Venus,* of course. Over and over. Is anybody reading anything else?" One steel finger tapped the volume. "You have read it yourself, have you not?" Izaak asked on a challenging note.

"Well, you know how it goes," Tunny said. "Things are rather frantic around here, what with the company's plans being disrupted and so forth. I've been meaning to get around to it."

"Get around to it!" Izaak groaned. "I suppose eventually you will get around to noticing sunlight and the stars."

"Why, I thought you were above any such gross physical things," Tunny said. This was the payoff. His throat was so dry he could hardly talk.

Izaak didn't notice. "It has proven necessary to make a re-evaluation," he said. "This book has opened my eyes as much as it has opened the eyes of the critics who first called my attention to its subtlety, its profundity, its universal significance and intensely individual analysis. Pilchard has written the book of our age, as Homer, Dante, and Tolstoy wrote the books of their own ages. He explores what is meaningful today as well as what is meaningful for all time."

"Bully for Pilchard."

"The conquest of space is, as the article in *pipette* showed, also the conquest of self. The microcosm opens on the macrocosm, which reflects and re-reflects the observer. This is the first example of the type of book that will be written and discussed for the next hundred years."

"Could be."

"None but an utter oaf would respond to this achievement as tepidly as you," Izaak snapped. "I shall be glad to see the last of you."

"Y-y-you're going away? Where?" (Hang on, boy, countdown to zero!)

"Mercury. Please notify Barsch and have my spaceship made ready. I have no desire to delay so important an experience."

Tunny sagged in his chair. "By no means," he whispered. "Don't waste a minute."

"I make one condition, that for the entire period of my service you send to me with the cargo ships any other works by Pilchard that may appear, plus the quarterlies to which I subscribe and the other exemplars of the literary mode he has pioneered which I shall order on the basis of reviews I read. They must be transcribed to metal, you realize, because of the heat."

"Sure, sure. Glad to oblige."

"When I return," Izaak crooned, "I shall be so uniquely qualified to criticize the new novels that some college will doubtless give me a literary quarterly of my own."

He moved toward the door. "I must go arrange for *Thunder Beyond Venus* to be transcribed on steelloy," he said.

"Why not tablets of stone?" Tunny muttered.

"That is not a bad idea. Perhaps I shall." Izaak went out.

When he was safely gone, Tunny whooped. For a while he danced around his office like a peppered Indian, until he whirled on the phone. Call Barsch and tell him — No, to hell with Barsch. Janet deserved the good news first.

She shared his joy over the screens. Watching her, thinking of their future, brought a more serious mood on Tunny. "My conscience does hurt me a bit," he confessed. "It's going to be a blow to Izaak, out there on Mercury, when his brave new school of literature never appears."

"Don't be too certain about that," Janet said. "In fact — Well, I was going to call you today. We're in trouble again, I'm afraid. You know that office and clerk we hired to pretend to be Wisdom Press, in case Izaak tried to check up? She's going frantic. Calls are streaming in. Thousands of people already, furious because they can't find *Thunder Beyond Venus* anywhere. She's handed them a story about an accidental explosion in the warehouse, but — What can we do?"

"Oy." Tunny sat quiet for a space. His mind flew. "We did run off some extra copies, didn't we?" he said at length.

"Half a dozen or so. I gave one to Arnold Roach. He simply had to have it, after seeing the other articles. Now he's planning a rave review for *The Pacific Monthly,* with all sorts of sarcastic comments about how *Entropy* missed the whole point of the book. Several more critics I know have begged me at least to lend them my copy."

Tunny smote the desk with a large fist. "Only one way out of this," he decided. "Print up a million and stand by to print more. I don't just mean tapes for libraries, either. I mean regular, bound volumes."

"What?"

"I have a hunch that commercial fiction has been revived as of this week. Maybe our book is crude, but it does touch something real, something that people believe in their hearts is important. If I'm right, then there's going to be a spate of novels like this, and many will make a whopping profit, and some will even be genuinely good . . . Lord, Lord," Tunny said in awe. "We simply don't know our own strength, you and I."

"Let's get together," Janet suggested, "and find out."

"Write about me as I am, warts and all."

One Rejection Too Many

PATRICIA NURSE

This story, Nurse's first sale, is told in letter form, which happens to be a device to which I am partial, though I myself used it only once and then only glancingly. I am a character in Nurse's story, which is always an attention-getter where I am concerned. Finally, I burst into laughter at the end. What more can I ask? Well, one thing! The ending did puzzle me in one respect. Who the devil is Arthur C. Clarke?

Dear Dr. Asimov:

Imagine my delight when I spotted your new science fiction magazine on the newsstands. I have been a fan of yours for many, many years, and I naturally wasted no time in buying a copy. I wish you every success in this new venture.

In your second issue I read with interest your plea for stories from new authors. While no writer myself, I have had a time traveler living with me for the past two weeks (he materialized in the bathtub without clothes or money, so I felt obliged to offer him shelter), and he has written a story of life on earth as it will be in the year 5000.

Before he leaves this time frame, it would give him great pleasure to see his story in print — I hope you will feel able to make this wish come true.

Yours sincerely,
Nancy Morrison (Miss)

Dear Miss Morrison:

Thank you for your kind letter and good wishes.

It is always refreshing to hear from a new author. You have included some most imaginative material in your story; however, it is a little short on plot and human interest — perhaps you could rewrite it with this thought in mind.

Yours sincerely,
Isaac Asimov

Dear Dr. Asimov:

I was sorry that you were unable to print the story I sent you. Vahl (the time traveler who wrote it) was quite hurt as he tells me he is an author of some note in his own time. He has, however, rewritten the story and this time has included plenty of plot and some rather interesting mating rituals which he has borrowed from the year 3000. In his own time (the year 5015) sex is no longer practiced, so you can see that it is perfectly respectable having him in my house. I do wish, though, that he could adapt himself to our custom of wearing clothes — my neighbors are starting to talk!

Anything that you can do to expedite the publishing of Vahl's story would be most appreciated, so that he will feel free to return to his own time.

Yours sincerely,
Nancy Morrison (Miss)

Dear Miss Morrison:

Thank you for your rewritten short story.

I don't want to discourage you but I'm afraid you followed my suggestions with a little too much enthusiasm — however, I can understand that having an imaginary nude visitor from another time is a rather heady experience. I'm afraid that your story now rather resembles a far-future episode of "Mary Hartman, Mary Hartman" or "Soap."

Could you tone it down a bit and omit the more bizarre sex rituals of the year 3000 — we must remember that *Isaac Asimov's Science Fiction Magazine* is intended to be a family publication.

Perhaps a little humor would improve the tale too.

Yours sincerely,
Isaac Asimov

Dear Dr. Asimov:

Vahl was extremely offended by your second rejection — he said he has never received a rejection slip before, and your referring to him as "imaginary" didn't help matters at all. I'm afraid he rather lost his temper and stormed out into the garden — it was at this unfortunate moment that the vicar happened to pass by.

Anyway, I managed to get Vahl calmed down and he has rewritten the story and added plenty of humor. I'm afraid my subsequent meeting with the vicar was not blessed with such success! I'm quite sure Vahl would not understand another rejection.

Yours truly,
Nancy Morrison (Miss)

Dear Miss Morrison:

I really admire your persistence in rewriting your story yet another time. Please don't give up hope — you can become a fairly competent writer in time, I feel sure.

I'm afraid the humor you added was not the kind of thing I had in mind at all — you're not collaborating with Henny Youngman by any chance are you? I really had a more sophisticated type of humor in mind.

Yours truly,
Isaac Asimov

P.S. Have you considered reading your story, as it is, on "The Gong Show"?

Dear Dr. Asimov:

It really was very distressing to receive the return of my manuscript once again — Vahl was quite speechless with anger.

It was only with the greatest difficulty that I prevailed upon him to refine the humor you found so distasteful, and I am submitting his latest rewrite herewith.

In his disappointment, Vahl has decided to return to his own time right away. I shall be sorry to see him leave as I was getting very fond of him — a pity he wasn't from the year 3000 though. Still, he wouldn't have made a very satisfactory husband; I'd have never known where (or when) he was. It rather looks as though my plans to marry the vicar have suffered a severe setback too. Are you married, Dr. Asimov?

I must close this letter now as I have to say good-bye to Vahl. He says he has just finished making some long overdue improvements to our time frame as a parting gift — isn't that kind of him?

Yours sincerely,
Nancy Morrison (Miss)

Dear Miss Morrison:

I am very confused by your letter. Who is Isaac Asimov? I have checked with several publishers and none of them has heard of *Isaac Asimov's Science Fiction Magazine,* although the address on the envelope was correct for *this* magazine.

However, I was very impressed with your story and will be pleased to accept it for our next issue. Seldom do we receive a story combining such virtues as a well-conceived plot, plenty of human interest, and a delightfully subtle brand of humor.

Yours truly,
George H. Scithers,
Editor,
Arthur C. Clarke's Science Fiction Magazine

Bug Getter

R. BRETNOR

Writers have their dislikes, and there is one dislike in which we all stand together. We care not that the Declaration of Independence says all people are created equal; we care not that the ideals of our great nation forbid prejudice of any sort; we care not that preachers tell us all are equal in the sight of God. In this one case, we stand as one and we hate as one. And I tell you that there are some misunderstandings that are made in heaven, as this story will amply demonstrate.

AMBROSIUS GOSHAWK was a starving artist. He couldn't afford to starve decently in a garret in Montmartre or Greenwich Village. He lived in a cold, smoke-stained flat in downtown Pittsburgh, a flat furnished with enormously hairy overstuffed objects which always seemed moist, and filled with unsalable paintings. The paintings were all in a style strongly reminiscent of Rembrandt, but with far more than his technical competence. They were absurdly representational.

Goshawk's wife had abandoned him, moving in with a dealer who merchandized thousands of Klee and Mondrian reproductions at \$1.98 each. Her note had been scrawled on the back of a nasty demand from his dentist's collection agency. Two shoddy subpoenas lay on the floor next to his landlord's eviction notice. In this litter, unshaven and haggard, sat Ambrosius Goshawk. His left hand held a newspaper clipping, a disquisition on his work by one J. Herman Lort, the nation's foremost authority on Art. His right hand held a palette knife with which he was desperately scraping little green crickets from the unfinished painting on his easel, a nude for which Mrs. Goshawk had posed.

The apartment was full of little green crickets. So, for that matter, was the eastern half of the country. But Ambrosius Goshawk was not concerned with them as a plague. They were simply an intensely personal, utterly shattering Last Straw — and, as he scraped, he was thinking the strongest thoughts he had ever thought.

He had been thinking them for some hours, and they had, of course, traveled far out into the inhabited universe. That was why, at three minutes past two in the afternoon, there was a whir at the window, a click as it was pushed open from the outside, and a thud as a small bucket-shaped spaceship landed on the unpaid-for carpet. A hatch opened, and a gnarled, undersized being stepped out.

"Well," he said, with what might have been a slightly curdled Bulgarian accent, "here I am."

Ambrosius Goshawk flipped a cricket over his shoulder, glared, and said decisively, "No, I will *not* take you to my leader." Then he started working on another cricket who had his feet stuck on a particularly intimate part of Mrs. Goshawk's anatomy.

"I am not interested with your leader," replied the being, unstrapping something that looked like a super-gadgety spray gun. "You have thought for me, because you are wanting an extermination. I am the Exterminator. Johnny-with-the-spot, that is me. Pronounce me your troubles."

Ambrosius Goshawk put down his palette knife. "What won't I think of next?" he exclaimed. "Little man, because of the manner of your arrival, your alleged business, and my state of mind, I will take you quite seriously. Seat yourself."

Then, starting with his failure to get a scholarship back in art school, he worked down through his landlord, his dentist, his wife, to the clipping by J. Herman Lort, from which he read at some length, coming finally to the following passage:

> . . . and it is in the work of these pseudo-creative people, of self-styled "artists" like Ambrosius Goshawk, whose clumsily crafted imitations of photography must be a thorn in the flesh of every truly sensitive and creative critical mind that the perceptive collector will realize the deeply researched validness of the doctrine I have explained in my book *The Creative Critical Intellect* — that true Art can be "created" only by such an intellect when adequately trained in an appropriately staffed institution, "created" needless to say out of the vast treasury of natural and accidental-type forms — out of driftwood and bird droppings, out of torn-up roots and cracked rocks — and that all the rest is a snare and a delusion, nay! an outright fraud.

Ambrosius Goshawk threw the clipping down. "You'd think," he cried out, "that mortal man could stand no more. And now — " he pointed at the invading insects — "*now there's this!*"

"So," asked the being, "what is this?"

Ambrosius Goshawk took a deep breath, counted to seven, and screamed, "*CRICKETS!*" hysterically.

"It is simple," said the being. "I will exterminate. My fee — "

"Fee?" Goshawk interrupted him bitterly. "How can *I* pay a fee?"

"My fee will be paintings. Six you will give. In advance. Then I exterminate. After, it is one dozen more."

Goshawk decided that other worlds must have wealthy eccentrics, but he made no demur. He watched while the Exterminator put six paintings aboard, and he waved a dizzy good-bye as the spaceship took off. Then he went back to prying the crickets off Mrs. Goshawk.

The Exterminator returned two years later. However, his spaceship did not have to come in through the window. It simply sailed down past the towers of Ambrosius Goshawk's Florida castle into a fountained courtyard patterned after somewhat simpler ones in the Taj Mahal, and landed among a score of young women whose figures and costumes suggested a handsomely modernized Musselman heaven. Some were splashing raw in the fountains. Some were lounging around Goshawk's easel, hoping he might try to seduce them. Two were standing by with swatters, alert for the little green crickets which occasionally happened along.

The Exterminator did not notice Goshawk's curt nod. "How hard to have find you," he chuckled, "ha-ha! Half-miles from north, I see some big palaces, ha, so! all marbles. From the south, even bigger, one Japanese castles. Who has built?"

Goshawk rudely replied that the palaces belonged to several composers, sculptors, and writers, that the Japanese castle was the whim of an elderly poetess, and that the Exterminator would have to excuse him because he was busy.

The Exterminator paid no attention. "See how has changing, your world," he exclaimed, rubbing his hands. "All artists have many success. With yachts, with Rolls-Royces, with minks, diamonds, many round ladies. Now I take twelve more paintings."

"Beat it," snarled Goshawk. "You'll get no more paintings from me!"

The Exterminator was taken aback. "You are having not happy?" he asked. "You have not liking all this? I have done job like my promise. You must paying one dozens more picture."

A cricket hopped onto the nude on which Goshawk was working. He threw his brush to the ground. "I'll pay you nothing!" he shouted. "Why, you fake, you did nothing at all! *Any* good artist can succeed nowadays, but it's no thanks to *you*! *Look at 'em* — there are as many of these damned crickets as ever!"

The Exterminator's jaw dropped in astonishment. For a moment, he goggled at Goshawk.

Then, "*Crickets?*" he croaked. "My God! *I* have thought you said *critics*!"

The Last Gothic

JON L. BREEN

I myself am a computer man. That is, I write stories about computers and I am enthusiastic about computers and I push them as the tsunami of the future. I like to quote one of my favorite aphorisms: "Anything that can be done by a machine is beneath the dignity of any human being to do." Except that someone sometimes asks: "What if computers could write books?" I push that aside with a ripple of laughter, but occasionally, in the middle of the night, I think about it and mutter uneasily to myself, "Well, not in my time!" As for Janet, after reading the story that follows, she asked darkly, "And just who — or what — is writing sf now?"

DAY BY DAY, Jorge Braun felt the death of fiction drawing closer. And it appeared that the gothic novel was to be the next casualty. Since 2005, almost fifteen years ago, all of them had been written by Edwina, a talented, creative, aging computer with twenty pseudonyms. The dwindling readership had forced the last of the human writers in the genre out of business. Once built, the computer was able to turn out novels very cheaply, demanding no advances, no royalties, and, until recently, very little editing. As long as Edwina kept producing, the massive Sheldrake Publishing conglomerate would keep publishing the novels for the small group of readers that remained, but any large outlay to refurbish the machine was branded non-cost-effective by the company's accounting department.

Balefully regarding his boss across a wide, gleaming, clutter-free desk, Jorge made one last appeal. "Mr. Sheldrake, I'm not convinced you'd lose money bringing Edwina up to snuff. Better sales and a resurgence of interest in the gothic might make up for it. But even if you did, wouldn't it be worth it to keep a whole category of fiction from dying? There are millions of elderly ladies out there who need their gothics."

"Jorge," said Sheldrake — after all these years, he was still pronouncing it "George" — "you've been a fine fiction editor for us, the finest fiction editor we've ever had."

Jorge didn't even try to suppress a groan. Sheldrake sounded like Henry Ford praising a blacksmith.

"You're a young man yet, Jorge, and I think you've outgrown fiction. And anyway, our fiction output will diminish year by year, and with it your responsibilities. I'm prepared to offer you a job in . . ."

"I love fiction, Mr. Sheldrake, and if fiction goes down, I go down with it."

Sheldrake sighed and leaned back in his chair. "Very well," he said. "Is Edwina really doing so badly? I haven't heard any complaints."

"Well, there are more and more anachronisms."

"Few readers notice those, and a little simple patchwork reprogramming should take care of that. You do have a budget, you know, Jorge . . ."

"A million dollars a year. Not much I can do with that. It's not just the anachronisms, though they're a symptom. I think Edwina is fed up, bored. Sometimes I think she puts in the anachronisms on purpose, to get attention."

"You're telling me you have a bored and willful computer?"

"It's very possible. Edwina is a creative artist, you know, not just some glorified calculator. If you could see the early attempts at computer-written fiction, Mr. Sheldrake . . ."

"I wouldn't know. I never read fiction." He said that with such pride!

"Well, it was pretty bad, ridiculous in fact. But we've come a long way. The computer fiction writer has a great deal of creative latitude. That's why our computer fiction has become so popular; it has to be something people can relate to. But with creativity comes personality, ego, consciousness of self, and a potential for mental breakdown. It's not just having the same old elements that's bothering Edwina, though I'm sure she'd appreciate some fresh programming. I think she resents having to write her books under twenty different names instead of signing them all Edwina Nightfall."

"You know why that's necessary. We can't publish twenty books a year under the same byline."

"Yes, I understand that, but Edwina doesn't. I think Edwina is going to go completely screwy, Mr. Sheldrake, if she isn't given a complete overhaul — cleaning, new parts, new programming from the bottom up. If she doesn't get it, she'll just crack up some day, and that will be the end of the gothic novel."

"Very sad, my boy, but aren't there enough gothic novels already? Why, in my youth, back in the seventies and eighties, they seemed to clog the bookstands. I thought there were enough of them to last any reader a lifetime."

Jorge tried to tell him that a fictional form dies if no new writing is done in it. It had already happened to the western and the formal detective novel. But of course it was no good, and an hour later he was back in front of Edwina reading her latest as it came sputtering out . . .

WHITHER THOU GHOST
a novel of romantic suspense
by Helena Lightcastle

Jorge shuddered. What could be more ominous in a gothic than a punning title? Maybe it had happened at last. Maybe Edwina was rounding that last bend. Jorge braced himself and read on . . .

The whole journey had about it an aura of foreboding. When the coach had only traveled a few miles from the inn, one of those new fangled horseless carriages had frightened the horses and it had been all the driver could do to keep the coach upright. Now, as the old stage rattled its way through the mist toward the village of Gootenshire at the foot of Devil's Mountain, at whose top was situated Pomegranate Castle, the autumn air chilled Gwen Dolan as she pulled her cloak more snugly around her shoulders. It was too dark to read the new book she had bought in New York, this so-called novel, *Pamela,* said to be creating a new literary form, but it had not interested her greatly, nor had the *Herald Tribune,* which recounted in gory detail Wellington's victory at Waterloo and Abraham Lincoln's nomination by the Republican national convention.

Times are surely changing, mused Gwen. Too fast? No. For a new era of women's rights was coming and Gwen longed to be emancipated. If only women had the right to vote, they would surely show those belligerent masculine politicians a thing or two. For the hand that rocks the cradle . . .

The coach lurched to a sudden stop, jolting Gwen from her reverie. Silly to be so nervous, she chided herself — the atmosphere is getting to you, under your skin, into your bones. But the castle, so bleak and forbidding against the October sky, must be quite homey by daylight, and so must this charming little village, nestled at the foot of the sharply rising precipice — Devil's Mountain, they called it. Whatever for? Gwen wondered.

The driver helped her down from the coach. They were in front of the Greyhound station, where Major Hawthorne's man was to meet her. She entered the waiting room, in out of the dark chill, and a friendly voice greeted her.

"Good evening, miss! Welcome to our village!" The waiting room was empty but for the rotund, mustachioed man behind the lunch counter. A warm and friendly man, she sensed. Someone to be relied upon. "I am Charles Evans Happychap, master of the Greyhound station, called Charlie by my friends one and all, and your wish is my command. What may I get you? Something hot to refresh you after your journey? A cup of tea perhaps?"

Gwen smiled. "I don't know if there is time. Someone is to meet me here — Major Hawthorne's representative. For I am the new governess here at Pomegranate Castle."

Charlie Happychap fairly jumped, and all color seemed drained from his face. He looked at the young lady, so fresh and pink-cheeked and lovely, her long black hair billowing about her shoulders, and he shook his head unbelievingly. "No, miss, it cannot be."

"Why, yes." Gwen was puzzled.

"You must not!" he almost shouted. Suddenly Charlie Happychap, with a quickness uncanny for a man of his bulk, darted from behind the lunch counter and ran out into the road. "Come back! Come back!" he shouted after the retreating stage. "Too late, too late," he moaned disconsolately and reentered the cheery waiting room.

"You shall stay here," he said. "You must stay here until tomorrow's stage comes, then leave the village forever. Under no circumstances are you to set foot inside Pomegranate Castle."

"Why, why not? It seems a good job, well paid and rewarding in other ways, the dream of a modern governess. Why should I not go?"

Charlie Happychap would say no more. He plied her with coffee and slices of anchovy pizza and they discussed current events: W. G. Grace's exploits on the cricket pitch, Sarah Bernhardt's farewell American tour, the impending Mexican war, Dr. Johnson's new dictionary. Charlie seemed renewed, but Gwen could not but wonder why he was so adamant about Pomegranate Castle.

A half hour after the coach had left Gwen at the Greyhound station, the door of that establishment crashed open and a tall, gaunt man in chauffeur's livery, his tightly drawn facial skin making a living death's-head of his baleful visage, entered the room. Charlie Happychap regarded him with ill-concealed hostility, determination spelled out on his jutting fat chin.

"You shan't have her."

A low, growling voice forced itself painfully through the pale, thin lips of the newcomer. "The master needs a new governess. For the master's young ones."

"And why does the master need so many governesses?" Charlie Happychap demanded.

"To feed the ghost," said the chauffeur, with a ghost of a smile.

Irrationally, Gwen felt herself shiver. Silly to fear this ordinary, simple servant, or his employer, probably a poor unhappy widower with children who must be raised. Still, some clarification seemed called for.

In a firm, steady voice, Gwen asked, "What do you mean, to feed the ghost? What ghost?"

The chauffeur would not answer. He held out a skeletal hand. "Will you come, miss?"

"She will not!" Charlie Happychap interjected.

"Of course I shall!" Gwen retorted, in a voice more decisive and confident than she truly felt. True, she thought, I know practically nothing about this Major Hawthorne, my new employer. But the very name had such a solidity and reliability about it. And where children need a governess, a governess must go. To them is not the blame for the follies and obfuscations of their elders.

She followed the emissary out to the waiting helicopter, leaving Charlie looking sad, his mustache drooping.

The castle was huge — surely no less than a hundred rooms of high ceilings, ornate chandeliers, and artificial cobwebs in every corner. Gwen kept staring above her, as she had at the base of that new Empire State Building that was the talk of Gotham.

The housekeeper's name was Mrs. Dalrymple. It sounded a friendly name, but the stern-faced party that bore it did not encourage girlish confidences with her slightly disapproving, though perfectly civil and correct, manner.

Gwen tried to make a friend of her. "Such a big house. It must be dreadful to keep clean."

"We manage. We have always managed."

"When will I meet the children?"

"The children are away," Mrs. Dalrymple almost snapped, and Gwen thought her cold and rather sinister stare looked almost accusing.

"Where?" Gwen wondered.

"They will not be your concern until they return, Miss Dolan."

Gwen started to say, "Make it Ms. Dolan," but bit it back. Mrs. Dalrymple was of another generation and would not understand. "Will they miss their old governess terribly?"

The housekeeper's stare was harder and colder still. "We do not speak of the old governess. Kindly do not mention her to the Major."

Major Hawthorne proved to be a handsome, nervous man of middle age, with a neat military mustache, a tic in his left eye, and a slight limp, his souvenir of the Battle of Shrewsbury. He darted about the room with undirected energy. Gwen detected deep wells of unplumbed depths lurking far beneath the surface.

"Miss Dolan," he said politely, "welcome."

That seemed to be the extent of his greeting. After a moment's hesitation, she asked, "When will I see the children?"

"Day. Two days. When they're back."

"May I ask, back from where?"

"I hire them out as chimney sweeps," he said. Did she detect a faint glint of humor in this troubled, haunted man? Or of something else?

"Candle," he said, handing her one. Then he gestured to Mrs. Dalrymple, who showed her up the winding circular staircase to her room. The chauffeur walked behind, carrying her satchel.

"And when do I meet the ghost?" she joked en route, her eyes twinkling bravely.

"Soon," said the death's-head, leering.

The walls of the bedroom were lined with paperback books. They seemed to be family products — Reynold Hawthorne and Renata Hawthorne were the names on their multicolored spines.

"His wife?" Gwen Dolan asked, a tear unbidden in her eye.

"The ghost!" the death's-head rasped at her and left her there alone, the small satchel of her worldly goods at her feet.

She slept in the large bed fitfully until four-thirty. A faint sound of clickety-clack had awakened her. From the next room, through the connecting door? She opened it and stole into the room.

In a dark corner, a hunched figure sat at the typewriter, a Tensor lamp illuminating his labors. As she watched, the stack of pages at his left grew, grew, grew. The figure typed as a man possessed. He was hooded, she noticed, and she felt an urge to see the face of this mysterious figure.

Softly she crept up behind him and snatched the mask from his head. The figure rose from the chair with a piercing shriek and turned on her.

"Governess!" he cried, his face not ugly as she had feared, but young, handsome, tortured. "My new governess!"

"Your new governess? No, Major Hawthorne's new governess. For his children."

"No, no, you are mine. A new governess to torture and terrify. But I cannot do this anymore. This is my ninety-seventh gothic. Ninety-seven! Hawthorne, damn him, is rarely here, jet-setting in his damned helicopter and doing Mafia novels and spy novels and, God help us, sex novels! But me, a ghost, a ghost, I do gothics, gothics, gothics. Liberate me! Save me! Burn this castle! Burn it down!"

"You are the ghost?"

"I am."

"I am a governess. The children are my province, and my duty is to them."

"They aren't children. They're midgets. Burn the castle! Save me! Save us all!"

"I cannot, somehow, believe this is happening."

"It is! It is!" He pushed buttons on his table and Gwen heard shrieking and creaking doors and mournful wails and knocking and clanking chains. "This castle isn't haunted. It's dead, played out. If Hawthorne were ever here, he'd know that. A hundred gothics to a castle is the world record, held by some woman with three names. No mere man with two names can equal it. I am tired. I long for rest."

Gwen pitied him but wished that he would not snivel so. He was not a real man, like Charlie Happychap, so solid and reliable and dependable: like the Major, with untapped reservoirs of depth and character pulsating under his brusque surface. Instead he was weak and indecisive.

"Why can't you be strong?" she lashed out at him. "Like Charlie Happychap?"

The face of the ghost twisted maniacally. "Happychap! Don't you know about him? The author of all your problems? But no, of course, you wouldn't know yet, would you? You never know, however obvious it is, that the lovable, helpful, simple, one-dimensional male friend is always the dark, smirking, lurking, mad villain. Why must you be so stupid and helpless, all you damned governesses . . . ?"

"You, poor ghost, are not my kind of man. I've known you for only a few moments, and already I am tired of you."

"I've known you for ninety-seven volumes, and I am tired of you," the ghost retorted, and viciously x'd her out.

The tape stumbled to a halt, and Jorge felt sure the end had come. But no, Edwina was trying again . . .

DARK HOUSE OF DARKNESS
a novel of romantic suspense
by Edwina Nightfall

Still not the greatest title in the world, but at least there was no pun . . .

Helena Brady brushed a stray lock of blond hair away from her eye and wondered if seeing the wanted poster of Jack the Ripper rush past outside the window of the Twentieth Century Limited as it roared through Colorado was some sort of an omen. But how could a job as companion for an elderly lady in the California desert be in any way dangerous?

She had chosen her traveling clothes carefully, not wanting to appear too ostentatious in her first meeting with her new employer. She had selected a knee-length mauve hobble skirt and a transparent middy blouse with a pattern of tastefully located deathwatch beetles, gleaming white bobby sox with violet spats over pale green Alsatian mukluks, a modest Salvation Army bonnet with pink chin tie, and a simple bison stole. Completing the ensemble were a dainty little shark's-tooth pendant, a shoulder-strap patent leather parachute bag, a Venus's-flytrap parasol, and a Naugahyde riding crop.

Jorge Braun pulled a switch and ended Edwina's agony. The end had come at last, and all that remained was to find some suitable memorial.

When night fell, the towering Sheldrake Building was black against the sky in unaccustomed darkness. One light burned in one window, in memory of the gothic novel.

A Benefactor of Humanity

JAMES T. FARRELL

*Some stories ago, I mentioned, in righteous anger, that enemy of humankind,
the critic. This story, however, brings up an altogether improbable variation of
the earlier thought. Can it be — I ask in a spirit of wondering disbelief
— that there are in the world featherless bipeds who resemble human beings
closely enough to fool the observer and yet dislike authors? No, no, it cannot be!*

THE OTHER DAY Ignatius Bulganov Worthington peacefully and happily
became *non est*. Known as Worthy Worthington, he was a great man, a great
American, and a great benefactor of mankind. He died a billionaire five times
over and was buried with many honors and mourned by all men. The flags of
the city and nation hung at half-mast; the President issued a eulogy of regret;
Congress held a memorial session and disbanded for the day; the National
Association of Manufacturers sent a floral wreath, as did three kings, six
dukes, two dictators, over two thousand police chiefs, and every book, magazine, and newspaper publisher in the world, including those in the Soviet
Union, Madagascar, Borneo, and Pleasantville, New York.

The funeral services were attended by thousands: These were described on
a national radio hookup, televised around the world, and Worthy Worthington
machines ground out newspaper obsequies, testimonials, regrets, eulogies,
laments, and obituary notices which were nationally and almost universally
described as worthy of the great Worthington.

Not a child lives in America who hasn't heard of the great name of this now
deceased greatness. His life, his example, and his contribution to the wealth,
security, peace of mind, and happiness of this country and of mankind can
never be praised too much, valued too highly, or forgotten. As long as mankind
inhabits this planet the worthy name of Worthington will be remembered,
reverenced, and revered.

Young Ignatius Bulganov went to a little red country schoolhouse hard by
a Baptist church in the land where the tall corn grows the tallest. He was not
a promising pupil. He couldn't read; he did not know how to write; and every

time he added up a sum, his addition was different from that of his teacher and from the *Stone Mills Arithmetic,* which was used as a textbook. He was known as the dunce. He never was graduated.

Unarmed, unprepared, but eager, he set out for the great city of New York, and there began the story of his great career and of his achievements and contributions. He got a job as a stock boy in a publishing house. Proud of his job, he did it well. He got to love books. He liked the covers on them, the smell of them. He liked to pile them on shelves and then to unpile them. He liked to lift them and to look at them in piles on the stockroom floor and the shelves. He liked to wrap them up and to unwrap them. He liked to do everything he could with them, except read them.

He lived alone at the Young Men's Christian Association and every night he dreamed about books. He made shelves for his room and filled these with books. Every night he looked at his books, touched them, felt them, counted them, and rearranged them. His fellow inmates of the Y.M.C.A. gave him the nickname of "the Book Lover," and he was proud of that. In later years, when he had become great, rich, famous, and honored, this was remembered, and a book was even published under the title *Worthy Worthington, the Book Lover.*

But just as he loved books, he hated authors. Every time he saw an author, he remembered how as a boy in a little red country schoolhouse hard by a Baptist church in the land where the tall corn is tallest, he used to be switched, birched, and in plain language, whipped, because of his inability to read books. Some author had written those sentences that he had been lambasted for because he couldn't read them.

But when he worked as a stock boy for a publishing house in New York, he came to see authors and in a sense to know them. The girls in the office all liked the authors and not him. And being normal and healthy, he wanted the girls to like him. The girls sometimes swooned about the masculine authors who came to the office, but they only called him Ignatz. And then, he soon learned that authors were not like he was. They didn't live at the Y.M.C.A. They were always causing trouble and getting into trouble.

One author got his boss, the owner of the firm, arrested because of a book he wrote. Another author was always getting drunk. And if an author wasn't getting drunk or causing the police to hand a warrant to the boss, then he was getting divorced. The authors who came to the office just weren't like Ignatius Bulganov or like the people he had known in the land where the tall corn is tall corn. They were always coming and going and never staying put, and they disrupted the whole work of the office. So more and more, I.B. disliked authors.

And he came to understand and learn that other people didn't particularly like them either. He heard complaints in the office about this author and that one. The girls complained. The editors complained. The owners of the firm yelled bloody murder about them. The wives of the owners complained. And the business manager, the bookkeeper, and the salesmen didn't merely complain — they screamed.

In those years, Ignatius was happy. He had enough to eat, a clean room to sleep in, and books to count and feel, touch, lift, pack, wrap, and distribute on shelves. He had no ambitions and would have been content with his job except for authors. They became worse and worse.

One day he overheard two of the girls talking. An author had just come in with the manuscript of a book and it had to be published. Business was bad, and the girls said that this book was going to lose money.

"Why are authors?" one of them asked.

This question struck Ignatz Bulganov's mind.

Over and over again that night in his room in the Y.M.C.A. he fondled his books and asked himself the question: *"Why are authors?"*

The next morning, as he was taking his cold shower, he asked himself why couldn't there be books, without authors.

Here was food for thought. And he nourished his higher faculties on this food.

That day at work, he idly went to a desk where there was an adding machine. He punched numbers on the machine and pulled out slips of paper. And there were numbers all added up correctly. He remembered how he had never been able to do anything like that in the little red schoolhouse. Just think of it, he had been whammed and whipped because he had not been able to add. And look at that machine. It added and never made a mistake.

Thus, Ignatius Bulganov Worthington acquired even more rich and highly nutritious food for thought.

Soon afterward I.B.W. went to the free night school, a youth seeking knowledge and opportunity. He had digested his rich nutritious food for thought and something had happened to him. He had become ambitious.

Well, the rest of the story is familiar to every schoolboy. Ignatius studied machines, machinery, arithmetic, statistics, engineering, and draftsmanship. And he worked on machines. And he invented the machine that revolutionized the life of mankind. He invented the Worthy Worthington Writing Machine. People thought him crazy. He was laughed at and jeered. But he triumphed. Just as once he had been able to add correctly by pushing buttons on an adding machine, so now he could write a book by pushing buttons on a Worthy Worthington.

Of course, the first years were hard, and it took time for him to get his machine accepted. But he had perserverance and stick-to-itiveness. So his machine was introduced into publishing houses, magazine offices, and newspaper editorial rooms. One machine, working an eight-hour day, could shed four books. And none of the books was gloomy. The policeman could read them without making an arrest and this saved the taxpayers' money, because the police were no longer needed to seize books and to arrest booksellers, authors, and publishers. The clergymen were grateful because they no longer had to write sermons about immoral books and could speak from the pulpit of God and Goodness.

And of course the publishers were happy. They had to take no authors to lunch, and they had to pay no royalties except a very small one to Ignatius Bulganov for the use of one of his Worthy Worthingtons. Their machines never erred and never produced an immoral or sad book. They whirred out works of joy and hope at a cost of ten cents a copy. Books became the cheapest commodity on the market. There was a tremendous boom in books. The publishers became millionaires. The nation became inspired. Joy and goodness reigned as though in the celestial spheres. And there were no more authors to cause trouble, to disillusion people, to lose money on bad books. The authors all went mad or became useful citizens. And Worthy Worthington married the girl who asked the question:

"Why are authors?"

He lived to a ripe age, left a fortune and a legacy of sunshine after him, and was eternally revered for having found a means to eliminate authors and to enrich the material and spiritual life of his country and his times. His remains lie in a marble tomb ten feet high, and on the door of this tomb, these words are graven.

HERE LIES WORTHY WORTHINGTON
IN
ETERNAL REPOSE

The Silver Eggheads

FRITZ LEIBER

It was psychologically essential to our sanity that we put Fritz Leiber's immortal chapter from The Silver Eggheads *right after the last story, and I am now beginning to see a pattern. Writers feel insecure. Why? I wonder. Surely they can find no fault with the genial publishers, the understandingly tolerant editors, the effusively kindly critics, the warm-hearted readers? What can make writers twitch so? What makes them look so gloomily into the future?*

R E S P L E N D E N T in their matching turquoise slack suits with opal buttons, father and son stood complacently in front of Gaspard's wordmill. No day-shift writer had turned up. Joe the Guard slept upright by the time clock. The other visitors had wandered off. A pink robot had appeared from somewhere and was sitting quietly on a stool at the far end of the vaulted room. Its pinchers were moving busily. It seemed to be knitting.

FATHER: There you are, Son. Look up at it. Now, now, you don't have to lean over backwards that far.

SON: It's big, Daddy.

FATHER: Yes, it's big all right. That's a wordmill, Son, a machine that writes fiction books.

SON: Does it write my story books?

FATHER: No, it writes novels for grown-ups. A considerably smaller machine (child-size, in fact) writes your little —

SON: Let's go, Daddy.

FATHER: No, Son! You wanted to see a wordmill, you begged and begged, I had to go to a lot of trouble to get a visitor's pass, so now you're going to look at this wordmill and listen to me explain it to you.

SON: Yes, Daddy.

FATHER: Well, you see, it's this way — No . . . Now, it's like this —

SON: Is it a robot, Daddy?

FATHER: No, it's not a robot like the electrician or your teacher. A wordmill is not a person like a robot is, though they are both made of metal and work by electricity. A wordmill is like an electric computing machine, except it handles words, not numbers. It's like the big chess-playing, war-making machine, except it makes its moves in a novel instead of on a board or battlefield. But a wordmill is not alive like a robot and it cannot move around. It can only write fiction books.

SON: (*kicking it*) Dumb old machine!

FATHER: Don't do that, Son. Now, it's like this — there are any number of ways to tell a story.

SON: (*still kicking it wearily*) Yes, Daddy.

FATHER: The ways depend on the words that are chosen. But once one word is chosen, the other words must fit with that first word. They must carry the same mood or atmosphere and fit into the suspense chain with micrometric precision (I'll explain that later).

SON: Yes, Daddy.

FATHER: A wordmill is fed the general pattern for a story and it goes to its big memory bank — much bigger even than Daddy's — and picks the first word at random; they call that turning trump. Or it's given the first word by its programmer. But when it picks the second word it must pick one that has the same atmosphere, and so on and so on. Fed the same story pattern and one hundred different first words — one at a time, of course — it would write one hundred completely different novels. Of course it is much more complicated than that, much too complicated for Son to understand, but that is the way it works.

SON: A wordmill keeps telling the same story with different words?

FATHER: Well, in a way, yes.

SON: Sounds dumb to me.

FATHER: It is not dumb, Son. All grown-ups read novels. Daddy reads novels.

SON: Yes, Daddy. Who's that?

FATHER: Where?

SON: Coming this way. The lady in tight blue pants who hasn't buttoned the top of her shirt.

FATHER: Ahem! Look away, Son. That's another writer, Son.

SON: (*still looking*) What's a writer, Daddy? Is she one of those bad ladies you told me about, who tried to talk to you in Paris, only you wouldn't?

FATHER: No, no, Son! A writer is merely a person who takes care of a wordmill, who dusts it and so on. The publishers pretend that the writer helps the wordmill write the book, but that's a big fib, Son, a just-for-fun pretend to make things more exciting. Writers are allowed to dress and behave in uncouth ways, like gypsies — it's all part of a union agreement that goes back to the time when wordmills were invented. Now you won't believe —

SON: She's putting something in this wordmill, Daddy. A round black thing.

FATHER: (*not looking*) She's oiling it or replacing a transistor or doing whatever she's supposed to be doing to this wordmill. Now you won't believe what Daddy's going to tell you now, except that it's Daddy telling you. Before wordmills were invented —

SON: It's smoking, Daddy.

FATHER: (*still not looking*) Don't interrupt, she probably spilled the oil or something. Before wordmills were invented, writers actually wrote stories! They had to hunt —

SON: The writer's running away, Daddy.

FATHER: Don't interrupt. They had to hunt through their memories for every word in a story. It must have been —

SON: It's still smoking, Daddy. There are sparks.

FATHER: I said don't interrupt. It must have been dreadfully hard work, like building the pyramids.

SON: Yes, Daddy. It's still —

BOOM! Gaspard's wordmill deafeningly blossomed into shrapnel. Father and son took the full force of the explosion and were blown to turquoise and opal bits. They passed painlessly out of existence, chance victims of a strange occupational revolt. The incident in which they perished was one of many, and it was being repeated at a large number of nearby places, fortunately with few further fatalities.

All along Readership Row, which some call Dream Street, the writers were wrecking the wordmills. From the blackened booktree under which Gaspard had fallen to the book-ship launching pads at the other end of the Row, the unionized authors were ravaging and reaving. Torrenting down the central avenue of Earth's mammoth, and in fact the Solar System's only, fully mechanized publishing center, a giddy gaudy mob in their berets and bathrobes, togas and ruffs, kimonos, capes, sport shirts, flowing black bow ties, lace shirt fronts and top hats, doublets and hose, T-shirts and Levi's, they burst murderously into each fiction factory, screaming death and destruction to the gigantic machines whose mere tenders they had become and which ground out in their electronic maws the actual reading matter which fed the yearnings and sweetened the subconscious minds of the inhabitants of three planets, a half dozen moons, and several thousand satellites and spaceships in orbit and trajectory.

No longer content to be bribed by high salaries and the mere trappings of authorship — the ancient costumes that were the vestments of their profession, the tradition-freighted names they were allowed and even required to assume, the exotic lovelives they were permitted and encouraged to pursue — the writers smashed and sabotaged, rioted and ruined, while the police of a labor administration, intent on breaking the power of the publishers, stood complacently aside. Robot goons, hurriedly hired by the belatedly alarmed publishers, also took no action, having received a last-minute negate from the Interplanetary Brotherhood of Free Business Machines; they too merely stood about — grim somber statues, their metal dented by the bricks, stained by the acids, and blackened by the portable lightning bolts of many a picket-line affray — and watched their stationary mindless cousins die.

Homer Hemingway axed through the sedate gray control panel of a Random House Write-All and went fiercely to work on the tubes and transistors.

Sappho Wollstonecraft Shaw shoved a large plastic funnel into the memory unit of a Scribner Scribe and poured two gallons of smoking nitric acid into its indescribably delicate innards.

Harriet Beecher Brontë drenched a Norton Novelist with gasoline and whinnied as the flames shot skyward.

Heloise Ibsen, her shirt now torn from her shoulders and waving the gray flag with the ominous black "30" on it, signifying *the end* of machine-made literature, leaped atop three cowering vice presidents who had come down to "watch the robots scatter those insolent grease monkeys." For a moment she looked strikingly like "Liberty Leading the People" in Delacroix's painting.

Abelard de Musset, top hat awry and pockets bulging with proclamations of self-expression and creativity, leveled a submachine gun at a Putnam Plotter. Marcel Feodor Joyce lobbed a grenade into the associator of a Schuster Serious. Dylan Bysshe Donne bazookaed a Bantam Bard.

Agatha Ngaio Sayers poisoned a Doubleday 'Dunnit with powdered magnetic oxide.

Somerset Makepeace Dickens sledgehammered a Harcourt Hack.

H. G. Heinlein planted stiletto explosives in an Appleton SF and almost lost his life pushing the rest of the mob back to a safe distance until the fiery white jets had stabbed through the involuted leagues of fine silver wiring.

Norman Vincent Durant blew up a Ballantine Bookbuilder.

Talbot Fennimore Forester sword-slashed a Houghton Historical, pried it open with a pike, and squirted in Greek fire which he had compounded by an ancient formula.

Luke Van Tilburg Wister fanned his six-guns at a Whittlesey Western, then finished it off with six sticks of dynamite and a "Ki-yi-yippee!"

Fritz Ashton Eddison loosed a cloud of radioactive bats inside a Fiction House Fantasizer (really a rebuilt Dutton Dreamer with Fingertip Credibility Control).

Edgar Allen Bloch, brandishing an electric cane fearfully powered by portable isotopic batteries, all by himself shorted out forever a whole floorful of assorted cutters, padders, polishers, tighteners, juicers, and hesid-shesids.

Conan Haggard de Camp rammed a Gold Medal Cloak-'n-Sworder with a spike-nosed five-ton truck.

Shakespeares ravaged, Dantes dealt electrochemical death, Aeschyluses and Miltons fought shoulder to shoulder with Zolas and Farrells; Rimbauds and Bradburies shared revolutionary dangers alike; while whole tribes of Sinclairs, Balzacs, Dumases, and authors named White and distinguished only by initials, mopped up in the rear.

It was a black day for book lovers. Or perhaps the dawn.

Adverbs

E.Y. HARBURG

WHERE and WHEN
   Are lost in space.
THERE and THEN
   Do not embrace.
So before we disappear
Come sweet NOW and kiss the HERE.

Dry Spell

BILL PRONZINI

Janet wasn't at all sure this story was funny. Tragic, she felt, was a better description. Cosmic tragedy, universal weeping, everlasting sorrow. She showed it to me, but I disagreed. In fact, I laughed heartily.

"Sure," she said. "You beast. It never happens to you."

Into the anthology it went, largely, I suppose, so she can hold me up to the world as the unfeeling monster I am, finding amusement in something so bitter.

The bane of all writers, John Kensington thought glumly, *whether they be poor and struggling or whether they be rich and famous, is the protracted dry spell.*

He sat staring at the blank sheet of yellow foolscap in his typewriter. His mind was as blank as that paper. Not a single idea, not a single line of writing that even remotely reached coherency in almost three weeks.

Sighing, Kensington pushed back his chair and got on his feet. He went to the small refrigerator in the kitchenette, opened his last can of beer, and took it to the old Morris chair that reposed near his desk.

I've got to come up with something, he thought. *The rent's due in another week, and if I don't get something down on that grocery bill I can forget about eating for a while.*

He sipped his beer, closing his eyes. *Come on, son,* he thought. *Just an idea, just one little idea . . .*

He let his mind wander. It seemed, however, to be wandering in circles. Nothing. Not even . . .

Wait a minute.

Now wait just a single damned minute here.

The germ of something touched a remote corner of his brain. It was a mere fragment, evanescent, but he seized it the way a man dying of thirst would seize a dipper of water.

Grimly, he hung on. The fragment remained. Slowly, inexorably, it began to blossom.

Kensington sat bolt upright in the chair, his eyes wide open now, the beer forgotten. His fingertips tingled with excitement. The coming of the idea was a catharsis, releasing the tension which had been building within him for the past three weeks.

It would be a science fiction/fantasy story, he thought, probably a novella if he worked it properly. He moistened his lips. *Now, let's see . . .*

Suppose there's this race of aliens plotting to take over Earth, because it is a strategic planet in some kind of intergalactic war they're involved in. Okay, okay, so it's hackneyed. There are ways to get around that, ways to play that aspect down.

These aliens have infiltrated Earth and set up some kind of base of operations, maybe up in the mountains somewhere. They're assembling a kind of penultimate cybernetic machine which, when fully completed, will have the power to erase all rational thought from the minds of humans, turning them into obsequious zombies. Wait now. Suppose these aliens have a portion of this machine already completed. This portion would be capable of reading, simultaneously, the thoughts of every human on Earth, and of categorizing those thoughts for the aliens to study. That way, if any human somehow happened to blunder on the scheme in one way or another — mental blundering as well as physical would have to be considered, what with clairvoyance and the emanation into space of thought waves, and the like — then the extraterrestrials would immediately know about it. And what they would do would be to train the full strength of this completed portion of the machine on that particular human, and with it eradicate all those thoughts endangering their project, thus insuring its safety.

Kensington was sweating a bit now, his forehead crinkled in deep thought. *Sure,* he thought, *it's a touch far out. But if I handle it right, who knows? At least it's a good, workable idea, which is a hell of a lot better than nothing at all. Now, how am I going to save Earth from this fate? It has to be in some way that is totally plausible, not too gimmicky, and . . .*

All at once the answer popped into his mind. *By God!* Kensington thought. *It's perfect! There's not a flaw in it!* He grinned hugely. *Those damned aliens wouldn't stand a snowball's chance in you-know-where if I set it up this way.*

He stood abruptly and started for his typewriter. The progression of the story was already flowing, plotting itself firmly in Kensington's mind.

He sat at the typewriter, excitement coursing through him because he knew, he could feel, that the dry spell was at an end. His fingers poised over the keys.

Quite suddenly, quite inexplicably, his mind went blank.

He pressed his forehead against the cool surface of his typewriter.

Why, he moaned silently, *why, oh, why can't I come up with just one little story idea?*

(Our Future Fans?)

PART VI

The End?

"I really hate the idea of the physical universe winding down, don't you?"

The Odds-On Favorite

E.Y. HARBURG

To make the longest story terse,
Be it blessing, be it curse,
The Lord designed the universe
  With built in obsolescence.
Each planet, comet, star, and sun
Enjoys a brief atomic run,
Erupting when its course is done,
  With cosmic incandescence.

Astronomers aver some day
Our solar star will blaze away,
There'll be a glorious display
  Of sunburst helium masses.
Our little planet Earth below
Will be a pyrotechnic show
Of blazing hydrogen aglow
  With thermonuclear gases.

Thank God, this great combustion day
  Is many billion years away
So, as philosophers all say,
  Why fret . . . why fume . . . why worry?
A billion moons will wane and wax,
Sit down . . . make out your income tax . . .
Buy stocks, be calm . . . enjoy . . . relax
  For God is in no hurry.

But oh, my friends, I have a hunch
That man may beat God to the punch.

"He's a nut."

"We've called you here today to announce that, according to *our* computer, by the year 2000 everything is going to be peachy."

Ed Nofziger drew this during the gas shortage of World War II. Now it's become futuristic — but let's all try to laugh anyway.

"Think the monkey will ever replace the man?"

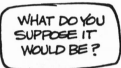

MS Fnd in a Lbry

HAL DRAPER

I don't want to leave you with a feeling of doom, so I will ask you to consider the following, which will not make sense to you till after you've read this marvelous story:

1. Suppose you eliminate everything that proves wrong.

2. Suppose you eliminate everything that no one wants to know.

3. Suppose you eliminate everything that makes no sense.

Well then, what's left? And are you worried?

From: *Report of the Commander, Seventh Expeditionary Force, Andromedan Paleoanthropological Mission*

WHAT PUZZLED OUR RESEARCH teams was the suddenness of collapse, and the speed of reversion to barbarism, in this multigalactic civilization of the biped race. Obvious causes like war, destruction, plague, or invasion were speedily eliminated. Now the outlines of the picture emerge, and the answer makes me apprehensive.

Part of the story is quite similar to ours, according to those who know our own prehistory well.

On the mother planet there are early traces of *books.* This word denotes paleoliterary records of knowledge in representational and macroscopic form. Of course, these disappeared very early, perhaps 175,000 of our yukals ago, when their increase threatened to leave no place on the planet's surface for anything else.

First they were reduced to *micros,* and then to *supermicros,* which were read with the primeval electronic microscopes then extant. But in another yukal the old problem was back, aggravated by colonization on most of the other planets of the local Solar System, all of which were producing *books* in torrents. At about this time, too, their cumbersome alphabet was reduced to mainly consonantal elements (thus: *thr cmbrsm alfbt w rdsd t mnl cnsntl elmnts*) but this was done to facilitate quick reading, and only incidentally did it cut down the mass of *Bx* (the new spelling) by a full third. A drop out of the bucket.

Next step was the elimination of the multitude of separate Bx depositories in favor of a single building for the whole civilization. Every home on every inhabited planet had a farraginous diffuser which tuned in on any of the Bx at will. This cut the number to about one millionth at a stroke, and the wise men of the species congratulated themselves that the problem was solved.

This building, twenty-five miles square and two miles high, was buried in one of the oceans to save land surface for parking space, and so our etymological team is fairly sure that the archaic term liebury (lbry) dates from this period. Within no more than twenty-two yukals, story after story had been added till it extended a hundred miles into the stratosphere. At this level, cosmic radiation defarraginated the scanning diffusers, and it was realized that another limit had been reached. Proposals were made to extend the liebury laterally, but it was calculated that in three yukals of expansion so much of the ocean would be thus displaced that the level of the water would rise ten feet and flood the coastal cities. Another scheme was worked out to burrow deeper into the ocean bottom, until eventually the liebury would extend right through the planet like a skewer through a shashlik (a provincial Plutonian delicacy), but it was realized in time that this would be only a momentary palliative.

The fundamental advance, at least in principle, came when the representational records were abandoned altogether in favor of *punched supermicros,* in which the supermicroscopic elements were the punches themselves. This began the epoch of abstract recs — or Rx, to use the modern term.

The great breakthrough came when Mcglcdy finally invented mass-produced *punched molecules* (of any substance). The mass of Rx began shrinking instead of expanding. Then Gldbg proved what had already been suspected: knowledge was not infinite, and the civilization was asymptotically approaching its limits; the flood was leveling off. The Rx storage problem was hit another body-blow two generations later when Kwlsk used the Mcglcdy principle to develop the *notched electron,* made available for use by the new retinogravitic activators. In the ensuing ten yukals a series of triumphant developments wiped the problem out for good, it seemed:

(1) Getting below matter level, Shmt began by notching quanta (an obvious extension of Kwlsk's work) but found this clumsy. In a brilliant stroke he invented the *chipped quantum,* with an astronomical number of chips on each one. The Rx contracted to one building for the whole culture.

(2) Shmt's pupil Qjt, even before the master's death, found the chip unnecessary. Out of his work, ably supported by Drnt and Lccn, came the *nudged quanta,* popularly so called because a permanent record was impressed on each quantum by a simple vectorial pressure, occupying no subspace on the pseudo-surface itself. A whole treatise could be nudged onto a couple of quanta, and

whole branches of knowledge could for the first time be put in a nutshell. The Rx dwindled to one room of one building.

(3) Finally — but this took another yukal and was technologically associated with the expansion of the civilization to intergalactic proportions — Fx and Sng found that quanta in hyperbolic tensor systems could be tensed into occupying the same spatial and temporal coordinates, if properly pizzicated. In no time at all, a quantic pizzicator was devised to compress the nudged quanta into overlapping spaces, most of these being arranged in the wide-open areas lying between the outer electrons and the nucleus of the atom, leaving the latter free for tables of contents, illustrations, graphs, etc.

All the Rx ever produced could now be packed away in a single drawer, with plenty of room for additions. A great celebration was held when the Rx drawer was ceremoniously installed, and glowing speeches pointed out that science had once more refuted pessimistic croakings of doom. Even so, two speakers could not refrain from mentioning certain misgivings . . .

To understand the nature of these misgivings, we must now turn to a development which we have deliberately ignored so far for the sake of simplicity but which was in fact going on side by side with the shrinking of the Rx.

First, as we well know, the Rx in the new storage systems could be scanned only by activating the nudged or pizzicated quanta, etc., by means of a code number, arranged as an index to the Rx. Clearly the index itself had to be kept representational and macroscopic, else a code number would become necessary to activate *it*. Or so it was assumed.

Secondly, a process came into play of which even the ancients had had presentiments. According to a tradition recorded by Kchv among some oldsters in the remote Los Angeles swamps, the thing started when an antique sage produced one of the paleoliterary Bx entitled *An Index to Indexes* (or *Ix t Ix*), coded as a primitive I^2. By the time of the supermicros there were several Indexes to Indexes to Indexes (I^3), and work had already started on an I^4.

These were the innocent days before the problem became acute. Later, Index runs were collected in Files, and Files in Catalogs — so that, for example, $C^3F^5I^4$ meant that you wanted an Index to Indexes to Indexes to Indexes which was to be found in a certain File of Files of Files of Files of Files, which in turn was contained in a Catalog of Catalogs of Catalogs. Of course, actual numbers were much greater. This structure grew exponentially. The process of education consisted solely in learning how to tap the Rx for knowledge when needed. The position was well put indeed in a famous speech by Jzbl to the graduates of the Central Saturnian University, when he said that it was a source of great pride to him that although hardly anybody knew anything any longer, everybody now knew how to find out everything.

Another type of Index, the Bibliography, also flourished, side by side with the C-F-I series of the Ix. This B series was the province of an aristocracy of scholars who devoted themselves exclusively to Bibliographies of Bibliographies of . . . well, at the point in history with which we are next concerned, the series had reached B^{437}. Furthermore, at every exponential level, some ambitious scholar branched off to a work on a History of the Bibliographies of that level. The compilation of the first History of Bibliography (H^1) is lost in the mists of time, but there is an early chronicled account of a History of Bibliographies of Bibliographies of Bibliographies (H^3) and naturally H^{436} was itself under way about the time B^{437} was completed.

On the other hand, the first History of Histories of Bibliographies came much later, and this H-prime series always lagged behind. It goes without saying that the B-H-H series (like the C-F-I series) had to have its own indexes, which in turn normally grew into a C-F-I series ancillary to the B-H-H series. There were some other but minor developments of the sort.

All these Index records were representational; though proposals were made at times to reduce the whole thing to pizzicated quanta, reluctance to take this fateful step long won out. So when the Rx had already shrunk to room size, the Ix were expanding to fill far more than the space saved. The old liebury was bursting. One of the asteroids was converted into an annex, called the Asteroidal Storage Station. In thirteen yukals, all the ASS's were filled in the original Solar System. Other systems selfishly refused to admit the camel's nose into their tent.

Under the stress of need, resistance to abstractionizing broke, and with the aid of the then new process of cospatial nudging, the entire mass of Ix was nudged into a drawer no bigger than that which contained the Rx themselves.

Now this drawer (D^1) itself had to be activated by indexed code numbers. More and more scholars turned away from research in the thinner and thinner stream of discoverable knowledge in order to tackle the far more serious problem: how to thread one's way from the Ix to the Rx. This specialization led to a whole new branch of knowledge known as Ariadnology. Naturally, as Ariadnology expanded its Rx, its Ix swelled proportionately, until it became necessary to set up a subbranch to systematize access from the Ix to the Rx of Ariadnology itself. This (the Ariadnology of Ariadnology) was known as A^2, and by the time of the Collapse the field of A^5 was just beginning to develop, together with its appropriate Ix, plus the indispensable B-H-H series, of course.

The inevitable happened in the course of a few yukals: The Ix of the second code series began to accumulate in the same ASS's that had once been so joyfully emptied. Soon these Ix were duly abstractionized into a second drawer, D^2.

Then it was the old familiar story: The liebury filled up, the ASS's filled up. Around 10,000 yukals ago, the first artificial planet was created, therefore, to hold the steadily mounting agglomeration of Ix drawers. About 8000 yukals ago, a number of artificial planets were united into pseudosolar systems for convenience. By the time of yukal 2738 of our own era (for we are now getting into modern times), the artificial pseudosolar systems were due to be amalgamated into a pseudogalaxy of drawers, when — the Catastrophe struck . . .

This tragic story can be told with some historical detail, thanks to the work of our research teams.

It began with what seemed a routine breakdown in one of the access lines from $D^{57 \times 103}$ to $D^{42 \times 107}$. A Bibliothecal Mechanic set out to fix it as usual. It did not fix. He realized that a classification error must have been made by the ariadnologist who had worked on the last pseudosolar system. Tracing the misnudged quanta involved, he ran into:

"See $C^{11}F^{73}I^{15}$."

Laboriously tracing through, he found the note:

"This Ix class has been replaced by $C^{32}F^7I^{10}$ for brachygravitic endorangana-thans and $C^{22}F^{64}I^3$ for ailurophenolphthaleinic exoranganathans."

Tracing this through in turn, he found that they led back to the original $C^{11}F^{73}I^{15}$!

At this point he called in the district Bibliothecal Technician, who pointed out that the misnudged sequence could be restored only by reference to the original Rx. Through the area Bibliothecal Engineer, an emergency message was sent to the chief himself, Mlvl Dwy Smith.

Without hesitation, His Bibliothecal Excellency pressed the master button on his desk and queried the Ix System for: "Knowledge, Universal — All Rx-Drawers, *Location of.*"

To his stunned surprise, the answer came back: "See also $C^{11}F^{73}I^{15}$."

Frantically he turned dials, nudged quanta, etc., but it was no use. Somewhere in the galaxy-size flood of Ix drawers was the one and only drawer of Rx, the one that had once been installed with great joy. It was somewhere among the Indexes, Bibliographies, Bibliographies of Bibliographies, Histories of Bibliographies, Histories of Histories of Bibliographies, etc.

A desperate physical search was started, but it did not get very far, breaking down when it was found that no communication was possible in the first place without reference to the knowledge stored in the Rx. As the entire bibliothecal staff was diverted for the emergency, breakdowns in the access lines multiplied and tangled, until whole sectors were disabled, rendering further cooperation even less possible. The fabric of this biped civilization started falling apart.

The final result you know from my first report. Rehabilitation plans will be sent tomorrow.

Yours,
Yrlh Vvg
Commander

(*Handwritten memo*) This report received L-43-102. File it under $M^{42}A^8E^{39}$. — T.G.

(*Handwritten memo*) You must be mistaken; there is no $M^{42}A^8E^{39}$. Replaced by *W-$M^{23}A^{72}E^{30}$ for duodenomattoid reports. — L.N.

(*Handwritten memo*) You damfool, you bungled again. Now you've got to refer to the Rx to straighten out the line. Here's the correction number, stupid:

Positively the end . . .